I0718721

Cover Design & Interior Format

DIANNA LOVE

TREOIR DRAGON CHRONICLES

OF THE BELADOR WORLD

VOL. 2

BOOKS 4 - 6

DIANNA LOVE

TREOIR DRAGON CHRONICLES

OF THE BELADOR WORLD

BOOK 4

PRONUNCIATION GUIDE

Note: A complete guide of unusual names, places and terminology for the Belador series is located on any Belador book page at www.AuthorDiannaLove.com but below are from this book.

aiteann – ah chin
Ainvar – AIN var (AIN rhymes with rain)
Brynhild – burn HILD
Casidhe – CAH sih duh
Cearcall na Sìorraidheachd – SEHR cull nah SEE ur RYE eecht
Dragani – drah GAHN nee
Eógan – OH un
Garwyli – gar WHY lee
gorse – GOERS (rhymes with course)
Gruffyn – GRUFF in
Imortiks – im MORE ticks
Immortuos Grimoire – im MORH tue ose gruhm WAAR
Jennyver - JENN uh vir
Joavan – joh uh VAHN
Josue – hoh ZOO eh
Ketche – KETCH uh
Lann an Cheartais – lahn nah KAIR tus
Luigsech – LOO gi sehk (g is hard like 'egg')
Maistir – MY stir
Mac Seáin – mac SHAWN
Medb – MAVE
Phoedra – FAY druh

Renata – REY not ah
Ruadh – ROO awn
Scamall – SKAH mull
Scáth Force – SCATH (like bath) Force
Seanóir – SHAWN ore ee
Skarde – SKARD
Sùilean – SOO lun
Talamh Dearmadta –TAHL am DUR mah tah
TÅµr Medb – TOWER MAVE
Timmon – tim MAHN
Tír na nÓg – TEAR nah nowg
Tzader – ZAY der
Yáahl – YALL
Zeelindar – ZEE lin dar

The past be carved in stone with lessons learned,
The future waits ta test those lessons,
The choices made today shall validate the past and
determine the future.
~Garwyli

LYDIA STONE WITH ATLANTA NEW Millennium News hurried to follow local citizens into a meeting being held in a three-story building in midtown, north of downtown Atlanta. She'd come alone, afraid a cameraman would create a disturbance. People were on edge with all this supernatural baloney. But it made for good stories.

A beefy young man stood at the front of the room with a wireless microphone. "Let's get started. We may only have a short time to meet if those ... things find out about this."

Rumbling erupted in the room, gaining steam.

"Hold it down," he ordered, quieting the crowd. "I'm building a team. I have six with me now, but I need more volunteers."

A man yelled out, "What are you going to do?"

"Take our city back. If you sympathize with these monsters, you best leave now. The rest of you, don't wear a costume. Don't post videos of them on social networks. Don't be out at night if you aren't on the team. Anything strange moves, it dies."

Lydia rolled her eyes. A vigilante group. Just what the city did not need. She had hoped to find someone to interview who claimed to have seen a supernatural. Too risky tonight. Turning to leave, she slipped away into an unlit lobby but paused at the door.

A tingle climbed her spine. She searched beyond the dirty glass. No one walked by. Lifting her eyes up a five-story building across the street, she watched a figure climbing the side with little effort. Another idiot trying to go viral on social media? Gray skin covered the unclothed body and silly horns stuck out from each side of its huge head. Four floors off the ground, the being turned to look around through glowing red eyes, then dropped to the sidewalk light as a feather and walked away. That's when she noticed the tail.

CHAPTER 1

WHAT HAPPENED TO ALL THE noise? Where were the jets and that loud helicopter?

Casidhe sat with her knees drawn up to her chest and arms wrapped tightly around them, rocking. Daegan said he'd come back. He wouldn't leave her alone on a mountain in Spain.

An unbearable silence pressed on her chest. Had Daegan survived the satyrs chasing him? Had he shifted into his dragon?

She stopped rocking. His dragon couldn't survive jets and missiles. What was going on? She grabbed her head, trying to keep the pounding from cracking her skull open. How would she know what happened? She wouldn't. Not if Daegan failed to return.

She couldn't sit in this dark hole forever. Daegan had been gone an hour, maybe more, since shoving her into their hidey hole. He promised to come back.

The sun hadn't risen yet, but it would soon. Maybe. She had no mobile phone or watch to use for obsessing over the time. Her crappy watch had not survived all the near-death moments since returning to this mountain last night. How long should she wait?

Bigger question was how would she return home to Ireland if Daegan couldn't make it back?

That would only happen if he died.

She'd never depended upon anyone to keep her safe, but she believed in him. That dragon shifter had been at her side through the crazy turmoil of reaching the oracle and going after the grimoire inside a hidden realm. Even when satyrs chased them around that world, Daegan had found a way to escape.

At some point, she started to believe he could do anything. Human military weapons could blow up even Superman. Shifting to his dragon would have been suicidal. A dragon couldn't outfly a jet, right? He must have stayed in human form and ... what?

She closed her eyes and fought to calm her breathing.

He had to be alive.

She didn't know what satyrs could have done to Daegan, but she'd seen the results of a missile blowing up a towering building the size of twenty dragons.

Daegan promised to return. Then he kissed her.

When he'd held her, she remembered every fleck of silver in his eyes and how his gaze had locked on her as if he couldn't tear himself away, then he'd broken something loose inside of her with his kiss. She'd avoided men for so long, always focused on her duties. One kiss and he ruptured the tidy life she'd convinced herself fulfilled her needs. Maybe mentally, but not emotionally.

He'd made her feel and want. She couldn't go back to being alone and living only to read another ancient journal.

That man kissed with more passion in one frantic moment than she'd ever experienced. She touched her lips and closed her eyes, reliving all the crazy emotions that swamped her at the touch of his lips. She'd been kissed before, or so she'd thought. Now, she lived for the moment to feel that again. He just needed to survive.

Oh, shit. Maybe that kiss had been a message?

Had Daegan been saying goodbye?

Her heart thumped wildly.

A fist of anxiety punched her chest, but she shook it off. Now was not the time to give up.

Dried leaves crackled nearby.

Casidhe sat up quickly, heart racing, and alert. What was that? She whispered, "Daegan?" No answer.

Where was he? She struggled to breathe and her heart beat as fast as a scared rabbit. She needed air. Now.

Moving her hand around in the darkness, she checked on the backpack for the hundredth time. Still there. She crawled out on her knees, pushing low hanging branches away from her face, and paused to listen before emerging.

Nothing. Just bleak silence.

Not even a noisy jet or helicopter. She had no one to call and no phone even if she did. Her heart fluttered fast as the wings of a tiny fly caught in a spider web. Not much of a family guardian now. She folded her arms over her chest and bit down hard, to keep from making the sound of a trapped animal. She stared at nothing in the thick darkness, fighting to keep her head together.

The sounds of nature trickled in, soothing her until she could catch her breath and think calmly.

Herrick did not raise a quitter. She'd fought to survive while a street kid on her own before he found her.

Do the same thing now. Live one minute at a time, then the next minute, and so on.

She ran cold fingers over her face, wiping her damp eyelashes. Time to buck up and face today. Not tomorrow. Just right now in this moment.

She drew in one cleansing breath after another. She could do this.

A soft glow peeked above the horizon, gifting her with the ability to see the outline of trees.

She pushed up to walk around and stretch her legs. Thick forest covered the steep slope sweeping away from her all the way down to terracotta roofs on bright white Mediterranean-style homes. Boats floated in a still cove beyond the picturesque village. Too far away for anyone to see her at the top of this mountain.

Time to think strategically and not about Daegan, who might be just fine. She should be figuring out how to save her own butt if he didn't return. She wouldn't be in this emotional state if she hadn't kissed him. What kind of fool got so personal with her family's enemy?

Her.

She'd been a fool. No, make that a super-sized fool. Actually, she'd behaved as a classic Casidhe-sized super fool once again around a man. Hadn't she learned anything from her one relationship back in college? A wise woman would have shut down that kiss the second his lips touched hers, or shoved him away, or yelled at him for daring to touch her so intimately.

Anything but standing there like a schoolgirl who had never been kissed.

A result of not having been kissed in a long time. Years. That didn't excuse losing her mind. She'd been mesmerized like a mouse entranced by a stalking cat right before being gobbled up.

Guilt tapped along her shoulders. What if Herrick had seen her kissing Daegan?

That would have been ugly.

She had to stop being a fool over a kiss. That's all it was and unworthy of angst.

Cool wind off the ocean rattled the leaves, drawing her to attention.

She'd never been one to sit still when she had books to read. Sounded like a great way to pass the time and not dwell on stupid actions she would not repeat.

Turning toward her hiding place, she stilled at the sound of a jet cruising the coast.

Not far behind, a large military-looking helicopter followed.

She picked her way to a higher point where she could see

the lights of more aircraft silhouetted against the brightening sky. The helicopter moved slowly, sweeping a beam of light over the water just beyond the cliffs.

If Daegan had shifted into his dragon, she hoped that dragon was as badass as she'd been led to believe by those who taught her the Treoir history. She hoped he outmaneuvered all those jets and technology capable of tracking a fly.

But if he didn't return ... nope, she would not go down that dark path again when she'd just climbed out of her head to a better place. Focus on the positive. They'd survived climbing a mountain, entering a tunnel where the ground fell away, and meeting with a spooky oracle. All that before they figured out a majikal code for passage into a hidden world.

Daegan now possessed the bronze box containing one-third of the grimoire pages.

She had the scepter the oracle expected for payment.

Mission accomplished, but at what cost? First Fenella vanished after walking out of the ancestral research centre. Now, Daegan had disappeared.

She slapped her head. Stop dwelling on things out of her control.

Once she'd fought her way back through the low-hanging branches again and scooted around until she had a place to sit against an uneven rock wall, she dug out her tiny LED light on a keychain.

She stuck her hand in the backpack. Her fingers landed on the scepter, a twenty-two-inch staff from the French Crown Jewels of the seventh century. She ran her finger over the enameled gold and pulled the staff halfway out to study the fat bird on top holding a man. Someone had stolen this from the tomb of King Dagobert I in Saint Denis Basilica.

Not a human thief, as many suspected, but a supernatural.

Leaning back, Casidhe pulled the scepter against her chest and held it close like a comfort stick. Could she wish on this like a majik wand and end up at home in Galway? That might be her best hope with only a driver's license in hand, no passport, and a rare artifact in her possession. Not to mention her powerful sword.

She might find someone in the coastal village below to help her, but she'd likely draw unwanted attention from law enforcement.

The sounds of the woods drew tension from her shoulders. Her eyelids drooped. She shook her head and blinked fast. What if the satyrs showed up and she didn't hear them?

What if Daegan returned?

She had to be vigilant. A soft breeze rustled the leaves. But it felt so nice to relax for just a moment. Her eyelids weighed a pound each. They fluttered closed. She shook herself awake again and lost her balance, falling sideways against her backpack.

Opening her eyes really wide, she tried to force herself to sit up.

Her body didn't cooperate.

She blinked again, murmuring, "Don't fall asleep. Don't ... close ... eyes."

Sleep pulled her under.

"Where are you, Daegan? Casidhe called out in the dark fog surrounding her. She heard a noise like someone groaning and walked in that direction. The fog billowed and shifted away from her until she saw a shadowy figure. She couldn't see his face, but the figure had broad shoulders like Daegan's.

She kept walking. The distance seemed endless. The figure turned to her.

Light touched his face. It was Daegan. His lips moved, but no words came out.

Her heart beat with the power of a war drum. "What, Daegan? I can't hear you." She took a step closer, thrilled to see him, but concerned. Something wasn't right. She tried to read his lips. Why couldn't he talk?

Panic pushed her to take another step.

He struggled to move toward her as if his muscles weren't obeying him. He was only ten feet away.

Her body slowed down. No. Keep going. She could barely move her legs. They felt wooden and heavy.

Darkness clouded her vision of Daegan again. She panicked and slashed her hands in slow motion to clear away the dark fog.

All at once, his face and body came into view again.

She could feel him close to her and started forward. Power hit her, like an explosion had suddenly detonated in her stomach, rocking her. What was happening?

"Where are you, Daegan?" she cried out.

He groaned a sound that stopped her. So much pain! Her stomach squeezed into a tight ball. She screamed, "Daegan!"

He moved forward from the shadows.

She reached for him.

His face twisted in agony. His entire body glowed bright yellow, the sickening color of the monsters.

She yanked back.

He shoved his face right up to hers with wild eyes a brilliant yellow. The pupils elongated and fangs dropped into sight. He screamed, "Ruunnnn!"

CHAPTER 2

THE DRONE OF LARGE HELICOPTER blades whined as the craft picked up speed, flying Daegan to some unknown location. Humans in black military-like uniforms surrounded him.

The cabin stank of sweat and fear.

No matter the weapons they carried, mortals feared the unknown.

He held his body still, no different than he had when they'd secured his wrists behind his back and shoved him inside the helicopter after the pilot had found a place to land near the cliffs.

He'd left the Luigsech woman behind, hidden high above, too far to have seen what happened to him.

Not the Luigsech woman, but Casidhe. He could no longer see her only as a Luigsech female, keeper of the Treoir history. She'd become important to him. He had to return to her. He'd accept his unknown fate if he knew she would be safe.

Had the satyrs returned to the hidden world they'd chased him from once he dropped the grimoire box at the cliffs? Or had they gone after her?

No, the satyrs had chased him because he'd taken the bronze box. He only recalled shifting into his dragon as he fell from the dropoff. Ruadh had been ready to battle, but his dragon had never faced a human weapon capable of destroying the earth, as Daegan had been told. Had Ruadh not shifted to save them on the way down, then landed on the cliff and immediately handed Daegan back the human body again, they might not have survived.

He'd had no hope for escape after the satyrs had spewed slime over the back of his body, which currently dried tough as a turtle shell and continued to spread.

Casidhe waited for him.

His chest ached with knowing she sat there watching for him.

She'd trusted him to come back for her. Every minute and mile of flying away from her gutted him. He should have had a plan to protect her no matter what happened.

He shouldn't have kissed her, but he would not take back that kiss for anything. He'd been driven to kiss her and now he felt her deep inside him where he'd never felt anyone else. Why would fate send him this woman now when he had no right to want more from her?

He didn't care about his needs. He wanted her off that mountain. He wanted her away from dangerous beings. He ... wanted her.

How could he survive letting her down? He'd fought alongside Beladors against powerful enemies over many generations, always there to keep them safe.

But he could not protect one wee lass right now.

His skin pulled tight across his back from the coating as it hardened. Before these humans had shoved a black sack over his head, he'd seen the coating on his arm taking on the same color as his skin. Tiny fibers crisscrossed, weaving into a rigid bond.

If they uncuffed him now, his arms would not bend.

At the rate the coating crept around his body, it would cover him in a day. Maybe less. Once the coating circled his neck and tightened as if shrinking, he'd have no way to survive even if these humans turned him loose.

Ruadh rumbled dangerously inside him.

Daegan had failed his dragon, too. Captured again.

One of the men sitting nearby whispered to someone, but Daegan's supernatural hearing allowed him to hear the words over the helicopter noise. "Think that guy knows how to call up the dragon?"

"I don't know. Did you see that damn thing?"

"Hell, yes. Scary monster. I wouldn't want to be out there in the ship with a dragon in the water."

Fools thought his dragon went underwater when they couldn't find Ruadh. They had been ready to kill his dragon, but they were someone's men following orders who believed they were doing their duty.

What about the Beladors? They had no one to protect them if he died.

The deadline to save Devon, a Belador facing execution from the Tribunal, had to be coming down to minutes. Daegan had no hope of escaping in time. He was gut-sick over the people he would let down. Beladors locked up in VIPER would be executed all because Daegan had not returned in time to meet with arrogant deities demanding he attend a Tribunal.

Innocent Beladors being judged unworthy to live because Imortiks had attacked them and slid inside their bodies. Those men and women now had less than two weeks before the Imortiks could take full control. A week Daegan had hoped to save them by finding all three volumes of the Immortuos Grimoire.

Here he sat helpless to protect his people and Casidhe, dammit.

Fury boiled his blood.

Ruadh banged around inside him.

Another male voice nearby said, "Hey, do you feel something weird? Like a pressure building in here?"

Frightened grumbling followed. Someone made a click noise, probably activating a weapon.

Daegan forced himself to settle as much as he could.

Crashing this aircraft would not save anyone and he'd kill humans who had not given him reason to take a life.

Not yet.

The pungent smell of fear lessened, leaving a strong wave of cigarettes in its wake.

He would not have allowed himself to be captured if not for the satyr coating and Imortik venom in his body shutting down his ability to move, shift, or teleport.

Or to reach one of his Beladors telepathically. No one answered his calls.

"You think he doesn't understand English?" one of the men asked.

Another one answered, "I have no idea. If he's one of those supernatural things, they may have their own language."

Daegan had taken on the only defense he could when these men dropped out of the sky to surround him with weapons raised to fire. They kept asking, "Where is that dragon? What did you do with that flying beast?"

Daegan had answered them with a blank expression.

They'd tried different languages on him.

He knew many languages, but remained mute. Let them think he did not understand their words. He had greater concerns.

As bad as the unknown situation he faced, he had no grimoire box after all he and Luigsech had gone through to find that and the stolen scepter.

Not Luigsech, but Casidhe.

She'd been Luigsech to him when he'd been angry over her secrets, angry about Tristan being captured, and angry over Imortiks attacking every time he turned around.

None of that had been her fault.

If Daegan were honest, none of that had been the true reason for using her last name to keep distance between them. He'd battled an attraction to a woman he hadn't trusted at first, but there had been more to it. Just breathing in Casidhe's scent had chipped at the wall he'd built to survive thousands of years locked in captivity.

He'd judged her to be a nonhuman stranger when they met. A dangerous mystery.

She'd become more than a stranger.

More than a resource.

But she could never be more than a friend to him. He clenched his hands, struggling not to roar in fury. For the first time in too long he was drawn to a woman whose energy called to his. His energy came to life around her, but he could not act upon the desire.

He'd never have a mate.

Dragons couldn't mate just any nonhuman, which had been the reason for arranged marriages long ago.

Maybe he should have accepted Brynhild when her father offered her to be Daegan's mate. That union would have built an alliance between their families, but he'd been arrogant enough to think he'd find a love match.

And to be honest, he'd never much liked Brynhild as a young woman.

She was nothing like Casidhe. He missed his little termagant so much it physically hurt.

Would she be safe all alone on that mountain?

When he closed his eyes, he could see her in his mind standing firm in the face of Imortiks, demons, and satyrs with her sword raised to do battle.

The whine of the helicopter blades changed. He felt them descend, but to where he had no idea. His best guess was they'd been flying for one or two hours. Based on where they'd picked him up on the northern coast of Spain, they had to be flying east or south. Would it be daylight yet?

Would Tzader or any Belador find out he'd been captured? Tzader had to know Daegan would have done all in his power to make the deadline to save their three Beladors from execution.

Death or capture were the only two reasons he'd fail to arrive on time. Since Tzader would expect Daegan to escape an enemy, his friend might believe him dead.

Only on the inside for now.

Someone must have opened a door. Blessed fresh air buffeted the interior. Men talked to each other in low tones, discussing how to move the prisoner from the helicopter.

Grief and disappointment clawed Daegan's chest. If he survived this, how would he face his people again after failing to prevent the deaths of innocent Beladors?

That damn coating on his skin kept digging in with tiny claws as it moved across his body and tightened. That hard covering inched forward from the back of his neck. Soon it would reach the front to form a collar around his throat and suffocate him.

Muscles across his back, arms, and legs drew taut as if they were being twisted and shortened.

Daegan picked up shouts from outside the helicopter somewhere below. Probably the landing spot. Men moved around inside, making noises about having weapons ready and who would exit first.

This military team reminded him of Isak Nyght's black ops soldiers in Atlanta, a human ally of the Beladors. Deadly fighters with weapons created by Isak's company to stun and kill nonhumans.

Voices buzzed with energy, both excited and apprehensive.

No one mentioned the name of their destination.

The helicopter settled with a hard thump. The sound of boots clomping around outside were joined by those jumping down from the cabin.

Daegan readied himself to be moved. Where would they take him? Some sort of confinement.

He and Ruadh had suffered thousands of years in TÅµr

Medb. He'd never intended to allow that to happen to them again.

I am sorry, Ruadh, he whispered telepathically.

Ruadh sent back, *Humans terrified. Air filled with sick smell of fear. We will kill them if they attack. We will escape.*

His dragon did not make empty promises and did not care if a human or nonhuman imprisoned them, but Daegan couldn't shift with the coating binding his body.

Still, Ruadh's words were meant to remind him they would not go down without taking others with them.

Daegan twisted his hands to give the raw skin on his wrists some relief. A futile effort, but at least his wrists moved.

The humans had not seemed to notice the thin layer of slime. Probably too distracted by losing sight of Ruadh to pay attention to Daegan's human form.

A hand clamped his arm.

Burning streaked across Daegan's skin.

Ruadh roared a vicious sound.

The hand disappeared. "What the fuck was that sound?"

Refusing to say a word, Daegan stood and turned toward the open air he could smell, but could see nothing beneath the black sack.

"Get back. He's coming out," someone outside the helicopter shouted. "Weapons up."

Daegan eased forward on his bare feet until his toes bumped the edge of the opening. He'd only been able to call up a pair of jeans to cover him when he shifted back from dragon form.

Remembering the height when he'd entered, he bent his head to avoid hitting the metal frame.

He tried calling out telepathically again. *I am Daegan of Treoir. Any Belador hearing me must tell Brina and Tzader I am captured.*

The sound never left his head, rolling around like a wooden ball banging the inside of his skull.

Barely bending his knees, he leaped out and dropped hard on a gritty unnatural surface. Pain shot up his legs and knees. He breathed through clenched teeth.

Someone ordered, "Turn to your right and walk straight ahead."

No one but his father had ever given him orders.

Every cell in his body wanted to revolt, but that would only cause Ruadh undue stress. Plus, he had no choice unless he wanted to die here with his eyes covered.

Following the order, Daegan took short steps, all the leg movement allowed by the coating.

Footsteps surrounded him and fell in behind him.

"Stop."

He waited as something in front of him made a whooshing noise.

"Move forward."

When Daegan complied, his feet touched cold metal. The whoosh happened again, closing off his fresh air. Probably an elevator.

Tristan had shown them to Daegan in Atlanta, but he'd preferred to avoid being locked inside the metal box. He sensed two humans with him as the unit descended slowly. The thumping of their hearts raced to see which one would beat the fastest.

If only he could reach Tzader, Brina, or Tristan telepathically, anyone who could rescue Casidhe.

Alone inside the dark covering over his head, he replayed her face, her eyes, and her lips in his mind. He could still taste her. The kiss had been impulsive, but one he would not regret.

Right or wrong, he longed to kiss her again.

He'd wanted for little early on in his life, but he'd never felt this crushing need for a woman as he did for Casidhe.

He'd never had any woman affect him the way she did. In foolish moments, he imagined keeping her with him to find out more about this attraction.

Casidhe's fear-drenched gaze would haunt him for whatever time he had left to breathe if he failed to send her help. She would know by daylight that something was wrong when he did not return. She was no shrinking female.

Lovely, resourceful, and tough, she might find a way home, but she had no phone and little money.

She did have the scepter they retrieved from the hidden world, but she had to hand it over to the oracle as payment for helping them find the grimoire box.

The box he'd lost going over the cliff.

One failure after another.

The grimoire could save his people, all nonhumans, and humans. They needed Daegan and that box to survive and force the Imortiks behind the death wall.

Please let Casidhe be safe from supernatural beasts. She could hold her own with humans and very likely best any who went up against her ancient sword.

"You think he really does not understand us?" one of the men asked quietly. He spoke English, but his words had a clipped Latin accent.

"Hell, I don't know," another man answered with an accent similar to that of Casper, a Belador ally from Texas. "Even a deaf mute will say somethin' when he gets hungry. If he don't talk then, not our problem, John. Our job is only to capture and deliver."

"You saw the red monster, did you not?" John asked nervously.

"Well, yeah. I'm sure one of them fighter jets probably filmed that beast."

"Then where do you think this ... dragon went?"

"Don't know, man. Heard someone say it dove in the water after two jets passed it. Must still be down there."

The elevator slowed and stopped. More whooshing noise and a sterile unnatural smell met him, reminding him of being inside buildings in Atlanta.

"Walk forward."

Daegan sighed at the endless orders, patience the only weapon in his arsenal at the moment.

Bootheel clicks echoed, sounding loud as if he walked through a tall space with hard walls. The elevator had descended longer than he would have expected to be one or two levels down.

"Hold up. Who are you?" a man on his right called out.

With no idea what was going on, Daegan stopped and listened for any hint of what might be happening.

Another set of footsteps approached from the opposite direction. A new male said, "I am to accompany him the rest of the way, corporal."

That voice sounded smooth with an odd accent, but what lifted the hairs on Daegan's head had nothing to do with the man's speech.

Daegan had caught a brush of energy.

Ruadh pushed hard under his skin. *Enemy.*

Daegan asked his dragon, *Which enemy?*

Do not know. Feels wrong. Ruadh sounded drained.

The corporal argued, "No, sir. Not unless you have orders from the top, in print, that override mine."

"I do have authority," the nonhuman replied. "Ask your superior."

That's when Daegan felt more than a brush of energy fly past him with the words.

When the corporal replied, he sounded drugged. "Yes ... you can take the prisoner to his cell. Carry ... on."

Mystery nonhuman spoke quickly and with power. "You will not recall meeting me, corporal. You and your subordinate will return to the elevator, take it back to the top floor, and forget you met me or say you handed off the prisoner."

"Yes ... sir." The men who had brought Daegan down walked away and left on the elevator, based on the familiar sounds.

The humans did not realize a nonhuman was among them?

Who had infiltrated this human operation and why?

What the hell was going on? Daegan had hit his limit of being fair. Casidhe sat alone, vulnerable to any threat and with no way home. He'd been led around by humans and now a nonhuman shows up?

The nonhuman said, "Begin walking forward and I will give you directions."

"Who are ya?" Daegan snarled, fed up with everyone.

"You are in no position to argue," the faceless intruder snapped back.

Power boiled inside of Daegan. Ruadh roared for release. The sound of walls shaking joined the floor vibrating beneath his feet.

Just like his dragon had reminded him, Daegan would not go quietly. Neither would he be controlled by another nonhuman. If this bastard had the power to do so, then he would be forced to show it.

Tension churned the air.

"Stop if you want my help."

As if Daegan would trust an unknown power for help? He did not sense fear so much as hesitation on the part of this stranger. "Answer me. Who are ya and what do ya want with me?"

His new captor did not reply.

"Only a fool would think I am harmless," Daegan warned in spite of the venom and coating his body fought.

If this stranger could teleport, he would have done so with Daegan by now. On his next inhale, Daegan smelled anise. Where had he smelled that before?

Power pushed back at Daegan.

Too bad this stranger could not see the mean smile twisting Daegan's lips. He called upon Ruadh to give him as much energy as he could.

Daegan's head began to grow and twist in shape, but not dragon yet.

The black bag ripped open enough to see with one eye.

With his head distorted and one eye able to see again, Daegan stared at a human glaring back at him.

The stranger hissed, "Stop. I have come with an offer."

Daegan's voice came out a dark gravel. "The answer is no. Ya hide yourself like a coward."

His boring face with dull-brown eyes, rough-chopped dirt-colored hair, and thin lips rearranged into something more disturbing and angry. "You think a dragon is safe from me? Attack me and you will regret your decision."

Daegan pushed energy even harder, flooding the space, and slapping this nonhuman's power back in his face. If it meant death, so be it.

CHAPTER 3

QUINN BENT, DROPPING HIS HANDS to his knees, weary of forcing his body to remain upright for so long. Weary of trying to do right by everyone yet failing the one person who needed him. The one person he should be with now instead of standing outside this bloody mountain housing VIPER headquarters.

Reese had stuck to her word and stayed at his building in downtown Atlanta until nine this evening.

Leaving one minute later meant she didn't believe he could protect her or their baby.

That hurt the most. He wanted a chance to get it right this time. A chance to keep both of them.

But she'd vanished with the use of a mysterious medallion she'd received from Phoedra's equally mysterious guardian.

Quinn had suffered about all the damn mystery he could take.

Loki would call him back into the Tribunal meeting any minute without a word of warning to face their arrogant demands. They fully expected Quinn to deliver Daegan right now.

Quinn had no idea what he would say this time. Tzader couldn't come here with his pregnant wife, the Belador Warrior Queen, so close to delivering twins. Brina's presence alone in Treoir drove the power for all Beladors.

Daegan hunted a volume of the Immortuos Grimoire in Ireland and also had to stop a rogue dragon shifter on a destructive binge.

That put Quinn as third in charge with the responsibility of Belador safety in North America. He had never hesitated to step up for his people. He'd managed to talk their way out of trouble more than once, but he had few options on how to solve this dire situation. The Tribunal deities meeting tonight demanded Daegan's presence to answer for a grimoire stolen from the VIPER vault. To suspect Daegan of that was insane.

Treoir's dragon king could not be found. Daegan replied to no telepathic calls from any of them. If Trey, their most powerful Belador telepath, and Tzader couldn't find Daegan, no one could.

Three innocent Beladors locked beneath VIPER mountain had no one to save them from execution except Quinn. The Beladors had been possessed by Imortiks, but their humanity was not lost yet. Not for two full weeks. The Beladors from earlier attacks had less than that now. Did the Tribunal care? No. Compassion was not in their vocabulary.

Quinn stared up at the night sky, searching for an answer.

None came.

Those deities would smell blood with Daegan unavailable.

Quinn's head was going to explode from the pounding between his ears.

Clyde's voice entered his mind. *Maistir?*

Quinn flinched, but caught himself before he snapped at the faithful Belador overseeing the protective building in Atlanta where Reese should be right now. *Yes, Clyde.*

Do you still want me to send out a team to search for Reese?

No, thank you. She's no longer in the city. Quinn had zero ideas about where she'd gone, but he'd bet a sizable fortune on her not even being in the state of Georgia. Maybe not in this realm.

Putting that aside as best he could, he sent back, *I'm going to be tied up a bit in the Tribunal meeting, but I'll be in touch once I return to the city.*

Yes, sir. Clyde's presence disappeared from his mind.

Quinn was in the wrong frame of mind to face an overbearing and demanding Tribunal, but as the Belador go-to person for verbal combat as well as leading physical battles, he had a duty to do. He flexed his shoulders and stiffened his backbone.

Loki and the other two had better be ready for him.

Quinn! shouted in his head.

He jerked back. *Tzader? What are you yelling about?*

Hey, sorry, man. Didn't mean to do that, but I don't have much time. Daegan has been captured by an international military force.

Fuck! Quinn had an extensive vocabulary, but could think of little else to describe the mess they were in right now. *I can only assume that means Daegan was unable to teleport away or escape somehow. Can we get him back?*

Tzader heaved a long breath. *I won't know until I talk to someone, but the fact that I had to find out about this from Isak Nyght's intelligence group, and not our Belador contact in DC, is not encouraging. It makes me think someone who is not an ally with America has him or ... a supernatural force.*

Wouldn't that just cap this bloody day? Quinn asked, *What does Isak think?*

Says he only knows what he sent me, but he's gonna keep digging. Had it not been for one of his men monitoring a private security group out of Spain, he wouldn't have had that at all.

Rubbing his forehead, Quinn explained, *I'll be yanked back into a Tribunal meeting any second now. Loki and company are demanding Daegan's presence.* Quinn quickly shared what had happened with Imortiks breaking into the VIPER vault and stealing the one grimoire volume.

Man, that's going to put Daegan over the edge when we find him. Tzader sounded pulled in six directions.

Quinn liked hearing "when" they found Daegan instead of "if." *Why didn't Daegan call for someone to teleport him out of there if he couldn't do it? Isn't Tristan in the Treoir realm with you?*

Hell, yeah, Tristan's here and he's close to popping a vein with Garwyli fussing over his screwed-up hand when all Tristan wants to do is go find Daegan. But you don't heal a cut-off hand in one day.

Appalled, Quinn asked, *Who cut off Tristan's hand?*

He bit it off while in gryphon form to free himself from spelled manacles Cathbad had clamped on him. Tzader's disgust at that druid burned every word. *Anyhow, Tristan has informed everyone here in Treoir he's gone as soon as we locate Daegan. As for not being in contact with us, I'm thinking Daegan can't hear us calling to him telepathically or he can't send messages, or both.*

Tzader paused and was probably running a hand over his bald head, something Quinn had noticed his best friend and former Maistir do when deep in thought. *I'll keep you informed as best I can, Quinn. Good luck with the Tribunal. I'm going with Tristan to find Daegan so we can teleport without leaning on Brina. If something is not a crisis, I'd rather no one call her for teleporting. She's been uncomfortable all day. We think the babies are coming soon.*

Quinn pinched his nose. Worst time for Tzader to be gone with Brina close to giving birth to twins. Any other time, Quinn would be taking Tzader's place so his friend could stay with his wife. *Sorry, Z. I would go with Tristan if I could get away from this Tribunal without our people dying, but Loki will execute all three Beladors held in VI-*

PER lockdown immediately if I dare to take a step away. He teleported me outside the mountain only long enough to try to locate Daegan.

Thanks, Quinn. Brina has Garwyli, Lanna, and Phoedra. They're hanging close to her. I'm going to do my best to get back quickly. Do what you can with the Tribunal, but if they kill even one of ours, deadline or not, Daegan will declare war and we'll back him.

Agreed.

Tzader's last words had just passed through Quinn's mind when his body was yanked and spun away with being teleported.

Evidently his time had run out and Loki wanted him back in the Tribunal realm.

When he appeared again, everything remained the same as before he left. Sometimes the deities became bored and redecorated the realm at any given time, but not today. Quinn still had the sensation of standing in a giant night-time snow globe that had not been shaken.

Loki, however, had changed to a new Armani suit, which must have been a strain, snapping his fingers and all. At least he did not have the horns that sprouted from each side of his head when he went into full god mode.

Quinn yanked his sarcastic inner bastard back under control. Giving in to the frustration boiling his blood right now would help no one.

His people, Daegan included, depended on what he said next. This was not the time to go to war with a group of gods.

Justitia moved her head to face him though a blindfold covered her eyes. He often wondered if she ever got tired of holding those scales of justice and put them down to take a break. Probably not.

Hermes plucked away on his lyre. He usually plucked out a droll Muzak-like selection of tunes, but right now it sounded more like a riff from a popular band's song about how the mighty gods smashed their adversaries into kindling.

So nice to have a soundtrack to impending murder.

Loki tossed a sparkling blue ball up and down from one hand. Light glittered in its trail. "Where is your dragon king?"

Quinn took a deep breath, ready to tackle round two with this bunch. "Tzader just informed me a European military force has captured Daegan."

Loki caught the ball and closed his fingers tight until it poofed out of existence. "Someone captured *his* dragon?"

Quinn heard equal parts disbelief and excitement in Loki's voice. "Tzader is on his way to find out if the force holding him is an ally of the United States. If so, he'll work through diplomatic channels to have Daegan returned. I seriously doubt *anyone* captured Daegan's dragon, definitely not humans."

Tiptoeing around not lying in this place could be deadly if Quinn made a verbal misstep.

Saying he seriously doubted something was not the same as claiming his statement to be truth, sparing Quinn from an immediate consequence here. He added, "Knowing Daegan, he went along with whomever has him to keep from harming humans or outing his dragon. Tzader believes Daegan might be somewhere he can't hear us call telepathically and it will only be a matter of time before he's released. In spite of all that has happened, Daegan and every Belador is doing their level best to keep from exposing supernaturals any more than we are at this moment with the humans."

Turning to Justitia and Hermes, Loki whispered something.

Quinn assessed Loki's reaction to the news as confusing. Did the trickster god think to take advantage of Daegan being out of pocket?

Loki finished speaking with the other two and turned to face Quinn.

Justitia said nothing.

Hermes nodded and lowered his lyre. He cleared his throat and spoke in an angelic voice created for singing. "While the news of Daegan's capture is unexpected, we still must deal with the prisoners."

A nerve twitched beneath Quinn's eye. He reminded himself that he was the North American Maistir over the largest supernatural force in the world. He had to restrain his anger and continue in a tactful voice.

"As soon as Daegan is free, I will bring him here immediately. In fact, our dragon king will want to address all of you himself. In the meantime, I think it only fair to stay any execution plans you have for our people in your holding cells as that would send the wrong message to your allies."

Hermes never acted emboldened, but Loki must have said something to get the musician jazzed up. "We are not babysitters."

Screw manners.

Quinn stepped forward, muscles tensing under his badly-rumpled suit. "No, you are *gods* and *goddesses*, who supposedly want to keep the human world intact. You have the ability to preserve life just as easily as end it. Not one of those Beladors locked up below VIPER did anything to incur your wrath or a death penalty. They were harmed while trying to protect the human world, which is where your followers live. You want followers, right? Then help us save this world."

Loki interjected, "We take offense at your tone, *Belador*."

Did Loki think calling Quinn a Belador instead of Maistir was an insult?

Hardly. He would always be a Belador first.

Squaring his shoulders, Quinn said, "I'm surprised you find my words offensive when I intended them as offering you the chance to realize we all have a common goal." He was too damned tired and emotionally spent to verbally battle with any grace when speaking to immortals willing to end a life with so little thought.

He pushed power into his voice. "Daegan is putting himself at risk to protect all of us. *Even* you three and the other Tribunal deities. Daegan understands balance. He believes we will all need to work together to rid this world of Imortiks to protect the humans and supernaturals."

Jaws dropped on all three perched on the lofty dais.

None of them considered themselves to be at risk.

Quinn had hit the point of no return, which happened when trying to have a reasonable conversation with three egotistical deities. "You'll understand if my words have an edge. I am *not* immortal. I need at least an hour, maybe two, of rest every three days and food, neither of which I've had for some time now. Our teams need me present to help them stop Imortiks, plus protect supernaturals from humans out to kill anything that appears strange. Standing here takes me away from my duties. But I will stand here and use my last breath if that's what it requires to get you to realize allying with Daegan and the Beladors is a huge benefit to everyone, including you. We *will* find a way to stop the Imortiks *and* put them back behind the death wall, or die trying. What other VIPER ally is offering as much?"

Justitia didn't smile, but her face softened with what might be considered amusement. "What benefit? As you said, we are immortal."

Quinn smiled, too, but not a happy one. His face would probably send children screaming at the moment.

All hint of humor vanished from Justitia's face. Blindfold or not, she missed nothing.

"You don't see a benefit?" Quinn asked in a chiding tone heavy with sarcasm. His shoulders bunched with the need to let out the anger tearing him up. He was good and fed up. "From what I understand, if an Imortik is powerful enough, he or she can take over *any* being. That's why deities and dragon families came together long ago to stop the Imortiks. They saw the wisdom in joining forces for a greater good."

Holding a smug expression, Loki shrugged. "I will admit we want those disgusting things out of this world and locked away permanently, but do not try to scare us with a threat to our existence."

Answering in an equally smug tone, Quinn said, "And here I thought you might realize everyone has a weak spot. I had hoped you'd prefer to continue as the top of the food chain."

When frowns puckered their foreheads, Quinn took advantage of his opening. "Let me put this in relevant terms. Did you not lose a grimoire volume from the VIPER vault? And to enter that vault doesn't a being have to possess the ability to teleport? If that is the case, then let's assume an Imortik entered the vault and is not one of your allies. If so, it would mean an Imortik overtook a body of someone capable of teleportation. The bottom line is that such an Imortik with that ability could enter this realm and other realms, which could be a threat to you as well, correct?"

Loki's expression soured.

Hermes stared with a dumbfounded look.

Justitia's lips twisted with a touch of temper.

Truth had a way of putting everyone on the same page. Quinn believed in the saying that misery loved company. He wanted every one of these three to feel his pain and that of all his people.

This time, Loki did not pause to share his thoughts with the other two on the dais before speaking. "What do you want, Quinn?"

Finally, an olive branch.

Quinn said, "Time. Give me another day to bring Daegan to you. He will be more willing to come in if you do not kill our people."

"And if we do terminate those infected?" Hermes asked, drawing a surprised glance from Loki.

The pause Quinn took before answering was intended to insure close attention to his next words spoken with precision. "If you do choose to kill even one Belador, then I suggest you call in every ally you have on speed dial. Daegan is furious about his people being in danger from Imortiks as it is right now through no fault of their own. I can only imagine his reaction to having three innocent Beladors executed."

Justitia flinched at that last comment. Good.

Loki became very still. A bad sign for an animated god who expected to be continually entertained. He spoke softly, but the sound could carry for a mile. "I must not be making myself clear. I do not allow anyone to threaten me or the rest of this Tribunal."

"I would never threaten any of you, Loki," Quinn qualified. "I have always held the highest respect for every god and goddess who participate in these Tribunals. I am merely trying to de-escalate this issue by pointing out how it could erupt with apocalyptic results. We have an opportunity to work together and protect all nonhumans who are aligned with VIPER as well as the humans. When I spoke of Daegan's reaction to losing any of his people, it was for you to consider the benefit of simply giving Daegan time to return so he can speak for himself."

Quinn drew a slow breath, allowing a pause for any negative reaction. When none occurred, he continued. "If once Daegan stands before this Tribunal, you take umbrage to anything he says, then I have nothing more to offer. It will be up to you and him to either come to an agreement for the good of all or ... not. If you execute our people without giving Daegan a chance to address the lost grimoire volume, then later find out all I've told you is true, will you not regret a hasty decision?"

Justitia stated, "If Daegan is captured, he may never return."

That was a truly frightening thought. "I am under the impression Tzader has an idea where Daegan might be and is going through diplomatic channels to bring him back to avoid any additional issues in the human world. An extension of time would allow you to call in others such as Queen Maeve, Macha, and Cathbad." Justitia's statement gave Quinn hope she would wait for Daegan to return if he could convince her to give him time. Quinn added, "If you extend the deadline for a day to allow our people time to bring Daegan home, I assure you bringing Daegan here will be my top priority."

Loki stared down at Quinn with cold eyes. "If it is possible to free Daegan through diplomatic channels, that should take no more than twelve hours in the human world."

Maintaining a composed expression when Quinn wanted to curse Loki for that god's determination to turn every situation into a battle pushed him one step too close to the end of his rope. "In that case, once you teleport me outside the VIPER mountain, I will inform Trey, Tzader, and others immediately so I may facilitate this more quickly."

No one on the dais spoke.

Quinn's body didn't so much as twitch. Shit. Loki was not teleporting *him.*

With a flick of Loki's hand, Evalle appeared facing Quinn and with her back to the Tribunal. Hands shoved out as if using kinetic power, hair wild, she was posed to battle someone or something.

She shook her head as if to clear her confusion. "What's

going on, Quinn?"

Loki's deep voice boomed, *"Turn around, Alterant!"*

Evalle's surprise fell away to worry for a second, but by the time she turned to face the Tribunal, she had her hard-ass look in place. "Yes?"

"What time is it in Atlanta right now?"

She frowned. "I can't say exactly, but I think we're close to eleven at night there."

"Take a message to Trey, Tzader, or anyone else who needs to know. The deadline for permitting the three Beladors turned into Imortiks to remain in our holding cells has been extended."

Her chest moved with the release of air.

Quinn wanted to send her a telepathic message that this would not be good news, but using unauthorized telepathy in a Tribunal meeting was unwise.

Loki smiled.

That wiped away whatever encouragement Evalle had felt. She asked, "What's the punch line?"

"Daegan has until eleven tomorrow morning in Atlanta to appear before this Tribunal. Until that happens, Quinn will remain here. If Daegan does not show up in time, we will teleport Quinn into a holding cell with all three Imortik Beladors to keep him company. At that point, Daegan can take his time arranging a meeting with this Tribunal."

Quinn's lips parted in disbelief. What if they didn't find Daegan by tomorrow?

Evalle turned to Quinn with a terrified look. "No! You can't do—"

She vanished.

Loki lowered his hand from teleporting her away. He gave a genuine smile so fitting for a homicidal lunatic who found this amusing. "If anything happens to those three Beladors once you are in their presence, Daegan will have no one to blame but himself."

CHAPTER 4

DAEGAN HAD REACHED HIS BREAKING point. He blew a stream of fire out the opening of the ripped bag on his misshapen head.

The nonhuman who still looked human disappeared.

That show of power had taken a load of effort. Daegan struggled to breathe evenly. His body ached from the coating growing harder across the back of his legs and arms. Venom continued to burn his insides. From his shoulders to the small of his back felt as if he wore a shell glued to his body and it was shrinking.

"That was impressive." The stranger popped back into view. He quickly added, "I ask for a truce until you hear me out."

"Then speak."

"If I do not get you into the holding cell soon, someone will check the monitor and question why you are not there. If they send a large team, I will not be able to stop them from taking over again. That will prevent any hope of escape."

Should he believe this stranger?

Just hearing the word escape shook Daegan's insides. If he could escape, he could get to Casidhe and his people.

"Please. I am not your enemy."

Ruadh rumbled at that, but said nothing.

Daegan had to live to escape. He hated going into any dungeon. Being locked up underground anywhere equaled a dungeon. Or a queen's throne room.

"You have less than a minute left to make it the last twenty feet," the stranger stated, clearly aware of Daegan's limited ability to move his legs.

Daegan walked forward the distance of one foot length at a time. Not to comply with this unknown being, but for those depending upon him. When he reached the cell, he continued moving on legs unwilling to stretch or bend. When he started to turn around, the stranger said, "Stop."

He stiffened. Hearing another order grated his soul. With the exception of King Gruffyn, his father, he had never taken orders from another being. If he had any other option right now, he would take it.

What was left of the bag on his head floated to the floor as his head shrank back to normal size when he pulled his energy back in.

He blinked, staring at solid gray metal walls with thick iron rods embedded.

An overhead light struggled to illuminate the area.

He drew in a slow inhale filled with the dank smell around him as if this place remained untouched by fresh air. But mixed in with that had been the hint of anise or licorice again.

Who was the supernatural being acting as a human guard?

The metal cuffs unlatched from Daegan's wrists, jangled, then were silent when they hit the hard floor.

He tried to pull his arms forward to rub them. One moved until even with the side of his body. The other arm remained behind him, frozen in place. The satyr coating kept hampering his movements.

Metal on metal squealed. That would be the door to this cage.

Every breath strained him. He moved his feet in inches until he had turned all the way around to face vertical bars. Iron bars? Each thick rod had been placed six inches apart. Horizontal crossbars ran every two feet from ceiling to cement ground. An eight-foot-wide by twelve-foot-tall section had been created as a door.

He stood in a twenty-foot-square box with a thirty-foot ceiling. Nothing appeared to be new or constructed for a human.

Had this been *planned* long ago for a dragon or some other supernatural creature?

Beyond the bars stretched a long hallway to what appeared to be the elevator used to bring him down here. Three more cage doors were spaced along each side of the hall. No sound came from those.

No one stood in the hallway.

Where had that nonhuman gone?

Daegan opened his senses. No energy trail. Cloaking?

He forced his fingers on one hand to close. His hands were stiff and the knuckles made bone-cracking sounds. Pain lashed his fingers. Blood dripped from where his skin ripped open.

Ruadh growled steadily, his anger vibrating.

Daegan spoke telepathically with his dragon. *Do ya think we can shift and break this coating loose?*

Ruadh did not answer right away. *Coating dried on skin like tortoise shell. Must be cleaned off. To shift is to kill you.*

Daegan couldn't sit or lie down even if this metal room had a chair or bed. No water as well.

Energy spun in the hallway on the opposite side of the bars.

Not a hard flush of power. More subtle and sly.

Would he finally meet the nonhuman who had used majik to take Daegan from his human captors down here? Did the humans even know Daegan still existed?

The same average-looking man appeared in the hallway. Not quite six feet tall with a soft middle and ruddy skin, he wore a black uniform matching those who had captured Daegan.

Saying those humans had captured him stretched the definition. He'd stood on the cliff waiting on these men to finish dropping on ropes from the helicopter.

Shoving the black-rimmed glasses up on his nose, the guy pretending to be human said, "I am here to talk to you alone."

Itchy and stinging coating crept around Daegan's neck from the back. How long would he be able to breathe once it completely enclosed his neck? He opened his senses, but could pick up nothing to identify the being speaking to him while hiding his identity with a glamour.

His visitor said, "No one can hear us. I must protect myself as well."

Daegan had yet to gain an answer to the only question that mattered. "Who are ya?"

Sighing softly, the stranger said, "I could be an ally."

Had Ruadh been right about calling this being an enemy? "I will not talk to an imposter who uses a glamour."

"You have few choices," the man pointed out in a smooth voice, one more cultured than that of the image he portrayed.

"Still, those choices are mine to make," Daegan debated, gritting his teeth as muscles tightened. "If ya are unwillin' to show your real face, I am unwillin' to say more."

"Do you not wish to escape?"

What a stupid question. Daegan still had a voice to unleash his anger. *"Ya waste my time with foolish questions! Ya must want somethin' or ya would not have brought me down here alive. Of course, I wish to escape. That does not mean I shall blindly step into a worse situation."* Though he could not imagine one at the moment.

His visitor glanced away as he mulled that over. The dull-brown eyes sharpened when they returned to Daegan.

"I had intended to expose my identity, but I wished to be sure of one thing first. You are Daegan of Treoir, the red dragon shifter, correct?"

Should Daegan answer that or not?

He considered the possible negatives of admitting such, but had a feeling someone in those jets and helicopters filmed his dragon.

Still, he had to take care. "What makes ya think I am such a bein'?"

The man pulled off his glasses and smiled. "I am the only one on the team sent to bring you in who does not think your dragon is in the ocean. I was not alive to see your red dragon fly free prior to Queen Maeve capturing you, but my ancestors made drawings of your beast. They told me how she imprisoned you in the shape of a dragon throne in TÅµr Medb. I believe I witnessed the one-and-only red dragon flying tonight."

So this nonhuman had been there the whole time? Maybe on the cliff, but Daegan did not believe this one had traveled in the helicopter with him.

Should Daegan confirm his identity to this unknown being?

Ruadh's voice whispered in Daegan's head. *To admit truth is no great risk.*

Daegan sent a quiet thank-you to Ruadh. He told his visitor, "I *am* Daegan of Treoir, *the* red dragon shifter."

The pudgy guy let out a long breath and nodded slowly to himself.

In the next moment, energy spun smoothly again. When the humming and blurring finished, a six-and-a-half-foot striking male with golden hair and too-perfect skin to be human stood before him. Soft light emitted from his body, creating a pale-blue glow around him, the kind driven by hidden power. His smooth black suit and sand-colored pullover reminded Daegan of wealthy men Tristan had explained were human power brokers in Atlanta. Boots with small heels added nothing to one of such height.

Daegan had guessed what being he spoke to by now.

The Fae's ears were not pointy, but the tops turned down in small wing-like shapes. A thin scar ran along his chin, flawing an otherwise perfect creation.

Daegan would take the scar over all that prettiness.

Ruadh growled. *Fae is not ally.*

Daegan replied silently, *I agree. As I have no option but to stand here, I shall hear his words.* Speaking out loud, Daegan asked, "Why is a Fae workin' with humans?"

"Do *not* call me Fae." The being all but spit after that snarl. "I am Faetheen from *Talamh Dearmadta.*"

Daegan translated. "Land of Forgotten."

"Precisely. Many of our people were once with the Seelie Fae until ... we separated. Now we live in a world alongside the human world. Specific members of our world can pass between both places. I am called Joavan. I have taken a great risk to show you my true identity."

Daegan's facial muscles tightened, but he discovered he could still arch his eyebrow. "'Tis not much of a risk I can see when I am the one imprisoned."

His father once told Daegan to never believe a Fae who spoke while hiding his or her true image. Once they revealed their true identity, their words would be accurate, but not necessarily trustworthy.

Did that hold true for a Faetheen?

Joavan said, "I insured you would arrive here safely."

"For what reason?" Daegan asked. "Why would ya help me?"

"With more supernaturals exposed every day, we all face being hunted. I have heard about the rift and that Imortiks are escaping. My kind does not want them walking this land."

"Your kind contributed to the creation of the first Imortiks," Daegan stated, curious to find out if Joavan would admit a connection to the history of Imortiks.

"True, but my Faetheen people are not of the group that joined a druid to create these monsters. My ancestors claim dragons once stepped in to lend their power and force Imortiks behind the death wall. I am here to facilitate their demise as much as I believe you wish it."

This had potential, but for how much in return?

And was this Joavan being honest about his true reason for approaching him or using the most obvious to gain Daegan's agreement?

Daegan clenched his teeth to keep from groaning over the pain stabbing deep in his muscles. His gut burned to find a way out of here. He could not get the last sight of Casidhe out of his mind.

Should he ask this Fae to go help the lass?

Two problems with that. One was to never ask a Fae for a favor and the second was that he could not trust this Joavan with her safety.

But standing here with no other option meant leaving Casidhe on her own far from her home and friends.

Daegan would push Joavan to see how he reacted. "I shall wait for my people to come."

Anger flashed through the aqua eyes, but for only an instant. Joavan held back his temper. "No one outside the tactical force guarding this area knows you were taken, much less where you are at the moment. Others will eventually, but it may be a long time before someone discovers how to enter this compound. You are fifteen floors beneath the surface. Even *you* do not know where you are located. I am your only hope for getting out of here."

Truth, but not all of the truth.

Again, what did Joavan want? "If ya truly wish to help me put down the Imortiks, ya would tell me where we are and call my people."

"I am willing to reveal myself only to you. I work alone. Far safer for me and those I protect."

Daegan would like to believe this meeting was as simple as the Fae claimed, but he could not so easily give trust. "I assure ya my people know I am missin'. We have one of the greatest nonhuman forces in the world and we ally with a powerful human group. I shall wait." Speaking those words had been difficult when this being, Daegan's only visible hope, could vanish at any moment. Plus, as much as he believed in his words, he truly doubted if his people had any idea of his location.

Joavan tossed his hands up and looked around as if expecting someone else to share his frustration, then turned back to Daegan. "Why would you refuse my offer to help you escape?"

"'Tis simple. While I do believe any sane nonhuman would wish to rid our world of Imortiks, I have yet to hear the true price of freein' me. If ya think to wait until I am willin' to agree to anythin', ya shall be disappointed."

For several seconds, they stared at each other.

Not a standoff so much as Joavan taking his time to reach a decision. "I do want you to do something for me in return for your freedom. It would be a fair trade."

When the Faetheen said nothing more, Daegan repeated, "I shall decide what is fair."

Joavan walked about, stepping lightly as if keeping his feet on the floor was a conscious effort and not a natural motion.

When he stopped, he shifted back to Daegan in a fluid movement. "I am trusting you with information you could use against me if you refuse to accept this deal. I say this so that you know we both take risks. I want you to find something missing. It is very important to our people and their future. I know where it is. I left my world to hunt for this, but I need a dragon shifter to do what I cannot. When

I received word the red dragon had escaped Queen Maeve, I left my world to enter this one and find you. There were reports of a dragon burning forests in two countries. I studied the human films. That dragon did not appear to be *the* red dragon of my ancestral images."

Daegan gritted out, "'Twas not."

"I knew for sure when I saw *your* dragon in Spain. I have connections in the human world. One managed to have me inserted into the human team sent to hunt you yesterday, which allowed me to be present when they captured you."

"Ya were not in the helicopter?"

Joavan wrinkled his nose. "I have other ways to travel." He frowned with confusion. "I am still stunned over the fact that you allowed yourself to be taken prisoner. Why did you not teleport away? This is why I was in no hurry to trust exposing my identity at first."

With the hard shell forming over Daegan's skin as fibers slithered around his chest to fully enclose him, he had to accept that he would not survive much longer.

The only potential aid stood on the other side of those iron bars.

But how much should he tell this being?

Daegan always taught his warriors to never share a weakness. Sound advice if not for silence ending with his death.

Forcing air through his throat, Daegan spoke mostly in a whisper at this point. "Before reachin' those cliffs and the water, satyrs from another world were chasin' me. They spewed a liquid over my back right before I went over the cliff and shifted. That coatin' began dryin' on my skin and turnin' into a fiber-like solid shell. I could not teleport. I barely managed to shift back to my human form. At this moment, the coatin' continues to crawl across my skin to areas as yet untouched. In all honesty, if I accept your agreement, I will not live long enough to fulfill any terms."

Joavan's face changed from cordial to horrified. He'd kept his distance until now and stepped closer, but not close enough to touch the iron bars. "Let me see."

Daegan had no reason to avoid showing this Fae the severity of his condition. If Joavan had wanted to kill Daegan, he could have used power before now.

Inching closer to the bars, which took so much effort sweat broke out on his forehead, Daegan turned to show Joavan the arm hanging rigid beside his body. He couldn't move his head to see his arm, but the look on Joavan's face told him how much trouble Daegan was in.

Cursing, Joavan gripped the back of his neck. "You say a satyr spit this on you?"

"Yes."

"I must ask one of our healers for advice."

Daegan rasped, "If ya are gone long, the trip may be wasted."

Joavan lifted his swirling-aqua gaze to Daegan. "I will be fast. If I can remove the coating from your skin, I will do so. If not, but a healer tells me our people can save you, then I will take you to them. That is, if I can tell them you are an ally."

Daegan squeezed out the words. "If I live, we shall reach an agreement."

The Faetheen eyed him for long seconds. Then Joavan dropped a sharp nod, took two steps back, and disappeared. It didn't seem as if he had teleported, but stepped out of this world.

Was that how he traveled between his home and locations in this world?

Stiff fibers crawled around Daegan's throat.

The tiny threads began forming the last inches of a solid collar from chin to shoulders, and tightening.

Daegan forced his neck muscles to fight back.

Stars sparked in his gaze.

His next breath wheezed.

CHAPTER 5

"WHAT ARE YOU DOING BACK in TÅµr Medb empty-handed, Erath?" Queen Maeve floated just above the floor with her arms crossed. She thought she'd made her orders clear to her Scáth Force.

Only a warlock begging to be made an example of would show up here without a volume of the Immortuos Grimoire.

"I beg your patience, my queen." The leader of her elite force trembled and sweat poured down the sides of his bruised face. He dressed in dark jeans, a pale-green collared shirt, and running shoes, all of which were as battered and torn as his skin. Every member of her Scáth Force dressed similar to the humans in the realm they infiltrated.

"Patience?" Queen Maeve snapped. "Why would you beg for something you know I do not possess?" Her long gold hair suddenly pulled tight, braiding itself into thick lengths, then wrapped all of those around her head.

Erath did not twist his hands as a maiden might, but neither did he stand confidently. "It is for the grimoire that I come to you with news of what we face. The Imortiks have taken over two of our Scáth warriors."

She lowered her arms and stared at him in disbelief. "How can that be? You are the strongest of my warlocks."

"I understand, my queen, but the Imortik master came for two of ours on his own. He sent a message that you should not hunt the volume he possesses, but search for the other two missing volumes."

She'd fully intended to do that once she had a way to view the human realm herself, but she'd been stuck in TÅµr Medb with no tool with which to scry since that disgusting dragon escaped. He and his disgusting Beladors destroyed the existing scrying wall.

Her new one would top anything before it once the majik had finished infusing.

Until then, she could not enter the human world blind.

Daegan would kill her at his first opportunity and those Tribunal deities wouldn't lift a finger to aid her.

She tapped her chin, thinking. "Does this Imortik master threaten me?"

"No," Erath quickly replied. "He claims he will return our Scáth Force warriors when you deliver a volume, just not the one in his possession."

"Does he plan to continue to take my followers?"

Swallowing hard, Erath nodded slowly. "Yes. I barely escaped an attack before coming here. I hid the rest of the team to protect them while I was gone. It will be impossible to continue patrols with these attacks. Our Scáth team is small for strategic reasons, but the attacks are draining us."

Daegan and Cathbad both had to be hunting the grimoire volumes.

Anyone of power would be, but she'd heard about Daegan cutting a deal with the Imortik master to find a volume. Daegan would not start a war with her, but he *would* kill her given the chance.

If the tables were turned, she would do the same.

She needed Daegan out of her hair so she could leave TÅµr Medb even for a short time to gain the upper hand.

Cathbad would be a greater problem. He'd use the grimoire volumes to destroy her or oust her from TÅµr Medb at the very least. With Imortiks taking over her warlocks, even two of her best from the Scáth Force team, she would be out of her most skilled followers in the human world soon.

If she did not manage to get her hands on at least one volume of the grimoire, she could lose everything, her life at the top of that list.

"What would you have me do now, my queen?" Erath asked carefully.

"Change your tactic from hunting the grimoire to shadowing those who lead the Belador forces. I want to know what they are doing about the Imortiks and any news on Daegan."

Erath kept his face neutral but worry vibrated the air around him. "I do have some information to report. The current Belador Maistir is gone at times. When that happens, Evalle Kincaid has been assigned to stand in for him. Her people have been busy chasing demons coming into the city from an unknown source. My team is hunting the demon source as well, but to use to our advantage."

She gifted him with a smile, which could be construed as a stay of execution.

Demons? Who could be behind an influx of those beings? She would know all once her scrying wall finished developing.

She ordered Erath, "Also follow anyone significant to the Beladors. That includes allies, such as the Sterling witch."

His face fell at her words. He squeaked, "The one with Witchlock?"

Adrianna LaFontaine carried an ancient witch power in the palm of her hand. A power she'd stolen.

"Yes, *that* witch." Queen Maeve would claim Witchlock the day she struck a final deal with the Imortik master. "Return to your team, Erath."

"One last thing may interest you, but I have no way to verify it yet." Hope climbed into Erath's voice at whatever he had to offer. "There are rumors on the human Internet system that a dragon has been spotted in Europe."

The humans didn't believe in majik, but trusted an invisible thing called the Internet. She gave him a pointed look of having her time imposed upon. "I know about the burned lands."

"This is different, my queen. My team has heard a rumor that will interest you. A dragon was seen late yesterday off the coast of Spain and a coalition of human military were involved. Speculation is that the aircraft were tracking a red dragon and ... they captured it."

Now that had been worth the trip here.

Erath should have started with noteworthy information first.

"Is that all, Erath?"

"Yes, my qu—"

She teleported him back to the location he'd last been before arriving here.

Well, well, well. Had the mighty red dragon been captured?

Floating up, she turned to her new scrying wall, a stone tapestry of two hundred and fifty-six crystals from quartz to tourmaline to indicolite and more. Each one perfectly chosen and placed to open the door into any life she requested.

No one would stop her plans now if the wall was ready.

Not even Cathbad.

That druid had pleased her in many ways before they faked their deaths to reincarnate in this era. They drank a spelled mixture developed together over their last year alive and fell into a deep sleep in a protected location. With wars erupting and enemies at every turn, they agreed to gamble on majikally reincarnating in the future with greater plans.

Why had Cathbad gone so far astray since reuniting in

this lifetime? What had captured his attention for him to think he did not need her? Did he really believe he was deceiving her?

She would have answers soon.

If her wall had been ready the first time she'd tried it, she'd have discovered what Daegan was doing in Spain. He had to be the dragon captured, but had that really happened?

And who was the auburn-haired woman with him in that quick glimpse?

Queen Maeve had tapped into her wall too soon before the power had finished pooling from the TÅµr Medb realm and her hidden Noirre majik supply. The first image had lasted only a second before blurring and turning dark.

This wall would either work or not.

She needed to know soon if she had to abandon her creation and start over.

Opening her arms wide, she lifted her hands and placed her palms near the surface. Energy crackled between her hands and the wall. Tiny bursts of lightning bolts shot out.

She closed her eyes and pictured the last location where she'd seen Daegan in the country now known as Spain. White houses with orange roofs had climbed from the ocean up the side of a mountain. With that image fixed in her mind, she prepared to engage *Sùilean*, the *Eyes* of TÅµr Medb.

"I request your vision, *Sùilean*. I wish to see Daegan of Treoir with a woman on the mountainside of my vision."

Power surged and swirled. Energy pulsed all around the tall stone walls of her private space, funneling some of this realm's life force into her scrying wall.

Cathbad believed himself so clever.

He had never considered tapping the energy of an entire realm along with Noirre majik to power a scrying device.

As Sùilean's energy coalesced, the center of the wall

came into focus, appearing ready to do her bidding.

Hard to imagine how anyone could expect this result from a simple scrying bowl. She'd been shown how to use her first bowl at ten years old, but abandoned it as too limited for her, even as a child.

The adults had scolded her.

Contempt had driven her to teach everyone that underestimating her would be dangerous. The next day, she sent a request to a dark witch she'd been observing through her scrying. She asked the witch to send her oldest daughter to become her handmaiden.

Furious at the idea of demeaning her nineteen-year-old daughter by such a request, the witch sent a scathing refusal to enslave her firstborn to anyone, and definitely not an arrogant child of little power.

The witch's beautiful daughter awoke the next morning to a face with no eyes and no nose.

Smiling at that wonderful childhood memory, Queen Maeve relaxed her arms and gazed at the lovely image of Spain's northern coast. As a reflection of her mood, her hair unwound and flowed happily around her face and shoulders.

She would no longer be forced to function blind of what went on in the human world.

No longer limited by second-hand information supplied by even her elite force in the human world.

Nothing could match seeing for herself. Since the moment she'd captured a glimpse of the Treoir dragon king with a woman while they hiked, Queen Maeve had been anxious to try this again.

Did the woman have anything to do with finding a grimoire volume? Why else would Daegan be there? He thought to find a grimoire to save his people.

Stupid lizard king.

Queen Maeve laughed and flames on the candles on the

stone walls around the room danced back and forth.

She would never waste that much power on saving minions when she had plenty to spare.

Daegan had always been a fool blinded by pathetic emotions.

She would see the day he returned to TÅµr Medb and she forced his dragon back into the shape of a throne. Her throne.

He owed her more than two thousand years this time.

First, she'd deal with Daegan.

Then she'd check up on Cathbad, another thorn in her side.

The world would be a better place without those two active.

She waited patiently for the wall to locate the place she envisioned. But it only revealed a rich green forest covering the steep ascent above the houses. Where was that lizard king?

Fisting her hands, she shook them at the wall. "Where is he?" Still nothing. She screamed, rattling the tower. Candles toppled to the ground. Fire burst from all of them.

The tall doors to her private area blasted open. Her guards shouted, "My queen. What can we do?"

Her head warped and her voice dropped two octaves. "Get out of my sight."

The men vanished and the doors slammed shut.

She hated for anyone to see her lose control of her shape. At least Cathbad had not been present to harp on it. Grabbing her head, she closed her eyes and calmed down. The tower settled into a peaceful hum, still fueling the wall.

The flames sizzled to nothing. Candles floated back up to pockets carved out of the stone walls and flames appeared again.

When she opened her eyes, she placed her palms back in connection with the wall and asked specifically, "Show me Daegan of Treoir wherever he is in the human world."

Energy spun and flowed, but nothing appeared.

He wouldn't be dead. If he'd been killed, her wall would find him even if his body or dragon had died unless his body was heavily protected from view such as inside a crypt. She took a different approach and pictured the mountain where she'd last seen Daegan. "I wish to see the woman with Daegan of Treoir."

Still nothing.

Fisting her hand, she stopped short of slamming the wall with a blast of power. This had taken too much work and energy to destroy.

Queen Maeve fine-tuned her request once more. "I wish to see the woman of auburn hair who walked with Daegan of Treoir in Spain within the past day."

The wall began swirling again as if searching.

A woman's face appeared.

"There! Stop!" Queen Maeve grinned with satisfaction.

She floated back from the wall to observe the entire image as it finished taking shape.

The woman being shown ducked under some branches and disappeared from view somewhere the sun had not risen yet. Enough to see when the woman reappeared again evidently still in Spain. She stepped out from a dark area in the trees to an exposed place, turning slowly as if sweeping her gaze over the land and sea beyond.

Was she looking for Daegan?

Where was Daegan?

If that dragon shifter had been anywhere near this woman, the scrying wall would have found him.

Daegan was not *there*?

If her scrying did not produce a current image of him someplace, then he was not out in the open. He was either hiding somewhere she couldn't view, like Treoir realm, or ... had he been captured?

Could this be any better?

Floating back to the wall, Queen Maeve placed the palm of her hand close to the churning surface again and held very still.

Details of the location filled her mind.

Why did this woman interest Daegan? It didn't matter.

Queen Maeve had a plan for her.

CHAPTER 6

Hidden realm in Haida Gwaii Islands,
British Columbia

REESE BARELY MOVED HER EYELASHES, careful to peek slowly at her surroundings from where she lay facedown in ankle-high grass. Had she made it to the destination she'd targeted or gotten tossed into an unknown world?

She'd only traveled through space and time once before to reach the elusive raven god. If not for the medallion hanging from her neck on a black leather thong and her clutching the disk like her last cookie before facing death row, she wouldn't have made it here this time.

That did not mean she would be welcomed with a smile and open arms.

Showing up unannounced on Yáahl's doorstep, so to speak, could end in more bad ways than she could count.

She'd had no choice.

Hard to imagine how this mirrored the first time she'd met this raven god. A wise woman of the Haida tribe had reached out to the Yáahl, asking for his help. Reese had been ten years younger, terrified, but just as pregnant as she was right now.

Back then, the man she thought she loved had taken off like a scared rabbit when he heard her baby news. He'd paused long enough to admit he was married and would pay for getting rid of the baby.

She'd wanted to strangle him. She'd used his money to travel cross-country to the wise woman.

This time?

Quinn offered her everything she'd longed for last time. He loved her, wanted the baby, would put his life on the line to protect them.

She had never felt more cherished or broken-hearted at his admission.

She might not have the most screwed-up life, but she had to be in the running for that award.

Opening her eyes wider, she searched the space around her. A gentle mist rose from the lake with a waterfall cascading into the pool. Giant red cedar trees circled a clearing filled with ankle-high grass and wildflowers. She hadn't realized the raven god had such a green thumb. She didn't remember wildflowers last time. The dusty twilight hadn't changed as if he couldn't make up his mind between sunlight and dark.

When she inhaled a calming breath, the crisp smell of pine filled her lungs. Just another fabrication of this realm.

An idyllic setting if this place belonged to a fairy godfather, instead of a tyrant.

Rubbing the medallion, she lifted the onyx disk the size of a silver dollar into view. One side had a raven carving and the other side the sun and moon. See? That proved he couldn't make a decision between day and night.

None of this would have happened if a monster hadn't raped her mother.

The tribe booted out her mother for getting pregnant by a *thing*. Even when Reese returned, no one could tell her just what *thing* had fathered her.

He'd cursed Reese's chance of carrying a baby to term or having any hope for a normal life.

Hard to blame the tribe now that Reese had realized her full potential of being a demon magnet.

She'd been surprised when Yáahl had agreed to help her ten years ago. If she'd only known how he had his own agenda in every little thing he did.

Would it have changed anything had she known when she met him?

Probably not.

She'd wanted protection from demons while she carried her child. In the end, Yáahl fulfilled his part of the agreement. He'd kept Reese safe throughout her pregnancy. The minute she delivered, their deal ended along with her baby's life. She'd begged until she had no voice left from crying and pleading.

He'd simply said, "I do not interfere with the normal laws of life and death."

Total lie. He interfered anytime it suited him.

Yep, she and Yáahl had history, none of it pretty.

Wind ruffled the tall grass and gently moved petals on the wildflowers.

She listened. Nothing flying around, not a giant raven anyhow. Pushing up, she surveyed the landscape for crows, his snitches.

The light breeze flowed, which would normally be odd inside a mountain. No one could find Yáahl's realm hidden in a Mosquito Mountain peak off the western coast of Canada.

Time and space were relative here, moving with no regard for the human world.

Thunder rumbled overhead.

Was the egomaniac making a grand entrance?

Fog hovering above the lake dissipated. No animals made a sound. No birds chirped. Not even a crow caw. Where were his minions?

She held her breath, gripping the medallion in her hand the whole time. Everything might disappear if she released the disk.

The raven god should be here by now.

He knew everything that went on in his realm and in hers.

More thunder erupted. The world around her darkened to twilight just before night. Wind surged and whipped her hair across her face.

A large shadow crossed overhead, swooping back and forth, wings outstretched as a raven the size of a human circled. The bird glided down to the lake. A massive boulder rose in the center of the pool, changing from rough-cut stone to a glowing pearl-white platform as it surfaced. Energy swept through the air, blasting her hair back off her face when the giant raven landed.

It immediately shifted into a tall, dignified male dressed in a black tunic and matching slacks.

His sharp cheeks, teak-colored skin, blunt nose, and straight black hair apparently hadn't changed in thousands of years. Two bean-like dark eyes stared out from a face resembling the indigenous people who once resided all over this part of Alaska.

Yáahl appeared to be in his forties or fifties.

In truth, that raven god had been around as long as the mountain shielding his realm.

"What are you doing here, Reese?"

She went on high alert when he failed to address her with his usual, "Welcome, xahlk'uts'." She'd been annoyed at the porcupine reference every time in the past, but wished he'd opened with it this time.

Add that to his pinched expression and her stress level did a high jump.

No point in delaying the inevitable. "I've come to ask for your help again. I am—"

"Pregnant." He spoke the word with power of a shot being fired from a cannon.

Reese tensed, wary of this Yáahl, an angrier one than

she'd ever faced before. "Yes. You of all people should know this was not my intention. I took precautions, but ... it still happened. I know you won't save my baby, but I don't want to endanger Phoedra, her father, or their friends by remaining near them while pregnant."

"How noble of you." His sharp tone and caustic words slashed deep, cutting her breath off.

This attitude topped anything she'd ever heard from him.

They had sparred over the years, devolving into sniping arguments at times. He'd belittled and criticized her often, but she gave as good as she got.

Still, she did not know *this* mean-spirited raven god.

Scrubbing a hand over her face, she tried to figure out what was going on. "I don't understand, Yáahl. I get that you like to bust my chops for any perceived infraction, but why are you giving me a hard time about something I'm already sick over?"

"What makes you think I am here to fix your life every time you have a problem?"

"Wait a damn minute. I've been doing pretty freakin' good on my own. I don't run to you with every little issue. In fact, I think I've done well by Phoedra, and that doesn't mean I don't love her or think she's a burden. She's not. But you dropped me in the middle of all that crap and I fought my way out. So don't act like I'm some sniveling teenager coming here when I break a fingernail."

Her outburst appeared to have zero effect on him. "No, you are worse. You're an adult who has had time to handle her own life. You wanted the return of your powers. You have them. You wanted to live by your own rules. You are doing such. Have you ever considered you might have a destiny in life other than to be a victim of your own actions?"

What. The. Hell?

Crows fluttered into the area. Ah, his army of informants. Some settled in the trees behind her and around the lake. More circled above as if keeping guard over Yáahl.

Did they think *she* was a threat to him?

Their silence creeped her out more than their usual cawing.

Reese stood and clutched the medallion with one hand. Rubbing a thumb over the round disk had become her own version of worry beads. Now was not the time to quit.

She'd come here with a goal. If it meant sucking up to this raven god and biting her tongue from lashing out at him again, she'd do it.

Speaking in as pleasant a tone as she could muster, she asked, "Are you going to let me stay until I deliver the baby?"

"No. This is not a maternity ward."

How could he hurt her so badly now after all the times they'd argued? That was the difference today. Sure, they'd had some nasty arguments, but he usually trounced her ego. He had never really gouged her heart the way he was doing now.

Her soul whimpered with each verbal strike. She'd known him for ten years and just believed he would always be there, even when he ignored her.

He had never outright rejected her.

More crows filtered down from above. Some landed near her to stand still in the grass.

Tears burned her eyes. She had nothing left to lose. "Why, Yáahl? Why are you treating me this way after I did everything you've asked of me over the years? Just tell me that."

"Ah?" He arched a smooth black eyebrow. "So you wish to hear someone else's thoughts."

Hadn't she just said that? She waited in silence, which had always been more productive before when they hit an impasse.

Angling his head in an elegant bird-like manner, he stared down his nose at her. "I provided you a safe haven at one time. I never said this would be available a second time."

She couldn't argue that point and kept her mouth shut.

"Do you claim you want to keep this baby as you did the last one?"

Why would he pour salt in a wound that never healed? "Of course, I want this baby, but I was a teen the last time who hadn't accepted the curse. I know what's going to happen. I want the loss to be mine only."

"So the father of this child feels no loss?"

Just keep jabbing a knife in her heart. "Yes, he does, but I've told him the truth about not being able to save my ... our baby."

Yáahl lifted a shoulder in dismissal. "If you want to keep this baby, then show enough backbone to save its life."

She jerked back from the power behind that verbal slap. Tears leaked from her eyes. She couldn't catch her breath.

This damned raven god, who possessed the power to play with people's lives, had witnessed what she went through last time.

He didn't lift a feather to help.

Crows continued to find branches in the trees. More flew into the realm and joined the flock until the cedar trees showed more black than green.

Her voice dropped to a low, nasty sound. "How dare you say that to me? I *begged* you to save my baby last time, *begged* you to trade my life for my son." A knot of anguish thickened in her throat from just saying the word *son*. "I said I'd do anything if you'd save that child."

"Good news," he replied in a taunting voice. "You won't have to beg this time and I won't have to listen to you whine the entire time." Yáahl's arrogance knew no limit.

"You bastard. If I could have saved a baby, I would have saved the first one." She vibrated with so much pent-up fury.

Some of the crows lifted off and flew fast around her.

"I do not think you were capable of doing so ten years ago, but you might be today."

She held her arms out. "I am *still* a freaking demon magnet. I am *still* cursed. What is different now?"

"Everything."

"*Argh!* I don't understand you."

He admonished, "That is only because you *choose* not to understand. Just as you *choose* not to figure out why you can't carry a child to term. Stop waiting for some unknown force to show up and solve your problem. Whoever cares the most for your child is responsible for his chance at surviving."

"His?" Chills raced over her arms. She had refused to even think about the gender. To do that would have made this baby more real than the nightmare she faced.

A baby boy. Her heart cried.

She couldn't go through this again.

Yáahl released a stream of air coated with irritation. "As always, focusing on the wrong point."

That jab sounded more like the Yáahl she had always known.

Did he think she could save her baby? If so, why hadn't he said so sooner?

She knew the answer to that.

Yáahl lived to be confusing and infuriating.

Also, if he really thought she could save Quinn's baby, why not allow her to stay here to be protected from demons during her pregnancy?

Yáahl had sucked her in again and she'd taken the bait.

He knew she couldn't birth a live baby.

Shaking her head at her foolishness for allowing him to

screw with her, she said, "Some things might change, but not you, Yáahl. You're still messing with my head the way you have for the last ten years." She clenched the medallion, her hand trembling.

Yáahl's gaze zeroed in on her fingers. His conversational voice dropped to bastard-mean again. "I gave you that medallion in case *Phoedra* needed anything, not for *you* to use at any whim."

Reese had taken in more than she could handle in twenty-four hours. If he discounted her worry over her baby one more time, she might use this medallion to teleport to his rock dais and rip out his throat.

He held the power in his hands to save an infant.

Now he accused her of showing up on a whim?

Eyes dark and fierce, he waved a hand in the direction of crows on his right.

That group took to the air, swarming back and forth, then flying in a circle as they descended around Reese. They closed in on her until she could see the tiny holes in their beaks.

She waved her hands back and forth, protecting her head, then slapped her hands over her eyes and cheeks.

No beak touched her, but she felt something bump her back and tug on the leather cord.

The cord fell loose, taking the medallion with it.

She peeked out as one crow flew away with the medallion in its beak and the leather cord trailing. That one flew over Yáahl, dropping the medallion in the raven god's open palm.

Yáahl closed his hand, then reopened it.

No medallion.

The crows returned to their perches.

Reese ran both hands over her hair, dragging her fingers back and forth in an effort to shed her anger. She took a deep breath and faced Yáahl again. "I would have handed the medallion to you had you asked."

"I saved you the trouble," he quipped, so full of himself.

She reminded him, "I won't have that medallion if Phoedra needs your help."

"You're not with her right now as it is, plus she is in a protected realm. Her father will not bring her back to the human world until he believes it is safe for her. So you see, she has far more protection than you could offer even with the medallion."

Yáahl had always been a master at shredding her ego.

His miserable minion crew snooped on everyone who interested Yáahl, then reported to him.

Lifting her hands up in surrender, Reese said, "Fine. You don't want me here. If you'll send me to San Diego, I can probably find a safe place to hide in the desert until the time comes. I still have some contacts there."

"You came here uninvited. You can find your own way home."

Her skin pebbled with the threat in his voice. "What does that mean? You're going to drop me on the side of a mountain with me pregnant and being a walking de-mon-magnet?"

"I would not do that to the Haida tribes."

"Then where are you—"

Wind spun up fast and turbulent.

Crows took to the air, cawing loudly.

All of them joined the wind, circling the lake, and blur-ring into a black fog hiding Yáahl from view.

She shouted louder. "*Where are you sending me?*"

Cawing and the wailing wind became deafening. She covered her ears. Her body flew up into the crow storm. Panic ripped through her chest. She'd never made him this angry. Where would she end up? Terror of the unknown had her gasping for air.

Her chest pulled one way and her limbs yanked back in

the other direction.

She dragged her arms in to wrap her stomach and protect her baby.

Then she flew like a tornado, her body spinning wildly in a gulf of screaming madness.

CHAPTER 7

"DRAGON KING!"

Daegan pushed one eye open. His stiff body leaned against the bars where he'd fallen onto one shoulder. Agonizing pain sent a shudder through him.

Joavan poured liquid from a pottery jug onto a folded square of cloth. "I do not know if this will work until we test a spot on your skin."

Moving one eye to Joavan, Daegan stared hard.

"I understand your hesitation, dragon king, but I have no reason to harm you and every reason to help you."

Daegan couldn't move his jaws. His voice came out rough as a demon's. "Do it."

Remaining back from the bars, Joavan flipped the rag toward Daegan. The cloth floated through the bars and landed on his arm, then coiled around and slid from shoulder to hand leaving a wet path behind.

Daegan's skin burned as if bathed in fire ants.

His taut muscles bulged.

Tears stung his eyes, but he slammed them shut.

Dragging in a desperate breath, Daegan hissed out, "Throat."

A wet cloth wrapped Daegan's throat and seared it just as much. With one hideous wipe around his neck, the cloth then washed the solvent over his shoulder blades.

It felt as if he'd shoved a hornet's nest onto his throat. Fire would not harm him, but this burning blazed against his skin.

Ruadh roared and battered his insides to get out. His dragon raged against the agony Daegan's human form suffered, but Ruadh would not shift if he thought it would kill Daegan.

If one died, they both died. Neither would intentionally force that fate on the other.

Finally ... the pain began to lessen.

Daegan drew in a gulp of air, then coughed it out. He pulled in air again and again, breathing as much as his lungs would allow for now. His right arm, which had been as unyielding as an oak tree, now bent forward at the elbow. The muscles moved freely. He lowered his chin to watch his bloody fingers flex and the cracks begin to heal.

The medicine worked.

Joavan lowered the jug and took a step back, waiting. The Faetheen held Daegan's life in his hands, because the coating still on his body began feathering down his arm again.

Swallowing hard against his thick throat, Daegan found hope in being able to negotiate. "Ya have yet to tell me what ya want?"

"My family lost everything when they walked away from *Tír na nÓg*. They created a safe haven for those who were not pure of blood and those who wished to live out from beneath the powerful Fae leaders. I am also of mixed blood and I want only to protect my people. I will only share what I consider necessary to save my people. One who lived amongst us was cast out for practicing dark majik. He was believed to be of druid and Fae blood, but he had no Fae blood. He snuck in and lived for many generations, never taking a mate honestly, only stealing a woman's virtue without honor. He never showed a true interest in our people. He could have continued that way for even longer had he not stolen a treasure. I waited a long time to mate and that may have slipped through my fingers with this theft, but more than that I must protect my people. Simply put, if I fail ..."

"If ya fail then what?" Daegan could understand the depth of the Faetheen's longing more than most. Failure to protect those who needed you most crushed a person's soul.

"I have shared more than enough. Suffice to say it is extremely important to return that amulet."

"Ya are sure this druid is at fault?"

Joavan smiled sadly. "I had a sister who was born of a different father, but she was all to me. The Faetheen do not have many children. Those of us in our world have even less children as our small community offers fewer chances for mating. Females are rare and special." He held himself erect, his eyes darkened to the color of deep water. "The night after this druid was cast out of our world, my sister died of a sudden illness. I believe he poisoned her to draw me away from my duty. I will find the treasure and return it, hopefully with the thief as well so he might face judgement."

This being could have said a lot of things which would not have had the impact of losing family. Daegan asked, "Why did the dark druid attack your sister?"

"This druid hated me. We were always in conflict, but I never thought he would harm any of our females. A traitor helped him gain entrance again after being cast out and to steal the amulet at a moment when all fingers would point only at me for dereliction of duty."

"Why would one of yours do this to ya?"

Joavan sounded bitter when he explained, "There are many reasons why some become traitors in any society. I do not wish to delve into those details."

"I would not deal well with anyone who betrayed me in such a way."

Joavan's lips curved in an unhappy smile. "The traitor

has paid for her part in all this."

Daegan could accept what Joavan had shared, but the Faetheen kept dancing around explaining what treasure was taken. "What is in this liquid?"

Had relief flickered through Joavan's gaze? Hard to tell with any kind of Fae, masters of facial expressions. "We have an elder healer who has lived far longer than many of my kind. He explained the liquid comes from a plant which grows only in our world. I have enough in this jug to remove the coating on your body. The healer warned me to use only a little at a time to avoid injuring your skin or body. This can burn severely if too much is applied."

Daegan had delayed this decision as long as he could. He believed Joavan had given him truth or as much truth as one of his kind would divulge. Daegan had to escape and get back to Casidhe while not dragging his people into whatever commitment he made.

He again considered bartering to help Casidhe first, but tossed that aside just as quickly. Daegan would trust her on her own before allowing any unknown being to catch Casidhe in a vulnerable position

Every second he spent delaying would cost him more effort to free his body from the hard-shell coating. Would the liquid have any effect on the venom still sliding through his body? Probably not.

Daegan took joy in each breath he drew, but pain still clawed his skin. "I will agree to go with ya to find this druid and regain the treasure. What exactly is the item we are huntin'?"

A tiny cheek muscle moved in Joavan's smooth skin. He held himself very still. "When we have a final agreement, I will share more details."

"How will we find this druid?"

"I know how to find him."

Daegan considered his reply. "Then what has prevented

ya from goin' after the treasure before now?"

"I have druid blood as well as that of the Fae. He will know the minute I am close to him. He will recognize my cloaking. I need someone who can get close enough to remove the ... treasure."

Daegan had a feeling they were talking about something a person held or wore. "Why a dragon shifter?"

The muscle stopped twitching, but suspicion glided through the Fae's expression. "We may not be able to leave with the treasure unless he dies first."

"Ah. Ya want someone to kill him."

Joavan shrugged. "I am not going with that intention, but I am also not opposed to his death. We will have only one chance to retrieve what he stole. For that reason, I require one with your skills and gifts."

Daegan decided to keep his lack of teleporting to himself for now. More discussion weakened his position until he could stand strong. "I give ya my word to help ya, but only if ya can free me quickly." Daegan would be shocked if Joavan asked for more than his word.

Supernatural beings of power lived and died by their honor.

Joavan pinched his chin with his thumb and finger, remaining in a thoughtful pose for several seconds. Lowering his hand, he gave a brief nod again. "I agree, but I am not able to open your cell door immediately. I looped a cloth around the bars to close it and the door locks on its own. I cannot pass through the iron bars around your area without harming myself, but I can send the jug into your cell with cloths for you to continue cleaning off the coating. One of the cloths is long enough to reach around you."
He held the jug and a stack of folded material in his two palms until they turned into a ball of sparkling lights that reshaped and flowed into Daegan's cell.

When the sparkling ball stopped inside the bars, it reformed into a wooden bucket with two hooks to hang from a horizontal bar at chest height. Four different lengths of yellow cloths formed and draped along each side of the bucket, one hanging to the floor.

Joavan held a thick rag he produced from nowhere. "I will send this one to clean the arm twisted behind your back. You will be free to use both hands."

Daegan nodded.

The rag drifted into his cell, dipped into the bucket, then floated to him and coiled around his left arm. Liquid fire wiped around and all the way down to his wrist and hand. He clenched this hand into a fist, fighting the urge to throw up or shout at the agonizing stinging.

Now that he could watch the solution working, it bubbled and sizzled.

Thankfully, that misery passed just as quickly. His body must be becoming numb to the pain.

Daegan pulled his left arm around and put a hand on the horizontal bar, pushing himself upright. He lifted the hand to his face, wiggling his fingers. "Thank ya, Joavan, but ya have yet to explain the part about my escape."

"I intended to do so," Joavan said. "No one else can see the pouch of liquid and cloths in your cell except us. I will not return immediately, because I require a little time to make arrangements for your escape. I can free you in four, maybe five hours. I know you wish to leave now, and I wish the same, but both of our lives will be far simpler if you allow me to arrange for you to be moved out of this cell. Freeing you is not as complicated when you are no longer behind iron bars."

"Four to five hours? I left someone hidden before I was captured, who waits for me to return."

Shimmering blue-green eyes lightened with interest. "Tell me who it is and where to hunt. I will find this person for you."

Daegan would not give Joavan one more thing to hold as hostage. Casidhe was resilient. She would be worried when he didn't return immediately, but she would wait. He hoped.

"No. This shall wait a few hours," Daegan groused.

"Very well, I will be off so I may return sooner. I am taking your word to mean you will not abandon our agreement the minute I free you."

"My word is my bond, Joavan. If ya free me and can take me to this druid's lair, I shall rescue your treasure."

Joavan smiled with a look of victory. His body glowed as a diamond struck by sunlight. He lifted two fingers and vanished.

Daegan hurried as much as he could to wipe the stinging liquid over his skin, but it took time. Every new patch he cleaned allowed him more flexibility and movement. He'd feared the cleaning liquid might run out, but the level in the bucket remained the same no matter how many rags he dredged through it.

He dropped his jeans to wipe his skin from feet to just above his knees and thanked the gods that fibrous coating had not climbed high enough to reach his genitals.

Pulling the jeans back on, he still had to remove more coating from his back to be able to twist and flex his body.

To maybe even shift into his dragon.

Before he left, Joavan could have used his majik to clean Daegan's back just as he had his arms. His failure to do so had not been an oversight, but intentional.

That Faetheen wanted to keep Daegan dependent upon him for as long as possible. Daegan would not hold such a sound strategy against Joavan. He would have done the same.

But that did not mean Daegan had any intention of waiting until Joavan returned to finish freeing his body.

He would make good on his promise to help the Faetheen, but not until after he rescued Casidhe. It felt as if they'd been apart an eternity. He shouldn't long for a woman this way, not when he could not follow through on his interest. He had to stop the Imortiks and now he had to hunt a druid.

More than all that, wanting Casidhe pricked his conscience. He had no intention of leading on Casidhe only to walk away when they finished finding the grimoire volumes.

Just thinking about leaving her dug around in his heart with sharp claws. He didn't want to walk away.

Too much venom and satyr spit had rattled his mind.

Reaching for the long cloth, he tried to wipe the dry cloth across his back just to see how much skin he could clean.

As he'd suspected, the material would not reach all the contours of his body. He tied the additional rags around the middle of the long strip of material in thick knots. He ran that over his body and felt satisfied it would work.

Soaking the knots in the bucket, he prepared for the worst pain yet.

As appreciative as he was to have Joavan's help, Daegan hoped to free his skin from this binding and not wait four or five hours to escape this cell. If the Imortik venom allowed him to teleport, he could reach Casidhe.

All of that depended on how well this next step went.

He lay on his stomach and apologized to Ruadh for what he was about to do.

With his arms stretched out in front of him and each end of the wet material held tight in his hands, he flipped the laden cloth onto his back, changed his grip, and pulled hard, dragging the saturated cloth from neck to waist.

Liquid flooded his back and sizzled.

Smoke steamed off of him and clouded the air.

He howled at his skin being stripped off.

CHAPTER 8

CATHBAD STROLLED OVER THE GENTLY arched mound of Newgrange in County Meath. He'd chosen this ancient location to face off with Sen so he could draw on Newgrange's power.

No one ignored Loki's call to attend a Tribunal.

Cathbad had. Too many possible traps there. Refusing to answer telepathically or show up meant the Tribunal would send their enforcer, Sen, liaison between supernatural beings and VIPER.

As a demigod, Sen believed himself above all except the Tribunal gods and goddesses.

To underestimate Cathbad would be Sen's last mistake.

Cathbad paused to observe humans milling around below.

Those inferior beings would become overly upset if they could see him walking on top of a structure older than Stonehenge. Many of them had likely traveled across the world to view this, the stones ringing the mound and megalithic art.

They could not see his cloaked presence.

Entering through the east opening, humans toured the passage tomb, but for what reason he had no idea. Who among them could appreciate the power thrumming through this giant mound? They had not believed in supernatural beings until Daegan exposed himself and the Beladors. From what Cathbad had seen of humans in Atlanta, they raced around either trying to photograph a nonhuman or kill one as a trophy.

So far, he'd heard of no trophy captures, but a number of missing citizens.

None of the humans had a clue of the dangerous beings they dared to poke. They saw supernaturals as an amusement, just as those below entering Newgrange found this powerful mound an entertainment attraction.

Each December, a lucky few entered ahead of the winter solstice to stand in the passage where they could observe sunlight shooting through the roof box on the eastern side. Illuminating the entire chamber with the brilliant display had awed many over the centuries, but the power of that light served only a few.

He'd been a recipient at one time.

That had been prior to joining the dark druids.

No regrets.

Someone below shouted at another person. A rude young man had walked in front of a couple being photographed.

Cathbad sighed. What was taking Sen so long?

That liaison normally teleported out immediately to grab anyone the Tribunal wanted. Loki had called to Cathbad quite a while back. Plenty of time had passed for Sen to arrive.

Different trios of gods and goddesses aligned with VIPER took turns overseeing judgement in Tribunals, but Loki had been hanging around for quite a while now.

He would not be happy to be ignored by a druid.

That trickster god never made requests.

Thus the reason Cathbad teleported away from his secret cavern in the Himalayas to protect that location and confront Sen here.

He could dodge Loki only so long, but what was up?

Not that Cathbad feared the god, at least not if he faced Loki alone, but he had too much going on to become entangled in whatever conflict Daegan had started.

Daegan demanding to have Tristan returned could be the only reason Loki had reached out to Cathbad about attending. Even though Tristan had escaped the cavern, Cathbad did not want to be dragged into a conversation, which would inevitably result in him also admitting he'd kept an ice dragon alive for all these centuries. Lying in a Tribunal meeting had devastating results.

Neither did he wish to attend a Tribunal with Queen Maeve present. He had no doubt she'd also be called in. Unfortunately, all of the supernatural world tied them together.

That would change in the near future.

Cathbad sighed hard and scratched the back of his neck. He had no patience for standing still. He'd allowed Sen more than enough time to show up. Time to abandon the confrontation. If Loki called him once more, which would be to determine Cathbad's location, Cathbad would have to consider the danger of Loki coming himself.

He could not afford to lose more time by standing here when he had to find Brynhild.

Once he dropped the cloaking, he teleported at the same instant to his mountain cavern in the Himalayas. Snow and a brisk wind slapped him as soon as he arrived on the ledge leading to the entrance. With the protective ward he'd created long ago now gone, the cave where he'd kept Brynhild for two thousand years had only a boulder blocking the opening.

Flicking a finger slowly, the boulder rolled aside.

He entered carefully, searching the soaring ceiling and every dark corner for the crazy female dragon shifter who might be hiding, ready to attack him.

Nothing had changed. Dampness clung to the walls where water drizzled down. Chunks of ice floated in the wide pond he had to walk around to reach the golden pile Brynhild had left behind.

She would be back for her hoard.

She was possessive and self-centered, if anything.

Admirable qualities, in his mind.

But she had not returned to take even one piece yet. Her shield still stood in warning to not touch her gold and other treasure.

Where was she? What prevented her from returning to claim her booty? The sooner she did, the sooner they could come to some agreement.

Once she flew away with a specific tray marked with her family coat of arms, he'd be able to track her by the spell he'd placed upon that serving dish. If he knew anything about that ice dragon, she would leave nothing behind that had belonged to her family.

He glanced around, confirming every part of the cavern appeared unchanged.

No point in staying.

With the ward down, Loki's telepathic voice came through clearly. *Where are you, Cathbad? I do not usually make two calls to anyone. You test my patience, of which I have none.*

Cathbad considered his options.

Loki had not come for him or sent Sen. Why not?

He didn't know, but he would play along to find out more. Cathbad replied, *Ya called before? I have just left a warded environment.*

Careful, druid. You are safe from the Tribunal consequence of glowing red if you lie, but you can be asked these same questions once here.

I assure ya I have been quite busy, Loki. If ya called out to me before now, why have ya not sent Sen?

Loki's silence held a disturbing undertone. *Sen was attacked by an Imortik. Healers are treating him.*

That surprised Cathbad. *How unfortunate for Sen. Have ya chosen a new liaison?*

No. Sen will return soon. His body was not overtaken, just injected with venom from more than one claw.

Trying to get ahead of this conversation and act as if he had no idea why the Tribunal would be calling him in, Cathbad asked, *Does this have anythin' to do with Queen Maeve?*

Why?

Loki would be excellent at playing cards. His voice gave away nothing.

Now was the time to go on offense. Ramping up some indignation for his voice, Cathbad said, *Do not take offense as my words are not intended to offend any of ya on the Tribunal at this moment, but I have no desire to attend a meeting where Queen Maeve is present. I do realize we are considered a partnership, which we had at one time, but it has been strained lately due to her loss of control. I prefer to appear when she is not present and not be cast into her corner simply due to our prior arrangement. I wish to speak for myself only.*

Loki's pissed voice barreled through the connection. *You two act like children.*

Cathbad did not have to fake outrage. He would not be lumped in with Queen Maeve's antics. He pushed power right back through the connection. *Ya hold me guilty by association whenever she loses control. We are not on the best of terms at the moment. I shall come when she is not there.*

Loki said, *I will deal with her first. When I call you again, I will not discuss another delay.*

Cathbad had to find Brynhild and Casidhe Luigsech before he got yanked into a Tribunal meeting.

That meant he'd have to risk entering the TÅμr Medb realm again to access Queen Maeve's scrying wall. She'd tried to kill him last time.

She'd found it amusing.

He'd drag her death out longer when the time came.

This time, he'd teleport into his library and hope she had not set a trap there for him. If he made it to that point, he'd cloak himself and enter Queen Maeve's private chamber undetected.

Women were creating unnecessary turbulence in his simple plans.

Cathbad still intended to partner with Brynhild, but once she served her purpose he could see no reason to allow that dragon to continue living as he once had intended. Hard to imagine, but someone like Daegan might mate with her and fill the world with more dragons.

No, she had to go as soon as he dealt with Daegan.

When his teleporting ended, he stood in his personal chamber in TÅµr Medb, which included a library built over many thousands of years. Though he had to admit Queen Maeve possessed a greater one of her own. His gaze landed on the empty spot where he'd withdrawn the book of *Before Ainvar* and taken it to the Luigsech woman.

Had she read the secret passage he'd warned her to not touch until he could be there to observe her read the text?

He'd find out as soon as he located her and the book.

When he did face her, she had better produce that book immediately and undamaged. Some writings were worth killing to protect.

He stood very still.

What was that odd pulsing surge he felt surrounding him?

Before he headed into the open areas of TÅµr Medb, he reached out with his senses. The tower seemed to be generating energy at a higher rate than normal. Had Queen Maeve harmed the realm?

He closed his eyes and clamped a hand on his forehead. The woman should be put in a spelled straitjacket.

Then dropped into an active volcano.

After he removed her head.

Now he felt better. He cloaked his presence and exited his chamber. Little activity stirred in the long halls leading to her chamber, but that was not unusual.

He wove his way slowly across the black marble four-foot-square tiles. Had she been decorating? He moved from one hall to the next until he reached the passage four-arm-lengths wide with a high arching ceiling. As he neared the guards always stationed on each side of the tall doors to Queen Maeve's chamber, he paused.

Neither guard moved, but they could not see him cloaked.

Cathbad listened for any sound from her chamber. Last time, she'd been shrieking at the top of her lungs. He sent a kinetic tick sound at the bottom of the doors.

Both guards jumped, looked at each other, then squatted with their ears against the door.

The one on the left spoke in a hushed voice. "I don't think she's back. She said not to let anyone in while she was gone."

The other one shrugged and whispered, "I'm not trusting anything. Let's get back in position and be ready for her just in case she pops in unexpectedly."

"Good point."

Both men pushed up straight and returned to imitating statues with swords.

Cathbad never trusted teleporting while cloaked. He knew of others who had serious mishaps and did not want to appear in her chamber lacking his full ability to protect himself. He backtracked to the last corner where no one saw him, dropped his cloaking and teleported.

When he reappeared in her private chamber, he stood in the farthest corner from her scrying wall. He started to cloak himself, then realized he was indeed alone.

Smiling, he walked across the room to where her new

scrying wall swirled with energy and levitated up to face the center.

When had this wall become usable?

It had to be recently or she would have shown up at the cavern if she'd used it to track him. Clamping his hands together, a thrill of discovery rushed through his blood.

As did a concern that she might have set a trap here for him. She would do that. Create a scrying surface with her power, then the minute he made a wrong move the wall would lock him in place.

He scratched his chin, hesitating to break a simple rule he'd lived by for many thousand years.

Never attack any being he did not know for sure he could conquer.

In this case, never touch something of Queen Maeve's if he did not know for sure he could survive the tampering.

Energy surged around the room again.

As it did, he watched a sizzle slide across the stone wall surfaces toward her scrying wall. Candle flames surged and danced until the sizzle passed, then the flames returned to normal.

When the crackle of energy reached the scrying wall, the swirling fog covering the viewing area spun faster.

His mouth dropped open.

She wouldn't have, would she?

Few things ever raised his pulse, but his heart suddenly beat twice as fast. He lifted a hand, extending it to the swirling energy, closer and closer until ... his fingertips touched the scrying wall.

Power burst away in every direction, but without making a sound.

He grinned at the gift that foolish woman had left him.

She'd powered the wall with ... he sniffed. Noirre majik and TÅµr Medb's energy.

Had she forgotten how he helped create this realm?

While doing so, he loaded the realm with his power so he could never be denied entry. She so rarely paid attention at all he'd done, and quickly claimed credit for everything here. After so many years, she'd forgotten and actually believed this realm belonged to only her.

Cathbad had never been so thankful for her narcissism and overblown ego.

He flattened his palm and laid it gently into the moving energy. "Hello, there."

The energy slowed as it surrounded his hand and ran up his arm to his shoulder, playful as a puppy excited for attention from its owner.

Foolish, foolish queen.

He stroked the scrying wall and smiled.

CHAPTER 9

BRYNHILD HAD PUSHED HER CLOAKING and her dragon as far as she could. To hide them required a steady flow of energy.

Her dragon had found a pasture with a large herd of cows to feed upon twice already and turned in that direction now. Might as well. She had to make plans soon to do more than glide through the sky all day and night.

She tired of flying while invisible.

Nothing would replace the feel of flying freely with her brothers and sister. Five dragons flying together brought villagers running from their cottages to wave and smile. Children shouted and raced after them, unable to remain shadowed by the quickly moving clan of dragons.

She loved the ability to cloak, but no one saw her magnificent dragon and watched in awe.

No one feared her.

The ice dragons had been loved.

Her father and mother had been admired for the powerful dragon dynasty.

That had been when dragon families respected each other. Her world had been perfect before Daegan of Treoir destroyed it. First he insulted her family by refusing to take her as a mate, then he became greedy, attacking dragon houses to start the Dragani War.

He had the most powerful dragon.

Why couldn't that have been enough?

No one knew she existed today, except that miserable

druid Cathbad and the disgusting red dragon.

She'd had her chance to destroy Daegan at the cliffs, and should have. That fool dared to insinuate they could mate now?

As if she'd have babies for a cruel dragon shifter?

Still, why had Daegan spared her life? She'd been very clear about killing him.

What game could he be playing today after what he'd done to her family and all the dragon families so long ago?

Her dragon turned toward the pasture in the distance, but kept flying at a leisurely pace.

Feeding had not been an issue, but she had nowhere to hide her dragon at night, nowhere she trusted to stay in human form.

Because of Daegan, she had no family, no friends, no home.

She had lived when all others in her family had died. Could anything in life be more cruel?

Men were cruel beasts.

Daegan had acted so nice to her. As if he had done her no harm. Stupid dragon shifter must have lost his mind after so many centuries imprisoned at TÅµr Medb. She'd heard the crazy queen had used majik to change Daegan's dragon into the shape of a throne.

That had been funny long ago. Brynhild and her siblings lifted mugs of ale to cheer Daegan's demise. Her family had been alive then. She'd thought the Dragani War would end with the red dragon captured.

But no. Daegan's reach had been far and wide.

Brynhild's dragon angled downward as they approached the large pasture with white-and-black spotted cows.

She should burn this land and turn more people against Daegan.

The times she'd pretended to be the red dragon, Cathbad had ridden on her dragon's back to use a majik glamour, altering the color of her dragon to a red shimmer. Humans were stupid. They could not tell the difference between her glamour and the real red dragon.

She'd burned another place on her own last night. Strange gray structures. Her ability to shoot fire was limited. When she blew fire that time, the place exploded. Her dragon had soared quickly out of harm's way, but Brynhild enjoyed the moment of freedom from her anger.

As her dragon descended for a meal, Brynhild remained quiet. She would have to make a plan tonight. Her dragon snatched up a noisy cow then flapped hard, turning in a circle to land farther up the hill where she would enjoy her feast.

Once the cow stopped mooing insanely it would be pleasant.

Just as her dragon straightened out, a whistling sound came from the ground on her left.

Fly up! Brynhild shouted telepathically to her dragon who dropped the cow and shoved her wings hard.

The cow exploded into tiny pieces. Some of the blood hit her dragon's tail and back legs.

She lost her cloaking.

Another whistle came from the same spot.

Her dragon swung her big head around to see something flying up at them.

Brynhild shouted to her dragon, *Down!*

Her dragon turned head down and folded its wings.

But whatever hit the cow, caught her dragon across the wing, burning and breaking bones. They went cartwheeling down.

When her dragon opened both wings, one flapped like a shirt hung on a line to dry.

Just before hitting the trees, Brynhild ordered, *Change back now!*

Shifted into her human form and armored only on her

lower half, Brynhild wrapped her good arm across her chest and tucked her head. Her body smacked into the trees that lashed her. She cried out in pain. Broken branches cut any exposed skin.

Her skin burned with every wound.

Then she hit the ground hard and grabbed her chest. Breathing was impossible. Sucking in one breath after another hurt so bad. But she couldn't remain there with someone hunting her dragon.

When she tried to stand, her left arm screamed in agony.

Get up and move, she ordered herself silently.

Rolling over shot pain everywhere and brought tears to her eyes. She heaved hard, dragging air in. Had to get up. Had to get moving.

Her dragon would have been far more damaged.

Healing the human body had always been quicker, but great balls of Arrius, she hurt. The ancient dragon had met his demise long before she was born and he'd been a monster.

Someone shouted and dogs barked. Not close, but not far enough away. She laid there, asking her dragon to send energy to her, but she had to straighten her arm. If not, she'd have to break the bone again later if she allowed it to heal crooked.

Not doing that.

She'd made up her mind as a child to heal any broken bones immediately no matter the pain.

When she could breathe better, she used her good arm to push up to her knees. Another couple breaths and she made it to her feet.

The voices and dog barking grew louder.

Stupid humans hunted a dragon.

She searched the ground for fallen tree limbs and found a fairly straight one the length of her arm. This one would be thick enough to work. After a deep breath, she pushed her arm flat against the closest tree trunk and shoved the tree limb against her arm.

Jaws locked, she kept her scream of pain inside and grasped her left wrist against the long piece of wood. With both gripped, she blasted ice over her arm and the limb, stopping at her wrist.

With her arm secured, she started walking with no idea where she headed, just away from the sound of men and dogs. She needed to eat a meal and shift to heal her arm.

Her dragon generated energy, pushing what she could through their body. Cuts on her face and body began to heal. Her hair felt like a squirrel nest, but she could not waste any power for that or clothes.

She would never admit to Cathbad that he had been correct, but she saw the value in learning how to meld into this new human world.

First, she'd need somewhere for her dragon to rest.

That would not happen if the hunters caught her before her arm healed. She could not shift into her dragon until she broke the ice wrapping.

She should not be fighting for her life against humans with powerful weapons. Daegan had warned her.

That did not make him her friend any more than that miserable druid. Thinking of Cathbad, she scowled under her breath. He lied about what happened during the attack on her father's castle and how he'd taken her to keep safe. She did not believe his accounting.

Cathbad had tricked her somehow and shoved her into a frozen pond for two thousand years.

Two. Thousand. Years.

Only to be stuck here with no family and humans able to kill a dragon.

To be alone with no family. No one.

Angry tears rolled down her face. When they hit the ground, ice formed beneath her steps.

She would see Cathbad again. When she did, she would convince him they could be allies. That she now understood what he'd been trying to teach her.

She would become the charmer, the manipulator.

Then she'd kill him for what he had done to her.

CHAPTER 10

PAIN STABBED DAEGAN'S BRAIN. HIS back throbbed and burned as if he'd doused it with acid.

Bile rushed up his throat. Breathing in fast gulps of air, he slowly opened his eyes.

He still lay on his stomach. How long had he been out?

Sweat poured down his face and dripped off his nose on the floor. He lifted his chin off the floor. No one here. Testing his arms, he pulled them forward to cross and prop his chin on.

He'd only thought the first treatments of that liquid had been painful. He couldn't describe the torture he'd put his back through. Nothing he or Joavan had done earlier compared to soaking his skin with that liquid and allowing it to remain pooled on his back.

He inhaled another ragged breath, glad he could still breathe at all. In fact, his chest moved easily. The smell of burned flesh sickened him.

What had he done?

Was there any skin left on his back?

Ruadh spoke to him. *The skin peeled off. I have been healing you.*

That meant his dragon had suffered as well. *I am sorry, Ruadh.*

I am not.

Why? Daegan pushed higher off the ground, stopping short at the sharp pain of moving his back muscles.

Ruadh explained, *We will be free to shift soon.*

Moving gingerly, Daegan struggled until he stood and leaned a hand against a horizontal bar.

When he could manage to test his reach, he moved his free arm around to touch his lower back and flinched. His fingers met ragged skin.

That liquid should be called Hell On Earth.

Did he have use of any powers?

He called telepathically to Tzader. *This is Daegan. Do ya hear me?*

No reply.

What about this room and underground location prevented him from reaching anyone in the Beladors? Or was Joavan behind keeping him isolated from his people?

Ruadh suggested, *Try to teleport.*

Daegan gathered his strength, taking his time to even out his breathing. Without any idea what was beyond the hallway outside his cell except an elevator, he attempted to teleport a hundred feet away to the end of the hallway.

He made it over halfway down the hall and reappeared. Teleporting had come up short and still took too long. Damn Imortik venom in his body.

The elevator motor began humming in the distance. Without keen hearing, Daegan would have missed the noise.

Hell. He teleported back and reappeared inside the enclosure, breathing hard at the energy that had taken.

Four men appeared at the end of the hall, heading his way. All wore black uniforms and each one held a personal weapon Tristan would call a small cannon.

None resembled Joavan's human image.

What was going on? Were these humans taking him somewhere now? Was this part of Joavan's plan?

All four stopped as one unit. The tallest had black hair cut short on the sides, a hooked nose, and flashed a surprised look at Daegan's hands. "Where are your chains?"

Daegan stared ahead, showing no sign of acknowledging the man's words.

That one turned to his left. "Who delivered the prisoner here, Croy?"

Croy pulled out his mobile phone, stared at it a minute, then said, "Uhm, it shows that *you* did, sir."

"*No, I did not!*" his leader shouted, clearly perplexed. "Review the video files for this cell once we deliver him. I want a name." Turning back to Daegan, the leader's gaze darkened with revulsion. "I don't care if you understand me or not. If you attack any of us, we will execute the shoot-to-kill order currently in force on you. We're taking you upstairs. Someone is here to see you."

When one of the men opened the door, Daegan kept his eyes ahead, not taking in the mess he'd made with rags or the bucket still hanging on the inside of the bars.

Joavan had said no one could see any of it except the two of them, which appeared to be true.

Daegan waited until one of the men gave him a universal hand signal to follow, then he stepped out of the cell and walked in the middle of the four.

These men were all human.

Just teleporting a short distance had boosted his confidence. He would find a way to escape now, Joavan or no Joavan. Once he did, Daegan was done with taking orders from anyone.

Hope flooded him with thoughts of his next steps. Would he be able to teleport once above ground, if that was their destination?

On the other hand, what if the person waiting to speak with him was Joavan in human form? That Faetheen might have taken the image of a superior officer who could simply walk out of the building with Daegan. Less chance of harming a human or himself if that happened.

He had to wait to see how this played out.

Ruadh silently offered, *We could shift and fight.*

Daegan sent back, *Their firepower is great. They would turn all of it on ya. I wish to escape without bloodshed, if possible.*

He entered the elevator plenty large enough for all of them as the elevator climbed slowly. When the doors opened again, the ride had not taken as long as the one to the underground cell. Daegan paid attention to the time required to make the trip up. He'd counted to himself during his first descent underground. When the elevator ceased moving, he doubted they had reached the surface level.

Croy and another man took the lead. Daegan fell in behind them with the other two following again. He needed a plan of action if the person waiting on him was an enemy. His only option would be to take down everyone, including the guards, and hope to discern the correct key to activate the elevator and reach street level.

That plan offered too many ways to fail.

Daegan's bare feet walked quietly over the sterile gray-and-black-speckled tile floor. Pale-gray walls on each side had an occasional panel the size of his hand next to a door with buttons, but little else. No decorative pictures or mirrors, nothing like the office buildings in Atlanta.

Of course, most of those were above ground.

Based upon what he'd learned of the world in the current era, this place reminded him of human prisons.

How far above would the next floor be and would that offer an escape to the street level?

Not yet. He'd have to leave that method of escape as his last option.

One guard whispered to his friend, "Did you see his back before he was taken to the holding cell?"

"Yes. His back had been scratched up some. Sure as hell hadn't looked like he'd rolled in hot coals. Wonder what happened to him down there and how'd he get his cuffs off?" the other guy mused.

While they were busy observing him, Daegan called out telepathically again, *This is Daegan. Do ya hear me?*

Yes, this is Tzader.

Hearing his friend's voice sent Daegan's heart thumping with hope. He fought to keep walking calmly and not give away his excitement. *Tzader? Where are ya?*

In the building where they are supposedly holding you, but I'm under armed guard. We couldn't find you, then Adrianna sent word through Trey that Isak Nyght had information on a red dragon spotted off the coast of Spain. When I got all the details, I contacted the Belador we have inside the American government to find you. He didn't know anything, but did some checking. He came back with a meeting he set up between me and your captors, but someone along the line betrayed us. These people were waiting on me to make contact. They did admit a team of multi-national coalition jets flying along the coast of Spain had captured someone connected to the red dragon that destroyed a power plant.

'Twas not me, Daegan declared, furious at another rogue attack that had nothing to do with Ruadh.

Tzader said, *You told me that and you know I believe you. If this is that Brynhild, like you think, we have to figure out what to do about her soon.*

Daegan curled his fingers tight then forced his hands to relax and kept his anger under control. Now would be a bad time to frighten the guards. Brynhild had to be stopped if she didn't end up shot by a jet or other human super weapon first. He dismissed the topic with, *We shall discuss the other dragon later. First, I must get out of here. What else do these people think they know about the red dragon?*

Tzader gave a terse snicker. *They keep asking if I know how long a dragon can stay underwater. What are they talking about?*

Daegan told Tzader about being chased by satyrs who spat a coating on him, which interfered with teleporting and telepathy. He explained, *The satyrs chased me until I lost my footin' and slid over the edge. I barely had time to shift before smashin' on the rocks. I shifted, but my dragon struggled to fly. Still, my dragon outflew them, which was no easy task even at night. We dipped out of view over the water then landed on a cliff and shifted quickly to human form. I feel the jets did not shoot at my dragon at first out of curiosity. When they could not find a dragon, they assumed he dove underwater.*

Daegan would definitely not test his ability to teleport now with Tzader's life at risk. He'd already cost Devon his life by missing the Tribunal deadline. Hope and denial forced him to ask, *Did the Tribunal kill Devon?*

No. Ah, shit, Daegan, I meant to tell you that Quinn bought a tiny amount of extra time.

Relief raced through Daegan so fast a chill skittered across his skin. One person still alive. If only he could have similar news on Renata. But she supposedly still had over a week left.

He just could not imagine the hell she would suffer until he freed her and the others.

Then there was Casidhe. Was she crouching in her hiding spot wondering *if* he would return? Was she even safe?

Daegan had to breathe a moment before he could reply even silently, *Thank ya for that news. I needed it.*

You're welcome, but I have to tell you that this is only a short reprieve. Switching back to the current problem, Tzader asked, *Are you pretty sure they didn't see you shift back to human form?*

I do not think they saw my change. These men have asked over and over about the dragon as if I have it hidden somewhere. I have not spoken to any of them. They think I do not understand their language.

Smart move, Daegan. Stick with that and let me see what I can do.

After a right turn, the hall stretched another seventy feet, then the lead guard opened a sliding door halfway down.

Daegan and the four-guard team entered a room with a light-brown carpet. It softened the bootheel clicks of the guards. He remained dressed only in jeans.

A long oval-shaped wooden table with the ends chopped off flat and polished to a high sheen centered the room. Bookcases of the same dark wood, pictures, and a large television screen covered the walls. No one sat around the table.

One human stood at the far end. He dismissed the guards that had delivered Daegan.

He held himself as one in charge would. "I'm Senior Agent Huntsen."

Daegan didn't acknowledge him. Instead, he maintained a blank expression and swept a gaze over every detail, including the lack of windows. Still underground.

Tzader stood in front of a seating area with two gray-colored short sofas and a low table between them. Arms crossed, attitude unwelcoming, and jaw rigid, Brina's mate wore a pale-blue button-down shirt in stark contrast to his rich-brown skin and black dress slacks. He'd rolled the long sleeves up to reveal thick forearms.

Daegan had battled him once with swords. With few worthy opponents in many years, he'd been impressed by Tzader's power and skill. That Belador fought with abandon when he'd first believed Daegan to be a threat to Brina. Long before finding out Daegan was her uncle born two thousand years before her.

Two guards standing on each side of Tzader were dressed in the same black uniforms and held large weapons across their chests.

Brina's mate lifted his head. Light shined off the bald

surface.

Daegan hated for Tzader to be here.

That meant others had to protect Brina.

Huntsen nodded at Daegan when he addressed Tzader. "Is that the one?"

"Yes. He is one of mine, a special operative I sent out to do reconnaissance to determine if the dragon stories were true."

Huntsen glowered in Daegan's direction, clearly unconvinced. "He has yet to tell us what he was doing in Spain or say anything for that matter."

Tzader spoke out loud to Daegan. "You can explain your assignment." Then he telepathically told Daegan, *Repeat what I tell you telepathically. I've been hiking those hills for two days, following up on a lead.*

Daegan cleared his dry throat. "I have been hikin' those hills for two days, followin' up on a lead."

Huntsen asked, "Why have you not spoken before now?"

Daegan continued repeating what Tzader fed him. "I was operatin' dark, no contact with anyone when I am covert. Your people were the ones who believed I saw a dragon. I did not say such a thing."

Ruadh snorted at that. *Smart lie.*

Daegan managed not to change his stern expression as he continued. "I did see somethin' suspicious, but lights from your aircraft blinded me before I could determine what it was."

"Your body was badly scratched when my men picked you up," Huntsen interjected. "What happened to you that caused those injuries?"

Daegan hoped no one had taken photos since Ruadh had healed some of the cuts when he sent energy to Daegan's back. "I ran up on a large cat in the dark. No idea what it was, but I did not have time to be bothered and would not risk a light to identify what attacked me."

Huntsen snapped, "You don't look so bad right now."

In response, Daegan turned to show his back.

Someone sucked in a fast breath.

When he faced his interrogator again, he glanced at Tzader whose eyebrows were drawn tight, but he said nothing.

Exactly what Daegan wanted from him.

Huntsen walked out from behind the end of the table and strolled until he stopped closer to Daegan. "One of my men reported a slimy coating on your body. What was the coating?"

Tzader paused in talking to Daegan, but Daegan had this part. "A healin' ointment."

Cocking his head as if trying to determine if he heard the truth, Huntsen pointed out, "I was told your skin appeared to have a hard-looking finish in places. What is this ointment?"

Tzader interjected, "That's proprietary. Are you charging my man with anything? If so, what are the charges?"

Huntsen flashed an angry and perplexed glance in Tzader's direction.

Tzader must have scented an opening. He spoke in the strong voice of a leader. "He did not interfere with your operation, according to what you told me before you brought him up. You said you had questions. He's answered them as much as he can without divulging classified information. Since we're all faced with this supernatural issue now, my man just happened to be in the wrong place at the wrong time. Had I known about the power plant attack sooner, I would have extracted him until we knew more. My country is pulling in all resources to figure out how to address supernatural beings and our elite force is one of the very best. I can't afford to have even one locked up out of fear of the unknown."

The two guards and Huntsen stiffened at the slight.

Yes, Tzader had called them out for being afraid and they had not liked the insult one bit.

Huntsen's voice dropped to a menacing tone. "We do *not* react from fear. We captured him because he was in the midst of an operation where multiple aircraft were tracking a dragon."

Tzader gave the guy a look that would make anyone feel foolish if they had no evidence.

Stepping away from the two guards, which was a good power move, Tzader shrugged. "Let's say, for argument sake, your people *did* see a dragon. Why didn't they shoot it down? They had artillery."

Daegan slashed a momentary frown at Tzader, who ignored him.

Huntsen blustered, "We intended to kill the beast, but my pilots waited for it to fly out to sea. They were being careful to avoid wounding it close to shore. The damn thing might have landed on nearby homes or attacked humans."

Making a show of dropping his jaw, Tzader said, "So you *lost* a dragon?"

Lips twisted as if he'd sucked on a lemon, Huntsen grumbled, "The beast went into the water and did not surface again. My jets can't follow into the water."

Ruadh made a happy rumble. *Stupid humans will never kill us.*

Daegan allowed his dragon a moment to gloat, but the humans would regroup and change their plans next time.

Returning to the other end of the long table, Huntsen flipped a hand in Daegan's direction. "Who exactly is this man?"

Tzader shook his head slowly. "He's already explained he's in dark ops. Asking the same question repeatedly will not result in a new answer. I'm not sharing his identity with anyone, just as I would be shocked if you shared the identity of the men on the team who brought him in. My man came willingly and harmed none of your people. You should be thankful. You have no idea just what he's capable of and you don't want to find out. He's of no use to me if he shows up in an international database. In fact, I expect you to scrub any photos just as I would in your shoes."

Daegan doubted Tzader believed this group would delete any images, but it sounded commanding to make that demand.

A tense silence followed while Tzader stood calmly with a don't-push-me expression covering his face.

Daegan couldn't be prouder of the man Brina had chosen to rule Treoir and the Beladors with her. Daegan would always watch over those and all they protected as a patriarchal dragon king, but there stood a man every bit his equal.

Huntsen directed his attention at Tzader. "What is the name of your group?"

"VIPER. Vigilant International Protectors Elite Regiment."

"Never heard of you."

Tzader opened his arms. "Then we're doing our job right."

"Who in American intelligence can confirm any of this?"

Huffing out a humorless laugh, Tzader shook his head. "Not a damn soul. Who can confirm your off-the-books operations?"

Huntsen said nothing.

"Exactly." Tzader stepped over to Huntsen. He produced a card without fishing in a pocket and offered it.

As Huntsen accepted the card and turned it over, Tzader said, "It has only a phone number. The person who answers that number can find me day or night. You will have twelve seconds once the call connects to state your name, your phone number, and why you want to talk to me. I'll be contacted immediately. If I find the reason valid, I'll be in touch. Oh, and if you think to trace that number, you'll only find a nasty surprise and no person answering a phone. Consider yourself warned."

Sliding the card into an inside pocket of his jacket, Huntsen asked, "What will you do if I deny releasing this one?"

Tzader lifted his eyebrows and shrugged. "Not a thing, but you won't like what he does if you fail to release him after he's given you a fair accounting of his activities in Spain. That's more than he would normally share, but we're all trying to be diplomatic with supernaturals appearing in this world."

Daegan hoped since he and Tzader had spoken telepathically he could teleport them both out if things turned deadly.

When Huntsen showed no sign of relenting, his men lifted their weapons, training one on Daegan and one on Tzader.

Daegan pushed his power out without moving a muscle.

Tzader slashed a look at Daegan, but said nothing telepathically. He merely gave a short nod of agreement to stand and fight.

The time for talking had passed.

CHAPTER 11

CASIDHE CAME AWAKE WITH A start and breathing hard. She had the scepter in a white-knuckle grip. She trembled from the nightmare and covered her mouth to keep from retching.

What happened to Daegan?

Had the satyrs killed him?

Had that damned grimoire box possessed his body?

No, just a dream. Please just be a dream. Her eyes burned with tears. Daegan couldn't be dead or possessed, could he? No, she felt him connected to her, still alive.

What? Where had that thought come from? She shook her head, pushing away the cobwebs from the disturbing nightmare.

He'd taken the grimoire box. The same one that had burned her hand, but he'd been able to carry it.

Now that she thought about it, why had he been able to hold the box when she couldn't?

Daylight peeked through the leaves way above her. She laid the scepter aside and scrambled out of the hole, needing to be out in the open. When she reached her lookout spot, she wrapped her arms around her body and watched the sun break over the horizon. What time was it now? Where was Daegan?

How long should she wait before striking out to find a way home?

She could wait a little longer.

The minute she packed up to leave, she might as well

admit Daegan was not coming back. That he might just be dead. Why did that idea hurt so bad when he was her family's enemy?

She'd kill for a shower and clean clothes. Her stomach growled. Add food and water to that list.

A tingling sensation ran up her spine. She'd experienced that when she'd caught someone watching her in the past. She backed away from the exposed spot. Feeling paranoid, she broke off a branch with leaves and did her best to wipe away evidence of her steps. Once she sucked into the dark hole where she'd been hiding, she found more branches and dragged those over to cover the entrance. Last, she ran her hand over the depressed grass while scooting backwards.

Sitting on her knees, she stared out at everything.

How could anyone be watching her here?

She pulled some dead limbs around and made them look as random as possible, then peeked again.

No one could see her here. Right?

Back deep inside her tiny sanctuary, Casidhe finished her half-bottle of water while she studied the scepter with her LED light. She'd never be this close to something priceless again.

The oracle had been correct. Humans would have never found the scepter.

Every minute of waiting for Daegan and not hearing him call her name pinched her heart, warning her he would not be back.

Her conscience shamed her over caring about him.

She was too freaking emotionally spent to argue with herself.

She shoved the scepter inside the backpack and sat back, defeated. Deny it all she wanted, but Daegan would have returned by now if he could have.

The thought of him not surviving hurt beyond belief.

She squeezed her eyes tight, forcing back tears ready to break free. She was not a crier and she had no one to mourn.

"Stop it!" she snapped out loud, refusing to wallow in grief when she had no proof he had died. For all she knew, Daegan might be in a better place than her at the moment.

Any place would be better than alone with no way home.

She wrapped her arms around her chest, trying to hold herself together.

If she hit a checkpoint and they searched her bag, the stolen scepter would land her in prison no matter the country once someone executed minimal research.

She had an ancient book of dark druids written in a language she felt certain no human could read, which would likely point a finger at her as a nonhuman as easily as allowing someone to see her eyes glow. She'd listened to the radio while driving to see the professor. America was in a panic over supernaturals.

Some people believed. Some did not. All were fearful.

She understood. If she switched places, she'd fear a being with hidden powers. Hell, she had a healthy fear of those like Cathbad.

With no resources and an obstinate sword that might or might not come to her aid, her chance of making it to Ireland did not look promising.

How had her life blown up so badly?

A tear escaped and ran down her cheek.

She should have followed Daegan to the cliffs and helped fight off the satyrs. When he'd told her to stay put, she'd thought she'd be in his way.

Now she'd wonder forever if she could have saved him from whatever he'd faced.

What about the dream she'd had where he suffered and turned a bright yellow? Had an Imortik overtaken him? She could rarely recall dreams, but this one had been terrifying. Daegan had struggled to breathe and seemed to struggle inside his own skin.

That made no sense, but dreams were often full of mixed images that she couldn't translate.

Somewhere between meeting Daegan that first night and now, she'd come to trust him on a basic level. He'd protected her every step of the way to the oracle and through the hidden world with the scepter and grimoire box.

He believed the satyrs came for them when he took the box from her. She couldn't hold the thing anyhow. The moment she'd lifted the bronze box, pain had pulsed from her fingers to her shoulder. Had that part of the grimoire been attacking her?

What had it done to Daegan?

Bile raced up her throat at that thought. She clamped her jaws and held back tears. What was going on with her emotions? She did not break easily, but ... she felt something deep for Daegan.

Had to be the nightmare ripping her apart.

Daegan would come back.

He would. To believe otherwise would crush her.

But it might not be soon enough and she couldn't sit here forever. She'd eaten the last of her crackers before falling asleep. Sitting here bemoaning her fate would not get her home. She took in the mess she'd managed to make with very few items.

Fenella would be giving her an *a-hem* sound.

Where was Fenella? Had she tried to call Casidhe's phone and gotten no answer? Was she somewhere safe? Wouldn't it be nice to walk into the ancestral centre and see Fenella sitting at her desk with a warm scone half eaten?

Sure it would, but Casidhe would want answers. Where had Fenella been? Why hadn't she answered her phone?

Or why hadn't she called Casidhe's mobile phone?

Casidhe began collecting her litter and books, shoving everything into the backpack. Her fingers brushed Cathbad's book of dark druids.

A little zing of energy zapped her.

She snatched her hand back.

Why not read it now?

She'd fought off every urge to read that section Cathbad had warned her to not touch until he was with her.

Screw that druid. He'd started her down this dangerous path.

Lifting the book, she sat back and clamped her LED between her teeth. Then she flipped to the section he'd referenced. She still couldn't decipher the text without her gift. Rubbing her hands over her jeans, she cleaned them the best she could. Even if this book did belong to Cathbad, it was still a treasure to treat with respect.

The text he'd indicated was in the middle of a page, so she backed up to begin reading from the prior page. She lowered two fingers until barely brushing the text, moving them left to right. Symbols changed and lifted off the page in golden shapes her gift allowed her to translate.

Based upon her first impression of the timeworn book with a tooled-leather cover and the title *Before Ainvar*, she believed this could be a historical accounting of someone's life.

But as she read this snippet of text, her fingers trembled.

The words spoke of a change in power when the time came to enslave humans. Supernaturals who refused to kneel to the dark druid would take their last breaths. One druid would rise above all others, powerful and impossible to defeat.

The dark druid Elder, or Seanóir, would rule. No other would stand above him.

Clearly a sexist group of deranged nonhumans.

Cathbad fit right in.

She took the LED flashlight from her mouth to keep from drooling and tapped it against her knee.

What did all of this mean?

Could Cathbad be the Seanóir? If so, why couldn't he read this section himself? Wouldn't the Grand Poobah of the druids be able to read a book about druids?

What about Ainvar? Was he still alive or had this title only meant to document the time frame for the claims inside?

Maybe Cathbad couldn't translate all of this. Would that mean he was trying to *become* the Elder of the dark druids? A druid had been involved with creating the first Imortiks.

Could all of this be connected?

That would depend upon the time frame for the rise of this mighty druid.

Her hand shook. At one time, she'd believed the greatest threat to this world and her family was the red dragon. Her heart pounded at what might be coming for everyone.

Fear for those she loved settled thick and heavy in her stomach. She swallowed and lifted the LED to stick between her teeth. She was in this far. No point in stopping.

She continued scanning, searching for as much information as she could find.

The Elder dark druid would remain hidden for many years, waiting for the majik to shrink and hide in this world, then step from the shadows and come to life again. Huh.

She read on. The day would come when dragons returned to the skies and turned the world into ashes.

When that happened, all would bow to the Elder, the only one to save those chosen to survive. She paused. Did that mean humans and nonhumans or only one group?

Did she really care since she had no desire to live under the thumb of a deadly druid?

The snap of twigs and leaves jerked her head up.

She swallowed, afraid to move and give away her position.

More noise, then a brownish-gray rodent similar to a squirrel but with a mouse face chased another just like it. They both had dark rings around their eyes. Dormice? Maybe. But not a human or nonhuman threat.

She closed the druid book and pushed it inside the backpack, which would weigh enough to throw her off-balance if she made a misstep descending this severe downhill trek.

Daegan wouldn't be here to snatch her out of the air before she tumbled down the mountain. With the thick forest covering this mountain, a tree might stop her.

She would be better off hiking without a pack on her back. Fewer questions about that scepter, too.

If Daegan returned, would he be upset if he found she'd left the backpack here?

Not if she did a good job of hiding it.

When, not if, Daegan returned. Got it.

He'd see it as a sign that she had survived and find her if she didn't return for the backpack first.

She shoved the LED into a pocket and secured the scepter with the books inside then pushed out of the hole on her knees. Hunting for fallen branches and twigs didn't take long. When she had an armful of evergreen and dead branches, she buried the pack beneath them.

Sitting back on her knees, she nodded to herself. "Not too shabby for someone who does not camp."

She'd stashed all her money, which was less than twenty dollars, and a single credit card in her pocket. She had a low limit on that card and had just charged the rental car. She'd never cared about the puny limit, because she generally paid cash for everything and bought nothing extravagant.

Even if she could buy an airline flight or boat ticket home, she had no passport or ID.

The less known about that the better.

As a stranger in this land, wandering around would draw the wrong attention. The quaint village down near the water appeared idyllic, but she knew nothing about Spain, including the language.

Maybe she could pretend to have amnesia.

She'd watched a documentary on how that was not as easy to fake as shown in movies.

After checking her hidey hole one more time, she stopped stalling and climbed out to recon the area. She'd stepped out a few times since daylight to search for any sign of Daegan. The world had been still as a stone until boats began moving around in the cove.

She couldn't make her feet take a step.

Much as she preferred to pick her way down this steep terrain without a backpack, leaving it behind worried her.

What did Fenella always say? "Ya fash too much, Cas. Make a decision and let it go. What is the worst that can happen if no one dies?"

Casidhe tried to swallow around the lump in her throat.

She would accept Fenella back with no questions just to see her friend safe again.

Same went for Daegan.

Please let him be alive.

She waited for guilt to pile across her shoulders at wishing well for the red dragon Herrick hated, but ... Daegan did not seem anything like what she'd been taught about a murdering red dragon shifter. The more time she spent around him, the more she struggled to hold onto her animosity.

That was her failing.

She'd never been able to dislike someone based upon another person's opinion if the person in question had done her no wrong.

But she'd been raised to understand Herrick's enemies and wanted to be loyal to him.

Daegan wasn't here at the moment so she could stuff those conflicting thoughts away for now.

Yep, she was stalling again.

Licking her dry lips, she tried not to think about needing water she didn't have. Backbone stiffened, she stepped all the way into an opening beneath a brilliant sunrise streaking orange across a wide blue sky.

Plenty of time to think about how to escape from Spain before she reached the village. Maybe a kind soul would allow her to borrow a mobile phone to call for help, which would mean contacting a Luigsech or Connelly squire family.

One small problem. She had none of those numbers memorized.

Fenella had been her go-to person when it came to contacting anyone.

Angling her direction toward the clearing where she and Daegan had first searched for a place to hide last night, she slid her hand into a pocket where she'd stashed a knife.

Still there.

She'd only been at this for five minutes when sweat formed on her forehead and energy lifted the hairs on her neck. She lacked the ability to maintain the ancestral centre accounting or to keep her space tidy, but she'd always had good instincts. Right now, those instincts warned someone was watching her.

The same feeling she'd had earlier she'd brushed off as being edgy.

When she made her next sidestep to move horizontally, she altered her course before turning downhill. That deposited her into an open space beneath a large tree ruling this part of the mountain. Her neck tingled again. She backed up against the wide tree trunk, pretending to rest already.

From this vantage point, she would be able to see someone tracking her downhill.

But nothing followed her beyond a soft breeze.

Had she been wrong?

Climbing down this freaking mountain would be easier if she didn't spook herself every ten seconds.

"Stop bein' so jumpy," she grumbled to herself and stepped away from the tree, emerging into the sunlight again.

She looked up and froze.

A woman appeared ten feet in front of her, directly in her path. Beautiful in an eerie way, long hair fell in flaxen waves to her waist. That could be hair extensions. Even so, this woman had perfect hair. She could be thirty, but Casidhe had a feeling that facial presentation was a lie.

Her inch-long black nails meant she didn't perform any job that required manual labor. Neither did she have mountain-climbing gear and that deep-green silk suit did not belong out here.

Final damning point?

This woman had appeared out of nowhere.

Call her paranoid, but Casidhe had a bad feeling about this. When nervous, she turned her mouth loose. "Hi. You went all out dressin' for an early mornin' climb."

"You will be entertaining," the woman commented. Her gorgeous face belonged on a magazine model, but human models did not have eyes that changed from green to brilliant gold.

Casidhe took a step back and glanced around. No easy exit. "Do I know you?"

An evil grin lifted the perfect lips. This woman looked down as if staring at a plump rabbit whose only use would be as a meal. "You are coming with me."

Casidhe's fingers itched for her sword, but her weapon remained hidden in the woods with the scepter. She would not expose any of that to this unknown woman.

Scratch that. Unknown supernatural.

Who could this woman be? When in doubt, Casidhe had a two-word basis for decisions. Screw it. She smiled back at the nonhuman with as much threat as she could muster. "Such a temptin' offer to get to know you better, but I'll be passin' on it. Have places to go, people to see, and all that. Be careful not to hurt yourself in those shoes."

The glowing gold eyes narrowed. "You no longer amuse me. Ready?" She snapped her fingers. "Silly me. Like I care if you're ready." She snarled the last words in a threatening voice that would scare a demon.

"What? *No!*" The world spun out of shape, slurring Casidhe's words.

When Casidhe's head stopped spinning, she'd been dropped, literally, in a huge space with rough-carved stone walls. She scrambled to her knees, searching her surroundings. A cave? No. The floor was covered in huge squares of black marble. Hard to describe this as a mere room. The ceiling seemed to go forever. Red candles of all sizes had been placed everywhere on ledges cut out of the stone walls as if someone had stood here and slapped them at random spots.

Shaking started in her knees and climbed to her arms. She crab-walked backward until she fell on her butt. Her breathing sped up. She'd need a bag to breathe into soon if she didn't get a grip.

Would a place like this even have a paper bag?

Panic dug in deep, grabbing hold of her confidence and slapping it around.

She glanced to her right and part of one wall had a huge space in a square shape where light shifted and moved in a swirling cloud, reminding her of a rough-shaped flat screen.

Where the hell was she?

"What were you doing with Daegan?" that same demonic voice demanded.

Casidhe squeaked and jumped around in an awkward break-dancing move. Her heart tried to beat its way out of her chest. With one look at this crazy woman, her heart would climb right back in and whimper.

The woman's long gold hair danced around her shoulders. Casidhe meant gold, too, as in brightly gilded locks as if the valuable mineral had been mined, spun into hair strands, then illuminated.

Gone were the silk pants and top.

Her gown appeared to be layers of red-gold butterflies and black flowers. When she stepped back and forth, the gown swayed, which would seem normal, but Casidhe could swear she heard the gown whispering and laughing.

Casidhe swallowed hard, trying to sound strong and failing. "Where am I and who are you?"

Crazy golden-haired woman lowered her cruel face close to Casidhe's and whispered, "I am Queen Maeve and you are in my realm TÅμr Medb."

CHAPTER 12

DAEGAN KEPT HIS ARMS LOOSE at his sides and begged the universe for his power to protect Tzader. He would not return to Brina without the father of her babies.

Tension held everyone still in an unspoken standoff.

Tzader called to Daegan telepathically. *Might want to back off the power push. Getting hard to breathe in here.*

Guards on each side of Tzader flinched but gripped their weapons, fingers moving toward the triggers.

Huntsen backed up a step at first then stopped and narrowed his eyes at Daegan. He spoke as if Daegan were not present. "Is he a nonhuman?"

Tzader chuckled a merciless sound. "Would you call a cyborg nonhuman? Daegan is a superior warrior it has taken centuries to develop."

Daegan managed to not snort. Just.

Huntsen rounded on Tzader. "Centuries?"

"In a manner of speaking, yes. The first prototype was nothing compared to the current model." Any sign of humor vanished when Tzader demanded, "Make a decision. Do we end this as allies or adversaries?"

Huntsen cursed then waved his hand in dismissal. "He can go, but if we find him in the wrong place at the wrong time again, I will not be as accommodating and he will not leave a free man. I'm sure we have ways to disconnect his battery."

"Understood." Tzader turned to Daegan. "Let's go."

"Before you leave," Huntsen added, "what can you tell

us about this nonhuman uprising in America? What do they look like? Hell, what are those beings?"

Tzader rarely showed his emotions, but Daegan had been around him long enough to know Tzader's goodwill had just been stomped on.

Treoir's sitting king turned back to Huntsen and stepped up close. "They look just like you and me. I have *some* information. We're running down what are believed to be eyewitness accounts. At this point, it appears many non-humans have lived among humans for thousands of years and appear physically identical. Those have been rumored to be protective of humans."

Rumbling broke out between the two guards who had lowered their weapons. One of them spit out the word bullshit.

Tzader stepped around to face the pair. "I only tell you what our intel has uncovered. There are some beings who look nothing like humans and are attacking the nonhumans as well as the humans. So if we start killing everything that goes bump in the dark, we may destroy potential allies. It would be foolish to believe humans outnumber nonhumans."

Daegan had no idea if that were true or not, but Tzader had given them something to think about.

Looking even less convinced than he had about Daegan, Huntsen said, "You should remember that I'm releasing your man without stirring up trouble for your group. In return, I would like to be informed of new developments about nonhumans in your country."

Face smoothed out to unreadable again, Tzader turned back to Huntsen. "I'm happy to share any intel I can. The more we all know, the better it will be for this world."

With that, Tzader stepped away from Huntsen and raised a finger for Daegan to follow him.

Four armed men escorted Daegan and Tzader to a vehicle in an underground garage. Tzader sent a message to Daegan. *Prepare to have a sack dropped over your head. They don't want us to know how to find this location again.*

Daegan sent back, *If they ever bring a powerful non-human here who takes offense to their tactics, they won't have a location left to call home.*

True.

Once inside a large SUV and with their heads covered, Daegan had reservations about leaving without talking to Joavan. If Daegan had been able to teleport out, find Casidhe, then teleport back, he would have done so.

He didn't need one more enemy, but he had no idea how to locate Joavan.

If the Faetheen could not accept what had happened, Joavan would never have made much of an ally anyhow.

After driving over an hour, the car stopped.

The black sack was yanked off Daegan, causing him to blink at the bright sunshine warming the road. He stepped from the backseat to find they were in the middle of no-where.

Scattered trees covered both sides of the narrow paved road.

He had more than one priority, but getting to Casidhe immediately topped his list. His heart seized with pain at a sudden rush of fear for her safety. How long had she been alone?

Tzader joined him and asked the driver, "Where the hell are we?"

That was not what Daegan wanted to hear.

"Our orders were to leave you somewhere safe, but not at your hotel where you might have been seen by a nonhu-man. We don't want any of them to know about our oper-ation."

Ruadh make a grumbly noise that Daegan took as a de-rogatory sound.

The guard shrugged indifferently. "My boss indicated you have the kind of contacts capable of producing a vehicle anywhere and at any time."

"I'll be sure to show your boss the same consideration should the tables ever turn," Tzader replied in a snarl.

Once the car drove off, Tzader grinned at Daegan. "Perfect. Now we don't have to find a place to hide before leaving. We're in France, by the way. This doesn't look to be a heavily traveled area. I wasn't registered at the hotel in Limoges where they picked me up. Just used it as a neutral pickup zone."

Daegan admitted, "I shall need Tristan. My teleportin' has ... problems. The venom is interferin'."

"Damn. I hate you being out here facing off with humans or nonhumans without all your powers. By the way, what the hell happened to your back? It's looking better, but still rough."

Daegan did not want Tzader involved with Joavan, but Tzader needed to know anything Daegan could share with him. "A nonhuman does know about Huntsen's group. They have no idea he is among them."

Tzader turned slowly to Daegan, black eyebrows furrowed. "Who? Or what?"

"'Tis a lengthy story I shall be happy to share it once we have time, but for now suffice to say I am callin' this bein' a potential ally as he helped me greatly."

"Did he do that to your back?" Tzader asked sounding appalled.

"Not really. The coatin' Huntsen mentioned came from a satyr chasin' me. The slime began to harden and spread from back to front. I faced suffocatin' to death had it completely circled my throat. When he brought me a solvent to remove the coatin', he warned to use small amounts. Then he left, sayin' it would take four to five hours to arrange pullin' me out of there so he could free me outside the buildin'. I was desperate to teleport out, which I could not do at all with that on my skin. I soaked rags and rolled the part of my back I could not reach on it."

"Damn, Daegan. Looks like it burned the skin off."

"'Tis growin' back. Healing shall be faster when I am able to shift." Daegan didn't care for being out in the open. He walked off the road and up into the shade of a scrawny old tree with sprawling branches. When Tzader joined him, Daegan explained, "This bein' says he is from *Talamh Dearmadta.*"

Tzader squinted in confusion.

"'Tis Land of Forgotten, a world alongside this human one. He can step between that world and this one."

"Never heard of them or that place."

"Nor I as well. His name is Joavan. I owe him aid in return for his help, but I must take care of our people first."

"You're not going to trust him, right?"

Daegan barked out a cold laugh. "I trust no one who is not currently part of our circle."

"Figured as much." Tzader nodded. "Back to what's next. You don't think you can teleport?"

"'Tis only for short distances and is not a concern if Tristan is available."

Tzader rolled his eyes. "Are you kidding? He's been making all of us crazy while we couldn't find you. He brought me here and wanted to come to the meeting, but I didn't want to risk that they might have had a nonhuman on their force who could recognize us. He was our backup off-site. I don't know how to tell him to find us, though."

"Wise decision to not take him inside with you," Daegan agreed. "Let me call Tristan. I can help him find us." Daegan reached out telepathically to his second, who replied quickly.

Boss! Hot damn. Are you free?

Daegan chuckled. *I am, but they dropped me off with*

Tzader in the wilderness. I am goin' to try to link with ya through this connection. Once ya feel it, follow that link and teleport. We are standin' next to a road in a deserted area.

Tristan said nothing for a moment. *Okay, boss, I feel a buzz of energy coming to me, but how do I find you?*

Daegan also felt the surge in the connection. *Reach for my mind. When ya make that connection, teleport.*

When Daegan felt Tristan's energy coming his way, he reached out with his power and grabbed Tristan's weaker buzz, then linked with him.

Tristan's grunt came through, then he appeared ... almost on top of Daegan who jumped back.

"Shit! Sorry, boss. That was ... pretty freakin' wild." His face split with a big grin at his accomplishment. "Hey, Tzader. Did he tell you what we did?"

Tzader smiled, "No, but whatever it was appeared to have worked. Next time, try not to knock each other out."

Ignoring Tzader's jab, Tristan stuck out the hand he'd been healing.

Daegan accepted his hand, careful not to crush new bones still forming and pulled Tristan into a hug as he would have with a friend from long ago. "I am glad to see ya mendin' properly."

Tristan had a warm smile that filled his eyes, letting Daegan know the hug meant more to him than the teleporting trick. "Yeah, well, I should have been back with you yesterday, boss."

"I am glad ya were not, Tristan, or ya might have been captured with me."

Tzader turned to watch a truck filled with hay roll down the road at a peaceful speed. "Let's cut out of here. I need to get back to Brina. Also, now that you have Tristan, I'm stopping Brina from teleporting so many people. Garwyli said the babies are coming soon and she's getting more exhausted every day."

Daegan said a silent thanks that Tzader could return to Brina and stay. "Tristan and I shall return to Atlanta soon. Inform Trey and Quinn no one is to contact Brina for any teleportin'. I am sorry ya had to leave her when she needs ya, and I shall visit my niece soon." Daegan backed up a step toward trees capable of hiding them from anyone driving by.

Tzader said, "Not a problem as long as we have you back safe again."

"Thank ya, Tzader. Ya wield words as skillfully as ya do a sword." Daegan shook Tzader's hand.

"You're welcome. Oh, hell. Wait a minute, Daegan. One more thing. Quinn needs you at the Tribunal like yesterday. Loki is still demanding to see you."

Tristan stood near Daegan, waiting for directions.

Daegan thought on how to manage what he had to do next. "Tristan, teleport Tzader back to Treoir then return here." He told Tzader, "Once Tristan and I find the Luigsech woman and insure her to safety, Quinn is my next priority."

"Where is she, boss?" Tristan stood with his hands on hips.

"I left her on a mountain."

Tristan lifted his eyebrows, but said nothing else.

Tzader scrubbed a hand over his face as if trying to wash the weariness out of his eyes. "You've been captured for a number of hours. You think she's still there?"

"I hope so." Daegan had a sick feeling about those satyrs. Had they returned to their world or had they found Casidhe? "We shall teleport there once Tristan returns from droppin' ya in Treoir, I intend to waste not one minute reachin' the Tribunal to aid Quinn." Daegan glanced at Tristan. "Shall teleportin' that much strain ya?"

"Nope." Tristan met his gaze. "I've had so much healing

in the last few days I'm probably super-charged. Ready, Tzader?"

"Yes."

Tristan had made no empty claim. He reappeared sooner than Daegan had expected. Much as he'd like to catch up Tristan on all that had happened, he couldn't spare another second before going to Casidhe. "This time, we shall link so that I may direct our teleportin'."

"I'm ready, boss."

Once they linked, Daegan took them back to the mountainside in Spain. Daegan blinked to clear his vision quickly when the teleporting ended. His insides were twisted over rushing to find Casidhe. With a quick glance, he recognized the spot as where he and Casidhe had landed after spinning away from the oracle.

The burst of Tristan's energy lifted Daegan's spirit, but also informed Daegan he would not be teleporting any great distance on his own for a while.

"Sure this is the place?" Tristan searched all around as if expecting something to dive out of the woods at them.

"Absolutely." Daegan turned to work across the steep wooded area to the low spot he and Casidhe had used as a place to hide. Hunting the world shielding the grimoire box and scepter seemed so long ago, but it had only been hours.

He followed her scent, heart pounding at the idea of seeing her again. He wanted her in his arms.

Crossing the last open stretch before reaching the cluster of trees where he'd left her, Daegan inhaled and froze at the tainted scent belonging to Queen Maeve.

Daegan called out in a harsh whisper, *"Casidhe!"* He rushed forward, pushing branches aside and falling to his knees to dive into their dark hiding place.

The closer he got, the stronger her scent grew and none of Queen Maeve's. His heart leaped with hope Queen

Maeve had not touched her.

Ruadh roared, *Queen Maeve has woman.*

Daegan knocked the last obstruction aside. His dragon had called it. No Casidhe. He sat hard, dropping his face into his hands and fighting the emotion choking him.

How could he keep failing everyone?

He'd told the lass he'd be back.

"Where are you?" Tristan shouted, snapping branches and plowing through the underbrush like a bull cutting a new path.

"I am here, Tristan." Daegan lifted his head, but his heart remained flat on the ground.

His second-in-command dropped into a crouch next to him and looked around the small pocket of space. "Is that her backpack?"

"Yes." Daegan forced out his next words. "She is gone."

"You have a hell of a time keeping up with that woman."

Daegan ignored the gentle jab. "I scented Queen Maeve outside. I believe she has Casidhe."

"*Shit!* She's got Luigsech?" Tristan shoved his hands in his hair, raking through it with agitated motions. "What are we going to do? Tzader said Quinn is hanging by threads." Tristan stilled with a thoughtful expression. "Wait a minute. How would Queen Maeve even know to come to this spot?"

Daegan's head came up. "No one should have. I shall tell ya more later, but the oracle sent us here from meetin' with her. When I say sent, she caused us to teleport even when I could not." He considered how anyone could have known to come here for Casidhe. "Queen Maeve must have rebuilt her scryin' wall, or used some other scryin' tool, and saw me here. She would not have known to look for Casidhe otherwise. I must get her back."

At Tristan's silence, Daegan swung his face to him. "Ya appear confused. What bothers ya?"

Tristan scratched his head and stalled. "I just, uh, noticed you were calling the woman Casidhe and sound like you've lost someone you care about. Has anything changed between you two?"

Daegan could demand Tristan not ask him a question like that again, but Tristan had become his friend and Daegan needed one more than ever right now. "Nothin' has actually happened between us, but I did kiss her. We have been through a great deal since ya teleported us to the place we started huntin' the oracle." He struggled to put his thoughts into words. In truth, he didn't really know how to explain what he felt for Casidhe.

Only that she mattered to him, felt essential, and every minute she remained missing ate a hole in his chest.

She'd trusted him.

He'd let her down.

Daegan sighed and shook off his painful thoughts. "She has become important to me. I should not think of her as more than a research aid, but I do. It makes no sense. I cannot encourage a woman who is not a direct descendant of a dragon if I wish ... if I wish for more."

"She's something more than human, though," Tristan pointed out.

"'Tis true. I cannot pursue anythin' with Casidhe," Daegan admitted, hating to give those words life. "Neither shall I allow Queen Maeve to think she can keep her."

Tristan blew out a fast breath. "But we need a plan. My bet is that Queen Maeve intends to use Casidhe to get to you."

Daegan's voice roughened with fury. "'Tis possible. That queen had best not harm one hair on Casidhe's head."

"If that is the case, you can't just go teleporting in there with guns blazing, boss."

Daegan cocked his head. "Guns?"

Grinning at first, Tristan turned serious and explained,

"Basically, I'm saying it would be suicidal to teleport in and attack Queen Maeve in her own realm. She may be crazy, but she's smart enough to know if she wants you she must take care of Casidhe. She knows if she so much as scratches Casidhe that you'll take TÅµr Medb—*and her*—apart. I know you're worried about Casidhe, but we have time to figure this out and come up with a good plan."

"Ya have a valid point." Pinching the bridge of his nose, Daegan considered all he had to do. He did not want to wait. He would like to bust into TÅµr Medb with guns blazing, but he had to be careful or risk putting Casidhe in further danger. "I must go to see Quinn and deal with the Tribunal. We have a chance to save Devon. The minute that is handled, we're coming back here to hunt for the grimoire. 'Tis still my only hope for returnin' Devon, Renata, and any others to their natural state. Of course, we must find where that Imortik is holdin' Renata and the others first."

Feeling a little less hopeless thanks to Tristan, Daegan scanned the small area, raking branches away from the backpack. He sat back and dug into the pack.

The books and scepter were still inside.

"I'll take the backpack." Tristan offered his hand.

"One moment." Daegan dug into the backpack and found where she kept her sword in a hidden sheath. His fingers touched the hilt. She left her sword?

He tried to pull the sword out.

The sword would not budge. Offering it to Tristan, Daegan pointed at the hilt. "See if ya can pull the sword free."

Tristan grabbed it and yanked. He yanked again. "How is it stuck in there?"

"I do not know, but I have a feelin' the sword will only leave the sheath for her."

"No way." Tristan lifted the backpack and walked hunched over to leave the hiding spot. He turned to Daegan, "So you found one of the books? I mean volumes."

Daegan followed him out. "Yes. 'Tis not a book as ya think of one, but a sealed bronze box with sheets of text inside, which I shall explain later. I had it in hand when I ran from satyrs. I could not teleport or shift until I fell off the cliff and the box was knocked from my hand. I shifted, but Ruadh could barely fly. 'Tis how I ended up captured. I must return to retrieve the box."

"Want to hunt for it now?"

"No, we must go to Atlanta for Quinn," Daegan admitted, feeling kicked in the gut. "I must think on the safest way to rescue Casidhe from TÅµr Medb before we return."

Tristan stared off at the ocean. "Do you think Queen Maeve knows Casidhe can find the grimoire volumes?"

Daegan recalled all that had happened on this mountain side. "I am not sure. I shall have a better idea when we return and hunt the box. If she saw me when I had the box, she might have gone to the cliffs to search for it. If that was the case and she found it, we may not be able to save anyone if Queen Maeve hands that box over to the Imortik master. I may have to enter TÅµr Medb guns or not."

"If you do, I'm going with you." Tristan would not budge.

Daegan stared at the cliffs where clouds the color of pewter gathered overhead, but the sun still burned brightly and would for a while. Searching now would be risky. Huntsen's people probably continued to watch this area for a dragon. Still, the sooner he had his hands on that box, the safer everyone would be.

Perhaps he and Tristan could look quickly ...

Trey's voice came into Daegan's mind. *Where are you, Daegan?*

In Spain.

A fat pause followed, then Trey said, *Tzader told me you were free. I just heard from Evalle that the Tribunal is holding Quinn until you show up. If you aren't there before eleven this morning in Atlanta, Quinn will have to face the three Beladors possessed by Imortiks locked inside VIPER. Based on what Evalle said, I'd get there sooner than later.*

CHAPTER 13

In Treoir Castle, inside Treoir realm

LANNA NIBBLED ON HER LIP, trying her best not to rage at anyone. That should be simple when sitting alone in a room.

Besides, if she made any angry noise *this* room would probably tattle on her to Garwyli. She normally enjoyed her time visiting with the kind old druid. She could spend days in this room if not for the task he'd given her.

His private quarters included this solarium, a room filled with books and personal treasures from one very long lifetime inside Treoir castle.

He was many hundred years old. Maybe a thousand? She didn't know. He answered no questions about his age. The powerful druid said he had rarely left Treoir over the centuries and preferred not to leave at all now.

Maybe if he took a trip and had fun he would be unable to think of ways to torture her.

She hated to disappoint anyone. Since discovering her unusual power, she'd made it her goal to help others and disappoint no one when they needed those powers.

She had to complete an exercise successfully or Garwyli would be disappointed. He'd been cranky lately. She wanted him to be happy. Then she could enjoy her time here, too.

No. She could do this.

Garwyli had promised to teach her how to teleport if she

succeeded at the tasks he gave her. Nothing would mean as much to her. She had figured out how to teleport only fifty feet and not always on target.

Lifting her hands, she turned the palms to face the ceiling. Then she focused on her palms and called up an image of a butterfly to form there as a hologram.

A translucent image began taking shape and ... it turned into a distorted three-dimensional image of a butterfly that would scare a child.

"Argh!" She folded her fingers into fists.

This should not be so difficult.

She had tried for a rabbit hologram only to close her hands when something hideous appeared.

Calling up a butterfly should be simple. She wasn't trying to create the real butterfly, just a holographic image.

Maybe creatures that flew and hopped around were asking too much for her first time. Once she understood the majik for this, she would know how to attempt animals.

A daisy should be easy, right?

She opened her hands again, focused hard on her empty palms and said, "I request a daisy to appear as a hologram."

White liquid formed and leaked through her fingers.

"Ack." She jumped up and flicked her hands to get rid of the slimy feel.

"What did ya kill that bleeds white?" Garwyli asked, shuffling in.

She turned to him, glad to see her hands clean and the white liquid disappear from the floor.

"I kill nothing." She crossed her arms, ready to be lectured on not focusing or not trying hard enough or not something.

He paused and lifted a bushy white eyebrow. He had a matching beard that fell to his chest and snow white hair just as long. He'd always been ancient since she'd known him, but seeing him use his hickory cane to bear his light weight bothered her.

She could not envision this powerful druid as feeble.

He asked, "How comes yar practice?"

She bit back an answer born of irritation. He'd been tutoring her every time she visited Treoir, but this time he'd increased the level of instruction. She'd also gained valuable insight from Caron, the Fae half-sister of a white witch in Atlanta. Caron had a short fuse if annoyed, but she'd come to the aid of the dragon shifter once and the Beladors had protected her witch half-sister. She'd also been the one to bring Lanna back from the edge after an abusive attack.

Caron had trained her first and given her challenges, but not frustrating ones Lanna could see no use for right now.

Garwyli waited silently for her reply.

"Are you angry with me?" She admired this old druid and wanted to show him her power.

He frowned and tilted his head. "Why would ya think such?"

"You dragged me away from Reese outside yesterday when she needed someone to help her, then you give me strange exercises. I appreciate all you show me very much, but I am confused."

Moving over to the window seat in front of tall panes of beveled glass, he sat and propped his hands on his cane. "I saved ya from makin' another mistake."

"What mistake?" Lanna asked, not hiding her annoyance. She helped people. How could that be a mistake?

"Ya cannot go around tryin' ta grant wishes every time someone ya care about is havin' problems. 'Tis not how ta use yar powers."

Lanna thought back and couldn't recall anything significant being said between her and Reese right as Garwyli walked up. "I do not grant wishes. I am not fairytale godmother."

"Ah, but ya wish ta be." His mild expression remained

the same.

"I do not." Her words sounded more defensive than confident. Why would he criticize her for offering aid where she could?

His pause gave his next words gravity. "Then why did ya agree ta what Reese asked ya ta do?"

Lanna's face heated with embarrassment. "We had private conversation. I swore to keep her words secret. Did you listen with majik?"

He didn't give her a direct answer. "'Tis important ta hold a confidence no matter what. I never want ya ta lose such a fine quality. I heard enough yesterday ta know ya agreed to aid Reese in leavin'. 'Tis not yar place ta interfere."

That stung. "I mean only to help with stressful situation, not interfere."

"What about Quinn? Do ya not care what he thinks?"

"*Of course I do!*" she shouted, slightly ashamed at raising her voice, but she would do anything for her cousin. Never question her commitment to family. Never.

"Then how do ya know what be right for him or Reese?"

Why would Garwyli make her feel bad about her good intentions? She held her tongue rather than utter words she'd regret.

"Good intentions do not equate wise decisions, child," he said gently.

Her lips parted in shock. "Did you read my mind, Garwyli?"

"I do not push into any mind, but once ya have lived as long as I have and yar majik has matured to the level of mine, ya will have to raise walls ta avoid hearin' thoughts shouted about near ya. That does not change what I said about decisions."

She walked over to where she'd set up a step for some physical exercise between frustrating attempts at the hologram. She'd never been much of a workout enthusiast, but found doing this helped her think at times as she tried to master her gift.

Taking a step up, she remained on one foot for a few seconds, then dropped to the floor and changed to step with her other foot. She was not ignoring Garwyli, but he had just accused her of acting without thought.

Lanna said, "You say I should not help Reese?" Another step up and down. She'd been having dreams, which were more like visions right before she woke. Dreams about Reese that bothered her deeply, but she did not know what Reese needed. Only that she ran from something that scared her.

She had visions of a castle with a dragon flying above it, too, but they were confusing. The castle was not Treoir and the dragon was not red. She would wait until she had a clear idea of what they meant before telling Daegan.

Garwyli broke into her thoughts. "I am sayin' ya must learn restraint. I was not angry with ya so much yesterday as with myself."

Lanna paused midstep and looked over at him. "Why?"

"Because I have become complacent and keep puttin' off my duty."

He said nothing more as she finished a series of steps. She turned and sat on the structure to face him. "What duty?"

"To train ya."

Smiling, she said, "You have trained me more with each visit. I welcome what I learn from you. I want to improve. One day, I will master teleporting."

Garwyli's eyes twinkled, then softened. "Ya will know so much more than teleportin' one day, child."

She leaped up, excited. "Truly? You do believe I will be able to teleport long distances?"

Garwyli pushed up from his window seat and tottered

over to her. He might look feeble, but that old druid still packed plenty of power. She'd felt it whipping around her yesterday when he had come for her at the castle entrance.

When he stopped in front of her, he lowered his voice. "Ya must do more than visit. Ya must stay here for longer periods ta learn all ya can."

"I will." She wanted the knowledge so much, but she didn't want to miss out on life back in Atlanta either. Quinn and the Beladors needed her help. She wanted to spend time with Evalle, Storm, Feenix ... all of her friends, but one male witch in particular.

She missed Kellman.

Scowling, Garwyli's face wrinkled in disapproval. "See? Ya jump ta answer and act when ya do not have all the information."

She shook off thoughts of back home in Atlanta. "What did I say wrong now?"

"Ya say ya will come back for longer periods, but ya do not know why or for how long."

He had a point. She could be impulsive at times. "I am just anxious to continue what I learn from you." She smiled, hoping to get them back on better footing.

He put his hand on her head in a grandfatherly show of affection. "I trust ya ta keep this confidence above all."

She felt the weight of his words to her toes. What could be so important? She nodded. "I will protect any words you share in confidence."

"Ya have a greater power than I have seen in one so young in many centuries. Ya must learn to harness that power for far more than what is asked of ya now. Ta do so will require bein' in Treoir for many months at times while we train. I have lived well past my years only because I stayed in this realm. 'Tis time I make plans for the future druid of Treoir, a greater one than me."

Lanna felt the blood drain from her face. "You think I

could be ... druid?" No one knew where her powers came from. Her mother had disappeared for the best part of a year then returned pregnant with no knowledge of who had given her a baby.

"I know ya are capable of bein' a druid. Ta be honest, ya have much more inside ya than the power I possess. All of Treoir and the Beladors need ya ta become the powerful female druid I see in ya."

Lanna tried to feel honored, but saw the freedom she'd just begun to enjoy slip through her fingers. She could not walk away when she heard what Garwyli had not said.

The old druid was dying.

As the shock of his words sank in, she started seeing a new possibility he had not. "I will think on this, Garwyli, but you of all know I cannot walk away from duty."

He should also realize she would not walk away from him. She would work harder at tasks and improve her power faster.

Now she had to save Garwyli.

CHAPTER 14

JOAVAN PASSED FROM HIS REALM of *Talamh Dearma-dta* to the human realm, standing in the gray interior many floors underground in Huntsen's secret compound. He expected to find a dragon shifter ready to finish removing the last of the hardening shell on his back.

Instead Joavan found an empty cell.

With the door open.

Not having to touch the iron bars allowed him to step into the cell where rags remained on the floor and the bowl of healing liquid still hung from a horizontal bar. The area smelled of burned skin. He assessed the mess on the floor.

Had Daegan soaked rags and rolled his back with them?

Joavan flinched at that thought.

He'd told the dragon shifter he'd return, but Daegan had clearly been unwilling to wait. Had he cleaned off all of the hardening film on his body?

If so, had he teleported away?

Probably not. There would have been no reason to open the cell door to teleport.

Why abuse his back to clean the slime coating away before Joavan returned? Did Daegan think to renege on their deal?

That dragon shifter owed him for this skin cleanser.

He would pay up.

Joavan called the bowl and rags to him, then he slipped from the cell. He'd been warned since a child to never try to move between worlds when surrounded by that much iron. It might work, but he had never wished to be the guinea pig for an experiment, as they said in the human world.

Once back in the hallway, he moved between worlds. He dropped off the cleansing material in his home realm, staying in his private quarters only seconds before he once again entered the human world.

This time, he appeared inside a hall closet on the same floor as Huntsen's office.

Before stepping out, he glamoured himself to appear human again wearing the black uniform of Huntsen's forces. With a glance in both directions outside the closet, Joavan emerged and walked until he stood next to the wall for Huntsen's office. With his supernatural hearing, he listened to a report being delivered to the stodgy leader. He needed to find out where they'd moved Daegan.

Nothing significant turned up in the report being given.

Then Huntsen said, "Keep looking into VIPER. I think that one we freed knows something about that dragon. His people sound convincing, but I don't trust any of them. I want a team assigned to look for anything they can find on that guy, Tzader Burke, and his mysterious dark operative."

"Yes, sir."

Joavan turned away, striding back to the closet quickly. He paused with a phone in his hand while the subordinate exited Huntsen's office at his back. Once footsteps turned the other way, Joavan glanced around to see the guard hurry to do the man's bidding.

Stepping back inside the closet, Joavan slipped between worlds again, which was not as simple as it sounded. Every time he crossed between worlds, he drained his powers. He could make one more crossing today, but might have to stay in the human world a bit longer before coming back to *Talamh Dearmadta*.

Not the most comforting thought.

Once back in his realm, he waited for his murky vision to clear. When it did, he left his private quarters and flashed to an arched wooden bridge with flowers growing along the railing. He crossed the bridge spanning water that trickled through a creek below. On the other side stood a quaint cottage belonging to the one person who might be able to find that dragon shifter.

He and Daegan had a deal.

Daegan would make good for his part or regret accepting help from a Faetheen.

CHAPTER 15

DAEGAN BLINKED AS THE TELEPORTING ended and quickly took in everything around him where the sun had yet to shine. Most prominent in the dark shadows surrounding him was a wall of rock on the mountain concealing VIPER headquarters. Tristan had done his best to teleport them, but the trip had been a bit rough.

Tristan possessed less power than Daegan.

More accurate to say Tristan possessed less power than Daegan when Daegan was free of Imortik venom in his body.

"Must be four or five in the morning to still be dark." Tristan turned his head, scanning the area. He wore Casidhe's backpack. "What's the plan, boss?"

Daegan had no real plan.

His life had been moving faster than Ruadh flying with a tailwind. He'd had no time to form a solid thought. "I shall call Sen to teleport us into the Tribunal. I have an idea to get Casidhe back."

"You do?"

"Yes." Daegan rubbed his gritty eyes that felt as if some of the satyr film had reached them, but that couldn't be. "Keep in mind, my idea may work or ... it could backfire."

Always onboard for whatever Daegan wanted to do, Tristan nodded. "Understood. Just so we're clear, don't even think about leaving me out here."

"I wouldn't. Ya are my only way to teleport out of a Tribunal meeting without dependin' upon Sen or Loki."

Keeping his voice quiet, Tristan said, "Loki would *love* to know about you not teleporting. We have to keep that under wraps until you get better."

Daegan agreed, but had his doubts.

Would he ever rid his body of the venom?

He had no time to waste and called telepathically to the liaison, Sen. No reply. Daegan called again. Second time he got a groggy Sen saying, *Call Loki.*

After standing there longer than they normally would while waiting to be teleported to a Tribunal, Tristan asked, "What's the holdup?"

"Sen told me to call Loki." Daegan didn't hide his confusion. "He sounded ... tired or sick."

Tristan's jaw had dropped. He closed his mouth. "Tired? A demigod who does nothing but the bidding of the Tribunal needs a nap? On the other hand, what the hell is going on with him to tell you to call Loki for teleporting?"

"I have no idea." Daegan held even more concern over what they might face in the Tribunal. "We shall see if Loki is accommodatin'."

Daegan called telepathically to the god. *Ya requested my presence, but your liaison is unable to teleport us.*

Loki replied, *Who is with you?*

My second, Tristan.

Daegan had second thoughts about Tristan entering the Tribunal realm with that backpack.

Before he could say a word, Daegan's body surged with the pull of being teleported quickly. When he reappeared, he faced Loki, Justitia, and Hermes.

Tristan had not made the trip.

That meant Daegan would have to admit he could not teleport out of this realm on his own. That limited his position when dealing with difficult deities.

A dark sky spread from side to side over this circular land, which stretched far and wide in every direction.

Twinkling stars filled the dark night sky above.

Quinn stood to the side, looking exhausted and bleeding anger. Regardless, he spoke up in a clear voice. "I request a moment to update Daegan on what has transpired here as I always strive to respect your time."

"Very well." Loki often dressed as he did today, as if he were a powerful businessman in Atlanta, when he was so much more dangerous. As usual, he wore a bored expression meant to belittle others.

Quinn added, "It will be telepathic, which will be much faster."

Hermes never paused in strumming a repetitive tune.

Justitia's gown never changed from the cream white material. In one hand she held the scales of justice. She lifted her other hand to intervene, but Loki said, "Go ahead. Since it will be so efficient, you have one minute."

Turning to Daegan, Quinn maintained his professional expression when he started speaking mind-to-mind. *They're blaming you with stealing the grimoire that was in VIPER's vault. I argued that you were not here, but out hunting a dragon impersonating you. While I hated to admit a second dragon was on the loose, it was the best excuse I had for you not being present.*

Daegan kept his face blank while he replied. *Tzader filled me in on much of this. VIPER might as well know about the second dragon since that is not goin' away. Have they questioned Macha, Queen Maeve, or Cathbad?*

No. I pushed for that early on—

Loki pushed power behind his voice. "We want the grimoire returned now, dragon."

Quinn flinched as if hit, but Daegan never moved a muscle until he turned to speak to the Tribunal.

"I assume ya speak of the one locked away in your vault. I would gladly hand over that volume if I possessed it. I do not. I am concerned over how ya allowed someone to steal the volume. I was under the impression the VIPER vault was impenetrable except for teleportin'."

Justitia said, "That was my understanding as well, but the Imortiks invaded VIPER headquarters. During that attack, someone broke into the vault."

Daegan allowed a silence to hang in the air before he asked, "How many beins' can access the vault besides the Tribunal members and your liaison?"

Loki and company looked affronted by that slight. He snarled, "We are not suspected of stealing."

Opening his arms wide in resignation, Daegan noted, "'Tis a bit narrow-minded to think only I could have accessed the vault, especially when I do not even know where the vault is located. Did Sen not recognize a power signature left from the bein' who entered? In fact, where is Sen?"

Justitia surprised Daegan by speaking when he'd expected Loki to be in charge. Her lips flattened. "Sen was nowhere near the vault when the attack erupted. He was battling Imortiks trying to reach your imprisoned Beladors."

Daegan asked, "Why did he battle the Imortiks?"

Those on the Tribunal dais stared at each other. Even Quinn sent him a mild frown.

For the first time since Daegan arrived, Loki's mouth curled with a smile. His sarcasm returned with his change in attitude. "I didn't realize you cared so little for your minions, dragon. If not for Quinn arguing nonstop, I would have had those three Beladors destroyed by now."

Face still calm, Quinn tensed at the casual offer to kill Beladors.

Daegan had been attacked by Imortiks, more than once, had put his dragon at risk time and again while trying to find at least one grimoire volume, battled a dragon determined to kill him who caused Tristan to bite off his own hand, and now Queen Maeve had captured Casidhe.

People were sorely testing him these days.

He didn't flinch at Loki's disgusting comment. Daegan's voice dropped low, drawing his power and dragon to the surface. "To jest about takin' the life of even one of my people is a dangerous action. I value every one of my followers and have been fightin' to save their lives, the lives of humans, and that of any other supernatural beins'. I questioned why Sen would have cared about Imortiks gettin' to those already sharin' their bodies with an Imortik."

Releasing a long breath, Quinn glanced at Daegan and gave a slight nod, which Daegan took as a positive sign.

Mouth twisted in a sour shape, Loki flicked a hand, indicating the insignificance of this dialogue. "Evidently Sen was caught up performing his duty and your people benefitted by his overachievement."

Daegan grunted a deep sound, part of which had come from his dragon.

Justitia returned to the original discussion. "We must have that grimoire returned."

Showing consideration for the one Tribunal member who would appreciate it, Daegan replied, "With all due respect, Justitia, we need more than to have one volume of the grimoire in hand. We must bring together all three grimoires to push the Imortiks back behind the death wall, then seal it."

Loki huffed out a breath. "You want us to believe you are actively trying to accomplish such a task?"

"Believe as ya choose, but that is exactly what I am tryin' to do. I left here to hunt a rogue dragon and, no, I was not able to capture that dragon. While gone, I discovered information which might lead me to one of the grimoire volumes hidden long ago. If I am able to make this happen within three weeks, less now in fact, I have a chance to save my people who have been infected. If we work together, we can push the Imortiks behind the death wall forever. I do not have details on how to accomplish that yet, but I shall. The longer I stay here, the less time I have to give us all a chance to save this world. Ya should be askin' others about the grimoire."

Loki's eyes boiled white hot. "Do not think to tell us how to do our duties. You are here to answer a question. Daegan of Treoir, do you have the Immortuos Grimoire volume locked away in the VIPER vault until yesterday, the volume your family originally hid?"

"No." Daegan crossed his arms and shook his head. "Ya know I speak the truth. I do not glow red."

Justitia sighed as if tired of the discussion. "Then you are free to go."

Loki yanked his head to her. "Not so quickly, Justitia." Ignoring her ire, Loki asked, "Daegan of Treoir, do you have any *other* volumes of the Immortuos Grimoire in your possession?"

"No." Daegan should be happy to have lost that box to be able to stand here and reply truthfully, but he would not sleep until Casidhe was freed and that grimoire box found. "Ya may ask me that question as many ways as ya choose, but ya will continue to receive the same answer."

Making a sound of exasperation, Loki grumbled, "Very well, you may leave."

"No."

Quinn sent Daegan a what-the-hell-are-you-doing look.

Shaking his head at Quinn, Daegan kept his attention on the Tribunal trio where Loki glowered at him. Justitia's lips turned down. Hermes paused in strumming and frowned as if someone had asked for a different tune.

Calling up two silver balls to toss into the air one after another, Loki appeared unconcerned. "I thought you were in a hurry to leave."

"I wish to offer an exchange."

The silver balls paused in flight. Loki angled his head at Daegan. His eyes asked if this was some trick. "What would an exchange involve, dragon?"

"I will inform ya as soon as I locate all three grimoires and bring ya the names of those who have opened the rift, if I can find them as well. I would prefer to deal with those behind releasing the Imortiks myself, but I shall defer to the Tribunal to serve justice if at all possible."

Still holding a suspicious expression, Loki said, "That is unlike you, Daegan. You must want something important to make such an offer. What do you want?"

Daegan had to be free to save his people and to stop the Imortiks, but the one thing pummeling his mind the hardest right now was saving Casidhe. For that, he had to make an offer that would intrigue Loki. "Do ya agree to this exchange if it is within your powers to deliver what I want?"

"*Anything* is within my powers," Loki bragged and smiled.

"Finding all three grimoire volumes may not be," Daegan said, tossing out a potential damp towel on the negotiations. He needed these three to realize something like the Imortiks might be a danger greater than all of them if they fought each other.

Loki's smile turned into a deadly sneer. "We agree, but if you fail to deliver those behind this Imortik outbreak to us, you will give us something *we* ask for in exchange."

That flipped this conversation the wrong way. He did not want to commit to an open-ended deal with a Tribunal lead by Loki. "What would the Tribunal request if I cannot deliver the one behind the Imortiks?"

Justitia turned to Loki as if to confer on this, but Loki's eyes gleamed with excitement. He knew exactly what he wanted. "The name of your mother."

Hermes hit the off-tune chord and slapped his hand against the lyre strings.

Justitia's jaw dropped.

Loki glanced at his companions on the dais. "What?"

Hermes shook his head and returned to strumming. Justitia closed her mouth and gave him a regal nod of her head. Loki had found an opening to determine the identity of Daegan's mother, which he had wielded as a weapon at times to keep the Tribunals in line. They knew she was a deity, but that was all.

Besides Daegan, only his father had known her identity and he had warned Daegan to never call upon her unless he had no hope of surviving. A last option and a dangerous one, according to King Gruffyn.

Daegan would have called to her had he been able to while trapped in TÅµr Medb. He and Ruadh had survived that torment. To give up her name to this group was unthinkable.

But to deny Loki these terms would prevent Daegan from gaining Casidhe.

Quinn didn't turn to give Daegan his opinion. He stood calmly with his hands behind his back, but his fingers clutched tightly.

The decision to accept that deal resided entirely with Daegan.

If he backed down now, he would save no one. "I agree *if* ya agree to keep my Beladors in your lockdown safe from harm and release them when the Imortiks are put down. I will take full responsibility for all of my people at that point if they are still possessed by Imortiks."

Walking around the dais, Loki ignored the two silver balls following behind him like puppies.

Justitia frowned and moved aside.

Hermes remained in his position with a clueless half-smile on his face for Loki.

Murmuring softly, Loki returned to his usual position on the left of Justitia. He flipped a finger forward and his silver orbs flew over his shoulder to land in one hand. "We will agree. If you do not uphold your part of divulging your mother's identity should this exchange not work out in your favor, any being connected to you in any way, Belador, ally, whatever, will be forfeited. Now, what is your request, dragon?"

Daegan always felt a heavy weight of responsibility on his shoulders, but the burden just tripled. "I wish to have Queen Maeve brought here for me to question. In addition to answers I need, I will ask a question just for the benefit of this Tribunal."

Loki's eyebrows drew together, but he shrugged. "I will call to her. I cannot force her to appear."

"You can if you tell her she is being given a chance to clear her name," Quinn suggested.

Loki acted as if he hadn't paid attention to Quinn, but after a slight delay Queen Maeve arrived, scowling at all of them.

"How dare you request my appearance," she shouted. Her head wobbled as if about to change shape.

Daegan hoped not. He needed her answering questions.

Usually soft-spoken, Justitia powered up her voice. "I will remind you, Queen Maeve, to not lose control here. We overlooked one time. We will not overlook a second."

Golden waves of hair moved around agitated until Queen Maeve snapped her fingers and the errant locks flew into tightly braided strands that wrapped around her head in an intricate style.

She eyed Daegan for only a moment then snapped at Loki, "What do you want?"

Loki had disposed of the silver orbs and crossed his arms. "You must answer Daegan's questions."

Ignoring Daegan, she spat out, "I do *not* answer to that lizard."

"You will give him answers today." Loki's tone implied

no room for argument.

Queen Maeve must not have noticed the trickster god's tone. "Why?"

Daegan interjected, "Because we are here to discuss a missing volume of the Immortuos Grimoire."

Turning unusually quiet, Queen Maeve lifted her chin. "I don't have that grimoire. There. Are you all happy now?"

"But ya do have Casidhe Luigsech," Daegan accused.

Queen Maeve's eyes flickered with excitement. What had he just given her? When she said nothing, he took it as much a confirmation as if she'd admitted out loud she had Casidhe.

Daegan shifted his jaw to loosen tight muscles. He needed patience to make this happen. "I want Luigsech returned to me. She is under my protection."

Face splitting with a grin, Queen Maeve turned to Daegan. "Come and get her, lizard."

Addressing the Tribunal, Daegan said, "Luigsech belongs to me."

Eyebrows lifted all around the room.

Clearly surprised, Loki asked, "What exactly does that mean?"

"It means Luigsech is a descendant of the squire family who kept historical records for my father's family. Unfortunately, she was unable to tell me anythin' to fill in the missin' years I spent as a prisoner in TÅµr Medb."

Queen Maeve didn't bat an eyelash at that accusation.

Daegan took a risk, since he did not know this for sure. "Queen Maeve used her new scryin' tool to observe me with Luigsech and she will use it on others." Ignoring the queen's gasp of anger, Daegan finished. "Queen Maeve kidnapped Luigsech, someone who researches ancient writin's, because she is tryin' to be the first to deliver a grimoire volume to the Imortik master who offered survival to any powerful bein' handin' him one volume."

Stunned, Queen Maeve said nothing.

Loki roared, "Is this true, Queen Maeve? Remember what happens if you lie. Turning bright red would be only the first consequence."

She balked. "I *have* heard of the Imortik offer. I did not kidnap anyone to find the grimoire."

Daegan knew then she had taken Casidhe to use as bait to capture him, but Queen Maeve could have later decided to use Casidhe to find the grimoires as well.

Justitia's voice deepened into a threatening rumble. "You would entertain annihilating the supernatural world for *what*? Power? Do you really think an Imortik would not possess your body?"

"*I am powerful!*" Queen Maeve shouted. "Those miserable beings wouldn't dare touch me."

Daegan had her. "So ya openly admit ya hope to accept a partnership from the Imortik master?"

"I did not say anything of the sort," Queen Maeve muttered in a guilty tone.

Loki straightened his shoulders and dropped his gaze down his nose at her. "You did not say anything *yet*."

Daegan would not allow Loki to pull the point of this meeting away from him getting Casidhe back. He suggested the simplest way to yank the Tribunal off Queen Maeve's back. "If ya wish to prove ya are not usin' Luigsech to find a grimoire volume, then teleport her here right now and let her speak for herself to clear ya."

Not a being in the Tribunal meeting made a sound, waiting to see what Queen Maeve would do.

She vanished.

CHAPTER 16

CASIDHE WALKED CIRCLES AROUND THE giant room in TÅµr Medb to keep her panic at bay.

Not working.

Queen Maeve had disappeared without a word, which might be a good thing if Daegan caught her outside this realm and forced the crazy woman to free Casidhe.

Not a realistic possibility, but Casidhe had no better way to keep her mind from a full-blown meltdown. Where was Daegan? Had he returned to Spain and discovered her backpack in the woods?

Or was he in his own battle to survive?

Energy burst into the room, knocking Casidhe off her feet. "Ow." She jumped up and rubbed her elbow. One look at Queen Maeve with her wild hair flying around and Casidhe tried to calm her racing heart.

No time like the present to go digging for information. "What am I doin' here?"

The woman's perfect eyebrows lifted. "You were captured. What gave you the idea you would be asking me questions? Are you one of those humans with mental issues?"

Casidhe narrowed her eyes, but stopped when she realized Queen Maeve had not realized Casidhe was not human. Had she held her sword and engaged this being in a battle, she would have given herself away before now.

She would also have likely died on the spot.

The professor had known Casidhe was not human, but

they had talked before they met.

Tossing her hands wide, Queen Maeve complained to the empty room, "How could she have been damaged so easily?"

Casidhe looked around to see who Maeve spoke to, but they were the only two inside this gigantic room surrounded in rock walls. When Casidhe turned to face forward, Queen Maeve had stepped close enough to spook her.

She jumped back.

Eyeing Casidhe as if she were a blob of mindless cells, the ruler of TÅµr Medb asked, "Your head isn't damaged, is it?"

Casidhe considered lying, but convincing this woman she was not capable of conversation might reduce her value to the point of termination. "I didn't hurt my head, no. I'm just a little surprised at bein' here. I'm *not* mentally damaged."

Did a smile on the face of someone clearly mental mean that Casidhe had saved her hide for a bit longer?

"Then answer my question," crazy woman ordered.

Wiping a hand over her head, Casidhe's exhaustion colored her words. "Not to be difficult, but what question?"

"What were you doing with Daegan?"

The queen never asked that question. What a loon.

When Casidhe took too long to reply, her body elevated off the ground six feet in the air. Her hands yanked above her head and an invisible force clamped each one, holding her in place. "Whoa. What's happenin'?"

Queen Maeve stared up at her. "You seem to have trouble paying attention. Now, answer my question before I decide it was a waste of time to find you."

"Okay, okay. Daegan asked me to search for information he needed, which I did and as you can see it didn't pay off." Until Casidhe knew what this woman wanted, she would try her best to convince her that she had only known

Daegan through a business arrangement.

Tapping a long black nail against her cheek, the queen asked, "What information?"

Mentioning the grimoire was a bad idea. "He wanted to know the history of his family. I think he might have suffered amnesia at some point in his life." She would not admit she knew Daegan had been imprisoned in this realm. Maybe right in this very room. Plenty of space in the middle for a throne.

The queen started walking in an odd figure-eight pattern. Her gown swished around, giggling like a child. "Did he ask you to hunt for a grimoire?"

Casidhe would have shrugged, but not possible when hanging like wet laundry. More importantly, she could not allow this woman to know Daegan had been hunting the grimoire volumes.

Hurrying to reply before something else happened to her body, Casidhe said, "No. That would have cost him extra." She held her breath as the queen reversed course and began walking in an oval pattern.

Was she OCD or just nuts?

When Queen Maeve finished her circuit, she turned toward Casidhe. "Were you waiting on Daegan to return when I found you?"

"Well, yes. He doesn't want to see my bill after leavin' my ass stranded on the top of a mountain. A deposit will *not* be coverin' that. Now that I'm in this place, I'm realizin' he must not be human. I read about dragon shifters, but ... didn't believe they existed. My world view has changed incredibly and not in a good way."

Queen Maeve studied her with a blank expression.

Casidhe knew that look on anyone. This woman did not believe her. No one was coming for her. She had to find her own way home. She asked, "Is there somethin' I can do to trade for my freedom?"

The woman gave her a look of amusement. "Originally, your only value to me was to bring Daegan here."

Excitement shoved through Casidhe, lifting the fear and worry she'd been dragging along. This queen really thought Daegan would show up?

Did that mean Daegan knew where Casidhe was being held?

"But we both know he isn't coming here," Queen Maeve added, dropping a bomb on Casidhe's relief party. Damn her.

Casidhe had to prove she was worth keeping alive long enough to give Daegan time to find her, but she did not have the floor.

"I understand you have expertise at researching ancient writings," the queen said, giving Casidhe the opening she needed.

"Sure. I find old books and text. I can translate a lot of ancient languages. People come to me to determine the value of a rare book or ask me to help find specific journals and other very old text." Casidhe offered a polite smile of pride.

Could this bitch even read?

"I have a task for you," the queen announced.

Casidhe's heart started doing the hallelujah dance, but she couldn't get her hopes up yet. "Sure. Great. What can I do for you?"

"Find a volume of the Immortuos Grimoire."

The same grimoire Daegan and Cathbad were hunting?

Casidhe wanted to tell Queen Maeve to take a number and step in line. Instead, she cocked her head in confusion. "A grimoire? Isn't that a book of majik? How old is the one you're huntin'?"

"What a waste of time," the woman snarled. "I'll just put you in the dungeon until I determine if you have value or not."

Oh, hell no. Casidhe could see being left in a dungeon forever. "I can find almost anythin'. Just give me some background and a chance to research. What have you got to lose?"

The woman's golden locks stopped swirling and settled across her shoulders. "So you were not hunting that grimoire for Daegan?"

"No. That would have been much simpler than tryin' to fill in his missin' years."

"Hmm." Swirly queen spun again, looking up as if she were thinking. She stopped and pointed a black nail. "The grimoire is in three volumes and was created during the time of dragons. Does that shock you?"

Was she being tested?

This Casidhe could do. "No. I told you I've now guessed Daegan must be nonhuman. I've researched deeply into that time period and into the Treoirs. I admit it was hard to believe dragons existed, but between Daegan vanishin' from Spain and some dragon burnin' up land in different countries, I'm a believer." Casidhe waited as her kidnapper smiled slyly, encouraging her to continue. "I would have actually been excited to look for a grimoire, had he asked me. His loss. If you can tell me more about it, I'll do my best to help you find the grimoire." Holding her breath, Casidhe watched for any indication the queen had realized she'd just lied.

"Why?"

So far so good. Casidhe explained, "I'm captured and bein' held in a realm and want to make a deal. If I find this for you, I'd like to go home. Then you supernaturals can continue on doin' whatever you do."

The woman smiled, then started laughing as she spun in place. Her gown laughed along with her. Her voice changed to one of a young woman. "Wait until they realize what I have." She acted as if Casidhe were a toy she'd found that no one else knew about.

Who were *they* she'd mentioned?

Arms aching, Casidhe said, "Think we could finish this with both of us on the ground?"

Without a word of warning, Casidhe dropped to the floor like a puppet whose strings had been slashed. She bent her knees at the last moment to cushion the hit.

A pain stabbed her from legs to spine. "Ouch, dammit."

"Don't be a baby." Queen Maeve turned serious. "What do you need to do your research?"

Well, at least it sounded as if Casidhe would be allowed to live while she researched. That should give Daegan time to find her, right? Maybe if he brought Tristan, the two of them could break her out.

Casidhe rubbed her back. "I would need my library in Galway. I have an extensive collection of very old and rare journals. Depending on how much information you can provide about the timeline for this grimoire, I may be able to narrow down—"

"No. Your library is nothing compared to mine," her kidnapper said.

What kind of library would this queen possess?

Why not yank Queen Maeve's chain to see if she would share anything significant. "That's fine. I'll work in any library, but I'll still need reference material from the time of dragons."

Then an errant thought hit her.

Cathbad and Queen Maeve were supposed to be partners of some sort.

Was Cathbad here? Would Casidhe run into him in the TÅµr Medb library?

She did not have his book on dark druids. If he showed up, he'd probably pop a vein. Or maybe she could convince him to teleport her to her backpack and escape this place.

That had flaws, too.

The minute he touched his book, he'd know she'd read the area he'd forbidden her from translating before he could be present.

She also had a scepter worth a fortune in the same backpack, which had to be delivered to the oracle.

Going to her backpack with Cathbad would be a bad decision.

The backpack might not be there if Daegan had returned to find her and took it with him.

Worse, the backpack might be there if Daegan had not survived.

The silence jerked her back to the moment. Why hadn't Queen Maeve said anything else?

Repeating her comment, Casidhe said, "I'll still be needin' reference material from the time of dragons."

Queen Maeve lifted her hands.

Oh, hell.

Casidhe teleported away and reappeared in a library larger than the last room. Books filled shelves standing twenty feet tall and stretching a hundred feet deep. Maybe more.

This place stole her breath.

Her heart thumped a wobbly beat though. She called out, "Helloooo."

Queen Maeve appeared and snapped, "What?"

Note to self to be careful speaking in here. Casidhe said, "I have not eaten or had water in a long time."

Grumbling as if imposed upon, Queen Maeve pointed to a table behind Casidhe where fruit, cheese, water, and some kind of cooked meat appeared. "Now what?"

How could she act as if Casidhe had asked for the moon? Casidhe bit back her angry reply and offered a compliment. "I admit your library is far larger than mine."

Queen Maeve gave her a smug look.

It felt an awful lot like men comparing sizes. Ugh.

Getting back to what she had to do next, Casidhe suggested, "I would be able to move more quickly if you pointed me toward the books regardin' dragons."

Without looking up at any bookshelves, Queen Maeve pointed a finger over her left shoulder twice then at the table. Two huge scrolls floated down and settled on the table like well-trained pets. She then pointed over her head at a high shelf and down at the table. A thick book with a wooden cover Casidhe guessed would weigh an easy twenty pounds backed off of the shelf and floated down to settle next to the scrolls.

Alrighty then.

Queen Maeve crossed her arms. "This should be all you need."

Casidhe really wanted to one up her and admit she'd been trained by the best of dragon families. She carried knowledge not found in any print form. But antagonizing the crazy queen of TÅµr Medb ranked right up there with free-falling without a parachute.

Both would be exhilarating and both would end with her death.

Casidhe turned to the table. "Thank you for the food, water, and books. I'll get started." She hoped these were not Cathbad's books. He seemed possessive of his.

"Do not waste any time. If I return and you have not found something sufficient, you'll end up somewhere not as comfortable until I decide what to do with you."

Message received.

Casidhe's next destination would not be as nice as hanging by invisible cuffs.

"I heard Daegan was killed," Queen Maeve whispered right beside her ear.

Casidhe gasped and jerked around with tears in her eyes. "No."

Queen Maeve stood too close, laughing. "I knew there had to be more going on than family research."

Busted. Well, as long as Casidhe could not change her reaction, she said, "I admit we became friendly."

"More than friends," Queen Maeve challenged then shook her head. "You must not have researched the Treoir family very well or you'd have known with whom you were dealing."

Why did that sound as if the queen knew something about Daegan that Casidhe did not? She stammered, "I … I don't understand. He was nice to me."

"Of course he was. Everyone of power is hunting the grimoire volumes, including Daegan. Whether he told you or not, he is. He was known as quite the rogue in his time and hasn't changed. Young women have always fallen victim to his charms. He had a chance to mate with an ice dragon shifter and turned her down."

Casidhe knew the ice dragon history, which gave some credibility to the queen's words. "Why are you tellin' me this?"

"Remember when I mentioned I originally wanted you to lure Daegan here?"

"Yes." Casidhe feared saying anything more. Her heart thumped wildly. She braced herself for the queen's next words.

"He's not dead."

"Okay." Not just okay, but Casidhe's entire body felt battered by that mean shock.

"Daegan is very much alive," the queen went on. "I left here when the VIPER Tribunal asked me to join a meeting."

Casidhe had heard about VIPER and the Tribunals, but not much on how they operated. "What was the meetin' about?"

Queen Maeve frowned. "Waste of time really. Daegan

was there lobbying to bring me in."

Casidhe's heart surged. He not only lived, but was trying to find her. She kept emotion from her voice. "What did he want?"

"He told the Tribunal I used my scrying wall to watch him and capture you."

"So he knows I'm here?" Okay, that sounded too anxious.

"Oh, yes. I expected him to demand your return."

"He didn't?" Casidhe was losing the battle to keep her emotions locked down.

Waving her hands around, Queen Maeve said, "No. I was quite put out. He only called me in to claim I was using his resource tool to hunt the grimoire. He tried to make the Tribunal agree that anything you found for me belonged to him. The Tribunal refused his request. Daegan became angry and said he would find the grimoire volumes on his own. Of course, he claims to want to save the world with them, but those of us in power know differently. We have all known that dragon a long time." Queen Maeve looked around as if done with that topic. "I think you have everything you need. Get busy."

She vanished.

Casidhe stood there with her mouth open. She made a keening sound she couldn't stop and hugged her stomach, dropping to her knees. She dropped her head against the table. Tears streamed down her cheeks and dripped on her knees.

Daegan knew she was here and hadn't even tried to get her back?

Her heart imploded. She covered her mouth to keep from howling like a wounded animal.

That bastard kissed her and played her.

He'd dragged her heart into this and stomped on it.

Her heart ached. She could still feel a connection. Probably something he intentionally generated so he could track her down again to find out if she'd located another grimoire. He'd acted as if he felt something for her just like she'd felt for him.

It didn't matter. Everything fit now. He'd abandoned her on the side of that mountain, assuring her he'd return and sealing that promise with a kiss. But he was free now and cared nothing about saving her. He probably had her backpack.

Oh, no!

She pounded her fist against the ancient wood table. Her books. The scepter. Her sword. Daegan had all of it.

She finished her pity party and sniffled. Fury drove energy back into her weary body. She climbed to her feet. Yanking a cloth napkin from the food tray, she wiped her eyes and face, then blew her nose.

Staring at the books so much like her sanctuary in Galway, she slammed the napkin down.

Her moment of weakness for a heartless dragon only interested in the grimoire was over. The next truth hit her between the eyes.

Of course Daegan had not returned immediately.

He had the grimoire he wanted.

Heaving a deep breath, she stepped over to take a seat. She would save her own ass. She would be the person Herrick and her family needed. If Daegan could shove her aside so easily and do his duty, whatever the hell that was, she could do the same but better.

He'd left her to fend for herself.

She would find another grimoire and use it to gain her freedom.

Then she would bring the wrath of Herrick to get her sword back or die trying.

That dragon would regret playing with her.

CHAPTER 17

REESE ROLLED DOWN A HILL, her head bouncing on the ground and her limbs slapping rocks and thick stems. She inhaled and sucked in dirt, then landed in water with a loud splash.

Dropping her feet down, she stood up in two-foot-deep water sputtering. Now she had water in her mouth to go with the dirt.

She rinsed her mouth and spit out the sludge.

Crows cawed overhead, but she could see nothing except black skies. What time was it in whatever place that miserable raven god had dropped her?

She drew a fresh breath and shouted, "*You outdid your usual asshat self, Yáahl!*" Let his crow minions take that message back.

Shoving wet hair off her face, she trudged out of the shallow creek onto a grassy bank and dropped to her knees, breathing hard. When she looked around, the creek was only twenty feet wide.

Did Yáahl even care about the locals in this area who would be at risk with a demon magnet in their backyard?

A wet demon magnet.

She flipped over and sat down, staring up as a cloud moved past a partial moon. The same sky she'd stared at as a child who believed in dreams.

Dreams were for human children.

She couldn't sit here forever. Might as well get moving and figure out what country she was in. At least it wasn't snowing, but in this day and age, a person with no money and no identification was SOL when it came to getting around.

Pushing to her feet, she took in her jeans and blouse that had been clean before visiting the raven god. Now her clothes and underwear were soaked with grit in uncomfortable places. She didn't need a mirror to confirm her hair disaster.

She had to be careful or someone would call the local authorities to pick her up as an escapee from a psych ward.

Considering that she had thought Yáahl would help her, she probably belonged in a psych ward. He could have teleported her to a familiar urban setting, but that might have strained his pinky finger. He couldn't even allow her a safe place to stay until the end of her pregnancy.

That miserable jerk had made it sound as if she whined to him all the time.

Twice. She'd gone to him twice to protect others as demons were more attracted to her energy than usual when she was pregnant.

Also to protect her child the first time.

Damn him for refusing her sanctuary, knowing what she faced and that she did not want anyone harmed just by being too close to her.

Did Yáahl think she'd just give up and hand her body over to be syphoned of energy by the first wave of demons to come for her?

No way. She would not go down without a fight for one thing. More than that, she would protect her child to the very end. He was still alive inside her. Until the time came to deliver, she'd insure this baby felt cherished then ... she dropped her chin. Her throat squeezed tight.

She couldn't think about losing her baby.

If she didn't redirect her focus right now, that single thought would take her legs out from beneath her.

Something whistled overhead and hit the water, sinking out of sight.

She jumped up and pushed her way through thick brambles and found a perfectly manicured golf course. A guy stood a hundred yards away with a golf club in hand. On her left, a green waited for someone with better control.

She stepped out on the course.

The man jumped into his golf cart and came flying up to her. "Did you see my ball?"

Was he serious? "Yes. It took a nosedive in the middle of the creek behind me."

He cursed. Fortyish with thinning red hair and a little pudgy, he seemed heartbroken. He must have never lost a ball before.

Sure.

He stared down his pointy nose, eyeing her from head to toe. "Did you fall in the creek?"

"My foot slipped," she hedged. Asking what country she was in would raise his suspicion. "I was trying to catch my dog and lost sight of him out here in the dark. I thought he came this way. I ended up running right through these bushes. Had no idea a creek was on the other side. I don't live here. I'm visiting someone." She made a point of looking around. "What's the name of this golf course?"

"Atlanta Country Club."

Heh. The raven god had dropped her in Atlanta. While she was glad to know she could find her way around, she would not thank him for dumping her close to Quinn.

A golf ball hit the top of the golf cart, sounding like a gunshot before bouncing off.

This place was dangerous. "Why are you playing at night?"

He gave her an indignant look. "It's close to five in the morning. I work in the clubhouse. Just getting in some practice." He looked back. "You idiot. Why didn't you call fore?"

Someone way back yelled, "That you, Terry? What the hell are you doing out here?"

"Me? I work here. What are you doing?"

This looked like a fight brewing.

"Sorry to hold you up." She backed away and started walking the perimeter of the course as they yammered at each other.

She was in North Atlanta and that creek probably flowed into the Chattahoochee River that ran through the greater Atlanta area. That put her twelve to fifteen miles north of the apartment she shared with Phoedra, who she hoped was still in Treoir realm. According to the all-knowing Yáahl, she was.

Going to that apartment would bring Quinn running the minute the Belador doorman called his boss.

Quinn probably had Beladors looking everywhere for her.

How was she going to explain leaving and coming back?

How was she going to keep him safe when he would refuse to stay away?

She mentally slapped herself to focus. She couldn't deal with what to do about Quinn right now. Ten years ago when she lived here, long before meeting him, she'd hiked an area due west of this country club. That might be the direction to take while she figured out plan B.

Plan A had been staying in evil raven god land.

She walked a ways to find an easy place to cross the creek then started trekking what she believed was west through the wooded landscape. If she kept going this way, she should find a business or industrial area around Windy Hill Road, somewhere outside the perimeter highway that circled Atlanta.

Then what?

A branch hit her in the face.

She swatted it away and the damn branch whipped back, hitting her again. Hands on hips, she stared down, gathering herself so she didn't attack a puny little pine tree in the dark.

Moving again, she shoved low branches aside and wiped wet hair off her face, feeling more in control.

Then a root as thick as her arm caught the toe of her shoe. She stumbled forward, going headfirst at the tree. Her hands broke her fall and saved her head from injury. She scratched the hell out of her hands.

Some women cried. She cursed.

Vividly.

The end result was the same. She felt better.

Stepping from beneath the tree, she wiped her palms off on her pants. Was she still going west? Had she ever been?

She had no idea.

The sound of cackling crows and wings batting the air came and went.

Screw Yáahl.

If she could channel Daniel Boone, she might figure out how to find her way and track a bear at the same time.

It would just be nice to know she wasn't walking in circles.

After moving quickly for another stretch, she still had found nothing to indicate her location. Tired and hungry, she squatted in a stand of trees to catch her breath.

A firefly blinked once then a moment later glowed again.

She smiled at a memory from the days when she sat outside watching them light up. Back when she'd been relatively safe sitting outside at night. Before she'd become pregnant and unleashed the sweet scent of her demon energy to monsters.

Hard to imagine anywhere safe now.

She didn't move for a moment, content to watch the tiny creature flying around, bringing joy to others just by lighting up. When she died, she wanted to come back as a firefly. No, she wanted to be a hummingbird. Those tiny birds flew like a cross between a fighter jet and a helicopter. Sure, they had predators, but something had to be insanely fast to catch that itty-bitty bird.

Yep, she'd be a badass hummingbird.

She stood and cracked her neck. Hadn't this area been full of hiking trails? She hadn't been around here for ten years. Maybe she remembered it wrong and had entered swamp land.

She hadn't even found a road yet.

Energy buzzed in her chest.

Uh oh. Something had found her. A demon.

She didn't even know which way to run. If she made the mistake of running back to the golf course, she would drag a vicious monster to those people.

Running in any other direction might have the same outcome.

Damn. This forest would not work in her favor.

She needed room to sprint and move for fighting a demon.

Breathing fast, she placed her hands on her stomach. "We're gonna fight our way out, Junior. I will protect you with my last breath, but no matter what happens I need you to know I love you so much. I would give up my life for you to live yours. If this doesn't go well, always remember I love you. Very much. So does your dad. He would have been an amazing dad."

Heat built quickly beneath her hand then dissipated.

Had that been Junior?

She smiled. Her boy was a badass, too. "Okay, let's do this."

She'd been so careful with her first pregnancy and hadn't brought her baby to life.

A demon had better be ready for the hell of trying to

harm her baby. Drawing in a series of deep breaths, she started walking, hyperalert to everything around her with her energy spinning up. More than sounds, she noticed the lack of birds tweeting or squirrels racing around.

Pay attention to natural animals.

Their senses were tuned to danger twenty-four-seven and had taught her a lot during her early days of fighting demons alone.

Something ran through the woods, breaking branches and howling.

Reese could not run and put humans in danger.

She turned to stand her ground.

Energy coiled and grew inside her. More than one set of footsteps pounded in her direction. Shit. She put her hand on her stomach, wishing she could be alone in this battle.

Red glowing eyes showed up first. A demon crashed through undergrowth, running insanely fast.

Reese rubbed her hands together, generating a crapload of power.

Two more demons followed that one, moving just as fast.

That just screwed her plan. If she hit the first one with a big load, she wouldn't have as much for the next two.

She needed them running in single file.

The first one stood over seven feet tall, no hair on its upper body covered in gray skin, all that glowing an ugly greenish hue. Thick hair hung from his thighs down. Couldn't have grown any hair to cover his dangly nether regions?

Glowing red eyes, one horn sticking out the back of his head, and swirling tattoos on his face came into view fast.

She sidestepped twice to her right.

All three demons altered their direction, falling into line. Better.

She revved up her energy ball and blasted it at the first

one. He lit up like a supersized firework mortar gone bad.

Demon number two slammed into the first one, lighting up and exploding into fire.

Hot damn. That worked.

Not so fast. Those two crashed to the ground. Demon number three jumped over those two as they turned to ash and kept running for her like a heat-seeking missile.

That demon wanted her energy the way crackheads lusted after cocaine.

"Hell, no. You aren't touching my baby," she yelled, balling her hands again, but not fast enough.

She threw what she had, knocking him sideways. He didn't go down.

Shit.

Scrambling away from him, she backed up fast, trying to gain ground for a chance to generate more power.

This demon stood only six feet, had a shock of glowing blue hair sprouting out from the top of his head, and a horn sticking out above each ear. Big cauliflower ears.

He regained his feet and hissed, turning to her. "Mine."

"Not my type," she shouted, still backpedaling.

He hunched his shoulders like a bodybuilder showing off, but his body started taking on more mass.

Not good. She ran at an angle, weaving through trees. She called up her energy, rolling her hands together. All she got was a small surge.

"Mine!" the demon shouted, coming for her.

"You remind me of a seagull."

He slowed down, confused.

Oh, great. Maybe she could make another movie reference from *Finding Nemo* and that would stop him completely.

He roared and raced for her again.

Reese almost smacked a tree straight on again. That would have knocked her out. The demon would think it was his birthday and someone delivered a Reese cake. She had nowhere to go and could not outrun him forever.

She was already suffering oxygen debt and gasping for air.

Turning to face him, she backed up until she bumped into a tree.

That miserable piece of crap slowed down and grinned. Big glowing-white incisors filled its mouth. "Mine."

"You have a piece of spinach stuck in your teeth."

He frowned, then shook his head and stalked her, coming forward with long strides.

Moving one hand above the other, she kept balling as much energy as she could and considered the best place to strike his body. Definitely a him. His erection pushed up through the cluster of hair between his legs.

Ugh.

Screw it. When he got within fifteen feet, she stepped into her throw and nailed his flag stick.

He screamed, grabbing himself.

Huh, demons weren't much different from human males when it came to their favorite personal toy.

The demon jumped around.

She would have run, but she had nothing left in the tank after the last two days.

When he stopped howling, he turned to her. No grin. No stalking.

He ran at her.

She raised her hands, calling for any bit of energy to feed into her fingers she could use when he made contact.

Got a trickle of power.

When he came close enough for her to smell his disgusting odor, something hit him. He flew sideways into a fat oak tree.

What had happened?

"*Look out, Reese!*" Evalle came running up with Adrianna, the Sterling witch, on her heels.

Jeans ripped, ponytail askew, and her khaki-colored short-sleeved shirt just as battered, Evalle held her hands up. She had the demon pinned with her kinetics.

Not quite as ragged looking as Evalle, Adrianna raced up with a glowing white orb the size of a baseball spinning above her open palm. She used her other hand to lash out at the demon.

He exploded into flames, then ashes dusted to the ground.

Evalle dropped her arms and looked around. "There are two more around here somewhere."

"No. I killed them," Reese admitted.

Adrianna lifted a delicate eyebrow at that. She wore snug-fitting black jeans and a blazing-red shirt tucked in. A few strands of her blond hair had fallen loose from the long braid hanging down her back.

How that woman managed to look put together while hunting demons, Reese had no idea. Respect.

Adrianna closed her palm. "Two demons when they were running almost like a pack? That's impressive."

For the first time in a long while, Reese felt something warm that had nothing to do with her energy. Admiration from a peer. "Thanks. I'd like to have that white orb you carry around, though."

"Actually, you might not." Adrianna smiled to soften her words. "It comes with its own headaches."

Evalle shoved hair off her face. "Ah, hell. I lost my cap."

"Storm will probably buy you ten to replace it," Adrianna quipped.

"Yes, but that one was broken in." Evalle turned to Reese. "What are you doing here? I heard you disappeared from Quinn's building."

"That's a long story." Reese scratched her neck. She started getting an idea about what she could do between now and delivering the baby. "Look, I'd appreciate it if you two would not tell Quinn I'm here."

Evalle and Adrianna said, "*No!*"

"Fine," Reese groused. "How about just don't go calling him immediately so I can catch my breath. It's not like I can move around Atlanta without him finding out." She clamped her hands on her hips.

"Did you two clear the air?" Evalle asked.

"Yes."

"I don't mean to pry, but does he know ... *everything*?"

"*Yesss.*"

Evalle frowned and looked away then back. "Good talk. What are you going to do now?"

"Have you found the being driving all these demons into Atlanta?"

Adrianna and Evalle shook their heads.

"I think I can help you find where they're coming from."

"Quinn would kill me," Evalle muttered.

Reese had to start right now taking the reins of her life. "Here's the deal. I can either wait around for demons to take me down or we can mount a team to find the source."

Adrianna glanced at Evalle. "I agree with her. It's not safe for her until we can beat down the demon invasion. The national guard has been called in to handle the chaos breaking out, but they're dealing with humans. We either stop the demons or the humans are going to panic more and that could cost the lives of nonhumans we care about."

"You both have good points." Evalle wiped mud splatters off her arm. "Are you going to your apartment?"

Reese shook her head. "I would put the humans there in danger and it takes too many Beladors to babysit me."

"What are you going to do?"

"I have an idea. Quinn won't like it, but he'll just have to deal."

CHAPTER 18

DAEGAN CLOSED HIS EYES IN defeat. How was he going to rescue Casidhe when he couldn't even teleport himself out of the Tribunal meeting on his own?

Opening his eyes, he found Loki, Justitia, and Hermes huddled in a discussion. He'd have thought Loki would be laughing his head off at Queen Maeve disappearing.

Had the prospect of that queen working with the Imortik master sobered Loki's arrogant attitude?

Quinn caught Daegan's eye. He mouthed the words, *Can you teleport?*

Daegan shook his head, rather than risk speaking telepathically.

Clearing his throat, Quinn said, "We've answered your questions." As the three on the dais turned to him, Quinn continued. "As soon as I am outside VIPER headquarters, I will inform my people to contact Trey before calling Sen to receive anyone they contain. That should insure there is no chance of Sen facing Imortiks unexpectedly again, at least from anyone we send in."

Daegan quickly followed up. "As ya can see, I showed ya Queen Maeve is indeed searchin' for a volume of the grimoire to use for a pact with the Imortik master. I am not. My only goal is to stop the Imortiks and return them to imprisonment, then find a better way to hide the volumes located."

Cheek flexing as if he chewed on his thought for a moment, Loki said, "If we determine at any point that you have tricked us today, a kill-on-sight order for every Belador will go live immediately."

"'Tis clearly your choice, Loki, but I have offered to be allies in this fight. I will only caution that ya speak to me, Quinn, or the current Maistir in North America before takin' any deadly action if ya wish me to keep ya informed and continue as an ally."

Justitia angled her blindfolded face to Loki, who paid her no attention. Sounding out of patience, he swept a hand across his chest. "This meeting is over."

Daegan's body flew into a spiral. If he could teleport, he'd pull out of it, but he had to wait to see what Loki had done to him and likely Quinn, too.

When the head-pounding spin ended, Daegan stood outside the VIPER mountain once again.

Tristan spun to Daegan. "How'd it go?"

Quinn appeared at the same moment and answered, "As well as can be expected from those wankers."

Daegan stretched his stiff neck and shoulders. "Not good, not bad. We gained an agreement to not kill our people in the holdin' cells, for now, thanks to Quinn's efforts."

Quinn waved a hand in dismissal. "I would have been happier if I could have managed this meeting without dragging you in there. If not for irritating Loki at the end, we would have been forced to ask him to teleport us."

"I wondered how you pulled off getting teleported out," Tristan said. "At least Loki still doesn't know about the venom in you."

"For now," Daegan amended. "They did bring in Queen Maeve. She all but admitted she has Casidhe, but when pressed she teleported out."

Tristan cursed vividly.

Daegan agreed.

Quinn released a tired sigh. "I need time to meet with our teams and insure no one calls directly to Sen. If they go through Trey, that should solve one problem, but it may mean our people are exposed to deadly situations longer. Depending on what you two have planned to do next, I'd appreciate it if Tristan teleported me to my secure building downtown."

"No problem." Tristan turned to Daegan. "You want to go with us or wait?"

While his second-in-command sounded stronger, Daegan did not wish to run Tristan's energy into the ground. "I shall wait here."

Tristan nodded, then he and Quinn disappeared.

Daegan called up two bottles of water, glad to see his power actually performed as expected. When Tristan reappeared, Daegan handed him a bottle. "Do ya feel up to teleportin' to Treoir?"

Tristan boasted, "Hell, yeah. I'm good, boss, really."

"I am glad ya are." Daegan gave his friend a smile of encouragement.

In the next moment, they teleported into Treoir realm.

And landed in the middle of an argument.

Petrina and the other Alterants who shifted into gryphons faced off with the Belador guards.

Tristan called Petrina his sister, though they only favored each other with glowing green eyes all the Alterants possessed. Tristan and Petrina had found each other while in captivity after being abandoned by their mothers who wanted nothing to do with strange children.

Petrina yelled at the guard, "I don't believe you. Find someone who can answer our questions."

Tristan groaned then said, "Why don't you ask me, Petrina?"

Guards turned, took one look at Daegan standing next to Tristan, and immediately fell into order.

Petrina and her motley group remained in their angry state. "Where have you been?" she demanded, storming over to Tristan. "First I hear you come back injured and rumors about losing a hand, then you're gone again."

Unfolding his arms that had been locked across his chest, Tristan held up his previously injured hand. "All healed up. I've been gone helping Daegan."

Her angry gaze slashed over at Daegan then back to Tristan. "We want to go to Atlanta."

Tristan bristled. "Nope, that's not happening."

"We're more powerful than Beladors." She swung to the guards. "No insult meant, but it's the truth. We should be there helping the teams."

Allyn, the lead guard, shrugged away the insult.

"No." Tristan shook his head.

Daegan stayed out of this. Tristan lead the Alterant gryphon clan and had final say over their activities unless Daegan requested their aid.

Petrina faced Tristan again. "Why not?"

"We're trying to keep as many of our people safe as possible."

"Exactly," she shoved back at him. "We've spent the last week creating housing and getting the families brought in settled here. We are *not* the families. We are warriors. Let us do our part to help or there may be no world left for any of us to go back to."

Tristan crossed his arms again. "Can we discuss this later?"

"No." She crossed hers with a look of mutiny.

"Dammit, Petrina, I don't want any of you exposed to Imortiks."

She waved her hands wildly. "What about the other Beladors in the human world?"

"We don't have room for everyone here," Tristan argued, but Daegan could hear defeat climb into his voice.

She slapped her hands on her hips. "Even more reason to clear up some space. You just don't want *me* to go."

Tristan grabbed his hair. "Okay, fine. No, I don't want you there."

She lowered her arms. "I understand and can appreciate your concern. I would feel the same, but we need to be a part of this and not treated like the red-headed stepchildren left behind." Her voice had softened. "Send us in pairs and we'll work as teams. Send each team with a Belador guide first so the other Alterants and Beladors will know that we will all fight together for a future."

If a man could look kicked in the groin without taking a hit, Tristan did. His gaze danced over to the Belador guards who stood at attention, but clearly listened to every word with keen interest.

Tristan stared at the ground then lifted his gaze to her and the other Alterants. "Okay. Please return to the gryphon village to wait for me to finish up with Daegan, then I'll come over and teleport the first two."

She smiled and lifted a thumbs-up to the group that cheered.

Daegan had never been ecstatic to enter a battle, but neither had he ever been left behind. These gryphons had joined him, Tristan, Storm, and Adrianna to rescue Evalle from a realm where the chances of leaving alive had been nonexistent.

He couldn't be more proud of them or Tristan, but he did worry about all of his people. Tristan would be distracted with his sister in Atlanta.

Petrina stood strong, showing the warrior she held inside.

Then she stepped over to Tristan and kissed his cheek, whispering, "Thank you. I will be very careful. I'm really proud of you." Turning away quickly, she told the group, "Let's go. We need to plan our pairs and schedule."

They followed her half the way across the beautifully groomed lawn, which stretched from the castle to a tree line. When they reached the trees, they shed their clothes and shifted into gryphons, then picked up their clothing bundles and flew away.

"Ya may dismiss the men, Allyn," Daegan said.

"Yes, dragon king." Allyn wheeled around to face his men and began issuing orders.

With that settled, Daegan and Tristan walked toward the castle. Daegan had to support Tristan in some way. "When ya speak to Quinn, ask to put your sister and the others in the lower risk areas of Atlanta, maybe even farther out."

"Thanks, Daegan, but she'll figure that out and yell about being disrespected."

Daegan paused, causing Tristan to stop. "Then ya tell her that although I am proud of them for steppin' up to help out, they have not been on patrol in the city at all. They will need a Belador guide for at least the first two weeks while they learn what is required of them. Then they will have to prove to Quinn or Evalle they are ready to go off as pairs. That is how I would integrate any new members of the team, just as we did with the ones who traveled from other countries to provide more Belador power where we needed them."

That reminded Daegan of Renata, which dropped a ball of regret in his stomach for not having found her yet.

Tristan's relief was palpable. "Thank you for giving my brain a shake. I should have thought of that since I'm in charge of the gryphons."

Putting a hand on Tristan's shoulder, Daegan offered, "'Tis difficult to think clearly when family is involved."

"Yes, 'tis," Tristan replied, joking.

Daegan laughed at his friend and walked up the steps leading to the castle entrance.

"Daegan?" Tristan asked before reaching the entrance.

Twisting around, Daegan said, "Hmm?"

"Do you need me right now?"

"No. I plan to be here long enough to check on Brina and talk to Garwyli, then I would like to return to Spain to hunt the grimoire box."

"As long as I'm teleporting two Alterants to Atlanta, I'd like to go see my friend, Mac. She might have information about the Imortiks from the guy she works for."

That was not the only reason Tristan wanted to see his young lady, but Daegan would not tease him. He wanted Tristan to take a break even for a short while. "Sounds like an excellent idea. I shall give notice before I need ya back."

Tristan's cheeks colored with embarrassment. "Thanks, boss. That would be nice." Then he walked out from the steps, dropped the backpack, and stripped. He rolled his clothes and boots into a bundle he shoved inside the backpack. Tristan shifted into a green-blue gryphon that snatched up the bundle in his giant beak, then took a running start and lifted into the air, flapping gracefully.

Continuing into the castle, Daegan called telepathically to Tzader. *Are ya with Brina? Is she up for a short visit?*

I am with her and she would be delighted to see her favorite uncle. We're in the solarium.

Daegan grinned. He was her only uncle.

He strolled through the entrance and turned to his left down an arched hallway. When he reached the solarium, he entered to hear Brina say, "I am strong enough to do it."

Tzader argued, "No you aren't, love. It's stressing you and the babies."

"My babes are strong."

Daegan sighed, both happy to not be in Tzader's shoes and envious to be in the same position, something that would never happen. Not when the only dragon shifter female wanted to kill him and did not interest him one bit sexually.

"*Uncle!*" Brina lay stretched out in an alcove where sunlight backlit the cut glass window, sending scatter flecks of light everywhere. Pillows were piled behind her back with one supporting her head. Her fiery hair and personality reminded him so much of Jennyver.

None of those large pillows matched the size of Brina's stomach. "Hello, favorite niece." Daegan pulled a chair over to sit next to her while Tzader paced and tossed worried looks at the woman he loved.

Brina let out a sigh and the effort sounded painful. "I wish for ya to inform my husband I am still able to teleport anyone who needs it."

Daegan took her hand and sandwiched her fingers between his much larger ones. Her skin had a slight increase in temperature, but she appeared healthy except for the dark circles forming beneath her eyes. "I never thought I would say this to ya, Niece, but I shall have to deny your request."

She lifted a surprised gaze to him. Her mouth opened into a small O.

Daegan lifted a hand to her cheek. "Ya know I would grant ya any wish, if I could, but right now I want the same as Tzader. For ya to take it easy and keep the babes content until the time comes. Ya have been an amazin' queen to our people and wife to Tzader. Ya have more than done your duty for now. 'Tis time to allow us to do ours. We need ya safe and healthy more now than ever. I feel selfish, but I wish for ya to birth the first babes I shall have seen born to our family. Ever."

Her face melted with compassion and tears leaked out of her eyes. "I did not know, Uncle. I forgot ya were younger than your sister, Jennyver."

"Yes, she gave birth here in Treoir, not at the castle where my da and I lived." Daegan swallowed the emotion clogging his throat. "'Twas a long time ago and I am focused only on today. Tzader wishes to be alongside me fightin' to save us, but his place is here with ya. I commend him for puttin' his family first. I need ya to do the same. Every Belador is excited for these babes to be born, but none more than Tzader ... and me."

She smiled then sniffled. "Ah, look what ya did to me. I'm a waterin' pot these days."

Tzader was at her side in an instant with tissues. "Here you go, love."

She blew her nose in an unladylike way and Daegan loved it. There was the Belador warrior queen whose presence in Treoir drove Belador power.

That power would only grow greater with two new babies.

After visiting with Tzader and Brina for a bit longer, Daegan stood to leave. "I shall return as often as I can. Do not worry between visits. I take Tristan everywhere and he has turned into a tremendous second-in-command."

"I'm going to walk Daegan out," Tzader announced.

"Go." Brina waved him off. "I know ya want to talk about stuff ya think will distress me. Ya fool me not."

Tzader kissed her and whispered something that had her laughing. As Daegan and Tzader headed for the door, two female Beladors dressed casually in lightweight shirts and jeans entered. Tzader must have called them telepathically to oversee Brina in his absence.

In the hallway, Tzader said, "I appreciate that, Daegan. I'm losing my mind trying to keep her resting without hovering."

Daegan slapped him on the back. "Ya are a lucky man then."

Tzader took a step and said, "I am. I never thought to be with her, much less watch her give birth to our children. I do wish I could be out with you, but nothing could tear me away from her right now."

"As it should be, Tzader. What did ya have to tell me?"

Walking with long strides, Tzader explained, "My Belador embedded in Washington, DC contacted me about an intelligence report on Huntsen's people."

"What do they want?" Daegan hadn't forgotten how he left Huntsen's compound without speaking to Joavan. Could the Faetheen be stirring up trouble while searching for Daegan?

"Huntsen's men are still off the coast of Spain hunting your dragon they believe is underwater, but they're also now hunting in France."

Daegan stopped. "Why would they be in France?"

Tzader's powerful shoulders bunched when he crossed his arms. "There was a dragon rumored to be in France killing cattle."

"That could be Brynhild," Daegan murmured. "Did the reports indicate the color of the dragon in France?"

"No word on that. My man just got a flash report that came through with the rest about Huntsen. Someone shot a missile from the ground."

Daegan's blood chilled. He may not want to mate with Brynhild, but neither did he want her killed. "Did they harm the dragon?"

"No word on that yet, which probably means no, but the dragon could have been injured." Tzader tapped his fingers on his arm. "Where are you headed next?"

"I must speak with Garwyli, then Tristan and I return to Spain."

"Bad idea," Tzader groused.

"I do not have a choice. One of the grimoire volumes is beneath the cliff where they captured me. We need all three grimoires to put the Imortiks behind the wall and save our people who have been possessed by the monsters. If I do not find the box, some other bein' eventually shall. Then we face this threat all over again if we manage to escape the worst this time."

"I hear you. Just be safe. Brina and I need you to see these babies as much as you need to witness new life in your family."

Daegan extended his hand. "I shall do all in my power to return safely, though I do believe ya have the more stressful job than I."

Tzader smirked. "Maybe." His gaze went back down the hall. "Brina's calling me."

"Go on. I shall keep in touch." Daegan kept striding toward the entrance then past the large foyer and down the next hallway. He often shouted Garwyli's name to find the old druid who came when he chose, but Daegan had just told Brina to rest. Shouting in the castle would not aid her.

Daegan stopped in the middle of the hallway and quietly said, "Garwyli, I wish to speak with ya."

Fifteen seconds passed, then a door opened and Quinn's cousin, Lanna, stuck her head out. "Daegan? You look for Garwyli, yes? He is here."

Daegan strode to the door and entered to find Garwyli sitting on a stool across from another stool with stacks of stones on the floor between them. "Am I interruptin' anythin'?"

"Yes, but yar presence is welcome." Garwyli used his gnarled hickory cane to stand. Slowly.

Lanna waited by the door.

The old druid pointed to a chair for Daegan.

"I will not be here long," Daegan said in polite decline for the chair. "I wish to ask ya about the grimoires," he started, allowing Garwyli to send Lanna away.

"I will leave?" Lanna asked in her charming broken English.

Garwyli said, "No, child. Stay."

She crossed the room to sit on the empty stool. This part of the castle appeared to have been lived in for a long time. Books were everywhere as were some cushions reminding him of how his sisters used a needle to decorate the material. The scepter in Casidhe's backpack would fit right in.

Garwyli had been training Lanna on how to use her powers for a while now. Maybe he wanted her to observe so he could use this conversation as a teaching moment of some sort.

Daegan directed his conversation at Garwyli as Lanna had not been around when much of the grimoire discussion happened. "I have a few questions. One is do we absolutely need all three grimoire volumes to imprison Imortiks behind the death wall?"

"As far as I have been able ta research, I do believe that ta be true." Garwyli sat with a heavy sigh.

Was the old druid feeling his age? Daegan would not ask him so personal a question until they were alone. "I have located one volume originally hidden by the ice dragon family."

Lanna's eyes widened. Maybe she did know something about the grimoires.

Garwyli spoke softly. "How did ya come ta find that one?"

"'Tis a long story I shall gladly share when I have time, but suffice to say I took your advice and located Luigsech."

The druid's white beard hid his smile, but his eyes twinkled. "I heard ya found her."

That's right. Tristan had been here for healing. "I convinced Luigsech to help me search for the grimoire volume. We traveled to an oracle who sent us in the right direction." Daegan wouldn't take the time to explain how he and Casidhe had tumbled from the inside of a mountain with the oracle to the top of another one in Spain. "I am thinkin' ya heard I was captured."

Garwyli nodded.

Lanna's eyes bounced back and forth, following the conversation.

Daegan had to share more so the druid would know he had not been careless with the box. "I left the Luigsech woman hidden on that mountain in Spain so I could draw satyrs away that were chasin' me."

Lanna's eyebrows climbed high. "Satyrs?"

"Yes. They were guardin' a hidden world we entered to retrieve the grimoire volume, which turned out to be a bronze box filled with sheets from the original scrolls."

"Ah! Now more of what I have read makes sense." Garwyli moved his hand, animated at that discovery. "I did not understand how the original text had been broken apart, especially during the era 'twas believed created. I thought ya would be lookin' for scrolls, which ya are, but not in a continuous piece. Where is the Luigsech woman now?"

"'Tis the problem," Daegan admitted, feeling as if he'd lost something more precious than the grimoire box. He rubbed his temple and grimaced at the pain of having no idea how to rescue her yet. "Before I could return to the woman, Queen Maeve found her by scryin' and teleported her into TÅµr Medb."

"Oh, no," Lanna moaned. "Is not good."

"Ya are correct."

She stood. "Is not what I mean. She must help you find someone."

Daegan stared at her with confusion. "As soon as I free her from TÅµr Medb, we must deliver a scepter we retrieved to the oracle."

Lanna slowly shook her head. "I have vision about Luigsech."

The last thing Daegan wanted to do was to be short with Lanna, but he needed to ask Garwyli more. "Maybe ya could share that with me another time, Lanna," Daegan said gently. "Right now, I am hopin' Garwyli has an idea of any weakness for enterin' TÅµr Medb."

"Vision is important," Lanna claimed, not budging an

inch.

Garwyli had said nothing, allowing Lanna to speak, but he stood. "Daegan, Lanna is very powerful."

"I know this, Garwyli, and it sounds as if her trainin' with ya has been good for her, but—"

Lifting a hand for silence, the druid said, "Ya should hear her out."

Out of respect for Garwyli, Daegan found his patience. "Go ahead, Lanna. What is important about this vision?"

"The woman Queen Maeve has captured shields information you will need to find truth of what happened to your sister."

Daegan reached for the back of the chair. It felt as if the room fell away. "What exactly do ya mean?"

Clamping her hands on her face, Lanna stared ahead straight. "Garwyli teaches me to read your family chronicles. When I touch words today your father wrote about his children, I see things. I have had visions about dragon and castle, but I am not sure if that is you or not. Your father wrote of Jennyver with sadness. I was sad, then I have vision of her ring broken in half." She lowered her hands and lifted her gaze to Daegan. "I see only one half."

Daegan started to interrupt her and explain that he'd found the half of Jennyver's ring, but Garwyli shook his head.

Lanna told Daegan, "In my vision, the woman you call Casidhe is there. She is key to finding half of ring you cannot."

When Daegan entered this room, he never expected to hear a word about his sister or her ring.

Maybe he had underestimated Casidhe's ability as a squire ancestor. None of this would matter if he failed to pull her out of TÅµr Medb.

Garwyli leaned heavily on his staff. "Ya asked for a weakness ta breach TÅµr Medb."

That snapped Daegan back on track. "Aye."

"Just like Treoir, realms generally only have one weak point."

"What is it?"

"The people. Yar best hope in getting in there and out is by utilizing someone else ta gain entry who can reach yar Luigsech woman and exit with her before Queen Maeve discovers an intruder."

That sounded like a logical plan, but entirely unrealistic with TÅµr Medb. "I shall keep that in mind, Garwyli." Daegan turned to Lanna. "Thank ya for sharin' your vision. I have one half of that ring." He paused at the surprise in her eyes. "If your vision leads to locatin' the other half of the ring, I shall be in your debt."

"No, Daegan. You owe me no debt." She glanced at Garwyli then back to Daegan. "Like you and Garwyli, I have duty."

Daegan might be wrong, but he caught a heavy meaning beneath the solemn words. He and Garwyli would have a longer conversation soon.

Leaving those two to her training, Daegan walked quickly down the hallway. He called telepathically, *I have completed my visits here, Tristan. We shall leave once ya return to Treoir.*

Daegan considered going to the dungeon to see if Skarde had found his tongue yet and tell him about Brynhild, but he rejected that idea.

Brina would deliver her babes very soon.

Skarde must be behaving or Daegan would have heard about any disturbance, especially from Tzader.

If Daegan shared about Brynhild or even pushed Skarde to speak, that might set off the ice dragon. He couldn't upset Skarde then leave.

Neither could Daegan go after Brynhild now, not with Casidhe still captured and the grimoire box to recover.

Once he saved Casidhe and his people, he would hunt down Brynhild and try to talk to her again.

If she survived the humans hunting her with weapons.

He pushed open the tall doors to exit the castle.

Tristan appeared on the lawn, spooking two guards walking by. He still wore Casidhe's backpack holding books and the scepter.

When Daegan reached him, he said, "You could have taken a little time to return."

Sounding relaxed, Tristan said, "I had finished my business in Atlanta."

Arching an eyebrow, Daegan asked, "Was it a satisfactory trip?"

"Very." Tristan gave him a smug grin.

Daegan returned his smile, happy for Tristan while longing for a more normal life. What would it have been like to have met Casidhe while only hunting information on his family? He would never know.

Returning to his task, Daegan said, "We head to Spain."

"Do you want to teleport to the place we found this backpack?"

"Yes. We go to that exact location first so no one sees us arrive, then we shall teleport beneath the cliffs where I hope to find the grimoire box."

"Maybe we can pop in, find the box, and pop out."

"I wish it would be that simple, Tristan, but Tzader informed me Huntsen's teams are still searchin' that coast for my dragon."

Heaving a deep breath, Tristan said, "Well, damn. If our lives were easy, everyone would want to be us."

CHAPTER 19

The Caucasus mountain range

SUNLIGHT SPEARED THROUGH THE WINDOW with a view of the Caucasus mountain range where clouds floated across the highest peaks.

Kleio folded her laundry, unwilling to ask her chambermaid to do tasks she could handle herself. A cool breeze swept through the open window and ruffled curtains she'd made for the windows. This castle had no glass over the window openings, but she enjoyed breathing fresh air and taking in the soothing view.

Nothing would quiet the uproar in her head though.

Not since her visit by the god Janus, who bade her goodbye with no plan to meet with her again until she completed a journey she had no clear path to follow.

She'd worshipped that god since their first meeting when she was a child.

Every word he spoke stayed inside her as if inscribed on her soul. His last words left her disconcerted.

"Your vision will change your path and your path will change the course of the human world. The world will either survive what is coming or burn into eternity. Do not return to speak to me again until you have completed this journey and the future is clear."

How could he place the burden of the world's future on her shoulders with no more direction than three sentences?

She would not see him again until she completed her

journey. He would be the one to determine if she had or had not.

Janus had not abandoned her, though, or she would no longer receive visions. In fact, she had been seeing more, but some visions were not as distinct as before. Some raised the hair on her arms without giving her a clear understanding of the image.

Stacking her clothes, she placed them in an old wooden trunk with tarnished hinges and a broken latch. It had been in this room when she arrived.

Standing up, she rubbed her tired eyes. She had not slept well and needed to fall into deep slumber to do her best.

With her eyes shut while she massaged them, a vision began to form in her mind of a sleeping young woman.

She held her fingers still against her eyelids, afraid to disturb the vision. This one had come to her once before, almost, only to fracture and vanish.

Focusing on every detail now, Kleio noted how the woman still appeared to float horizontally.

A lovely shade of red hair fell around her shoulders, set off by the stunning green gown. She came from money, but there was no bed beneath her. No furniture in her room. Just a foggy smoke billowing around her.

Nothing alerted Kleio to the location of this woman.

She had a pretty face, maybe in her twenties or possibly thirty, but her chest did not seem to lift with taking a breath.

Had the woman died?

A tiny motion drew Kleio back to her face. An eyelash twitched. Had that really happened?

Kleio held her breath, waiting to see if she'd imagined that movement—

"Seer? Where are ya?" Herrick bellowed outside her door.

The vision shattered.

Kleio lowered her hands and opened her eyes. She shook her fist at the closed door. "What do you want, Herrick?"

"Open the door. Ya forbade me from touchin' it when closed."

Dropping her head back to stare at the heavy beams crossing her ceiling, she said a prayer for patience. She lifted her head and crossed the room to the door she pulled open. "I was meditating," she lied.

"I thought ya meditated in the other room where we cannot disturb ya." Herrick stood a head taller than her and dressed in his standard jeans and pullover, rich blue today. He scratched at his thick golden beard, which could use a trimming, but that was not her duty. Neither was putting up with his moods when he had not flown as a dragon for days.

In no mood to argue, she asked, "What do you want?"

"Have ya had more visions about the two in Ireland?"

She went on alert. "Did you send word to remain in County Galway would put them in danger?"

His gaze shifted away, unwilling to meet her eyes. "Yes."

He told part truth and part lie at the same time.

She rephrased the question. "Did you tell Fenella and Casidhe about my warning?"

"I have done my duty. I only ask to know if ya have a new vision or not. I will leave ya alone." He turned to leave.

"You did *not* tell Casidhe, did you?" she guessed.

Without turning back, he said, "'Tis my castle and my land. Do not think to question anythin' I do." He walked down the long hall and descended the stairs.

Kleio closed her door and leaned back against it, her heart beating rapidly.

Janus expected her to choose a path, not just interpret visions for one man.

If she continued in the role of Herrick's seer only, she would face no conflict and remain in her esteemed position, but Herrick would be the only one informed.

He would choose how that information was utilized.

He would be in control of destiny for others.

She began to understand what Janus meant about holding the future of the world in her hands.

CHAPTER 20

RAIN HAMMERED DAEGAN THE MINUTE teleporting ended. He shuffled his feet to keep from sliding down mud streaming between rocks.

"What the hell?" Tristan sidestepped as he appeared.

Daegan lifted his hands to create a kinetic barrier above them. He shouted, "Push up your kinetics so I can free my hands."

Tristan shoved his hands up and nodded.

When Daegan dropped his arms, he pointed at Tristan, covering him and the backpack in a dark-gray rain slicker with a hood Daegan had seen in Atlanta. Then put the same on himself. The second slicker took a little longer.

Some power seemed to be returning, but slow to build up.

"Ready?" Tristan called out.

"Yes." The slickers that stopped at their knees would blend them into the storm better and keep water from constantly washing into their eyes.

Tristan lowered his arms. "Should be afternoon here, but feels like night."

Rain pounded Daegan's head and shoulders. Lightning crackled, followed by a distant boom of thunder.

A jet flew along the coast in spite of the weather. If not for his hearing, Daegan would not have heard the engines. The distinctive *whomp, whomp, whomp* alerted him to a large helicopter also searching the coast. Those men were relentless.

"We should probably leave the backpack up here some-where," Tristan called out.

"Good thinkin'."

"Same place?"

"Yes. If Queen Maeve did not find the pack when she took Casidhe, then I would think it to be safe there again."

"Be right back." Tristan teleported away and made fast work of hiding the backpack in the dark hole then popped back into view. "Ready to go treasure hunting?"

"I am concerned about the helicopter movin' slower than the jet," Daegan warned, giving voice to his worry. He did not want Tristan injured again. "We shall go and I shall cloak us, but I do not trust my powers entirely right now."

Tristan stood with his hands on his hips, staring out to where a large ship sat off the coast in the turbulent sea.

"We'll figure it out. I'm ready when you are, boss."

"First teleport us to the cliff so we may choose a landin' place among the boulders below."

"Got it."

When Daegan's vision cleared this time, wind drove the rain across from left to right and whipped their slickers around. The crisp scent of salt water and fresh rain filled his senses. He told Tristan, "Follow me to where I believe I went over the edge."

When Daegan stopped, Tristan leaned forward to look down. "I'm thinking we try for those two big rocks closest to the wall."

Daegan made a quick observation. A tingling sensation started in his arms and flowed through his body to his legs.

What could that be about?

Tristan said, "Heads up. We're going down there."

The trip down was fast and rolling waves crashed against the largest rock formation the moment Daegan appeared, forcing one foot to hit air. He used kinetics to push against the towering wall of rock and dirt below the cliffs to hold himself steady.

Tristan appeared next and had his hands out fast doing the same shuffle. Using his kinetics, too, he shouted, "Where do we start?"

"Should be in this area. I shall cloak an area to include these boulders and fifty feet to each side." Daegan paused when that strange sensation increased to a vibration. He could not bother with it right now. "See how there are so many rocks piled close to the wall? The weather was calm when I dropped it. If the box is here, I hope it was caught in the pockets of those stones." He completed the cloaking just as the sound of an approaching helicopter stilled his movements.

What if his cloaking did not hold?

Tristan looked up. The cloaking dulled images.

A long helicopter like the one that had carried Daegan to Huntsen's compound moved slowly overhead but farther out to sea. Good thing or they might see the water pausing and flowing around an invisible wall. If he had his full power, he could stop the water and knock it back. This was actually better.

Tristan stared at Daegan as they both stood very still while the craft continued on.

"I was ready to teleport us away," Tristan said, heaving out a long breath.

"It appears we are safe from detection for now." Daegan cast a look around. "The cloakin' seems to be slowin' down the water breakin' over these rocks."

"You still got some mojo," Tristan muttered while squatting to look around.

Daegan found moving from rock to rock difficult, but not impossible. He could use his kinetics to maintain his balance. That vibration skittered over his skin.

Could that have anything to do with the box?

Tristan shouted, "Shit!" He slipped off his rock but teleported right back soaking wet. He shoved hair off his face, leaving wet strands poking out in every direction.

That blasted helicopter had turned around and was searching the coast slowly again.

Did they think a dragon sat at the bottom of the sea, ready to fly up in the air at any moment?

Daegan waited as the helicopter passed overhead, then the jet returned following the helicopter. Another jet flew a similar path farther out. Beyond that, the ship remained pointed into the wind.

This would not work. They were making no progress and couldn't as long as they had to worry about aircraft.

Waving Tristan to his rock, Daegan said, "We need time to search and I have an idea. First, can ya see down into the pockets?"

"Not really." Tristan snapped his fingers. "I could teleport to Treoir and get a flashlight."

Daegan did not want to push Tristan's teleporting more than necessary only to discover they had drained him if they needed Tristan's ability in an emergency.

But Tristan had given him an idea. "We have somethin' closer."

"What?"

"Casidhe has a wee light she calls an LED. 'Tis in a pocket on her backpack."

A large splash broke over the top of the cloaking, jarring them both.

Tristan shouted, "Give me a minute to look and I'll be right back." He returned in seconds and held up the LED flashlight.

Daegan explained, "Once I step out of the cloakin', I shall shift into my dragon and—"

"What? No, boss. They're hunting *you*."

"I know this, Tristan, but while I cannot teleport far, I

am able to shift and fly. I will only be in dragon form for a short time, just long enough to draw them farther down the coast. Once they are away from here, I have an idea to make them search a new area."

Tristan had flipped on the LED, pointing it down. He had a sick look on his face. "What if you can't get back?"

"I shall call to ya and ask ya to link with me to teleport again. We must find that bronze box and take it somewhere safe then come up with a way to pull Casidhe from TÅµr Medb."

Daegan would not rush Tristan to agree. He treated Tristan as a peer, which he was.

Tristan asked, "What if I shift into *my* gryphon? That would draw them away."

There were no words for how much Daegan cared for his friend, but that idea would only increase their problems. "Huntsen's people would then have two flyin' supernatural beins' to hunt. Also, I believe the red dragon flyin' is the only reason their people would leave this area. I shall be fine, Tristan. I am not fragile."

"Hell, Daegan. I didn't mean to insinuate that. I just ... hell, don't get killed, okay?"

"Now ya insult Ruadh."

"No, I ... " Tristan sputtered, then realized Daegan had been teasing him. "I would never insult that powerful dragon."

Ruadh rumbled a contented sound inside Daegan.

Waving off Daegan, Tristan said, "Go on. I'll call you if I find anything."

Daegan said, "Teleport me to that pile of rocks fifty feet away."

When Tristan complied, Daegan exited the cloaking, but left it intact for Tristan.

With no aircraft nearby, he immediately shifted into his dragon. Ruadh shoved off, flapping slowly and staying low over the water. When his dragon had flown halfway out to the ship, he slapped his tail hard enough on the surface of the water to create a large splash.

Then he flew up at a sharp angle.

Whatever equipment those operatives had in place on their ship and airplanes had hopefully captured what appeared to be something very large flying out of the ocean.

Ruadh went higher and higher.

Daegan asked telepathically. *Are ya truly healed enough to do this, Ruadh?*

Yes. We are strong. His dragon picked up speed and flew a wide arc. When the jets and helicopter turned toward his dragon like sharks after blood, Ruadh flew toward the cliffs, then banked hard to turn east, taking advantage of the strong wind pushing the storm.

Now able to utilize a tailwind, Ruadh flapped like crazy, pumping powerful muscles and flying through rain coming down in sheets along the coast.

Lightning fingered and rippled across the black skies.

When the jets neared, Ruadh shot straight up into a driving rain, which could not harm his thick hide, and drew the aircraft in to follow him as he took them on an undulating series of spins and turns.

Ruadh had flown around the curve of the coast, taking them out of visual range of the ship. Daegan suspected the ship and aircraft had technology to track him.

In their desire to take down his dragon while Ruadh twisted in tight circles and flew in different directions, the jets had ended up flying almost at each other. They now appeared to have regrouped, spreading out as if a new plan were afoot.

Daegan hated to ask this, but he had no time left. *Do ya feel up to a swim, Ruadh?*

His dragon roared and a burst of flame shot from his jaws. *We are not fish.*

I know, but it would keep them huntin' ya once we surface and shift again into the human body as a speck in this black sea.

Ruadh gave a gravelly sound of irritation, but in the next breath Daegan's dragon made a point of flying high again, but farther out as well.

This next move would be disastrous if Ruadh dove into a shallow area.

The jets did not get suckered in this time.

Gaining distance going high, Ruadh flipped over without warning and dove as something shot past him.

Had that jet unleashed a weapon?

If so, those in charge had likely decided to kill the dragon rather than risk losing it again.

Ruadh tucked his wings, gaining speed as he dove at an angle, which would allow him to break the surface with a massive splash for effect. Daegan could feel the jolt to his dragon's body as Ruadh shot into the sea, smooth as a mighty arrow.

They were sliding into deep water at the same angle.

With the speed his huge dragon had entered, they might be diving fast.

Too fast.

Daegan said, *Give me the body back and I shall try to teleport out of here.*

Ruadh replied, *At surface.*

His dragon would not risk shifting with Daegan so far beneath the surface he could not reach air quickly enough.

Just as Ruadh slowed their descent and lifted his head to begin rising, a powerful explosion hit the water right at his tail. Heat boiled around them. Sparks shot through the water.

The blast shoved his dragon forward, flipping Ruadh out of control deep in the water as if a giant had lifted the ship and smashed it down on his dragon.

CHAPTER 21

DAEGAN CAME TO HIS SENSES and shouted telepathically, *Ruadh! How bad are ya hurt? Give me the human body. 'Tis lighter. I shall make it to the surface.*

Ruadh didn't respond. Not even the sound of a growl. Nothing. Had the blast knocked out his dragon?

Whatever that jet dropped into the ocean had been unlike anything Daegan could imagine.

Ruadh floated lifeless under the water.

Daegan's head throbbed and he could feel the pain ripping through Ruadh's tail and body.

Calling up all his power, Daegan tried to force the change, something he'd never done. If he did not shift into his human form fast enough, they might fall to the bottom and drown in the middle of a shift.

Ruadh groaned. His massive body bucked hard and bowed in on itself.

Daegan stopped trying to force the shift. *Ruadh?*

In a pained voice, his dragon said, *Wait.*

Ruadh's wings moved up and down slowly as if flying through mud, straining to force the huge wings to keep moving. Each thrust lifted the dragon higher and forward, driving them out to sea more.

After several tense moments, Ruadh's body floated just beneath the surface. His dragon said, *Now.*

Daegan had only to be ready as Ruadh pushed energy into the shift.

In seconds, Daegan floated facedown and naked in cool

water. He rolled over and spit out salt water, coughing to catch his breath. Rain battered the water harder than before, stinging his exposed skin.

Black clouds hung low in the sky and thunder pounded the heavens.

His body shook from all he and Ruadh had just gone through. When his aching lungs calmed down, he lifted his head to search the black skies.

Jets swarmed between him and the cliffs. A helicopter swept slowly over the water, shining a bright light as they hunted a dragon.

Ruadh had moved them far enough out to sea to not be noticed in the dark swallowing late afternoon.

Once again, his dragon reminded Daegan how they never quit, no matter the situation.

He wished to float here forever. No Imortiks, no responsibility, and no arrogant deities.

Even if such a life was offered, he would not accept it.

His soul longed to find Casidhe. He wanted to see Brina's babies. He wanted to do right by the Beladors and protect them now the way he couldn't long ago.

They were all his family to watch over.

What had Lanna meant about Casidhe knowing how to find the other half of Jennyver's ring?

He didn't know. What he did know was that Ruadh had been with him from the beginning and was always with him when he had nothing else.

Unwilling to spare the breath to speak out loud, he told Ruadh telepathically, *Ya are the best dragon ever to fly in this world or any other. My father and the goddess blessed me with more than the human side probably deserved.*

Ruadh stayed quiet at first, then replied, *We are strong together. I would share a body with no other.*

That was a major compliment from his dragon.

Returning to the problem at hand, Daegan explained, *I*

shall try to teleport up onto the land first, Ruadh. If that turns out well, we go to Tristan next.

Yes.

Daegan lowered his legs to tread water. He found he had to prepare himself in case this did not work. He had never doubted himself so much. When he'd first lived in this world, he'd had the mightiest dragon and had been considered a formidable warrior in human form.

The Imortik venom and the slime that hardened on his skin had both managed to undermine his confidence for the first time ever. He hated to feel even a tiny bit weak.

His father had always told him there was a gift in every lesson.

Daegan had a hard time finding any gift in hesitating to trust his powers.

Ruadh's deep voice boomed in his head. *Teleport. We will survive.*

Daegan smiled. It was always good to have a dragon ready to kick him in the arse. He inhaled and exhaled a couple fast times, then teleported.

CHAPTER 22

WHEN THE TELEPORTING ENDED, DAEGAN stood on the edge of a cliff, teetering forward. He waved his arms wildly to throw his weight backwards and landed hard.

As if this body had not been through enough tonight already?

Groaning, he had to lay there until the dizziness passed, but the screaming sound of a jet approaching forced him to sit up. Bile clogged his throat. Rolling to his feet, he went scrambling for cover behind a boulder.

This must be how a human feels when unable to teleport away from a threat. Humbling to say the least.

The aircraft flew over. Daegan had seen those jets enough to know that one moved at a slow speed. While he caught his breath, he called up jeans, a long-sleeved pull-over, and boots. All soaked in seconds. He stood, watching as the jets and helicopter remained in this area.

So far, his plan had worked.

No time like the present to give teleporting another try.

He called out telepathically, *I am alive and on land, Tristan. Have ya found anythin'?*

Glad to hear from you, boss. Nothing that looks like a box yet. Can you get back on your own? The aircraft did exactly what you thought and followed Ruadh down the coast.

Yes, they seem to be stayin'. Daegan didn't mention that the jets were likely still looking for the body of an injured or dead dragon to float up. *I will teleport to the place where I shifted.*

The short distance should have worked, but Daegan landed over half the way, then tried it again.

He ended up on the outcropping of rocks grouped near Tristan and breathing hard. His eyes adjusted to see the tiny light shining near the base of the cliffs. Daegan entered the cloaking.

Tristan lifted a hand, indicating he saw Daegan, then teleported to him. There was more room on this outcropping than those single boulders where Daegan wanted to search.

"Sorry, boss." Tristan stuck the light between his teeth the way Casidhe had and wiped water off his face. "I kept thinking my light would reflect off a flat and shiny surface. That area has enough rocks to hold a heavy box in there. Still, when the tide came in, it may have lifted that box and taken it out to sea."

Daegan had to consider all possibilities, but the box had been heavier than it appeared and ... his hand began to warm and tingle again.

He opened and closed his fingers.

"What's wrong with your hand?" Tristan asked.

"The whole time I carried the box, my hand and arm felt as if the limb burned inside. When I released the box, that feeling went away and I could shift. I felt an unusual tinglin' in my hand when we first teleported down here, but my hand is burnin'." He looked up at Tristan. "The sea could move the box away, but I do not think it went far. We may be closer to it here."

"We can use you like a divining rod." Tristan grinned.

Daegan shook his head, glad to have the irreverent young man with him again. "We shall see how useful I am."

Tristan shined the light as Daegan moved around. His

hand would heat more, then he'd make another step and his hand cooled. They were hit by waves nonstop.

Daegan sensed his cloaking had begun to weaken.

A particularly large wave almost knocked Tristan off his feet. The cloaking had failed.

After another ten minutes, Daegan growled. "'Tis as if the bloody box is jumpin' about as a flea on a dog's back."

"No kidding." Tristan pushed wet hair out of his eyes. "I don't get it. We haven't moved out of a tight diameter for the last ten minutes. It should be right there where your hand was very hot a few seconds ago."

"I believe the cloakin' has faded, Tristan." Daegan glanced out to sea and up in the sky. "But the aircraft still search the new location."

"No problem, boss. Why don't you forget about the cloaking and save your power? I'll start over there next." Tristan pointed at a rock six feet away.

Joavan appeared where Tristan pointed. "Hello, Daegan. Did you forget about our agreement?"

"Whoa. Who are you?" Tristan lifted hands, ready to use kinetics.

Joavan wore his glamoured look of dull human.

Daegan said, "'Tis fine, Tristan. Ya remember me sayin' I'd explain what happened when they captured me?"

"Yeah."

"This is Joavan, a Faetheen. I will fill ya in on everythin' later." Turning to Joavan, Daegan said, "I will only talk to the real person."

Joavan glared at Tristan and made no move to drop his glamour.

Daegan growled at the Faetheen. "Tristan is my second. He goes where I go and he knows what I know. Show your true self if ya want my help."

Tristan shot Joavan a suspicious glance, but spoke to Daegan. "Why is he here?"

Joavan dropped the glamour, exposing his taller form and male beauty. He wore the same clothes as he had earlier and glowed. "I am here to collect on a debt. Why are your eyes glowing green?"

"Asks the person whose entire body is lit up like a night-light," Tristan kicked back at him.

Joavan smiled and tilted his head, acknowledging Tristan's point.

Daegan had no time for this Faetheen, but he had to explain what happened. "I intended to find ya, Joavan, but I was not about to turn down bein' freed from Huntsen when my people came for me."

"Understandable, dragon. Still, you should be willing to fulfill your part of the deal right now."

Daegan had to be careful not to allow Joavan a chance to gain the upper hand here or he'd be forced to walk away from the grimoire box and finding Casidhe. "While I am more than willin' to return the favor for freein' my body from the deadly coatin', I am huntin' somethin' here I must find immediately, then I need to free one of mine who was captured. Then I will go with ya."

Waves crashed around them, but none splashed the pile of rocks where they stood. No rain entered this area either.

Was the Faetheen responsible for creating a protective space?

Joavan continued standing with his hands behind his back in a pose similar to the Belador guards when at attention. "We all have problems, Daegan. That is why you struck a deal with me. I concede that you found a way out of the cell before I returned, but without the salve I brought from my people you would not be alive right now."

Tristan slashed a concerned look at Daegan.

Daegan could not argue Joavan's point. He just needed Joavan to work with him. "I do owe ya for keepin' me alive and I fully intend to help ya. I only need time to locate a box I dropped out here the night they caught me and to rescue a woman held prisoner in TÅµr Medb through no fault of her own. Queen Maeve saw the woman with me and believes she will find one of the Immortuos Grimoire volumes for her. The woman cannot do that without my help."

Joavan cocked his head as if he'd heard an interesting tune.

Daegan pressed harder. "The minute it is clear the woman is unable to locate a grimoire volume, Queen Maeve will kill her."

"I understand your dilemma, Daegan. Someone you care about is in jeopardy. I have people in jeopardy as well. I will save you some of that precious time, because I have the box you hunt." Joavan pulled his arms forward with a palm open on one hand.

The bronze box floated above his palm.

Tristan cursed.

"I need that box, Joavan," Daegan snapped. "I have little more than two weeks to save my people and all other nonhumans, as well as humans."

Offering an expression of confusion, Joavan said, "See? You keep expecting me to work with you when you have yet to do your part for the salve."

What could Daegan say to reach this being?

"I have a time frame, too," Joavan shared calmly. "If we work together, we can accomplish everything."

"Ya did not free me from that cell. That was part of the deal, too."

Joavan's face morphed into one of restrained anger. "It does not matter. I have the box."

Seeing that grimoire box in his hands was almost as bad as the sea taking it. Daegan implored, "We will all die without that grimoire box. Our only hope is to find the other two and put those three together to lock Imortiks behind a death wall forever."

"I would miss visiting this world, but my people would survive in our world." Joavan's aqua eyes were stone-cold.

Daegan had to accept that he was up against an immovable force. "What will it take for ya to hand me the box, Joavan?"

"Retrieve an amulet and the box is yours."

Not until he had Casidhe out of Queen Maeve's claws. Daegan nodded. "I will agree, but I must free the woman first."

Joavan waved that off as inconsequential. "Spiriting a woman out of TÅµr Medb is simple."

Daegan quirked an eyebrow. "Ya can do this?"

"Yes."

Tristan asked with a bit of suspicion, "How do we free the woman?"

Joavan shook his head slowly while the box hovered above his palm. "I will tell you exactly how to rescue her when we are in agreement. See? You may gain more than you bargained for."

"In more ways than one," Tristan muttered darkly.

Daegan hadn't slowed down for days and hitting this brick wall called Joavan drained the last of his patience. "In other words, ya will not help me save her until I take care of your problem? How can I trust ya to hand over the box and help us free the woman after I fix your problem?"

Joavan's too pretty face twisted with fury. "Trust? You mean in the way I trusted *you* to be in your cell when I returned after my people had healed you?"

Daegan's back still ached from being flayed open by the liquid, but he could not blame that on Joavan. He'd done the damage to himself. "I already explained why I was not in the cell when ya returned. In my place, would ya have not left with your people?"

Joavan didn't want to admit it, but his eyes conceded Daegan's point. "Let's not *quibble!* I did not have to tell you I found the box. I only did so to save time and convince you to leave here immediately. You should thank me for saving you the trouble. If I agree to hand over the box after you retrieve the amulet, I will not allow a debt to go unpaid. It is against our way."

Tristan stood with his arms loose, prepared to fight, but Joavan did not attack physically. His words dove inside Daegan to twist his soul. Leaving without that box would be disastrous, but Casidhe needed him just as much. She had no one who even knew where she was, much less how to save her.

Daegan was not above humbling himself to save another. "Then I give ya my word I will go with ya to find your amulet right away if we can rescue the woman first. 'Tis not an unreasonable request when ya said yourself to free her would be simple."

Joavan stood perfectly still, breathing slowly. "You misunderstand me, dragon. I said I would trade the box for taking the amulet from the druid, not the box *and* saving the woman. If you refuse to go with me now, I will take this box to my world where it will stay forever. I will use it however necessary to protect my people. You go with me now to yank the amulet from the thief and I will trade either this box or the woman's freedom. Not both. Which do you choose?"

Blood rushed through Daegan's head, pounding in his ears.

Choose between the grimoire box or Casidhe?

DIANNA LOVE

TREOIR DRAGON CHRONICLES
OF THE BELADOR WORLD
BOOK 5

CHAPTER 1

DAEGAN'S DRAGON RAMPAGED INSIDE HIM. Ruadh wanted blood.

"What will it be, dragon? Make a choice," Joavan shouted over the roar of a storm hammering the cliffs of Spain's northern coast towering above them. The Faetheen lifted his hand where the grimoire volume Daegan and Casidhe had risked their lives to retrieve floated above his palm. "This box ... *or* the woman?"

As if Daegan could turn his back on Casidhe and leave her imprisoned in TÅµr Medb?

Pain ripped up his insides and muscles across his chest expanded, pushing him closer to shifting. He crouched, feeling the bones in his face crack as his mouth pulled out of shape. "How can ya expect me to be choosin' between a woman's life and the future of all other livin' beins'? I shall not turn my back on a woman who has risked much to save others, but neither shall I give up that box."

Joavan leaned forward, eyes glittering. "I could leave now and never care about the consequences to your world. You should have presented saving the woman as something you wanted when I came to offer you aid to escape imprisonment."

Daegan flexed his fingers, wanting his claws around the Faetheen's throat. Holding back from shifting into his dragon physically ached.

We win all battles with Fae, Ruadh declared telepathically.

Daegan's power boiled, anxious for a target. *Yes!*

Boss? Are we gonna shift and throw down with this guy? Tristan asked telepathically.

Daegan glanced at his second-in-command standing on a boulder next to him. Soaked pale-brown hair flattened against his head, jaw stiff with anger, and just as ready to jump in.

Ruadh spoke again, but only to Daegan. *No battle is too great if you do not lose what you fight for.*

That stopped Daegan's mad thoughts as fast as flying into a wall.

What would he lose?

Casidhe. His people, innocent humans, everything he'd fought to protect. What was he thinking to shift and attack Joavan? He hadn't been thinking. Daegan shoved a hand through his wet hair and gripped the back of his neck, breathing for a moment before lowering his arm.

He sent a silent message to Tristan. *No. I cannot gain the box or save Casidhe by attackin' Joavan.*

Daegan forced his body to pull back from the edge of shifting. Muscles tightened and twisted back into shape. He grunted with the strain.

Wind howled around the cloaking protecting them from the sea where dark had fallen.

Ruadh normally voted for complete destruction of an enemy and would kill this Faetheen if Daegan gave the order. But his dragon knew him as well as Daegan knew Ruadh. This had been a rare time when his dragon had been the one to caution him to be sure of his next step.

Daegan had never lost his ability to think clearly in the midst of a battle. But Casidhe lived in his every thought. Nothing would soothe him until he yanked her from TÅµr Medb and into the safety of his arms. Call him selfish, but Daegan's insides ached with the need to save Casidhe above all.

He could not make the mistake of allowing an enemy or a dangerous ally to know how important she felt to him. If he did, Casidhe would become a bargaining chip to be used against him by every adversary once he freed her from Queen Maeve's clutches.

If he freed her.

Not if. He would find a way.

Every minute Casidhe spent in TÅµr Medb and out of his reach clawed at his need to protect her.

Far better to convince this narrow-minded, half-blood Fae of her importance for stopping the Imortiks. Daegan could not save her if he did not win this battle, but neither would he forsake his people or the humans.

He told Ruadh, *Ya are correct and stopped me from makin' a bad mistake. I must find a way to renegotiate my deal with the Faetheen.*

Daegan could not deny the importance of the liquid solution Joavan had brought from a healer to prevent a coating spewed on him by satyrs from hardening over his body. If not for the Faetheen's help, he would be dead by now.

Sucking in his pride to deal with Joavan, Daegan said, "I do not take savin' my life lightly. I only ask ya to work with me so that we may both succeed." It took all Daegan's effort to ignore the arrogant pose Joavan struck.

His dragon roared, angry with Joavan and wanting to turn the Faetheen into ashes.

That was the dragon Daegan had known and loved his whole life.

Joavan had claimed his people would be safe if he went back and took the bronze grimoire box with him to his hidden world.

Daegan doubted that as truth.

He could not allow the grimoire to disappear with Joavan. Without all three grimoires, no one could force Imortiks behind a death wall again.

Tristan sent a new telepathic message to Daegan. *Want me to poke at Joavan to see if we can make him reveal a weakness?*

The Imortik venom in Daegan's body still drove spikes of pain through his head at unexpected moments, and right now, that spike felt thick as his fist. He was thankful to have Tristan and his dragon with him.

It cannot hurt, Daegan replied silently to Tristan. *If Joavan were so confident about disappearin' with the box, he would have done so by now. He clearly needs help, but I believe the stubborn fool is determined to make me choose because I left the lockdown cell before he returned.*

Understood, boss. Clearing his throat, Tristan called out, "How can you expect us to retrieve some necklace when we're trying to protect the future of the world for all of us?"

Joavan's face distorted into major pissed. "Some *necklace*? The *Cearcall na Sìorraidheachd* is not a *trinket!* It bears the *Talamh An Asraon* diamond valued above all by my people. I must have that to protect them."

Tristan lifted his hands, palms out. "Hey, chill. I'm just trying to understand why we can't get the woman now, which will make it easier for us to focus all of our attention on what you want. Then once Daegan gets your amulet and you hand over that box, all of us can go about our business. Why do you want to fight about this when we could solve one problem quickly?"

While Tristan drew Joavan's attention for a moment, Daegan took that opportunity to sort through the few conversations he'd had with Joavan. As he did, an idea began to form, but he'd only get one chance to try it.

"Hey, boss. Incoming," Tristan muttered, looking over his shoulder to the east.

Daegan glanced around at the sound of a large helicopter approaching. Far away, a bright beam shined down along the coast. They were hunting his red dragon. If the machine stayed on course, it would fly right over them.

Joavan flashed a look in the same direction and shouted, "They can see nothing in this cloaking."

Turning back to face the ignorant fool, Daegan argued, "The humans shall notice how the water is flowin' around the cloakin's invisible barrier and breakin' against a wall they cannot see. A jet dropped an explosive device on my dragon earlier while we were underwater right before I returned here."

Tristan's eyes popped at that. "You okay?"

"Yes." Daegan slashed his gaze back at Joavan. "They may do the same here if they find somethin' unusual. I say we teleport up on the mountain where no one is searchin' for a dragon."

Joavan had a moment of indecision while the helicopter noise grew louder. "I will drop the cloaking. You will teleport all of us. Do not leave my sight or I am gone."

Daegan's teleporting could not be trusted with the venom interfering. Rubbing his pounding forehead, he quietly asked Tristan, "You up for this?"

"Oh, hell, yeah. I'll take you up then I'll come and grab him."

Daegan hesitated, worried Joavan would vanish if they left first.

Water suddenly crashed over the rocks, soaking the three of them. Joavan shouted, "What are you waiting for? The helicopter will be here in less than a minute."

Tristan said, "Hang on, boss."

Daegan spun away in a blur of teleporting. When his eyes focused again, he stood fifty feet from where Tristan had hidden Casidhe's backpack.

Tristan blinked into view then out of sight again. In ten seconds, Tristan reappeared with Joavan shouting.

"We were supposed to teleport together!" The Faetheen shoved dripping hair off his face. "Do you not care about this?" Joavan lifted his open hand where Daegan's grimoire box floated majikally above it.

The helicopter continued searching the coastline, but far enough away now it was no threat.

Daegan replied in a hard voice, "We took a risk huntin' a place to land first or ya might have been dumped on the side of the mountain. Ya would have accused me of doin' so to knock the box from your hands." But the fact that Joavan had waited for Tristan's return, reinforced Daegan's budding idea. "I have made a decision."

"Finally. I was not staying any longer," Joavan warned.

"I understand and I wish to make good on my agreement to help you." Daegan felt Tristan's eyes on him, but he trusted Tristan to follow his lead. He did not want to be distracted by telepathy.

Allowing a victorious smile to curve his lips, Joavan asked, "Did you choose this box over the woman?"

"No." Daegan crossed his arms and spoke with confidence born of hope. "I have realized that if ya know how to rescue her from TÅμr Medb then another Fae, who is an ally of the Beladors, could do so just as easily. I only need a moment to send for the Fae woman. Once she comes here and receives the details, she can take care of savin' the woman. Then we are free to search for the amulet."

"What? *No!*" Joavan shouted. He clamped his lips shut. It didn't matter.

Joavan had confirmed Daegan's belief that this Faetheen would not want a strange Fae involved. Not after Joavan's people had run from the Fae. Also, as a half-Fae and half-druid being, Joavan might fear going up against a more powerful pure-blood Fae.

Especially if he had never fought one.

"Wait. What am I thinking?" Joavan shook his head and

sounded relieved when he spouted, "You must know you should never ask a Fae for a favor."

"I do know this, but 'tis not askin' for a favor if one is owed." Daegan walked away toward a high point where he could watch airplanes fly across the vast sea.

"*Stop!*" Joavan stepped toward him.

"Stop what?" Daegan asked innocently. "We need to get movin' so that I can find your amulet and take that box to my people. We waste time."

Inhaling deeply through his nose, Joavan stood there stiff as a board. He exhaled slowly. "Do not call a Fae here. My people are at risk until I find the amulet. A Fae might try to enter our world while I am not there to protect them."

Daegan glanced past Joavan to Tristan who lifted an eyebrow and nodded in respect. While Daegan appreciated the show of support, this idea had not worked yet.

Not until Casidhe stood here free of Queen Maeve.

Holding his arms out in supplication, Daegan gave an exasperated reply. "I have a way to save the woman and fulfill my agreement to ya, Joavan. If ya do not care for my idea, what do ya propose?"

Lifting his chin, Joavan said, "I will show I am the bigger person and save the woman, but once she is free, we leave to find the amulet. No more arguments."

Throbbing eased in Daegan's head. He'd allowed the Faetheen to save face and hopefully rescue Casidhe, too. "What is your plan for gettin' in and out of TÅµr Medb?"

Joavan frowned, tapping his chin. "This box will be safer if I put it away before saving the woman."

"I want to know where that box is *every* minute," Daegan demanded.

"Do not judge me so poorly when I have been the one to uphold my end of our deal," Joavan lashed out. "When I returned to your cell, I had planned to make a formal agreement, which would have saved us these issues. If we agree now on the specific terms, I will place a spell for the box to reappear as soon as you have fulfilled your part."

After giving that offer consideration, Daegan nodded, but not because he trusted Joavan. Daegan added, "Or the box shall appear if ya *fail* to fulfill your part."

Frowning, Joavan stared at Daegan, taking his time to decide. "I intend to do what I say, so that will be fine."

Tristan asked, "Do you need someone to hold the box while you two execute this plan?"

"Hardly," Joavan snapped. "You are not an objective party." He bent his knees and dropped down as he lowered his palm to the ground. Using his other hand, he pushed invisible energy at the box until it slid onto the grass. When he straightened again, he told Daegan, "You stand on the other side of the box."

Daegan complied.

Joavan cupped his hands above the box. "I offer Daegan, dragon king of Treoir, my aid to facilitate the rescue of ... " Joavan paused and gave Daegan a pointed look.

"Casidhe Luigsech, a historical researcher," Daegan supplied.

Joavan continued, "Casidhe Luigsech, a historical researcher, from where she is imprisoned in TÅμr Medb. Once she is safe, Daegan agrees to then retrieve the amulet known as *Cearcall na Sìorraidheachd*, or Circle of Eternity. As soon as the dragon king of Treoir completes this task, he will receive the Immortuos Grimoire volume beneath my cupped hands. Should he fail to take the amulet from the druid who stole the treasure, the Immortuos Grimoire volume is forever forfeited."

When Joavan paused, Daegan gave him a narrowed-eyed look. "You do not clarify which druid."

"I prefer not to mention his name." Holding his cupped hands in place above the bronze box, Joavan added, "To fulfill Daegan's part of this agreement, he must take the amulet from only one druid I lead us to as soon as we leave this location. Does that satisfy your concern?"

Daegan nodded. "Go on. Add the rest."

Acting put upon, Joavan added in a half-hearted voice that suggested his words were ridiculous, "Should I, Joavan of the Faetheen, fail to uphold my end of the agreement, the dragon king of Treoir will receive the Immortuos Grimoire volume to do with as he wishes." Joavan closed his hands as if wrapping them around a ball. He lifted his fingers to his lips and whispered. When he finished and opened his hands, gold, silver, and red sparkles bounced between both curved palms.

He said, "Open your hands, palms facing up, and place them side by side, Daegan."

Daegan hated to be touched by anyone's majik, but he'd survived the satyr coating and had a feeling he'd face worse before finding all the volumes. He opened his hands.

Joavan poured the flickering sparkles onto Daegan's palms. He could feel nothing from the sparkles.

"Close your hands once, then open them and pour the spell onto the box," Joavan instructed. "That will bind the two of us and the box into one agreement."

Daegan opened his hands.

Now blue, silver, and gold, the sparkles dusted down over the box.

The grimoire vanished.

Blood drained from Daegan's face, leaving him light-headed. "Where is it?"

Joavan backed up. "Do not shout at me. The box is hidden from both of us until our agreement is satisfied. I cannot call it to me. You cannot call it to you. It is safe. Do you not worry about Imortiks being drawn to that box while we travel?"

The Faetheen sounded so reasonable Daegan had to take a leap of faith just to move ahead. "In that case, how good is your plan for pullin' Luigsech out of TÅµr Medb?"

Joavan cupped his jaw with his fingers as a sour look twisted his lips. "It is an excellent plan ... but I'm sure you know plans are always perfect until they meet the enemy."

CHAPTER 2

CASIDHE SLOUCHED AGAINST THE ELBOW she'd propped on the heavy wooden table in the TÅµr Medb library. Turning another page to read with bloodshot eyes, she couldn't stay on task. At home, she'd lived for days lost in reading. The books stacked on the table around her now felt like a yoke closing slowly over her neck.

Even that was not as bad as being cast aside.

Why had Daegan made her feel wanted only to turn his back on her?

A tear slid down her cheek and landed in a fat splat on the page she'd had open too long. How could she damage a written artifact this way? She jumped up and used her shirttail to carefully dry the wet spot. Finished saving the page, she sagged to her chair and propped her elbows on the table to support her aching head.

What had she ever done to deserve landing in a realm with a crazy queen? Abandoned by a man she'd started to trust. A man who had sent her heart cartwheeling.

She wiped her eyes with her sleeve and sat up straight. No more tears for Daegan. Just accept the truth. That gobshite had used her to gain the grimoire volume and now he was done with her.

She'd believed him when he said he needed all three grimoires. She'd believed that kiss. She'd believed they had a future of some sort.

Stop it, she shouted inside her head.

Blinking her dry eyes to focus, she sucked in a long

breath and carefully turned another fragile parchment page. The material crackled as it moved in a book so old majik probably held it together.

That wouldn't be farfetched either.

She couldn't imagine any material in this library defying Queen Maeve by daring to disintegrate, especially pages older than dragons still alive today.

Her gaze tripped over to the glass of water that continued to refill when she drank the level down. A half-eaten tray of cheese, meats, and fruit hadn't automatically replenished.

Her eyelids drooped. She'd love to put her head down and catch a nap.

"What are you doing?" a brittle female voice snapped in the quiet space.

Casidhe jumped at the sharp words echoing through the cavernous library.

Queen Maeve stood to her left at the end of the table in all her outrageous appearance. A striking beauty from a distance, but up close her eyes were dead and mean, her crazy hair changed color on a whim, currently a mix of silver and reddish gold, which fit just fine with a gown the color of blood, if blood sparkled.

There stood the reason Casidhe couldn't catch a nap, not with an insane queen zapping in and out of here. "My eyes are blurry. I was trying to—"

"I do not care about your whiny excuses. I asked what you were doing. How close are you to locating a grimoire volume?" Queen Maeve actually floated at the end of the table.

Hours ago, when Casidhe first entered TÅµr Medb, everywhere she looked had overwhelmed her. After living on the edge of panic for so many hours, exhaustion had beat the nerves out of her.

Not to mention having her hopes for being saved crushed

by a dragon shifter that had duped her.

She just wanted to curl up somewhere to sleep and nurse her wounded heart.

When Queen Maeve left earlier to face Daegan in that Tribunal meeting, Daegan knew for sure the queen held Casidhe prisoner. Had he asked if she was healthy or injured? No. Had he offered something in exchange for her freedom? No.

He hadn't even tried. That cut the deepest and said the most.

He'd merely argued that anything Casidhe and Queen Maeve found belonged to him.

She'd only mattered to him as long as she could help him hunt the damn grimoire.

How could he just forsake her on that mountain?

Had she meant anything to him at all? Even if he didn't want her for any other reason, surely he could use her skills. Maybe he only needed one grimoire volume unless every single thing he'd said were lies.

"Are. You. *Listening*?" Queen Maeve snarled.

Twisting to face that woman, Casidhe let out a long sigh. "Yes, I'm listenin'. I need material from around the time the original grimoire was created." She decided to test the crazy queen. "I'm thinkin' it would be when the *first* red dragon lived."

Hate permeated the beautiful face of this vicious queen. "How can you be interested in that lizard after he turned his back on you?"

Just shove that knife deeper, bitch. Casidhe kept that thought to herself and put up a strong front. "I don't give a rat's ass about any red dragon and definitely not the one alive today. I *am* lookin' for material from a specific period of time, which is why I referenced the first red dragon. If your books don't go that far back, no problem."

Queen Maeve shot up into the air, paused, and floated

from left to right, pointing a long black fingernail at the spines of different books. When she'd drifted ten feet over, she crooked her finger in a "come here" indication.

A wide burgundy-colored book slid out.

No, not a book, but a wooden chest with tarnished metal adornments at the corners.

Casidhe's pulse jumped at the possibility Queen Maeve actually had a book from the time of the original red dragon.

Why? her conscience argued.

She didn't have the energy to carry on a debate with her mouthy conscience. Information was power in her world. She had to survive to help Fenella. The best way to survive here would be by making herself irreplaceable. No one else could come close to deciphering the information in those ancient books.

When the queen floated back down, she waved a hand in a sweeping move at the stack of books on the table.

The books shifted quietly down the long table. Pages on the book in front of Casidhe flipped closed, followed by the cover, then that book joined the others.

Dust floated about after all that movement.

She sneezed and heard no "*gesundheit.*" No surprise there.

With the table surface now clear, Queen Maeve opened her hands and the chest floated down to land in front of Casidhe. The queen uttered a short blast of sounds under her breath. She could be speaking words in some language, but Casidhe didn't recognize them.

Wide as her shoulders and a foot tall, the chest turned to face her, then the latch snicked open. The lid continued rolling away from her to reveal a stack of papyrus scrolls, which some scholars called rolls.

Casidhe closed her eyes and inhaled the earthy scent of history from thousands of years ago penned by scribes. If not for being in a dangerous realm, she would stay here for as long as the queen allowed her to research.

But her window of safety would run out soon. Her stomach twisted with anxiety over what would happen at that point.

The queen had been popping in more often.

Casidhe lifted her gaze to Queen Maeve. "I'll start on this immediately."

A taunting smile lifted on Queen Maeve's evil face. "You really think you are capable of deciphering *those* rolls?"

Warning signals went off in Casidhe's head. She hedged, "I won't know for sure until I review them, but I am pretty good at ancient languages."

Leaning forward, Queen Maeve dropped both hands on the wood surface. Her smile widened. "I doubt you have ever seen a text like you are about to read. This language belonged to a supernatural being long gone from this world. I captured six translators. All human squires. The last one had been the only one who could translate parts of it." She straightened to her full height again. "If you read any one of those rolls entirely, I will consider freeing you if we are able to locate a grimoire with that information."

No other words could have rattled Casidhe from her sleepy doldrums and lifted her hope until she realized the queen had said *we*.

She glanced at the stack of six rolls darkened to a mocha-coffee color by age and curled her fingers. She couldn't wait to get going. Not that she would hand someone like Queen Maeve a volume of the Immortuos Grimoire, but she might have a better chance of escaping if she left TÅµr Medb to hunt for a volume. Knowing this queen, she'd probably be locked in a cage the whole time.

It didn't matter. If she found anything the least bit useful, she'd talk it up to convince Queen Maeve for a chance to return to the human realm.

That plan had holes. Still, better to have a plan with holes than no plan at all.

It wasn't as if Daegan cared if she lived.

Her throat tightened, but she would not waste one damned tear on that cold-hearted shifter. She'd been a fool to care about him at all.

"If you cannot read any of it," Queen Maeve continued, "you will disappoint me, which would be unfortunate as I am not one to offer second chances."

Casidhe gulped. She got that message no problem.

Failure equaled death.

Queen Maeve snapped her fingers. An hourglass appeared, floating in the air. She twirled a finger in a circular motion. The glass flipped over and sand began running.

Really fast.

The queen warned, "You have until the sand runs out to show me your value."

Mouth open, Casidhe stared at the spot Queen Maeve vacated in the next second.

There couldn't be thirty minutes in that hourglass.

Less every second she wasted.

Her hands shook as she reached for the first scroll from the chest and placed it on the table. She carefully unrolled the papyrus and cringed. The roll was so brittle it might break.

If she damaged any of these, she might as well cut her own throat and save herself from being tortured.

Translating had a way of settling her nerves by focusing on something she could accomplish. As she scanned the strange markings, Casidhe understood why Queen Maeve had found the idea of her reading this text humorous.

Rubbing her hands on her jeans, Casidhe lifted two fingers as if saluting then lowered them to move across the text on the manuscript.

Nothing happened.

What? Where was her power?

She glanced around, worried the queen would be hovering above her, but no. She was still alone.

Casidhe glanced at the hourglass emptying too quickly and tried not to panic.

She placed her left hand on the left edge of the roll to steady herself and moved the two fingers over the text again.

Golden letters began to lift and reshape into words she could read.

She jerked her left hand up in a fist pump of excitement and ... the gold letters disappeared.

What? That made no sense.

Opening her left hand, she carefully placed those fingers back on the end of the roll and the golden letters lifted once more. That was new and something to keep in mind.

The strange symbols had been scripted in lines parallel with the top and bottom edges and eighteen inches wide. She raced over each column, reading as quickly as she could.

Nothing in this mentioned the grimoire.

The scribe wrote about the era leading up to a conflict between humans and nonhumans. Huh, she hadn't thought about how the same thing happened long ago just as chaos erupted now in America with nonhumans being exposed.

Rolling up the left end of the scroll and moving it in that direction, she revealed two more columns of text.

The scribe began writing about the dragons. Earth dragons, ice dragons, and the red dragon, but not Daegan. Long before he and Herrick had been born.

There were other dragons, too. Some very old.

She stopped at one part, not believing what she read.

The dragon families had been allies for centuries and

the duty of keeping peace had fallen to the red dragon, which no one could defeat.

That echoed Daegan's words.

She read on. There had not been just a simple agreement. The kings of every dragon clan created a document and each king took a blood oath to uphold their alliance. The most powerful dragon shifter of each house also swore their part in protecting peace.

They wanted their families, plus their nonhuman and human clans to thrive and live free of fear.

With all the dragon families supporting the alliance, the benefits had been amazing. Every clan raced in to fight alongside another clan in times of trouble.

Talk about significant peace talks.

No one would start a war with another dragon house when they were all willing to fight together against invaders like marauding Vikings.

She sat back, feeling smacked between the eyes.

She'd been taught Daegan had started a war to wipe out all of the dragon families. Based upon what she'd just read, no dragon shifter would break his blood oath.

The consequences of such a move would band all the other clans together to attack that one dragon shifter, his king, and his clan.

Even the infamous red dragon might not have survived a joint attack. Of course, the first red dragon had been born of a dragon shifter and dragon-blood mate.

Daegan had come from an unknown goddess and his dragon-blood father.

Herrick's family had possessed five dragon shifters in their house alone.

Why had the dragon clans battled each other during the Dragani War when it sounded as if the families had lived in peace for a long time? The history she'd been taught presented Daegan as the worst kind of villain.

A tiny noise snapped her out of research mode.

Cathbad stood on the other side of the table.

CHAPTER 3

CASIDHE JUMPED UP.
Lifting a finger quickly to his lips, Cathbad indicated for her to be quiet. Then he waved her around the table to him.

Should she call out for Queen Maeve?

Or go with Cathbad?

How was either of those a good choice?

She glanced at the hourglass with a thimble of sand left.

Cathbad looked up and his face erupted with worry. He teleported around the table and appeared next to her.

Casidhe backed up. "What do you want?"

"Hush or we won't get out of here. Give me your hand."

"Why?"

"I don't have time to argue. Give me your damn hand."

"No."

Cathbad looked as if he'd go ballistic any minute. He whisper-shouted, "What is wrong with you?"

She hissed back, "I'm tired of everyone yankin' me around."

"What are you doing here?" Queen Maeve screamed from ten feet off the ground.

Cathbad grabbed Casidhe's arm and the world turned somersaults. She screamed, tumbling wildly as they teleported.

Then all the chaos in her head stopped at once.

"Casidhe!"

Her hearing muffled the word as if she had a head cold.

She wrapped her arms around her chest where she knelt on grass barely visible in the darkness. The air smelled fresh and wind cooled her hot skin, but she might throw up from disorientation.

Rain dinged the top of her head and wind whistled, slapping hair against her face. She croaked out, "What?"

Someone lifted her to her feet and hugged her. "Ya are safe."

Was that Daegan's voice?

Sure felt like his big body holding her.

Lifting her gaze, she ignored the worry etched in his face and backed out of his arms.

He stared at her in surprise.

Did he really think she was so easy?

She slapped him with a loud crack. "How could you leave me there? How could you ... wait a minute." She grabbed her head. "And now you're workin' with *Cathbad*? You *bastard!*"

Just as her hearing cleared to pick up the sounds of birds in the trees behind Daegan, everything muted again. No water or wind touched her. "Did you cloak me? Let me out of here."

Daegan rubbed his cheek. "Ya have a hell of a punch for such a wee lass."

Her heart trembled at hearing him call her a lass again.

No. She would not be charmed by him this time. "You think I'm jokin'? I hate you." Those words hurt to say, but she'd pushed him out of the space he'd been taking up in her heart and mind.

Daegan wiped water off his face and ran his hands over his hair, letting out a big sigh. "'Tis clear ya have somethin' to get off your chest. Say it."

"You bet I do, buster." She jammed her hands on her hips and leaned forward. "I sat here and waited for you."

"I know. I—"

"Shut. Up. I'm talkin'." She caught a breath and continued. "I climbed out of that hidin' hole all night lookin' for you. At daylight, I stepped out and ran into Queen Maeve who teleported me out of here." Her eyes burned with anger and hurt. She clenched them shut, wishing for her sword. Her eyes flew open. "Where's my backpack?"

"We have it nearby. 'Tis safe."

"You left it out *there* with Cathbad?" she screeched.

He covered his ears. "If ya would give me a chance to—"

"No. You had a chance in the Tribunal and blew it."

His expression shifted from pained and contrite to confused. "What is this ya speak of?"

"Yeah." She nodded and stepped around, not caring if she bumped into his stupid cloaking. Too dark to see much around her. "Queen Maeve told me when she came back how you were only concerned with gainin' possession of whatever she had me find out about the grimoire."

"'Tis not what I said," he argued in stern words.

She whipped around to face him. "Easy to say now."

Daegan's eyes darkened to pewter and his pupils elongated.

Ah, hell. Would she finally see the red dragon?

Would it be the last thing she saw before his dragon turned her into ashes?

Daegan's voice sounded more dragon than human. "I made a deal with the Tribunal that may cost me somethin' I have *never* allowed to be traded just to force them to call in Queen Maeve. I informed the Tribunal she had kidnapped ya to find the grimoire, when I knew full well she intended to use ya to capture me. That did not matter. I was comin' for ya one way or another, but I had hoped to force her to hand ya over in the Tribunal to free ya sooner. Once the deities realized what she was up to with huntin' the grimoire, she vanished."

Why did it sound like truth when he explained his side of what happened? Her damn heart and conscience teamed up against her demanding to hear him out.

He looked away and ran a hand over his mouth, muttering to himself. When his gaze lasered back to her, his eyes had calmed down to human-looking again and held a warmth she missed. "Casidhe, I would not have left ya here if I had thought I would not return." Pain and disappointment rippled through his words. "The satyrs spewed a coatin' on me that started turnin' hard. I could not escape the human military who caught me on the cliffs. I could not teleport or send a telepathic message. If I could have, I would have sent my people for ya."

Should she believe him? "How did you escape?"

"'Tis a bit of a story, but I had help from someone known as a Faetheen, whose people gave me a salve to stop the coatin' from killin' me."

She couldn't prevent her hard swallow at hearing Daegan had been close to dying. She might be pissed, but the idea of this world with no Daegan hurt in a way she couldn't explain.

Continuing, he explained, "My people found where I was bein' held. They negotiated my release. My power has been damaged by Imortik attacks so I could not teleport. 'Tis why I had Tristan take us to the oracle's mountain. As soon as I was free, Tristan and I came here first to find ya. When we went to where ya left the backpack, I knew immediately Queen Maeve had been here. I believe she has her scryin' wall workin' again and watched us. I am sorry she took ya, lass."

She exhaled a trembling breath. She'd been alone here all night after that heart-stopping kiss, then captured and threatened. Every part of her wanted to believe him and stop hauling around this anger.

Would she be a fool to believe him?

He stepped forward. "I would not lie to ya, lass. Nor would I ever leave ya somewhere, not even TÅµr Medb." He put his hands on her shoulders. "I would have gone there to trade myself for ya if I had no other way to save ya."

Warmth soaked into her skin. Her heart flipped all about in a happy celebration. She wanted to touch him and feel his warmth up against her skin, to have him use his hands to help her forget the terror of being trapped in another realm.

Believe him or not?

If she got this wrong, she'd never forgive herself. Daegan had either just told the truth or he'd set her up for a bigger emotional crash.

She still had questions he'd failed to answer. "But why are you workin' with Cathbad?"

Daegan smiled and his handsome face went up a hundred notches in appeal. "'Twas not Cathbad, lass. A Faetheen glamoured Tristan to look like the druid."

Thinking back on the few seconds she'd faced off with the druid in TÅµr Medb, she realized what had seemed odd. "He didn't sound like Cathbad."

"'Twas no time to fix his speech. We told Tristan to say as little as possible since the queen might hear."

Her shoulders relaxed with the weight of betrayal lifted and her heart sighed. When she looked up at Daegan, his gaze locked with hers.

Those silver eyes held a longing that rivaled hers.

He muttered, "I cannot wait another second." Then he lowered his head and kissed her.

His mouth swept over hers like a gentle wave, then it crashed harder at the end. She clutched his shoulders, holding him close, determined to keep his body tight aginst hers. Energy built in her middle and fed to her limbs. When it reached her fingers, she felt a snap of electricity.

He lifted his head. "What was that?"

"Our powers seem to be talkin'." She smiled.

"Let them." His big hand cupped her face and his mouth lit a fire in her womb, sending a raging wake-up call to her hormones.

She had never felt this pull from another man, definitely not that idiot from college who claimed her body heated up too much during sex. Wasn't that the point? To get hot?

She'd bet every book in her precious library Daegan wouldn't make that complaint.

His hands gripped her carefully, but he was not letting her go. His every move reassured her he had meant what he said and would have found her no matter where she went.

She needed to be wanted and missed. She needed to be important to someone.

Not just someone. To Daegan.

She'd been lonely for so long she'd chastised herself for being attracted to the first man to care about her in a while. More like forever. But this didn't feel like desperation to leap at a sexy man who happened to be convenient.

This was passion.

This was real.

She wrapped her arms around his neck, pulling him closer. He lifted her off the ground, holding her with an arm around her waist. His other hand raced along her face and shoulders, touching her with care as if she were his whole world right then.

She'd never been that important to any man.

She'd fought for what little space she could find in Herrick's family.

Something told her this might be a once-in-a-lifetime man.

Dragging her fingers through his wild hair, she wrapped her legs around his waist, hugging up against a very turned-on dragon shifter.

He shuddered and moved his hand to her bottom, holding her against him.

His kiss had pushed away the world. Nothing mattered but this moment. When he slowed, he pecked kisses on her forehead then her cheek. She ran her fingers over his chin where a beard had shown up.

Daegan leaned his forehead down to touch hers. "I was destroyed with worry for your safety. Ya trusted me and I could not come to ya or send someone. I died a hundred times in that cell thinkin' I would never see ya again to know ya were safe. I would never hold ya again."

For a normally tight-lipped dragon shifter, Daegan shocked her by sharing those feelings.

Was this moment just as unusual for him? "I should never have doubted you, Daegan."

"'Tis easy to do when stuck in a realm where ya have no idea escape is possible, lass."

Even after she'd yelled at him and abused his handsome face, he forgave her that easily.

She allowed her arms to drape loosely on his shoulders with her hands clasped behind his neck so she could lift her head. "Still, I will not be so quick to give up hope again."

He didn't speak for a long second, then vowed, "As long as I have breath in my body, I shall not break a promise to ya, lass. It pains me to let ya go, but I must fulfill an agreement to the Faetheen who has helped me twice now."

Lifting her head, she studied his tense face. "What do you have to do?"

"His people lost an important amulet. He needs a dragon shifter to take it from the thief. Once I have fulfilled my part of our deal, I shall come for ya. Then we must hand the scepter to the oracle. I may need help with the grimoire again. Until I come for ya, I am sendin' ya somewhere safe."

Huffing out a long breath, she scratched her head. "When will you understand that you can't dictate what I do?"

His eyes darkened again, but in irritation this time. "I am not tellin' ya what to do, but protectin' ya."

Ancient hardheaded man. She squirmed around. "Let me down. I can't talk to you when you've got a log shoved between my legs." She'd said that in a teasing tone. Had she embarrassed the arrogant dragon?

He leaned in and whispered, "'Tis only a log because of your sweet scent." His eyes twinkled, but he knew he'd one-upped her.

Score a point for Daegan.

Lowering her to the ground, he groused, "Ya make it difficult for me to drop the cloakin' while my jeans are taut."

"As if that's my fault?" She tossed him a saucy look.

He shrugged. "'Tis your fault, but I forgive ya. Does not change that we are stuck in here until I can walk out."

She stared up at the muted sky then back at him. "Think of somethin' else."

"Not possible with ya so close."

More points for Daegan. He'd managed to make her feel sexy when she had to look like a witch and had never been proficient at flirting. She hit on the perfect idea. "Why don't you think about usin' that log on Queen Maeve?"

His face lost all joking. "'Tis not funny. In fact, 'tis a disgustin' thought."

"*Aaand* ... you're all calm again," she said with a pointed look at his crotch. "You can thank me now."

He leaned close to her ear. "I prefer to make ya pay for a vision I cannot burn from my mind." Then he kissed her cheek and nipped at her ear.

Thankfully, her body did not show the effect that sexy dragon shifter had on her when he dropped the cloaking. Not unless someone could see her hard nipples.

Jets flying along the coast came into view, then storm clouds and trees close by sharpened again when Daegan revealed their presence.

"Hi, Casidhe."

At the sound of Tristan's voice, she turned to her right where the northern coast of Spain overlooked the ocean. A man, who she guessed to be the Faetheen, stood next to Tristan.

"Thanks for getting me out of TÅµr Medb, Tristan." She added a smile, then glanced at the very attractive male beside him. "Thank you, too."

Tristan chuckled. "Glad you didn't hit me with something when I surprised you."

She laughed. "I really thought you were Cathbad. I was too rattled to realize you didn't have his Irish accent."

"You have a lovely laugh. I am Joavan," the stranger said, walking over and picking up her hand to lift to his lips.

Like an idiot, she just stood there in shock.

He got shoved aside before his mouth had a chance to kiss her skin. Daegan snarled, "Do not touch her."

Recovering from his sidestep, Joavan glared at Daegan. "She appreciates what I did where you do not."

"'Tis 'cause I do not want ya kissin' *my* hand either."

Joavan made a hacking noise. "You are in no danger of that ever happening."

She cocked her head to give Daegan a what-the-hell look over that move, but her silly heart found his covetous action endearing. She didn't know exactly where she stood with Daegan, but he clearly would not tolerate another man touching her.

Fair enough. She'd turn evil if another woman touched him.

Daegan then placed a possessive hand on Casidhe's shoulder, which drew a surprised look from Tristan.

Clearly not caring one bit, Daegan asked Tristan, "Do ya still have the room in your friend's hotel?"

"Yes. It's a perpetual deal."

"'Tis safe?"

Scratching his chin, Tristan nodded. "I'm the only one who can teleport in and I'm pretty sure scrying can't see inside *that* room. I can make sure she has everything she needs."

"What?" Casidhe ducked away from Daegan's hand and wheeled on him. "Are you really makin' plans for me without askin' what I think? Again?"

Daegan made a noise that came out part exasperation and part exhaustion. On a closer look, she noticed the deep lines around his eyes and mouth, but she could not let him get away with his high-handed approach every time.

"Did I not just tell ya I wish for ya to be somewhere safe while I go to make good on my word with Joavan? 'Tis a nice place from what Tristan has shared. Ya would be comfortable." After grumbling a moment, Daegan added, "I only need a day to do this, lass."

Joavan's mouth opened. "One day? I do not know how quick this will be."

"*Quiet!*" Daegan ordered. "'Tis not your conversation." When he spoke to Casidhe, his voice softened. "I want ya to go to Tristan's place. I shall come to ya as soon as I have fulfilled my commitment. I am askin' ya, not tellin' ya."

He had a way of needling under her skin when he became contrite, something she doubted many witnessed with Daegan. "I will go under one condition."

Daegan covered his eyes and muttered, "What now?"

"Hey. Don't be an ass about this when I'm meetin' you halfway," she chastised him. "I'm not askin' for the moon. I will wait if I can go to wherever Fenella's phone is when you return."

Lowering his hand, Daegan gave her a smile filled with

understanding. "I promise to make this happen."

"O-*kay*, we are finally in agreement." She slashed a look at Tristan. "Are you my ride?"

"Yes, ma'am."

Casidhe spun around, looking in the direction of the dark spot where she and Daegan had hidden in the woods. "Where's my backpack?"

"Stand by." Tristan vanished for five seconds and reappeared holding her backpack out to her.

"Thanks." She took it from him and slid her hand in the backside far enough to touch the hilt of her sword. Still there.

Daegan watched her. "All is as ya left the pack."

That meant the scepter and books were inside, confirmed by the weight. She gave him a quick nod, then slipped her arms through the straps and latched everything until the pack settled properly.

A rumbling growl came from Daegan.

She jerked her head up. "What's that?"

"Nothin' to be concerned over." Daegan had a hard head when it came to something he wouldn't share. "Take care of the pack. We still have a debt to pay, but ya shall be taken to Fenella's phone first."

She gripped a strap on the backpack, wanting to talk to him more about how they were going to deliver the scepter to the oracle. Now was not the time or place with that Joavan guy listening.

"We'll figure it out," she offered, hoping to ease his worry. Shifting her attention to Tristan, she lifted her eyebrows in question.

Tristan told Daegan, "May need a few minutes to make sure everything is set after we get there, boss."

"'Tis fine."

Casidhe stepped over next to Tristan who grinned at her. "Ready?"

"Yes." As teleporting started, she glanced at Daegan. His dark eyes stayed with her until the last second as teleporting distorted her world.

CHAPTER 4

PULSATING VIBRATIONS DRAGGED RENATA FROM sleep again.

She gritted her teeth when a sharp throb raced through her, slithering across her skin and stabbing hot pokers into her mind.

Her body trembled and shuddered more every day as the Imortik entity inside her kept clawing for a better hold on her body and mind.

Her fingers tingled. Sometimes numbness started in the tips and climbed to her wrists, searing every inch of the way beneath her skin.

Today was different. No numbness. Just that steady pulsation of heat shooting through her, then cold freezing her when the heat receded.

Sweat ran down her face, into her eyes, then dripped off her forehead. Splat. Splat. Splat.

Her body had been draped over a wide strap hooked to chains running down from the ceiling. Did that help the monsters gain control faster? She couldn't make her legs or arms move.

How was Roberto? She stuffed her mind with any memory of him every second that still belonged to her. His heart would be crushed if she did not return.

Would he ever know the truth?

Tears trickled out her eyes and joined the sweat.

Splat. Splat. Splat.

Her body shuddered hard. She groaned, doing her best

to stay quiet. Don't draw attention around monsters. Sniffing, she smelled the other bodies. Whenever she could catch sight of the others, some moved a little and some never did.

All the bodies glowed at different levels of bright yellow.

One person started shouting yesterday. Or had that been today? She didn't know. When she'd looked, the man's glow had tripled until she thought he'd swallowed the sun.

The master had him taken down from the sling, then he compelled the man to do as he said. At least it looked like compelling. She didn't know much about how all this worked.

The fully converted Imortik had walked away with a dead gaze.

She lifted her eyelids just enough to peek, cautious to not make eye contact with the master. He was not here based on what little she could see and the lack of noise. That one complained and shouted all the time, always angry at someone he'd made a deal with and now regretted it.

He had episodes where he howled and jumped around, pulling at his long brown hair then he'd scream in agony. He'd rip out chunks until his scalp bled. When his teeth chattered, he forced out words that sounded majikal. Must have worked.

Within moments, he'd stop jerking around, fall to his knees, and wail like a little boy who had just skinned his knee.

She smiled every time. Sympathy must be reserved for decent humans and nonhumans, not a crazed monster. Her tangled hair hanging hid her face from the sides, but she never smiled very long, just enough to feed her soul a cookie.

Her eyes rolled up. No, no, no. She'd seen that happen to the guy who was taken down. She shook her head to jar her brain.

Splat. Splat. Splat.

Stupid Imortik master suffered seizures from the Imortik steadily taking over his body. Based on something he said once, she believed he'd been an Imortik for more than two weeks. She hoped it was not two weeks for her yet.

The master and his partner talked as if they had a plan to return the master back to his original state, whatever that had been.

Timmon, the Imortik Master. Who had he been before this?

And why did it sound as if he'd done this to himself on purpose? Who would willingly become an Imortik?

During his occasional conversations with a partner, Timmon lamented a rash decision that must have sounded exciting when laid out by an insidious manipulator. *Become a master today and rule the world tomorrow, just sign here.*

The partner only visited in hologram. He clearly did not trust Timmon to not shove an Imortik inside him just to equal the playing field.

Who was his partner?

Was he a man, woman, or it? The last time sounded male, but it had sounded female before that.

If she knew anything about the partner's identity, she'd send that name telepathically to all the Beladors.

Of course, if she could do that, she'd send out an SOS to her people. Once a Belador heard her, they would find her. Her people would use any resource to save her, Devon, and others captured. What had happened to Devon? Her heart whimpered when she thought about him and Roberto. She had to stop allowing emotions to affect her.

Emotion had played a role in pushing others to concede life to the Imortiks quicker.

She fought to stay strong, even if only in tiny moments.

None of her telepathic messages had gone out. They stayed in her head, but she kept sending them anyhow.

Just in case.

Three words that breathed life into her hope.

Calling Beladors, she started and paused to take a breath even though she shouldn't need it for telepathy. Sometimes simply thinking drained her. She continued with the same mantra she sent every day.

This is Renata. Tell Trey, Daegan, anyone who is looking for me. Slow inhale and exhale. *The master moved us to a ...*

Her mind struggled to pull the words together.

Moved us to a building. Warehouse maybe. Old metal walls. Tall. Windows at top, some cracked. Smells like ... Another breath. *Engine oil and gasoline, solvents. Humans. Sun rises in front and sets in back. Quiet outside. Always silent unless ...*

"*Where are you?*" the Imortik master shouted.

Renata didn't flinch. The Imortik master knew exactly where she was, where everyone was in this building.

"Stop calling me all the time!" the partner's voice boomed. Yesterday that voice sounded like a woman. Today it had a manly baritone again. Why keep changing it? Did these two worry any Beladors might get word out?

They should worry.

She would not stop trying to reach Trey.

Timmon whined, "*The seizures are worse!* Make it stop."

"I can't do that in hologram form."

"You hide behind that. You compelled me to not say your name. You're using me!" Timmon started crying. "I can't do this. You're stronger. You should do this."

"If you could do my job, I would take your place, but you can't. Just the fact that you can't handle an Imortik proves that."

Renata blew gently to move hair from her eyes, trying to see the being in hologram form. Too blurry.

"I can't do this for another week," Timmon whimpered. "I want my body back. I hate this thing inside me."

See? Another opportunity to smile. Renata hoped whatever lived inside Timmon was ten times worse than what she fought, but seriously doubted it.

"Stop acting like a child," the partner ordered.

Lots of sniffling followed, then Timmon said, "I have an idea how to move up our timeline."

"I'm all ears, Timmon."

"You could take some of the ones close to completing the transformation and start a major battle. Force the Beladors, warlocks, everyone to move faster and produce the grimoire volumes."

Quiet permeated the building until the partner released a loud sigh. "No."

"*Why not?*" Timmon screamed.

"That screws the timeline for us to open the death wall all the way and might cause nonhumans to join forces. That's the last thing we want. Instead of sucking it up for one more measly week, you'd be stuck that way for months, maybe longer. Want that?"

"No." Timmon's glum word came out so low Renata would not have heard him without her Belador hearing. He muttered, "You're safe. You come here as a hologram and leave me to do all the dirty work."

"As if I'm not out there facing just as much as you? I have more powerful people after me. You would not fare well in my position."

Timmon made a derogatory sound. "I'm not just dealing with nonhumans when I'm outside this building. There's a group of humans out there with weapons that can obliterate me."

"That's not going to happen. You're a demigod, Timmon. Act like one."

"I can't," Timmon shouted.

That man had two levels. Yelling and whimpering. But Renata had a new piece of information. Demigod, huh? That just meant he was more dangerous than she'd thought.

"What do you mean you can't?" the partner scowled.

"You miscalculated. This thing is eating my body."

Sounding compassionate for the first time, the partner said, "I hate this for you. I've been working on a plan, too. Give me a chance to put it into motion and maybe motivate everyone to find the damn volumes faster."

"What are you talking about doing?"

"Stir up more chaos. That's working right now. Humans are taking up arms against nonhumans. Queen Maeve has someone in her realm actively hunting the grimoire. That fucking dragon shifter has the resources to locate a volume. He hasn't been in Atlanta for too many days now. He wouldn't leave his Beladors to face all this insanity alone unless he was getting close to finding a grimoire. That chump thinks he'll use it to stop our Imortiks."

Timmon whispered, "I don't want to face that bastard again."

"You sent the dragon running last time. You made him expose the nonhumans. You bested him," his partner praised.

"It wasn't easy. If an Imortik takes over *that* dragon's body, we are doomed. There's no way I could stop him once the Imortik rules his mind and dragon."

"We are not going to let that happen. The rift is opening in other places, but not as wide as ours. Daegan will likely kill those Imortiks, but you injected venom into his body. Yours is a strong venom. Just with that, he's not going to be one hundred percent, but if he's popped with more, he'll be even easier to handle. That's all we need to manage him."

Renata's face crumpled. She swallowed the cry wanting

to rip out of her throat. Not Daegan. The Beladors needed him.

She needed him.

He'd said he'd come for her.

She believed him. That kept her going.

The partner continued trying to appease Timmon. "Give me some time to work behind the scenes. Don't panic if I can't show up the minute you call. I'm not going to be handy every minute. Keep in mind, the more humans we turn into Imortiks will divide the Belador attention between stopping Imortiks and protecting their own people. This will work. We just have to stick to the plan."

Timmon shuffled around, whining, "What about all these demons? They convert quickly, sometimes in one day, but I can't control that many at one time. I had to kill some."

"I've had to kill a few, too," the partner admitted. "To be honest, I have no idea who's behind the demons but that's a bonus for us. Like you said, the demons change into full Imortiks fast. More bodies for our army."

Her arms trembled. She had to stay strong and not give in to the scream of fear climbing her throat.

It was getting harder and harder to stay focused. A voice whispered through her mind. She choked on her fear, eyes watering as she tried to stay silent. Desperate, she asked in her mind, *Are you a Belador?*

Not a word.

Please!

The silence filled her with more terror. Was she going crazy before the Imortik took over her body? She listened for a bit then drifted off until Timmon's voice yanked her eyes open.

"You need to get this done in two days," he demanded.

"Or what?" His partner dropped that demand with the crash of an anvil hitting the cement floor.

"Or I'll call in a power to save me," Timmon threatened. "I am not doing this alone any longer."

"*Don't* call her." Timmon's partner issued the warning in a low tone. Words intended to not be ignored. "Trust me on this. One mistake and we will never be free of her."

Timmon grumbled, "I won't call her. Just get this crap moving. I'm exhausted battling with myself. This miserable Imortik is doing its best to push me out and break free."

"Do *not* allow that to happen!"

"You think I don't know that?" Timmon screamed. "You have no idea what I'm going through!"

"My life isn't perfect either. Hasn't been for a long time. Let's do this and no one will ever deny us anything again. Turn more Imortiks and get them ready to battle."

"I'll do my best," Timmon mumbled, dragging his feet as he moved around. Then he tensed and spoke in a voice an octave higher than his. "Rise, Imortiks, and take your place."

Tortured human voices moaned then began screaming.

Poor Timmon. He needs our help.

Renata froze at the high-pitched voice so clear in her mind. Not a Belador. She struggled against the bindings holding her and yelled, *"Noooo!"*

We will help Timmon when the time comes, the voice assured her with utter confidence. *Together we are strong, Renata.*

CHAPTER 5

DAEGAN STARED AT THE SPOT where Casidhe had stood only seconds ago.

He missed her already.

His conscience climbed up to ask what he was doing with her. He'd never doubted his decisions, but this didn't even feel like a decision when his head couldn't keep up with his body. How could he explain how his body ached the minute she was out of his sight?

Her energy connected with his. That was the only way he could explain the strange buzzing that happened whenever they touched. What power did she possess?

His power was drawn to her as much as his body wanted hers.

Could she be of dragon blood?

If so, no one would know better than her. She was a squire of a dragon family. She had the ability to trace any ancestral lineage. He could not keep trying to convince himself that she could be a mate.

But if that was the case, could he keep encouraging her affections? Easier said than done. He longed to be with Casidhe in a way he'd never wanted another woman.

He trusted Tristan without question, but … Daegan couldn't shake the feeling that she was *his* to protect.

"What is going on with you two?" Joavan asked.

Daegan had forgotten the Faetheen. He shot a warning glance at Joavan, who should stop annoying him. "What is your plan once Tristan returns?"

Accepting he'd been shut down, Joavan replied, "We must teleport as close as possible to the location. Then you will cloak us."

"Why?"

"Why what, dragon? Teleporting or cloaking?"

"Both. Why do ya need me to do those things? Ya can move around as easily as we do and ya proved ya have cloakin'."

Joavan grumbled, "If I travel between worlds in my normal way to reach this druid, he would know as soon as I appeared and attack me before I could stop him. As for cloaking, he would sense my cloaking as well."

Daegan found his explanations weak. Why would a druid be so easily alerted to Joavan's cloaking and not Daegan's?

This Faetheen held back too many details.

Tristan reappeared holding a bag of something succulent smelling. "Brought you some food, boss. Figured you haven't had time to stop. I also explained about how this guy made you choose between her and the grimoire so she'd know what we're dealing with."

Joavan scowled at him. Tristan smirked.

Daegan's stomach grumbled again. His dragon needed a more substantial meal, but this was more than either of them had had in a while. "Thank ya." He took the sack and opened a wrapped hamburger, something he had grown to enjoy.

Tristan added, "Casidhe insisted I not leave without bringing something back for you."

Joavan glanced between them. "Did you not think of me?"

Crossing his arms, Tristan turned to the Faetheen. "Why would I? You said you pop in and out of here from your home realm. Does no one feed you there?"

Devouring the hefty hamburger, Daegan smiled, mouth

too full to speak.

"You keep saying we waste time," Joavan complained to Daegan. "I am ready."

Tristan gave a quick look at where Daegan was with this meal and replied, "Well, I'm not ready. I'm handling the teleporting. I can't do that blind. Where are we going?"

"I will tell you—"

Lifting a hand, Tristan cut him off. "Stop. You can't expect us to help you if you're going to keep us in the dark the whole time."

Tristan's energy pulsed out hard with that reply, surprising Daegan.

Finishing his last bite, Daegan didn't interfere. He had not felt a rush of power like this from his second-in-command before now. Tristan continued to surprise him in the best of ways.

Joavan sulked in angry silence, then his gaze drifted to Daegan. "Does he speak for you, dragon?"

"He does when necessary. He is my second-in-command above all my forces. Ya would do well to respect his position if ya wish for me to gain the amulet."

Tristan's hard demeanor never changed.

Pride surged in Daegan at seeing the young man begin to believe in himself as much as Daegan's faith in him.

Not happy one bit, Joavan admitted, "We go to a remote location on an island. We must arrive far enough away to not alert the thief, then move in close until we can corner him. He will not have the amulet out in the open."

Tristan asked, "You say he's a druid. How powerful a druid? What are we going up against?"

"Very powerful. He has used majik to slow his aging. He will appear as someone around sixty, but he has lived for as long as this dragon shifter."

Daegan went on immediate alert. "What is his name?"

"Ainvar."

"I have never heard of him." Daegan couldn't decide if he should feel relieved it was not someone of Cathbad's level or concerned this druid could be worse.

"Few have known his name. Even less have met him." Joavan paused, staring off for a bit, then his arrogance returned. "It has taken a great deal of work to figure out where he hides on that island. I will tell you more, but we must go now."

Finished with the meal, Daegan wadded up the bag and opened a palm where he called up a flame to burn the paper until tiny ashes floated to the ground.

He would not have thought so small a meal would give his stomach relief, but it did. Even Ruadh had quieted. "Where is the island ya speak of?"

"Do you know the Shetland Islands north of Scotland?"

Tristan piped up. "Of course, we do." Then he spoke telepathically to Daegan. *Scotland today is the north end of the big island east of Ireland we call the United Kingdom.*

Daegan replied the same way. *'Tis the land of the Britons, or it was in my time.* He spoke out loud to Joavan. "Is he hidden on that island?"

"He created the *Caisteal Taibhse* over a thousand years ago."

"Cash what?"

Joavan pronounced the words again. "That is Gaelic Scottish for Ghost Castle. The inhabitants avoid that area. They believe it to be cursed. They claim the castle is not seen for months at a time, then on a moonlit night, the translucent shape of a mighty structure wavers into view. They blame all missing cattle and sheep on it as well as young women who disappear. Locals believe the women were taken for a sacrifice by an ogre who lives there."

"Is that all?" Tristan asked sarcastically.

Daegan reminded Joavan of their agreement. "Ya are

certain this druid has the amulet? I am only committed to deal with the first druid ya point to as the thief."

"I am sure."

Tristan had an uncomfortable expression on his face. "We need a specific image of the location for teleporting."

Joavan held up a finger, asking for silence. He held a palm out and in the next moment a holographic image of a desolate looking land appeared vertically on his palm.

Daegan eyed the image. "Ya believe a castle is going to just appear there?"

"No. That is where we will arrive, which allows us the ability to sneak up on the druid. There is a partial moon this evening, enough to see the castle."

"What if the castle does not appear?" Daegan had not agreed to sit on an island for days.

"It will." Joavan closed his hand and the image disappeared. "This is why I was willing to heal you. I have a small window of time."

Tristan asked Daegan telepathically, *Do we trust this guy?*

No, but he has no reason to heal me only to walk me into a trap. He could have stood by as I died in the cell.

You have a point. Tristan spoke out loud. "Everyone ready?"

"Yes." Joavan edged closer to Tristan yet stayed an arm's length away.

"You have to put your hand on my shoulder, Joavan."

"Why?" The Faetheen angled his head to look at Daegan. "He does not."

"That's because Daegan is driving this train and I have no intention of explaining how that works. If you want to go with us, you have to put your hand on one of our shoulders."

Joavan gripped Tristan's shoulder, clearly not willing to touch Daegan.

Sending a last telepathic message, Daegan told Tristan, *I have the place Joavan showed us in my mind. We shall link again, then teleport.*

Okay, boss.

Daegan generated power and linked to Tristan, then pushed the image into Tristan's mind.

Tristan mouthed the word, *Wow.*

CHAPTER 6

WAITING ON DARK TO FALL this far north of the equator had squeezed the last of Daegan's patience to nothing. Joavan called this barren land Shetland Islands. Daegan recalled flying over these islands long ago, thinking little about them back then. Being in the midst of summer meant lands in this part of the world managed on extremely long and tepid darkness for more than half the day.

Cold bit at the exposed skin on his face, neck, and ears, which bothered him little since his dragon generated heat. Squatting down on Daegan's right, Tristan had said little else since teleporting to this barren land far from any village. His wind-burnt face and red nose barely protruded from the hooded buffalo-fur cloak Daegan had provided in addition to a thick wool shirt, leather pants, and rugged boots.

Daegan wore similar clothing in solidarity with Tristan.

If they were hiking or battling, the air would not be so cold, but sitting for hours allowed the chill to seep into a being's bones.

Tristan's bright green gaze met Daegan's, but he spoke over his shoulder to the Faetheen crouched behind them. "How much longer before we see the Ghost Castle?"

"It must be dark enough for the moonlight to shine on the structure." Joavan tightened the bulky gray scarf around his neck with glove-covered hands. By making a quick stop in his world, he'd acquired his own outfit of a coat made from the pelt of a black bear. The cloak fell to his knees above black leather pants, thick boots, and a black skull cap of soft leather. He looked ridiculous, but Daegan didn't care if he showed up naked as long as they got this task done tonight.

He owed a debt for his life and saving his dragon from dying. Once that debt was paid, he hoped to never see this Faetheen again.

"So there is definitely a building here," Tristan pushed, sounding just as out of patience. "Not just a mirage, right?"

Mirage? Daegan frowned at yet another strange word he assumed must mean some majikal vision.

Wind buffeted all three of them, blasting sand everywhere. Joavan slapped his hand over his eyes, squinting. "Yes. The building will not seem real from where we view it. Once we are inside, you will touch stone and see the actual castle."

"And you believe we can just teleport in?" Tristan's terse voice gave away his lack of belief.

Joavan once again dodged a direct answer. "We must enter from above."

Daegan ground his back teeth every time that Faetheen sidestepped the truth.

Tristan quipped to Daegan, "Is he talking about the battlements?"

Daegan smiled at the memory from days ago of visiting the castle where he'd once lived and tutoring Tristan on terms from his life thousands of centuries ago. "Yes. More important 'tis a chance to encounter guards in that area. Ya are certain there are none, Joavan?"

"Yes, yes, yes. Do you two always ask questions so many times?"

Smirking, Tristan said, "Only when we don't trust what we've been told."

Daegan grinned.

"I have no idea how you two get anything done with so little faith," Joavan groused. "No men guard the top of the structure. This druid has no need for the type of protection lesser nonhumans would utilize."

Tristan twisted to look back at where the Faetheen had taken a warm position behind where Daegan and Tristan's bodies blocked the wind. "Did you just insult us? I only have a gryphon, but he's the freakin' red dragon."

Daegan's dragon rumbled a deep, threatening sound in support of Tristan's words.

"I did not mean to insult anyone," Joavan quickly let everyone know. "I am anxious to find this druid and make him pay."

The underlying feeling of being tricked raised its head again. Daegan's sharp tone could cut through steel. "Make him pay in what way?"

Joavan went mute.

"I have never killed without reason, Joavan. Do not expect that or ya shall be disappointed."

"I did not ask you to kill anyone," the Faetheen muttered.

"Then we are in agreement," Daegan declared, shutting down any more talk of vengeance.

Again, misgivings about what Joavan had not told Daegan pushed at him. His dragon spoke silently. *Fae hides much truth. We fly into deadly storm blind.*

Daegan sent back, *I agree, but I have no way to argue without seein' the trouble.*

You did not agree to keep Fae alive. We protect ours.

Ruadh always put their survival, and now Tristan's, above anything else when going into a potential conflict. Regardless of what Joavan claimed, Daegan had never known a powerful being to leave himself exposed with no additional guards.

Daegan would not turn his back on Joavan unless the

man forced him to walk away. Should harm come to him and Tristan, Daegan would feel no guilt over turning Ruadh loose on the Faetheen.

Night finally settled across the area, though this dark gray was not as black as deep night in Atlanta.

A cloud drifted across the moon.

Daegan sensed tension from Tristan as they all prepared for the moon to shine down on the barren land. Moonlight peeked out from the cloud, dancing across a still-empty landscape.

Daegan's stomach dropped when nothing came into view. "'Tis not here," he complained.

"Wait," Joavan whispered sharply.

Tristan curled his ungloved fingers. Puffs of white clouds appeared with each slow exhale.

"There," Joavan murmured in a relieved voice.

Daegan blinked and squinted as a castle began to waver into view. Though it resembled his da's and other castles from his past, this one was not as large.

Sounds whistled through the air. Soft howls.

What could be making that noise?

The moon vanished behind a cloud again, blocking the light and hiding the castle's translucent shape.

Joavan said, "It is time to go."

"Teleport?" Tristan asked.

"No. We need to move closer on foot so you can see the castle better during the next lighting."

Pushing up to go first, Joavan ran hunched over for thirty or forty feet at a time, pausing behind a boulder or wall of rock that jutted out.

Daegan followed with Tristan beside him. He did not understand Jovan's reasoning. Why should they run closer when they could teleport?

Once Joavan had covered over two hundred yards, he waved Daegan and Tristan behind a large pile of rocks where he dropped to his knees breathing hard.

Daegan squatted, searching for any indication of the castle.

Tristan asked, "Is it always so cold here in the summer?"

"Not this bad," Joavan admitted. "This is the only area so frigid now because of the druid. The unusual drop in temperature supports keeping locals afraid to come here."

A string of clouds passed by the moon until light glowed continuously again.

The castle image returned and wavered. The name Ghost Castle fit what he saw.

Joavan put a hand on Tristan's shoulder. "Now we teleport."

Daegan wanted to push the Faetheen again for more details, but the suspicious being would have shared more by now if he intended to do so.

Tristan's bright green eyes turned on Daegan. "You ready to go, boss?"

Joavan tensed at that question but said nothing while he stared holes into Daegan.

"Yes." Daegan focused hard as soon as the teleporting started. He could not risk coming out of the disorientation slowly. As soon as his feet touched the battlements, he blinked hard to clear his vision and prepared to meet the enemy.

No one greeted them.

He had been expecting Joavan to have lied just to keep moving toward the amulet.

Daegan would not apologize.

He still had a feeling Joavan held back something important. "Where to now?"

Joavan should be happy at their progress, but his eyes filled with concern. He hissed, "Be quiet." He kept looking around nervous as a mouse in a cage with a cat. Did he expect to see those guards he'd sworn did not exist?

A hideous screech sounded from far away.

Tristan froze, eyes moving from side to side.

Joavan's face lost color. "They are here."

A giant beast flew up from the side of the castle and over their heads.

It blasted fire down across the empty land.

Daegan shouted, "'Tis a wyvern. Largest I have ever seen." He tossed his cloak aside, shoved off his boots, and called up Ruadh. His dragon forced a fast change, breaking bones and stretching muscles. Beside him, Tristan had shed clothes just as quickly and unleashed his gryphon. Though not as tall as Ruadh, the gryphon grew and expanded to a formidable size. Translucent scales covered gray skin from the eagle-shaped head down to the body of a lion with huge wings.

Ruadh opened his jaws and blasted fire fifty feet in the air, warning the wyvern. Tristan's gryphon bellowed just as loud.

Before flying off, Ruadh swung his giant head around to face a shaking Joavan. Daegan spoke through his dragon. "Do not dare leave this spot."

Ruadh took two steps away and leaped into the air.

Tristan's gryphon followed, flapping hard to keep pace.

The wyvern made a big turn and leveled out, flying right at them. Similar to a dragon, this beast had only two legs and Daegan had never seen one with eyes the color of hot embers. Nor had he encountered a wyvern as large as his dragon.

A second wyvern screamed from behind them.

Tristan spoke in Daegan's mind. *I'll take the second one. I'll let you know if I need help.*

Ruadh swung his big neck to look at the second wyvern.

A bit smaller than the one they faced, but still larger than Tristan's gryphon and blowing fire, too. That was just as unusual.

Swinging his head back to the oncoming battle, Ruadh flapped his wings with powerful strokes and made loud huffing sounds. Daegan's dragon was not tired.

That was a furious sound Ruadh often made right before ripping into an opponent.

The wyvern coming for them blasted fire.

The distance shortened with every fierce flap of wings.

Heat reached Ruadh's head.

Daegan's dragon would not flinch.

Ruadh opened his jaws and unloaded a storm of fire at the wyvern, knocking the beast straight up in the air and over on its side. They had not flown high, so the wyvern landed hard on the unyielding ground, bouncing and rolling until it slid to a stop. One wing remained outstretched and the other bent under its body.

That was simple enough.

Well done, Ruadh.

The only thing his dragon said before banking around hard was, *Gryphon.*

A fist squeezed Daegan's heart at what he saw.

Halfway to the castle, the second wyvern had Tristan's gryphon on the ground with blood flying.

Daegan called to Tristan. *We are comin'. Can ya get up?*

Tristan didn't answer.

Ruadh flew harder, straining every muscle and roaring at the wyvern pinning Tristan's gryphon.

That wyvern rolled to the side with wings tucked before Ruadh came close enough to torch the beast.

As they flew past at a blazing speed, Tristan lay there in human form, blood everywhere and not moving.

Daegan told his dragon, *We must land to see that Tristan is not dead.*

Ruadh released a fifty-foot explosion of fire and fury, fought to turn in a tight circle, then fanned his wings and shuddered to a hard stop close to Tristan.

Daegan called again telepathically to Tristan.

No response.

Let me have the human body, Ruadh.

His dragon argued, *One wyvern lives.*

We shall shift back immediately if that one returns.

Daegan changed to his human form, but the shift had been rough. No matter how hard Ruadh fought to make it fast, they still had Imortik venom in this body.

Daegan dropped down to Tristan. The minute he touched Tristan's chest, his second sat up fast, eyes wild, and yelled, "It's a trick! The wyverns have majik."

In the silence, more than one set of wings flapped a rapid pace heading toward them.

Two beasts were coming in fast.

CHAPTER 7

DAEGAN SHOUTED, "ARE YA INJURED, Tristan?"

"No." Tristan stood up and pointed. "The one I fought stabbed me with a claw. Something majikal. I couldn't move or send you a message. Then it covered me with blood. If we fight them, I bet they both have that crap in their claws."

Ruadh demanded, *Shift or die.*

The wyverns had reached them and hovered above their heads, flapping slowly now and making deep cawing sounds.

Naked against the cold, Tristan whispered, "Think they're holding us in place for someone else or something worse?" His teeth chattered.

"Possibly." Standing naked as well, Daegan couldn't feel his lower extremity, but he also could not expend energy clothing them. "If we shift together or separately—"

Tristan finished, "They'll c-c-catch us in a vulnerable position e-e-either way."

Ruadh pushed energy through Daegan's body for heat, but he stopped his dragon. *We must save our power, Ruadh.*

Daegan hurried to find a way out of this, but his gut said Ruadh was right. They had to shift. Putting on clothes would also inhibit another shift.

A loud sound boomed from the castle.

Yet another wyvern leaped from the wobbling image of the castle.

Tristan huffed out a blast of white air. "Shit. That

m-m-monster looks like the granddaddy of-f-f these things. These two are holding us ... " He couldn't get the words out.

"For their alpha," Daegan finished. His teeth chattered now, too. Ice coated his eyes. Like Tristan, he used a hand to shield his groin area.

"R-r-right."

If not for the Imortik venom, Daegan could shift fast enough to attack those two above them. But without that blast of power, he would sacrifice his dragon.

Tristan's skin turned blue. "I'm outta ideas, boss." His voice became sluggish and thick. "Think it might be time for your ace in the hole?"

"My what?"

Swinging a desperate look to Daegan with frost forming on his eyebrows and lips, Tristan uttered, "Your mother."

If Daegan died here, he could save no one.

But call in a new unknown powerful player? Even he had no idea how his mother would react. He might bring death more rapidly.

The wyverns above them dropped to the ground on each side of Daegan and Tristan, blocking any escape.

Ruadh roared. *Teleport both. Change both.*

Daegan asked Tristan, "Can you teleport?"

"No. I tried."

The monster wyvern flapped slowly. Each swipe of its wide wings swirled snow dust and brought it closer.

One of the wyverns guarding them puffed a short blast of fire when it cawed a loud happy sound to the approaching beast.

Ruadh roared to break free and kill them. *Imposters!*

That's when Daegan realized his dragon was correct. These were not dragons, but beings altered by majik. In his time, a wyvern would never attack a dragon.

These two had majik in their claws, but they didn't have

Ruadh's ability.

Deagan's dragon only needed the power they'd had since birth.

Ruadh had said, *Change both.* Daegan now understood what his dragon was raging about. He told Tristan, "Link with me and turn to face the wyvern behind us so we're back-to-back."

No hesitation from Tristan. Daegan felt Tristan's power reach out fast for his.

Daegan blasted all the force of his power back at Tristan who groaned.

"We shift as one," Daegan ordered. *"Now!"*

Ruadh needed no encouragement to force the fastest shift Daegan could recall in some time. The energy to do so came from joining with Tristan's healthier body.

Tristan made a pained sound amidst the loud popping of bones, but their beasts both stood in seconds.

The startled wyverns guarding them flapped backward a couple steps.

That was the moment Daegan and Tristan needed.

Ruadh reared back and blasted nonstop fire at the wyvern they faced.

From the side, Daegan saw Tristan's gryphon mimic Ruadh. His gryphon torched his wyvern with more fire than Daegan had seen from the gryphon before.

Both wyverns screamed in pain and fell over in burning piles.

A roar of anguish reached Daegan just before the giant wyvern bore down on Ruadh, who had leaped around to face the threat. Tristan's gryphon took advantage of the fast attack by ducking beneath a stream of fire coming their way. As the wyvern flew over, Tristan's gryphon leaped up, hitting the back half of the monster wyvern.

That sent the beast off-balance, beating its wings to stay upright.

Ruadh leaped into the air, flew straight up fast, then arced down.

Tristan's gryphon stood and made vicious sounds, wings out, beak open, prepared for the wyvern attack.

Daegan called to Tristan. *Do not move or attack. Wait for us.*

Okay, boss. To Tristan's credit, he did not even look up and kept his gryphon in a threatening stance.

Ruadh's roar jerked the wyvern's head around, twisting its neck to look up. Daegan's dragon wanted the enemy to know who brought death to end its days.

When the wyvern leaped into the air, Ruadh could have burned him, but his dragon flew into battle, claws out.

Daegan would not deny Ruadh his chance to vent rage and battle one-on-one.

The wyvern tried to catch Ruadh's neck. His dragon had no soft spot. The large beak slid off Ruadh's scales, then the wyvern broke loose.

It fought to fly higher. This one was wiser than the smaller wyverns still smoldering on the ground.

This one climbed and climbed, then turned to head down and catch Ruadh still flying up. It thought to shift all that weight downward fast and drive Daegan's dragon into the ground.

That might have worked if Ruadh had not fought other dragons from the time Daegan first shifted. All of those dragons had tried many strategic battle moves on his. And lost.

Ruadh showed his cunning by flapping even faster, fly-ing upward to catch the wyvern by surprise. Claws out, Ruadh latched onto the wyvern wings, stealing its ability to maneuver. Still, the wyvern found places to rip open with sharp claws.

But Ruadh possessed a second set of claws and slashed the wyvern's underside, shredding the soft tissue until the beast stopped biting Ruadh.

When the body hung heavy in Ruadh's claws, dragging them to the ground, Daegan's dragon released the wyvern and flapped slowly away to remain airborne.

They watched as the big body slammed hard, shaking the ground.

Tristan came into Daegan's mind. *You both okay?*

Yes. Shift back.

Will do, but I need clothes and boots, boss.

Ruadh landed immediately and gave him the human body. Daegan bled from a few wounds, but the time Ruadh had spent flying gently after the battle allowed his dragon to heal the major wounds. Daegan could tolerate the rest.

He clothed Tristan then himself, surprised when he managed to cover both of them so quickly this time. But he still felt the hum of Tristan's energy mixed with his and running through his body.

Tristan ran his hands over his hair, knocking water crystals out. "Da-yam! That was one hell of a power punch."

"I agree. With the Imortik venom still in my body, Ruadh and I could not have shifted so quickly had we not linked."

"I've never shifted that fast or had that much fire come out of my gryphon. Good thinking, boss."

"'Twas Ruadh's idea."

"No shit?" Tristan gave him an amazed look. "Tell Ruadh, I'll be his wingman any time he wants."

Daegan frowned. "Wingman?"

Tristan laughed. "It's like being your dragon's personal second-in-command."

Ruadh made a warm rumbling noise Daegan loved to hear and feel the few times it had happened. He told Tristan, "Ruadh is honored by your offer."

"Awesome." Looking around, Tristan said, "These two aren't dead, but they won't fly any time soon. That big one hasn't moved yet."

"I doubt that one is dead either as 'tis not a natural being. I believe the druid took wyverns and cooked them into these creatures with a load of majik." Daegan turned to face where the castle should be. "'Tis time to unlink from ya. We shall save that move in case we need it again."

Tristan grunted at the change. "What now?"

"Now, I find a Faetheen and choke the truth from him." Daegan lifted a fist in the air. He lowered it and watched until the castle came into view again. "Ready to teleport?"

"Hell, yes." Tristan grinned.

CHAPTER 8

EVALLE SAT ON HER KNEES next to Adrianna behind two fallen trees. She felt something on her arm and brushed at it frantically. She should be glad the demons had been emerging from this wooded area west of Atlanta where there were fewer humans, but if one more crawly thing landed on her, she was pulling out her spelled dagger to smash it.

Turning a wry smile on her, Adrianna shook her head. Blond hair slicked back in a ponytail and no makeup, she still looked runway ready. "You kill demons two at a time, race into any danger to protect your people and humans, but a tiny critter gives you a cardio workout?"

Evalle straightened the special

 sunglasses that hid her glowing eyes the color of a baby lizard, which would give away their location this time of night. She muttered under her breath and swatted something on her neck. "I hate the great outdoors. Give me city backstreets in the darkest night any time. This place has too many critters with too many legs."

"*What's wrong, ladies*?" Isak Nyght's voice rumbled quietly in their comm gear.

Before her witch friend could bust her, Evalle said, "Nothing, Isak. Anything over your way?"

Isak led a badass bunch of human black ops team with incredible toys, some of which could take down nonhumans. The first time Evalle met Isak, they were both after the same demon. He took an interest in pursuing her, but

Storm had laid claim to her heart. Isak hadn't been all that interested when he found out she was not human.

"*Nothing to report. In fact, it feels too quiet,*" he replied. "*My men just dropped off Reese and Casper near your area. They're approaching from the south. Be ready.*"

"We're on it," Evalle replied.

A long sigh filled her ear with the tiny comm unit. "You should say *copy that,* so we know exactly what you mean."

She pulled her lips back and pretended she had Isak's throat in her hands shaking him.

Adrianna snorted a laugh, then crab-walked over to a huge oak tree where she stood, stretching her neck and shoulders.

Evalle's super hearing picked up the sound of approaching footsteps. She turned to Adrianna who immediately lowered her hands, ready to cover their backs.

Reese emerged first, lifting a hand to wave.

Evalle lifted her chin in acknowledgment.

Casper and Reese dropped to their knees next to Evalle. Reese looked right at home in this setting with short boots, a black T-shirt, and jeans that Evalle had picked up from Reese's apartment. She'd shoved her auburn hair out of the way with a green headband.

Casper always had the look of a cowboy just off the range regardless if he wore jeans with chaps or a tuxedo. He had an easy smile until someone crossed him and enough muscle to back it up. He pulled out a comm unit and handed it to Reese.

She frowned and kept her hands to herself. "I suck at using that stuff."

"We need to be able to talk to you, cupcake," Casper pressed, still offering the set.

Reese made a *pfft* sound. "Okay, but if I lose your toy, I don't want to have to buy it."

As she stuck the part in her ear, Isak's voice came

through everyone's comm. *"Then don't lose it. I had these communication devices made special for our nonhuman partners so we don't blow out anyone's ears."*

She made a face at no one and stuck her tongue out. "Okay, okay. They're expensive."

Evalle felt the need to share what a headache Isak could be. "He wants radio talk, Reese."

"Ah." Reese changed her tone to sound like a trucker yammering on a radio. "Ten four, good buddy."

Isak grumbled something about it being impossible to teach them proper radio dialogue.

Laughing, Evalle covered her mouth to keep quiet, but she'd take this ragtag group of unprofessional supernatural fighters any day. She reached up and touched a button on her comm, serious again. "Okay, he's off our circuit right now."

Reese's eyebrows lifted. "You mean you can dial him out whenever you want?"

"Yep, but we need to be in touch. Isak brought the fire-power today."

"He brings it every day," Adrianna added, joining the group. "Hi, Casper. Haven't seen you in a while."

"Ah, hell, I was out west helpin' with a little ol' troll problem," he drawled in the southern accent he dialed up when he needed it.

Evalle gave one of her favorite Belador allies a fist bump. "Good to have you back, cowboy."

He winked, the rogue. She gave him a you-know-better look, but Casper was all talk with her. He'd never seriously try to poach another man's woman. She'd known him for a while, long enough to realize he could flip the switch on that Texas drawl to sound like someone else if that's what the mission called for. He also shared his body with a highland warrior from the fifteenth century after lightning struck him while at an old castle in Scotland.

Reese had been grinning at them, but her eyes widened and her smile flattened. "Heads up, everyone. I have energy waking up inside me."

"Comm going wide again." Evalle touched hers and informed Isak of what Reese had said.

"*Can she give us an idea of direction?*" Isak asked.

All business now, Reese said, "If we came in from the south, then I'm sensing demon energy northwest of me. I'd call it ten o'clock from our position."

"*Copy that,*" Isak replied. "*We'll head your way and find a closer backup point.*"

Evalle's jaw dropped at how Reese nailed the direction of potential demons. When Reese smirked, Evalle remembered what she needed to find out. "Uh, did you get in touch with Quinn?"

"Nope. He'll find me when he slows down for a minute." She shook her head at Evalle, as in don't go there.

Evalle hated this moment. She hunted demons by herself and with Storm just fine, but the responsibility of other people had her on edge. She'd never realized how much pressure Tzader had carried when he'd been the North American Belador Maistir and then when Quinn took over.

She would never fill their shoes.

The job of keeping Quinn's woman safe might kill her, but Evalle would not allow a demon to drain Reese of her energy. "Okay, listen up, team. Reese and I will take that side." She swept her hand from eight-to-ten o'clock. "Adrianna and Casper, you watch our backs, because Isak and his team should be coming from over there, around three-to-five o'clock."

"Look at you talking operational and all," Adrianna teased.

"Don't push it, witch." Evalle checked her spelled dagger sitting in the sheath right where it should be. She used to never think twice about it, but this whole interim Maistir gig was making her paranoid she'd slip up and someone would die. She had to keep Reese safe even if the woman was a fearless demon killer, which only added to her stress.

Where the hell was Quinn?

Reese should be his problem.

Evalle resorted to hand signals since she had no Beladors in this group. She'd sent a Belador with Isak just in case they lost electronic communication and she had to reach out telepathically.

As she moved to her left, Reese followed close behind and whispered, "Where do you think the demons are coming from?"

"Not sure, but a Belador team took down two demons in separate places little over a mile from here."

"Did Storm track them?"

Evalle's Skinwalker mate and new husband was known for his ability to track nonhumans as well as natural beings. She shook her head and kept easing around. "Storm is with another team in the city hunting demons there, so Adrianna and I tracked the two taken down in this area. Isak's intel indicates there's a well around here. I'm sort of wondering if they're being pulled out of that hole."

"Not to discount your theory, Evalle, but demons don't just come up out of the ground. Some being creates them."

"I know," Evalle scowled, dropping behind cover at a new spot. What the hell? She was winging this crap.

"Not criticizing you. I know you've killed your share of them." Reese quieted and knelt next to Evalle. "Just saying I've met more demons than most. They come in all shapes and sizes, but finding the origin isn't impossible."

"No insult taken." Evalle stretched her neck then to search around them. At the odd silence, she flashed a look at Reese, noting the tight pull of her mouth. "What's wrong?"

"We're close." Reese stared hard straight ahead of them

and nodded. "There."

That's when Evalle squinted, realizing the dark area she'd scanned past a moment ago was actually a deep fifty-yard ally through the trees and about fifteen feet wide. She couldn't wrap her head around weather and time creating that tunnel. Thick brush and vines grew up each side.

Nothing natural about any of that.

What had caused a tunnel to form out here in the woods?

The first demon to appear far back in the dark tunnel had bright red eyes and ivory fangs. She could handle that without too much trouble. It probably went a buck-eighty in weight. Its head swung from side to side, exposing a single horn sticking out the back like a bone ponytail. His skin was dark as a walnut with orange patches.

"We can take him," Evalle murmured.

"He's not the only problem," Reese said on a long exhale.

Evalle swung her head to Reese whose face had lost a shade of color. "Are you okay?"

Isak called into Evalle's ear, "*Give me a sit rep!*"

"What?" Evalle hated this radio mumbo jumbo.

Reese explained, "Situation report. I learned the lingo from listening to Navy SEALs at night when I hunted demons in San Diego." She told Isak, "We're in the ten-to-eight position. One tango coming, but I'm pretty sure we have more on the way. Many more."

Snapping her attention back to the tunnel, Evalle's skin chilled at the small demon army marching out of the black hole at the back of the tunnel.

Two of them had to go over ten feet. Shit.

Isak said, "*Moving around to intercept.*"

Reese pulled the earpiece out and shoved it in her pocket.

"What are you doing, Reese?"

"I'm not getting blood on his gadget and someone

talking in my ear will distract me. You should back up about twenty feet to catch anything I miss." Reese stood and started rolling one hand around the other one.

"Oh, hell no." Evalle lifted her hands to use kinetic power. She took in Reese making an invisible ball of glowing dough. "What are you doing?"

"Trying to make smaller energy balls. I used too much last time and would have been attacked if you and Adrianna hadn't shown up."

As if waving a bloody steak at a hungry wolf, the first demon zeroed in on Reese.

"Move away," she ordered Evalle.

Evalle had no time to argue something she wasn't going to do. "Shut up."

"Is this about me and Quinn?" Reese slashed a quick look of annoyance at Evalle.

"Yes, dammit. You, Quinn, and the baby. So, either get out of here or shut up and kill demons. I am not leaving you here alone and that's about me facing my best friend."

Three demons started running. Two more had finally caught the scent of Reese's demon energy and picked up their pace. The last one was larger and lumbered along.

When the first demon screeched and launched itself at Evalle, she shoved her hands up and smacked it with a kinetic blast.

That one went flying over the heads of the next two and slammed into the pack behind them.

Reese said, "Clear the wall. I'm ready."

Evalle dropped the kinetic barrier.

Reese side-armed a throw at the demon on the right coming at her. Her strike burst a hole in the demon, which exploded into flames before the body turned to ash.

Evalle yanked out her spelled blade, jumped up on the rock they stood behind, then went airborne, shoving her free hand down to employ kinetics to flip her in the air. She landed behind the demon still heading for Reese. In two steps, she shoved her dagger through the top neck bone and the skull.

The demon's head flopped to the side.

She yanked the blade out and finished the cut.

"Watch your back," Reese called out.

Evalle spun, flipping the dagger to a better handhold as she did. Four demons were coming like a spooked herd of buffalo.

Reese appeared next to her, hands balling again.

"Get back, Reese."

"No. We've got this."

Evalle pushed up a kinetic wall, stopping the next two demons to reach them. The majority of that bunch were running so close, they all slammed into each other, falling back. Then one jumped up and attacked another demon, ripping a horn off its head.

"Hey, that'll work," Evalle said, feeling positive about all this for the first time.

"Drop the shield when I tell you, Evalle."

"Are you nuts?" Evalle ignored Reese and kept shoving the kinetic wall as she headed into the tunnel.

Demons ran into each other, beating the field of energy they couldn't see and gnashing at each other. One clawed the face off another one.

Reese ran up beside her. "I need the wall down so I can throw a strike."

That sounded like an exceptionally bad idea. Evalle kept forcing her wall forward. "No, Reese. You don't know how many you can take out at one time, do you?"

"A lot more if you'll drop the damn wall."

"Okay, fine. Ready?" Evalle pressed the demons deeper into the dark hole.

"*Now!*" Reese shouted.

When the invisible barrier ten feet in front of them vanished, piled up demons fell forward.

Reese rolled a fire ball of energy like a pro bowler.

The power struck the first two and flashed across their bodies. They screamed and burst into flames that jumped across the pack with the demons so tight. In a matter of seconds, the fire turned all of them into ash.

Reese lifted her fingers in the shape of a pretend gun and blew at the tip of her index finger.

"You're a bucket of laughs right now." Evalle would make Quinn pay for not being here to deal with his baby momma if he dared to question why she'd pulled down a kinetic field protecting Reese.

"Lighten up, Evalle. It's bound to get worse before it gets better."

"That's just what I want to hear." Taking the lead, Evalle walked over the piles of ashes that stirred beneath her feet. She'd lived her life in the night and didn't fear the dark, but a buzz racing over her skin warned she headed into an unfamiliar danger.

Reese whispered in a cautious voice, "Uh, we need to go slow. My internal power pack is generating energy. We're getting close to demons again."

The tunnel turned to the right and ambient light sifting from a partial moon through the trees gave Evalle a moment of relief. At least she'd be able to see what they faced and possibly have more room to function.

Isak's voice floated softly into her ear. *Where are you, Evalle? We don't see you where I expected.*

She explained quickly about the demons they took down and how she'd gone about seventy yards and they were now turning in the direction he had been before. "Back track and meet us there."

"Copy that."

Reese snagged the back of Evalle's shirt.

Evalle stopped. "What?"

"This energy is acting different. Almost like it's going haywire. I don't know what that means."

"Just stay behind me, Reese. I know you don't like being sidelined, but I'm responsible for this entire team and I need you to work with me."

"I hear ya. Keep going. I'll be right here."

Lifting her hands to activate another kinetic wall ahead of them, Evalle eased out of the tunnel and into the semi-lit area filled with waist-high fog. That was odd. She hadn't seen fog any other place out here since arriving.

Were they close to some river?

Even so, wasn't it too hot for a fog or mist? She took in everything from one side to the other. Nothing. She continued going forward until both of them were out of the dark tunnel.

Something, or someone, had sent demons into that tunnel.

While standing in one spot, she turned in a circle and spoke softly. "Keep your back to mine so we can cover all sides."

Reese spoke softly. "I'm on it."

Light brightened the fog to the right of the tunnel opening.

As if pumping air into a deflated body, a demon began to rise out of the mist and kept going until it stood ten feet tall. Two spiked horns stuck out from mangled black hair covering a fat head. Its eyes were wide and narrow as if it could only squint, but a red glow seeped out the opening. That one had no neck and a chest as wide as a car hood.

"We got a big one." Evalle called up more power and enlarged her kinetic field to keep it from jumping over the wall. That was assuming this one couldn't leap tall buildings in a single bound.

Stepping over to stand beside Evalle, Reese began rolling her hands around again. "I can pull up enough energy to take one down."

"We should wait on Isak and his team."

"This fog makes me wonder if they can find us. They should have been here by now."

Shit. Evalle couldn't argue her point. In fact, neither Isak nor Adrianna had said a word through the comm unit since Evalle and Reese stepped into this heavy mist.

Monster demon started for them and the mist parted as if ordered. Giant hands tipped in claws as long as her fingers hung from massive arms.

"I'm ready, Evalle." Reese's ball of energy glowed in a crackling fireball.

Evalle's heart slammed her chest. She could not let this thing get to Reese or her unborn baby. "I will give you five seconds then the kinetic wall goes back up."

"That's not long enough. I need time to choose the best moment to strike."

"That's all you're getting!" Evalle snarled.

"If you raise the wall too soon, the fire will hit *us*."

Raising balled fists, the demon let out a hideous shriek.

"Now, dammit!" Reese yelled.

Evalle slammed her hands toward the ground, yanking her kinetic power down. No fireball shot from her sidekick to the demon. "Reese?"

More spinning of hands.

The demon ran at them with heavy steps that shook the ground.

"Reese!"

Evalle's sidekick stepped forward as the monster closed to six feet away and grinned, showing off its jagged fangs.

CHAPTER 9

EVALLE CURSED AND CALLED UP her spelled dagger. Reese spun more power as the demon came in hot and went airborne to tackle her. At the last second, she shoved that fiery ball of energy at its chest and dove to the side, dodging sharp claws.

But the demon slapped a hand backward at her. Then flames engulfed the massive form right before it hit the ground and plowed up dirt.

Silence followed suddenly when everything stilled.

Releasing a pent-up breath, Evalle shook her head. How had Tzader and Quinn handled the role of Maistir without losing their minds?

Reese let out a yelp of pain and grabbed her arm.

"Let me see." Evalle stayed where she was and kept an eye on the burning demon still flipping around and making odd noises.

When Reese reached Evalle, she turned to the side and uncovered her upper arm. The claw had dragged a deep slash six inches long.

"Hell, Reese. That's bad, but it could have been far worse if the demon had gotten more than a single claw on you. Keep watch while I bind this." Evalle used her dagger to cut the bottom of her cotton shirt and ripped a strip she used to wrap the wound mainly to pull the skin together. Blood still oozed from the cut. Reese should be able to heal this.

The writhing demon burned bright and fast, leaving a

big pile of ashes. A stench smelling like sewage hung in the air.

"Thanks," Reese croaked out, holding her arm again.

Evalle spoke into her comm unit. "Isak? Adrianna? Anyone on our team hear me?"

Not one person replied.

"I hear you."

Evalle jerked around at a man's voice coming from the direction where the demon had appeared. She groaned. "Who the hell is that?"

Grimacing in pain, Reese whispered, "I don't know, but my energy became normal when the demon appeared. Now it's all jacked again. He must be the reason."

Not the most encouraging news.

Lifting her kinetic field into place once more, Evalle worried she'd used too much power and her wall might fail. Speaking out of the side of her mouth, she asked, "Have you got any more mojo?"

"No. That demon was so large, I wasn't sure I had enough to throw it and have the same result. That's why I had to hit him with it when he was close."

Fog moved around the man now silhouetted with a bright glow at his back. He might be an inch or two over six feet. When he moved forward, the fog swirled around him like a pet anxious for attention. The mist glowed as it came into contact with him, illuminating the alabaster skin on his face. Not white like a human, but white as cadaver bones. His shoulder-length hair and eyebrows were silver, but his eyes were a dark blue, almost black. He had peach-colored thin lips as if someone had used a crayon on a black and white photo to give it color.

He only had eyes for Reese.

"Who are you?" Evalle called out, kinetic shield in place.

"I am I-zubrrali."

Evalle shrugged in Reese's direction. "Not ringing a bell for me. What about you?"

"Nope." Reese raised her voice. "Your reputation must not precede you. We've never heard of you."

He smiled, a weird looking expression as if he had to affect it. His voice held awe. "I did not believe it was true, but there you stand."

That smooth, yet creepy, voice lifted hairs on Evalle's arms. His tone could lull a prey into believing he was the most reasonable person around as he lifted a blade to slit your throat.

Reese quipped, "Let me guess. You're a demon maker and you found out I've been breaking your toys. You should keep your distance. I'm not in a good mood after that last piece of shit scratched me."

Evalle murmured an atta-girl at Reese while keeping her attention locked on whatever being they faced as he walked slowly toward them. He showed no concern of ending up injured.

Fine by Evalle. She wouldn't hesitate to do the injuring.

He stopped his advance thirty feet out and put his hands in the pockets of his silver slacks. He wore a matching tunic with a mandarin collar. The loose material reminded her of silk. If he weren't so strange looking, he might be attractive in a creepy way.

"Is it true?" he asked Reese, still ignoring Evalle.

"Is what true, dickhead?"

"That you are pregnant."

Something just changed in this game. Evalle risked a quick glance at Reese who had stalled with a dumbfounded look covering her face.

A flash of power erupted on the far left behind him.

I-zubrrali turned casually at what sounded like Isak's demon blasters shooting into the fog.

Why would Isak take that risk to shoot blindly when she

and Reese were in here?

"*Who. Are. You*?" Reese demanded in a shaky voice.

He turned to her, cocked his head, and grinned. "You should ask Ketche." Then he vanished along with the mist.

Reese released her arm and her jaw dropped.

The sound of male voices shouting as they headed in from the left surprised Evalle. She'd expected Isak to enter from the right. "Here comes the calvary, Reese. Is the comm working now, Isak?"

"*That shooting wasn't us. Get out of there, Evalle!*" Isak shouted.

Six armed men stalked into the now clear area with weapons lifted in Evalle and Reese's direction.

Evalle yelled, "Look out!" as they fired.

She dove to the left and Reese leaped the other way.

Those blasters sounded like the ones Isak's men used to decimate demons.

Spinning back to her feet, Evalle shoved up a kinetic wall, stopping the second round of fire. "Stop, you idiots!"

"Shut up, nonhuman."

She knew where she stood. Something to kill as easily as a demon.

Reese's jaw muscles flexed with gritting her teeth. She lifted her bad arm and started balling up energy, but not much.

Power struck Evalle's kinetic field, driving her back a step. "You don't have power and we can't harm a human, Reese."

"I'm going to try to hit their weapons."

Isak's voice rang out in Evalle's comm. "*Fire!*"

Bullets rattled the air ahead of the Nyght team emerging from the forest on her right. His men were shooting the unknown humans attacking.

"*No!*" Evalle yelled for everyone with a comm unit. "They're humans."

Men on the left jerked backward, falling in a pile and shouting in pain. The weapons dropped from their hands as if their muscles didn't work.

She shut down her kinetic shield. "*Don't kill them, Isak!*"

Reese muttered, "What a shit show."

Isak barged into the clearing and shouted, "Everyone stand down."

"Little freaking late for that," Evalle complained, walking over to meet him.

"They're not dead, Evalle. Those were rubber bullets. Swapping ammo delayed us, but we couldn't use the stun charge on our demon blasters. That might have given some of these men a heart attack."

She watched the attackers in question as two of them struggled to their feet. One held an arm against his chest and the other one limped.

"If the bullets weren't real, why do they look hurt?" she asked softly.

Isak snorted. "Rubber bullets hurt like a mother and sometimes break bones. We intentionally avoided center mass. We aimed for their limbs." He lifted his voice in the direction of the two men standing. "Who's in charge?"

"I am," the first man with sandy-blond hair and beard answered. Probably in his thirties and definitely fit, he wore a dark-blue uniform and black boots. No insignias, nothing to identify this team.

Isak lowered his handgun, which looked as if it belonged in a science fiction movie. "I'm Isak Nyght of Nyght Armory. Identify yourself."

"Pass."

Adrianna and Casper came running into the scene, stopping short. Evalle angled her head in Isak's direction to indicate he had the floor.

Adrianna nodded.

"Why can't you reveal who you work for?" Isak asked,

his tone wrapped in suspicion.

"Because they follow my orders," a new man replied as he emerged from behind what Evalle assumed were his soldiers. He walked past all of them, not even pausing to check on their injuries. But he did take a position standing between his men and Isak. Beefy and taller than Isak, who towered over the rest of the men present, the stranger had dark wavy hair, short on the sides, and teak-brown skin. His nose and mouth reminded Evalle of someone Hawaiian or Polynesian. Samoan? Maybe.

He wore dark pants and a light-blue collared shirt tucked in. Everything natural in appearance, but he reeked of power.

She had no way to let Isak know, but one look at Adrianna's narrowed gaze told Evalle her witch friend knew and stood ready to protect their team.

Isak repeated his original question. "Who are you?"

"I am Palaki and these are my men you have harmed."

Isak had so much swagger he even spoke with it. "They were shooting at these two women."

The sandy-blond-haired guy said, "We killed two demons that came out of a fog right here. It disappeared by the time we stepped in and found those nonhumans."

Isak asked, "How did you determine they were nonhumans?"

Evalle smirked at the strange soldier.

He stalled a second then pointed at Evalle. "That one used her powers."

"Not until you tried to kill us," she countered, glad she'd worn her sunglasses today or her bright green eyes would have marked her immediately.

Scoffing, Isak said, "Who trained this bunch? They shot at two women they *assumed* were nonhumans." Not giving any of them a chance to come up with more excuses, Isak directed his words at Palaki. "Regardless of what brought your men here, I stepped in to prevent them from killing these women."

"Why?"

Hair stood on Evalle's neck and arms at the cold question. "Why would you try to kill us when we did nothing to you?"

Palaki shifted his cool gray gaze at her. "Because neither of you are human. You have no place in this world."

She gave him a nasty smile in return. "Oh, really? In that case, neither do you. In fact, just what exactly are you?"

Isak flicked a tiny glance her way but showed no reaction.

Palaki had no words to return. It was as if he thought animals were barking at him.

Reese snarled, "We were out here killing demons. What were your men out here to do?"

"Kill *any* nonhuman," Palaki answered without a care.

Adrianna stepped forward. "You're what? One of Queen Maeve's Scath Force warlocks? Or some crazy demigod who wants to rule the world alone?"

"I am a wizard who should not be tested." That gray gaze iced over. He shifted it to Isak. "You are human. Why are you helping these beings?"

Evalle watched Adrianna's reaction to his answer. Isak and Adrianna had been an item until Isak's mother was captured by preternaturals. He'd been so rattled by her kidnapping, he walked away from all of his nonhuman friends. Now he wanted back in, but Isak had hurt Adrianna deeply and she'd shut her heart to him.

Offering a smile that carried a warning, Isak said, "My men and I are partners with the supernaturals protecting humans. We don't kill indiscriminately, not even humans who attack a being without reason."

Palaki remained still as if thinking. "This is the only warning you and your partners will receive. I am tired of the damage caused by reckless nonhumans. Now one has released Imortiks. I intend to rid the world of nonhuman problems."

Evalle interjected, "That would be great if you worked *with* us and didn't attack our people. You're a hypocrite and have no more value than any other nonhuman standing here. We're not monsters like those demons. I'm a Belador—"

"I know what you are, Alterant."

As if he could insult her? She'd been insulted and beaten down by the best, starting with family as a child. She'd risen out of every flame thrown at her to be where she stood today.

"Yes, I am an Alterant gryphon of the Beladors." She enjoyed the flicker of surprise in Palaki's face when she added gryphon. He didn't know as much as he thought. "I'm also the Maistir over North America right now."

Still hard for her to say that with a straight face.

"Damn right," echoed around her team, giving Evalle a shot of support she appreciated.

She would not let up. "Beladors have been protecting humans for thousands of years. Where were you and your human team all that time? Oh, wait, let me guess. Sitting on the sidelines until you got your feathers ruffled."

Palaki developed a tick at his eye. "I have watched from afar, not interfering with the human world. Your presence alone has altered this world."

"For the good," Isak stated firmly. "If your men draw down on any of our people, human and nonhuman partners, without reason, they should be prepared for more than rubber bullets next time."

Palaki countered, "You should consider yourself warned that being human will not protect you if you stand with nonhumans." With that, he turned to his men and started issuing directions to help the ones still down. He must have used majik, because even the worst one injured got to his feet and walked away.

Adrianna stepped over to Reese. "Do you need help healing?"

"No, thanks. The wound is already closing up. I just needed some time for my energy to burn off the crap from that demon."

Evalle swiped sweat off her face and told Isak, "They're gonna be a problem. We'll have to up the size of our teams just to watch our own backs."

"I know. I'll add another team to work on keeping Palaki and his people under surveillance. I need to know anything your people can tell me about him. Hopefully, we'll have enough resources between us to send your people support when we have a tip Palaki's men are headed your way." He twisted, looking over at Adrianna and Reese.

Mostly Adrianna.

Evalle felt bad for Isak, but she also wanted to smack him for hurting Adrianna. "Okay, team, let's pack up and get out of here."

Casper had been standing to the side with arms crossed over his chest. "What about the demons?"

Evalle murmured, "We know where they're coming from."

"What?" Adrianna and Isak asked together. Their gazes danced back and forth at each other while trying not to connect.

Reese frowned at Evalle.

In the stilted silence, Isak ordered his men to head back to their vehicles.

Evalle hated this Maistir gig more by the minute, but she had a duty just like everyone else. Quinn needed her help. He'd taken a load off of her by insuring Beladors and their allies patrolling this part of the country were as safe as possible. Until he could return to full Maistir duties, she had to buck up and do her part.

That meant not blurting out she knew the source producing demons before talking to Reese first.

Isak would call that a debrief.

Poor Reese had so much on her as it was and a new load of mental turmoil just trying to figure out who that weird guy was and how he knew her.

Evalle owned up to her mistake. "Sorry, Reese, sometimes shit comes out of my mouth."

"Not your fault, Evalle. I just need some time to process all of this."

"What's going on?" Adrianna asked, stepping over to them.

Reese growled like a bear in hibernation being awakened. "I think I know who is creating demons."

Eyebrows shooting up, Evalle asked, "You do? Who is that being?"

"Pretty sure it's my father."

Evalle's stomach squeezed into a ball and dropped. "*Reese!*"

Everyone stopped talking and stared.

Reese looked up slowly, face pale with rage. "I will kill him. Don't get in my way."

CHAPTER 10

BRITTLE COLD WIND BUFFETED DAEGAN and Tristan while they waited for the moon to illuminate the castle again.

Daegan had suspected Joavan hid details, but the slippery Faetheen had set them up. His father had warned him to avoid the Fae, any type of Fae, but the supernatural world did not always allow for simple choices.

"I don't see it, boss." Tristan shoved the fur hood off his head. His skin had color again.

Daegan should leave, but he did not want Joavan showing up when he least needed that headache and he couldn't risk losing the grimoire box.

No, he would find Joavan and settle this now.

The translucent castle shape waved into view.

Daegan nodded. "Teleport us, Tristan."

In seconds, Daegan's boots stood upon the hard floor of the battlement once again. He swung around, checking for any unexpected attack.

Tristan arrived at the same time and twisted to search as well. He paused and stared out at the dark landscape they'd just left. "See what I'm seeing?"

"Yes." Daegan had noticed the missing wyverns immediately. He also noticed what was missing from where they stood.

No Faetheen waited.

Daegan roared, *"Joavan!"*

The Faetheen appeared. "What?" he hissed. "Do you

have to yell?"

"Where were ya?" The battle Daegan had just survived deepened his voice into a rough guttural sound intended to warn any who crossed him.

Joavan lost his snippy attitude. "I was close by."

"I told ya not to move from that spot."

Sounding impatient and irritable, Joavan looked away then back. "Why are you upset? I would only have gotten in the way. I was very close, on the other side of the veil between our worlds." He huffed out a grumbling sound. "I do not fight dragons and wyverns. That's why *you* are here."

Finally, a sliver of the truth from this being.

Tristan stepped up beside Daegan, just as bruised and cut, but his second remained silent.

Shaking his head, Daegan told Joavan, "No. I am here to retrieve an amulet. Ya said nothin' about any flyin' beasts."

"I had no doubt you would be powerful enough to handle yourself against any obstacle."

The miserable cur had known the whole time that Daegan and Tristan would face fierce threats. "I could leave now and owe ya nothin', Joavan."

The Faetheen's eyes flared with anger but fear too. "You would be breaking your word," he argued in a weak tone, which admitted fault as much as his actions.

"Ya lied to me outright when I asked ya about guards. In our world, that breaks a deal. Had I lost Tristan, ya would be takin' your last breath."

Tense silence dropped hard between them.

Joavan held his hands up with palms out. He dropped his head once in agreement. "You are right. I should have told you there was a chance, only a chance, we would run into some barrier."

"'Twas Tristan and I, who fought those beasts, not ya. Why would ya hold back information and put us in danger?"

"This won't sound good, but it's the truth. I feared you would not come at all."

Tristan blew out a stream of air and ran his fingers through his hair. "What's so important about this amulet to risk our lives? And don't give us the crap you've been spewing."

Daegan sent a silent message to Tristan. *'Tis the right question. I had been willin' to do my part and repay him for savin' my life, but I shall not continue without good reason.*

Joavan's frown of despair said he knew he was caught and had no chance of going one step farther without coming clean. Jaw muscles flexed in his cheek. "Our people are all Fae with mixed blood, outcasts. But it is possible to be a pariah among even them. I am my mother's bastard child. I should not be allowed to enter the Faetheen world, but when she agreed to mate with the king she would only do so if he claimed me as part of his court. I had to work to earn my place, which is right below his two blood sons by my mother. I overheard my half-brothers plotting to kill the king and take over. I could tell no one. Who would accept my word? I would have humiliated my mother."

Tristan's face revealed no change from the stony expression he'd held since Joavan returned. He glanced at Daegan then back at Joavan. His second understood the power of silence to force another to keep talking until the truth tumbled out by accident.

With a quick look at Daegan and Tristan, Joavan seemed disappointed no one commented. "Though younger than me, my half-brothers enjoy their resemblance to the king and hate me. They hate whenever I'm included in a discussion or decision. I began watching my back two years ago when I started experiencing accidents. I know they were behind it, but they used the subtle attacks to claim I was not capable of the position I'd been given. I had no idea they were setting me up for something far worse. The amulet was stolen on my watch."

"You were the only person guarding it at the time?" Tristan inquired.

"Not exactly. I was in charge of the guards who protect the king and queen as well as the amulet. The night the amulet went missing, I received a message my sister was ill. When I arrived, she could barely speak, and my mother was not there for her only daughter. I called for healers and sent word to the queen. The amulet was stolen while I was gone. The guards on duty had been killed. My half-brothers accused me of being an accomplice to the thief, claiming I might even have poisoned my sister. They told their father he was wrong to trust me, that I intended to claim the kingdom, maybe kill the king and queen. I could not be at my sister's burial. I have ways to enter and leave, but I wish to clear my name."

Joavan took a moment, staring in the distance. "No one will come near me and I am unable to reach my mother." His smile had a bitter twist. "I have been given a deadline to return the amulet."

"What is this deadline?"

Shaking his head, Joavan said, "I will not give you more ammunition to use against me. I will only say the time frame is not long and narrowing by the day. If I fail to return the amulet in that time and prove my innocence, the window of moving between this world and mine will close and I will be stuck here for a year, if not forever."

"'Tis not so bad in this world. Ya might have fewer enemies," Daegan pointed out.

Joavan huffed out a derisive laugh. "I am able to survive during a short wait to return to my world again as a respected member, but if I fail to deliver the amulet, the king will officially cast me out. My power will no longer be tethered to my home realm. Without that, I will slowly weaken and be at the mercy of my enemies as I wither."

Daegan had wanted to strangle Joavan, but without Tristan's aid here and others back home, Daegan could be in a similar situation.

Still, that did not pardon Joavan's reckless actions by withholding pertinent information.

Tristan crossed his arms and waited on Daegan's decision.

Joavan watched both of them for a bloated moment. He shook his head as if disappointed. "I have told you the truth. All you have to do is teleport away and I will end up in this world with no support. I cannot regain the amulet on my own."

Tristan asked Daegan telepathically, *What do you think, boss?*

To be honest, I wish to rattle Joavan's bones, but I also want to pay my debt. What about ya?

A mild smirk touched Tristan's lips. *I'm in for whatever you want to do.*

Joavan had flicked his gaze from Daegan to Tristan and back to Daegan, perhaps realizing they spoke mind-to-mind.

Drawing in a slow icy breath, Daegan said, "Here is my offer. Lie to me again, even a lie by omission, and we shall leave ya to face any consequences alone."

Joavan nodded. "The truth only."

"Do ya expect any more barriers, as ya call them?"

"I don't know. Before you yell at me, I did think something would come out when we arrived, but I had no idea it would be wyverns. Ainvar knows we are here by now. I do not expect him to open a door and invite us in at this point."

"Just how do we get to the druid?" Tristan eyed the Faetheen as one would an annoying bug. "We aren't teleporting somewhere we have no visual on."

Joavan smoothed the damp hair away from his face. "No teleporting at this point. We have to enter over there." He pointed at the middle of the area where Daegan saw no door, but he waited for Joavan to explain further.

"There is a door. Once we enter, we take stairs down to find him."

The lack of an obvious entrance still bothered Daegan. "Have ya been in this place before?"

"No. I found this through a dream-weaver fairy."

Tristan scrunched up his face. "A what?"

"They are small beings with unusual powers."

"I've heard of fairies, just not of dream-weavers."

Inhaling a slow and deep breath, Joavan blew out a white cloud ruffled with frustration. "I can explain those later. For now, I will tell you what I know of locating Ainvar here."

Daegan had not finished. "Ya have two hours to take us to the druid or expect to continue alone."

The desire to shriek at Daegan came to life on the Faetheen's face. "Then we best get moving." Joavan walked away to the center of the area where they stood.

Tristan shrugged and followed.

Daegan kept watch over their backs until he reached where Joavan bent down and placed both hands on the ground. The Faetheen stayed that way for a full minute as he whispered frantically.

A line formed around his hands three-foot square, which began to take dimensional shape as a hatch or trapdoor. Wood planks joined together, framed in heavy metal around the edge. Two half-round holes large enough for hands appeared on opposite sides.

Joavan cupped the holes, grasping the hatch and lifting with a grunt.

Daegan took the wooden covering from him and set it

aside.

In the gaping hole now exposed, wide stairs in a circular pattern appeared and descended into darkness.

Stepping back, Joavan pointed down. "I told you I knew how to enter."

"'Tis good. Ya shall go first."

Joavan's jaw dropped. "Me? I am not the power here."

"We shall be close by, just as ya were while we fought wyverns."

Mumbling curses to himself, Joavan stepped down, placing his foot carefully and testing his weight. He kept his hands on each side of the opening until he had dropped too far to maintain any grasp.

Tristan cupped his jaw, staring down. "Should we put that lid back in place?"

"No. I have a feelin' no wyvern type of beast shall follow us. If somethin' else appears in there, we should have the same advantage and disadvantage. Ya go next but stop if Joavan disappears at any point."

"Got it." Tristan lowered his body down and began taking the steps.

With one last look around, he saw no flying beasts or other threats. If the druid had more traps or defenses in place, Daegan hoped his words to Tristan would not be proven wrong.

CHAPTER 11

DAEGAN KEPT JOAVAN'S HEAD IN view as the Faetheen continued to descend the endless circular stairs. The dank smell seemed natural, as if this structure had been on the Shetland Islands for as long as Joavan claimed.

What kind of majik could maintain the ghostly look from outside?

Tristan asked, "What if these steps never end, Joavan?"

"There will be an end."

Daegan couldn't put much faith in the Faetheen's confidence. What if some deadly surprise waited once they were deep inside here? Could Tristan teleport the two of them out?

At that point, Joavan would be on his own.

A noise came from Joavan.

"What is he sayin', Tristan?"

Speaking over his shoulder, Tristan replied softly. "Something like 'found it,' but I can't be sure."

"I have located another passage," Joavan clarified in a short-tempered reply.

Or had that been fear boosting the tension in his voice?

Joavan pushed against a wall and a section gave way.

Light flowed into the stairwell.

As soon as Joavan passed through the opening, Tristan stepped down quickly and paused, facing out at the new space.

Daegan closed the distance to him. "What do ya see?"

"Nothing but an empty room. My gut says it is not empty. Joavan's waiting about ten feet away. What do you want to do, boss?"

"We must stay close. I fear the moment ya pass through the door, a wall may form to trap us."

"That could definitely happen."

Daegan could not remain here, but he hated the unknown they would leap into. "When I say go, jump. I shall be right behind ya."

Tristan nodded.

"Go."

Daegan and Tristan went through so close one might have been a shadow of the other.

The opening to the stairway solidified, just as Daegan had suspected, but he and Tristan had passed through safely.

He'd had it with druids harming his second-in-command.

The large area had an uninspiring grayness to it from floor to walls. Light flowed down from above, though Daegan saw no windows. Nothing made a sound besides their combined breathing.

"What now, Joavan?" Daegan murmured.

"We wait."

Tristan growled at the untrustworthy Faetheen.

Energy pooled into the room, circling the three of them. Daegan considered sending Tristan out, but his second had made it clear he wanted to be right here.

Just as Daegan respected Tristan's decision regarding the other Alterant gryphons wanting to fight alongside Beladors in the human world, he could not ask Tristan to leave now.

Beneath Daegan's feet, the gray stone floor changed to a polished white marble with black and gold veins. The marble spread out beneath Joavan and Tristan and moved toward the walls of the cylindrical room. Where were the sharp angles Daegan had seen outside this castle?

Four detailed sculptures of a huge hand and arm formed in stone stuck out of the wall. Each hand clutched the base of an elegant black hammered-steel torch as long as Daegan's leg

When the marble finished spreading and touched the base of the continual wall, large cuts of brown-and-black stone began stacking along that base. The stones continued piling to the ceiling.

Daegan tilted his head back.

Stone blocks climbed over fifty feet above his head, but he never saw an actual ceiling. Just darkness where he'd seen light earlier.

The torch glow failed to reach any higher.

He dropped his head back down, studying every movement in the room as a hawk would any blade of grass disturbed in an open field.

Between him and the far wall across the hundred-foot-wide space, a hole opened in the marble floor from the wall to a third of the way back, revealing a black pit five feet deep in the void.

Flames burst up head-high above the marble then settled down into a vibrant pile of glowing red coals. Every chunk larger than Daegan's head.

Fifteen feet above the searing pit, a thick dais floated twice the width of Daegan's arms from fingertip to fingertip and clear as glass.

A man appeared there. Not quite six feet tall with long light-brown hair and unnaturally smooth olive skin, as if he'd sanded away every tiny wrinkle. Not even a beautiful goddess had skin that flawless.

His too-perfect face reminded Daegan of mannequins he'd seen in store windows. Another thing of this era Tristan had explained.

Where Daegan had found Joavan too pretty to be a warrior, this druid did not feel natural at all.

Until he stared into eyes that had seen many centuries. There might be no wrinkles around the druid's pale sea-green eyes, but that gaze did not boast of robust health.

Still, those eyes were familiar.

This deadly being had devised a way to emulate immortality if he'd lived as long as Joavan indicated.

What amount of majik had that taken?

Garwyli had lived far longer than he would have normally if he'd spent his entire life outside Treoir realm.

But this castle was no realm.

Ainvar wore a regal robe of black with sparkling clear jewels woven into the material so that firelight gave the cloak life with any movement. He held a white staff in one hand with a glass orb on top. The glass held a black adder with red eyes curled inside. Its tongue flicked out once.

Lifting his staff, Ainvar demanded, "How dare you enter my castle and harm my guards?"

Nothing in the druid's whiny speech indicated his background, though based upon the designs on his clothing and his name, Daegan surmised he faced a Celtic druid.

Daegan replied, "We were told ya had no guards."

"I do not care what you have been told. You were not invited to visit my castle."

Flames from the pit shot high, putting a sharp point on his words.

Joavan jumped in. "I am here for the amulet, Ainvar. How could you take the power of *Talamh Dearmadta*?"

Ainvar's mouth twisted into a wry smirk. "To come here and accuse me of such means you are an even greater fool than I remember. I have no amulet."

"*Liar!*" Joavan shouted on the edge of hysteria.

Daegan growled the rough sound of his dragon.

Tristan leaned over to look past Daegan at Joavan. "We went through all that for this crap?"

Joavan's eyes bulged. Any minute his head might explode. He shot a dismissive look at Tristan and turned on Ainvar again. "Admit it. You stole the stone to kill the king."

Appearing unconcerned, Ainvar frowned with indifference. "Why would I do such a thing when I have a place of my own? Unlike you, I *choose* not to live under his miserly rule."

Joavan's hands opened and closed nervously. His panic became a living thing, filling the air. "I must have that amulet back. You have put me in an untenable position. You know what I face!"

Ainvar tossed an uncaring shrug at Joavan. "You have wasted your time coming here. You have no proof I have this stone you claim."

Daegan told Joavan, "I do not see how ya plan to solve this argument. I see no amulet around the druid's neck or in his hand. If he took it, he could have hidden it in a thousand places."

Joavan's body vibrated with fury and underlying terror. His aqua eyes were wild when he whipped around to face Daegan. "Do not go anywhere. I must have the amulet. I told you I needed a dragon and you agreed to take the amulet from him."

"What?" Ainvar roared. He lifted his staff and shook it. "You brought a dragon here to kill me?"

Joavan waved his hands around and shouted at Ainvar. "What did you expect me to do when you stole that jewel on my watch? You knew what you were doing, the trouble you would cause me." He paused and added in a shaking voice, "You made my sister sick. She died."

"I am not guilty of those accusations, you little bastard." Ainvar's mouth opened to reveal the sharp teeth of a beast. "I will not allow you to sully my name this way."

Daegan couldn't believe this mess. He had pushed himself just to do this out of honor. He owed Joavan for the cleansing solvent, but this debt could not remain open-ended.

Tristan gave Joavan a worried glance and took a step away. "Dude. Calm down before your head explodes. You might have the wrong guy."

"*No!*" Joavan shouted. "I will kill anyone who thinks to convince me Ainvar is not at fault."

Daegan snarled, "'Tis enough! Threaten my second again and it shall be your last words."

"I am done with all of you," Ainvar called out then started wailing, like something gone crazy. His body lifted off the dais.

The pit below him fired up with flames roaring.

Ainvar pointed his staff at a torch. The hand and arm in the wall broke free, moving from side to side. A nine-foot-tall ogre attached to that arm stepped through the wall to stand on one side of Daegan's group. The torch burst with power and changed into a sword fit for that monster.

Three more times Ainvar pointed at torches, bringing three more ogres to life. Big heads for thick bodies. Wide jaws with long fangs and each one had steel-plating for armor covering it from chest to thighs.

All four surrounded them, not making a move.

"Well, fuck," Tristan muttered.

Spinning the tip of his staff in a circular motion, Ainvar continued speaking in a strange language.

Daegan said to Joavan, "We are leaving. Yet again, ya did not tell me all the truth."

Joavan latched onto Daegan's shirt and yanked. "You must stay!"

Daegan slapped his hand away. "Our agreement is over." He turned to Tristan as a massive steel chain net fell over all three of them.

"Tristan, teleport now!"

"I'm trying, boss. Not working."
Daegan roared.
The glass dais exploded.

CHAPTER 12

REESE SCRUBBED THE FILTH OF fighting demons off her skin, thankful for the place Storm had people make inhabitable last night. That man had some serious business power besides being a Skinwalker.

Evalle had hit the jackpot with him.

Not because of the buildings he owned and what had to be a pretty solid bank account, but because he lived only to have her as his mate. His number one priority was Evalle's happiness.

And her mate's happiness was Evalle's top priority.

Every woman should be so lucky.

She didn't envy Evalle's relationship. Seeing anyone so happy lifted her heart, but it always reminded her of what she'd never have. If she didn't carry a demonic power inside of her, she could have a happy life with Quinn.

She'd asked Evalle to pass along the number of Reese's new mobile phone to Trey, the Belador who coordinated their team communications by telepathy.

He'd give that number to Quinn for sure.

But surprisingly, she hadn't heard a peep out of Quinn, which hurt even though she'd told him to stay away. She wanted him safe.

Still, a phone call would be nice.

That was entirely insane. Why would any man want to be with her when she told him to stay away, but longed to be with him? In fact, she'd like to have an all-nighter with him. One that involved no sleeping.

Being pregnant drove her crazy thinking about sex.

Ironic that sex would be at the top of her mind when that's what got her in this jam.

She dried off her body and felt a little thickening in her middle. Really? She turned sideways to the mirror to see if she really had a baby bump coming on.

There it was, a tiny rise.

Happiness flooded her. "Hi, Junior," she cooed and rubbed her belly gently. Heat flared under her hand. She grinned until she lifted her gaze to the mirror.

"Crap. You look like hell." She grabbed a brush to untangle her wet hair and changed hands. The wound had healed over, but she still had a sore spot on her arm. She brushed her hair so it would dry less feral looking and used cream all over her body.

Evalle might have helped in supplying creams and other female items for this apartment, but Reese had Storm to thank most of all.

He had people who had people doing things for him.

She walked out of the simple bathroom Storm had apologized for, which she reprimanded him over. She didn't need anything fancy, just somewhere to live until ...

Grief hit her unexpectedly and a tear slipped out. She cupped her stomach, drew a couple breaths, and shoved the darkness away.

She and Junior were going to have one hell of a ride until the time came to deliver. She'd save her grief for when she had nothing else to hold.

Walking into the main part of her studio apartment created in a single-story building once used as a machine shop, she smiled at the king-size bed with a tall headboard against the far wall. That would have been plenty, but it came with matching end tables, a low chest of drawers, and an armoire. All of it beautifully refinished mahogany.

Storm must have an affinity for fine antiques.

No windows in the room for security.

She still couldn't believe how much his people had done in one night. She had a complete kitchen with a stainless-steel refrigerator, gas stove, dishwasher, and double sink. Dishes, utensils, anything she needed to be self-sufficient, plus the freezer in her refrigerator had been stocked.

But the four-seater table with high-back chairs and a vase with blue flowers gave it the feel of home as much as the braided wool rugs.

She'd rather have those than something more upscale.

After putting on underwear and one of the oversized T-shirts she'd requested for sleepwear, she headed to make a cup of tea.

I-zubrrali.

She now knew the name of the person who first destroyed her mother's life, then hers. What exactly was I-zubrrali? He had to be more than someone with majik to produce that many demons and of all types.

She'd known sorcerer's and powerful warlocks who could create demons, but even they kept to creating less than three types of demons.

Had that bastard come to Atlanta because he'd heard about her? All those demons were killing people because of her. That didn't even count the demons being turned into Imortiks and succumbing within a day.

She had to stop him to protect others.

Her stomach heated. She patted her belly. "I know, Junior. We're gonna do it together."

But she'd finally realized her energy hadn't just been wonky. I-zubrrali had latched onto her power. What would happen next time? Would she be able to kill the being that created her?

Or would he harm her baby?

Her fingers tightened on the cannister with tea bags. It started shaking. She put it down and leaned on the counter, struggling to breathe. Her dreams were so simple.

She wanted to live.

She wanted to hold her baby.

She wanted Quinn to be with her when she did.

Gripping the counter, her arms shook. She had asked nothing of life, but to just live it in peace.

Pounding on the door jerked her up and around.

"Reese." Quinn spoke her name in a calm tone, but that meant nothing. He had to be furious with her.

She covered her face. One more painful conversation to go.

"Reese, open the door."

Should she let him in or have this conversation through the door? If she opened it, she didn't have the power to keep her hands off him. What message would that send?

He would not let her out to hunt demons.

Quinn would stand here forever to protect her.

Deep inside, she wanted that so much, but she knew her destiny and her fate. She would not drag Quinn through it all.

He knocked again. "Open the door, Reese. Now." He sounded civilized, but she heard the savage edge under his words.

She walked over to the door and leaned her forehead on it. "Can we just talk here?"

"No. You owe me to open this door. I would rather not damage it after all Storm went through to have a solid steel door installed."

Quinn had been talking to someone to know that much.

Time to grow a pair of lady balls and face him.

She undid the double latching system and whispered the word Storm had given her to open the ward for sixty seconds if she needed to let someone in.

As soon as she pulled the door open, Quinn blasted in. He hooked his hands under her arms and pulled her to him, then kicked the door shut.

His mouth owned her the minute their lips touched. She gripped his shoulders. Her heart thumped at a happy pace, feeling alive again. She wrapped her legs around him and kissed him back, giving her all to this moment.

Quinn paused, breathing hard as if he'd just fought twenty demons. His body trembled.

She understood. He struggled with bone-deep fear ... for her. She'd never seen him so vulnerable, not even when he'd told her he loved her and wanted the baby.

Quinn grabbed a breath. "I'm not going to ask you why you didn't tell me you were back. I'm only going to tell you one thing."

Reese could barely speak. "What?"

He lifted wounded eyes to her. "I want you." He inhaled deeply, scenting her. "I want you with every part of my being. I need you. I'm willing to be with you on your terms, just don't..." His voice broke. "Don't push me away."

She needed him more than her next breath. How could she say anything but, "Okay."

He kissed her again, deeper, but more slowly. His large hands cupped her bottom, then he walked until her back met a wall. With her pinned in place, he pushed her panties aside and dragged a finger through her damp heat.

Giving in meant no more pushing him away.

As if she would stop him now? "More," she demanded.

Her panties ripped and fell away. His kiss deepened and turned feral. This was a side Quinn kept in check. She moved her hips and urged him on. He pushed a finger inside, driving her insane.

She could look at this man and be ready.

Long fingers stroked her.

She arched, so close, so ready, so right fucking now ready! Then he pushed her over the edge into oblivion and drained her body of the stress and anxiety she'd had for company.

When she kept saying his name, he rained gentle kisses down her neck. He wouldn't let up on that finger, drawing out every aftershock.

His other hand massaged her extra-plump breasts.

She shook with relief.

Cupping his neck, she pulled his mouth back to her lips and kissed the man whose touch burned to her core.

She slumped against him. "That all you got?" she mumbled.

"Only you would challenge me when you can't stand on your own."

"Standing is overrated."

He sprinkled kisses along her shoulder. "Hold on, sweetheart."

The sound of his voice roughened by need brought her hellion hormones back to life. She wrapped her arms around his neck.

A magician couldn't have matched Quinn's ability to shuck off all his clothes from the waist down. She bit his neck and licked it.

He pushed up against her heat and her muscles decided to come back to life. She moaned, "Please don't stop there."

"No chance." With her still against the wall, he used his hands to tease her breasts until she could barely take it. The girls had been on edge for days, begging for attention.

Quinn slid inside her, but not all the way.

She dug her nails into his shoulders. "Yes, yes, yes."

He whispered all the ways he wanted to have her as he went deeper with every push. She wanted to stay right here, joined with him where nothing mattered but his warm body and gifted fingers.

He rubbed both nipples at once, pressing harder with each move. She kissed him, loving him, showing him everything she felt inside.

He started moving faster and she met his rhythm.

"I need you, Quinn. Need all of you," she pleaded, hanging on tight, wanting everything he could give her. Her orgasm ripped through her. She clamped her muscles tight.

Quinn's incredible control snapped. He slammed into her, pushing her to another height, then he called out her name in a roar with his release.

Her legs dropped from where she'd been locked around him. He caught her legs, holding her up.

Quinn would always be there to catch her.

He would always be her safe port in any storm.

She rubbed her cheek against his damp one. Her future might suck, but this right here was all she needed at this minute. She'd face every minute and every day as it came to her and not whine about the future, not with this man at her side.

He turned his head. His lips brushed her temple. "I've missed you. I crave being with you. I can't breathe when you're not near. I love you and never want to let go."

That broke the damn of emotion she'd been holding back to keep herself intact since finding out she was pregnant.

She cried hard against his shoulder, her entire body shaking.

He backed away from the wall, holding her against his chest. Then he kicked his shoes off and settled on the bed where he rubbed her back until she calmed to only sniffling. Reaching over to the nightstand, he snagged a handful of tissues and handed them to her.

Wiping the worst of her breakdown away, she blew her nose. How sexy was that?

He laughed and put her tissues aside, then helped her sit up. "I tried to do what you asked, but—"

"I know, I came back and screwed it up," she admitted.

"No." He brushed his fingers over her face, pushing away loose hairs. An endearing smile lifted his lips. "It wouldn't have mattered if you came back or not. I was saying I tried to do the honorable thing and respect your wish that I stay away, but I started putting people in place as soon as I could so I would be free to find you."

"That wouldn't have been possible." She kissed him and pulled back to see his face.

He gave her the look of confidence she admired about him. This man believed he could do anything. "To get you back, I intended to call in every favor owed to me in the human and supernatural world, and I have compiled a lot of favors in all my years."

There was the man every woman should have. A protector who would never stop until those he loved were safe. A man whose love had to be earned and valued for the incredible gift it was.

She'd never love another man. Ever. Quinn was it for her.

But she still feared him being close. "I need you safe."

"I will be, and you as well. I command an army of Beladors. We have a dragon and powerful allies. We will overcome the Imortiks."

She'd like to believe that, but she had serious doubts only because the Imortiks were gaining power and now her damned father was helping them by producing demons.

But she would not ruin the moment with her negative thinking. That didn't mean she couldn't set guidelines. "Before we do this, I have terms."

"Of course you do." But he'd uttered that in a light tone with no malice.

Sniffling one last time, she lifted her chin. "I want to hunt demons. I'm the best one for locating them before they spread out to eat a human or be turned into an Imortik. Plus, we found their maker today."

"So I heard." No smile and all grim.

"I don't want to talk about him right now, though," she admitted.

"As long as you fill me in before I leave here, I won't ask for more this minute."

She wanted to laugh at her trying to negotiate with the master of negotiation. "Agreed. Just know that I'm not suicidal to go off on my own. I love this baby and ... " She swallowed, determined to not be a weepy woman. Her voice thinned. "I want to love this baby every minute possible. I'm not thinking about the birth, only a life right now. If that bothers you—"

"No. I want to share this time with you." He leaned in, kissing her lips then her forehead. "But I also want to be with you when you give birth, no matter what happens." His Adam's apple rode up and down hard. His eyes glistened. "I want to be there for you and for our baby."

She swiped a tear off her face and whispered, "For our son. It's a boy."

He looked like he may break, but not her powerful Quinn. He seemed to know that she needed his strength now more than ever.

Running his thumbs over her cheeks, he said, "Let's name him."

Dammit. More tears. She only cried with her babies. After another round of tissues, she nodded. "I've been calling him Junior, because I want to have good memories of this baby. We do need a name."

"Horatio." Quinn said that with a straight face.

"What? No!" Her fighting side rose up and stomped away her squall fest.

He laughed and pulled her to him. "We will find a name."

The sexy, crazy man was just jerking her chain. If he could rise to the occasion and show a positive face in her moment of darkness, she could step up too. Gifting him with a smile that she hoped showed how much she loved him, she reached down and grabbed hold of his attention.

Quinn jerked and muttered a curse under his breath.

She grinned like the devil she was being.

He asked in a sex-roughened voice, "Give a man a heads-up next time, sweetheart."

"How about if I just give you some head ... period."

"You do have great ideas, but I should shower first."

She stroked him. "This place has a big shower."

"I am indebted to Storm for all he has done for you, but if you want anything, no matter what it is, I would like to take care of it."

Pausing her hand, she quirked her eyebrow. "I don't need anything else except ... you."

He kissed her soundly. "I would stay in a hut without electricity or running water to be with you."

She chuckled. "Let's not get crazy here, babe. I'm all about air conditioning and indoor plumbing."

By the end of the shower, she felt energized. How that could happen after more sex made no sense.

Quinn had dried off and was dressing again when he stopped all motion.

She knew that look. Somebody called him telepathically.

When his movements resumed, he sat at one of the dining chairs to put on his shoes. Then he surprised her by admitting, "Evalle just called. One of the teams think they've found a large demon nest northeast of the city."

"Hmm." She waited to give him any more response until he dared to keep her back from helping Evalle. Reese pulled on her jeans, boots, and a lightweight shirt, preparing for the argument about to ensue. She loved this man without question, but he had agreed with her terms.

Quinn stood and offered her his hand. "Ready?"

She beamed with pride over him backing what he said

with actions. "Yes, and so is Icarus."

"That's a nonstarter name." He gave her an appalled look she laughed at, then he pulled her to him and kissed her sweetly. He drew in a deep breath and let it out slowly as if releasing tension. "I am terrified to take you out there, but I love you and want to be the person you need right now more than the person I think you need. I trust your judgement to tell me when you can't do this. Until then, I will be there fighting alongside you and ... Eckard."

She poked him, drawing a laugh from Quinn. When he quieted, she got up close and warned, "I love you, too, but our child will never have a name that sounds like a defunct drugstore."

CHAPTER 13

FED UP WITH EVERYONE, DAEGAN shifted into his dragon.

The chain net expanded and grew with Ruadh's body.

Ainvar's stone ogres started shouting and raising their fire swords, waiting on the druid's order.

Ainvar had landed on the marble between the net and the fire pit.

Ruadh opened his jaws and blasted fire, blowing a hole in the chain net large enough to walk through without bending over. Daegan's dragon continued blasting fire in long streams as it turned from side to side. He extended a wing over Tristan for protection, but not Joavan.

Daegan had no problem with his dragon's decision.

Joavan screamed and backed up to the dragon, hiding his face from the fire storm.

Ainvar shouted and called up one majikal weapon after another. He sent a battery of swords flying at Daegan's dragon while the ogres waited. They would probably be the second wave of attack.

Tristan stepped forward and shoved up a kinetic blast between Ruadh and the swords from the druid. The weapons hit the invisible wall and bounced back at Ainvar who ran from side to side, dodging them.

The druid tried dousing Ruadh with a wall of water dropped from above.

Daegan's dragon blew the water back up in the air and held it there churning and bubbling with the power of his fire.

The druid ordered his ogres to attack.

Ruadh angled the water to the side and closed his jaws, allowing the water to spread out as it fell.

Boiling water covered Ainvar's ogres. They dropped their swords and ran around out of control, yelling as their stone skin turned red as raw meat. Daegan had not expected that.

When Ruadh finished destroying the center of the net all the way around, the rest of it clanged as it fell to the floor.

Ruadh flipped the last part off his spiked head.

He turned on Ainvar who shouted a series of strange words.

The ogres bodies became stone again and they returned to the walls, which sucked in their bodies, leaving four arms and hands. The fire swords they clutched returned to torches.

Talking with Ruadh's voice, Daegan said, "I am done with ya two arguin'. Settle this *now*."

Ainvar recovered himself to speak with power. "There is nothing to settle. He lies."

Joavan jumped away from where he'd been hiding. His eyebrows were singed and his clothes in tatters. "*No!* I need the amulet. He has it!"

Ainvar turned toward Joavan and lifted his hands, clearly going on attack.

Joavan jumped into battle mode, raising his hands.

In his dragon's voice, Daegan shouted, "If anyone attacks anyone, my dragon shall burn ya both and devour your ashes. He would not eat ya, because neither of ya are a worthy meal."

Ainvar tossed his hands up. "I cannot produce what I do not possess. How much simpler can I explain? You break into my home and damage my security, then expect me to accept your accusations." He shot an angry glare at Joavan. "You are the worst son I ever had."

"You are a horrible father. I did not ask to carry your blood. Now you put me in a position of being cast out of my home."

"You should not have joined the king's court. You would not be in this position."

Daegan asked for his human body back. When he shifted, he clothed himself in furs and leathers of his youth. "Have I had to go through all of this for a bloody family squabble?"

"This is no squabble," Joavan shouted. "The amulet is all to my people."

Ainvar scoffed. "They are not your people. They're a bunch of misfits and you happen to find a place at the top of a mixed-blood pack. You act as if you lived with the Fae. You have made a huge mistake. I do not have the amulet."

Joavan finally spoke in a calm tone. "Then you will die."

Tristan let off a long stream of air that ended in a disgusted sound. "What the hell do we do now, boss?"

Daegan held his hand up before Joavan or Ainvar could say another word. "We solve this now. Before ya start firin' questions at me, be silent while I solve this problem."

"How?"

Turning his head slowly, Daegan walked over and shoved his face an inch from Joavan's. "I can prove the truth. If ya do not remain silent until I tell ya to speak again, I shall leave ya to face Ainvar and his wyverns."

Joavan nodded, lips pressed tight.

Swinging away from Joavan, Daegan told Tristan, "Keep an eye on these two while I call to someone."

"Will do."

Ainvar's face almost developed a wrinkle from worry.

"What, Ainvar?" Daegan asked.

"Do you plan to use telepathy?"

"I do. What of it?"

The druid sighed heavily. "A moment." He lifted his hands and whispered words for a while.

The air suddenly crackled and sparked.

"Go ahead," Ainvar grumbled.

He must have had a ward preventing telepathic communication, which had possibly interfered with teleporting. Daegan hoped that meant Tristan could now teleport out.

Daegan crossed his arms and stepped back to allow the father and son pain in his backside to remain in view. He called to Garwyli telepathically. *I need your help, druid.*

What ya be needin'?

I have a dispute between a part-blood Fae called a Faetheen and a druid, who happens to be his father. I need a way to solve a dispute. Daegan explained about the amulet and where Joavan lived. *Can ya come here? I can send Tristan to teleport ya.*

Where are ya?

Shetland Islands near Scotland.

Garwyli said nothing for a moment. When he did speak, he surprised Daegan. *I shall come in hologram. I wish for my physical body to remain here at Treoir.*

An inkling of worry trickled down Daegan's spine. After what he'd seen of Garwyli earlier at Treoir, he had deep concerns for the old druid. Tzader had traveled in hologram from time to time simply to stay close to Brina, because he'd had no way to enter the castle back then without dying. That had been thanks to Macha, a heartless goddess.

But this felt unusual for Garwyli.

Would the druid be able to wield any power should such be needed? Brina and Tzader had possessed that ability while in hologram. Perhaps Garwyli could as well.

In fact, now that Daegan thought it through, he should have suggested the holographic travel as the safest way to have Garwyli intervene.

But when Daegan had a moment, he would find out exactly what was going on with his dear old friend.

He told Garwyli, *Thank ya. That would be most helpful. Once I leave here, I intend to have satisfied a debt I must pay.*

Very well, dragon. Give me a moment before we appear.

When Garwyli appeared, Lanna stood beside him.

Ainvar blinked and blinked again. "*You* still live?"

Garwyli stood with his hickory cane. "Aye and no greater a surprise that ya do as well. How is it ya have not aged, Ainvar? Yar skin is smooth as marble. Does not appear natural."

"As if any of us are natural?" Ainvar smiled with a sly look. "Who are you, little girl? A sacrifice?"

Tristan shouted, "Shut your perverted mouth."

Daegan ordered, "Direct your questions at *me*, Ainvar. Understood?"

Lifting a delicate hand to gain everyone's attention, Lanna said, "Yes, I am a girl, but I am no child. Do not speak down to me again. Is not wise to test me."

Ainvar's ego wouldn't let him back away from that challenge. He called up his energy, which ran around him, growing into a cloud of black and orange crystals.

Lanna looked at Garwyli who only nodded once, no expression.

Lacing her fingers together in front of her as if listening politely to someone while not moving another muscle, Lanna's power flooded the room and shoved Ainvar off his feet.

He landed on his backend, flapping his arms wildly and making indignant noises.

Daegan even took a step back, amazed at what she could do while not physically present.

Tristan grunted as if he'd taken a hit to his chest. He turned around. "Where's Joavan?"

"I am here, dammit." The Faetheen climbed off the pile

of chain net where he'd been blown.

Taking in everyone, Lanna said, "I am Garwyli's student. That is small example of the many things he teaches me."

Tristan chuckled and winked at her.

Joavan came limping back. "What is this thing you brought to put on a show?"

Daegan turned on him and caught the Faetheen by his throat, lifting him off the ground with one hand that trembled from anger. "If ya or Ainvar say one more disrespectful word to her or Garwyli, this meetin' is over. When I say over, I mean my dragon's fire shall be the last thing ya see in this life. I am tired of dealin' with ya and your father."

Joavan's face turned red from lack of air.

Daegan dropped him.

The Faetheen landed lightly and rubbed his throat, muttering, "I do not claim him as father."

"I do not care. We are on the verge of solvin' the question of your bloody amulet if ya two can behave like honorable men."

Joavan quietly stepped past Daegan to stand alone, but not far from the circle of Tristan, Ainvar, Garwyli, and Lanna.

When Daegan stepped back into the group, he asked Garwyli, "Do ya and Lanna have a way to sort out this problem?"

Lanna's eyes sparkled happily with being included.

Daegan would have to take some time with her when he returned to Treoir. He had been underestimating this young woman, but he didn't believe anyone else knew much more about her power than he did.

Maybe not even her cousin, Quinn.

Garwyli knew exactly what being he trained, which was why he'd brought her. Treoir's druid said, "'Tis simple. Everyone must tell the truth. Ta assure that does happen, each of the two arguin' must produce somethin' they do not wish ta lose." His wrinkled gaze turned to Ainvar. "Ya know what I speak of, Ainvar, correct?"

"Yes."

"Ya agree with this method?"

"Yes."

"What about me and what I think?" Joavan complained.

Garwyli angled his head in the Faetheen's direction. "From what I understand, the dragon king has listened ta all ya have said and ended up without a solution. Do ya have a better idea than what I am suggestin'?"

Face covered in angry lines. Joavan huffed out, "No. Let's just do this."

"Very well." Garwyli announced, "Ya each place somethin' of great value on the table."

Tristan asked, "What table, Garwyli?"

"The one Ainvar shall call up."

Puffing out his chest for the benefit of Garwyli, Ainvar lifted his hands and used his power to deliver a beautifully detailed dark wood table six feet long.

Daegan wanted to laugh for the first time. That old druid from Treoir was using Ainvar's ego to make him burn power unnecessarily.

Garwyli tilted his head toward the table. "Nicely done, Ainvar."

"Was simple."

"What will ya put upon the table, Ainvar?"

Joavan stared at Ainvar, who had a moment of hesitation before he pulled out a dubh knife.

Daegan asked, "What is the value of the knife?"

Smiling, Joavan jumped into share, "That knife can kill Ainvar."

"Very good." Daegan turned to Joavan. "Ya must match the level of that knife in value."

Ainvar crossed his arms, sliding his hands into deep

sleeves. "How will ya match mine, Joavan?"

A vein on the Faetheen's temple jumped. He reached inside his jacket and unclipped a pin, which he placed on the table reluctantly. Lifting his hand away slowly, he crossed his arms.

Neither of them was happy.

That made Daegan very happy, because it meant they both had skin in this game.

When Ainvar's gaze dropped to the pin, his lips parted. His voice filled with awe. "Is that ... your mother's?"

"Yes, but you will *not* win it."

Garwyli reiterated the details of the dispute exactly as Daegan had explained it. Then he asked, "Do ya both agree 'tis correct?"

Joavan and Ainvar said, "Yes."

Garwyli held his translucent hand over the table. The knife and pin slid together, meeting in the middle.

Daegan noted how both Joavan and Ainvar tensed.

He didn't believe one over the other, especially after Joavan had withheld information time and again.

Such as being Ainvar's son.

Still holding his hand in place, Garwyli began speaking in a commanding tone that belied his age. "Should the owner of the knife or the owner of the pin speak untruthfully, the item of the one who lied shall go ta the victor. Specifically, if Ainvar lies, his knife shall go ta Joavan, and if Joavan lies, his pin shall go ta Ainvar."

The Faetheen nipped at his fisted knuckles nervously.

Ainvar stood calm, his strange eyes fixed on the knife and pin.

Garwyli asked, "What is in question ta be decided here?"

Joavan pulled himself up and spoke as someone of authority now that he'd calmed down. "The *Cearcall na Sìorraidheachd* was stolen forty-eight days ago and must be returned to protect my home world. Our king and queen are in danger until this is returned. My sister became very sick with a mysterious ailment. I was called to her bed, leaving other guards on watch over the amulet. It is never left alone. Dead guards were found in a pool of blood. Ainvar had been seen in the area even though he was cast out of *Talamh Dearmadta* over a year ago. I believe he stole the amulet, but he claims he does not have it."

Garwyli turned to Ainvar. "Do ya have the amulet?"

"No. If I had the amulet, I would use it to kill that miserable king, but never the queen."

"Why not the queen?" Daegan asked.

"She is my mother," Joavan interjected dryly.

"She was my mate first," Ainvar countered with bitterness.

So that explained a bit more about the conflict here. Daegan arched an eyebrow in Garwyli's direction.

The old guy sighed.

Joavan's gaze jumped from Daegan to Garwyli. "I have not lied. Neither have I accused Ainvar of killing my sister, but—"

"What, Joavan? Do not accuse me of such."

"*Shut up!*" Daegan ordered and the torches quivered. He'd shown far more patience than someone such as Joavan deserved, but he fought nonhumans in all places. He did not care for the Faetheen, but would prefer to not leave here as enemies. He had enough of those. "I am sorry for your loss, Joavan, but we must settle this about the amulet."

Shrugging, Ainvar shook his head. "I have not lied."

Garwyli asked, "Do ya know where the amulet is, Ainvar?"

Daegan would have thought Garwyli tossed a wet cat on Ainvar when the castle druid shouted, "That was not the question. I have answered. We are done."

Thankful to have a druid like Garwyli and not Ainvar,

Daegan demanded, "Where is the *Talamh An Asraon* diamond? Ya play with words."

Ainvar produced his staff, which had been missing until now, and lifted it in Garwyli's direction.

Garwyli snarled and raised his free hand.

Lanna whipped around and moved in front of Garwyli, shoving a hand up. "Do. Not. Dare."

Daegan rushed backward as he called up Ruadh.

Ainvar held his staff pointed squarely at Lanna.

Tristan threw a kinetic blast at the druid's staff, but the power bounced off.

With Ainvar distracted by Tristan, Ruadh lowered his head quicky with jaws open and closed them around both druid and staff. His dragon lifted all of it off the ground.

Ainvar screamed and whacked the inside of Ruadh's mouth with the stick then he started calling out something that could be a spell.

Daegan spoke to Tristan telepathically, telling him what to say.

"Listen up, Ainvar and Joavan," Tristan shouted. "Daegan said produce the amulet or die. He's fed up with both of you."

Joavan held his hands up in surrender, fear shaking his words. "I will stand by whatever Daegan decides."

Ainvar whined, "I will produce the gem. Free me from this beast."

Daegan told Ruadh, *Put the druid on the ground, but keep him locked inside your jaws.*

Ruadh lowered his big head until Ainvar's booted feet touched the marble.

Ainvar sounded as if he yelled in a tunnel. "Let me out!"

Daegan continued sending his messages through Tristan who told Ainvar, "Hand over the amulet or my dragon shall bite you in half."

Shrieking wildly, Ainvar's skinny arm shoved out between two large fangs. He gibbered a chant in a panicked voice. Nothing appeared on his palm. After a moment of silence, he tried again but slower, calling out a string of strange words in a trembling, but clear voice.

A dazzling necklace with a giant blue diamond hanging from the center appeared on his palm.

Ruadh raised a claw and snagged the necklace from Ainvar, then opened his jaws.

Ainvar scrambled away like a frightened crab, wiping his face over and over. His skin had gone chalk white and wrinkles began to line his face, which was covered in dragon saliva.

Power rushed through the room.

Daegan stood in human form and dressed again. He held the necklace with the rare diamond in his hand.

Joavan let out a deep whoosh of air. "Thank goodness."

When the Faetheen started toward Daegan, Ainvar said, "You will need that to close the rift and put the Imortiks behind the death wall, dragon. Hand it over to Joavan and you will never see it again."

Joavan froze. "No. That is not true."

Sending a look Garwyli's way, Daegan asked, "Does he speak the truth?"

Heaving an unhappy sigh, Garwyli admitted, "I do not know everythin' about the Immortuos Grimoire or the Imortiks yet."

Unbelievable. Daegan had no reason to believe either Joavan or Ainvar.

Tristan suggested, "Want me to grab Storm, boss?"

Lanna brightened. "Yes. Storm will do this."

Daegan nodded.

When Tristan disappeared, Ainvar and Joavan started shouting at each other.

If Tristan hadn't returned so quickly, Daegan might have released Ruadh one more time. But he needed to conserve their energy until he cleared the venom from his system.

Storm appeared next to Tristan and swung a vicious look at the two people he didn't know, Ainvar and Joavan. "What the hell is going on? You pulled me away from battling beside my mate."

Daegan cut to the heart of the matter. "Thank ya for comin'. I shall make this as fast as I am able." He ordered Ainvar, "Repeat what ya just said about the amulet and the Imortiks."

Ainvar spilled it out word for word.

Storm snapped, "Truth."

Hell, now what was Daegan going to do?

"That is mine, Daegan," Joavan broached in a firm voice. "We have a deal."

Daegan could not give in to Joavan so easily. "I need this to close the rift and put the Imortiks back. Do you plan to bring the amulet to me when the time comes?"

"That was not our agreement."

"Then let's make a new deal for the return of the amulet after I finish closing the rift."

"No. I'm taking it *now*!" Joavan took a step as Tristan moved to stand beside Daegan.

Storm stepped up on the other side.

Closing his fingers around the amulet, Daegan said, "I give my word to return it after the Imortik death wall is closed. 'Tis more than ya would do."

Joavan raised his fist, shaking them. "You broke our deal."

"I have not." Daegan had begun to realize he had a chance to flip this agreement on Joavan, which would only be fair after the Faetheen had lied time and again to him and Tristan. "If ya think back on every word we both spoke, ya said I had to retrieve the amulet. Ya never said I had to hand it over to ya."

Ainvar chuckled. "This is quite interesting. Make Joavan admit he has lied to you about everything. He cares nothing for the king who hates him. Joavan wants the amulet so he can rule Talamh Dearmadta."

"That's not true."

But Daegan heard a crack of guilt in the Faetheen's voice. Glancing at Storm, Joavan backed away. "Not true. I want to *save* the king."

Storm drew in a deep breath and exhaled slowly. "Lie"

"Who are *you* to declare truth or lie?" Joavan turned on Storm, who flashed red demon eyes at him.

Daegan had to settle this. "We could stand here for days provin' over and over again how Storm is a natural walkin' lie detector, but I know he is. He does not have time to waste any more than I do. I fulfilled my part of the deal. Ya owe me the grimoire box."

"No."

Ainvar belly laughed. "That's precious, Joavan. Go ahead and break your word, Fae-*theen*. See how that turns out."

Cocking his chin at Ainvar, Joavan stated, "It is not up to me. We made an agreement. The box will go to him if he fulfilled his part or to me if he did not. I say he did not."

"Lying again," Storm declared.

"Damn you. Stop talking," Joavan yelled.

Daegan sliced a look at Storm whose only reaction was a bored sigh.

Garwyli spoke up. "If that be so, Joavan, then prove Daegan did not uphold his end of the deal by statin' the specific words he gave ya ta claim the box."

Daegan held his breath. He was pretty sure about what had been said, but he did not want to lose the grimoire box by having forgotten one important word.

Standing there in a ball of anger, Joavan lowered his voice to a dangerous tone. "I do not have those words. He knew the whole point of this was to return the amulet to

Talamh Dearmadta. You make a grave mistake, dragon."

"I have given my word to return the amulet once the death wall is sealed with all Imortiks behind it, Joavan. Do not make this worse than it is." Daegan stood firm.

"I cannot wait that long and survive."

"Lie," Ainvar murmured.

Storm said, "Yes."

"You are such a jerk, Joavan," Tristan groused. "We're all trying to save everyone in this world and all you care about is you."

Ainvar mused aloud, "Ah. You do not know the Faetheen. They do not worry about others, only themselves."

"You will pay, too, *father*." Joavan just kept issuing threats.

Daegan told Tristan, "Take Storm back to Evalle. This has gone much longer than I expected." As soon as those two vanished, Daegan turned to Garwyli and Lanna still in hologram. "Thank ya for comin'. I shall visit later and discuss more."

"As ya wish, Daegan. Ya have only ta call when ya need us."

Lanna lost her bright-eyed look now replaced with worry as she watched Garwyli.

Daegan would catch her away from the old druid on his next visit to Treoir.

With those two gone, Daegan asked Ainvar, "How does this gem stop the Imortiks and close the death wall?"

"Wouldn't you like to know?" Ainvar vanished, but without his knife.

Fury wafted from Joavan with every step he took forward and snatched the knife up then the pin. With a balled fist and tight muscles protruding from his neck, he warned, "Ainvar is *not* your friend. He will *not* help you! Not the way I have. By tricking me with turning words around, you have lost a powerful ally and gained a deadly enemy.

Believe me when I tell you I will get that amulet back before any death wall is closed. For failing to do right by me, I will help none of you stop Imortiks."

Daegan's fury topped everything. This Faetheen had lied to him, walked them into a trap, and now thought to threaten him? "Joavan—"

The Faetheen disappeared.

CHAPTER 14

AINVAR STEPPED FROM WHERE HE'D hidden in his castle, close enough to observe the dragon shifter and Joavan argue before Daegan's number two man returned everyone vanished.

That dung beetle, Joavan.

Ainvar would never forgive himself for having bred that one.

He called up power to hide the translucent castle image even in moonlight. Let the locals think it had disappeared. None would risk coming to this area for another year or two.

Maybe not at all.

He'd chosen this spot to create the Ghost Castle, as the locals called it, for a reason. He had buried a sorcerer here back when no one could traverse this land.

The power came from having buried the female sorcerer alive.

Joavan had just cost him the amulet, for which Joavan would pay with his life. Did he think Ainvar would spare his own child's life? Stupid son. Ainvar could have more children if he chose, but based on that one mistake, another child would not happen for a century or more.

Walking quickly, he crossed the marble now covering the entire floor of the antechamber. As he strode, he reached inside his robe and ran his fingers along the black opals strung on a chain of twisted rhodium links.

Power hummed through his fingers and into his body.

Waving a hand ahead of him, an arched passage opened in the curved wall and resealed after he stepped through. He'd created the antechamber just for unexpected visitors. Joavan must feel smug about bypassing the wyverns then finding a way inside.

Ainvar had prepared for such an occurrence hundreds of years ago, but he had not expected a dragon tonight. Having just returned from a visit to America again, he'd shown up at the castle just in time.

Had he not been present, that dragon might have killed one of his wyverns.

Ainvar gripped his staff hard. The glass ball at the top vibrated with energy and the adder came to life, hissing. He eased his hold and ran a loving hand over the glass. "You are not needed yet, Tabia. Rest."

The adder curled tight again, becoming still.

Waving his staff from one side of him to the other, a room with crystals arranged in a circular wall two feet high and forty feet in diameter appeared on a floor of malachite. The wall had one small opening for entering the circle.

As he passed through, an altar rose from the center, pausing at the same height as the crystal wall.

Hundreds of candles in all shapes formed along the top of the crystal wall, flaming all at the same time. Stepping to one end of the altar, he lit a sage incense, then did the same at the opposite end.

With several deep inhales, he felt his body relaxing.

Lifting his staff and free hand, he called out, "Lady Of The Dark."

Slowly, she appeared in an ethereal form of a serpent as tall as Ainvar and with a woman's head shielded by a hood of golden skin similar to a cobra's flare. Eyes closed, she said nothing, moving from side to side in a trance-like state.

"Are you not glad to see me?" he asked with a smile.

Green-gold eyes opened with black reptilian irises. "What do you wish?"

"You did not answer my question, sweet one."

She spoke as if dead. "You call for me. I come to you. My happiness has never been part of our arrangement. Only that I provide information."

He grumbled, "I ask so little of you. When was the last time we spoke? Ten, maybe eleven years ago?"

She said nothing, just continued to move back and forth.

"What have you been doing to stay busy?" he asked, taking a dig at her.

"Your amusement carries a sickness."

Shaking his head in frustration, he said, "I have spent time in North America recently."

"This I know."

He added, "I could not be more pleased with the Imortik activity in progress."

"What of the humans who suffer?"

Waving off her comment, he said, "The ones that matter to you will be safe. Imortiks are escaping in a steady stream from the rift. I need to make plans for the big day when the wall comes down."

Her steady gaze offered no reaction. "You no longer have the amulet," she pointed out, once again showing him her knowledge.

"I know where it is and will be until that moment. As long as the dragon king of Treoir has it in his possession, that miserable son of mine will not get his hands on it." Ainvar chuckled at his quick decision to expose the value of the amulet regarding Imortiks.

A true stroke of brilliance on his part.

But then, only a few druids had managed to live as long as he had. Garwyli lived because he remained in a protective realm.

Unfortunately, Cathbad had returned from the dead, the

cur.

That pushed him back to what he would ask next. "While in North America, I discovered Cathbad still lives. I must find Cathbad and I don't mean at this moment. I need to know where he will be most often or at a specific time and place. Also, does he still possess the book *Before Ainvar*."

She closed her eyes and turned her head up while weaving back and forth in a mesmerizing motion. Her golden hood enlarged to twice its size. Her lips opened and she blew out a thin stream of reddish-gold fog.

When she stopped, the fog took on the shape of Cathbad's face.

Cathbad's head rotated to show his profile.

She lowered her chin until the top of her head was at the same level as the top of his, then she pushed her head into the smoky outline of his.

When she did, his eyes became solid and his eyes blinked.

She stayed that way for what seemed a half hour but had probably only been ten minutes when she withdrew her head.

Cathbad's smoky image vanished.

Her hood shrunk back to the usual size as she turned to face Ainvar. "Cathbad has a cavern in the Himalayan Mountains."

Ainvar fought to hold his patience. "I will never find that without more specifics. Even if I could, I do not wish to go traipsing across thousands of miles of mountains."

She closed her eyes, swayed a little, then opened her eyes. "Cathbad calls in dark druids for a meeting. If you are alerted, you will find him there."

"That *bastard!*" Ainvar shook his fist, his voice booming against the walls. "Does he think to unseat me as Seanóir?"

"No."

"He better not," Ainvar muttered.

Her lips lifted a tiny bit at the corners, but she never smiled. "Cathbad believes he is Seanóir by default as no one believes you still live."

The audacity of that druid after Ainvar had helped him and Queen Maeve fake their deaths. Of course, Ainvar had offered his aid only to get those two out of the way. He'd thought with a little luck they'd never returned.

Catching her expression, he cast a furious glare at the halfling he'd saved from death along with her children long ago. He warned, "Take care you do not find joy in anything that angers me. I still hold the future of your children and their descendants in my grasp."

Her face became stoic again. "I take joy in nothing."

"You would also do well to improve your attitude when we meet again as we will be speaking often now. In fact, I would prefer you not come to me as a serpent. It's distracting."

"Then call me by my name next time, Ainvar."

He had the oracle exactly where he wanted her and smirked. "This I can do. See how agreeable I am, Zeelindar?"

CHAPTER 15

BRYNHILD LIMPED FASTER, HOLDING HER iced-over broken arm to her chest so it didn't flop around. So many dogs howling. How close were they?

She could fight off dogs, no matter how many, but not that weapon used to knock her dragon from the sky. Plowing through thickets, she finally reached a place where the undergrowth was not so deep. But she quickly found out why when she rushed into an opening and stopped short of falling into a river.

Below her, a raging river battered every rock in its way, dragging limbs larger than her body that dared to fall in.

She'd been herded to a spot with no exit.

The dogs were getting louder with each beat of her heart banging inside her chest.

If she shifted into her dragon, she'd have to rebreak her limb, but that would be better than dying. The sound of human machines flying overhead killed that idea. They would attack her dragon with the same weapons, or greater ones.

With no time to waste, she decided on the river, then looked to the right to see if it spilled into a calm pool.

In a short distance, the river disappeared over a waterfall.

Her dragon rumbled, wanting to be freed.

The dogs closed in.

Unwilling to sacrifice her dragon, she jumped, landing hard in the water then tumbling over and around with her arm covered in ice dragging her down.

She'd had seconds before going over the waterfall, curled in a ball, and hoping against all odds she would not be smashed to pieces. The world fell away beneath her. She kept the scream inside as she dropped like a dead body into the churning water, spinning viciously. She kept turning, trying to find the surface. Don't panic. She chose a direction and started kicking her legs hard, hoping she was right. Her lungs screamed in pain. She broke the surface, gasping for air, and fighting to keep her arm still partially iced from dragging her under again. The water finally calmed. She rolled to her back to float and a strained laugh of relief broke free.

She had survived a waterfall in her human form. No one would catch her.

She turned in time to crash into a huge boulder that knocked her out.

The cold water brought her back as she sank again.

Forcing her legs to drive her upward again, she watched where she headed this time. Dizziness turned everything around her into multiple images.

She blinked while swimming with one arm and kept kicking, angling toward the bank.

The water moved peacefully and a gentle current pushed her along. When she made it close enough to the bank, she dropped her legs and stood in waist-deep water. The fierce river had tried its best to kill her. She dragged her exhausted body to the bank and fell on her face, heaving deep breaths. Soaked hair covered her face. Her head began throbbing.

When she could think clearly, she struggled to sit up. Shoving all that hair out of the way with one hand had her thinking about using her power to deal with her hair.

No, she could not waste energy on an insignificant annoyance.

Lifting fingers on her good hand, she touched her temple where a lump had risen. "Ouch. Do not be stupid," she scolded herself.

Her dragon made more noise, much louder this time, rocking her insides.

She whispered, "I do not know if I can hide us as a dragon."

Shift and heal, floated through her mind.

If only it would be so simple. She could tolerate the pain better than putting her dragon at risk with no way to fly. She could endure the throbbing in her arm a little longer. She told her dragon, *Be patient. I will find place for us to rest and shift away from enemies.*

Her trip down the waterfall had damaged the ice splint she'd put around her arm. As the last of the ice melted away, the bone had begun to heal straight. She left it alone, but every move sent agonizing pain from her wrist to her shoulder.

She took a step. Her left foot burned with pain.

She looked down to see it angled the wrong way and groaned. Calling up her dragon's healing energy, she remained still until she could put weight on it.

For all the water she'd just battled through, she had no way to take any with her to drink later. Limping forward, she had no idea where she headed and just hoped she was not circling back to the hunters.

Some hours later, she found an old building by almost walking into it in the dark. Many boards were missing. It smelled of horses and filth. Uncaring, she collapsed on the dirt and passed out.

Something crawled on her face.

She blinked awake, squinting against daylight seeping in through many more holes than she'd realized last night. She reached up to capture what tickled her skin, pulled back a small spider, and dropped it on the ground.

Water. She needed to drink water but saw none in here.

Once she could get to her feet, she almost fell again. That foot would not support her much farther. But her broken arm had healed.

She murmured to her dragon, *I am sorry*. Leaning against a wall for support, she bent her knee to allow her a firm hold on her foot. Breathing in and out fast several times, she wrenched the foot back into position with a loud crack and wailed in pain.

Her dragon roared inside her, slamming her ribs.

Tears streamed down her face. She only allowed tears when alone. No one would ever see her weak.

Sniffling and breathing hard, she said, "Yes. It is time." She rolled over on the knee and leg she could put weight on and called up her dragon.

She'd only thought the foot was painful.

Her poor dragon struggled to break free during the longest shift she'd ever suffered through. Skarde had once told her how he and Herrick had experienced difficult shifts after being badly damaged in battles.

She'd scoffed at him that she would not ever have difficulty with her power.

Where was Skarde today to taunt her for being a fool?

Even Herrick, who she had never been as close to as Skarde, would be a welcome sight.

When her dragon finished shifting, she stood on legs struggling to carry their weight.

She had stayed human to minimize the repair and because her dragon could not straighten a bone. After thanking her dragon for pulling them through the shift, she could feel energy pushing through the huge body from head to tail.

Her dragon would heal much faster with food.

Eating cows had gotten them attacked.

It was up to her to take care of them once her dragon could heal as much as possible.

An hour later, her dragon carefully flapped each wing and shifted weight to the damaged limbs. She smiled to herself and sent telepathically, *I have always said you were superior among all of the ice dragons. I will do better watching out for us. Let me have body and find place to rest.*

The change back to her human form was slow, but not as tormenting this time. She walked barefoot across the dirt floor of the building.

Ick. She hated dirty feet.

Time for clothes. She called pants and a simple shirt from the pictures Cathbad had shown her. She still wanted to kill that druid, but these clothes made more sense to move around in the human world. Searching the building, she found an old trough that held a shallow amount of rainwater. Not the cleanest water, but first she drank her fill by ignoring the taste, then washed her feet and covered them in something humans called sneakers.

She saw nothing sneaky about them, but they did feel comfortable.

Which way now?

With no idea of where in the world she'd slept, she struck out in the opposite direction from which she'd arrived last night. Her body functioned, but after trudging a while, her stomach growled, and she couldn't draw enough saliva to spit.

The sound of a quack caught her attention. Then another. She turned in that direction, using her new footwear to sneak through the woods. A short walk brought her to a pretty pond with ducks floating around making happy noises.

Dropping to her knees, she leaned over to cup water and stopped at the sight of her face and hair.

Had Medusa been this scary?

With no idea of who she might meet, she manually

twisted her hair into a tight knot at the top of her head. Not attractive, but better than being seen as a monster. She drank water to appease her growling stomach, then peeled out of her clothes to wash in the pond.

A bath could do wonders for the soul.

Dressed again, she felt better and picked up her pace. Her foot complained, but it worked correctly.

She crossed gentle hills and found her way through pockets of trees to emerge from a dense forest. In front of her, a large pasture came into view. It was connected to another field where a white house stood on the far side of what appeared to be a garden.

An old man walked behind a metal structure pulled by a horse similar to field workers of her time growing up. The horse was thick and strong.

Her dragon perked up, sending her one word. *Food.*

CHAPTER 16

CASIDHE GLANCED AT THE DIGITAL clock in the kitchen again. Just after midnight. How much longer before Daegan returned? The air around her felt empty without him. She hadn't known him only a few days ago and now she couldn't keep him out of her mind.

That man could kiss the socks off a woman.

But they wouldn't have time for any kisses. As soon as he returned, she had to go find Fenella.

Daegan had promised to share everything his people had on Fenella's phone. She expected to teleport to the location of her friend's phone.

If it circulated, Fenella had to be safe, right?

That was only if her friend still possessed the device.

But if that were the case, Fenella would have called.

Casidhe wanted to scream. No matter how many ways she tried to convince herself Fenella was safe, logic blew up every argument. Fenella would have contacted her by now if she weren't in danger.

Daegan would help her save Fenella. That was the only reason Casidhe agreed to wait. He would not let her down.

She dumped the used tea bag into the trash and carried the warm mug to the living room of Tristan's hotel room.

Who kept a private hotel room? Before he finished introducing her to the man in charge of arranging for her to stay here, who was a troll wearing a human glamour, Tristan had rushed around to make sure she had food and understood how to get anything else she needed.

She'd gotten a quick glimpse of The Georgian Hotel when he walked her down to the front entrance and showed her emergency exits.

Then he asked her to please not leave the room or he couldn't guarantee her safety.

Even with all the uncertainty in her life, she enjoyed a little thrill every time she glanced out the window of the second-floor room. She actually stood in America. Right outside her window glowed the marquee lights of the famous Fox Theater in the city of Atlanta. She'd read up on that theater in one of the magazines he had delivered to her room.

People walked around, living normal lives.

She longed to experience normal. Not that she didn't appreciate her power to translate. She loved her connection to the preternatural world, but envied people with simpler lives.

Envy was an ugly color.

Now wasn't the time to be a Negative Nancy. She wasn't stranded on a mountain all alone. Tristan swore his good friend would keep her safe.

A troll watched over her.

Life continued to get stranger by the day.

She placed her tea on the end table and sat on the sofa next to where she'd dropped her backpack. The books in her pack were spread around on the sofa and end table. But nothing in those books held her attention at the moment as much as what she'd discovered in TÅμr Medb.

Either some of the information she'd been taught about the ice dragons and Daegan's red dragon had been wrong or the book from Queen Maeve's library had been deeply flawed.

Her instinct about books worried her.

She had more faith in those old texts than what someone told her, or she had until this conflict of faith. Why would the squire families have given her wrong information, though?

That twit queen would lie to Casidhe in a flash, and had, but ancient books generally documented what actually happened. Whenever in doubt, she had always hunted down a second confirmation, such as another book with corroborating text.

Or a valid source, like Professor Redmond, would confirm or discredit whatever she had a question on. Maybe the professor would speak to her again if she ever made it back to Galway.

Her home seemed so far away. An ocean away.

The top of the scepter poked out of the backpack.

Casidhe had read pretty much everything in this place. She normally enjoyed hours of reading, but she needed to get moving and do something productive.

Her mind wouldn't stop asking the same question over and over. When would Daegan show up?

She touched the plump bird on top of the scepter, tapping her fingers against the cool gold as she thought.

Those last few seconds with Zeelindar, the oracle, kept playing through her mind.

Did they have a deadline for delivering this treasure to her? How would she know? When Casidhe asked how to alert Zeelindar when they found the scepter, the oracle had said, "I will know."

Those were the last words Casidhe heard before a power spun her and Daegan to that mountain in Spain.

Clearly, Zeelindar did *not* know everything or she'd have sent word to deliver the scepter by now, right?

Gripping the short staff, Casidhe lifted it from the pack and leaned back against the sofa. She mused aloud, "How do we gain the oracle's attention? Do we say, here ya go, Zeelindar? Or should Daegan and I climb that mountain again?"

Ugh. That was one memory she did not want to replay or repeat.

Daegan had been amazing. She would never have made it to the oracle the first time without him preventing her from freaking out over clinging to the side of a sheer drop-off.

Anyone would have had heart palpitations over that.

He'd gone through so much to reach the oracle, then battled satyrs to gain the scepter and grimoire box only to have his life threatened by the coating. He'd come for her on the mountain and fought to bring her out of TÅµr Medb.

Given all that, her conscience weighed heavy as an elephant sitting on her shoulders.

She'd accepted the worst about Daegan without question and from someone as unreliable as Queen Maeve. That put a dent in Casidhe's confidence when it came to trusting her decisions. She'd jumped to the wrong conclusion before gaining the truth.

Maybe she should have given Daegan more credit and not believed an evil being who had imprisoned him for thousands of years. Sadly, in that moment, everything the crazy queen said confirmed Casidhe's deepest fears.

She'd expected to be let down. She expected the enemy of her family to play on her emotions and use her. Why? Probably due to Herrick being less than excited about her last visit, but she couldn't blame this on him.

She'd suffered bouts of guilt over allowing Daegan to kiss her and slide inside her heart.

Had she been blaming Daegan for making her care about him?

Pretty screwed up.

Years of loneliness had affected her more than she'd been willing to admit. Daegan's touch had been so much more than anyone in the past. His kiss had shaken her and challenged all she'd believed. She'd been trying to avoid admitting she was failing Herrick by befriending Daegan.

Then she failed Daegan by misjudging him.

Where did she go from here?

The more time she spent around Daegan, the more she wanted to stay around him. What was the possibility of that even happening?

It didn't matter. She had to do a better job of being fair with Daegan and not judging him against a history she'd been taught that might not be entirely correct.

So much to think about and no one to talk to and help her figure out how to move forward. She needed Fenella, her best friend.

It would be nice to have her own phone back in hand.

Tristan said he'd pick up her phone from the techs and bring it to her when he returned, but he'd had to rush back to support Daegan.

Raising the scepter to hold in front of her, she asked, "Where are you, Zeelindar, oracle of the mountain, and keeper of all knowledge? I have the king's scepter and it was no easy task to bring this back to the human world." Call her insane, but it felt good to talk about what she and Daegan had been through.

"We did survive Hadrianna's world, although satyrs chased Daegan out and spit something nasty on him. He—"

Energy spun up in the middle of the room between Casidhe and a recliner on the other side of the narrow coffee table. The shimmering miniature tornado grew to Daegan's height and began to fill in with colors, then a translucent form took shape.

Zeelindar stood there. Not so much a hologram as appearing ethereal.

"Why have you called for me?" the oracle asked.

"Did I do that?" Casidhe squeaked, sitting forward. The oracle had not threatened her in any way, but everything about Zeelindar scared the bejesus out of her.

"Yes. You disturb the rhythm of the universe when you make a request. You may not think your words are heard, but they do land at someone's ear. You asked where I was and here I am."

This put new meaning on being careful what you put out to the universe.

Casidhe cleared her throat. "Uhm, we found your scepter."

"So I see."

The oracle's tone pretty much called Casidhe Queen Of The Obvious. She lifted the scepter. "Here."

"I cannot take the scepter with me when I travel in astral projection. What of the grimoire box?"

Why would the oracle ask about the box after they managed to save the scepter? Frowning, because it irritated her that after all Daegan had been through that Joavan had him out facing another threat. "We could have gotten out with just the scepter, but the minute we touched the grimoire, all hell broke loose. Satyrs chased us until Daegan found a way to break out. They—"

"I do not want every detail, just an answer."

What a crabby person. "Okay then, here's the short version. We found it, lost it, and now a Fae type of person has the box." Shouldn't this oracle know all that?

Zeelindar's calm presence changed in a snap. The air around her turned dark as a storm and her golden eyes swirled with black then they changed to a fiery orange with white irises. "You *lost* the grimoire volume?" She didn't shout but the room trembled.

Was this woman, oracle, whatever criticizing her and Daegan after all they'd been through? What investment did *she* have in the grimoire box?

Casidhe dropped the scepter on the sofa, stood, and jabbed fists at her hips. "You must want the long version.

We were lucky to survive and get out of that place with both the scepter and the box. Satyrs chased Daegan to the cliffs. They spewed some kind of coating on him that started hardening and almost killed him. He's out there right now risking his neck to repay a Faetheen who helped clean off the coating and who also grabbed the box after Daegan was captured."

Heart pounding out of control, Casidhe would not let this oracle rail at her after all Daegan had suffered.

The dark swirling energy continued. Hmm. She might need to dial back her anger.

Casidhe tried for peace by not yelling at the oracle. "Uhm, so, Daegan *will* return with the grimoire box." She sure as hell hoped so and moved ahead to get attention away from the box. "What do you want us to do with the scepter?"

Slowly, the dark air lightened until she could see the oracle again and not just those scary eyes.

Zeelindar lifted a finger on each hand to her temples.

Had Casidhe given her a migraine?

The oracle began whispering something.

Blowing out a stream of air, Casidhe sat again and dropped her hands to the sofa. The oracle had the power to blow up her hotel room. Tristan would not be happy to find out someone came to Casidhe here, but in fairness to security, the oracle had not entered in person.

Casidhe pulled her hands to her lap and entwined her fingers. She'd just sit hear quietly until Zeelindar either had more to say or forgot she existed.

Preferably the latter.

When Zeelindar lowered her hands, her eyes returned to what Casidhe had come to realize as her normal look of gold swirling with black. "You two must be together to deliver the scepter."

"Why?" Casidhe regretted opening her mouth the minute that popped out. What happened to not drawing unwanted attention?

Ignoring the question as if it had been a gnat flying around, Zeelindar said, "When you are together and possess both the grimoire and scepter, you will receive my message. Do not reach out to me again."

Energy spiraled up once more, then it shrunk until no larger than a candle flame and blinked out of sight.

Casidhe fell back, body exhausted as if she'd just run a marathon around the perimeter of this hotel. That woman would drain a nuclear plant.

She looked over at her now-cold tea. She needed sleep more than she needed caffeine. Staying awake while she waited might get her into more trouble, plus she'd need to be rested for wherever tracking Fenella's phone would take her.

Getting up, she stuffed the scepter into her backpack, but left the books piled around. She carried the pack still hiding her sword to the bedroom. She hated to wrinkle a bed so perfectly set up with a million decorative pillows she'd never get back in the correct order, but her body begged to crash there.

Someone with more decorating taste than her had mixed aqua-blue, tan, and white colors in a way that would fit for a man or a woman.

She placed her backpack next to one of the nightstands then carefully tossed the decorations into a pile beside the bed and left only pillows for sleeping.

After shedding all her clothes except a T-shirt and panties, she closed the bedroom door to prevent any embarrassing mishap and pulled the heavy drapes together. Tristan wouldn't come in here without knocking. He'd shown her nothing but respect.

She stretched out between the sheets, muscles happy to be on a soft bed, but her brain wouldn't shut up.

What was happening to Daegan right now?

What would happen when she saw him again? Would he kiss her again? Should she let him if they were parting ways once they delivered the scepter?

Her eyelids drooped. She yawned.

No more kissing.

She had to stop making bad decisions.

Getting involved with Daegan topped that list.

Sleep pulled at her.

But she wanted ... one more kiss.

CHAPTER 17

DAEGAN AND TRISTAN ARRIVED AT the same moment on the mountain in Spain. He'd linked their powers again to preserve Tristan's as much as he could.

He stood in knee-high grass growing in land still dark, but close to sunrise. "I have no idea if returnin' here shall matter, but I wish to go to the spot where we last stood with Joavan."

"That jerk should have set it up for the box to reappear wherever you were," Tristan griped. He looked out from the area they'd chosen to shield them from popping into view should a human happen by.

Tristan pointed uphill. "Weren't we over there?"

"I believe ya are correct. We shall walk."

"I'm good to teleport us, boss."

"Save your power. Ya do not know when ya may need it." Daegan led the way in a hurry. When he reached the next rise, he stopped and looked around.

Tristan studied the spot. "Yep, this looks familiar from the few times I've been here."

"Damn." Daegan rubbed his head that kept a dull pain. He had been going for many hours and battled, plus shifted often. The strain and Imortik venom were beating him up inside. He'd return to Treoir soon and rest there, but not seeing the box had drained what drive he'd had left.

Disgust filled him. "That bloody Faetheen."

Tristan asked, "How can we find the box?"

"We should not have to do so based on the words Joavan and I spoke." Daegan scratched the back of his neck while he stared at the spot where he felt certain he'd last seen the box.

What would make that box appear?

With nothing to lose, he said, "If ya are here, grimoire box, show yourself as I have fulfilled my part of the agreement with Joavan."

Tristan smiled, looking amused. "Maybe that will ... *oh, shit.*"

A glimmering rectangle shape took form, becoming solid until the grimoire box appeared on the ground.

Daegan had not thought that would work since Joavan had failed to share any directions on how to retrieve the box. But in all honesty, he had also failed to pin the Faetheen down on details. He would take care not to make that mistake again.

"What are you waiting for?" Tristan asked. "It's right there."

"The Imortik venom inside me recognized the box last time. I could not shift, teleport, or call out telepathically. I experienced a burning sensation from hand to arm and 'twas only for a few minutes while runnin'. I am thinkin' of the best way to transport that box without harmin' either of us."

"Okay, that had to be why Joavan floated it above his hand." Tristan snapped his fingers. "I've got an idea."

Daegan nodded, sure he had the same thought. "We use kinetics to carry it."

"Right. But we still have to put it somewhere safe for the time being. Where would that be?"

Relieved at the box appearing, Daegan could now think calmly. "I must ask Garwyli if it would be safe at Treoir and not threaten anyone there. If we take it to Atlanta, I fear the box might call to Imortiks." Daegan telepathically said, *I have a question, Garwyli.*

What be it, dragon? came right back.

I have recovered the grimoire box and need a place to keep it safe until time to use its power for stoppin' the Imortiks. I do not want to risk hidin' it in the human world. Would this box be a danger to anyone in Treoir?

After a pause, Garwyli said, *I have a place ta store the box. Send Tristan ta where ya and I met last time. He and Lanna will know where I hide the volume then Tristan will report back ta ya. I see no problem havin' the volume in this realm as there are no Imortiks here.*

Very well. I shall send Tristan to ya. Finished with Garwyli, Daegan spoke out loud. "Carry the box to Garwyli. In fact, teleport directly into the first room of his area. Do not show the box to anyone else. I shall wait here."

"You got it, boss." Tristan turned to the box and looked confused on how to get it in the air.

Daegan pointed fingers at each side of the bronze box and used kinetics to lift it. Once he had the box high enough, Tristan slipped a palm beneath it and generated kinetic power to float the box.

"Joavan's got nothing on us," Tristan quipped. "Be right back."

When he disappeared, Daegan found a place to sit down and draw his knees up. He crossed his arms and propped them on his knees then dropped his head down.

It seemed he'd just rested a moment when he heard, "Boss!"

Daegan yanked his head up.

"You good? I didn't mean to be gone so long but it took a bit to put the box away."

Daegan got to his feet. "I am fine."

"That may be, but you look rode hard and put up wet."

When Daegan cocked an eyebrow at that, Tristan said, "You look wiped out, exhausted, ready to crash."

"I will rest once I check on Casidhe and make good on

sending her with ya to Fenella's phone."

Tristan twisted his neck one way then the other as if loosening muscles. "I have a bad feeling about that."

"Why?"

"Last I heard, our tech people had located the phone, but it was moving around one small area."

"And?"

"They say no calls have been made on it to Casidhe the entire time we've had her phone in our possession. It's as if someone has the phone but isn't using it."

"Why would that be strange?"

Tristan chuckled. "You've never had a mobile phone. Today's world loves their phones to text or make calls on all day long. There's something odd about the lack of activity with that phone even though it seems to move around."

"I should go with you and Casidhe when you take her."

"Nope. I'm doing that on my own while you rest, see Brina, the babies if they're born, whatever. It won't take me long to teleport Casidhe and I won't allow her to walk into danger."

Had anyone else suggested that, Daegan would have shut them down immediately, but not this man. Tristan would protect Casidhe with his life just as Daegan would and Tristan made valid points.

Daegan had to eat and rest so he could hunt the second grimoire volume. It had to be in Atlanta, but he had no way to pinpoint where.

That meant the oracle had been correct when she said he'd be back to see her again. When they handed over the scepter, he would ask for how to find the second grimoire.

Then he would find out who was behind the Imortik attack on VIPER. Could the Imortik master have two volumes now?

A frightening thought.

"I agree with ya about goin' to Treoir, Tristan. Still, I

need time to see Casidhe before the two of ya depart."

"You'll have plenty of time. I have to get the phone from our people and I promised Quinn I would check in whenever I was in town to keep him up on what we're doing, plus take his report to you."

"That would be excellent."

Tristan didn't waste time teleporting.

Daegan felt off-balance as he appeared in a strange room. A nicely furnished room empty of any living being. Fear flooded his thoughts. "Where is she?" He couldn't hide the panic in his voice after she had vanished so many times. Power gathered around, preparing to attack a threat.

"She's here, boss," Tristan said quietly as he appeared. "Bedroom door is closed. She's probably sleeping."

Relief almost took him to his knees. "I trusted ya had her safe, but ... "

"But you've been through hell for days and need a break. Why don't you shower and catch some rest while I'm gone? Shouldn't take more than an hour."

"Do ya think to fool me so easily?"

Tristan chuckled. "Not really. I was hoping you'd surprise me and agree." He smiled with compassion. "You're not gonna save or lose the world in an hour. The minute you return to Treoir, everyone is going to need your attention."

Wiping his mouth with a hand, Daegan gave in. "Very well. Do not allow me more than an hour. I want your word."

"You have it. I will always do whatever you ask," Tristan said in a solemn voice, which gave Daegan a twinge of guilt for having questioned him.

"Go on. I shall be here." Daegan tried to sound more lighthearted than he felt.

"Shower is in the bedroom." Tristan looked as if he wanted to say something else but disappeared instead.

Daegan stared at the door, torn between rushing in to be with Casidhe again and holding himself back from acting so rash.

Shaking off the thoughts he was too tired to sort out, he quietly opened the door, exposing the dark room. His eyes adjusted to locate the bed where he identified the sound of delicate snores.

Poor lass had to be just as tired as him.

He crossed quietly to the large bathroom with a standing shower. Daegan had taken showers in Quinn's special building in downtown Atlanta set up just for the Beladors. Another modern convenience he appreciated. While he scrubbed his body, he envisioned walking into the bedroom to find her awake, hair tousled, and with a sleepy smile on her face.

The way she'd look if she'd just had sex.

He groaned. One thought of her turned him hard.

In spite of how she'd joked with him on the mountain, the lass would likely take offense or fear him if he left the bathroom in this condition and startled her.

Twisting the handles, he endured an icy shower. That ruined the relaxing hot one from just before, but he could now manage his body by the time he dried off. He called up a pair of shorts made of soft material.

When he turned off the bathroom light and opened the door into the bedroom, Casidhe still slept soundly.

He longed to be near her and struggled with the notion of walking out to rest on the furniture he'd seen in the other room.

His body would hang off both ends of the longest piece.

The bed she slept on swallowed her small form. He could stand here and debate or he could give in to his need to rest close to her.

Walking over to the bed, he smiled at her curled up in the middle with her back to him. The lass had taken over half of the bed, but he had enough room on this side. He first moved her backpack to a corner where it would be out of reach.

If his little termagant became riled, she went for her sword.

He slipped between the sheets and turned on his side toward her while maintaining a proper distance. Every deep breath drew in her natural scent and soothed his battered soul. He touched her reddish blond hair, so silky between his fingers.

They had met under the worst of conditions. Much as he still harbored anger at Joavan, the Faetheen had helped with rescuing her from Queen Maeve.

Daegan would have given anything in that moment to save her. Joavan should not have lied to him. In spite of how the Faetheen acted, Daegan would return the amulet once the Imortiks were behind the death wall.

Perhaps they still had a chance to be allies.

If that did not happen, an amulet would save no one. The being who had teleported into the vault in VIPER headquarters would be difficult to stop.

The steady sound of Casidhe breathing and sleeping close enough for him to protect loosened Daegan's chest muscles. He rolled over on his back and put his hands behind his head. He'd slept that way for many years during battle with his fingers near the hilt of his sword.

Daegan dropped off, falling into deep sleep for a short while until he realized a warm arm was draped across his chest. His heart caught up with his observation and started beating fast.

Casidhe had rolled over at some point and hugged her body against his. He pulled his arms down, placing one carefully around her back.

Her full breasts pressed against his skin, heating his blood.

She snuggled closer and rubbed against him. His discipline would not hold up against her sweet assault. He wanted to lift her soft lips to his and taste her.

He wanted *her*. Simple as that.

But to take her and possibly not see her again would be an insult. Just the idea of being apart from her sent waves of longing through him to wrap her up and spirit her away to Treoir.

He could do nothing until he found out what power she carried and if he survived the venom from his first Imortik attack.

Still, at the moment, he would trade much for a simple kiss.

She moved her leg up onto his body, brushing her knee over his hard erection. He sucked in a sharp breath.

He could think of few tortures so difficult to survive as having Casidhe's warm body this close and not touching her everywhere. Not driving into her heat and making her his.

He found the edge of her shirt. He slid his hand beneath the material and ran his fingers gently over the smooth skin on her back.

She moaned and wiggled around, forcing him to bite back a curse.

Then her warm lips pressed against his skin pecking kisses.

He grinned. The termagant was awake. She moved again and he lost his smile. "Careful, lass. 'Tis only so much a man can endure."

In reply, she kissed him more and crawled up on top of him.

Clasping her hips, he held her still before he lost all hope for control.

Soft lights from the streets outside dusted her skin in the dark room and touched her sultry look.

The vixen ran her hands from his chest to stomach and moved her heat against him, as if he were not already hard as a battering ram. Hair tousled from sleep and full lips curved in an easy smile, this lass possessed a beauty all her own.

She ran her tongue over her lips. "Hi there."

Drawing a finger along the shape of her cheek and chin, he said, "I missed ya."

"Really?" Her eyes brightened at his admission.

How could she doubt his words when she sat upon the proof? But he missed *her*, not just her body. He feared once they made love he would be done for, unable to walk a step away from her.

Another reason he could not cross a line right now.

His life would not be his own until the world was free of Imortiks. He would not have Casidhe living in fear for her life any more than the others he protected.

One of her perfect eyebrows lifted. "Are you not ... *interested*?"

His heart pounded like a fist hammering on a locked door of a building on fire. "Ya have to ask if I want ya?"

She lifted a shoulder in answer, surprising him with her show of vulnerability.

"Lass, I want ya more than I can put in words, but I cannot have ya."

Her eyebrows dropped low and she sounded hurt. "What?"

Brushing his knuckles along her smooth cheek, he smiled. "Ya are beautiful and I would be humbled for ya to share your body with me, but a man who cares for ya does not accept what ya offer without serious intentions. If once I finish all I must accomplish, ya still want to give this a try, I am more than willin'. But ya have to know it would change everythin'."

They stared at each other for heavy seconds.

"What do you mean?" She cocked her head and nibbled on her lip.

"I would not treat ya so casually as a woman to never see again. I would only touch ya if ya were mine to keep."

Sitting up, her face struggled with confusion and something else Daegan couldn't identify.

Clearing her throat, she scrubbed her hands over her face. "While I do not offer myself to just anyone, I am not holdin' you to marriage or anythin' like that. This is not two thousand years ago. I've been with one other man, but only one."

Daegan's blood churned. "Who?"

"Oh, Daegan, it was back in college and a mistake. We did not spend much time together. He complained about sex. I disappointed him." She drew circles on his chest.

"He was doin' it wrong," Daegan replied dryly.

She lowered her gaze to his chest and murmured, "I might disappoint you."

"Not possible."

Eyes the color of an endless sky lifted to his and flickered with disbelief. Then she jabbed his chest with her finger. "How can you possibly know?"

He caught her finger and held her gaze while his heart thudded at having her this close. He slowly pulled her finger into his mouth and sucked it.

Her lips parted and her eyes widened.

Giving her finger a lick, his eyes held hers captive and his chest rumbled. "'Tis not my first time either, lass. If a man knows what to do, the woman shall enjoy the mating immensely. That was no man but a boy ya met."

Her smile could wake the sun. "Now I really want to do this with you."

"When I know we can be together for more than one night, I shall show ya all that ya have been denied."

"Cocky. I like that about you, dragon."

Mouthy wench. "I like ya. I like how I feel around ya. 'Tis the first time since escapin' from TÅµr Medb I see a glimpse of the future I want."

Her eyes glistened, then she blinked the tears away before they could fall. "I wish you wanted to take us on a test ride right now," she muttered and moved around as if getting comfortable.

He hissed. "Lass! Take care."

Easing down to cross her arms on his chest and prop her chin on her arms, she said, "I have spent a lot of time alone. No man has interested me the way you do. With all we've been through, I don't know when this opportunity will happen again." She stared down for a few seconds then lifted her gaze to him. "I have denied myself so much for so long I thought to ... I want to let go for once."

"I know what ya say and to give in would be so easy, but then I would be livin' with my guilt if this Imortik problem kept me from returnin' to ya." Daegan swallowed his disappointment, but he could not do this for the very reasons he stated. He brushed his hand over her hair. "I vow to ya if once this is over and I am free to live my life, nothin' shall stop me from comin' to find out if ya are still willin'."

Her eyebrows drew tight. "I will be ... if someone else doesn't come along."

He flipped her on her back so fast she gasped. Bracing himself on his forearms, he breathed hard in and out, fighting the struggle to keep his hands from her. "I am tryin' to say I shall not treat ya as a loose woman. I care for ya, lass. I want so much more with ya. If another man touches ya, he shall forfeit that hand."

Pushing up on her elbows, she whispered, "You aren't a Renaissance Man, you're an original. I was only teasin'." She lifted up and kissed him.

He held his control in a strangle grip. His arms shook from wanting to pull her to him and do so much more, but he kissed her, moving his mouth over hers and enjoying her sweet taste. She hooked her arms over his shoulders, rubbing that body against him. His deprived groin would never be the same.

Sitting up, he lifted her with him. She locked her legs around his hips and sat back on his knees. His hands found their way under her shirt to hold her full breasts.

He caressed her nipples, feeling the hard tips form.

She made a needy sound that sent heat zinging through his groin.

His energy spun up, reaching for hers. Their energies hummed all around them. He had no idea why that was happening.

Her fingers clutched his neck and hair. "I don't want you fightin' Imortiks."

Kissing her a long time, he eased apart. "I shall be fine as long as I know ya are safe. Ya must promise me to not take chances." Leaning forward, he kissed her cheek. "Ya are someone I never thought to have in my life. I shall find a way for us to be together."

She held his face to hers. "Really?"

"Aye.'Tis hard to imagine livin' without ya, lass."

Her face softened and her eyes misted. The longer he stared at her, the more difficult he found it to move away from this woman who had stolen his heart, but he had to leave soon. He kissed her again. "We should dress. I fear Tristan returns soon."

"I need a shower."

He stood up and lifted her to her feet, watching her all the way to the shower. When the water came on, he could think of nothing except how much he wanted to run his soapy hands over her body.

If he did not find something new to think on, he would be unable to wear jeans. But he was never using the image with Queen Maeve that Casidhe had suggested on the mountain.

He'd cut off his own member before being forced to service that crazy being.

By the time Casidhe dried off, dressed, and stepped from the shower, he'd donned jeans, a long-sleeved shirt, and boots.

Casidhe headed out of the room, speaking over her shoulder. "I'm going to make some tea for us."

Daegan had seen the lasses drink tea in Treoir. He was not much for the brew, but if it made Casidhe happy he would drink whatever she made for him.

Tristan's voice came into Daegan's mind. *I'm teleporting into the hotel room in five minutes.*

I shall be waiting for ya.

Daegan should go with Tristan and Casidhe. That should not take long then he would teleport to Treoir once he and Tristan found a safe place for Casidhe to stay.

As he walked out to meet Casidhe in the kitchen, Tzader called him telepathically. *Brina has been in labor for a while, but the healer says our babies are coming. Brina asked that you be here. Can you do that, Daegan?*

Yes. Tristan is arriving any minute. I shall come immediately. He felt a surge of happiness and disappointment.

He could not pass up the chance to be there when the babes were born, but that meant he could not join Tristan and Casidhe.

She walked out of the kitchen just as Tristan appeared in the large room. "Whoa. Scared me to death, Tristan. Glad to see you, but you should be careful poppin' in unannounced." Her guilty gaze jumped to Daegan.

"Tristan called to me a few minutes ago to inform me he would be teleportin' in," Daegan explained.

"Oh. That's fine." She smiled at Tristan. "Want some tea?"

"Thanks, but I have to teleport Daegan first, then I'll be

right back to get you."

Her lips parted with hurt. "Where are you goin'?"

Daegan did not want to leave her this way. "Give me a moment, Tristan."

"No problem, boss."

Walking over to Casidhe, Daegan gently turned her toward the kitchen. She walked ahead of him then stopped and spun around with her arms crossed.

He cupped her shoulders. "I had hoped to go with ya and Tristan to find Fenella's phone, but I am needed for somethin' urgent in Treoir Realm. I do not want ya waitin' any longer. Ya have been patient and 'tis time ya went to the place my people located your friend's phone."

She uncrossed her arms and frowned. "I understand."

Placing his palm on her cheek, he leaned down and kissed her. "I shall see ya as soon as I am free again. Tristan shall take ya wherever ya need to go and contact me immediately if ya run into trouble. I trust him with my life. 'Tis the only one I would trust with yours."

Nodding, she said, "I'll be fine. Hurry back." She lifted up and kissed him. "Go. Do whatever you need to and be safe."

"No harm comes to me in my family's realm."

If that was so, why did he have a strong misgiving about going there?

Or was it about leaving her?

CHAPTER 18

CATHBAD TELEPORTED INTO THE TRIBUNAL realm, ready to go on the attack first. If not, these deities would destroy him within minutes with one simple question.

The surly trickster god, Loki, glared down from the dais where he stood beside stalwart Justitia and Hermes, who never seemed to play much of a role here. This trio of powerful beings had been here often lately when VIPER had other deities willing to play judge, jury, and executioner.

This place needed new blood.

Cathbad pushed power into his voice. "I have somethin' I wish to make clear before ya start in on me with your questions."

"We do not allow anyone to qualify when or how we ask questions," Loki shot back. Energy boiled in a blue glow around him, but without disturbing his custom-tailored suit, shiny shoes, and perfectly styled black hair.

Someone had enraged that one recently for him to pop off so quickly when Loki generally liked to play with his prey.

Even Justitia had a pissy twist to her lips.

While Hermes plunked his lyre and stared off at nothing, Justitia spoke up. "We do have questions and little patience."

Cathbad powered up his attitude, showing no weakness. Never let Loki scent blood. "I am here to respond just as I said I would be. I merely wish to sort out a confusion to save us all time."

"How admirable of you, Cathbad. Quinn of the Beladors showed the same concern for our time." Loki's tone soured. "Forgive me if I find all this deference for inconveniencing us a bit suspicious."

The longer they bantered, the more this would disintegrate. Cathbad jumped ahead, getting to the meat of what he had to say. "When ya call me in to discuss a situation, I am always lumped together with Queen Maeve. While I did reincarnate with her, we have parted ways. I do not wish to be held responsible for her actions. 'Tis the only point I wished to make."

Hermes turned a surprised expression on Cathbad.

Angling around, Justitia lifted her chin in Loki's direction with eyes covered with a white cloth. Justice with impartiality, blind to wealth, status, or power. She whispered something to Loki, who kept his gaze on Cathbad, but nodded.

Music started up again.

Cathbad ignored the looney musical god, wishing he could cloak Hermes along with his annoying instrument just to enjoy some quiet.

"How can we know you are not involved with Queen Maeve, Cathbad?" Loki hadn't questioned Cathbad's words since no one dared to lie in a Tribunal. Regardless of power, lying in this realm would turn a being a bright red and death would follow not far behind. Loki had just poked around to find out Cathbad's game.

"'Tis simple if ya think about what I have done in recent months."

That drew frowns on all three of them.

Now that Cathbad had their attention, he kept going. "I have been comin' here and playin' peacemaker every time Queen Maeve stirred up trouble. I brought Quinn's child back from TÅµr Medb and helped VIPER allies take down Veronika *after* Queen Maeve had sent someone to aid that witch in escapin' VIPER lockdown." They should be kissing his feet for preventing that particular witch to run loose. She'd planned to use Witchlock on the world, supernaturals included, had Adrianna not yanked the power from her during a battle.

Cathbad kept going, unwilling to give up his chance to speak. "I was not informed about Queen Maeve's machinations nor was I involved in her stupid plans. That action alone on my part caused a great fracture in our relationship. I left for a while to think about how to move forward. 'Tis why I was not with the queen when ya called to me and why I wish to stay clear of her. We have met a couple times since then, none of which have ended well."

Justitia lifted her free hand that did not hold the scales of justice. "Are you aware of Queen Maeve hunting the Immortuos Grimoire?"

"Yes, but I only just discovered that durin' a recent visit."

"Are you helping her?"

"Absolutely not. That was another bad row we had." Cathbad affected a pained expression. "Ya have witnessed when she loses control. I promise ya, 'tis far worse when she is in her own realm. No one can stop her when she goes on a rampage."

Loki stepped away, staring off to his right, then turned around, walking with his hands behind his back. He paused to meet Cathbad's gaze. "You are saying you did not help her capture someone to hunt the grimoire?"

Ah. Now Cathbad understood the underlying friction. What had that crazy queen done now? "I do not even know who she captured. Who is it?"

"Casidhe Luigsech."

Unbelievable. Queen Maeve had found Casidhe?

Cathbad would deal with that later. With everyone

watching, he shifted his face into a shocked expression. "Did she now? 'Tis news to me. I had no idea of that kidnappin'."

With the no-lying consequence, he didn't have to *sound* believable, but he had. He'd been so busy hunting Brynhild, he had not spent time trying to find Casidhe.

The oversight had worked in his favor.

Loki crossed his arms and lifted a finger to his chin.

Justitia no longer frowned. Her lips softened but stopped short of smiling.

The idiot on her other side never even paused from strumming a tune meant to be heard alone.

Cathbad wanted to keep the attention on Queen Maeve and not allow the two with a mind up there to ask him pertinent questions about hunting the grimoire himself. He asked, "Are ya sayin' Queen Maeve has found one of the grimoire volumes?"

"No." A small word from Loki spoken with emphasis. "Do you know who Casidhe Luigsech is?"

Just as Cathbad had feared, the two of these three paying attention would zero in on specifics that could hang him. "Aye. While gone on my sabbatical, I visited the mound of Newgrange in County Meath. I heard Daegan of Treoir had been to see a woman who is an ancestral research specialist in Galway, Ireland. I assumed he hunted information on his family, but this sounds as if he also hunts the grimoire."

There was no tie between Cathbad's visit to the great mound and Daegan visiting Casidhe, but every word had been true. He'd presented the information in a simple way to allow this audience to make the connection he intended.

When no one spoke up, Cathbad returned to circling the discussion so that he disengaged himself from Casidhe in their eyes. "I have my differences with Daegan, but I doubt he looks for the grimoires to use them to rule Imortiks. Queen Maeve is another story."

Justitia frowned. What had her upset?

Queen Maeve should be the obvious answer.

Cathbad had to continue to distance himself from her for his own survival.

He continued to bring his tone down to polite and understanding to prevent those on the dais from becoming overly defensive. "As ya can see, this is why I wanted to clear up any confusion about me bein' joined with Queen Maeve. I tire of cleanin' up her problems. I ask as we go forward ya accept that I am only responsible for my actions. Do ya have any more questions?"

"Only one," Loki said. "Do you think Luigsech can locate any of the grimoire volumes?"

Taking his time as if he had to give the possibility serious consideration when he knew the truth, Cathbad pinched his lip a moment. "'Tis possible. If Daegan found her and Queen Maeve found her, that makes me believe Luigsech may know things no one else does."

"Daegan claims a second dragon is pretending to be his red dragon flying around Europe burning lands. What do you say?" Justitia had given Cathbad no warning before unloading that dangerous question.

Loki had been half listening as if deliberating on something, but her question snapped his attention to the discussion.

Cathbad didn't ponder on this one. He frowned and dropped his jaw, then closed his mouth. "Daegan believes more than one dragon lives today? Ya must be jokin'."

Loki speared him with a long stare. "We have not been in a joking mood for a while."

Sighing loud enough to make an impression, Cathbad said, "Daegan may not be huntin' the grimoire after all. He may have somethin' else in mind. Such a story is ... bizarre. Never in history since his birth has there been another red dragon. We all know about his mother bein' a goddess, just not her identity. I have never heard of a second red dragon bein' born. Hard to accept such a claim today by Daegan."

"Just because Daegan believes something does not make it true," Hermes interjected. Loki and Justitia must no longer be shocked when that nitwit spoke. Neither one showed a reaction.

"'Tis correct." Cathbad had never expected support from that corner.

"I have nothing more at this time," Loki said, sounding very much like he wished to end the meeting.

As Cathbad had stood here talking about the dragon imposter, he realized his priorities had changed.

He had to locate Brynhild and take her out of sight. If these three ever found out he'd kept a dragon alive for two thousand years and glamoured her recently to pose as the red dragon, he'd face a worse consequence than lying in a Tribunal.

CHAPTER 19

DAEGAN APPEARED ON THE GROUNDS leading up to Treoir castle where guards were positioned to protect the castle from any attack.

They protected the next generation of Treoirs.

His skin pebbled with thrill over a moment he'd thought never to witness.

Arriving at the same moment, Tristan stepped up next to Daegan. "Are you set, boss?"

"Yes. I shall be here for as long as possible. Brina asked that I be present for the birth of the babes and she is in labor."

"I'd stay if I could but give Brina and Tzader my best. I'll check in on them when I return."

"I shall do so, Tristan. I want ya to remain with Casidhe until she is somewhere safe. I do not wish for her to return to her home, but I expect her to fight ya on where she chooses to go."

"I won't leave her until I know she'll be safe."

Daegan put a hand on Tristan's shoulder. "I have no doubt. Your head is clearer than mine when it comes to her." He didn't mind admitting that to his second-in-command.

"We all have an Achilles heel about someone, boss." Tristan didn't smile when he added, "She may be yours just as long as she doesn't put you at risk."

The warning wasn't lost on Daegan. He merely nodded, unable to say anything when he had no idea what to do about Casidhe. He had gone farther than he'd intended with her, but he could not find the strength to walk away from her.

Tristan snapped his fingers. "By the way, before I came to get you, I teleported Petrina and Bernie here. They'd just finished their patrol." He chuckled. "They were whipped but excited about being a part of the team. I haven't seen Petrina that happy in a long time."

Daegan waited as Tristan seemed to gather his thoughts.

"I haven't done my best by our gryphons, boss. I know they understand when I have to be gone, but as soon as we figure out this Imortik thing, I'm going to start spending more time there to work out how to give them a better life. They've been waiting to be told what to do for so long, it will be nice to get their perspective and turn them into a better functioning unit but happy people, too."

"'Tis a wise plan, Tristan. Please tell them I shall visit soon as well so I can let them know how important they are to me. I, too, often think we keep them safe here, but they are not children to be told to stay home." Daegan noticed more guards filling in around the castle. "Time must be nearin' the birthin'. Go on and take Casidhe to the place of Fenella's phone. I trust ya without question to keep her safe."

"You bet, boss."

As Tristan disappeared, Daegan suffered a moment of wishing to be the one to watch over Casidhe just as much as he wanted to be here for Brina and the babes.

He meant what he said about trusting Tristan to do anything he could.

Mentally giving himself a shove, Daegan hurried up the steps to the castle. He entered then turned right at the wide hallway, moving quickly. At Garwyli's quarters, the door swung open as he lifted his knuckles to tap.

Lanna stood there smiling. "Is time for babies. I am excited." When Daegan stepped back, she took off walking in long strides on her short legs.

Garwyli stepped out behind her with his twisted hickory cane. "I told her ta wait until they call us, but she jumped up and said the babes were comin'. She has a powerful sense about her."

Daegan wanted to run after Lanna, but offered, "Would ya like to teleport, druid?" His power increased while on Treoir to aid short teleporting.

"Aye, dragon. I know ya be just as anxious as that young lass."

Smiling, Daegan teleported them to the sitting area in Tzader and Brina's suite at the far end of the castle. They arrived just as Lanna rushed in.

She stumbled. "I must learn to teleport." Then she glanced around at the empty room. "Where are friends?"

Daegan explained, "In my time, only the closest friends and family were present. Most of those are fightin' Imortiks in the human realm. Brina and Tzader will be pleased to see us."

Lanna had started backing away. "Me? I am not important."

Sighing, Daegan pointed to a comfortable sofa. "Yes, ya are. Have a seat."

When she took the spot he'd indicated, he chose one of the larger chairs for himself. Garwyli tottered over to an identical chair on the opposite side of the sofa, which swallowed his frail body.

Daegan had grown a deep affection for the old druid, thinking to have him for many more years. The possibility of losing him at all, but sooner than expected, was too painful to think on with no idea how to save him.

Lanna had clasped her hands on her lap, but nerves had her fingers moving around.

"What are ya two workin' on today?" Daegan asked,

hoping to lessen the anxiety in the air.

And why did they have anxiety? Did Lanna and Garwyli think the birthing would be difficult?

Lanna stopped twiddling her fingers and looked to the old druid, who nodded at her.

Daegan respected the relationship those two had and that the young woman deferred to Garwyli for when to share her training.

Sitting up, Lanna brushed her blond curls with black tips away from her face. "Garwyli has great patience. He teaches me basic things when I wish to do big things." She smiled at the druid, who chuckled. "He dangles giant carrot to make me work hard. I want to learn to teleport but must understand smaller parts of majik first."

Daegan sat back. "Teleportin' is nice. Have ya tried it before on your own?"

"Yes, I move from one room to second room in TÅµr Medb."

Daegan leaned forward with his hands on his knees. "What were ya doin' there?"

"I traveled with Evalle and Tristan to TÅµr Medb when they try to save gryphons Queen Maeve compelled to attack Treoir."

"They took ya to TÅµr Medb?" Daegan found that hard to accept. He'd only heard bits and pieces of that attack.

"Not exactly. I hide in cloaking and stand close to them."

Garwyli lifted a bushy white eyebrow at Daegan as if to say, "See what I must try ta tame?"

Lanna paused. "Why do we not hear Brina?"

Garwyli lifted a hand, stalling more questions from Lanna. "She asked that I ward the room ta prevent any noise she made."

"'Tis a natural noise, druid," Daegan said, not happy anyone would stifle his niece.

"She said it had been too long since a babe was born

here and did not wish any of us thinkin' she was dyin'."

Now Daegan worried along with Lanna about the quiet. What if Brina did have a problem? She would need their most powerful in the room. Daegan started to call telepathically to Tzader when Tzader opened the door and stepped out.

His dark skin had lightened two shades.

Daegan's heart hit the floor. He stood. "Tell me."

Gripping his head, Tzader said, "It was one hell of a battle, but we have two children." A tear ran down one cheek.

Lanna jumped up grinning and clapping lightly. "I am so happy for you both. When can we see babies and Brina?"

Good thing Lanna could talk. Daegan had lost the ability and his eyes burned.

Garwyli made it to his feet. "Congratulations to you both. Do ya wish ta remove the sound ward?"

Wiping his face with his forearm, Tzader sniffled. "Yes, Garwyli. Thank you. They have strong lungs." He laughed a tired sound.

At that moment one of the babes showed off those strong lungs.

Everyone in the sitting room laughed.

Beyond Tzader, Daegan could see two women bustling around in Brina's bed chamber. One was a Belador healer and midwife who had been brought to Treoir just for this birth.

Daegan dashed away dampness on his cheeks. His father would be proud of his descendants and those of the Belador warriors who had served him. Daegan gave the bitter-sweet thought a moment, then pushed away any sadness.

Treoir had new life.

Garwyli said, "Do ya feel the new power?"

Tingling rushed across Daegan's skin. His dragon rumbled quietly, but energy spread through his body. The Imortik venom still burned through his blood, but he had a fresh burst of power to combat the poison and possibly return to teleporting anywhere soon.

Tzader held his arms out. "Damn. I haven't even thought about what bringing in new Treoir lives in the realm would do to our power, to all the Belador power."

Looking from face to face, Lanna asked, "How much new power?"

Why did she sound so anxious?

Daegan said, "Not huge, but every Belador will enjoy a small surge as a gift shared by all from these births."

She smiled as if that answered her question, but Daegan picked up a sadness about her. He would ask her more later.

Tzader turned around and softly called out, "Ready, love?" Then he stepped aside. "I present our family."

Daegan strode immediately to the door and entered. He smelled all the natural scents of having given birth that might bother others.

Not him.

He hoped this would happen again and again. Walking quietly over to Brina, he knelt next to the bed.

Pale from her exertion, she gave him a watery smile. "Look, Uncle. We have a family, because ya saved us from Macha and other threats. I can never tell ya how much I love ya, but every day these two take a new step I believe ya shall see it."

A rush of love flooded Daegan. His heart swelled with so much happiness it almost hurt for him to feel part of a family again. These beautiful babes would be the future he'd never thought would happen.

He cleared his throat, but emotion still made it difficult to speak. "I love ya just as much, Niece. I vow to protect your babes, ya, and Tzader with my life for as long as I am here."

Tzader walked up and took one of the babies. When Daegan stood, Tzader handed him the tiny bundle. "This one is a boy."

Hands trembling, Daegan took the infant wrapped in one of the blankets he'd seen Brina working on when she would be still. He held the tiny child and inhaled deeply.

This was the reason for every battle he fought. So that his family and the families of Beladors, allies, and humans could live in peace to raise their children.

Tzader picked up the other twin and handed that child to Garwyli who said, "I thank ya for the honor, Tzader, but my old arms may fail me. Would ya allow Lanna ta hold her?"

"Of course, but I never said this was a girl."

The old druid smiled beneath that pile of white beard.

Lanna stepped up and accepted the baby with reverent quiet so unlike the constantly chattering young woman. "She is beautiful. Both are incredible."

"Thank ya, Lanna," Brina said, then moved around in the bed to get comfortable. Tzader was there in an instant to help her. Brina announced, "We have named them. Daegan holds Ronan."

Daegan tore his gaze from the boy. His voice came out in a whisper. "'Tis my da's first name."

"We know," Tzader said, taking Brina's hand in his. "We're naming our girl Caoimhe after Brina's great-and-then-some grandmother."

Daegan's eyes burned again. So unbefitting a warrior, but he would not deny his honest emotions. His voice trembled. "Jennyver's middle name."

"Yes." Brina smiled with pride. "Garwyli has been teachin' Lanna to read the Treoir chronicles. She found your sister's full name."

"I would have told ya," Daegan admonished with a

smile.

"Would not have been much of a surprise then, would it?" Brina beamed like the cat that caught the canary.

Holding his words until his voice would not embarrass him, Daegan said, "Ya do your ancestors a great honor. Ya have blessed this castle with lovely bairns, but ya have blessed me with a gift of the best way to honor my family long gone. I shall hold this day dear forever."

Before long, Tzader announced Brina needed rest and to feed the babes, ushering everyone out.

At the door, Daegan turned to him. "I shall be gone a lot until this Imortik trouble is handled. After that, I hope to be around to dote on the bairns. Try not to worry. Ya take care of your family and allow me to take care of the rest."

"Thanks, Daegan. I would be at your side if Brina and the babies did not come first above all for me."

"As it should be, Tzader. Do not feel any guilt. We all have duties. If we are all successful, we shall have peace again."

With that, Daegan caught up to Garwyli and Lanna walking back to the druid's quarters.

At Garwyli's door, Lanna said, "I would like some air. Do you have something for me to practice now?"

Waving her off, Garwyli continued in the room. "Go on. I need some time ta study the chronicles."

She closed the door and put a finger to her lips then pointed for Daegan to head for the front of the castle. At the doors, she continued outside and down the steps, smiling at the sound of guards cheering. She waved to them.

Daegan paused to announce, "Tzader shall be out soon to tell ya more, but he and Brina have two beautiful bairns. Ya should be very proud of your queen and king."

More cheering. Daegan's chest filled with happiness. The last week had been hellish. He'd almost lost Devon and others, who were still not safe, but Daegan was not finished yet either.

Of all the bad in this world, that moment with Brina's babes reminded him of how much more good filled this world than bad. He had to find a way to save humans, his people, and all others willing to support peace.

Lanna never slowed down, treading quickly across the open field covered in grass to the trees a far piece away.

He'd thought she wanted to talk. Maybe she only wanted air and exercise after all.

When she finally turned to face him, she lifted a serious expression he rarely saw on this one. "We must speak. Too many ears around castle."

He understood. "'Tis good to step away. I wished to ask ya why ya came with Garwyli to the castle where ya met Ainvar. Do not take that to mean I did not appreciate your presence, but ... is somethin' wrong with the old druid?" Daegan hoped his fears would be unfounded. Much as Tristan had become a close friend, Daegan found himself going to Garwyli as an advisor, who filled the place once held by his father.

The young often needed the older ones more than the older ones needed the youth.

"You do not insult me. Garwyli is aging."

"I can see such, but 'tis a natural result of bein' here so long. We are fortunate to have him. If he trains ya to aid him, I find that wonderful."

"You do not understand, Daegan. He trains me to ... " She closed her eyes and pinched her nose, struggling to finish her words.

Daegan sensed a maturity in her recently he'd not noticed before. Whatever she tried to tell him had to be the reason.

Lowering her hand, Lanna lifted her chin in a strong pose. "Garwyli trains me to take his place."

"What?"

"Is true. I do not share his confidence on this. He said if I need to talk to someone you are best one. Others must not know all he trains me to do." Her mouth closed in a tight line.

"What is wrong, Lanna?"

"He says his body is tired and his power is weakening. He claims I am the one he has waited for to take his place as druid." Her voice broke at the end.

Daegan cupped his forehead, wishing for different words. If Garwyli believed what he told Lanna, no wonder he brought her with him to face Ainvar. This young woman carried far more power than anyone had realized.

Not true. They all had recognized her power, but not to the depth that Garwyli had comprehended. Caron, the Fae who helped Daegan's team the day he escaped TÅµr Medb and had taken it on herself to train Lanna a little at first, had to have known as well.

He wanted to be happy for Lanna, but his heart hurt at the idea of losing Garwyli. Selfish on his part. The old druid had stayed in this realm for many generations. He might be tired, but ... Daegan did not want to lose even one of his people.

He asked Lanna, "What does he need from me?"

"I am the one he needs. I train hard, but I need more time before ..."

Daegan lifted his hands in surrender. "Tell me ya do not speak of his death comin' soon."

"I do not have vision of him. Not yet. I only know what I feel. His power is like leak in bucket. Water seeps out. One day, if no new water, bucket will be dry."

Now Daegan understood her reaction earlier. "'Tis why ya asked if everyone would receive new energy from the births."

She nodded.

Daegan had no idea how to help, but he would find a

way to do something. "What ya are sayin' is Garwyli fears ya may not be trained in time for his passin'?"

That had been hard to ask.

Her eyes widened. "Yes, but is not all."

What could be worse? "I do not understand, Lanna."

"I must be ready to help close death wall."

Daegan started shaking his head. "I do not want ya anywhere around that wall when the time comes, Lanna."

She shook her head back at him just as vigorously. "Is not your decision, Daegan. You will have choice. I go to help with wall or Garwyli must be there." She held up a hand, stalling his argument. "If Garwyli leaves Treoir realm at any time, he will die immediately. Being here is only place he can live longer. You need me, but I must know more before I am without him."

The pleading in her voice told Daegan she would do anything to keep her mentor and it had little to do with her majik education. Lanna had become very attached to Garwyli.

Understandable. Daegan did not want to lose the old druid either. Once he found more grimoire volumes, he'd intended to sit with Garwyli and have the druid teach him the next steps to take.

He would have to trust Garwyli's choice in Lanna, but he would need some demonstrations of her ability first. She'd shown her power at Ainvar's castle, but to close the death wall while trying to shove Imortiks inside would be a far greater challenge. Daegan could not face taking her close to this deadly risk without knowing for sure the power she wielded would protect her if he could not.

As if Daegan had agreed to the plan, Lanna continued explaining, "Garwyli say we must have at least me, you, another dragon, and a very, very powerful deity."

Another dragon? Had it been this difficult to close the wall the last time? Probably since all three dragon shifter families joined with powerful deities to stop the first Imortiks.

"I shall have to think on the dragon, but I would like to believe we can find a deity to coerce into helpin' us."

She corrected him. "Not just any powerful being. Specific one."

Disgusted at the possibility of Macha or Queen Maeve being called in, Daegan asked, "Which one?"

Lanna frowned. "Garwyli say I will know when time comes."

Daegan needed time himself to think on all of this, but he noticed Lanna's sadness. Was that about something more? "I am worried about Garwyli, too, but is anythin' else wrong, Lanna?"

She immediately stuck a phony smile in place. "No."

He would not push her to say more when the young woman was taking on so much responsibility. "I feel sure between myself and Tzader, we can help with Garwyli."

"Please do not repeat my words to anyone. I tell you only because I am sure you will not speak to Garwyli of this. He did not forbid me from sharing with you, but we must protect his confidence. We owe him much and that is small."

"I understand and shall always respect his wishes. Ya may trust me to hold your confidence. Feel free to seek me out when ya need anythin'." Daegan wished to draw away all her sadness, but he knew from experience that difficult times made them all appreciate the good times even more.

So many things had happened to remind him of all he'd once lost and all he now had. It sent his thoughts to the dragon in his dungeon.

Daegan had to see Skarde before leaving Treoir. He felt guilty over Skarde not knowing his sister, Brynhild, lived. Daegan had just enjoyed the best moment of his life with the babies. He knew how Skarde felt after being imprisoned for two millennia.

Lanna said, "Do not go to dragon."

Cocking his head at her, he asked, "Did ya just read my mind?"

"No. I have visions. More since staying here and working with Garwyli." She paused and stared unfocused for a moment, then cut her eyes at him. "I must speak of one more thing. I have visions of ring I do not understand."

Hearing her speak of Jennyver's ring again lifted fine hairs on Daegan's neck. "What confuses ya?"

"I told you Luigsech woman will help you find other half of ring, but I have vision of ring very still, then vibrating. Why?"

Crossing his arms, Daegan told her what he knew. "As I understood it, my sisters were given rings with a natural break for separatin' a ring into two halves. If they were kidnapped, they would leave one half at the spot from where they were taken. The other half would vibrate, growin' stronger as it neared the half the kidnapped sister kept in her possession. We were to use the half left behind to track either sister if they were taken against their will."

"Do you have part of ring?"

He reached into a pocket and dug out the half of Jennyver's ring he'd bonded to his body with majik so he would not lose it during a shift. He handed Lanna the ring.

She stared at the carved metal. "This is half I see in first vision. In new vision, this jumps around."

Was she telling him the ring would react if it came close to the other half? That he would find his sister? If he recalled correctly, his sister would have to be alive for that to happen.

But with no other half calling to this one, he might eventually only find bones.

Closing her hands around the ring, Lanna shut her eyes. Her lips moved with silent words. After a minute, she opened her eyes and her hand, giving the ring back to Daegan.

He smiled and shoved it in his pocket.

"The ring will talk to me now," she declared. "I will understand more."

What should he say to that? "Thank ya for anythin' ya can share, Lanna. I must see to a something before I leave again unless ya need anythin' else."

Releasing a delicate sigh, she told him, "Dragon hates you."

Now he understood why she'd said not to go to Skarde. "I know. 'Tis because someone convinced his family I started the Dragani War before he was captured. He knows as little of that time as I do. I wish to give him a reason to talk and start convincin' him I am not his enemy."

"Garwyli teaches me I do not know everything. I must not assume to make anyone else's decisions. Be safe, Daegan." She headed back to the castle.

He tried to shake off the ominous tone of Lanna's words.

Her power could not be questioned, but Garwyli had her training so much he might be overwhelming the young woman.

Facing the castle, Daegan flexed his arms and back. Time to test his power, which should be strong enough to face that dragon now.

He teleported to the dungeon where Skarde's dragon slept.

CHAPTER 20

CASIDHE LIFTED HER ARMS TO steady herself as the teleporting ended on a hill covered in wildflowers. Still, she liked traveling that way.

"Looks like our people picked a good place for me to teleport in unnoticed." Tristan stood calmly, seeming unbothered by that trip. He wore her backpack. She'd offered to carry it and he'd given her one of those not-happening looks that reminded her of Daegan. Many of his considerate and protective actions reminded her of Daegan's.

Tristan's gaze moved constantly from side to side.

She searched the long hill flowing down to a road and drank in the fresh air coming off the ocean. She didn't know how his people had determined this place would allow them to arrive unseen, but it had worked.

She waited for Tristan to move. "What are you lookin' for, Tristan?"

His gaze paused on her. "Just keeping watch."

That sounded as though he expected danger. "You think there are Imortiks here in Scotland?" That thought turned her stomach.

"They could be anywhere a rift opens. Probably not any here since our people would have reported them, but I'm also watching out for Cathbad. Let's try to make this a quick trip if possible, okay?"

"It should not take long to walk to the village and find the location if you can track it on your phone."

"I can."

Tristan had returned her phone fully charged right before they teleported. Casidhe had immediately checked for any missed call from Fenella. None. She'd thought about calling the number again, but what was the point when they were about to find Fenella's phone?

As they walked down the hill, she toyed with the delicate earrings Fenella had given her. Wearing the jewelry had kept her friend close to her.

Keeping up with Tristan's long strides, she attempted small talk. "I envy your ability to teleport. I can't believe I was in America a few minutes ago."

"You wouldn't envy how I received that power." He gave her a polite smile but returned to surveying the area.

"Why?"

He must have noticed how many extra steps she took to keep pace and slowed down for her. "I was locked inside an invisible spelled cage in South America. It kept me imprisoned, but any other supernatural and wild animal could enter. I had to constantly fight to survive."

She stopped. "What? Who did that to you?"

He turned to her. "Technically it was someone I call a friend now, but the goddess Macha had been behind the whole thing. It's a long story, but some immortal warriors coming to kill Beladors broke me out by giving me a witch highball with their blood in it. I'm *not* immortal though, just to be clear."

Her jaw dropped. "You're not a Belador?"

"I am, but it's been a long journey reaching the point where I'm now proud to be one." He waved her to keep walking. "Anyhow, I ended up with the ability to teleport. It's gotten stronger recently, which has been good."

She didn't push him to talk any more. It seemed to distract Tristan. He took keeping her safe to heart. She wouldn't make his job any more difficult.

They'd left the hotel room so quickly, she hadn't had a

chance to tell Daegan about the oracle coming to see her, but she'd share all that when she saw him again.

Her heart did a happy twirl just thinking about him and that he would come to her as soon as he was free again. Short of dying, Daegan would not break his word.

She knew that now.

Tristan used his phone to navigate the old roads, some made with cobblestones. He did an impressive job of never appearing lost while turning time and again, pausing at a narrow passage on his left, which was more alley than street. Casidhe followed him, taking note of the doors to homes in this alleyway. She smiled at the few people milling around outside visiting and one man walking with a bag of groceries.

Tristan made yet another turn that took him to a small courtyard in front of a single home with no one outside. Tristan turned to her. "This is it."

She stared at the door. How long had she been demanding to be brought here? Her feet wouldn't move. "Your people are sure Fenella's phone is here, right?"

"They are. I saw the tracking myself. Her phone is in this location and never moves any farther than a hundred yards from this spot, always ending up here in the evenings." His gaze traveled over the structure, the brightly-colored flowers in pots, but not back to her.

She had a case of nerves. Why?

Casidhe repeated, "The phone moves around."

"Yes."

"And you said no one has made any calls at all on it."

"Exactly."

Something did not make sense, but she couldn't put her finger on it. This was not complicated. Someone had Fenella's phone. It might have been found if Fenella had lost it on the run or it could have been stolen.

Either way, she had to leave here with her friend's phone

so she'd have a starting point for hunting Fenella.

Now was not the time to get cold feet. She'd been so excited to reach her friend, she hadn't thought about the moment of confronting whoever had Fenella's phone.

She finally realized what really bothered her.

Why would Daegan allow her to go to a stranger's home to confront someone over a lost or stolen phone? Why was Tristan standing back and not stepping in to inquire about the phone first?

Wringing her hands, she looked at the door then back to Tristan. "What is it I don't know about all of this?"

He stared over her head and sighed. "We discovered all we could. Our people have detected no danger here. I wouldn't allow you to walk up there alone if I thought there was any risk. You did not want us to interfere, so we haven't." Lowering his face to hers, he said, "Go on, Casidhe. Knock on the door. I'm right here."

Tired of mysteries. Tired of waiting and just plain tired, she walked over and rapped her knuckles on the wooden door.

"Comin'," someone called from inside.

The door cracked open to reveal Fenella with a half-eaten scone in one hand. Her friend's jaw dropped. She tried to close the door.

Casidhe broke free of her shock and shoved her boot in to block the door.

"I can explain, Cas!" Fenella shrieked.

All at once, Casidhe took in this impossible image of Fenella casually having a scone while she'd battled to find her.

Casidhe shoved the door open.

Fenella stumbled back, fear blowing across her face.

A gruff-looking man with graying red hair and standing a head taller than Fenella asked, "Fen? Ya need me?"

"No." Fenella pushed him back inside. She stepped out

and closed the door, leaning back against it.

Heart pounding in her chest, Casidhe shook her head. Scotland. Fenella's home. Everythin came into focus with blinding speed. Casidhe had waited and worried for so long. Now, she struggled to breathe past the pain racking her. Fenella had never been in danger.

This was the moment Casidhe had anticipated hugging her friend and dancing around to celebrate that they both had survived. Not trying to process a betrayal her mind could not understand.

Casidhe's heart whimpered. How many times had she though for sure if Fenella was safe that she would call?

"I'm sorry, Cas."

Those three words shoved a knife through all Casidhe had believed about her friend and her life.

"Why, Fenella? I have gone through things you can't imagine and made deals that put my life in constant danger to find you while you sat here eatin' scones." Casidhe tried to sort it all out in her dazed mind, but there was no understanding this. She demanded, "Who *are* these people?"

"Family. The MacConnaughs."

Family. That word ripped a hole through Casidhe's heart, shredding her. "The MacConnaughs, you say? Your family is *supposed* to be Connell, but that name traces back to MacConnaugh, doesn't it?"

Fenella gave a short nod, her gaze wary.

Did Fenella realize how this looked from Casidhe's perspective?

Did it even matter?

Casidhe had thought she and Fenella were family. Emotion stuck in her throat. She wanted to shout obscenities and cry at the same time.

When Fenella looked over Casidhe's shoulder with a suspicious glance, Casidhe followed her gaze.

Tristan had stepped fifteen feet away and stood with his

back to them, watching the area and giving her privacy. Casidhe turned back. "I am shielding my power, which should allow us privacy."

"But who is he?" Fenella dared to ask in a suspicious voice.

Cold anger filled Casidhe. "That's *my* friend."

Fenella's mouth rounded in surprise.

Casidhe would tell her nothing more. Being humiliated this way by the person she'd believed to be more than a best friend crushed her soul. "Just tell me why, Fenella? Why would you do this to me?"

Crossing her arms, Fenella lifted her chin, showing the strong woman she often hid with her bubbly personality. "I received a message the night I left ya to go pick up goats. 'Twas from ... *him*." She glanced at Tristan again then came back to Casidhe. "He said to leave at once and call no one on the phone. Not even ya. Said it was too dangerous for either of us."

Casidhe wrapped her arms around her stomach and bent at the waist.

Herrick. Every word slashed her into smaller pieces.

Tristan called over, "You okay, Casidhe?"

She'd never be okay again, but she straightened up and found her backbone. She nodded. "Yes, thank you."

Casidhe looked up at the clear sky, because she could not meet the eyes of someone who had deceived her love and trust. The person she'd considered a sister only to find out Casidhe had been nothing more than part of a job.

Pinning Fenella with a look meant to warn her not to lie, Casidhe said, "Why did *he* not send a note to *me*?"

"I doona know. The seer told him of danger." Fenella couldn't meet Casidhe's gaze. "I never meant to hurt ya, Cas," Fenella whispered, her voice breaking. "I have been told what to do and what to say all my life, treated the same as ya."

"*No!*" Casidhe snapped, sizzling anger spreading through her body. "*Not* the same as me. You were kept safe and treated as the family you are."

Casidhe had been nothing more than a tool, because Herrick did not send *her* a message of warning. He had not tried to keep *her* safe.

And Fenella had known the truth the whole time.

The only direction Casidhe had received from Herrick since day one was to study everything about dragon history she could get her hands on, go to college to broaden her knowledge for historical research, and go to Galway to live while maintaining minimal contact with the family. He'd given her a duty and she'd taken it seriously.

She had dedicated her life to hunting for Skarde, because Herrick had obsessed about finding his brother.

Family. She swallowed hard and it hurt. She'd never been family and never would be.

Just an orphan brought in to be his trained monkey and sacrificial hunter, because he'd done nothing to protect her from recent threats.

Only Daegan and Tristan had.

Her friends. New friends. Real friends.

Fenella's hard shell ruptured. She burst into tears. "I doona know what be happenin'. I was warned to stay away from ... the homestead, or the advisor would have me locked up. I only did as told."

The homestead was Herrick's castle and the advisor his seer.

Integrity forced Casidhe to keep Herrick's life confidential even now. Not for him, but for herself. Fenella and the others might not have honor, but she did.

Casidhe took a step back and huffed an angry laugh. "You expect sympathy from me? Really? You grew up in the bosom of family while I fought for every inch of my tiny spot. You sat here, perfectly content even as you knew

I'd be racin' to find you and keep you safe."

The magnitude of this betrayal threatened to fold her in half. Her knees wobbled and her chest ached as if she'd been stabbed repeatedly.

Something she'd missed until now struck her.

She pinned Fenella with a furious gaze and kept her hands clenched in fists. "I just realized why you go by the name Connell. It's not your real name, is it? I was never told when that name changed to a more modern one."

Fenella looked away and said nothing.

"Dammit, Fenella." Heartbreak pummeled her hushed voice. "I was sent here with a real squire name while you were given an alias. He did that to protect *you*. I was clearly bait for... "

Fenella's eyes flashed with horror that Casidhe would finish her sentence. It was so clear now. Herrick had sent Casidhe as bait for the red dragon and it had worked.

When Casidhe said nothing else, Fenella's face softened then crumbled. Her eyes filled with remorse and her lip trembled. "I didn't agree with any of it. I loved—" She sniffled. "I *love* ya."

"Don't," Casidhe ordered, backing away. "Just don't."

Love. What was that? She thought she'd found it with Herrick's group even though she'd had to dig what she clung to as love out from under everything he'd piled on her.

She'd thought she was doing all this for *her* family.

She wasn't even a Luigsech.

Her hands shook from anger and misery.

She was done with Fenella. There were no more words to say, but this was not over. She didn't trust Fenella to give her the correct time of day much less any truth about Herrick.

Still, she would try once more.

"A last question, Fenella, and do not think to lie," Casidhe said in a dead voice. "Do you know my true identity?"

Leaning against a wall of stacked stone, Fenella wiped her eyes and cheeks. She pulled a small cloth from a pocket.

Casidhe had always teased her about being part magician, pulling whatever she needed from a pocket.

Maybe she could find Casidhe a new heart in there.

"No. He told no one."

Of course, he kept it secret. Casidhe was nothing more than a gifted reader he'd probably spent tons of money hunting.

She reached up, fumbling to unhook both earrings. She dropped them on the ground then turned away and walked to Tristan.

Fenella cried out, *"Cas! Please!"*

Tristan glanced at Casidhe with worry etched in his face. "Ready?"

"Yes. Let's leave from here and go to the ancestral centre. She's the only one who will see us, and I don't care."

He teleported her away from Fenella calling her name.

When they reappeared in the centre, Casidhe still shook from hurt and the greatest disappointment she'd suffered. She'd last been here only a few days ago. Felt like an eternity since then. Smelling her precious library did nothing to ease her pain.

This had been her sanctuary forever.

Her happy place.

One big lie. Just like her life.

"Are you sure you're okay, Casidhe?" Tristan asked again gently.

She stilled and looked up into Tristan's eyes. He would let her cry on his shoulder.

But if she broke now, she might never pull herself together. Sniffling, she stepped over to the desk and grabbed a wad of tissues to blow her nose. She would not have a full-blown meltdown in front of Tristan. He'd done enough for her.

Clearing her throat, she pulled her shoulders back. "I'm fine."

He lifted an eyebrow to challenge her lie.

Heaving an exhausted sigh, she admitted, "I have badgered everyone to find Fenella. I've lived in a state of panic that I would never see her again. All she had to do was make one phone call. One stinkin' phone call. You do that much for a stranger. We've known each other longer than many people have been married. I never suspected what feels like an unforgiveable betrayal at all. Not from her."

"Sucks to be lied to by anyone, but even worse when it's someone you care about."

True, but Tristan didn't know the half of it.

Herrick had done far worse than lie to her, he'd used her to lure in the red dragon. He might be thrilled to know how well his plan had worked except for her caring about Daegan.

She'd been unwittingly playing her part in his scheme perfectly.

"I'll take my pack." She lifted the backpack from Tristan and lowered it to the floor. "Thank you, Tristan. Please tell your people I appreciate them findin' her. I won't need anythin' else right now. Thank you for totin' me to Scotland."

Tristan stuck his hands on his hips in a stubborn pose. "Daegan is concerned about you going to your cottage or staying here where someone like Cathbad could get to you."

"I must keep my library safe." Safe from Cathbad for one, but there were others. She waited for him to argue.

"Does that mean you plan to leave it here?" he asked.

"Hell. No. This place does not belong to me. It belongs to ... Fenella's people." If only she felt as confident as that had sounded. She couldn't walk away with no idea if this would all be here when she returned. Even so, the idea of moving hundreds of rare books, scrolls, and other research material brought her another step lower emotionally.

"Then let's do this," he said, sounding encouraging.

"Do what?" She cringed. That had come out somewhere between glum and sullen when he'd been nothing but nice.

He grinned with his arms open wide. "I'm the best moving company you're ever going to find."

"You're goin' to help me move *all* this?"

"Sure. If you have a place to put your shelves, I can teleport a couple at a time with the books on them." He stepped away from her to survey the rear area filled with her books. "I could probably move more at one time, but some might get bounced around. I don't want to risk damaging any of your books."

She couldn't believe what he was offering. After the heartbreaking meeting with Fenella, Casidhe had been ready to wallow in her hurt.

No time for a pity party when she was being offered a way to save her treasures.

Where could she put her books?

Not any of the squire houses associated with Herrick, that was for sure.

She racked her brain, but in the end had to admit she'd been so isolated and dependent upon Fenella and Herrick's choices, she had no backup plan.

Nowhere to take her books besides Herrick's castle.

That was definitely not happening.

He might have an explanation that would repair the damage she suffered, but she couldn't come up with a reason she'd accept right now. Thanks to her trust in Herrick, she had no cottage of her own, no place for her precious books, nothing.

She nibbled on her short fingernails, hating what she had to admit. "I'll have to stay here in the centre for now. I have no safe place to put my library, Tristan."

He walked around then stopped. "I have an idea of a good place to store them until you have a new location, but ... "

She lowered her hand and turned to Tristan. Hope fluttered in her chest. "But what?"

"I have to gain permission first, which I feel certain I'll receive, but you wouldn't be able to go with me when I delivered the books."

"Why not?"

"I would put the books in the Treoir realm. Our Belador queen just gave birth so Daegan will not allow anyone unauthorized to enter that realm, especially with the Imortik threat."

Casidhe stopped listening to anything else after he said the queen had just given birth. What the ever-lovin' hell?

Daegan had kissed her. And more. She was going to be sick.

"Casidhe? You don't look so good."

Her eyes burned and she choked out her words. "That bastard's mate just gave birth and he ... kissed me?" She would not admit more.

Tristan's dumbfounded expression just pissed her off more. Was that lack of morality the norm with Beladors and Treoirs?

"Oh, shit," he muttered.

"I was thinkin' somethin' a bit stronger." She crossed her arms to keep from knocking things over. This day sucked beyond all belief.

Tristan gave her a crooked grin.

Steam might come out of her ears any minute. "You think *that's* funny? Have you men no honor?"

He held up a hand and tried to wipe the smile from his face. "Brina is our Belador queen—"

Ah, great. Now Casidhe knew the name of the woman

she'd played an unintentional role in hurting.

"—and Tzader is our Belador king. Daegan is more of a patriarchal dragon king who watches over Treoir and the Beladors. Brina is *not* having Daegan's children."

Her lips moved to talk, but only one word slipped out. "Oh." Why did she keep defaulting to the worst about Daegan?

Because a lifetime of being trained to distrust Herrick's enemy would take some undoing and being betrayed by the only people she *had* trusted her entire life had done a number on her head. From now on, she would judge everyone based on how they treated her regardless of what Herrick and his squire families had told her.

All that knowledge. How much of it had really been true?

She could never dismiss the conflicting dragon history she'd found in Queen Maeve's library, especially not now.

When Casidhe had time to think harder on all this, she'd likely realize more emotional damage.

The new Casidhe started right now. She'd still make mistakes, but they would be *her* mistakes.

"Just to be clear, Casidhe, there is no more honorable man, human or supernatural, in this world than Daegan." Tristan's quiet words were loaded with respect for the dragon shifter he admired.

"I hear what you're sayin', Tristan. I need some time to rest and sort out things in my mind, but I won't have that time until these books are safe."

"As I was saying, the one place these books would be safe is Treoir realm. I realize trust is a bitter taste right now based on what happened with Fenella, but Daegan would protect your books, as would I, and either one of us would deliver them whenever you asked. No supernatural would dare to enter that realm even if they knew how to find it."

Could she do this? Could she trust people she'd known

less than a week?

She'd trusted an entire clan for most of her life.

See how that turned out? She'd always questioned why it was so hard to fit in and feel at home with Herrick. She'd worked every minute to make herself worthy, but she'd never had a chance.

One look at Tristan's sincere expression and his steady gaze warmed her soul and gave her faith.

In comparison, she'd never had to prove herself to Daegan and his people. They'd accepted her and valued her ability, then protected her. She had no words for how good it felt to not be alone to figure out her next step.

She had nowhere to take her library. What would happen to her library if Herrick figured out that a Belador had helped her find Fenella, which exposed his deceit? He'd become angry and might take everything out of here, especially if she and Fenella were no longer working at the ancestral centre.

Casidhe had spent ten years building this library and a reputation.

The losses kept piling up.

Should she send her books to a realm she couldn't enter?

If Daegan had wanted her library, he could have teleported it all away at any time. In fact, Daegan and Tristan had shown her more compassion in a week than a family of people she'd spent her life around.

She wouldn't be mobile as long as this library remained exposed to every person who could teleport in or break down the door.

Squaring her shoulders, she lifted her clear gaze to Tristan. "If my books go to Treoir, then for some reason I can't find you or Daegan, how would I get them back?"

"All you'd have to do is contact a guy in Atlanta known as Trey McCree. I'll give you his phone number. He can reach any of us from Daegan down to the newest Belador. But I'm pretty sure you'll be hearing from Daegan once he finishes his business at home and sees the new babies."

Drawing a deep breath, she couldn't stall any longer. "Okay, please move my books to Treoir."

"Stand by for a moment while I find out where they go." Tristan's gaze lost focus, just staring at nothing. He nodded his head slightly as if listening to someone, then glanced at her. "Our druid has a huge space in the castle. He said he'd happily open an area for your books. No one enters his rooms without permission. He's a great old guy." Tristan stepped into the back area.

Casidhe followed him. "What do you need from me?"

"If I take two bookcases at a time, will the order matter?"

"No. I suggest you take out all the middle ones first, then we can see how the cases around the walls are anchored."

"Good idea."

Tristan held his arms out and turned his hands as if he were cupping the sides of something. When he lifted his hands, one of her heavy cases elevated a few inches telekinetically, then followed Tristan's movements to end up in front of the case that had been beside it.

Tristan and the first load of her books vanished.

She grabbed two books from the closest shelf and hugged them to her chest, starting to hyperventilate. Was this separation anxiety? How did women ever let go of a child the first time if it scared Casidhe this much to watch her books disappear?

She calmed her breathing. Time to make changes, starting with trusting Daegan and Tristan. Nodding to herself, she put the books back and patted them. She could do this.

It took a half hour of Tristan teleporting back and forth, plus figuring out how to disengage the cases around the walls. Two had been anchored, which required a screwdriver.

Majik had limits on occasion.

When the back had been cleared of all books, Tristan returned the last time and pulled out his mobile phone. He opened his photos. "This is the picture I took of your books in Treoir. I'm sending it to you." He tapped a couple things and her phone dinged.

She opened the photo. "Thank you." How had he known she'd need something to reassure her the books were safe?

"Now we have to find a place for you to stay," Tristan pointed out. "I'll take you to your cottage then ... a hotel?"

"I have a hotel in Galway I had intended to stay in while gettin' my cottage fixed. And before you warn me about movin' back into the cottage, I'm not doin' it right now. I've got a lot on my plate for the next week or two."

"That's good." He looked at his watch. "You ready?"

"Yes. I spent the time while you were teleportin' to clear out my desk. I've got what I need in my backpack." She'd never considered the possibility of being fired and having to clean out her desk, but that's how this felt.

Who would she be after today?

Poor Tristan had been teleporting everywhere for her. She had to do something nice for him when she could figure out what.

At the cottage, she scratched her head, stalling for time to figure out what she could let go. She couldn't move all of her possessions out.

While she forced herself to select the things that had to go, Tristan asked, "You know dragon shifter history, right?"

She laughed sadly to herself, picking up a picture of her and Fenella she put back down. "I know what I've been taught and what I've read."

"What about the ice dragons? Didn't they have a big family?"

She had reached for her small cache of jewelry and stopped. Why would he be asking about ice dragons? She had plenty of bones to pick with Herrick, but she would not share anything that put his clan in harm. She was not that person.

Tristan's steps from the hall stopped at the door to her bedroom.

Lifting a bracelet, she did her best to sound casual about the ice dragons. "I know a good deal about them. Five dragon-shifter children. All died in the Dragani War. Such a shame."

"What if any of them survived? No one thought Daegan survived and he was in a realm all this time. Isn't there a chance one of them might have also landed in a realm?"

Words of Herrick's seer tumbled through Casidhe's mind. The seer had a vision of Skarde traveling between two great clouds, which could have been realms.

Folding clothes to stuff in a tote bag, she shrugged. "It was pretty amazing that Daegan lived this long, but where else would another dragon be? I don't even know how many realms are out there."

"Quite a few. We rescued one of our Beladors who had been kidnapped and imprisoned in a realm with other flying creatures. She's an Alterant gryphon like me."

Casidhe stood upright and angled her head at him. "What other flyin' creatures?"

"I remember wyverns, gargoyles, hard to say how many different ones were captured, but the person in charge came from when Daegan's father King Gruffyn had lived."

Cold foreboding shivered over her skin. She'd heard nothing about this. "Who was that man?"

Tristan scratched his chin, looking up as he thought. "Like the king's accountant or something."

"A steward?"

He snapped his fingers. "That's what they called him.

Anyhow, he cut some deal with a god King Gruffyn's people were not supposed to worship and landed in that realm. Sounded like a bad joke where he had asked to live forever and the god stuck him in a realm." Looking around, Tristan asked, "Is there anything not involving your personal belongings that I can pack?"

She gave him a smile of appreciation. "No. I'm almost done. I'm not takin' much." As she continued pulling together clothes, she couldn't let go of what Tristan had said.

Did Daegan know about an ice dragon? Skarde had vanished when he went to the Treoir castle after the ice dragon clan had been attacked, killing their sisters. Herrick believed King Gruffyn had done something with his brother.

What if the steward had figured out how to capture Skarde?

What if Daegan had brought Skarde out of another realm?

Lot of what ifs, none of which were very credible.

She needed more information, which she wouldn't get until she spoke to Daegan again, but she had one question for Tristan.

Before she could ask, Tristan offered her consolation. "I'm sorry about your friend. I could tell you were shaken by finding her safe and with her phone when she hadn't tried to reach you."

Shook up? More like devastated, but Tristan was being polite to allow her some dignity. He had no idea how deep that wound ran.

She maintained her fake smile, but her flat tone couldn't be fixed. "I'm disappointed in ... Fenella and her people, but I'll live."

He said nothing, but what could anyone say?

Lifting the tote bag straps to her shoulder, she took a last look around. "That's all I'm goin' to drag with me right now."

"I'll carry the backpack," Tristan offered.

She didn't blink an eye. "Sure, thanks."

As Tristan prepared to teleport to a place near her hotel, she asked, "If an ice dragon had survived all these centuries, do you think Daegan could find that dragon shifter for a family? I'm askin' because in this day and age with supernaturals comin' out, I may be asked to hunt ancestors of a dragon family."

"If another dragon shifter survived, Daegan would be the first one told with our international resources."

She didn't feel the thrill of getting close to finding something she'd hunted for many years. Not now. This time she asked for her benefit. She worked for herself starting this minute.

"What would Daegan want in return if he could help a dragon family find a livin' dragon shifter?"

"I don't know." Tristan lifted a shoulder. "If it was a friendly situation, Daegan would help for free when he's not trying to stop Imortiks. He would protect any dragon shifter living today."

"Why? The ice dragons were his enemy."

Tristan studied her.

She did her best not to squirm.

He said, "Daegan tried to protect every dragon clan and hold the peace back when they all lived. He was doing his best to figure out who had been pretending to be his red dragon and pit his allies against him when Queen Maeve captured him. His entire life back then was about protecting the clans and keeping peace."

Conflicting information warred in her mind. "You believe that even without having lived back then?"

"Yes. I trust Daegan with my life and would give up mine to keep him safe. I trust him that much."

She'd have to untangle truth from possibility from downright lies to understand what really happened long ago. She couldn't do that until she sent Tristan on his way so she could plan her next move.

She wouldn't have the help of squire families to travel this time.

CHAPTER 21

BRYNHILD WOKE UP AND QUICKLY looked around. Where was she this time?

Hay. Lots of hay. She crawled across the pile she'd been laying on and grabbed hold of a post and pulled herself up.

A horse neighed.

That's right. She'd decided to talk to the farmer instead of allowing her dragon to eat the man's horse.

Hungry, her dragon's voice rumbled through her mind.

"I know," she muttered, running her fingers through her hair. "I am sorry. We will find food." She had to do something about this mess piled on her head. She no longer had the luxury of using energy to deal with her hair.

The pants and long-sleeved cotton shirt the farmer gave her early this morning were wrinkled, but not dirty. He'd wanted to know what happened to her.

She'd said, "I am not from this country. Someone kidnap me, but I escape. Have walked far." That explained her messy look and injured arm, but the broken bone had healed last night.

Extending her arm, she felt a pinch of pain. Not bad, though.

That was why she suffered fixing a break immediately. After being battered around in the water and losing her first attempt at repairing her arm, she'd feared having to do it all over. She'd been fortunate the arm had healed straight.

Someone pounded on the barn door. Had to be the farmer. Josue. He looked old as the land she stood upon.

She grabbed her hair in a thick wad and twisted it into a knot on her way to the door.

When she pulled the thick wooden door open, Josue held a steaming mug in gnarled hands. He offered it to her. "Café?"

She accepted the warm mug of black liquid and sipped it, scrunching up her nose. "Taste bad."

"I am not so good as wife with cooking. Best I make."

He had a strange sound to his words. That must be how locals in France spoke English. He reminded her of an old blacksmith who had also been a widower. She'd enjoyed watching the man create tools and weapons in her father's forge long ago.

That had to be the reason she softened her words to this man.

"Is not bad, Josue. Just ... different." She added a smile, something she rarely shared these days. Her life had little to be happy about. No family. No friends. No idea what it took to get around in this world and keep her dragon safe. Cloaking only did so much.

"You want see police?"

He'd tried to get her to talk to the police earlier when she'd limped across his field. She'd shaken her head and said she preferred to not expose herself and allow her pursuers to find out she'd survived.

Josue had grunted his understanding, then clothed and fed her.

She could not let her dragon eat his only horse. The horse neighed again at that moment. Her dragon grumbled heavily.

Josue backed up and stared at her chest.

"I am sorry. Stomach makes noise, but I am fine."

His wrinkled forehead creased with suspicion.

Now was as good a time as any to leave. "Thank you for food, clothes, and sleep." She stepped out of the building with him backing up to give her room.

Sunshine warmed her skin. "What time here?"

"Morning. Not yet noon. What about danger?" he asked, concerned about her leaving again.

"I will be fine. I go to next village."

"*Mantes-la-Jolie*?"

She had no idea what he had said, but assumed he'd spoken the name of a village. "Yes. That one."

Waving her forward, he hobbled around the barn and walked to the road. She kept up with him. At the dirt road, he pointed to the right and gave her directions.

Just to get away, she nodded, but had no idea what he had said.

He dug in his pocket and pulled out several folded pieces of colorful paper. He held out his hand for her to take it.

She stared at the paper, trying to determine if she should take it.

"*Argent*." He made a motion of handing the paper to invisible people. "For food."

This was the man's form of payment. She took the folded bills, not sure how to feel about someone giving her money for no reason. She'd lived well as a revered dragon shifter in her father's kingdom, never wanting for a thing.

She'd been nothing but alone, angry, and confused in this world. She'd spent last night plotting multiple deaths.

But this man with so few possessions, who toiled the land by hand, had a generous heart to share with a stranger.

She gave him a bow as she would an ally to her father. When she lifted up, she found him surprised. Then he bowed to her.

A laugh bubbled out of her.

He grinned, showing off all three of his teeth. "Go safe."

She waved and struck out down the road, feeling more at peace than she had since discovering she'd outlived her entire family. Anger only drained her. She would put more effort into finding her way in this new life and not fighting everyone.

Only those she needed to kill.

After she had walked a few miles, she left the road in search of a place to shift into her dragon with no one watching, then cloaked them.

This time, as her dragon flew around, they searched for a much larger farm with thousands of cows in different sections. What she needed was a section with cows roaming free. When she located that, she had her dragon land in the pasture and sit very still.

They waited for maybe an hour before a cow wandered close enough to extend her cloaking around the cow. Her dragon blew a coating of ice over the cow.

The beast mooed then stood perfectly still.

With the closest building two pastures away, her dragon ate quickly while Brynhild kept them hidden.

Now that her dragon was full, their healing intensified.

She nudged her dragon to fly again.

Soaring through the blue sky would never get old to her, but now she had to dodge those human flying machines. When she saw what she believed to be the village the farmer had pointed her toward, her dragon slowed. She would not call this a village. Too large and developed.

She found a spot to land and shift into her human form. With her energy restored, she clothed herself with nicer pants than the farmer had given her and a shirt of soft material, both pieces she'd seen other women wear. No shoes with tiny spiked heels this time. She had never been small and needed no additional height.

She chose the flexible sneakers again. If only she had time to go back and take her hoard out of that cavern, but Cathbad couldn't be trusted not to set a trap for her. She had nowhere to hide it yet either.

First, she would figure out how to fit into the human

world like any other woman, then she'd come up with a plan for outwitting that druid.

One that included cutting off his head.

Thinking of painful ways to kill him relaxed her.

She walked around for a while and paused at times, sensing someone watching her. If Cathbad were here, he would show himself soon. His ego would not allow him to hide from her.

By the end of the day, she'd seen a magnificent cathedral, restaurants, businesses, and observed many women. Men who smiled at those women did not show her the same interest.

They stepped away as if she had leprosy.

She had been a sought-after female in her world. A well-regarded dragon shifter. Favored daughter of her father, even if her two sisters did not agree.

A wave of hurt and loneliness washed over her. She would never see her sisters or brothers again.

She had not one friend in this world.

Her sisters would have figured out how to dress and act in this world faster than her. She would never have admitted that back then, but they lived for clothes, parties, and to be chosen as a mate.

Brynhild had not wanted Daegan as a mate, but he had not allowed her the chance to save face by her rejecting him first.

The bastard.

When another man hurried past her, Brynhild paused to think and decided to make the first change in her new life. She backtracked to a place where she'd noticed women entering earlier with long hair then walking out with a whole new appearance. She could hide among humans with the right hair and clothes.

After a confusing discussion with the woman in charge about the paper she carried, the woman took one slip of paper and handed Brynhild back more paper. She washed Brynhild's ratty hair and massaged her head then tried to brush out the tangles.

Brynhild held up a hand for her to stop.

She dug through several magazines from a nearby table and flipped pages quickly. When she stopped, she stabbed her finger at the image of short hair as blond as hers.

The woman's eyes widened. "You want your hair *that* short?"

"Yes. Do this."

She thought the woman would refuse her request at first, but an hour later, Brynhild walked out of the shop feeling ten pounds lighter. She could do this on her own with majik next time.

The woman offered to apply makeup and Brynhild turned her down. She only needed to hide her face from those around her when she used majik to add kohl to her eyes and color to her lips.

With all that done, she walked the streets, taking in so many strange things. Everything had changed in thousands of years. Even the tantalizing smell of food had her wanting to eat in spite of having fed her dragon. She found herself studying every detail of people she encountered just as she would an enemy.

Now men turned their heads for another look when she passed, but she ignored them and their odd need to whistle. She was no dog to rush over to a man.

She took a seat at a small table under a covering outside a restaurant late in the day. Many people ate outside on the street.

That sensation of being watched rippled down her spine.

Her dragon slept but would rise in an instant.

She endured another conversation about the paper money from a server, who waved off the money. Did that mean she would eat and drink for free or pay later? If the paper was not enough it would be the server's fault. She'd tried to show him what she had to offer.

People moved along the walkways, laughing and carrying small boxes the size of their hands they spoke into.

Men took their time giving her long looks as they sauntered around.

One had caught her eye, but he continued on.

How did women and men join in this time? She might not understand the world today, but she still knew what her body enjoyed. Unlike her sisters, she had not been excited about marriage. She would never let Daegan know he'd saved her by turning down her father's marriage proposal.

If he'd had any honor, he would have waited for her to turn him down.

She'd watched her brothers and preferred the freedom men of her time had possessed. In fact, she found it encouraging to see women today living life on their own terms. She'd enjoyed her share of men and booted them out of her bed the next morning if they made any sound of wanting a mate to stay home and have children.

No one would stop her from fighting battles, the one place she felt alive.

Wind ruffled her short hair. See? Another freedom.

No woman in her time had worn short hair unless they were being punished. She smiled over her new look. She would find her way and become a power to be respected and feared in today's world.

She'd been sitting there enjoying her wine and meal of thin ham and cheese on succulent bread for a while. The sun would give up soon and disappear. A pleasant breeze fluffed up napkins and sent crumbs to the ground for birds ready to peck.

A man sitting on the far side of the outdoor dining area caught her attention. Even with him sitting, she could tell he would be tall. She liked a man she could meet eye to eye when standing. His short hair and his narrowed gaze gave him a daring look, but his pants and jacket were modest. What an interesting conflict in appearance.

He caught her watching him and smiled.

She lifted an eyebrow at him. Was this how men and women joined up by meeting at a place to eat? He lifted her spirits and woke the woman inside who missed being in the arms of a competent lover.

She would not go to him. She sat back, lifting the wine glass to her lips and swallowed slowly.

His smile slowly vanished, replaced by a look of hunger. His throat moved with a quick swallow as if she'd surprised him.

Men should not know a woman's every secret.

They must earn those hidden parts a woman revealed and not until she found the man worthy. Brynhild kept her smile hidden but studied him boldly. She was no shrinking woman who had been coddled. She liked a challenge.

They stared at each other for another ten minutes.

She wanted him out of the shadows so she could see his face better. In the past, she had been excellent at reading a man's intent by his eyes.

She ignored him to eat the last of her food and finish her wine. Would he follow her once she left?

When the server returned, she handed printed paper used as coins to him. He stared at the paper in disbelief. She prepared for some conflict over payment, but the sexy stranger appeared next to her table. He spoke rapidly in what she assumed to be the local language, taking back her paper in exchange for paper he handed the server.

She expected a problem, but the server cleared the table, thanked her, and vanished.

"May I sit?" the man asked in the most proper tone.

"Yes. Was paper wrong?"

He sat across from her, taking up all the space around

him just by the force of his presence. He had a handsome face and smiling eyes. "You did nothing wrong, dove. You offered a much larger bill than required for the cost of this meal. I take it you are not from France."

She shook her head. Why would he call her dove?

"I intervened to keep the young man honest."

The server returned with two glasses of wine and placed one in front of Brynhild.

She lifted her hand to stop him. "I did not order."

"I did, dove. I would like to get to know you." He lifted his glass as the server left. "Cheers."

She lifted hers. "What is this *cheers*?"

"It's something we say when we touch glasses. It means the same as a wish for health and happiness."

Clicking her glass with his, she took a long swallow.

His eyes never left her neck. Up close they had some blue mixed in with whiskey colors.

She enjoyed a smug moment of being in control again for the first time since waking in that cavern. Cathbad did not stand over her, lecturing her as if she were an idiot. She'd warned him she was no child and he should not test a warrior dragon shifter.

Over the next two hours, she and the stranger drank lots and lots of wine. Brynhild had always been able to hold her mead with the men of her time, but she did experience a pleasant light-headed sensation.

Not ready to end her best day ever since waking in this world, she considered one more glass of wine. Perhaps this human would become a favorite toy for a day or two while she learned many things from him.

"We are done here," he announced, placing paper on the table.

Her heart dropped. He thought to walk away from her now?

"Don't look so sad, dove. It's getting too busy here. I'd

like to go somewhere more private." His eyes offered intriguing things in this private place.

"Why?" She was not being coy, just curious. Coy was for young maidens.

He paused, looking out over the city. "I have been alone a long time and have had a few encounters with women who amused me, but you ... " His intense gaze returned to hers. "I have never met one so sure of herself. You don't amuse me. You fascinate me. This place has become too loud for a private conversation."

"Where would we go?" She sat back. This would be the first step in him earning more from her.

His lips tilted with a humble smile. "I am not the best with words for wooing a woman. For that reason, I speak my mind and accept whatever you say. I wish to invite you to have a glass of wine on the balcony of my hotel not far from here. You will have a gorgeous view of the city at night." He stood and offered her his hand.

She hesitated a moment and caught the pain of embarrassment flash through his gaze, then she took his hand.

He smiled, drawing her to him as they stood eye to eye. Placing the back of his hand on her cheek, he whispered, "I doubt any view will match the one I have right now. I know that may sound like phony line you have heard from many men, but I am sincere. I fear you walking away to find someone more worthy."

This man understood her.

Heat coiled in her womb at his light touch.

She had missed this mating dance with men. She wanted the stranger and would have him.

"Show me this balcony," she ordered in a husky voice. "I wish to see ... more."

He sighed, sounding happy she'd accepted. Walking her down the street, he turned at a street she had not seen, then he continued, taking another turn. When he angled off the walkway to a covered entrance to a building, a man dressed in a formal black outfit opened the glass door and gave them a nod.

The world swirled around her from the wine. She could burn off the lightheaded feeling if she changed into her dragon, but why? She could handle a human without any help should he think to lead her into a trap.

They passed through a palace-like place with people behind a counter making tapping sounds when not speaking to strangers standing on the other side. The cool air did not feel natural. Her soft shoes were silent crossing the marble. He pushed a button and walked her into a box that began rising.

What was this thing they rode in? She did not ask and embarrass herself. She could learn more on her own.

Or from this man if tonight turned out as she hoped.

"I love this city." He lifted her hand in his and kissed her knuckles. "I hope I have the chance to show you more."

She allowed him to lure her to him with his pretty words but did not want to make any promises.

He lived in rooms just as stunning as downstairs with thick rugs, soft-looking sitting furniture, and lots of glass for walls. Walking to the glass wall, he pushed one part aside, leading her to his balcony. The view had not been overstated. Lights sparkled across the city spread out before them. She could see the huge cathedral she passed on the street from here.

He called it Notre Dame while telling her about the city as they walked. The man sounded as if he had the information about surviving in this world she needed.

She might stay right here in this city for a while, learn all she could, then find a place to store her treasures.

She might even end up with a friend if he did not disappoint her.

After enjoying another glass of wine while he pointed

out interesting spots to visit, he took both glasses and put them aside.

When he turned back, his hazel-blue eyes twinkled. "I have not enjoyed myself so much in so long. I thank you for such an evening."

Yet again, she wondered if this meant he would go no farther. If so, modern human men would be a great disappointment. She had been willing to hold back her dragon energy and not burn this one when they mated, but she might burn him for leading her on and quitting.

He cupped her chin and leaned in to kiss her but paused before their lips touched.

He waited for her permission?

A man from her time would have known by now he had permission. Tired of dancing around the whole point of this, she leaned in, kissing him.

His arms went around her back, pulling her closer. Strong muscles rippled beneath his shirt. He hid his physique beneath the simple clothes.

She ran her tongue inside his mouth. He smiled, kissing her back.

Now he understood.

She grabbed each side of his shirt and ripped the buttons off.

"It's going to be like that, huh?" he asked with a lift of his eyebrows.

She shrugged. "I am hungry."

"Oh, dove, so am I." He kissed her with authority this time and she shivered. His hands pushed up beneath her blouse and touched her breasts. She wore nothing under these garments, because she had not reached that point in her studies.

Also, because her breasts expected freedom, too.

His thumbs brushed over her nipples. "You are exceptional."

She shivered at his touch. Finally, a man who appreciated her, one who had skill with his hands. She ran her greedy fingers up and down his chest. He had the build of a warrior, not the soft men she'd seen so often while walking around the city.

She ached for this one to be between her legs, to feel all of him. Running one hand down, she cupped his hard length.

He bit her lip lightly and groaned. His tongue played with hers, moving in and out, driving her into a frenzy. He unzipped her pants and the material pooled at her ankles. She stepped out. His fingers brushed back and forth through her heat.

She clenched hard and demanded, "More."

He stroked her and pushed inside, teasing her to reach for her release. She clutched his shoulders, going up on her toes, and moving with him. "Yes, much more."

He grabbed her at the waist and picked her up, nibbling on her nipple.

"Hurry," she demanded as he carried her into the room.

Lowering her feet to the soft floor covering, he spun her around and bent her over the tall back of the long seating piece.

Yes. This was what she wanted. She enjoyed the anticipation of what he would do and stretched her arms out. Her fingers gripped the hard shape beneath the cushions to keep her from going all the way over.

Spreading her legs, he reached around and cupped a breast. His other hand slid in from beneath to draw a finger through her damp heat at a pace that sent tremors through her.

After so many years, she could not remember past matings.

This felt vulnerable and exciting at the same time.

He whispered, "I need you, but I want you ready."

"I am ready." Had she yelled that?

"Not yet. Close." His fingers between her legs changed rhythm, pushing two inside of her. He taunted her nipples, driving her mad. Her body came apart. She shook with a release that kept going. He would not stop until she slumped.

He caught her around the waist, pulling her back to his chest and kissed her ear. "Now, you're ready, dove."

She smiled, still enjoying the aftermath. "That was ... exceptional."

He chuckled then scooped her up and carried her to the front of the long seating where he dropped her onto thick cushions. She did like the new furnishings in today's world. So much softer than those of her time.

"What is this furniture?" she asked, sounding very at ease. Being in control had that effect on her.

"An over-stuffed sofa. You are truly the most enticing woman I have ever met." He removed clothes as he spoke, revealing a staff she took her time admiring.

"I like this." She stroked a hungry glance to his chest and lower.

"The sofa?" he asked with a teasing lilt to his voice.

"Yes." Her gaze lingered on his manhood standing proudly. "Like everything I see."

He dropped down, knees on each side of her hips. Lifting a hand, he brushed hair from her eyes. "I just realized what a cad I am. I should have asked this long ago, but what is your name?"

"Names are not important." She had not cared what he called himself while trying to decide if she would have him. Names were words, a value only to shallow people.

He didn't say anything, just leaned down to thoroughly kiss one breast then the other. "Your name is important. I want to savor this memory in case we have only tonight."

She twisted his hair between her fingers, feeling her body hunger for his again. This time, she would have him begging for more. "I am Brynhild."

"That's lovely," he murmured, kissing her chin, then her neck and pausing at her breasts to lift his head. "I am called Joavan."

CHAPTER 22

"I NEVER THOUGHT I'D SAY I'M tired of killing demons, but I'm done for tonight." Evalle leaned against the foundation holding up a bazillion-story high-rise building in Buckhead. Looking up to count the floors would hurt her neck.

Adrianna looked no better than her, which was saying something about that woman. Shoving wet blond hairs off her forehead, the witch ran her hands to her ponytail she tightened, then she let her arms dangle. Probably from fatigue.

Looking in each direction down Peachtree Street, Evalle huffed out a tired laugh. "I have never seen this road in any part of Atlanta without traffic this close to business hours starting."

"Fighting demons in front of humans will do that. That one bunch didn't even stick around to film it."

Evalle pulled out her phone and found a text from Storm. He worried when she was out so close to daylight. She'd normally be home by now, but not this week. She replied she'd be home soon. Before shoving it into her back pocket, she noted the phone had only two percent charge left. She could charge it in Adrianna's car.

Stretching her stiff muscles, Evalle felt torn over using Reese to help them. "I know Quinn doesn't want Reese out in this mess, but we almost found that demon maker again. Looks like Quinn and Reese have reached some agreement. I don't like putting her at risk either, but she seems determined to find and deal with that I-zubrrali."

"True. Do you really think that's her father?"

"I don't know, Adrianna, but Reese seems to think so. I thought I had the worst sperm donor in the universe. She may have me beat."

Adrianna stifled a yawn. "Let's head to my car."

"If I have enough power left, I'll call Storm now. If not, I need a quick charge from your car."

"You know he's probably cooking dinner and pouring wine, ready to make you forget all your pains. Why call him out when I can drop you on my way?"

"I'm dirty as hell." Evalle brushed at her BDU shirt that had so many tears the khaki-colored material hardly covered her.

Adrianna waved off her concern. "That's what detailers get paid to clean up. Don't knock them out of work."

"Since you put it that way, glad to donate to the economy." Evalle lifted away from the wall. They walked to the parking deck a block away where Adrianna's sexy ride waited on the top level.

A pickup truck pulled out before they entered, surprising Evalle that anyone was still in the parking decks after all the commotion on the street ten minutes ago. Humans normally scattered when a supernatural battle started. At least, humans not with a black ops team hunting her kind.

When they reached the top level, Evalle sensed a vibration in the air and lifted a hand for her friend to stop. "You feel that?"

"No, what was it?" Adrianna unclipped her keys from her belt.

"Weird buzzing." Evalle started moving again, but slowly, and looked around.

Adrianna continued to her sleek Lamborghini, pressing buttons on her keychain to make the engine crank before she got within thirty feet.

A bright-yellow body climbed over the four-foot-tall wall that prevented cars from driving off the parking deck.

"Adrianna," Evalle said quietly.

Already backing up, Adrianna killed the engine to her car and said, "I see him."

Kill her, screamed in Evalle's mind. She grabbed her head. "Shit. It's a Belador-Imortik. He yelled in my head."

Help me, Evalle. Help me, moaned over and over. The Belador-Imortik dropped to his knees, shaking his head back and forth. He knew her, but she didn't know him.

"I can't kill him, Adrianna."

"I know, but we have to be careful not to let the Imortik that has him grab us. Remember how the Imortik jumped from the troll to Devon's body before the troll tossed him off that building?"

"I know. We need help," Evalle decided.

"Much as I know you hate to deal with Sen, that's the only way we're going to save this Belador. Do you know his name?"

"No. Give me a second." Evalle called out telepathically, *What's your name, Belador?*

The guy lifted his head and crazed glowing eyes stared at her. A demonic voice growled out loud, "Do not talk to him. He is mine."

Evalle had no time to waste. "You watch him while I make the call to Trey to get dickhead here." Because of Trey being mobbed with telepathic calls, she opened her phone and typed a fast SOS text.

Trey sent back, *I'm on it*. Then her screen went blank.

Sen could find anyone he wanted in this city just by giving him a name.

The Belador-Imortik stood again and started forward.

Evalle shoved up a kinetic wall between them.

Adrianna said, "I might be able to stun him with a small shot of Witchlock, but I can't be sure what it will do with any Imortik."

"Let's leave that as a last option." Evalle braced her feet as the man ran forward and slammed her wall, shaking her arms with his power. When he fell back on the pavement, the guy grabbed his head, crying telepathically. *I don't want to die. I have a wife and baby.*

Evalle repeated that to Adrianna then called out loud, "We're gonna save you from the Imortik. Just hang strong."

The guy lifted insane Imortik eyes to her again. "The master will kill you."

"Bring it!" she shouted back and slammed each boot down to release the blades around the sides of her heels. She might have to cut him a little, but she'd find a way to knock him down until Sen got here to take that Belador to VIPER.

Daegan had made a deal with the Tribunal.

They couldn't kill anyone until Daegan said so unless he failed to deliver the person behind releasing Imortiks to them. Too complicated for her. All she cared about was saving this guy right now.

Energy flushed all around her. "Sen's here." She glanced to her right at six-and-a-half-feet of misery and called out, "We've got him pinned down and just need you to transport him to VIPER."

Sen curled up his lip. "I should have known better than to come here. I don't have room or time for your crap."

"Then make room!" Evalle snapped back. Sen had always hated her for some unknown reason, but she would not allow him to make another Belador pay for his attitude toward her. "Aren't you a demigod? Doesn't that fall under your job description?"

The Belador-Imortik jumped up and slammed the kinetic wall again. Her arms shook.

Adrianna shouted, "Come on, Sen. Deal with this."

"You should have said so right away." He flicked a finger at the man and power lit up the yellow figure in a bright glow. He fell backward and stopped moving.

"What the fuck!" Evalle yelled and ran over and knelt next to the smoldering body. She lifted the guy's charred head. "You killed him, you bastard! He had a wife and kid."

"The witch said to deal with it. You don't like the results, be more specific."

Evalle hugged the guy, murmuring, "I'm so sorry."

Adrianna launched into Sen. "You really don't care what the hell you do to any living being, do you?"

"Why would it matter to you, witch?"

Placing the man back on the ground, Evalle turned to see Sen's arms crossed over his thick chest and blue eyes glowing. "Did you do that just because you hate me so much, Sen?"

"That's exactly why," he bragged with a smirk. "Look at the upside. I'll probably have room for the next one you people try to pawn off on me."

Evalle fisted her hands. "Daegan is not going to accept this."

Adrianna shoved her hands on her hips. "We're all sick of your shit. We're trying to stop Imortiks, but not kill all of our own while doing it. I could have knocked him out without killing him."

Sen rounded on her, voice deepening. "If that's so, why didn't you?"

Adrianna got a wild look in her eyes, one that should not be on a witch who controlled Witchlock. She spoke in a low voice chock full of menace. "Maybe I should give you a demonstration of how that would work."

Evalle felt a wave of energy blast past her. "Uh, Adrianna, we don't need a demonstration." If her friend lost her cool with Witchlock, she might take out a couple city blocks. And Evalle.

"Shut the fuck up, Alterant," Sen snapped at her. To Adrianna he said, "Let's be clear. I don't give a fuck what body an Imortik jumps into. I've been told to kill Imortiks. End of discussion."

As Adrianna walked toward him, her signature control crumbled with each angry step. "You're a disgusting being."

"Do something, witch. I would love it."

She opened her hand and energy spun in a white glow the size of a baseball.

"Adrianna, we're good," Evalle said, trying to take the tension down a notch. A flicker of light outlined the eastern horizon. Daylight was coming and Evalle had to get out of there. First, she needed to call in someone to take care of this Belador's body. She couldn't do anything until those two powerful beings calmed the hell down.

"No, we're not good, Evalle. He just murdered a Belador and thinks it's funny."

Evalle took a step toward Adrianna. She hated what Sen had done, but Daegan would have to deal with VIPER's liaison.

Sen's gazed dropped to Adrianna's spinning ball of Witchlock energy. He had enough survival sense to back up.

Power burst all around them in a bright glow.

"I hope like hell that's Daegan," Evalle muttered, but turned to face a being she'd never seen before. He had blue-black hair that did not fit with the chalky skin. His thin lips belonged on a chicken with the missing chin.

Those swirling white eyes with red centers were the problem. That gaze screamed of power.

Energy hovered in a dark cloud around his copper-colored robe marked with black symbols all down the center.

The Adrianna vs Sen dustup paused with them two steps apart.

Sen amped up his nasty tone. "Who the fuck are you? I've had it with bullshit today."

"How dare you kill Imortiks!" the supernatural shouted.

The entire parking deck shook and rolled as if they stood at the epicenter of a 5.0 earthquake.

Evalle danced around to keep her footing.

Adrianna closed her hand and executed her own sideways two-step.

Pointing at the dead Belador-Imortik, the new being bellowed in a craggy voice, "You shall pay for showing off to your girlfriend."

"My *what*?" Sen's jaw dropped.

Adrianna looked at the guy as if he'd called her a sleezy crackhead.

Evalle glanced at the horizon, lightening by the second. They had to move this along before her time ran out.

As if talking to a child, Sen said, "There is no more room at the inn, dumbass. I've been told to kill Imortiks when I see fit."

The copper-robed being lifted his hands high and roared. Then he flicked one hand at Sen and the other at Adrianna.

They both disappeared.

CHAPTER 23

CASIDHE PEDALED HER ASS OFF on the bicycle she'd rented. She'd exited Galway quickly and hurried through the countryside to the small village of the ancestral centre once Tristan left her hotel.

She'd feigned exhaustion, which wasn't hard to do when she needed a good night's rest. But that was the key to sending him back to Daegan before she grabbed her backpack and took off.

Once she reached her village, she didn't stop until she turned off the main road and weaved her way to the side door at the rear of the building.

This one normally stayed bolted from the inside, but she'd unlocked it while Tristan had been teleporting her books to Treoir. She still had momentary panic when she thought about her library not even being in this world.

Propping the bike against the wall, she looked around. No one came back here very often and not so close to dark. She opened the door, walked the bike inside to prop out of the way, then bolted the door again.

Thanks to Cathbad, the door to the once-secret tunnel still flopped open. Adjusting her backpack, she stepped into the tunnel with her LED light in hand and pulled the door shut behind her. With the latch broken, it swung open.

Her abs had a workout while she made the long walk to the hollowed-out-tree exit. But she would not leave that way and risk anyone following.

Besides, she'd have to cross a lot of fields to get anywhere. She'd scouted the tunnel years ago and found another way out, but it would be some work just getting that part open.

First, she had to clean out the tree storage.

She kept only a few things here, one being the screwed-up looking ring Herrick had given her to protect. What importance did this ring hold? It didn't even seem to be complete, as if the ring had been one of those puzzle rings that had to be put together.

She'd convinced herself for ten years that he'd given *her* something precious to show her how much he cared.

Now she looked at everything with suspicion and clear eyes.

She lifted the black velvet pouch holding the ring. This jewelry had a story and she'd bet it was connected to the red dragon in some way. While she now tried to keep an open mind when it came to things concerning Daegan such as the Dragani War, she fully intended to filter every word Herrick said from here on out.

Every time she recalled finding Fenella hiding safely with her family, Casidhe felt a punch to her stomach.

No stranger could ever hurt her any more than those she'd believed to be family.

Clutching the bag, she had so many questions. She'd searched for the history of this ring but had found nothing.

Herrick knew the history and sent it with her for a reason, not as a gift.

She was not cherished. She was not family.

She'd worn the odd ring on a chain around her neck during her college days to prevent it being stolen from her dorm, but she always worried she might lose the ring if her chain broke without her noticing. To be honest, she had never understood the value of what appeared to be a partial ring as if it had been made in two parts joined all the way around and one side broken off. Turning up the velvet bag, the silver links of the chain pooled in her hand along with the ring piece.

She hooked the clasp behind her neck and dropped it all inside her shirt.

Herrick had a lot of explaining to do.

With a last look to insure she left nothing she'd worry about, Casidhe backtracked a third of the way down the tunnel. She'd found this offshoot by accident many years ago while curious about everything to do with the centre. She'd felt a wisp of air while pausing here before she got into shape to walk that distance bent over. Not as easy as it might seem.

Running her hands over the rough stone now, she moved a foot at a time to her right.

When she couldn't find the indentation to use as a handle, she started to move her hands faster, trying not to panic.

If Daegan went to her hotel and discovered she'd left, he'd hunt her. Tristan had said Daegan might be a day or two taking care of issues in Atlanta, but she didn't think he realized the vow Daegan had made to her in Tristan's hotel room.

Her heart clutched sharply at not leaving him a note to keep him from worrying, but she couldn't risk it. Daegan had ways to find her. Nothing she said would convince him to stay put where he'd be safe and she really had no idea how to explain what she was doing. She could only hope to reach a squire house and get word to Herrick. She'd wait a day, which would expose if Daegan came for her right away. He would not sit back and watch.

Not now.

He'd knock down any doors between them. If he did, she'd convince him to leave. He would do as she asked as long as she came back to explain herself.

By day two, she would take off to reach Herrick's land.

Herrick would not expose himself if Daegan followed her, which would prevent those two meeting. If Herrick did not meet her in the canyon, she would walk to the warded castle and wait until night to slip through the ward. That should keep those two from a bloodbath.

Asking him to not follow her would be like asking a giant tree not to fall after a tornado ripped the roots out of the ground.

She'd dug out Fenella's cash jar at the centre while waiting on Tristan going back and forth to Treoir. It was only fair. Casidhe had taken only what she needed to travel fast and left the rest.

She had been conditioned to believe all money came from Herrick and all money she earned belonged to him. Fair enough. He could pay for this trip.

With some luck, Casidhe would return to the hotel before Daegan mounted a search for her.

That would be a very fast turnaround, but she had no intention of staying at Herrick's castle once she got her questions answered.

Her fingers dipped into a hole in the rocks and clutched a familiar feeling metal.

That had been the easy part. Removing the covering not so simple.

After a lot of grunting, swearing, and sweating, she managed to pull the rocks away and open the metal shield enough to push her backpack in. Then she squeezed her body through.

Dragging the cover back in place was probably a futile effort, but it might slow down someone if they followed her. She'd sent Cathbad's book along with the other ones she'd been carrying to Treoir with Tristan by hiding those among the other volumes.

That seemed to be the best way to keep that evil druid off her trail, but who knew? If Queen Maeve had not discovered what Cathbad had been up to, he would have the benefit of her scrying wall Daegan talked about.

Casidhe sat in the dark, heaving breaths and wiping sweat from her face.

Knowing it was too small for him, Daegan would come down this tunnel to find her.

He'd scent her and use his force to open the wall to this offshoot even if she'd tried to hide it. She had to get moving. Regardless of what Tristan had said, she'd been around Daegan enough to expect him to teleport in today to check on her.

She had to escape everyone and travel to Herrick without any other dragon shifter or supernatural following.

That would end in a bloodbath.

If not for that, she'd have asked Tristan to teleport her close to Herrick's castle.

Hefting the backpack into place, she killed half a bottle of water, stowed the rest, and lifted her LED light. This tunnel had not seen activity in a long time. She'd taken a long, dirty day to find her way to the end just to be sure it provided another exit point.

That had been ten years ago.

She hoped the boots with her jeans stuffed in the top meant staying dry. She recalled one low spot with water to her ankles. She wore layers of a tank top, short-sleeved cotton shirt, and a long-sleeved flannel shirt. The temperature remained moderate down here, but she'd need clothes where she was going and could only pack so much.

In the first seventy yards, she perspired heavily in spite of the cool air and moving slowly. She should reach the exit in another fifty or sixty yards, but the ground had begun to slope down.

That should mean the ground would begin to rise soon.

She splashed into water.

No problem. She shined her LED down only to find

black liquid. She took another step and it dropped an inch. Not so bad, but if this became any deeper, her nice clean socks and jeans would be wet and dirty. Roots had grown through the opening and followed the wall. Not too surprising after a century, but she hoped roots had not caved in some of the tunnel.

Fifteen slow steps ahead, her boot dropped into a hole, sending her into waist-deep water before she could pull the other foot around.

"Dammit!" She moved the left boot forward and found the other side of the caved-in spot.

"No problem. Stay calm and pull hard," she whispered to herself when she was anything but calm.

She leaned forward and yanked her right boot but couldn't move it. Her heart thudded so loud in her ears she expected to hear an echo.

Had mud sucked her boot down?

She wiggled her toes, trying to pull her foot from the boot. If that happened, she'd still have to figure out how to free her shoe. It felt like her boot was trapped under something. She ran her light around the walls and found lines of roots on the right side running down into the water.

"*Come on!*" she shouted. "Give me a break."

That might have been the wrong thing to shout at the universe. If she broke a leg, she wouldn't get out of here.

She kept working her foot back and forth, lifting up, and in different directions to back out of whatever had her caught. Best she could figure, her foot had slipped through an opening between two roots.

This was not working. Maybe she could chop the root off. She reached over her shoulder, grabbed her sword by the hilt, and yanked.

The blade would not come out of the sheath.

After three more hard yanks, she dropped her head. That sword was ridiculous. Dragging in a deep breath, she rasped out, "I need help, *Lann an Cheartais*."

She tried again.

The sword wouldn't budge.

Her mobile phone would not work down here.

What if Daegan didn't come to check on her for a day or two? Or couldn't find her?

She yelled at the top of her lungs, *"Stop screwin' with me! I have had it."*

Light shined from behind her.

She lifted a trembling hand over her shoulder and curled her fingers around the hilt. "Please, *Lann an Cheartais*."

The sword slid free, its glow tossing off light as she pulled it over her shoulder. Staring at the weapon, Casidhe said, "I just want to cut some roots. I don't want to lose a foot in the process or cut myself and bleed to death."

She jabbed the blade tip down in the water.

CHAPTER 24

DAEGAN TELEPORTED INTO THE DUNGEON under Treoir castle, suffering a moment of guilt over having not told Skarde about Brynhild. If the ice dragon before him had not rocked the castle so much he disturbed Brina close to her birthing, he might have.

Far back inside the dark cave, Daegan had created a lair for Skarde's dragon. The ice dragon rose and stared down his scaly snout at Daegan with fury seething.

Daegan said, "I have good news for ya. Brynhild lives."

The ice dragon's eyes opened more, then pinched almost closed again.

Skarde's dragon slapped his tail against the walls of the cavern, making the whole place shake. Eyes flaming with cold-blue anger glared at him.

"I warn ya one time only, Skarde, to not shake the castle or carry on as an overgrown bairn. I come to ya in good faith to share news I would think to please ya." Daegan waited as Skarde's dragon looked away then back at Daegan with doubt replacing anger. But hope lived in those eyes as well. "Ya do not believe me? I have no reason to lie. My dragon fought hers. Ya are not the only one who suffered for thousands of years in another realm. I was imprisoned in TÅµr Medb the same time."

A flicker of surprise moved through the ice-blue dragon eyes.

"'Tis true," Daegan continued, determined to take this small opening and widen it. "I went to TÅµr Medb to see my sister, who Queen Maeve claimed had become very ill. 'Twas a trick. Queen Maeve caught me in her realm where she held the most power and had a beast attack me. I shifted into my dragon. A great mistake in hindsight. She was ready and placed a spell on my dragon, forcin' it into the shape of a throne. 'Tis where I spent all these centuries."

Skarde sent no words telepathically to communicate, but his dragon's tail had stopped moving around as if agitated.

Daegan waited for something, anything from Skarde to confirm he accepted what he'd heard, but no. Releasing a frustrated blast of air, Daegan asked, "How can ya not believe your sister lives? Ya were trapped in the Scamall realm as a young man and would still be there had I not teleported ya here. Ya do remember Cathbad the Druid, do ya not?

No reply, but the slight lift of the ice dragon's head could be a yes.

Ruadh spoke in Daegan's mind. *Ice dragon is not ally. Sees us as enemy.*

Daegan understood his dragon's words, but Ruadh did not care about coaxing someone to act logically or behave with honor. His dragon only cared about saving Daegan and his people when it came to other dragons. But Daegan had once been the glue that held every dragon family together as allies.

He wanted that for the few dragon shifters still living.

He continued to educate Skarde on what had happened in his absence from this world. "Cathbad and Queen Maeve did somethin' majikal to fake their deaths long ago and slumber for thousands of years. They recently were awakened or reincarnated, but they live today. I have heard different versions, but I was there when they both appeared again for the first time before I escaped. I tell ya this so ya shall know how Brynhild can be here just as we are."

Daegan kept a close watch on Skarde's dragon's every move. As he'd talked about Cathbad, the ice dragon seemed to show interest.

He continued, "I do not know everythin' about what happened to Brynhild as she was in no mood to talk with me the one time we met. What I do know is Cathbad recently captured my second-in-command of our forces. The druid took my man to a cavern where he'd been keepin' Brynhild hidden inside a ward."

The dragon eyes staring at Daegan glowed bright with anger. Good. Maybe he was getting through to this hardheaded dragon shifter.

Daegan added, "My man helped Brynhild escape, though she almost killed him."

The ice dragon smiled.

Daegan shook his head at how hard he had to work to get this dragon to accept he and his people were helping Skarde and his sibling. "From what I was told, Cathbad had placed Brynhild's dragon in a frozen pond inside that cavern for two thousand years. She has endured bein' imprisoned somewhere just as we had to endure bein' trapped in realms not of our choosin'."

Still not a word from Skarde when he could speak mind-to-mind even if his voice might not work.

Daegan might be fighting a no-win battle. If so, he'd have to figure a way to take Skarde out of this dungeon so his dragon could fly. Leaving a dragon locked away like this went against everything Daegan believed in.

But he could not risk allowing Skarde to fly around Treoir if the man was not willing to talk to him. So little to ask.

"What must it take for ya to realize there are few of us around, Skarde? I am doin' all I can to protect those still livin'. I allowed my dragon to be injured just to avoid killin' Brynhild's dragon. I shall not keep puttin' my people and dragon at risk if ya are not goin' to step up and work with me."

Skarde's dragon turned away.

Stubborn bastard.

Speaking telepathically this time, Daegan shouted, *Dammit, at least talk to me. Brynhild spoke to me and it cost her nothin'.*

Silence and more silence.

Daegan scowled. "I shall return, but do not expect me soon." He made a move to leave.

Wait. The single harsh sound whispered through Daegan's mind. Skarde's rough voice would make sense for someone who had not spoken to another being in thousands of years, even telepathically.

With arms loose at his sides, Daegan waited, but the ice dragon spoke no words out loud. "Ya test my patience, Skarde. Ya should recall I have none with an enemy. I have shown ya all I can in hopes we can once again be allies. I do not like to leave ya here, but I cannot trust ya around my people if ya do not at least talk."

Daegan had said enough. He crossed his arms and returned a flat stare.

I will talk, flowed into his mind in a painful raspy sound.

Still, Daegan held his tongue. He had to see a sincere effort before he took another step in Skarde's direction physically or verbally.

The ice dragon lifted one leg after another as he stepped from the lair at the back of the dungeon, moving its large body forward. Blue reptilian eyes blue as ice chips never moved from staring at Daegan. The dragon's breath blew out in white puffs.

Daegan stood ready if Skarde made an aggressive move.

He'd warned this dragon shifter once already to not attack him again. When Skarde buried Daegan in ice one time, Daegan had called up his red dragon's hot energy and melted it. He'd left the ice dragon sitting in a lake of water while it slowly drained over several days as a reminder.

What do you want, red dragon? Skarde asked when his dragon paused in moving around.

Speaking out loud, Daegan said, "I wish to speak to ya in human form, man to man."

After a tense moment, the ice dragon's head swayed from side to side in an agitated motion more so than denying Daegan.

Could Skarde still shift into human form?

White foggy puffs blew out from the dragon's snout, flaring again and again.

In a soothing tone, Daegan said, "Shiftin' to human may seem impossible at first, but ya can do it. When I escaped TÅµr Medb and broke the curse on my dragon, I had help from my people. At that moment, I wanted freedom more than anythin' and called up my human form with no problem. I do not believe ya shall become stuck between forms, if that troubles ya."

Skarde's dragon lifted his head and stared over Daegan's head for a long time.

Daegan waited, not rushing the dragon shifter. Hope sat like a lonely stone in his chest.

Energy stirred around the ice dragon. Power built and swirled until it blurred the lines of Skarde's dragon. Bones cracked with loud pops.

Daegan grimaced. Slow shifts were painful.

The silver-blue dragon began to shrink still slowly at first, then all at once the cloud of energy expanded and disappeared, leaving a man standing in its place.

Seeing Skarde as a man just younger than Daegan took him back so many years. His heart pounded at facing someone alive from his past.

He'd been too shocked about Brynhild to feel this rush of excitement, but there stood a living part of his history. Naked and too thin, Skarde still looked the same as Daegan recalled with his scruffy blond beard, white-blond hair, and deep-blue eyes always full of suspicion. There stood someone whose family had been allies of Daegan and his father.

Emotion flooded his mind and senses. Daegan cleared his throat. "Hello, Skarde."

Skarde licked his lips, which were dry and cracked, then opened his mouth. "I do not understand ... this." The words sounded as if he'd swallowed broken glass.

"I shall explain all I can. I have had some time here and people giving me aid to adjust. I offer the same aid for ya."

"Why?"

Daegan sighed with disappointment. "Brynhild believes I started the Dragani War. I did not. I was on my way to see your father to join forces so we could figure out who was behind pittin' dragon clans against each other. I told ya I went to see my sister in TÅµr Medb first and ... my life ended there. I never saw my da or anyone else alive again, until now."

"Your red dragon ... " Skarde drew a couple breaths and his words so much like Brynhild's with a Nordic influence, but in a deeper voice, came out. "Dragon seen burning our lands, killing our people."

Holding back his frustration, Daegan asked, "Did ya see my dragon with your own eyes?"

"Reports."

"Someone was tryin' to make a dragon appear to be red like mine. In fact, Cathbad used majik on Brynhild without her permission to give her the ability to blow short blasts of fire when he took her from the cavern. He even glamoured her dragon to look red. I am thinkin' he could have been behind the Dragani War as he lived when we did."

That clearly confused Skarde, who grimaced. "Where is Brynhild?"

"I do not know. She fought me and flew away. I did not want to fight your sister. Instead, I stayed back to help my man who had been injured."

After a few more long seconds, Skarde asked, "Do you have family?"

"I have my father's descendants here in Treoir but lost everyone else from my past." Daegan would not share how the ring in his pocket had begun to move around and vibrate at times. Neither of the ice dragon siblings would care if Jennyver lived.

Queen Maeve had gloated when his other sister living with the evil queen died. Daegan did not doubt that death.

Skarde stood perfectly still with a sad look in his eyes. Perhaps he did recall how their families had all been friends at one time.

Daegan asked, "Do ya need me to clothe ya?"

Lifting an eyebrow at Daegan, Skarde asked, "Why?"

"I cannot take ya outside around my people if you cannot clothe yourself when ya shift to human. There are families about."

"You would take me out of here?" Skarde asked with the awe of a dying man finding out he would live.

"Aye. 'Tis been most important to me. I only waited for ya to talk to me. I need your word ya shall not harm any of mine."

Skarde licked at his lips, frowning. "Why would I harm an innocent?"

Why indeed. Daegan took this as a positive sign. "I do not believe ya would and hope ya do not believe I would now or would have all those centuries ago."

"How many?"

Daegan angled his head with confusion. "How many what?"

"Centuries."

"Two millennia."

Color washed from Skarde's face. "No."

"'Tis true. 'Tis also true that ya, I, and Brynhild live today. I shall help ya find your sister."

Nodding as if having a conversation with himself, Skarde said, "I would like to leave." His face showed the strain of clothing himself in leather pants. He left his feet bare and wore no shirt, but Daegan said nothing.

He had to give a man room for pride.

In the next moment, Daegan teleported Skarde to the center of the wide lawn leading to the castle.

Skarde took in the castle, the guards, and a group of mothers and children of Belador families brought to this realm to protect. The women appeared to be entertaining the children in the shade of old trees.

"I see little difference," Skarde muttered.

"Treoir has changed some inside the castle, but nothing like changes in the world of humans. Do ya wish to allow your dragon to fly? The exercise would be good. When we return, I would like for ya to share a meal with me and allow me to introduce ya to some of the others." Daegan would not expose Brina and the babies to anyone, but he'd like Tzader's impression of Skarde, as well as Lanna's and Garwyli's.

"Yes. I believe I can shift again much faster."

Giving Skarde a quick nod, Daegan explained, "I shall teleport us to a mountain top to give your dragon a high place to fly from."

"Yes."

Sighing at the effort this took, Daegan did not want Skarde shutting down again. "I do ask that ya talk to me as we fly."

Skarde nodded.

Ruadh rumbled heavily. *Not ally.*

Daegan sent back, *Give him a chance. To be alone so long is difficult for anyone. Skarde has no family or army here. He would be foolish to attack us.*

Ruadh quieted, but Daegan still sensed his dragon's misgivings.

He enjoyed a stronger press of power in Treoir and teleported the two of them to a high mountain he'd visited multiple times.

When the ice dragon shifter appeared again, he shook his head as if to clear it, then looked around, ready and alert.

Shucking off his pants, Skarde shifted to his dragon.

Daegan had been ready and shifted quickly into Ruadh, then lifted off to be flying first. Once Skarde changed, his dragon took a couple hops and leaped from the mountain, flying perfectly.

Seeing that did not surprise Daegan. Skarde had been in dragon form when Daegan rescued him from the Scamall realm. No reason for his dragon to have any difficulty here.

Daegan started the telepathic conversation. *'Tis nice to find two people from my life before being captured, Skarde. I am willin' to help ya and Brynhild settle in this new world if ya work with me.*

I have nothing to offer the red dragon.

Trying not to take offense at Skarde's tone, Daegan said, *Ya have much to offer. Supernaturals are bein' exposed to humans in this new world. Peace has never been more important.*

The ice dragon flew too close to Ruadh, who roared and maintained his position, knocking Skarde's dragon back.

Skarde yelled, *What are you doing?*

Daegan grumbled to Ruadh, *I do not want conflict when the ice dragon flies too close. I am tryin' to gain an ally.*

Ice dragon aggressive.

Daegan would always take Ruadh's side, but he wished for a chance to build a bridge with Skarde. *No dragon would handle what we went through, certainly not Skarde's. Can ya try to do this for now, Ruadh? I would appreciate your help.*

I fly. I fight. You talk.

That was pure Ruadh.

Daegan followed as Skarde's dragon angled one way then the next, likely testing his wing strength. He told Skarde, *Your dragon must be more careful to not fly into mine. If he cannot manage here, he will bang into tall buildings in the modern human world.* Not that Daegan planned to take Skarde out of Treoir any time.

My dragon is excellent in air.

Daegan dismissed Skarde's defensive tone. His dragon flew with the red dragon, known as the most powerful in their time.

Still was.

Leaving Ruadh to keep pace with the ice dragon, Daegan shifted back to explaining more about the new world. *Ya shall not have to worry about the human world yet. Ya are safe here.*

The only sound that followed was that of the wind rushing across Ruadh's wings.

After a long silence, Skarde asked, *Do you intend to keep me here?*

At the moment, monsters known as Imortiks are escaping from a rift into the human world. They take over bodies and have taken over Belador bodies. Treoir is the safest place for a dragon for now, was all Daegan would say.

Ruadh banked hard to the right, following the ice dragon.

Daegan gave up talking. It would be easier once he sat across from Skarde sharing a meal.

They flew in silence until Skarde's dragon noticed the Alterant-gryphon village where some of the members gathered as if discussing something.

Where did you find a clan of gryphons, Daegan?

Surprised at the question, Daegan replied, *'Tis a long story I wish to share when we take a meal.*

As the dragons flew closer, some of the Alterants stared up in surprise at seeing them.

Daegan spotted Tristan with his sister, Petrina. Tristan glanced up for only a moment and returned to what he was discussing. He probably listened to reports from gryphons having experienced their first patrol duties in Atlanta. Petrina talked with her hands flapping around.

Tristan had to be proud of his sister. She would have everyone down there ready for duty in no time.

One of the gryphons took flight, drawing Daegan's attention. He told Ruadh, *Keep an eye on that gryphon. I do not want it close to—*

Skarde's dragon folded his wings, dropping fast.

Ruadh whipped around to follow, but the ice dragon had a jump on them.

Daegan yelled, *Stop, Skarde! Do not touch anyone unless ya wish to die.*

I am dead, Daegan. Brynhild does not live. My brothers do not live. None of my family lives and the woman I loved is dead. But you have everything.

Ruadh folded his wings too close to the ground.

Daegan yelled telepathically, *Gryphons, shift now! Fly out of the village.*

Two shifted immediately into gryphons.

Tristan jerked his head up. Petrina dragged her gryphon friend, Bernie, who looked shocked senseless and stumbled in her wake.

Skarde's dragon blasted a load of ice at the gryphons heavy enough to crush humans.

Ruadh opened his wings, ending his fall painfully, and blew short blasts of fire at Skarde. Any more might pass Skarde and kill the gryphons below. Daegan's dragon pummeled Skarde's dragon with strike after strike until the ice dragon made a hellish cry and flapped wildly.

Ruadh flew down close and hooked giant claws in the ice dragon's neck and flapped powerful wings hard, yanking Skarde's dragon off course from the gryphon village. As soon as they cleared the village, Ruadh stopped flapping and dropped his full weight on Skarde's dragon now falling fast toward towering trees.

Daegan warned, *Take care not to break your bones, Ruadh.*

His furious dragon said nothing. At the last moment, Ruadh released Skarde's dragon and shoved off, sending the ice dragon body crashing into trees and breaking limbs. The sheared-off sharp top of one tree impaled a wing.

Arching up and flying fast, Ruadh blew out a stream of fire fifty feet in the air and roared at his victory. He banked around and flew toward the village. From a distance, piles of frozen rubble and collapsed cabins dotted the normally tidy area. Most of the gryphons had shifted back to human form and were frantically digging through razor-sharp piles of ice.

Ruadh said, *I told you.*

Ya were correct, Daegan conceded then swept a gaze over all the gryphons as he took head count. He stared at the village with a sinking feeling.

Where was ... ?

Daegan shouted, *TRISTAN!*

DIANNA LOVE

TREOIR DRAGON CHRONICLES
OF THE BELADOR WORLD
BOOK 6

CHAPTER 1

SWEAT RAN DOWN THE SIDE of Casidhe's face in spite of cool air in this dark underground tunnel. Standing in chest-deep water and facing the possibility of dying here jacked her pulse out of sight. She hadn't left a note at the hotel for Daegan to shield him from the danger of meeting up with Herrick. She did not want a battle of those two dragons. Unfortunately, she'd told Tristan she needed some time to herself.

Daegan would be honorable and respect that, dammit.

"No whinin'," she muttered, tired of standing in water.

She'd gotten herself into this and would find a way out. Moving her booted foot again, she wiggled it beneath what felt like a crisscross of roots trapping it.

Her routinely insubordinate sword had surprised her by finally sliding from the sheath after another obligatory begging. The blade pointed down, now glowing underwater. One would think that would illuminate the black hole, but she could see nothing past a few inches beneath the surface. All she had to do was cut enough roots to free her boot, then finish trekking the rest of this tunnel to the escape point.

Not a big deal, right?

More sweat trickled down her face.

Her backpack pulled on her shoulders as if it held big rocks when she'd only packed clothes and other necessities for traveling.

Not even a heavy book this time.

Had she made the right decision in sending her books with Tristan to a realm she couldn't enter?

Her books were safer than her at the moment. Good point.

"Stop stallin'," she grumbled, which did little to fill her with confidence.

If she jabbed wrong, the razor-sharp blade with a cranky attitude might slice through her boot and take her toes off.

She blew a breath upward, knocking a damp lock of hair from her eyes and poked the sword slowly around her feet. She tapped around, feeling for an opening for the tip.

Nothing yet.

Maybe she should have taken her normal escape route she'd used for years, but every supernatural person looking for her could pick up her energy trail, her scent, or whatever, to follow her. Someone with a larger body than her average size would have a tough time following the main tunnel, but it would be even more difficult to reach her here.

That's why halfway through the main tunnel, she'd broken loose the dirt and rocks covering the entrance to this off-shoot from the primary path.

She'd told no one about this alternate route for the ten years she'd lived in Galway.

Not even Fenella.

Casidhe hadn't hidden anything about the tunnels from her friend. The woman did not like to be in a small place and feared darkness. Avoiding conversation on it seemed considerate.

Shoving harder, her sword skipped off toward her leg.

She froze.

Her leg felt intact. She took a deep breath and kept moving the tip around six to eight inches from where her boot felt stuck. Panic rattled her chest.

She could die here.

Would anyone care if she never showed up again?

Not Fenella. Maybe not even Herrick if he had decided she was disposable.

Her stomach soured with the lingering hurt of betrayal.

Fenella had been her closest friend for ten years. Her *only* friend.

No more. That's why Casidhe needed to reach Herrick's mountains before Fenella sent a message through the squire family system to him.

Fenella's family, not Casidhe's. She had never been part of any family. Only someone trained to do Herrick's bidding.

Light from the sword dimmed.

Shoot. "Okay, I'll try harder," she pacified the sword, which had a mind of its own at times.

Taking a couple deep breaths of dank tunnel air to steady her grip, Casidhe changed her hold on the hilt and prodded around her boot with more effort. She slowly pushed her muscles, silently begging the damn sword for help.

Evidently the sword approved. Light glowed really bright beneath the surface.

If she lopped her toes off, she should be able to grab them when they floated up.

Pressure on top of her boot backed air up in her chest. What was the sword doing?

She pressed down a tiny bit and the root moved down on her boot. The sword blade must be right on top of *the* root. Easing the blade to her right, she tapped a couple times.

That confirmed what she thought as the tapping didn't put pressure on her boot again.

She hoped.

Only one way to find out for sure.

Closing her eyes to enhance her sense of feel, she started sawing up and down over the root. After a couple minutes, it felt as if she made no indentation.

Was the root dead and petrified?

Her shoulders drooped. She could not stop now. Moving the tip around, she tried to find a place to pry the root aside so she could wiggle her foot free of the boot. Not ideal, since she would face continuing without one foot protected against the chewed-up floor of the tunnel, but that beat staying here.

A distinct sound of rocks hitting the ground way behind her stopped her motion.

She'd been focused on her task and failed to pay any attention to noises. There shouldn't be sounds down in this tunnel except water dripping and her exertions.

She held her breath, listening.

The bare clacking of rock on rock sounded again. Was someone down here?

Her heartbeat took off like a rabbit trying to outrun a mountain lion. She tried to stay quiet while putting renewed effort into stabbing the damn sword around to free her boot.

"*Cassssidhe,*" sang through the air in a whisper. The voice sounded male.

Chills raced up her arms. Who was in the tunnel with her?

Heart pounding furiously, she jabbed the sword down hard. Missed her toes, but still failed to break any root.

"*Cassssidhe.*" The whisper gained strength.

Her body trembled and her hands jerked the sword. "*Cut the root!*" she hissed at the sword and shoved the tip down again.

The blade slid off the root.

She wanted to scream.

Gripping the hilt with white knuckles, she begged, "*Please,* please cut it." Once more, she jammed the sharp tip down and the blade kept going into the root. Now it was stuck.

Oh, hell.

"*Casidhe!*" the angry male voice shouted. "Bring me my book!"

She knew that voice. Cathbad.

What would he do when he found out she'd sent his book to Treoir with Tristan?

She wiggled the hilt back and forth, trying to free the sword. It wouldn't move an inch and wouldn't pull straight up. Damn irritating weapon.

"Ya need to come to me, Casidhe. I know ya read the section I warned ya to not read without me. 'Tis fine by me. Now I can call ya to me."

Could he do that?

Hell, yes. He was a druid thousands of years old.

She had to get out of here fast, which was pretty much impossible without power.

Furious, she hissed at the sword, "Either help or get out of the way, dammit."

Light glowed brighter beneath the water. The sword yanked down hard, pulling her shoulders to the water. She strained to keep her chin dry. She couldn't even pull her hands from the hilt.

Well, hell. She'd pissed off an ancient sword.

All of sudden, the sword eased up. She pulled it gently as she raised her body upright.

She turned her boot back and forth, working it free of the roots now that a big one had been cut.

"I am not jokin', Casidhe. I would prefer not to bang yar head, but I have no control over how my power drags ya to me, only that it will obey me. Ya have until the count of ten to convince me ya are comin' back, but no more. I am out of patience with everyone at the moment."

Go to him voluntarily or get dragged by majik? Screw that.

Cathbad shouted, *"One!"*

As soon as the blade cleared the water, she waded forward, her boot free and foot still inside it.

"Two."

Her body moved faster than she would have believed possible for slugging through the rocks and mud. Terror would do that to a person. The uneven ground tossed her off balance.

"Three."

She swallowed the urge to whimper. What would he do to her? Now she could walk, but only bent over.

"Four."

Her legs and back muscles burned, but she would not stop. If she felt herself go backward, she'd try to use the sword to brace her.

"Five."

The sword stopped glowing.

Of course. She shoved the blade into the sheath in her backpack, leaving her arms free to pull her through a narrow opening.

Her body stopped suddenly. The blasted backpack got stuck.

"Seven."

Wait. What happened to six?

Wiggling out of the straps, she turned and yanked, dragging her pack through the opening. Rocks and dirt fell loose from above.

"Eight."

The next steps were slow and difficult through areas she had to turn sideways to pass through. The backpack needed to slim down, but that wasn't happening. She dug in her heels and leaned back as hard as she could.

"Nine."

Tears burned her eyes. Fear gave her another burst of power. She leaned forward then threw her body backward toward the exit, pulling with all of her weight.

The backpack broke free.

She landed on her bum.

A cracking sound rippled overhead. Then another.

"*Ten!*" Cathbad roared.

CHAPTER 2

Treoir realm

STUNNED, DAEGAN STARED THROUGH RUADH'S eyes at the gryphon village covered in piles of ice. Where was Tristan?

Ruadh blared a roar that shook the trees.

Ice exploded from one side of the village.

Tristan's gryphon burst free and screeched furiously, answering Ruadh.

Daegan felt a jolt of relief unlike anything he'd experienced in a long time.

Hurry, Ruadh, Daegan urged telepathically.

His dragon flew a tight circle, dropping as he did until his giant wings flared. Wind from his approach blew sheets of ice crystals away, but piles of jagged ice remained.

The gryphons in human form rushed away to clear a spot for Ruadh to land.

Frozen water covered their wooden cottages and the ground. Those in human form were stunned silent. Two gryphons that had managed to fly away now returned, landing on top of the ice. They attacked chunks of ice with their claws to start clearing the cottages.

Tristan changed back to human form. Daegan clothed him in his normal jeans and T-shirt attire. Tristan turned to shove piles of ice away from where his gryphon had broken free of the ice.

Daegan shifted, clothing himself as he ran over to give

aid. Tristan must have shifted into his gryphon as the ice hit and tried to protect Alterant-gryphons.

His sister, Petrina, and Bernie were not anywhere to be seen.

Tristan shoved ice piles aside with Daegan clearing more just as fast.

Daegan could have had Ruadh melt the ice, but he feared endangering anyone beneath it. "How many are buried?"

"Petrina and Bernie are right here, not far under." Tristan used kinetics to lift a tall pile of ice now dripping as it melted. He tossed that fifty feet away in an open spot then heaved a deep breath at the site of Petrina.

Tristan pulled his sister free first, hugging her to him.

She gasped for a breath, heaving hard. *"Bernie!"*

Daegan saw a leg sticking out between her ankles. "Ya may have been sittin' upon him, lass." He grasped a large section of ice, breaking it free from the pocket shielding Bernie.

The Alterant-gryphon's bright green eyes were wide open, but not moving.

Relief washed through Petrina's face. Her deathly pallor regained some color.

She dropped down and patted his cheek. "Bernie. Wake up, Bernie." Then she lowered her lips and blew air into his lungs.

Bernie's arms reached for her. His mouth formed a smile.

She lifted away and chuckled. "Come on, Sleeping Beauty." She offered him a hand, pulling the skinny guy to his feet.

Daegan assessed the damage. Those two suffered a few cuts, but Petrina held her left arm close to her chest. Wounds on Tristan's back oozed blood through the dark gray T-shirt Daegan had given him.

Guilt slammed Daegan's middle.

Petrina rounded on him. "What the hell was that?"

Tristan put a hand on her shoulder. His green eyes glowed brighter than usual with a promise of retribution for harming his sister. "I will deal with this."

She pulled back and wrapped her good arm around the injured one. Water from her soaked short hair ran down her angry face. "No. This is not on you. That dragon attacked our village."

Daegan spoke up, powering his voice so all would hear. "Petrina is correct. 'Tis my fault and I apologize to all of ya. As ya know, I've kept that dragon in the dungeon since we returned from Scamall with him. I would not allow him to leave until he spoke to me in person or by telepathy. That happened today and ..." Daegan shook his head. "I believed he was ready to be among people of this time. I had no idea he would mentally break and attack anyone. I assure ya he will return to the dungeon and remain there."

Shoving wet hair off her forehead, Petrina lifted her chin. Feminine green eyes flashed with the need for vengeance. "Why don't you let *us* teach him a little lesson first?"

Tristan hadn't taken his eyes off his sister.

Daegan sympathized over the terror Tristan had suffered. It could be no less than the moment he thought he'd lost Tristan as well as the others.

Though he'd been fortunate to have Tristan at his side since coming to Treoir, Daegan still knew little about the backgrounds of Tristan and Petrina, something he would remedy once the Imortiks were stopped. Tristan had shared how he first met Petrina in what he'd called the equivalent of a foster home run by a nonhuman. Tristan had decided to protect the fierce young woman even before he became an adult, creating a bond stronger than that of blood siblings. From the anxious look in Tristan's eyes, Daegan's second-in-command never expected his sister to be in danger on Treoir, and she shouldn't have been in this realm.

While Petrina did not carry the same family blood as Tristan, she had the heart of a warrior just like him.

Daegan explained, "While I would enjoy seein' the ice dragon face all of ya to pay for his dishonorable action, I have much to deal with in Atlanta and other places. I wish to lock him in the dungeon immediately. I do not wish to leave Treoir without him secure. How badly are ya hurt, lass?"

She scoffed. "Nothing my gryphon healing won't take care of quickly. Tell that dragon our gryphons are tougher than him."

While Daegan was proud of her, Petrina and Bernie had blood stains on their clothes. Even with gryphon-healing, bones had to be set, plus he would not leave without knowing his people were cared for.

He started to issue orders to see the healers, but held off, allowing Tristan to handle this as he saw fit.

In Tristan's uncanny way of knowing just what to say at times, he interjected, "Bernie, if you don't have a broken bone, I'd like you to shift and fly Petrina to the castle healers so they can set her arm to heal straight."

Stick-thin and gawky, Bernie might not intimidate anyone in his human form, but he held a formidable gryphon inside of him just like the others. With one look at Petrina's arm, his bright green eyes turned murderous. "That dragon hurt you, Petrina?"

She growled under her breath, clearly not happy with lots of attention out here among her peers. "An edge of ice hit my arm. You have anything broken?"

That young man looked at Tristan's sister as if she were the goddess of his dreams. Bernie had no intention of appearing weak in front of her.

"No, I'm fine. Let me shift and get you to the healers."

For a moment, Petrina appeared ready to argue, then let

it go. "Okay, let's do this." She walked off with Bernie. He shed his clothes, wrapped them up for her to hold. Then he shifted into a magnificent gray and orange gryphon with a golden head.

Daegan had been told of how the ones with golden heads, like Evalle, were considered special, but he had no idea why.

Tristan's gryphon did not have that unique head color, but every gryphon here would follow him into battle.

As Bernie's gryphon flew away with Petrina, another gryphon named Ixxter walked up. He had a bruiser's voice. "What about all this ice?"

Daegan surveyed the area. "Everyone move back from the heavy sections of ice. When I shift, my dragon shall melt it."

Every member of the village backed up quickly from the ice as if it were a bed of vipers, but more as a show of respect for Daegan's dragon.

Tristan moved to stand next to Daegan's dragon.

Ruadh lowered his big head close to the ground and huffed out short bursts of fire. Ice melted and ran through the land to a creek running alongside the village.

With the gryphons taken care of, Daegan spoke to Tristan telepathically. *I shall return as quickly as I am able.*

Tristan nodded and started issuing directions for cleaning up the village.

Ruadh hunched down and pushed up, flying toward the area where they'd left Skarde's dragon. Once Daegan realized the ice dragon intended to attack the gryphon village, Ruadh had blasted Skarde's dragon, knocking the beast away from the village. Then Ruadh drove Skarde's dragon down, shoving it into the tops of sturdy trees.

One tall evergreen with a sharp stub where the top had broken off had impaled the ice dragon's wing.

That would not be healed by the time Daegan found

him.

Ruadh located the ice dragon's body among smashed trees and told Daegan, *Ice dragon not ally. Deserves death.*

Daegan understood his dragon's uncomplicated thinking when it came to those considered enemies, but Daegan could not be so cut and dry when it came to killing any being while injured. He argued, *I may need this dragon to negotiate a truce with Brynhild.*

Both ice dragons dangerous.

Daegan agreed to a point, but if he could convince them Ruadh had nothing to do with starting the Dragani War, he would not have to battle those two dragon shifters constantly.

If Brynhild realized she had family, she might want a future where they did not have to fight the red dragon.

Daegan told Ruadh, *Skarde and Brynhild are not allies yet, but if I kill Skarde I shall have to battle Brynhild again. This time to the death. Peace reigned before because dragons worked together. I wish for the chance to have peace again. To have fewer enemies, not more. Maybe even to have more power to call upon with these Imortiks.*

Ruadh said nothing more as he circled the broken silvery blue dragon trapped in the forest.

Daegan said, *'Tis time to free the ice dragon's wing from the tree.*

Gliding around the spot with slow wing flaps, Ruadh found a place to land. He walked through the dense forest, breaking tree limbs as his huge body forged an opening. When Daegan noticed the base of the tree staked through Skarde's dragon wing, he waited to see if Ruadh had a plan.

Ruadh burned the lower half of the tree.

Skarde's dragon groaned a loud noise filled with pain and misery, then sprayed ice water to prevent the fire from climbing the tree.

The tree trunk dropped down and sideways as the lower

half turned into ashes. What was left toppled over, crashing against other trees.

Skarde shouted curses in Daegan's head.

Daegan ordered, *Silence. We must pull your wing free.*

Ruadh used his snout to lift the ice dragon's wing high enough to clear the broken stub. With one look at the ripped-up wing, Daegan saw no way the dragon could heal that damage soon.

Speaking through Ruadh, Daegan ordered out loud, "Shift, Skarde."

The ice dragon flopped over with bones sticking out at odd angles from the wing and shifted. Skarde's human body was covered in a patchwork of bleeding wounds, but nothing as awful as his mangled arm.

Skarde sagged and gently held the top of his arm against his body. His pain-filled eyes lost their arrogant glare from earlier.

In the wake of Ruadh pushing through the wooded area, they now had a clearing of sorts.

Daegan shifted into his human body, ready to verbally rip Skarde to shreds for harming his people. He clothed the man with a pair of jeans.

The sound of flapping wings drew Daegan around.

Tristan's gryphon flew in fast.

Daegan expected Tristan to return to his human body as soon as he landed, but the gray gryphon with clear scales hit hard, shaking the ground and emitting snarling sounds. The gryphon started forward with all focus on Skarde.

Daegan intervened with a bump of his shoulder, startling Tristan's gryphon.

Speaking telepathically to his second, Daegan said, *Do not kill him, Tristan.*

The giant gryphon head swung low to him. *Petrina could have died! Not just her, but all of the gryphons still in human form.*

I understand.

No, Daegan. This dragon has no conscience. He doesn't deserve your understanding. He doesn't deserve to live. Time to make him pay.

Ruadh spoke in Daegan's mind. *Agree with gryphon.*

Tristan's gryphon flapped to leap over Daegan, screeching a war cry at Skarde, who took a step back. The gryphon flapped enough to stay in the air with claws out.

Daegan ignored his dragon and lifted his hands to stop Tristan's gryphon from getting past him. *Wait, Tristan. I share your feelings. I feared losing ya and wanted to kill Skarde, too.*

Why didn't you? Tristan had never sounded so raw and ready to rip an enemy apart.

Please. Come back down, Tristan. Daegan more than understood, he wanted justice as much as his second. Guilt would stay with him for a long time over the mistake he'd made in judgment today. One that his people had paid for. He struggled even now to see the bigger picture in spite of arguing with Ruadh.

Tristan's gryphon landed, but stomped from side to side making angry chuffing sounds.

I am sorry about Petrina. I know ya want to kill Skarde and I share that feelin', but we may need him.

Tristan's gryphon swung his head at Skarde, who stood still, watching for an attack. *We don't need him. He's a coward.*

I shall not argue that point. I wish to not add to my list of enemies and ask him questions about the time after Queen Maeve captured me. This may be my only chance for information. 'Tis selfish of me, I admit, but I have few other ways to gain this.

After a brittle silence, Tristan replied telepathically, *I won't kill him. Not right now. Please step aside, Daegan.*

When Daegan complied, Tristan's gryphon opened his

wings wide and moved forward in a threateningly posture, towering above the ice dragon shifter.

"Daegan," Skarde demanded quietly, never taking his eyes off Tristan's gryphon. "Get your gryphon under control."

"'Tis my second-in-command. Ya owe him blood for harmin' his sister." Daegan would allow Tristan to put some fear into the ice dragon shifter if Skarde failed to show contrition and humble himself with an apology.

Skarde spoke louder, showing a total lack of concern for his future. "Your gryphon is no match for my ice dragon once I heal. I do not fear him."

Why would he goad Tristan?

Daegan needed to knock some serious sense into this one.

Tristan's gryphon released a loud battle cry, then blew fire out horizontally above Skarde.

Shocked, the ice dragon screamed. When the smoke cleared, Skarde had no hair or eyebrows and bloody patches on his head.

He stumbled backward, his mangled arm still clutched against his chest. He stared up in horror at the gryphon.

The gryphon shifted, leaving Tristan in human form.

Daegan clothed him immediately in jeans and a gray T-shirt once more. He remained silent to allow Tristan the moment to have his say. That was the least Daegan owed his friend after bad judgment on his part had resulted in an ice dragon flying freely in Treoir.

Veins stood out in Tristan's neck when he shouted at Skarde, "*What the fuck is wrong with you?* What kind of worthless piece of shit harms innocent people? Including a *woman!* You're disgusting."

Skarde's eyes glowed bright blue with anger and tears. His voice shook. "You do not know what my life has been—"

"News flash. I don't give a flying fuck what your life has been like." Muscles in Tristan's neck bulged. He curled his hands into thick fists. "My life sucked for a long time, but I have *never* hurt an innocent being and I *never* harmed a woman. Only a spineless coward does that."

"I am an ice dragon," Skarde shouted back. *"Don't you dare call me a coward!"* His body trembled, probably from shock as much as anything else.

"Words mean nothing. Actions tell the truth." Tristan blew out a harsh rush of air, hooked his thumbs in his front jean pockets, then spit on the ground in Skarde's direction. "What are we doing with this piece of crap, boss?"

Skarde shouted, "You have no say—"

Daegan roared, *"Shut! Up!* He has far more say than ya. I agree with his words. I gave ya a chance to fly and ya attacked my people. Ya are fortunate my dragon did not burn ya to ashes as your dragon's wing was pinned on a tree."

Skarde stood there vibrating. His face turned deep red and he yelled, "Go ahead. Kill me!" Misery loaded in those four words.

"I'm all in on that," Tristan tossed back at him with a negligent shrug.

"Not you. The red dragon."

Tristan sneered at him. "Why should the red dragon waste any energy on killing something no more important than a tick?"

"This tick buried your village in ice!"

That snapped Tristan's tight leash on his control. He roared and punched Skarde, knocking him on his ass. "You're screwed in the head, Skarde. I bet you can't even heal that broken nose."

Skarde lay there moaning and clutching his damaged arm. Blood poured from his crushed nose. He muttered unintelligible words that ended in a curse.

Daegan felt time pressing on him constantly. "At the

moment, ya may be of use, Skarde, but if it turns out ya no longer hold a value ... " Daegan lifted his shoulders. "Then I shall grant your wish. I have no reason to continue feedin' someone who is a danger to my people."

Skarde struggled to turn over and push himself to a standing position. His skin had a greenish sickly hue. He laughed, edging close to an insane sound. "You would starve me to death instead of a sword to my gut?"

"I want first dibs if you change your mind about letting him live, boss," Tristan offered in all seriousness.

Daegan nodded, but said, "Thank ya for restraint, Tristan."

"Restraint? He *burned* me," Skarde argued.

Ignoring the ice dragon, Daegan continued, "'Tis time to teleport him to the dungeon."

"*No!*" Skarde shouted. "*Do not leave me alone! I will fight the gryphon now!*"

Tristan cupped his ear. "Did you hear anything, boss?" He glanced at Daegan. "Me neither. Ready?"

"Yes."

Skarde started babbling. "I will talk. Do not—"

Daegan reappeared inside the dungeon with Tristan and Skarde as the ice dragon finished, "... force me to stay here alive." Skarde wore only jeans on his lower half, but to clothe him more would only get in the way of healing his body.

But Skarde's last words rang in the empty dungeon. Daegan finally realized this ice dragon *did* have a death wish.

He had no sympathy for someone who harmed innocents, but he recalled wishing for death after weeks and weeks turned into years of being captured by Queen Maeve.

Speaking to Tristan telepathically, Daegan said, *I need a moment. Watch my back and use your body to block his view of what I am doin'. Skarde knows to not shift until his arm has been set or the arm heals crooked.*

That dragon is getting nowhere near you, boss. Tristan waited until Daegan had walked over to the side wall before he stepped in front of Skarde.

CHAPTER 3

DAEGAN STUDIED THE AREA WHERE he'd installed a bed, chair and table plus other amenities earlier for Skarde to reside comfortably in the Treoir dungeon. His attempt at providing a habitable environment for the ice dragon shifter had been met with obstinance. Skarde had never used any of the furnishings created for a human due to remaining in dragon form since arriving here.

Pausing to glance over his shoulder and check on Tristan, Daegan continued to create a spot to better contain Skarde. His second-in-command had his part handled.

Tristan stood with legs apart and hands at his hips. He provided a wall to block Skarde's view of Daegan while doing a commendable job of not strangling the ice dragon.

Skarde shouted at Tristan, "Meet me when I am healed, and you will beg for mercy." Oddly, Skarde shrank back, eyes wild, and wrapped his good arm around his body. He shivered and clenched his teeth, a mad man with a dragon inside.

That was a deranged dragon shifter. Daegan had failed to see more than he'd wanted, too anxious to gain an ally. Someone who knew his past and might fight alongside him today.

He shook his head at how he'd been blind to Skarde's demons. The fool tried to push Tristan to attack him even now. Skarde had no idea of the steel backbone and honor Tristan possessed.

"I'm down with kicking your ass, ice boy, but not until

I'm allowed to fight to the death," Tristan retorted with casual indifference meant to insult a dragon shifter.

Forcing his words through chattering teeth, Skarde scoffed, "You are a fool to believe your gryphon's little puff of fire can harm my dragon."

"Have you looked in a mirror since my little puff of fire?" Tristan asked in a taunt. "In addition to the gift of fire, you might have noticed I can also teleport."

Daegan paused in forming a word for his ward to take in Skarde's reaction.

The ice dragon shifter pulled back, shaking his head. "No. The red dragon teleports."

"Joke's on you, dipshit. I teleport, too." Tristan leaned forward and dropped his voice with a hard edge. "I'm not like any other gryphon. If we ever get the chance to face off, I have a few other tricks. I'll be waiting to dance on your head, asshole, and teach you to never attack my gryphons again."

Once Daegan had a basic containment ward in place, he called to Tristan. "Bring Skarde over here. I shall straighten his arm."

"I bring myself," Skarde ground out in a shaky voice reeking of agony. He might have a death wish, but he didn't want to spend his final hours in pain. He limped past Tristan on wobbly legs. Sweat ran from his face and his skin had a pasty quality.

"Tristan, I shall need a splint and cloth for wrappin'."

"I'm on it." Tristan disappeared.

Pointing at the chair, Daegan waited for the dragon shifter to sit. "I shall make this quick, Skarde, but 'tis painful no matter how the arm is set."

"As if you care how much pain I suffer when you won't kill me and let me escape this hell."

"I had cared at one point, but not after seein' ya attack the gryphons, many of whom were in human form." Daegan fought back the need to bellow at this bastard. Being sick in the head did not forgive Skarde's heinous actions. "I treated ya well. Why did ya attack my people?"

Skarde's head hung forward. He muttered in an agonized tone that made no sense. Sounding exhausted with fighting inside his head, his voice lost all arrogance when he lifted his head. "I have never harmed innocents before now. You cost my family everything, then I am captured by your father's steward and spend thousands of years in the Scamall realm." He lifted his head. "You speak of honor? You and King Gruffyn had no honor in the Dragani War. Now you live like a king yourself and I ... have nothing."

"Ya believe I started the Dragani War," Daegan ground out, tired of being accused of what he'd tried to prevent. That war had taken *his* family and *his* people when Daegan could not be there to protect them. He challenged, "Ya never saw my red dragon, did ya? I know ya did not because Brynhild did not see my dragon either. Ya only heard the stories and ya convicted me of a crime ya had no evidence I committed. My red dragon held the peace for years. The last thing I wanted was war."

Skarde's eyes tried to hide his shame but failed. He still argued, "I do not believe your words. You left your family to face the Dragani War alone, which your father deserved, but not the others. Here you are again with family on Treoir. You live a gifted life again."

Tristan returned with his arms full of bandages. "Tell me when you want this."

Daegan wished to continue the argument but had little time left. "I am waitin' on Skarde."

Breathing rapidly, Skarde clenched his jaw and lifted his bad arm supported by his other hand.

Taking in the mess of bone, muscle, and skin, Daegan chose the best two points to grip lightly for straightening his arm. "I need the splint first." Gripping the mangled arm, Daegan quickly pulled the bones in line.

Skarde yelled a raspy scream. His eyes rolled with a wild look, but he remained conscious. He clenched his jaw hard. Muscles in his neck and cheek flexed while he breathed in and out rapidly. Sweat rushed down his face and neck.

Tristan leaned in to clamp the splint in place.

Skarde groaned with every movement.

Daegan took the long, narrow cloth draped over Tristan's arm and used it to wrap the splint from shoulder to hand. Skarde's jaw muscles bulged. He made guttural sounds. The pain had to be excruciating, but he was being shown mercy when he least deserved it.

With the cloth tied off, Daegan motioned for Tristan to back up.

Daegan followed him and lifted his arms, whispering words he'd been taught long ago. "Ya shall stay here until I come for ya again."

Skarde's eyes widened as his gaze followed Daegan's hands. "What are you doing?"

"Placin' a ward around ya. Everythin' ya need is inside and ya will be fed. This ward shall keep the castle quiet while I am away."

"*No!*" Skarde stood, weaving where he stood. Sweat poured down his face and chest. His voice shook with fear. "I cannot do this. I ... I must shift to heal."

"Ya can heal just fine in human form, though not so quickly."

Skarde's angry voice died to a weak demand. "Do not leave me here unable to shift. My arm and head will have scars if I do not change into my dragon."

"Thought you wanted to die? Now you want to have a pretty corpse?" Tristan took an aggressive step toward Skarde.

Daegan held up his hand, a request for Tristan to wait.

When his second stood down, Daegan spoke in a gravelly voice. "The ice dragon clan I knew long ago stood strong as one family and with allies. Not one, male or female, would have attacked an innocent group. None of the male dragon shifters would have injured a female the way ya did with not a concern for if ya had killed her."

"I did not kill anyone," Skarde grumbled.

Daegan roared, "Ya should be protectin' those without our powers. Ya shall wear your scars to remind ya when ya had no honor. 'Tis a small penance for the destruction and injuries ya caused but know this. My dragon will not stand down a second time."

Tristan sent Daegan a telepathic message. *Tzader is looking for you. He says Lanna has asked you to see her before you leave Treoir.*

Glancing at Tristan, Daegan gave a short nod, then slashed his gaze at Skarde. "I have done all within my power to keep ya alive. Ya had better hope by the time I return again I have found a reason to continue feedin' ya. Otherwise, your future shall lay in Tristan's hands."

Skarde jerked his gaze from the floor to stare at Daegan in defiance. He snarled, "You are one to speak. You start a war then leave your family to fight it. You accuse me of hurting a female yet you left your sister defenseless. Where is *your* honor?"

"Do not speak of my family," Daegan shouted, hating that he'd allowed Skarde to know he'd struck a raw nerve. "I treated ya well after freein' ya from Scamall and savin' your sorry life. Ya wish to be enemies? So be it."

Skarde kept shouting and screaming, "I was there when you were not. No red dragon showed up to save his people. You know that. Their blood is on your head!"

Daegan had angled his head at Tristan, who teleported them immediately.

As they reappeared near the outer wall of the dungeon,

everything Daegan had learned since being freed weighed heavily on his heart. Skarde's damning comments rang inside his tired mind. Daegan took a moment before entering the castle wall and placed his hand on stone carved many centuries ago. Just being in this realm, on this land, soothed a damaged part of his soul. His heart and soul were torn between his first life and this second chance he'd been given.

Turning his head to Tristan, he admitted, "I have been too understandin' with the dragon shifters. To find even one of those from my time twisted my thinkin'. I must begin to accept them as the enemies they are determined to be and let go of what I cannot find out about the past."

Tristan lifted a hand to his face and rubbed his forehead. "I'm pissed as hell at that asshole in the dungeon, but I can see how you would want to save dragon shifters who had once been your allies."

Daegan took in Treoir and all it meant to him. Not just a castle with people and Belador guards. Not just a protected realm, but ... everything he never thought to have again, starting with Brina, Tzader, and their bairns. Then Tristan and his gryphon clan, Evalle, Quinn, every Belador, and their allies.

He'd escaped the damned to live a new life.

Perhaps it was time to let go of the old, no matter how much that thought hurt.

Tristan looked out over the Treoir land for a moment then came back to Daegan. "I didn't get why you tried so hard to protect dragons that hate you. Not at first, because I wanted to kill anything that attacks you or our people. I've had some time to think about it since that day on the cliffs when you met Brynhild. That's when I realized how hard it must be to hide your dragon from the world and have none of your kind around." Frowning at some hidden thought, Tristan shook it off. "I'll stay open to the idea of saving the dragon shifters if they show a change of heart to play nice.

Skarde is probably already regretting what he did. Petrina will heal and I'll get over the urge to kill that ice dragon, eventually, but Skarde's not going to live long if he doesn't get his head out of his ass."

Just when Daegan had sunk as low emotionally as he could after putting his people in harm's way, his chest eased with Tristan's admission. Daegan's lips twitched with almost a smile. "Ya are correct. I shall have to remember that phrase about his head."

Tristan gave a quick grin. "Let's go see what that little terror wants."

Daegan started for the castle. "Little terror?"

"One of these days when you get to see Lanna riled up, cover your head. Her power is crazy."

"I have just witnessed her power with Ainvar."

"Oh, hell no. *That* was a *reserved* Lanna." Tristan laughed. "She was once trapped in a basement beneath a building in Atlanta with a room full of innocent humans and two young male witches, one of whom she has a crush on. Even so, she would not stand by and watch one person die. When the warlock kidnappers threatened to kill everyone, Lanna got upset. That unleashed her power without her in control. It created a thunderstorm inside the basement and shook one of the largest buildings in that area of Atlanta."

Daegan's lips parted. "'Tis true?"

"Oh, yes. I don't know what she's been doing with Garwyli, but I hope that old druid can teach her how to manage her powers. She's sweet and protective. Nothing stops her from racing into danger, no matter how great the threat. Makes Quinn nuts all the time."

Daegan could imagine Quinn trying to keep his tiny cousin safe from danger and the world safe from her. As Daegan took the steps to the castle entrance, his mind went to his own family. He thought back on Skarde's comment about Daegan not protecting his family.

Skarde had mentioned Daegan's sister, in fact. That could only be Jennyver.

Why would that ice dragon care?

Daegan shook his head, cursing himself for falling into an emotional trap Skarde baited with the right words. That ice dragon only thought to strike at Daegan by poking a raw wound.

Nothing more.

CHAPTER 4

CASIDHE COULDN'T SEE A THING in this black tunnel, but she knew a cracking noise had to be bad.

The ceiling broke free.

Rocks and dirt crashed to the floor.

With a death grip on a strap, she dragged her pack and scooted backward as fast as she could in the midst of dirt showering her. She'd made it fifteen feet when the crush of dirt and dust flying around finally stopped.

Where was Cathbad?

The silence rattled her almost as much as the cave-in. She dug out her LED light.

Rocks and dirt had piled up to the ceiling.

Her body wasn't being dragged through all that by Cathbad's majik.

She drew her knees up and dropped her head on her crossed arms. Coughing to clear her mouth and lungs, she wiped her lips on her sleeve. Then she just sat there, drained.

If Cathbad walked up right now, he wouldn't need majik to contain her.

The tunnel collapse and crazy druid had taken five years off her life.

Sitting up, she ran both hands over her hair. Her clothes were wet and filthy. No telling what her face looked like.

The ring!

She clawed at her neck, caught the chain, and lifted it to see the ring dangling there. Thank goodness. She fed the chain back inside her shirt.

What happened with Cathbad? Not that she wanted to be yanked through this tunnel like a ragdoll, but she didn't think Cathbad made empty threats.

Why hadn't his majik worked?

She got to her knees and pulled the backpack into place on her back. Then she made it up on her noodle legs and continued her stumbling march to the end of the tunnel offshoot.

What if she ran into another cave-in?

Could she dig her way out before she suffocated?

She'd crawl across that bridge when she came to it. Cathbad worried her more than another wall of rocks and dirt right now. He believed he could call her to him. Why?

As she struggled another twenty feet at a time, she ran what he'd said through her mind again. *I know ya read the section I warned ya not to read without me. Now I can call ya to me.*

He had to be referencing the *Before Ainvar* book.

He thought she still had the book with her, giving him a way to use it against her. Relief slapped her silly over the simple act of sending the book with Tristan when he tele-ported her library to Treoir.

Sure, there was a chance she'd never see her books again, which physically hurt to think about. But she would have been at Cathbad's mercy if she hadn't given up her precious archive.

She'd been bent over so long, she'd stopped looking forward, just held out one hand so she didn't run into any-thing. After all this time in pitch black, suddenly seeing her scuffed and dirty boots surprised her.

She lifted her head.

Tiny shafts of daylight pierced the tunnel from thirty feet away. Adrenaline rushed through her shaky body. She took off on all fours, hurrying to reach the hole before it vanished.

With her life, that could happen.

When she reached the opening, she tried to push through, but a tangle of vines grew there. That's why the light had not been solid.

She squinted, trying to see through the weave of thick wooden twists. She could make out nothing that would orient her to what waited outside. On her next breath, she dragged in a lung full of fresh air.

She'd made it this far.

Vines were not stopping her.

But that meant pulling out her sword again. What was the chance her sword would cooperate?

She wouldn't even speculate.

Reaching over her shoulder, she lifted a little at a time until the sword swung free and over her head. "Thank you, *Lann an Cheartais,*" she cooed to the sword, hoping it wanted out of this tunnel as much as she did.

Sucking in a long breath, she exhaled, calming her nerves first, then lifted the sword to swing down. She felt the first chop vibrate all the way up her arms. She kept whacking at the vines. *Lann an Cheartais* did not melt through them like it had the root, but neither did the sword refuse to cut.

Was cutting wood and vines an insult?

When she had enough of a hole for her to push through, she put away the sword and began shoving tree branches aside. She still could not see clearly beyond this point with a cluster of leaves on trees and skinny vines blocking her view.

But it smelled fresh and clean.

The only thing she recalled from the last time she'd climbed out of this tunnel ten years ago was a gentle sloping hill.

Pushing the backpack ahead of her, she yanked it away

from sharp edges grabbing at the tough material. Her arms wanted to quit, but she held on and worked her entire body out the toothy hole.

Then the backpack weight dropped, yanking her arms down fast.

She lunged out of the hole, figuring the backpack would knock weeds and branches out of the way, breaking her fall. Then she'd walk down the slope.

Nope. The universe had other plans. Her world dropped away. She fell ten feet before she hit wet ground with a thud. Her body slid and rolled madly down a hill. She yelled and held the backpack in a death grip. It bounced all around, slapping her.

Eyes closed, she kept her fingers locked around the strap and hoped it did not break. Finally the flipping around and rolling ended. She flopped on her back, staring up at a bright blue sky with clouds shaped as cotton puffs.

Bruised and cut, she wanted to just lie here panting. That would make it easy for Cathbad to catch her. At the moment, he had no idea where she had exited the tunnel. She tried to force herself to jump up and take off. Not happening.

The window of time for that druid to find her dwindled.

"How am I going to cross thousands of miles when I've barely made it a hundred yards from the tunnel?" She waited just in case someone felt like hurtling advice at her.

Nope. After another moment of talking herself into moving, she struggled to her feet.

Hefting her backpack into place once more, she reached for the silver chain around her neck, bringing it up again to confirm she hadn't lost the ring in her tumble.

All at once, the running from druids, being captured, then betrayed by Fenella hit her hard. Could she make this journey and face a hostile Herrick?

She had to go to Herrick alone, but she'd love to have

Daegan at her side again.

She missed him. Missed his unspoken support for anything she needed.

Her heart wanted more time with him, but he'd been right to not become intimate with her. Now that she'd had a chance to think on it, she couldn't feel free to make that choice to share herself with Daegan until she met with Herrick. She intended to go her own way, but not before Herrick answered for all the years he'd misled her and she made it clear she was done.

She wanted to have her say before they parted ways. He owed her that much.

Then she'd have to walk away from the clan. The idea of leaving all she'd ever known sickened her, but she'd never truly belonged. Not really.

Still, it would hurt worse than a dagger to her chest.

She could not start her own life until Herrick explained why he'd let her believe she was part of his clan. She'd give him a chance to tell his side.

She also wanted the truth about the Dragani War.

So many questions she'd wanted to ask and hadn't for fear of backlash. Was Herrick immortal or had that ward played a role in him surviving all these centuries? Her squire tutors had warned her to never ask that question. Why?

From what she'd pieced together over her many years of research, most dragon shifters lived three times as long as humans. What about Daegan? He'd been born of a goddess and king with dragon blood. Was he immortal?

While she would not trust any words from Queen Maeve again, that woman had a serious library of material dating back before the Dragani War. So many things in those scrolls had contradicted what Casidhe had been taught. Words that painted Daegan as the force protecting the dragon shifter clans.

All of them, which included the ice dragons.

She needed the truth and facts before making any life-altering decision now waiting in the back of her mind.

Feeling a spurt of energy, she headed to her next destination.

She pulled out a water bottle and an energy bar, chewing the nutty mixture and guzzling water with each step. She had a few miles to cross before she could thumb a ride. A farm truck would let her jump in the back, which would give her a chance to catch some rest.

The only downside would be walking across open fields.

Queen Maeve could see her with that scrying wall.

Cathbad might have his own scrying unit.

Did everyone but her have one?

She glanced up to see where the sun sat in the sky. Had to be around one in the afternoon. A lot of things could happen before she reached the airport.

Maybe she should wait until dark, but Daegan had some person who could use remote viewing.

No, the longer she put off reaching the road, the more she killed her chance at escaping.

CHAPTER 5

KLEIO LEANED AGAINST THE OPEN window. The view of the Caucasus mountain range in the afternoon from the second floor of Herrick's castle never got old. Good thing or she'd feel trapped living in a remote castle shielded by a dragon-shifter's ward.

She'd had a disturbing dream last night she couldn't shake.

Dreams were normally easy for her to understand, and more often than not, an indication of something she should focus on to incur a vision.

This one had been in fragments with no clear meaning.

A disturbing dream even without a clear meaning.

Different faces she could not identify and in strange settings, which reminded her of a time long before she'd been born. Possibly from as far back as Herrick's early life. The turbulent actions and images had brought her wide awake at dawn. In hopes of learning more about the dream, she'd tried to sleep again only to be denied.

Herrick's pet griffon vulture, Stian, flew across the vista, gliding from time to time. Her gaze followed the bird a moment then drifted away to watch the castle workers below. If she did not know better, she'd think she'd gone back in time. All parts of this castle lived as Herrick had thousands of years ago. All except her area and even those changes had been modest.

Two children raced around playing with sticks and the dogs below.

She'd never wanted a child of her own. If she had, she doubted Janus, god of beginnings and transitions, would have chosen her to do his bidding for this world.

The first time she met him she was but a child herself. He was an imposing being she should have feared, but she'd experienced a reverent level of admiration the first time in his presence. Over the years, he became mentor and parent, raising her as much as developing her gift.

If she were honest, which she always strived to be, she'd admit a bit of hurt at the idea of not being visited by him again until she completed a journey she had yet to truly see. She replayed his words daily, focusing on what he required of her.

Your visions will expose a threat, free a life, and cost a bond.

Every day brought the possibility of each declaration. Every word had a deep meaning.

Your vision will change your path and your path will change the course of the human world. The world will either survive what is coming or burn into eternity. Do not return to speak to me again until you have completed this journey and the future is clear.

Uncrossing her arms, she walked over the stone floor of her simple room furnished with a bed of thick dark wood. She often studied the symbols carved in the headboard, but had no idea what they meant. Herrick had refused to explain them.

Nothing appeared to be evil or demonic, so she let it go as she did so many times with Herrick.

He upheld his part of their agreement, so she pushed only when something mattered.

The mahogany armoire against the far wall belonged to her and matched the low chest moved here at the same time. Herrick had thought the screen in the corner and the basin she had to fill with water would suffice for her personal needs. No.

Demanding a private bathroom had caused Herrick no little frustration. He'd tried to tell her how he preferred the clan live naturally as he had growing up.

She'd explained the definition of a deal breaker. She was not clan and did not care if others wanted to live in a primitive way. Then she'd reminded him how he had agreed to provide her living quarters equal to her current life when they first met. Except for her bathroom, she'd lived as sparsely as a monk.

Herrick had been so excited to gain her agreement to live at his castle, he'd failed to realize the modern convenience most women would expect.

Washing her face at the basin, she patted it dry and hung the towel on a rack.

She glanced in the mirror at her red-and-gold brocade skirt and long-sleeved white blouse. In a humdrum mood this morning, she'd left her black hair loose to cloud around her head and shoulders, but now was the time to get busy. With efficient moves of having worn her hair only two ways for years, she braided a long black length, tied the end, and tossed it all over her shoulder.

Going through her normal routine had done little to ease her mind over the dream.

Nothing would until she opened her senses for a vision.

She hadn't been able to pinpoint the exact location of the setting or why that mattered, but those details felt important.

One woman in particular from the dream interested her.

Kleio listened for any noise outside her room and heard none.

She opened her door to the hallway and checked that no one headed in her direction. With the only access to her room closed again, she lifted a heavy timber into the slats provided. That prevented anyone from entering uninvited.

Even Herrick.

Across her bedroom and to the right of the window, she entered a room all were forbidden from entering, except her. Herrick often grumbled about being barred from any part of his castle.

When he did, she merely waited out his rant.

He'd storm off afterward and she wouldn't see him for at least a day.

Now that she thought about it, he'd left the castle early this morning in dragon form without a word to anyone. No one would dare question him. Herself included.

After her last visit from Janus, she now questioned her failure to give more consideration to Herrick's habits.

He never remained absent from the castle more than two days. That in itself had been mysterious years ago when she first made this her permanent residence. Based on silent observations, she began to realize upon every return, he visited his lair immediately or very soon. The castle had been built against a mountainside thousands of years ago by one of the ice dragon ancestors. Herrick forbade anyone from passing from the castle into a large cavern inside the mountain the castle abutted.

No one ventured near his lair, or more specifically, his dragon's lair.

In recent months, she'd sensed something unusual in his secret area and made the mistake of bringing it up for discussion.

His response had been quick and vicious. Keep her nose out of things that did not concern her.

Herrick had a temper best not triggered.

Still, Janus had handed her a heavy responsibility to do more than inform Herrick of visions about him and his people.

Even that had proved to be a recent disappointment.

Last week, she'd rushed to tell Herrick of a vision where

danger shadowed Fenella and Casidhe.

What had he done?

Warned Fenella.

Kleio had another vision of danger chasing Casidhe. She demanded to know if he had contacted the young woman.

Herrick walked away without answering.

He'd sent no word to Casidhe.

Kleio paused to confirm the half-burned candles from her last visit had not been disturbed. There should be no reason for change, but she could not risk entering a trance only to find some being had been here and left her a trap.

She took a spot in front of the low altar, kneeling on the soft rug. After lighting the two yellow candles placed at corners of the altar, she brought to life the three purple candles arranged in a half circle in the center.

Sitting back on her knees, she inhaled deeply of scents meant to relax and enhance her experience while in an alternative state of mind.

As her mental pathways opened, she brought up images from her dream and lost herself in observing every detail.

She'd gone far back into time again. So strange when the journey Janus had spoken of would happen in today's world. This was not the time to analyze, but to take in every detail.

Sunlight slipped behind the horizon, throwing the last shadows across a castle high atop a hill and the land leading up to it. Nothing of this setting reminded her of Herrick's castle nestled deep in the Caucasus mountains.

Two different castle structures, in fact.

Clanging of metal against metal drew her to the people.

Some men fought in pairs using massive swords, but appeared to practice only. They wore groin covers. Sweat poured down their tanned muscular bodies. Women dressed in natural wheat-colored peasant gowns of brown and cream with white blouses. They carried baskets of clothes, cooked over open fires, and visited in small groups.

Kleio drew in the aroma of some meat being cooked in a stew. Some women cared for children also in simple clothing from a medieval time.

A noise in the distance caused the entire area to pause and look past the castle at something Kleio could not see.

Whispers erupted. Wide eyes stared intensely with fear.

But she heard the loud roar of a beast and hard flapping of giant wings.

Someone shouted, "*'Tis not our red dragon!*" They all ran to grab children and hurry for the castle, screaming they were under attack.

The image spun and blurred.

Kleio struggled to hold herself in the moment. She had never been thrown from a vision, but this one pushed her away.

How could that be?

She called upon her powers and forced her way back inside the vision, battling the energy blocking her. Her body tensed and she leaned forward hard as if fighting a powerful storm.

Clenching her teeth, she pulled her hands together as she had when Janus had told her to behold the woman she would become. The woman she'd seen in a mirror with horns curling from her head had worn a black gown and gripped the hilt of a sword with the blade pointed down.

Energy flooded her.

The storm calmed, allowing her back into the vision.

Sweat trickled down one side of her face. She ignored it, intent on staying put and riding this vision to the end. She had never faced so difficult a time trying to reach for a vision.

As her sight cleared, Kleio observed a new setting. A young woman knelt in a chapel with walls of stone. Screams and shouts sounded far away. Was this a chapel inside the castle from earlier?

Red hair of autumn colors fell to her waist in waves as she prayed. Her beautiful gown of subdued green had been sewn by the best of dressmakers. Based on the style and richness of the material, this woman likely held a high position in the castle.

Just outside, someone screamed, *"Runnn!"* Then more voices picked up the shouts of danger.

The red-haired woman glanced over her shoulder, eyes flashing terror, but she returned to praying.

Who was she?

A large figure entered the chapel, remaining hidden in dark shadows.

The red-haired woman lifted her head, but remained on her knees. She did not turn to face the intruder when she spoke. "Leave me. This is a place of worship."

The dark figure still said nothing.

She twisted her hands together and swallowed. Tears ran down her cheeks.

The world blurred again with flashes of fighting and people begging for their lives. So much pain and heartache.

Kleio gripped her chest, unable to prevent the agony from sliding inside her. She struggled to breathe. She begged for relief, caught up inside the vision, then finally ... silence and darkness.

Releasing a strangled breath, Kleio grabbed her head and kept her eyes closed as she pulled herself together. She searched for the connection again and again, then gave up.

Time had taught her the visions either come or they don't. She could not recall when she'd had so much trouble with any vision. Murmuring comforting words to ease her galloping heart, she cupped her hands to her chest and lowered her head.

She had no idea how much time had passed when a vision nudged her to pay attention.

She lifted her head, but kept her eyes closed.

An image began to form.

No castle or people.

She pushed to her feet and stood erect as if drawn to do so. Then her body floated in a smoky ether, which pulled her forward. Remaining calm had come so easily in the past, but those visions were nothing like what she had experienced today.

Should she pull out and protect herself?

Janus expected her to be his warrior with sight.

Her hands trembled at standing strong. If she'd wanted a simple life without facing the unknown, she would never have become a seer for Janus.

That admission did nothing to build her confidence, but neither could she turn back. Not now. Not when it felt as if she were on the brink of something important.

Lights glowed and dimmed in the cloudy world she continued to be drawn through. She found no origin for the lighting. The smoke swirling around her appeared only as wide as her bedroom, but it seemed endless until her body stopped moving.

Part of the smoke reshaped into hands, nudging her forward.

Her skin chilled. She had never experienced that sort of touch during a vision. Remaining calm tasked her greatly.

Evidently satisfied with her position, the ghost-like hands withdrew.

Where was she? She stared at a wall of haze that ebbed and flowed.

On occasion in the past, she'd had to wait for long periods until a vision reached the point of revealing itself. She'd come too far in this one to become impatient.

Time swam around her.

Lulled by the gentle movements in the room, she started when the ghost hands shook her.

Heart thumping fast, she sharpened her attention. Clearly, that appeased the filmy hands, which left her once more.

An ocean of thick and iridescent fog swirled this way and that until it subsided and began spreading out.

When the fog thinned, she faced a rock wall.

After all that anxiety, her energy flattened with disappointment at this dead end.

What else could she determine about this vision?

Moving around the room, she searched for some identifying factors besides feeling as if she floated in a cave. Fire burned from torches on the walls. On the other side of the room, steps appeared to ascend in an exit.

She tried to float there, but her body would not move.

Where were the ghost hands when she needed them?

Air chilled across her skin. She sensed a change behind her and managed to turn only to find the stone wall still there.

This vision had drained her. She needed to leave and heal her energy.

The seer started to withdraw from the vision, but filmy hands on her arms stopped her. This couldn't be. She had never been held captive inside a vision.

Chills covered her skin.

Unable to break away, she stared as the stone wall began to turn translucent ... then transparent.

More smoky air appeared.

This time, the fog dispersed a bit.

What was going on?

Helping hands pushed her forward until she saw an unclear image of a young woman sleeping on the other side.

Maybe not asleep with skin too pale for life.

Why had the body not deteriorated if she were dead?

If this woman was from the medieval time Kleio had been viewing, she could have died of anything from childbirth to a plague.

Or was that an altar her body had been laid upon? Had she been sacrificed?'

Dark energy began to rise around the woman.

Something felt wrong, very wrong. Kleio had never run from a vision, but she turned away.

She had to remain calm and not panic.

Those hands pulled her around to face the young woman again whose face and body came into focus better.

A gown the color of moss and sewn for a female of importance clung to her body. Red hair fell in waves over her shoulders and off the side of her altar.

Kleio could not breathe.

The young woman from the chapel turned her head to Kleio and begged, "*Help. Herrick is killin' me.*"

CHAPTER 6

CASIDHE HOISTED HER BACKPACK INTO place, fastening the straps as she stood on a sidewalk in downtown Luxembourg, Belgium. She watched people flow around her as smoothly as an unremarkable rock in a river beneath streetlights pushing away the dark night. She hadn't expected to arrive so late, but it would have been longer if she hadn't flown most of the way inside a cargo plane.

And she wouldn't have managed to travel without documents had she not tapped her friend who boxed her up to fly in the pressurized area of a freight jet.

She'd tried to sleep, but it wasn't the most comfortable flight. Once she reached a squire house here, she'd get some rest.

A tingle raced up her spine. Again.

Call her paranoid, but she'd felt eyes on her since leaving that tunnel in Galway. No one approached her before she reached Shannon airport and her contact there hadn't blinked an eye. She had to be suffering anxiety from lack of rest and an overactive imagination.

Maybe her stalker antennae had broken with so many people after her lately.

Vibration hummed against her chest.

Dammit. Not that again.

She turned her back to anyone watching and reached inside her shirt to hold the stupid ring until it calmed down again. The thing had scared her bad when it vibrated as the airplane took off from the airport in Shannon.

So now she'd have to pacify a nervous ring on top of dealing with a stubborn sword?

She'd worn this ring on a chain in college and after. It had never twitched. What the heck had this thing jumping around?

And what did *that* mean?

Just another pitstop on her way to Crazyville.

When the ring quieted, she dropped the silver chain inside her shirt again.

She fell into step in the midst of people spread along the sidewalk. On her left stood a string of three-story-tall buildings of old-world architecture. She'd bet historical locations were on every street. Across the narrow street, cafe umbrellas covered diners and those only enjoying a glass of wine.

She caught a whiff of kriibsen. Her mouth watered and her stomach rumbled, but she could not spend money on the succulent crayfish dish. Whatever the squire family shared with her would be much appreciated.

People jostled her as they passed on quicker feet.

She had pushed her legs enough today. Every step so far had been an effort. If her freight airline contact had not been on duty, she'd have had to wait until he showed up at work tomorrow or the next day.

She'd found him taking a late lunch nearby. Once she cooked up a story about having to take off without a local squire family packing her in a crate with all the supplies she'd need, her contact had been great, as usual. He'd taken one look at her dirty clothes and shoes and hustled her to a friend's nearby business where she'd cleaned up in the bathroom while they built her crate.

She'd never wondered how he managed to pass her crate through when needed. After today, she had the feeling he and his friend might smuggle on a regular basis and not just for a dragon shifter.

At the next corner, this part of the city opened into a plaza with more cafes and a couple food trucks. Pulling out her phone, she checked the time. After ten at night. How long would food trucks stick around?

Why waste time worrying when she just needed to locate the squire family? If she let paranoia rule her life, she'd never make it to the Caucasus mountain range.

In the next block, the crowds began to thin.

Food trucks seemed to be shutting down.

In another ten minutes, she wouldn't get much choice.

Her stomach nudged her to take a bird in hand and eat now. Not a wise choice. Stick to the plan and hurry up.

She pulled out one of her two packages of crackers left and munched while following the map on her mobile phone. She still had to reach Tegernsee, Germany, another five to six hours by car from here. Too expensive. She'd have to ask the squire family for help even if they had not been designated for travel aid.

She had enough money to live on for a week and would have had more in hand if she'd visited her cottage. Fear of meeting Cathbad or Queen Maeve had killed that possibility.

Not to mention the demons and Imortiks.

Daegan had explained how they were more prevalent in the city of Atlanta in America right now. There may not be a rift here, but hanging around to find out would not be smart.

Cathbad showing up in the tunnel had proven she'd been right to err on the side of get-the-hell-out-of-there-quick.

Suspicion clawed at her neck.

Pausing, she pretended to tighten the strap on her backpack. No supernatural came flying at her.

Betrayal had eaten away at her confidence.

She'd trusted Herrick and Fenella for years, believing she lived inside a close-knit clan. It surely had been close-knit, but she'd fallen through a gaping hole in it.

Pushing on, she thought about her upcoming meeting with Herrick. Could she be misjudging him? She'd jumped to conclusions on Daegan only to learn she'd been wrong.

She'd been so angry and hurt when she saw Fenella, she couldn't think straight. She'd lashed out mentally at everyone involved.

Not the seer, who Casidhe had never trusted.

That was exactly why she hadn't slowed down to consider the seer's possible role in all this.

Now that she thought back on her conversation with Fenella, had the woman been trying to tell her the *seer* was behind all of this?

Herrick could be overbearing about finding Skarde. He'd been so crazed lately, he seemed to heed the seer's every word even more than normal and could have easily been manipulated.

That seer had been at the castle a long time.

Anyone in her position of power could influence Herrick's every decision.

Had the seer convinced him to use Casidhe to catch the red dragon? Huh. Maybe. If so, damn her.

Casidhe would not betray Daegan, the man who held her heart, but neither could she be with Daegan until she could tell him the truth about everything in her life.

That would not happen until she freed herself of any obligation to Herrick.

All this mental gyration brought her back to her original plan to reach Herrick as soon as possible.

A young man riding a skateboard came too close, forcing Casidhe to step off the sidewalk. He shouted his apology in Dutch without slowing down.

Shaking off the reckless board rider, she hurried ahead, glad to see she was closing in on the residential area for the local Connell squire family. She wouldn't mind catching a meal and some rest until leaving at daylight. No one should have to drive her to Tegernsee in the middle of the night.

She got lost twice then unlatched the pack and dropped it to the ground when she reached the apartment building. Exhausted, she pressed the buttons on a panel to call the family.

"*Deich anseo.*" *Ten here.* The unit number spoken in Irish by this woman was a normal way of answering.

So far, this fit what Casidhe expected.

She had the right place.

Smiling so she didn't sound as irritable and tired as she felt, Casidhe said, "Would I be speakin' to Anna Hugh?" Hugh had been used as a pseudonym for the Connells when Casidhe traveled to protect the families in case someone overheard her.

She had always prided herself on being part of the squire families, and until now, had believed the false name shielded them from fortune hunters.

Now everything in her life took on a different meaning.

She'd been sent out with the last name Luigsech to act like a glowing beacon to draw in the red dragon.

One good point? That had been the reason she met Daegan.

"Aye," the woman answered slowly.

"Wonderful. I am Casidhe of Hugh from the north. I'm in town for a short visit and researchin' information on Dimma MacNathi." Dimma had been the scribe who penned the *Book of Dimma* in the eighth century. Using his name was code for Casidhe requesting shelter and travel help from any squire family and had been for the past ten years.

She'd been taught different codes for multiple situations.

Anna's words shot out terse and sharp. "Ya have wrung

the wrong number. Ya want food, the trucks still run at this time. I know nothin' of some Dimma." The woman hung up.

Casidhe stared at the button unable to speak. Her skin crawled with feeling exposed all of a sudden. Worse than exposed. She felt cut adrift in a sea of strangers.

Had someone sent word to turn her away? Who? Fenella? Why would Fenella or anyone else deny Casidhe safe passage to Herrick?

Had Herrick done this?

She might be angry at him, but he'd been the one to say over and over that family and clan came first. Both must be protected by all of them at all times.

Hurt burned deep at another confirmation she was not family, but she'd always believed she belonged to the clan.

What the hell?

This was the correct address and the woman had acknowledged the Hugh pseudonym.

Herrick and Fenella had told Casidhe if she ever ran into trouble while traveling, all she had to do was knock on the door of *any* Luigsech or *any* Connell squire family on the list. Out of the twenty-nine families in this part of the world, she'd memorized addresses for seventeen scattered along the trip from Galway to Herrick's castle.

This Anna had rejected her even though she never even opened the door. A Connell family. Actually, the original name of Connell had been MacConnaugh.

Tears stung her eyes. The seer would push her out for sure.

Casidhe could see it all so clearly now.

Kleio had probably seen Casidhe traveling to the castle in a vision. She would know how to get word out to anyone she chose. The seer could have sent word to turn Casidhe away as if it had come from Herrick.

What would Kleio do when she realized Casidhe would

not be deterred?

Not after all this.

Casidhe had an even greater journey ahead of her now. She'd make it with or without help from the chain of squire families. No one would prevent her from reaching Herrick and allowing him a chance to explain all of this.

No one would stop her from protecting him if the seer ruled his thoughts.

At least she hadn't accused Herrick of anything yet, not like she had Daegan. He'd forgiven her. She missed Daegan and longed to be with him, but that would end up with two dragon shifters battling to the death.

Daegan would come out of worry for her safety.

Her heart did a flip over knowing someone cared that much for her. She couldn't wait to sort all this out and get back to him. And she meant to have answers on everything, including what Herrick knew about her background and power.

What to do now?

She had never met this particular Connell family in Luxembourg, but she'd stayed with the Luigsech family in Tegernsee. Plus, she'd seen them recently while returning from Herrick's castle.

That family would open their door to invite her in.

But now she had to find a way across borders without a current passport.

Her stomach growled.

She could handle being hungry or tired, but not both at the same time. Food would invigorate her and help her think through her next steps. Backing away from the tarnished button panel for the apartment units, she hefted her pack again. It weighed more with every step on her sore legs.

When she reached the business area again, one glance depressed her. Small cafes were shuttered for the night. A rat raced out of a dark shadow with a cat chasing it.

She grabbed her chest and backpedaled fast. Then felt like an idiot.

She couldn't make this trip if she started jumping at everything that moved. She had a sword when she could coax it out of the sheath. She had the number Tristan had given her for some guy named Trey in the US, but that would be if she had no other option and needed help.

She trudged toward the corner where she'd made the last turn, backtracking her steps until she reached a street with a little activity.

Her gaze landed on a food truck in a spot that had been empty when she passed by the first time. It seemed to be the only one illuminated for business. Her resident paranoia urged her to hunt up a bar or restaurant, but nothing in sight for two blocks showed signs of life or being open.

She strolled over, taking her time approaching the tall box truck rehabbed with a serving window on this side. Two men speaking French argued whose fault it was for being late tonight. Ignoring them, she stepped close enough to read the menu board hooked on the side.

Whatever they cooked smelled like a stew of yum. Her stomach growled painfully this time.

A tall young man with the thin build of a runner appeared at the open window where orders were taken. He had a thick pile of blond hair on top and short on the sides. Maybe mid-twenties, he wore a white chef's tunic with stains, a tall white hat that had been starched, and a smile of perfect teeth.

His bright teeth struck a contrast with his almond skin and curly light-brown beard. He spoke light-hearted English. "You look hungry, yes?"

His shorter partner with a wide body and bald head faced the grill. "So clever, Ferrand. Only hungry people walk up to a food truck."

Ferrand turned to his left and hissed, "Shut up. First we are late because you fail to pick up supplies on time and now you insult our first customer."

"Only customer," his grill cook shot back. "Is too late to come out tonight. Should have stayed home."

"Tell that to man we owe money on truck!" Ferrand drew a long breath and released a loud, exaggerated sigh. He turned coffee-brown eyes with thick lashes on her. "I am sorry. Please. Let me feed you. What would you have?"

Watching those two go at it like a married couple had loosened the tight muscles in her shoulders. Even the muscles in her face gave in and allowed her to smile. "Are you ready to cook? Sounds like you just got here."

"Yes, yes. This one." Ferrand flicked a thumb in the cook's direction. "He only needs to light grill. We have *Carbonnade Flamande*. Is made of finest beef and my personal favorite beer. No one makes this better."

The surly cook slung an irritable look at Ferrand, who did not turn to acknowledge it.

To preserve their partnership or whatever deal they had, Casidhe glanced at the menu, but decided she was too tired to think. "I would love a bowl of your *Carbonnade Flamande*."

"Excellent choice. I tell truth. We make the best."

His cook corrected him over his shoulder. "*I* make the best. You make problems."

Ferrand clamped his jaws together and ground out a sound of warning.

Casidhe paid and included a tip. Not extravagant, but enough to show her appreciation.

While the cook made lots of banging noise while preparing her order, Ferrand asked, "Where are your friends? We are very behind tonight. We need more business."

Great question. Where were Casidhe's friends?

She counted two right now. Daegan and Tristan.

She'd also like to have them with her to share a meal. She missed Daegan more than she'd believed imaginable. She'd never felt this lonely. It was all because Daegan had climbed inside her heart to take up residence and now was nowhere near her.

Clearing her throat, she said, "I'm only visitin' for a day. Business trip. Nothin' social."

"Ah." He frowned. "Is terrible. You are young and pretty. You should be here for romantic trip. Oh, wait a minute!" He snapped his fingers. "I remember you. Is good to see you again."

What? Her brain had lost the ability to argue so she smiled at the flirt in hopes of moving this along. He probably said that to every female who wandered up.

He waved his hands as he talked. "You will enjoy city. You must stay. This is most beautiful place to—"

"*Order ready!*" the snarly cook shouted.

Shoulders drooping, Ferrand turned to his cook. "Wrap the food tight so it stays warm. She must find place to sit and eat."

The cook slapped down a large serving spoon, making a loud racket. He wrenched around to face Ferrand. "I warn you over and over. Do not think to boss me."

Ferrand shouted at him in French.

Casidhe caught enough to know Ferrand considered the cook a child and a huge mistake to take into business with him. This sounded like an ongoing conflict.

Their words devolved into cursing with the two of them inches apart.

Was she even going to get her food?

The angry cook threw his serving spoon, a towel, a long-handled flipper, then two more towels at Ferrand who batted them away.

All except the last towel. It was soaking wet and hit him in the face.

The door on the back of the truck opened and banged the side.

What the hell?

Ferrand jumped up and ran after the cook, shouting madly. For a heavy guy, the cook covered half a block fast then told Ferrand to have sex with himself.

Unbelievable. Can't one freaking thing go right?

Casidhe walked around to the back of the truck where the door hung wide open. Both men had disappeared, but she could still hear them shouting in the distance.

Good thing for them she was no thief, but she'd paid for the food and wanted it. She waited a minute, heard more yelling and what sounded like a fight.

Would the police show up?

She did not want to be around for the authorities to question everyone and ask for her out-of-date passport. Climbing up a short set of steps that appeared to fold away for driving, she hurried to the cooking area. Food had been wrapped, but not put in a bag. She lowered her backpack, which kept banging the sides of the narrow area, and hurried to find a bag. She snatched the first one up she found and shoved the hot food inside, then stuck it in her backpack.

Sirens sounded in the distance.

Her pulse beat like a war drum.

No one here would bail her out if those sirens were coming for the men from this food truck.

If the police went to where she'd heard the men fighting, she'd have time to leave the area.

Yanking her backpack up to put on her back outside where she had more room, she turned and faced Ferrand.

His cook stood quietly behind him.

Oh, shit.

"I only grabbed my food," she explained.

Ferrand stared at her saying nothing. What was going

on? Then he smiled, but not the charming one from before. This one belonged on a weasel.

She reached into her backpack for the sword.

Something bit her arm. A dart. Her fingers wouldn't grip the hilt. Everything around her wobbled.

She looked up.

Ferrand's sidekick entered the truck and stepped up next to his friend.

The ring buzzed against the skin on her chest.

Her eyes rolled up in her head.

CHAPTER 7

EVALLE SQUEEZED HERSELF AS SMALL as she could to hide in a dark corner. She pushed her dark sunglasses into place. Now would not be the time for some human to see her unnaturally bright green eyes.

A blade of sun just making an entrance at daylight slashed past one corner of her hidey hole. Not much protection from the sun, which would turn her into a charcoal briquette, but better than being caught completely exposed on the upper level.

She still couldn't believe a supernatural had captured Sen and Adrianna. A demigod and the most powerful witch Evalle had ever met once Adrianna took control of Witchlock. She had to find Adrianna. Sen could pound sand, but not her friend.

First, Evalle had to save her own butt. Her phone had died, so that was out, but she had another option.

She called the Belador team coordinator telepathically, *Hey, this is Evalle.*

Trey replied, *Where are you? I just texted you. Storm is about to rip this city apart to get to you before sunrise.*

My phone died. She smiled. That was her Skinwalker mate and Trey wasn't joking. Storm would tear through any world to find her. She gave Trey her location, then added, *Find Quinn and send him. A being I've never seen showed up and snatched Adrianna and Sen.*

What?

Yep. We've got demons coming from all directions and

more Imortiks every day, now this. I want Adrianna back more than anything, definitely more than butthead, but ... much as I hate to admit it, we need both of them. With Daegan and Tristan out of pocket, Sen and Adrianna are two of our best weapons on the street even if we have to badger Sen to do his part.

Got it. I've sent a text to Storm. I'll contact Quinn next. You gonna be okay until then?

Sure. I found a dark corner to hole up in. Trey withdrew from her mind. Her home with Storm was in a downtown Atlanta building not far away. Maybe twenty minutes in early-morning traffic if he hadn't taken off in the wrong direction first.

People were starting to enter the garage down below. Evalle's sensitive Alterant hearing picked up every sound. Engines rumbled into the street-level parking, which would fill up first. People were talking.

Evidently the scuffle she and Adrianna had survived with two demons and an Imortik, which had driven frightened humans away a half hour ago no longer worried them.

Either that or curiosity seekers were showing up.

Evalle could not leave this corner until Storm showed up and cloaked her from the sun. He should be here before people began parking on this level.

A garbled noise like a cross between a snarl and something guttural out of a horror movie drew her attention around and up.

Sickle claws then hairy arms appeared to crawl down from the level above.

Well, hell.

The demon attached to those appendages stuck its head into view. Corkscrew horns protruded from coarse brown hair covering each side of its head. The demon dove toward her level. It flipped and stuck the landing on two feet as long as her forearms.

She clapped. "That's a ten no matter what anyone tells you."

Its head angled to one side then the demon opened a mouth full of needle-sharp teeth.

Pinned in the corner, she quickly shoved a kinetic blast, knocking the demon backward. It rolled head-over-ass all the way across the deck, slammed into the short wall, and flopped down. Shaking its head, the demon sat up.

Glowing red eyes turned her way.

Then the six-foot-tall demon spawn of Big Foot stood and started forward. Its lower jaw hung open. Jagged fangs dripped saliva.

Yuck.

No problem. She could slap the demon around with kinetics until Storm or Quinn showed up.

That idea flew out the window at the sound of a vehicle from down below climbing the one-way ramp at the far end of her level. How could she keep humans safe from this thing while stuck in the shadows?

When she checked the demon, it had heard the same thing and abandoned having her for a meal.

She threw kinetic hits to slap the hairy body, but it zig-zagged until too far away for her to make a direct hit. Sweat pebbled on her forehead and drizzled down her neck. That monster would kill any humans coming this way.

She called up her spelled dagger.

The demon slowed before reaching the ramp and waited like a predator preparing to attack easy prey.

Evalle pulled her arm back and shouted, "Here I come. You want me or not?"

The demon twisted around.

She whipped her arm forward and released the blade. It zinged through the air, but the demon had enough time to lift an arm to knock the blade away.

"Shit! Why couldn't that work like in the movies?"

The sound of the vehicle's engine grew louder as it neared the top of the ramp. A human would see the demon any second now.

Please let the occupants stay in the vehicle and not run away screaming.

A demon would love an easy chase.

She couldn't believe it when the engine revved. Tires squealed, racing forward. A Jeep blasted into the parking area and drove the demon into the wall at her end of the structure. Contact made a nasty crunch.

The driver's door flew open. Black hair pulled back with a leather thong and with teak-colored skin thanks to his Native American genes, the man of her dreams rushed over to her. "You okay, sweetheart?"

She smiled. "I am now, demon smasher. How's your Jeep?"

"It'll live." Storm pulled her into his arms and hugged her close. His heart pounded like crazy.

Nothing scared this man except losing her.

She felt the same way about losing him.

Colors dulled as his cloaking fell over them. She'd fought every battle alone from the moment she escaped a basement she'd been locked inside as a small child until she turned eighteen. After she escaped and ended up in Atlanta, this incredible man crashed into her world.

Sen had brought in Storm to catch Evalle in a lie and put her away. That hadn't worked out well for Sen.

Storm's kiss cured any problem in her world. When he lifted his lips away from hers, he brushed the loose hair off her face and palmed her cheek. "Where the hell is Adrianna? She promised me this wouldn't happen."

"Not her fault, babe. You're not going to believe what happened. Some weird being showed up and took her." Evalle nodded at the disbelief in his face. "Took Sen, too. Thought they were a pair."

Storm frowned in disbelief. "Clearly a being who doesn't know either one of them." He glanced around at the still-empty parking deck where sunlight streaked through the open areas. "You can tell me all of this once we deal with the demon. Stay close so you're protected from the sun. I'm going to widen the cloaking to include the demon."

They walked over to where the demon remained smashed between the Jeep's grill and a solid cement wall. Black liquid oozed from its mouth with every rattling snarl.

Storm squatted down. "Who do you belong to?"

The demon hissed at him, but its glowing red eyes drooped with agony.

Sighing, Storm tried again. "You're dying. I can put a spell on you to stay exactly as you are in constant pain while we find your creator. Or I can end this fast."

A limp hairy arm flopped to the parking deck. The demon's bright eyes rolled around then landed on Storm. It wheezed every breath. More black gunk leaked from its nose, but it tried to talk. "I uh ..."

Storm waited patiently.

Evalle asked, "What about civilians coming up to this level?"

"I caught a security guard and told him to keep people from coming up. Told him we suspected a demon up here. I had no freakin' idea that was true. I just wanted to get to you without any interference."

"I-sha-uh ... " the demon garbled and spit out.

Impatient, Storm asked, "What?"

Evalle jumped in. "Wait a minute. I think it is trying to tell us." She asked the demon, "Is your maker I-zubrrali?"

Its eyes opened wide with understanding. "I ... bar... ee."

Standing up to face her, Storm asked, "Is that the person Reese thinks is her father?"

"Yep. That's probably all we're going to get from this

one."

Holding his hands above the demon still pinned between his truck and the wall, Storm murmured a string of words in a rough voice Evalle recognized as him chanting.

Bright demon eyes dimmed then the lids closed. When it drew one last breath, the demon poofed into dust that swirled away.

Storm had treated that creature more humanely than it deserved since it would have ripped her or a human apart and eaten every piece. Possessing demon blood from one half of his genetics, Storm could destroy demons without a second thought, and had done so when necessary. But he had his own code of honor, regardless of his roots.

Once Storm had the ashes cleaned up, he assessed the front of his Jeep. "I can get that fixed with no problem."

"Evalle! Where are you?" Quinn shouted, running toward them.

Jeans covered his long legs eating up ground with Belador speed. He'd been dressing down from his normal business suit look to work with the patrols. Tall with fair hair and an aristocratic profile, he wore a black turtleneck like a younger, deadlier version of Steve Jobs.

Storm stepped outside the cloaking and held up a hand. "She's safe. I'll bring you in the cloaking when you stop."

Quinn slowed a few steps out then stopped, breathing hard. As soon as he was inside their secret shield, he asked, "What happened?"

Evalle rarely saw Quinn so panicked, but he and Tzader had taken her on like big brothers when they found her. She could take down nonhuman monsters with no help on night patrols, but those two men had been her only shield against powerful Tribunal beings, including Sen, before Storm stepped into her life. She gave Quinn a bullet-point report, something she'd been learning to keep as brief as possible. With teams reporting to her as the interim Maistir, she now understood what a pain it was for someone to tell the entire story instead of significant highlights.

As the actual Maistir, Quinn listened intently. "We must find Adrianna and Sen. Preferably before the Tribunal realizes their enforcer is missing."

"No kidding. Got any ideas?" she asked.

Storm crossed his arms, dark eyes intent on every word said. "Can Reese help us track them?"

Evalle glanced at her mate. "Uh, Storm ... "

"What, sweetheart?"

Quinn lifted a hand. "She's trying to be polite, because she doesn't know that I found Reese and we talked."

Evalle let out a heavy sigh of relief. "Finally. Did you two work things out?" Not really her business, but she needed to know what to do if Reese showed up to help hunt demons again.

"We did. We're good." Quinn's face relaxed into a smile.

"Okay." Evalle nodded. "So she's not demon hunting any more, right?"

"Wrong. We've reached an agreement. I intend to keep her with me when she goes out on patrol, but she wants to do this."

Storm's eyebrows lifted at that declaration.

Evalle grinned. "So glad to know I'm no longer the only one responsible for keeping her alive. We appreciate her help, but she's making me crazy when she comes out with the teams."

"Understood," Quinn allowed. "I still want her protected if I'm not present."

"You can bet on it." Evalle gave him a thumbs-up. "Just glad you're sticking around for a while. We need you." She had never wanted to lead anyone, just doing her best to stay alive and keep her people and loved ones safe.

"Back to Reese," Storm said, reminding them what they had going on. "Do you think she can track Adrianna and

Sen?"

Quinn cupped his mouth. "I doubt it if they teleported, which is what it sounds like."

Storm quietly argued, "But what if it wasn't teleporting? Didn't Reese see where your daughter was taken through a bolt hole?"

"She did," Quinn replied in a thoughtful voice. "Good point. We should at least determine if it was teleportation or if the being used another way to exit."

Horns blew with the traffic getting heavy down on the street. Evalle interjected, "We need a way to get Adrianna's car out of here. I don't like leaving anything of hers here, not with the way unknown supernaturals are showing up. I have no idea if they could use something of hers against her or us."

"Where is it?" Quinn looked around, ready to take off immediately.

"Next level up. The body of a Belador is also up there."

Quinn stopped short. "What happened?"

"Sen." Evalle cleared her throat. "A Belador climbed up to the top level. He was yellow with glowing eyes. We were trying to contain him to be picked up. Adrianna has been careful not to use Witchlock around a being we might save whose in the grasp of an Imortik. That's the only reason she was willing to wait on Sen once I sent a text to call him in."

Quinn cursed. As an empath, Storm picked up on Evalle's misery. His warm gaze consoled her.

"Exactly," Evalle agreed with Quinn. "Our Belador struggled to talk to me telepathically. He managed to tell me he had a wife and child right before Sen killed him." She fought back the sting of tears. The Beladors would watch over his family forever, but that would not replace a husband and father.

She pushed on. "When Sen showed up, he started

mouthing off about not having room for our crap. I questioned why not since he's a demigod. All this happened as I still had a kinetic field holding off the Belador-Imortik attacking us. Adrianna shouted for Sen to do something ... so he killed our Belador. Adrianna lost her shit. Sen said the death was her fault because she wasn't specific when she said to deal with it, but he also admitted he did it because he hates me. Those two really got into a shouting argument, then that being showed up and snatched both of them."

"Why?" Storm asked, a permanent frown of confusion on his face as he listened.

"Well, the weirdo was really upset anyone had killed an Imortik. Sen mouthed off at him. Adrianna just happened to be standing too close to Sen. The being accused Sen of showing off for his girlfriend and they all disappeared."

Quinn had a look of someone who saw a dancing turtle with his own eyes and still couldn't believe it.

Evalle lifted her eyebrows. "Yep, this is crazy stuff."

"Can we get inside Adrianna's car?"

"Doubtful. It was locked when she was grabbed."

"Let me see if Trey can contact Tristan to come here and teleport inside Adrianna's car. We must leave the car where it is at the moment, though. Reese might do better sitting in the driver's seat without anyone else sitting there after Adrianna."

While Quinn stared off as he called out telepathically, Evalle turned to Storm. "I need to go up there, too."

"We will. My truck will still run." His truck also stayed warded against the sun. He put a hand on her shoulder and squeezed. "We'll get Adrianna back."

Evalle believed Storm would do all possible to save their friend, but she struggled to commit to his confidence.

Quinn's gaze came back to Evalle. "Trey is contacting Tristan. Why don't you two meet me on the top level? I spoke to one police officer below and warned him no one should come up here, that it was a crime scene and more APD would be coming soon. I'll call one of our Beladors in the Atlanta Police Department to send officers to keep humans below this upper area."

"Sounds good." Storm walked Evalle over to the passenger side, then jumped in, and backed the Jeep away from the wall.

When they reached the top level, Quinn was exiting the stairwell and speaking into his mobile phone. He shoved the phone inside his jacket and strode over to where the dead Belador remained.

Evalle's stomach lurched.

Storm parked next to Adrianna's fire-engine-red Lamborghini. Once he had Evalle out and cloaked again, she told him, "See if you can help Quinn, okay? Then stay outside the cone-of-silence, so we don't have to put everyone inside here."

"I will." He gave her a quick kiss and left. The minute he did, his body changed to an unfocused image as if she stared through murky plastic.

Quinn knelt next to the body, looking as heartbroken as she felt.

Storm said something to Quinn, who stood and stepped back. Then Storm dropped down and placed his hands on the man's chest. Storm's lips moved. In the next moment, a yellow glow bulged around the body. Storm's face muscles flexed, and he seemed to be snarling his words. The glow shrank back inside the body and vanished.

Had he pinned the Imortik inside?

She'd completely overlooked what had happened once the Belador died. Had the Imortik been trapped until Storm began freeing the man's spirit? Based on what Evalle knew about her mate, that's what he probably did first.

Why hadn't the Imortik been able to break free? Maybe

because the Imortik had been trapped inside a nonhuman body that died before the yellow monster could take over.

So many things they did not know about Imortiks. For example, did all Imortiks function and react the same way?

After another moment of Storm talking calmly, a frosted covering seemed to wrap the body. That must be some form of preservation.

Quinn used kinetics to move the body to the side where the short perimeter wall tossed a shadow over it. He joined Storm as they walked back to Adrianna's car.

"Where is Evalle?" Quinn looked around until Storm pointed to where she stood near the car.

"She's right there."

Tristan appeared so close to her she jumped. He looked the same as always in his dark gray T-shirt and jeans, but different too. He had a quiet edge to him now as if his time with Daegan had begun honing him, and in a good way.

Quinn quickly explained what was going on and nodded at where Evalle stood, invisible to all of them.

"Got it." Tristan bent at his waist and looked inside the low-slung car. "Let's try this." He vanished. His big body appeared in the passenger seat to avoid messing with anything Reese could. His too-big-for-exotic-cars body looked like sushi-grade tuna stuffed in a sexy can.

In another couple seconds, the door locks popped open and Tristan climbed out. He handed over a key. "Is that all you need, Quinn?"

"Yes. How did you find another key for her car?"

"Adrianna had one stuffed on the visor. It's not like she worried about anyone stealing *her* ride."

Storm asked, "How's Daegan doing?"

"Still has venom in his body, but being in Treoir gives him a super-charge. He took that damn ice dragon out of the dungeon to fly the island."

"He did?" Quinn sounded both surprised and apprehensive.

"Daegan's patience was beyond belief. First, he saved that ice-dragon-shifter jerk and created a safe place for Skarde's dragon and his human form. Skarde never shifted and the bastard wouldn't talk until today. Once Daegan got him talking, he thought he could turn Skarde into an ally. In a show of good faith, Daegan took him out to fly with the red dragon. That ice dragon took off unexpectedly and attacked the gryphon village."

Evalle shouted out loud, "*What?*" No one heard her. She repeated it telepathically to Tristan.

Tristan cringed and looked in her direction. "Damn, Evalle. How about not shouting?"

Storm's eyes darkened at the tone Tristan had taken with Evalle, but she deserved it.

She sent an apology to Tristan telepathically. She knew not to shout in someone's mind, but a freaking dragon had attacked her friends.

Quinn asked, "Was anyone harmed?"

"My sister had her arm broken and Bernie got banged up, but the healers have set her arm and gotten them healing faster. I was in the village and had half-shifted to protect Petrina and Bernie when I got pummeled with a load of ice." Tristan's green eyes fired up more with talking about his sister. "Some of the cabins buckled. We'll fix that. My gryphon had a damaged wing, but I've been in Treoir for a while, so I healed immediately, especially with the push of power from the new Treoir births."

Quinn smiled. "I noticed a push of energy and figured Brina had given birth. I take it everything went well."

Evalle sent to Quinn, *I noticed it too and never even considered the births.* She smiled. *That is so freaking cool.*

Tristan smiled, taking some of the edge from his face. "Yep. Daegan will tell you all about it once we stop the Imortiks."

Quinn glanced at Storm who gave a head tilt in agreement. "Understood. Thanks for coming here, Tristan. I think that's all we need."

"Before I go, anything you want me to report to Daegan?"

Quinn pulled out his phone and started typing a text. "I don't. I need to check on the car I sent to pick up Reese. You may want to talk to Evalle."

Tristan looked in her direction again.

Evalle called to him telepathically. *Just tell Daegan we're fine.*

Tristan cocked an eyebrow. *How is Adrianna and Sen missing fine?* He lifted a hand. *Let me rephrase that. How is Adrianna missing fine?*

Quinn took off and disappeared in the stairwell.

It's not, Evalle admitted. She could not lose one of her closest friends. *But you two can't do anything about Atlanta or this world until you find the grimoire volumes. Do you think you'll have what you need in six days? Isn't that how long we have before we lose Devon and the others? We don't even know what happened to Renata.*

To be honest, Evalle, I've teleported to so many places at different times of the day that I'm losing track of time. I'll tell Trey to send us a daily reminder. We're working to return as fast as possible, but it will help to have updates on how much time we have left.

Holding onto hope was the most difficult thing when facing impossible odds, but no one ever succeeded by giving up. She had to get Tristan headed back to Daegan. *Thanks for being here every time we need it, Tris.*

Tristan looked down then raised a humble face to her. *You got it.* He vanished before anything else could be said.

Would that Alterant-gryphon ever be comfortable with being thanked or complimented? Maybe not, but he'd come a long way since the first night they met when he tried to kill her.

Muted screams erupted down on the street below.

Hell, what now?

Storm ran over to the edge and looked down. *"Quinn? You need help?"*

"What's wrong?" Evalle shouted, but not even Storm could hear her in this cloaking.

CHAPTER 8

FROM INSIDE THE TINTED WINDOWS of a sedan, Reese watched the angry faces of humans shouting at her, *"Monsters! Get out of Atlanta!"*

Those people didn't even know who, or what, she was, did they?

A fit young man drove the black car Quinn had sent for her. Just like all the other Beladors who had driven her, he remained calm and held an obvious confidence, but the steering wheel creaked under his fingers.

She seriously doubted that tiny sign of stress was from fear of a human crowd. More like concern about delivering her unscathed to his Belador Maistir.

She asked, "Is this car bullet-proof?"

"No, ma'am. The Maistir wanted you picked up immediately. I was closest. We didn't have time to send for an armored car. Please don't be concerned for your safety."

"I'm not." Could he hear the lie in her voice?

Her car moved closer to the parking deck entrance where APD worked to keep citizens out. One woman ran forward and beat her fists on the windshield.

An officer pulled her off and directed her to stand behind a line created by yellow crime-scene tape.

Reese had her doubts about the strength of that tape against a mob.

A thick-bodied man with a wide face and long hair to his shoulders yelled, "If you're going up there with demons, you're not human. *Stop murdering our people! Stop hiding the truth!"*

She maintained a stoic face to avoid agitating the crowd more. How would supernaturals, as well as their families, survive in the human world after this?

Would all of them be hunted?

Would humans ever believe that many, like her, protected humanity from really dangerous predators?

Still, that man had nailed one thing. The supernatural community was doing its best to keep all knowledge about their people from humans. For now, anyhow.

At some point supernaturals would have to face the world and come to an agreement on how to coexist with humans. With chaos and violence erupting across the city and spreading beyond, now wasn't the time to say, "Yes, we're the boogeymen you always hoped didn't exist. Here are cookies. Can we be friends now?"

She had a stranglehold on the strap of the seatbelt crossing her chest. A movement ahead of the car drew her attention.

Quinn appeared outside the parking deck at street level with his gaze locked on her car.

The angry mob surged.

Gut-wrenching fear grabbed her throat. She jerked forward. *"Quinn!"* Grabbing the shoulder of her driver, she ordered, "Go help him or let me out so I can."

"The Maistir forbade me from leaving you alone in the car."

Gripping the door handle, she yanked with all her strength. Locked, of course. If she'd been a Belador, she could have broken it off or kicked the door open. Nothing gave way.

"Here he comes," her driver announced in a soothing voice that failed to lower her blood pressure.

Reese twisted around.

Quinn broke free of hands grabbing at him. He angled

his head to look up at the sky, or maybe the top of the structure, and shook his head at someone.

By the time she gave up twisting her neck to see what he saw, the rear passenger door lock clicked.

Quinn yanked the door open and dove inside, locking it again. He leaned over, cupped her head, and kissed her temple. "You okay?"

"Sure. Why wouldn't I be when you're out there swimming through a riot?"

"I heard what they were yelling at you." Hurt dimmed his blue eyes.

She leaned over and gazed into the rearview mirror with a cocked eyebrow.

Her driver acknowledged her silent accusation with a shrug. "It's my job, ma'am."

"Call me Reese and I'll let it go."

He flipped a quick look at Quinn, who nodded.

"Very well ... Reese."

She leaned back, ignoring the jeers outside, which began to fade as they entered the lower parking level.

Quinn had been relaxed and smiling at her place before taking off to come down here. His haggard face now wore the strain of life as a Belador leader.

He brushed a wild curl from her forehead. "Remember, we have a deal."

"I know. But I'm not fragile."

"Elroy might be," Quinn suggested with a straight face.

"*That* is never going to be his name." Reese placed a protective hand over her middle, but smiled at Quinn's attempt to lighten her mood with another goofy baby name.

His gaze raced over her as if he wanted to commit every hair on her head to memory.

She lifted a hand and tried to finger-comb her wild reddish-brown hair, which could probably scare a demon right now. She'd had no time to freshen up when he'd asked her to help.

He caught her hand. "You look amazing." He kissed her knuckles as the car climbed another level.

In three words, he'd made her feel attractive no matter how she looked. "You're sweet even if you are losing your eyesight. Fill me in so I can get up to speed fast."

When the car paused on the next to last level, Quinn jumped out and retrieved a dagger. The crowd noise rumbled through the open door, but had dulled considerably.

As soon as they reached the top level open to the sky and parked on the opposite side of Adrianna's car from Storm's Jeep, trepidation churned Reese's stomach.

What if she could not find Adrianna or any lead?

How many times had she told herself in the past to only focus on what she could do right now? Got it.

She jumped out the minute the door lock disengaged before anyone could open her door. Taking in the shiny red car and Storm, she asked, "Is Evalle at home?"

"No," Quinn answered as he joined Reese. He handed Storm Evalle's dagger and pointed at an empty spot between Storm and Adrianna's car. "Evalle is standing there where Storm cloaked her."

Oh. Reese gave Evalle a wave.

Quinn said, "Evalle sees you and hears you, but we can't see or hear her except with my telepathy. She wants the window opened on this side of Adrianna's car so she can hear what you share."

Reese hurried over to the driver's door of Adrianna's car.

Quinn followed her and leaned in to use a key to open the passenger window, then pulled his body out. "As I explained on the phone, if you can't find anything, that's fine. We think sitting in Adrianna's seat will give you the best chance at being able to view where she went."

Reese climbed in and got comfortable. Holy moly.

She'd never even sat in a car this expensive. The seat fit her like a glove.

Okay, enough ogling Adrianna's sexy ride.

Reese placed her hands on the steering wheel and dropped her head back with her eyes closed.

In thirty seconds, her remote vision opened up. She watched silently as Adrianna and Evalle went on a new patrol from here, fought demons, then returned as light started highlighting the eastern horizon.

When they came back up, she had a front row seat to what Quinn had told her happened when the two women arrived on this parking level.

A bright yellow guy climbed up to this level from the far side. Imortik. Wait, not just an Imortik.

Evalle identified him as a Belador.

Reese's fingers tightened on the steering wheel. She leaned back, not wanting to get up close to the yellow being as the crazed man ran at Evalle and Adrianna. Evalle held him off with a kinetic shield.

Reese started talking. "Evalle and Adrianna are trying to save the Belador, but also stay away so the Imortik gripping his body doesn't jump into one of them. Evalle texted someone, then ... Sen showed up. She wants him to transport the Belador to VIPER."

Nibbling on her lower lip, Reese shook her head. "What a piece of work. Sen's giving Evalle a hard time, saying he doesn't have room ... whatever. Jerk. The Imortik-Belador is slamming Evalle's kinetic wall. Adrianna snapped at Sen to deal with it. He ... *oh, shit*! You bastard, Sen. He killed the Belador." Tears burned her eyes. "Evalle is holding the dead guy's head. Adrianna is getting up in Sen's face. She's really pissed, and Sen is egging her on. Adrianna's furious. She's walking over to him, reading him the riot act."

Reese took in everyone and continued. "Evalle looks

worried about Adrianna and is trying to calm her, but her witch friend and Sen are locking horns. Uh … that's not good. Adrianna brought out her Witchlock energy. It's spinning above her palm."

Reese clenched her clammy hands, wishing she could throttle Sen. What a miserable demigod. She breathed in and out, slowing her panic. "Sen is … " Reese jerked back against the seat, trying to get away from the being that appeared. She muttered, "Whoa. What kind of being is that? Power. Lots and lots of dark power is covering the deck. Tall guy. Maybe seven foot, but skinny. Like he got stretched. Bony hands. Milky skin, whiter than a cadaver. Black hair, maybe dark blue. Boring face. Thin eyebrows, thin nose, thin lips. Swirling white eyes, glowing like molten energy. Blood-red centers."

Squinting to figure out a small detail, she murmured, "Tattoo on his cheek. Looks like ... a skull?" She leaned forward. "Dark energy flooding around him. His robe is shiny gold. Maybe copper. Black symbols float over the material. He's yelling at everyone about the dead Imortik, blaming Sen for showing off to his ... *girlfriend*?" Reese's voice went up with her surprise.

She continued, "Guy must be on crack to think Adrianna and Sen were an item." She flinched. "A black cloud opened and swallowed them."

Reese cupped her head, working to stay in the moment as Sen and Adrianna vanished into a dark cloud. When everything came into focus again, she muttered, "That's weird. Sen and Adrianna are floating horizontally behind the tall being. He might be towing them with majik. The black hole is opening into a foggy tunnel, sort of. Is he entering a room? Too dark. Everything blurry again. Oh, wait, they're still moving. Now ... Adrianna is in a dreary stone place like a medieval dungeon with her hands chained above her head. She's facing Sen, but her eyes aren't open. She's breathing, though."

Reese sat still for several minutes, waiting on something more. Then the being reappeared in another room. He shrugged out of his robe, now wearing a pale green button-down shirt and jeans.

She leaned in closer. What in the world?

He waved a hand casually at the room without looking up from where he stared down at something on a normal office desk. The room brightened with light glowing from some location or fixture out of her view.

This room did not fit with the dungeon at all. This space appeared too contemporary. She scanned every wall, surprised by the pictures and the modern window above his head.

The being stilled then lifted his head slowly. He turned to stare straight at her and flicked a finger in her direction.

Light exploded in her face.

She screamed. Had that bastard blinded her?

Quinn was there, pulling her from the car and into his arms. "Reese, what's wrong?"

She blinked and widened her eyes, thrilled she could see the parking deck. She lifted her gaze to Quinn. "I'm okay. That asshat flicked power at me. I thought he blinded me."

Quinn had been worried, but now looked stricken. "Did he hurt you?"

"No."

"What about—"

"Jethro is fine," she assured him, offering a smile to ease his panic.

Shaking his head, Quinn groused, "You scared the crap out of me. I'm glad ... Royston feels okay."

"Dream on." She pushed apart.

Storm joined them, explaining, "Evalle followed me to this side and wants to ask some questions." Storm gave Reese an assessing look. "We both want to know if you're okay first."

"Yes. What else did Evalle want to know?" Reese turned that question to Quinn who would talk to Storm's mate telepathically.

"What about the tattoo? Evalle said she never noticed one."

Reese fretted, "I'll have to draw what I can remember, but the best I can describe it is a skull covered in designs or carved with designs. Something tribal, but not like Native American." She sighed. "I don't know."

Storm asked, "Did the designs remind you of Egyptian tribal or Celtic?"

"Not really. It's as if you drew a square and kept drawing the line toward the center so it repeats the shape of the square as it shrinks in size, then repeats again. Reminds me of adult stress-relief coloring books. Does that make any sense?"

Storm's forehead drew tight with thinking. His gaze lit with an idea. "Could it be Aztec or Mayan?"

She snapped her fingers. "Yes. That's what it reminded me of from art I saw often in San Diego when I lived there."

Quinn asked, "Could you tell what kind of realm they're in?"

Reese propped an elbow on the car's roof. She took her time, trying to be sure of what she saw. "This may not make sense, but I really studied the last place I saw him. When he came back from that dungeon, he made light glow in what appeared to be a normal room or more of an office space, based on the furniture and windows." She moved her gaze from Storm to Quinn. "This is going to sound so freaking weird. I saw a picture of the city, Atlanta at night, on one wall and local sport teams' paraphernalia scattered around. I think Adrianna and Sen are right here in the city."

CHAPTER 9

ADRIANNA LICKED HER DRY LIPS and squinted against the throbbing in her head, specifically her forehead. What had that strange being done to her? Who was he?

She struggled to shake off a dull sluggishness and come fully alert. Stone walls that belonged in a castle surrounded her. Real stone chunks that appeared to have stood for ... eons. No window. Long room with more chain stations, all just as stained and aged as the walls.

Where had she ended up thanks to Sen?

Her arms and shoulders ached from being lifted above her head. She sat on a cold floor and the place smelled damp and putrid.

Across from her, Sen slumped with his arms up in the air, too. Bastard. Served him right for killing that Belador, but she had done nothing to deserve this. She wished the weird being would finish what he started with Sen.

Be nice for someone to show Sen how he treated others.

Angling her head to the side, she peered at her hand that held Witchlock and slowly opened her palm.

The energy came to life.

Then it began to jut out of shape from its normally round look as if stabbed from the inside. Energy pulsed out in one direction then sucked in and poked out in other directions. Her energy should be a spinning ball of energy and not making a high-pitched noise as if trying to break free.

She snapped her hand shut.

Witchlock had ... shrieked? That was ... not just new,

but worrisome.

A raspy groan dragged her attention to the demigod of her nightmares, who slumped with his legs outstretched on the same dirty floor.

His shackles glowed for an instant. She looked up at hers, also glowing, then it stopped.

Not a promising sign.

Did that crazy being have a way to constantly renew the power in the shackles?

Sen's chin touched his chest. He made another groggy sound.

"Wake up, jerk," she snapped at him.

Lifting his head, he showed off a black eye. "What, bitch?"

"It's witch, not bitch," she ground out.

"Pretty sure I had it right the first time." His acidic tone felt like sandpaper dragged over her skin.

"How'd you get that black eye?" Not that she cared since he deserved ten of them if he had ten eyes.

"First attempt at escaping."

When had he tried to escape?

"You can't heal a black eye?" she gloated. "Karma can be a mean bitch."

"This is healed for wherever we are." He ran his tongue inside his mouth and spit a tooth out to the side.

Lovely image.

She waited to see if he'd say more.

He yanked at his chains, muscles bulging with the effort. He snarled a deadly sound. Still plenty of fight in Sen. He banged his head back against the wall and his arms sagged as far as the chains would allow. "Something is pressing against my power. Yours too probably. You'd have seen how I got my black eye if you hadn't passed out."

"I don't pass out. Try again, Sen."

He lifted his gaze and shook his head then stopped and

pinned her with a smirk. "Our captor slammed you from the back with a hit of majik and you landed against that far wall. You have your own black eye. We match."

"Ugh," she muttered, not happy to have anything in common with him. That black eye would explain her banging headache. Being the bigger person in this room, she offered, "Much as the idea of doing anything with you revolts me, we should work together to get out of here."

He jerked one chain and leaned forward. "Don't like me, huh? Big surprise being a Belador suck-up and bestie with a fucking Alterant."

She hated even breathing the same air as Sen. This demigod had done his best to put Evalle away more than once. He kept an extra load of hate in reserve just for Adrianna's closest friend.

No one could figure out why. Even after all Sen had done to her, Evalle would not attack him except in self-defense.

"What?" Sen growled without looking up.

Adrianna waited until he lifted his bludgeoned face again. In spite of being a demigod, Sen had been locked into slavery to the Tribunal and now sat here battered and imprisoned. What did that make the being who captured them?

Genuinely curious, she angled her head to study him. "With all the nonhumans out there, what did Evalle do to land on top of your hit list?"

He huffed out a sarcastic sound. "Trust me, she isn't at the top, but close."

"But why her at all?" Adrianna waited, but he said nothing.

She'd feel a twinge of sympathy for someone who seemed to have no friends. She'd heard he'd been in charge of VIPER security for more than a few centuries. From what she could see, he had to perform whatever task the

Tribunal handed him without question.

She had nothing better to do than keep prodding him. "I'd ask if you have even one friend, but I seriously doubt you're capable of any type of relationship."

He flashed a furious glare at her, then looked away.

Had she really struck a sore spot?

What would he do to her? Not much if he could not at least teleport by now. Otherwise, he'd be gone by now.

This place and the shackles might slow Witchlock, but she doubted any being could shut down the ancient power. "Come on, Sen. Surely you have the energy to answer one question."

Grounding out a sigh, he rolled his head to face here and snarled, "What? You still nagging me about that Alterant bitch?"

She smiled at his aggravation and gave a single nod.

"She breathes my air."

What a stubborn rock. Couldn't he just talk? "Do you fear her? Is that why you can't admit the real reason?"

Sen lifted his head fully this time. His hands fisted and the chains banged the wall. His blue eyes glowed hot. "Careful, *witch*, or I might not find you so amusing."

She'd definitely hit his pissed-off button. Not stopping now, she changed her tone to serious. "See, I'm not buying you got up one morning and decided to hate Evalle for no reason. That's shallow, even for you."

Sen's eyes continued to burn bright. "You want to know the truth?" he asked in a soft voice that would chill a monster.

She lowered her chin and let her power flood her eyes, then answered in a deep, inhuman voice. "Oh, yes. I'd like to hear the answer to one of the great mysteries of our time."

Angling his head to stare at the far wall, he breathed slowly for a moment as if trying to decide if he should say anything. "I've been stuck at VIPER as enforcer for the Tribunal one thousand years, sixty-eight days, twelve hours, fourteen minutes, and ... whatever else since we were taken."

Wow. She hadn't expected that length of time, which meant he was at least a thousand years old. But how had he ended up *stuck*? Since Sen had decided to share this tiny bit, she remained quiet to see how far he would go.

"It should have ended at one thousand years, but then fucking Evalle came along. This miserable drudgery of dealing with lesser beings would be over now if Tzader and Quinn hadn't taken her in like a little sister. Damn Beladors." His voice had dropped to a guttural sound.

"What did Evalle do to you, Sen?" He acted as if he hadn't heard her. "*Tell me!* What changed? Grow a pair for once and tell the truth!"

When he swung his face to her, his eyes were feral and glowing. His fingers curled so tightly, blood ran from his palms. "No one could figure out what to do about that Alterant when she was the only one running around free. Goddesses and gods do not like when unknown beings with serious power show up. Before my time was up, the Tribunal requested another hundred years of my *service*." He spit out the word service as if keeping it inside would poison his tongue.

Adrianna had clearly hit his trigger button. Her heart tap-danced in her chest at how Evalle had never had a chance. She'd done nothing more than exist.

Holding her gaze with his unyielding one, Sen snarled, "One more day answering to VIPER and the Tribunal was too much. I could have ended my time *right fucking then!*" Looking away, his lips curled back and his voice matched that of a mad animal. "If VIPER had given Evalle a hundred-year sentence the one time they locked her away, I could have disappeared even then."

While Adrianna could now understand, and maybe even sympathize a grudging bit with Sen's position, she could never justify such a decision. Lock an innocent person away for a hundred years just because she had been born?

"Why couldn't you fix the problem now, Sen? The Tribunal knows Evalle isn't going to slaughter humans or nonhumans at will. You could ask them to free you from this obligation instead of continuing to blame your misery on Evalle."

Sen looked incredulous for a second then laughed a dark sound. "You really think it works like that with deities?"

She heard the bitterness and couldn't argue with him. If she'd been forced into a position like his, she'd hate it, too.

But she wouldn't punish someone else the way he'd gone after Evalle. "I don't get it, Sen. Who forced someone with *your* power to be a servant to the Tribunal? How could anyone do this to you?"

Silence reigned for a stretch, then he admitted, "The Tribunal agreed to take me on as a *favor*."

A god or goddess had handed him over to the Tribunal, which meant Sen had no ally dominant enough to go up against the being who placed him in servitude, and for so long.

She mused, "A thousand years is ... mind-boggling."

Sen scoffed, "A hundred years to anyone in the Tribunal is like a week to you inferior beings."

"Says the half-human being," she countered.

He glowered. "I don't claim that half. I'm above humans and the rest of you."

"There you go again, trying to snub me when I might be able to get us out of here." When he continued to just stare at her with dead eyes, she added, "Or don't you want to leave?"

Sen's deadly eyes narrowed. "I'll get out *without* your help. Don't expect me to drag you with me."

Considering what happened to him in the past, creating more enemies in the supernatural world was not wise, especially right now with Imortiks running wild. Unable to shrug with her hands chained above her head, she mirrored his detached emotion with her voice. "Fine. That will make my escaping so much easier *without* you. But remember that I offered. You had a chance to form an alliance. It makes me wonder why you would pass up the opportunity to escape imprisonment."

"It's simple." He pulled his lips back, exposing all his white teeth, in a smile meant to send vicious animals whimpering away. "I'm not owing anyone else again, and *never* someone beneath me in the power structure."

Then what power held him here? She pressed on. "If you're so above everyone else, why are those shackles keeping you from teleporting?"

Sen yanked on the shackles and the room shook like they sat at the epicenter of a major earthquake. "Why don't you shut the fuck up?"

Dark energy rushed through the room.

Their kidnapper appeared on the right of where Adrianna sat. Would he give her water if she asked nicely?

He stood with his hands behind his back in a proper way. Same wacked-out gaze, but the red turned into pinpoints. She could do without his smile filled with pointy teeth.

"I am Tenebris."

Her Latin was not the best, but she believed that name meant dark or darkness. Wonderful.

Unlike when he initially yelled at Sen in fury, Tenebris now sounded as if he'd been sent by a superior to catch them up on today's schedule. "The time has come to answer questions. Before either of you consider trying to ignore me or remain silent, I will share what happened to the last being who dared to deny me."

He held his hands in front of him eighteen inches apart

with his palms facing each other. A growly sound came from deep in his chest. He moved his hands apart until his arms were stretched wide to each side of his chest.

The filmy shape of a body formed slowly.

As the image sharpened, so did the scent of old blood and decay.

Adrianna breathed through her mouth and tried not to throw up. One leg had been ripped from the socket of the figure. Fingers appeared cut from each hand. Blood that had dripped from an empty eye socket had dried on the naked woman's cheek.

Her other eye stretched wide in terror.

She blinked.

Adrianna held back a scream of horror that she still lived. Any reaction would not save this woman.

The female's mouth opened, but no words came out. Just grunting. She had no tongue.

Adrianna turned her gaze away.

Sen shouted, "Fuck you if you think you can do that to—"

Light flashed through the dungeon room.

Adrianna blinked to clear her vision. The gory image was gone along with Sen and the kidnapper.

Her heart slammed her chest. She fought to keep her wits about her.

A long painful howl in another area. Now, she felt true sympathy for Sen. She had to find a way to get them both out in spite of his attitude. If that bastard Tenebris tried torturing her, she doubted Witchlock would allow it any more than she would.

Howling turned into a scream that crawled across her skin. She gripped the chains holding her wrists to keep from unleashing Witchlock, the consequences be damned.

But Witchlock might just destroy the world around them as well as everything here. She never wanted to kill innocent people who had no idea what went on in here.

She would never like Sen, but after finding out what drove him to be cruel, she had a sliver of empathy.

Releasing the chains to let her arms swing from them again, she opened her palm where Witchlock began spinning. Her powerful ball grew to the size of a canalope ... then lost shape again. She'd had this power long enough to know when something was very wrong. How would she get out of here without Witchlock?

Her heart screamed at the thought of never returning to her home and friends. To never get a chance to set things right with Isak. She called on Witchlock to calm and work with her. Without this energy, Tenebris would win. She kept sending her power in soothing waves, anything to gain control of Witchlock.

Seconds ticked by. She started to smile at the energy rolling into a ball.

The Witchlock's energy grew double in size and warped out of shape. Energy lifted her hair and sizzled across her skin.

She tried to close her hand and put Witchlock to sleep.

Her fingers stopped halfway. She gritted her teeth and forced her hand muscles to work. Her hand and arm shook. Veins stood along her forearm. Her fingers turned white.

"No, Witchlock. *Stop!*" she shouted at the ancient energy.

CHAPTER 10

BLURRED IMAGES SWAM THROUGH CASIDHE'S mind. She fought through her mental fog and ... fell unconscious again.

Something irritated the skin on her chest.

She blinked a heavy-lidded eye open and kept blinking until she could see through both. Now if she could just process a thought. The hum of an engine vibrated through the floor she laid on.

A truck.

She had enough information for now, but she couldn't turn or move her body. They'd tied her hands and feet. Kidnappers. More mental tips kept flooding in. Stale smell of food lingered. The food truck in Luxembourg.

Ferrand. Mean cook. Both phony.

That asshat Ferrand had stuck a needle in her neck, which explained the cottonmouth sensation.

She tensed, twisting her head at painful angles to look around. Where was her backpack? No! Her heart sank. What had happened to her sword?

Maybe her sword would attack whoever tried to use it.

But the scepter!

She had to have that priceless treasure. Would these two know what they had? Were they even kidnappers? Who were they contacting for ransom?

What if they contacted no one? Her skin chilled at the possibility of being caught up in human trafficking. Please, please, no.

She needed to hang strong. Thinking about being sold was not productive.

Adrenaline burned off the last remnants of sluggishness. She had to escape these two. They hadn't attacked her physically, so far. If they did plan to ransom her, that wouldn't last a minute past realizing they'd grabbed the wrong woman.

She had no value.

That hurt to admit, but who would pay to get her back?

Daegan. Hope lifted her spirits. She might be able to convince these two to call Trey at the number Tristan had given her. Daegan would stop at nothing to find her. He'd deal with these two as well. She didn't want a bloodbath, but neither did she want to end up as a human sex slave.

Or had they captured her for someone else?

Who?

Were they supernatural bounty hunters? She dropped her head back, sick at that thought. Had Cathbad, Queen Maeve, or another player put a price on her head?

Her only hope was reaching Daegan. He would come for her.

Had he gone to the hotel in Galway and discovered her missing yet? Tristan indicated his boss would be busy for a day or so, but Daegan had a way of showing up sooner than expected. This would be a perfect time for his impatience.

She closed her eyes, thinking back on how peaceful and happy he'd looked when she woke to find him in her bed at the hotel. She couldn't recall a happier moment in her life. Watching him stare at her with warmth and eyes filled with caring. He'd been happy to see her and had been unhappy to leave her.

Never in her life had she felt so coveted.

Why couldn't she have that every day of her life?

She had no idea how far this would go with Daegan, but

she was all in. She wanted more with him.

Daegan made it clear he wanted more, too.

He'd vowed to give them a chance once he protected the world from Imortiks and could pursue her with honor. He was her perfect man. Sexy as hell, a force nothing could stop, and gentle with her.

She'd have to explain how she ended up in this part of the world. With the way she'd been betrayed by her people, she had a hard time worrying about answering Daegan's questions honestly. He deserved her answers more than Herrick deserved the loyalty she'd shown him for her entire life. She'd explain to Daegan how she needed a couple days to first deal with something, then she would tell him everything he wanted to know about her.

Daegan was reasonable.

She'd deal with Herrick, then call Tristan's guy the minute she found a place for her mobile phone to function.

She had no phone at the moment.

That brought her back to escaping.

Maybe Daegan would bring in the person he'd used before to track Casidhe. Someone who used a remote viewing gift to search for her.

The ring on the chain laying on her chest buzzed, irritating her skin.

What was with the ring and why had it started acting up today? Or yesterday. What time was it?

She ignored the itchy feeling on her chest she couldn't reach. That was the least of her worries right now. Herrick needed to explain the ring, too, when she arrived.

If she ever got to the Caucasus mountains.

How long would she have to wait? She licked her dry lips and called out, "Hey. Can I have some water?"

The men might not have heard her raspy voice over the engine noise.

How long had she been unconscious? She should feel

rested, but the drug left her drained.

The truck took a sharp curve, jerking her body sideways. They drove up, climbing an incline. A tire dropped into a hole and back out again, bouncing her body against the hard floor.

She yelped.

Out of the darkness, her backpack fell across her legs.

She had momentary relief, but would her pack still contain everything?

Her stomach growled and clenched. When would this freaking drive end?

Minutes crawled along until the engine groan decreased and the truck slowed.

Wish granted, but to be honest, she wasn't ready for whatever they did next. Her pulse kicked into high gear. She had to prepare for an opening to fight her way out. Her fingers had gone numb. She bent her fingers to close and open them, working the feeling back into her hands.

Pain needled through her fingers.

The truck bounced off of a somewhat smooth road onto a rough surface and stopped with a jolt. The passenger side door opened and closed. Then the rear door opened.

There stood Ferrand, not looking any happier than her.

"Why are you doing this?" she demanded.

Silently, he stepped up into the kitchen part of the food truck. He untied where she was bound to the truck and lifted her to her feet. Then he freed her hands and legs.

The door was open.

She rushed out and dropped to the ground, stumbling to her knees. She pushed up, disoriented by the dark. Clouds drifted past a partial moon, giving her some light.

Swinging around, she searched the landscape for any indication of where she was. No lights from a house or building. Rolling hills. Open pastures. Trees in the distance.

Why would he stop here?

She should run.

Not without her backpack.

She whipped around to hurry back to the truck and fight for her possessions.

Ferrand tossed her backpack to the ground at her feet, jumped down, closed the rear doors, and returned to the cab without a word.

As soon as the passenger door slammed, the truck drove off.

What in the world? What had this all been about?

Casidhe stood there staring at the truck until it disappeared around a curve. If those two had not kidnapped her for their benefit, then who was behind this?

She dug out a bottle of water, glad to see all her contents were still intact. She even had the bowl of food still wrapped up. Might as well eat it. If they wanted to kill her, they'd had plenty of time.

Had the Connell family she'd contacted pulled strings to get her removed from their city? How would they know she'd go to that food truck?

It had been the only one on the street then.

That seemed even more odd now.

She ran it all back through her mind. That Connell person could have been alerted to Casidhe flying in and had her watched.

Then when Casidhe asked for a meal, Anna told her food trucks were still about and sent her away.

Low and behold, a food truck appeared.

Everyone had a limit and Casidhe marched closer to hers every minute.

She'd always been impressed by the network of squire families. Not so much at the moment as she'd witnessed how they could be used against her just as easily as to help her. The idea that Fenella must have sent word up the line to other Connell squire families sickened her.

She lost her appetite and shoved the half-wrapped food back into the pack.

Lifting the backpack, she shrugged it into place again and tucked the half-empty bottle into a side pocket.

Where was she?

Wait! Her phone.

She dug into the place she always kept her phone and found the device in three bashed pieces. They'd intentionally broken her phone and left it for her to find.

No way to call that Trey guy to reach Daegan or use her phone to determine her location. She started walking uphill. Not because she wanted to torture her calves, but she needed a high point to give her a hint at where they'd dropped her.

After walking a slow incline a couple hundred yards long, which felt like a mile up, she saw the twinkling lights in a village spread across a valley.

But her heart kicked up as predawn light crept over a mountain range behind the village, outlining the uneven top.

An odd outline formed in the middle of the ridge.

She'd seen that before and knew this area!

Picking up her pace, she continued over the crest and down the road, begging her aching calves to hang with her a little longer. She slowed when she spotted a gnarly tree with no leaves that hooked toward the road like an old man bent over. Rushing ahead, she broke out a grin at the sight of a mailbox with vines crawling up the old wood post. A small flag of Germany waved from where it had been stuck in the box.

She knew the people who lived here.

Her heart thumped wildly with relief.

Those men had dropped her in Tegernsee and not too far from a Luigsech squire family. One she'd visited recently.

Maybe the Connells had pulled back from her and left

Casidhe to the Luigsechs. She didn't understand why or being kidnapped, but she couldn't wait to get with familiar faces who might know more.

The dirt road that peeled off from the main thoroughfare took a twisted path uphill again.

She shifted the backpack and walked with renewed determination. Funny how a taste of hope could infuse new energy into a tired body.

Excitement drove her to walk briskly, ignoring her aches and pains. Soon, she'd be inside a cozy cottage with a sweet middle-aged couple and their two children. They would still have food left over even with dinner having passed a long time ago.

The stew Ferrand had given her soured in her stomach.

If the Luigsechs just welcomed her into their home, that would fill her soul.

She rounded the last curve and the quaint house sat at the base of a tall hill. The same hill she'd run down the morning Herrick had dropped her off on a plateau overlooking the Tegernsee Lake.

Trees growing for many generations surrounded the home and a mix of flowers filled tidy gardens.

She hated to wake anyone, but these people rose early and would be understanding about her unexpected visit once she shared her circumstances. She lifted her knuckles to knock on the weathered wood door and listened for any sound.

Someone mumbled. Footsteps thumped over a hard floor to the door.

Casidhe stood away, waiting for the woman or her husband to look through the peephole.

The husband groused, "What do you want?"

Casidhe took a breath and gave the same password, using Hugh as her last name again. She finished with a smile.

He didn't answer at first, but spoke to someone, probably his wife. When he came back, he cracked open the door and kept his voice low. "Go to the top of the ridge and wait."

Her hope hit rock bottom. "Is something wrong?"

He looked past her and lifted his finger to his lips. "Must be quiet."

More was going on than she realized. She nodded. "Will you bring food and a blanket when you come up? I just need a little rest then I'm ready to be on my way."

His eyes held no warmth as she'd seen the last time. He nodded and closed the door.

Suspicion chewed up her insides, but she could go no farther without help. If she tried to ask more questions, would she end up shipped out of here, too?

She would do as he said and wait. Until he proved he would not help, she had to give him a chance to talk away from his family. That was fair to ask of her, now that she thought about it. He hadn't acted mean or rude.

Not like Fennella, who had clearly shut off all Casidhe's options for traveling.

Casidhe swung around and headed for a path, which would take her up to a flat stretch of land higher up.

Herrick's dragon had dropped her there when he'd flown her as far as he could on her way home last time. If this Luigsech family could not help her arrange for travel with someone, what then?

She finished the climb and reached the flat ground where she walked over to drop her backpack at the edge facing water. Sitting, she pulled up her knees and felt all the effort from tonight hit her hard. She crossed her arms over her knees and put her chin down. Wind ruffled waves below, forming white curls. All that adrenaline and hope oozed away.

She'd been on her own all of her adult life, but this felt like a deliberate shunning. Her heart couldn't take much more. Fenella had betrayed her. The seer, Herrick, or both had betrayed her.

No wonder that Daegan had captured her heart.

But he'd also pulled back. She understood. They came from two different worlds. Even she didn't know where her power and gift had originated.

Daegan hadn't wanted to go too far with her, but he'd made his feelings clear. With all that had happened to her, she had a man who would cross the world and fight the kraken to protect her. Warmth spread inside her at that realization.

She'd see him again soon. Not just see him, but she'd kiss him to the point his control would snap, then she'd have him right where she wanted him.

In her bed.

She would figure out what was going on at Herrick's castle, have her talk with him, and clear the air. She'd have to tell him about Daegan. Herrick would not understand, but then she didn't understand why she'd been treated as no more than a lure for the red dragon.

Her lips twitched, wanting to smile. She'd caught Daegan and he was hers now.

Maybe once she and Herrick had an honest conversation, she could then go to Daegan and ask about Skarde. Everything inside her said Daegan would be reasonable. If he had Skarde or knew where Herrick's brother was, Daegan would hand him over. With another dragon pretending to be the red dragon, she could see how Daegan might have teleported Skarde to Treoir and kept him there until he found the imposter.

Just who was that imposter?

She'd let Daegan explain how he'd come to have Skarde, if he did indeed possess Herrick's brother. Something told her he did, but she couldn't honestly put her finger on why she believed it.

No matter what, once Casidhe left Herrick's castle again, she intended to tell Daegan that Herrick lived and spill her entire life story. All that she knew of it. If what she'd read in TÅµr Medb was true, the red dragon had stood by every other dragon family at one time to protect the clans. There had been no stories about Daegan hunting treasures for his hoard.

There had been plenty of stories of him fighting to protect the lands.

He had been the peacekeeper.

That fit the man she loved.

She sat up. *Loved?* Whoa, she was jumping ahead. Yes, she felt deeply for Daegan, but ... she had to think about love. That had never been on her radar her entire adult life.

In her mind, love was a forever commitment.

What about spending the rest of her life with Daegan?

She stared at the water that rippled here and there. Her heart and mind joined forces.

Forever with Daegan would be wonderful.

Her energy rumbled again. She placed a hand on her chest. What was with that sound?

A bird flew over, squawking.

She smiled, watching as it disappeared.

Now was not the time to get ahead of herself. If Daegan could help her hand over Skarde, she might get Herrick to end a secret war he'd been waging against the red dragon his whole life since moving to the mountains.

He had to be tired of carrying all that anger.

Wasn't his number one goal to find Skarde? He'd sent Casidhe through the university then set up her and Fenella at the ancestral centre just for that reason.

The more she thought on that particular point, why would Herrick sabotage Casidhe *now* when she had the best chance at finding Skarde?

Maybe he wasn't behind any of this.

His seer just might be driving all this interference. Kleio could have sent a message to Fenella as if it had come from Herrick.

That would explain the doors closing in Casidhe's face.

Herrick had no reason for subterfuge.

He held the ultimate power over Casidhe and his people. All he had to do was send word he wanted her to stay in Galway. The longer she sat there thinking on the squire family rejections and not receiving a warning about danger as Fenella had, the more Casidhe believed Kleio could be trying to keep her from the castle.

Why? Had the seer received a new vision on Skarde? Did she know where Skarde was and wanted to be the one to hand over his brother?

Had she come up with a way for Herrick to kill the red dragon? Still, why get Casidhe out of the way?

Casidhe sat up. Her hands shook and her palms became damp. Had Kleio seen Casidhe and Daegan together and kissing in a vision?

If so, Herrick might believe Casidhe to be a traitor.

She slapped a hand over her eyes. Between beings with scrying walls, remote vision, and Kleio, Casidhe had no way to keep anything in her life a secret. She lowered her hand, eyes blinking away the sting of tears.

Why couldn't Kleio give her a break?

Damn her. Casidhe would ruin the seer's plan if that was going on. She'd save Herrick from the seer and tell him what she suspected. She needed a chance to talk to him far from Kleio to figure out if Herrick had been poisoned against her.

Wind slid over her, ruffling loose hairs. Her skin pebbled in warning. She knew better than to ignore her sixth sense.

Who watched her?

No one out at sea unless they had a telescope, but she'd

left herself vulnerable from behind.

She reached into her backpack and jumped to her feet in one smooth move, turning with her sword ready to defend herself.

A tall and muscular dark form walked toward her.

Was it Daegan?

He shoved a hood off his head.

Not Daegan.

CHAPTER 11

ENTERING THE TALL DOORS TO Treoir castle, Daegan angled toward the hall on the right, which led to Garwyli's quarters. Blood still surged through his body after having dealt with the gryphon village. He wanted to go there and see for himself that his people and their homes were taken care of, but he accepted Tristan's assurance that repairs were being managed.

If not, Tristan would not have teleported away to help Quinn open a car in Atlanta. Daegan would find out more on that when he returned.

Standing in the center of the castle, Daegan restrained himself from shouting for Garwyli. He risked disturbing Brina and the babes, even though they were far away, tucked deep inside her and Tzader's private family area. Also, with the old druid moving slower these days, Daegan did not want to cause Garwyli any undue stress.

As the druid's young protégé, Lanna feared Garwyli's days were running out and the druid would leave her to take his place. The young woman had a tender heart for everyone she considered hers to protect. But she struggled with the thought of losing Garwyli for more than losing a tutor. The old druid had become far more important to her.

Daegan understood. He could not bring himself to accept that the old druid might pass soon. He needed Garwyli's wisdom and advice with the Imortik crisis, but more than that, he needed Garwyli alive and smiling. He needed his friend.

The door to Garwyli's area opened as Daegan approached.

He'd become accustomed to Lanna sensing his presence and opening the door, but the druid stood there this time peering down the hall.

Daegan slowed his steps as the druid stepped out. Garwyli's white beard and hair reached his waist, all of it bright as snow on a sunny day. He always appeared in a simple robe, the one today a pale gray with a tasseled belt tied at his middle. His rheumy eyes shined with warmth, but that old druid could put the fear in a fool with a glare.

Closing the door softly, Garwyli tapped his cane ahead of his steps. When the druid reached Daegan, he tottered on past him with a wave of his hand to follow.

Daegan stayed with the druid, who slowly led him through a series of short halls until Garwyli paused in the middle of one walkway. He turned to a marble wall on his left and lifted a crooked finger. He drew an arched opening.

The stone wall vanished, exposing a garden Daegan had no knowledge of and a feeling no one else could access without this druid present.

Garwyli entered with Daegan right behind him.

The minute Daegan took two steps inside, he felt a mild sizzle brush his skin. He had the sensation of life pulsing through the brilliant flowers of every color framed by deep green leaves on some and softer greens in other areas.

Trees stood tall with wide branches stretching overhead as if protecting all who stepped beneath the leafy wings. Birds sung softly and tiny creatures chattered, all of it blending into a pleasant hum of life.

Daegan opened his hands with his palms facing up. Tiny blue zings of energy skipped across here and there.

He glanced up to find Garwyli seated on a wooden bench carved with Celtic symbols. The old guy breathed deeply with his eyes shut, his face calm, and his gnarled hands propped atop the cane standing in front of his robed knees.

"Sit, dragon," Garwyli said in a congenial tone without opening his eyes.

Daegan strode over to the bench, smiling at the old guy's joy of using dragon as his name. "'Tis quite a garden. Energy flits around as a butterfly huntin' a flower." Daegan took a spot on the eight-foot-long bench. As he surveyed the lush surroundings, his gaze paused at where they'd entered.

The arched opening had returned to solid rock again.

Garwyli opened his eyes and faced Daegan. "Ya have been patient ta not press me for more than I had been ready ta explain."

"Ya owe me nothin' ya wish to keep to yourself, druid."

The old guy smiled at the moniker that had become a sign of their close friendship. "I know Lanna has told ya I am trainin' her ta replace me."

There it was. Garwyli admitting the end of his days.

Daegan's eyes stung, but he would not make this more difficult for his friend by revealing the pain cutting him up. Still, who would blame him? He had only recently gained this extended family and cherished each one. The possibility of not seeing Garwyli in the halls every time he returned to the castle sucked the joy from this moment.

"'Tis more than facin' my mortality some day in the future." Garwyli took his time forming his thoughts. He admitted, "I created this garden long ago ta rebuild my energy as I aged."

"I feel the energy in here on my skin." Daegan's gaze picked up every little movement. Nothing in this garden appeared to be dying, not even a leaf. He swallowed, hoping this meant they had a way to save his friend. "Ya should come here more often."

Lifting a hand to stall what Daegan was clearly suggesting, Garwyli said, "When I first began ta absorb the energy here, blue lightnin' strikes would flash all about the garden, raisin' the hair on my head."

Now Daegan understood what he saw. This was not the powerful garden of so many centuries past. Even this garden would slowly die.

Garwyli's fingers moved slowly as if he heard a sound only he could detect. "This garden has done its duty as I have done mine. 'Tis why I need ya ta know Lanna is ... "

Daegan prodded, "Is what?"

Garwyli shook his head as if struggling for words. After a long silence, the druid frowned at some thought and continued. "Tzader and the others who travel ta the human world often tell me of many unusual human discoveries. One is called a supernova."

"'Tis an odd word." Daegan seemed to always be learning of something new in this world.

Garwyli stared off at nothing, still in a thoughtful pose. "Over many thousands of years, humans have discovered much about what exists in the sky. They find planets besides the one they live on. Stars in the sky possess tremendous power deep inside at the core. I have no idea how all this happens and might not be explainin' it correctly, but if energy in a star runs out, the star explodes. A supernova is a very, very powerful and bright explosion. They say ta understand how giant the star was ya must think of a planet one million times the size of earth explodin'."

Daegan could not comprehend anything of that nature nor why they were discussing it. "I do not understand what ya speak of."

Garwyli's eyes crinkled. "I do like bein' able ta outwit ya."

Chuckling, Daegan sighed. "Aye, ya have earned that right, but to be honest, 'tis easy to outwit me about today's world. Now explain what tree ya beat around in words a simple dragon shifter can understand."

Tapping a crooked finger on the top of his cane, Garwyli said, "When my energy is no more, my passin' will be much like a small star not even the size of Earth. 'Tis ta be expected. But should we lose Lanna, we lose a supernova."

Chill bumps lifted on Daegan's skin at what he realized Garwyli said.

The druid angled his head at Daegan with a challenge in his eyes. "She is the future of the Beladors, humans, Treoir, and many worlds besides ours. She has grown more powerful since I first met her, which was not long ago. She must be trained for her benefit and that of the people she is determined ta keep safe."

Daegan considered the significance of what Garwyli shared. "Ya do know she considers *ya* one of hers, do ya not?"

"Aye." The druid sat quietly for a bit, then added, "She wants me ta stay forever even though she knows I am not immortal."

Daegan had been thinking on this and suggested, "'Tis written in the chronicles how to use the river of immortality runnin' beneath the castle."

Shaking his head slowly, the druid said, "'Tis been there the whole time I have lived in Treoir. I never wished ta live forever. I have had my time. I shall not die today or tomorrow, but when I leave, ya need someone ta take my place. Someone more powerful than I would ever be for the way the world is changin'. Ya need Lanna."

Daegan took his druid's words to heart and agreed with Garwyli's thinking, with one exception. Had anyone asked Lanna if she wished to walk away from her life outside Treoir? The lass was barely an adult. Would this life mean she would never marry or have a family? Did she want that?

These things would be better discussed once Daegan could remain in Treoir longer than a few hours at a time.

He would find out what Lanna wanted.

Garwyli would always put duty first, just as Daegan had, but now he wanted Casidhe to share his life.

How could he want a future with her while denying Lanna the same choice?

There was much to think on, but he had to leave here soon.

Even so, he would not rush Garwyli who had asked so little of him before. "What can I do for ya, druid?"

"Do not allow Lanna ta drain herself tryin' ta save me. 'Tis yar duty ta protect her, even from herself."

Daegan would fulfill Garwyli's wishes no matter how much it hurt the day he'd have to say goodbye to his old friend or how much Lanna would hate him for stopping her from using her powers to save Garwyli.

Every decision he made affected more than one person.

How had his father managed it? Daegan had fulfilled his duty as the protector of King Gruffyn's lands as well as all the other dragon clans allied with them. He would never be the king his father had been, which was why he had no plans to rule Treoir, only to protect it.

"What weighs on yar mind, dragon?" Garwyli asked, always seeming to sense what others were going through.

"I am thinkin' how my father was a just and fair king, who watched over all our people and made good decisions. I was never trained to be a king. 'Tis why I am glad for Tzader and Brina, who will rule together."

"'Tis not what bothers ya," Garwyli argued.

Daegan could not dance around the druid and win. "I must make the right choices and decisions. I made a bad decision earlier today and it resulted in my gryphons bein' harmed. Those injured are healed and their homes will be repaired, but a greater mistake could cost many lives of humans and nonhumans."

Garwyli tapped his finger a bit. "Yar da would be proud

of ya. He would not expect ya ta know this minute what is yet ta be learned."

Daegan frowned, not finding help in his words. "I understand this, but to make decisions without knowledge is to risk much. To risk myself and dragon is one thing, but 'tis much at stake today in our world. The burden lies with me to do right by all, as it should." Daegan propped his elbows on his knees and dropped his chin down to rest on his folded hands. "I believed I was bein' right by the ice dragon to take him out to fly, but he attacked my people. They trusted me to not release an enemy in Treoir, the most protected place for all our people. I failed them."

Sighing loudly, Garwyli turned to him. "Ya can only do what ya know ta be correct this day. Then do the same the next day and the next."

Daegan had carried so much alone for so long, it felt good to share his inner thoughts with the person who would not judge him. "I did just that in the past and left my family unprotected." His words fell off with his darkest admission. "I fear repeatin' such a mistake today."

The druid studied his wrinkled hands and spoke with a quiet reverence. "'Tis simple, Daegan. The past be carved in stone with lessons learned, the future waits ta test those lessons." He lifted his eyes weighed down with wrinkles and surrounded by bushy white eyebrows. "The choices made today shall validate the past and determine the future."

Daegan soaked up all Garwyli said and rolled each word around, taking all this wise druid said to heart.

Garwyli was explaining how a decision made today would prove who Daegan had been in the past as well as who he would be in the future.

If so, he had been right to give Skarde a chance to gain his freedom. The mistake Daegan had made was in not insuring all others were safe.

He should have been the only one to face Skarde's attack.

Skarde and the other ice dragons had believed the lie that Daegan's red dragon started the Dragani War. Showing Skarde kindness had been a step toward convincing him Daegan was not his enemy.

Or based upon Garwyli's words, to have not given Skarde a chance to become an ally would have validated the ice dragon clan's belief from the past and would have insured they remained enemies in the future.

Daegan could only make choices he believed to be in the best interest of his people and their world when pressed to do so and insure his people remained safe as possible when he took a risk.

He was not perfect, would never be, but he could perform his duty. His past had given him wisdom to use in this world.

A weight lifted from his shoulders at realizing he could do this and find a way for his people to live in peace.

Evidently Garwyli had said all he wanted. He rose slowly and tottered to the wall.

In two strides, Daegan stood right behind him. This time, when Garwyli lifted a finger to draw an arched opening, the wall sizzled as stones vanished.

The old druid's skin had a new flush to it as he left. He would be here for a bit longer.

On the way to his quarters, Garwyli waved a hand for Daegan to go ahead. "Lanna wishes ta speak with ya."

Concerned, Daegan asked, "Ya do not wish to join us?"

"Nay. 'Tis time ta visit the babes." His voice carried the joy shining in his eyes.

"I enjoyed our talk." Daegan teleported the druid to the end of the long hall leading to Tzader and Brina's private quarters without asking his permission. When Garwyli reappeared, he turned to Daegan and wagged a finger then went on his way.

Stifling a laugh, Daegan headed for the area where Garwyli trained Lanna.

She stood outside the door with her arms crossed. Lines of worry marred her smooth, but pale, skin and tight mouth. "Where does he go?"

"He wishes to see the bairns." Daegan reached the door and waited for her to step through.

"Oh."

"Why do ya sound concerned, lass?" Daegan entered and closed the door.

"Garwyli goes off alone sometimes and ... I worry for his safety."

"I am not Storm, but I know when I do not hear all the truth." Daegan stood in the middle of the room. His gaze tracked over the small and large items added by a wise man who had spent many generations here. Lanna had put her stamp on the area too, proven by the light feeling in the space. He turned to her, wondering if she'd tell him the truth.

Guilt piled up in her eyes before she glanced away. "I speak truth that must be said."

"Lanna," Daegan started gently and waited for her gaze to lift up to his. "Garwyli has been here a very long time. He has his secrets as do all of us. Allow him the room to do as he needs. He will not leave without makin' sure ya know first."

A slight flush filled her cheeks, but she had even more of a pinched look. She wore her fear and stress with dignity. He hoped they both had more time with Garwyli.

She walked over to a tall window looking out on the lawn stretching from the castle to a dense tree line. She tucked her small arms across her chest, then turned around to lean against the window and face him. "The ring speaks to me now."

This young woman had the ability to toss him sideways with a few words. "Ya mean the half of my sister's ring I gave ya to hold?"

"Yes. But messages are confusing. Garwyli tries to help. Is no good. He tells me to discuss with you."

This young woman might be a powerful being, but she lived inside a human vessel, which could crack wide open from strain. She was determined to do her duty, no matter what was asked of her. Pressure from the strain poured off her.

How could he ask more of her when she carried enough burden? "Lanna, I appreciate your help, but ya have a lot to do here. This can wait."

She lifted striking blue eyes too mature for one her age. "I understand you want to help. No one can take away what I feel. If you do not talk to me about ring, I add that to worries."

Damn. He had to trust her the way Garwyli did, but he would spend more time with her once he could return for longer periods. "Tell me your questions and I shall do my best to aid ya." Daegan had waited so long to hear anything about his sister, his palms became damp and his heart pummeled his chest. Could this tiny cousin of Quinn's be the one person to answer questions about his family?

Straightening away from the window, Lanna seemed to push off her sadness about the druid and focus on the moment. In that moment, an incandescent power bloomed twice her size, sparkling.

Then it was gone as quickly.

He began to understand what Tristan had been trying to tell him and what Garwyli called a supernova level of power.

Lanna opened her palm and extended it to him. "I wish to hold ring again."

Daegan fumbled trying to pull the ring out fast enough

and hand it to Lanna. He was a fool to stand here, heart racing with anticipation of finding his sister who had not been immortal.

Explain that to a heart still yearning for his family.

Lanna held the ring sandwiched between her palms and closed her eyes. Light leaked from her hands as if she had captured a small sun.

"Ring vibrates," she murmured.

"Yes," Daegan confirmed. "Not much, just now and then."

Her blond curls with black tips moved about then lifted around her head as if current surrounded her. She opened her clear eyes. Her hair settled again. Had she just released some pressure?

She explained, "Ring wants to be whole. This half searches for other half and one who possessed complete ring."

He couldn't hide the anxiety in his voice. "My sister, Jennyver. Do ya think that means my sister lives?" Yes, that was a stupid question, but he had to ask it. Garwyli berated him any time Daegan dismissed someone from the past as dead. The druid often asked Daegan how he and Skarde could still be alive.

Lanna only allowed, "I do not see her in this world."

This was why Daegan argued with Garwyli when the druid tried to convince him to think positively about finding his sister.

Every time Daegan got his hopes up his heart cracked open again. He muttered, "'Twas foolish of me to think she still lives."

"Is not what I say," Lanna snapped, sounding short-tempered. Then she caught herself. "I am sorry. I worry about ... things. If sister is alive or dead, I would see her. I would know."

The confidence of this lass awed Daegan. "I shall do a

better job of listenin', Lanna. What can ya tell me?"

She walked around, gripping the ring in one hand and waving her other hand as she spoke. "I am not sure. Is strange. I feel ring yearning for her. Sister is somewhere ... vision blurry like thick fog ... " She stopped and shook her head. "I do not understand location."

Fog could mean his sister had passed into the afterlife. Daegan suffered another bout of discouragement, but he would not give voice to negative thoughts here.

Opening her palm, Lanna extended her hand for Daegan to take back the ring. Light no longer glowed from her hand.

He pushed the ring into a pocket. He'd kept the ring on his being with majik even when he shifted. "Thank ya, Lanna. I will take all ya told me to heart." He started for the door.

"I read your father's chronicles each day."

He stopped and swung around. "I recall you aidin' Brina and Tzader in locatin' the family names. So ya know how to read the Treoir writin'. 'Tis impressive."

"Garwyli teaches me. I know much, but not all words," she explained with humility. "I read king's words about gifting daughters with special rings and how ring breaks apart for daughter to leave one half if kidnapped."

"'Tis true. I mentioned that to ya on my last visit."

"Yes, but you do not listen to your words." She held his gaze with the steel-blue eyes of a tutor who commanded a student's attention.

Where was Garwyli when Daegan needed an interpreter? "I do not know what ya mean."

"I find note your father wrote later in chronicles. He said rings live and die with daughters."

"Yes, 'tis also what he told me when I was young." Lifting his shoulders, Daegan admitted, "Much as I try, I do not understand how this half of Jennyver's ring is callin' to the other half. That would seem to mean my sister is still alive. Yet, I see no possibility of such unless she is hidden in a realm and still possesses one half of the ring. If so, how can one half know to hunt the other half if she is not in this world?"

"I share all my visions with Garwyli."

Daegan fought to keep his emotions locked down. "And?"

Lanna cocked an eyebrow at him. "Garwyli said to pull a stone apart with my fingers would be easier than opening your mind to possibility your sister still lives. I try to show you what I know, not what I want or do not want. Truth only."

Daegan stared at the floor. "'Tis the right of it. My mind has a difficult time acceptin' what I cannot see with my eyes. I envy your gift of vision." He felt a deep weariness every time he opened himself up for more disappointment. "Allow me time to think on all of this. I shall return or send a message if I have a question ya might be able to answer."

Giving him a sweet but tired smile, she offered, "I do not wish to raise hopes only to disappoint you. I will do all in my power to search more and help if I am able. Did you ask Luigsech woman about ring?"

"I haven't had a chance, but I will."

"She is important."

Daegan once again noticed the maturity Lanna had gained just by spending time with Garwyli. He felt Casidhe's importance, but Lanna meant with regard to finding the other half of Jennyver's ring.

Could Casidhe figure out what happened to his sister with her resources, such as that professor?

Only she would know.

He'd tried to convince himself again and again that Jennyver was not alive and to stop chasing an empty dream.

Lanna had said, "If sister is alive or dead, I would know.

I would see her."

She had not seen Jennyver dead.

For the first time since he escaped TÅµr Medb and be-gan hunting for his sister's burial site, Daegan questioned Jennyver's death more than her being alive.

CHAPTER 12

BRYNHILD TOSSED BAGS ON THE sofa when she walked back in from a full day of searching for everything she needed.

Joavan was proving to be more helpful by the hour.

She called over her shoulder, "I will shower. Alone."

"You wound me."

"You will hurt more if you do not listen." In the bedroom, she pulled off the soft shoes, then dropped the black pants and gauzy shirt. In the large bathroom, she glanced at the mirror, admiring her necklace of bones sharpened into points.

Joavan had not been impressed.

He did not have to be, only her.

She removed her new jewelry and took her time under the hot water in the bathroom of his hotel room. He called it a suite. Such an easy man to spend time around and helpful in this new world. He could stay with her as long as he became no problem. She rinsed the shampoo from her hair, feeling more like herself for the first time since entering this new world.

Everything in this time was strange.

She missed her family and longed for the freedom to shift and fly whenever she wanted.

Never had any human been a threat to her dragon before.

Those flying machines with weapons were unlike anything she could imagine.

Once she'd dried off and pulled on one of the two robes Joavan had explained the hotel supplied, she smiled with appreciation at her new shortened hair. So easy to towel dry and walk away. Opening the door to the main area, she stood there, searching for Joavan. He had not given her reason to suspect he could be a threat, but she trusted no one out of her sight.

"There you are, dove." Joavan stepped in from the patio overlooking the city with a glass of wine in each hand. He wore the other hotel robe. "I took the liberty of ordering enough food for you to choose whatever pleases you."

"That is acceptable." She took a glass and sipped. "Today was good. We did much."

"You're a pro in the stores."

"I found it easy once I understand more." She'd kept mental notes of everything Joavan did from paying people to the words he used.

Cathbad thought to bury her in books.

Nothing would ever match being able to learn while living in the world. She sniffed the food, turning to find a table covered in upside down metal bowls.

Joavan stepped around the table, lifting each metal covering as he called out different dishes. Always ready to please her.

She did not trust him one bit.

She wanted no man clinging to her. Definitely not a human.

But she liked having him around for the time being.

"Come. Eat while it is hot." A smile drew his lips up, showing off his attractive face.

Strolling over, she took a seat and stared at the different eating utensils arranged with napkins. She had never been shy about eating and wasn't now, but neither did she want Joavan to think she was untrained.

The point of spending last night with this man had been

to gain information and learn how to blend in with the humans.

And to enjoy sex. Humans were such simple beings.

How difficult could this one be to keep around for a while?

Joavan began serving meats, a strange vegetable called broccoli, sauces, and bread. She moaned with happiness over the bread. Her mouth watered at the succulent smells. Cooks in her time had created great feasts, but they would have been in awe of this food, too.

While she ate, Jovan talked about all the things they could do tomorrow.

When he wiped his mouth with his napkin, she mimicked him.

"But first, it is time to tell you who I am." Joavan placed his napkin to the side of his dish.

She shrugged and smiled with confidence. "I know all I need to know." He had a nice body and was adept at kissing. He seemed intelligent enough to fit her needs.

"Oh, but you don't, dove."

"Please. I am not a woman who desires a mate. I will not become a servant or breeder for any man. Do not waste energy trying to impress me to change my mind." She stood and smiled to please his basic nature of being a man ready to rut. "I did enjoy last night. Has been a while. You entertained me much."

He pushed his chair back and stood. "I'm glad you enjoyed our time together and we *may* do that again."

His words made no sense. He *might* have sex again? Only if she desired such, because he was unimportant. She dipped her head in his direction. "Then we are in agreement."

He lifted his hands, placing the fingertips together in a mirrored form in front of his chest. "I know of the red dragon."

Suspicion shot up her neck. He had tricked her. She backed up, arms and legs bulging with a coming shift.

"Please do not shift into your dragon, Brynhild. Give me a chance to share everything I know."

Muscles in her shoulders and neck tightened. She was sick of men lying to her. "I kill anyone who allies with the red dragon."

Her body mass surged.

"*Stop! Please.* I am no ally of that bastard!" Joavan shouted.

The rope on her robe fell open. She stood there heaving short breaths.

"I tell you the truth," Joavan said, voice calm. "I will tell you everything if you give me a chance. I have not deceived you."

She wanted to scream at him that he had, but recalled how he *had* given his name last night. To be honest, she had not asked for more. Slowly, her body began to shrink, but her dragon was not happy and railed to get out.

Silently, she told her dragon, *Wait. We will hear him out. If we do not like his words, we will destroy him with our energy.*

After another moment, she pulled her robe into place and tied the belt. "You have one chance to live. Take care with the words you choose. Start with how you know the red dragon."

Joavan showed no sign of relief, except for the tense muscles in his neck softening. "I met Daegan when the human military captured him. He suffered with a coating on his body from satyr spit. The coating was hardening and killing him. I gave him a solvent to clean the coating off then he backed out of our deal after I saved his life."

She opened her mouth and roared at him. "You are no ally of mine if you protected the red dragon from death!"

"You miss my point. I am no ally of the red dragon at

all. If I had not needed his help, I would not have helped him in the first place. I learned from my mistake. I wish to partner with someone who will help me take that dragon down."

Crossing her arms, Brynhild asked, "Why would I partner with a human, witch, or whatever you are to have conjured a cure for that coating?"

Joavan smiled then disappeared.

She started and spun, looking for him everywhere. When she turned back to face the table, he reappeared.

"I am no human, Brynhild. I am Faetheen with both blood of a Fae and a druid. I needed help regaining a priceless jewel for my people. They must have it for protection. Daegan got his hands on my people's amulet and kept it."

Brynhild's interest perked up, but should she trust this being, especially someone with druid blood? She could use a guide in this world. Humans were so fragile, even the men. She would likely kill one no matter how hard he tried to stay out of her way.

This man, this Faetheen, would not cling. He wanted to make Daegan pay for deceit. She wanted to destroy the red dragon.

That could be considered mutual goals.

Joavan lifted his hand, drawing her from her thoughts. "I can see you need proof you can trust me. Every minute you have been here, I could have taken you to my realm where I went a moment ago."

Her hair bristled with her anger. "Do not ever threaten me again and expect to take another breath."

Joavan chuckled. "If you think about it, I have been in more danger from you had you decided to shift while here. Why would I threaten a dragon shifter, especially one I wish to join forces with?" He lifted an eyebrow, making it appear as a simple question. "I merely wanted to show you how I could have taken advantage of you last night, but did not." His smile turned wicked. "I do admit taking advantage of your exquisite body and would welcome another invigorating evening."

His charms did not work on her and would never control her. "I decide when I want sex. Not now."

"I like a woman who knows what she wants. I only ask that you give me a chance. If you are willing to work together, we can both succeed at our goals."

His words echoed Cathbad's, but that druid had deceived her from the start. She did not believe his lies about how she ended up in that cave.

Should she take a chance with Joavan? He had to tell her more first. "What majik do you possess to help me?"

He waved her toward him as he turned to walk out to the balcony. When she stood next to him and a light wind caressed her skin, he said, "Do you see anything in the sky?"

She took in the wide blue expanse. "Birds."

"I was able to find you after a human military group shot your dragon down."

Her fingers gripped the rail tightly.

"I got there right after they'd shot at your dragon. I then went with the trackers until they got too close. That's when I used my powers to send them in a different direction. I reached you just as you jumped in the water and followed you from the bank."

She lifted a hand from the rail and cupped her mouth, then asked, "Why did you not show yourself then?"

"Are you serious?"

"Yes!"

"You had just been attacked and were injured. If I'd shown myself, you would have killed me."

She had to admit the truth of it. "Go on."

"I stayed with you until you reached this city. While you wandered around, I arranged for this hotel room then took my time approaching you. I wanted you to choose to come with me."

"If I had not?" She turned on him, waiting for what his plan would have been.

"I would have eventually approached you to discuss the red dragon, but it would have taken longer." He leaned over and kissed her cheek. "Now, let me tell you what I can bring to the table. I have infiltrated a human military agency to access their human resources, which is how I heard reports of a dragon spotted in the air where they found you. I can enter and leave that group whenever we need it."

"You think these humans can find the red dragon?" She had her doubts, but she did not think Daegan was as clever as her and certainly not more so. He just had more warriors to help him.

Continuing in his thoughtful tone, Joavan explained, "The humans have something known as satellite images."

Brynhild frowned. "What?"

Pointing up at the sky, he said, "Satellites are machines thousands of miles in the sky that take pictures as the equipment circles this world."

"The gods have machines?" Her eyes pinched to small slits.

"No, the humans. People today are very advanced. I saw pictures of your dragon and Daegan's in a battle over the sea on the west coast of the island now called Ireland. You had the upper hand until his dragon pulled a dishonorable trick."

She still stung from that loss. "Yes. He has no honor."

"It was clear to me then that you wanted him dead. Having a Faetheen partner with access to human resources will expedite your wishes."

She had no idea what "expedite" meant, but took the happy expression as a sign he offered to give her what she wanted.

Smart man, he did not push, but gave her time to think

through everything he said. She could not get to Daegan without help, not in this new world. To do that, she wanted more than Joavan offered. She wanted the knowledge Cathbad kept promising, but not in small doses the stingy druid offered.

She did not want to sip from a cup. She wanted a barrel to draw from whenever she thirsted for more.

Joavan would show her how to blend in with humans.

He would uphold his promise ... or he would die.

Turning to lean back against the rail, she glanced at Joavan. "I want to be invisible when in human world."

He angled his head and his eyebrows dropped low over his eyes. "You don't mean you want to vanish, right?"

"No. I need to change face sometimes. To look different." Her beauty would stand out now that she no longer appeared as a street beggar.

"Ah! That's what I thought. You wish to walk among the humans as if you were one of them and change your face and appearance sometimes. We can do that easily."

"Yes, that. I must be able to find Daegan without his Beladors alerting him."

"He's been leaving his people to hunt for a grimoire volume. We can find him either alone or with his second-in-command. His name is—"

"Tristan," she supplied. "Cathbad captured him. When Cathbad left, I made Tristan help me."

He blinked. "Doesn't he teleport?"

"Yes. I made him teleport me outside cave, but he was under my control. I shifted and flew him to cliffs where I think Tristan called to Daegan."

"You have far more talent than just being a dragon shifter, dove."

Though his voice held admiration, she turned a sharp gaze on him. "Nothing is more important than shifting into dragon. Now, tell me how we kill Daegan."

"I am ready to do that, but I must get my people's diamond back from him."

She stalked away, waving her hands. "Everyone expects me to allow the red dragon to live. *No!*"

"Brynhild," Joavan said in that soothing voice.

She did not want to be soothed. She wanted to end Daegan's life. "What?"

When he remained silent, she turned with hands on hips. "What, Joavan?"

"One question so that I know how to fulfill your request and return my diamond. Do you wish to kill Daegan quickly or make him really pay for the things he's done to you?"

"You do not know what he has done."

"I don't need to, dove. What would give you the most satisfaction?"

She considered his words. What would give her the most satisfaction? To make Daegan feel the deep pain of loss that burned in her chest. The red dragon had not seen his family killed and his home destroyed.

All her family died because of trusting the red dragon.

Joavan's words sounded too much like Cathbad's. Like the druid, this Faetheen needed something from Daegan, but Joavan had played no games with her so far. He had not exposed his true identity last night, but she had not asked. She respected how he'd been careful in approaching her.

A wise man. She had no patience for fools and admitted, "I wish to make Daegan suffer greatly before he dies."

Joavan smiled and opened his arms. "Now, that's the way to think."

"What is this diamond you want? Will Daegan have it with him at all times?"

The Faetheen told the story of where he lived in another world alongside this one and how a druid had taken a necklace with the diamond, which protected his people. She did not understand how a stone could protect someone, but that was not important.

She only cared about how to get to Daegan.

Joavan walked as he talked, his hands waving around and his voice heavy with emotion. He stopped and stared up. "Daegan knew I had to return the amulet for the protection of my people. I must have it back, and soon." Lowering his arms, he turned a sad smile to her. "That is all, dove. Any suffering on Daegan's part on your behalf is a bonus."

Brynhild felt energy rush through her, spreading happiness to every part of her being. She would no longer be lost in this world, waiting for every new threat.

She would be in charge. No one would dare cross her again. She had plenty of enemies between Cathbad, Daegan, his Beladors, and the humans with giant weapons, but she had never been anyone's prey.

Joavan would answer her every question and turn her into a modern-day dragon shifter, capable of destroying Daegan. Plus he would watch her back with Cathbad hunting her.

That druid would not allow her to escape him so easily.

When Cathbad showed up again, she would make him regret having shoved her into an ice pond for two thousand years.

"I don't know what is going on inside that gorgeous head of yours, dove, but I am ready, willing, and able to fight at your side."

She smiled, unable to stop herself, and quietly strolled over to him.

His eyes flashed with curiosity, but the man had backbone. He stood there, allowing her to make the next move. She moved close enough to smell the warm scent flowing from him and lifted an arm to drape over his shoulder.

They stared at each other until he whispered, "What would you have me do first?"

She slid her hands down the taut muscles over his chest and pushed the robe open, giving him a smile filled with desire.

His eyes darkened with hunger.

Men were so easy to tame.

Her voice dropped to a husky sound. "You will satisfy my need for someone to show me how to live in this world and ... " She stroked him during the long pause. "In other ways."

Eyes steady on her, he lifted a hand and ran the back of his fingers down her cheek. Then his hand slipped inside her robe to cup a breast. "You have not seen anything yet. Last night I had to behave as a human. Now, you will know the beast I can be."

Did he think to impress her in bed? Men were always foolish to put so much value on sex.

She would allow him to do his best. After all, why not make the most of this man while she had him with her?

Still, she would have to be very careful around Joavan. He had a hidden world and the power to pull her in with him. She had no doubt of his ability to back up his words.

He had also sought her out for his own needs.

Joavan would balk at any attempt to kill Daegan until he had his diamond in hand.

He believed his goal was greater than hers, which she would allow ... for now. Once she had all she needed from him, they would part ways, diamond or not.

Joavan moved his lips close to her ear. "Where are you, dove? You are not here with me."

She studied his striking face for a man. Not a warrior, by any means, but a wise one with gifts. "We must find the red dragon. Once we do, you will have all my attention." She could not spend hours in bed while Daegan flew around free.

Pulling his hand away from her breast, he withdrew

from her in every way. "Will you kill him?"

"Not yet," she lied. She would allow no one to stop her from destroying Daegan.

His relief was immediate. "I can find him," Joavan stated, not even boasting. Just confident.

"We must take care of what is important first, then we play as much as we want," she mused with a soft smile, which did its job.

Joavan grinned. "I do love how you think. We find Daegan first. Then plan how to hold something over him. I will take back my amulet and aid you in taking down the red dragon."

She continued her indulgent smile. She needed no one's help, not a Faetheen's. If Joavan did not get what he wanted, she would rid herself of two annoyances at once.

CHAPTER 13

THE STALE AIR IN THE ancestral centre in Galway carried a hint of ancient books and the woman known as Fenella.

And the faint scent of coconut from wilting gorse flowers the lass had a fondness for.

Daegan took in Tristan's glum face. "Casidhe was not at the local hotel nearby where ya left her. She was not at her cottage. Nor does she appear to be here." On previous trips, he'd raced around shouting her name.

Not anymore.

He had come to his senses when she was close … or not. When her energy and heat were nearby, all of that called to him and soothed the beast inside him. Not Ruadh, but Daegan's driving need to be with her.

"I hate to say this, boss, but—"

"Do not tell me I have lost her yet again," Daegan grumbled, pressing his fingers to his temples. As much as she calmed him when nearby, he turned into a prickly bear when he could not find her.

Both of Tristan's eyebrows climbed his forehead and he fought a smile. "Good news is that we've always found her. We can do it again."

"Neither of us will fit through that tunnel without a struggle, but we shall have to start there." Daegan passed through the opening from the front reception area to the rear of the building. Panic hit him at the sight of an empty room. "Where are her books?"

Tristan explained as he followed Daegan. "You didn't want to talk until you found her or I'd have told you about helping her move her library. She didn't want to leave her books here alone and couldn't stay here safely."

Having that pointed out did little to ease Daegan's irritation. "Ya could have mentioned somethin' as we searched the cottage."

Tristan said nothing. He tried to smother his amused look, but failed.

Daegan angled around and snapped. "I find nothin' humorous about any of this."

"Sorry, boss. I'm just, uh, ... "

"Say it, Tristan." Daegan's mood darkened by the moment. Casidhe could be in danger this very minute and Tristan found this funny?

"I like seeing you happy." Tristan had said that so sincerely.

What had happened to his second? "Do I *look* happy?"

"Not a bit." Tristan chuckled. "What I meant was it's nice to see you so taken by Casidhe and her totally into you. I get that you can't bond with a woman who doesn't carry dragon blood, but with so few dragons to choose from, especially when the only female is a homicidal nutjob, can't you be with a woman like Casidhe and not bond your energy?"

All the anger seeped from Daegan. He clutched his forehead. "I do care deeply for her. I could not allow myself to become so close with a human, but Casidhe possesses a load of energy. Hers reaches for mine when we are together." Lowering his hand, he sighed heavily. "'Tis the truth she turns me into a ravin' idiot when she runs off. I am not sure I shall survive this lass."

Tristan bellowed out a laugh and slapped Daegan on the back. "I understand only because I have my own strong female to keep up with and survive. But I wouldn't trade mine for anything."

Daegan's face relaxed into a smile. "I have never been in such a dilemma before. She runs me ragged, but I do feel alive when I am with her as I have not in many a year."

"As it should be, boss. You're allowed to feel human even if you aren't." Looking around, Tristan said, "She's definitely not here. You two still have to see the oracle again and we aren't any closer to shoving Imortiks behind that death wall."

All good points that Daegan should be making. Serious now, he strode to the rear of the building where her hidden door swung inches from the back wall. He pulled it wide and a sizzle of energy popped then a scent smacked him.

Daegan snarled, "*Cathbad!*"

"Shit." Tristan raced up to him. "Think he's still here?"

"*I do not know!*" Daegan stuck his head into the cool tunnel and shouted, "*Casidhe!* Are ya there?"

His voice echoed.

Fear would drive him mad. He had to find Casidhe. He roared, "*Cathbad! Ya will face my dragon!*"

Still nothing.

Desperate to find her if he couldn't hear her, Daegan wildly opened his energy and let it flood the tunnel, reaching for Casidhe's. If he did not find her, he would teleport in blind. He could not let Cathbad take her from him.

Tristan doubled over and disappeared.

Daegan backed off his flood of power. He shouted, "*Tristan!*"

His second reappeared and went to his knees, holding his head.

Daegan dropped down with a hand on his shoulder. "What happened to ya?"

"Tried to teleport to the middle and hit a wall as I started to reappear. I bounced back here but I don't know how."

"How could you teleport in without knowin' where to

stop?"

Tristan stood with Daegan lifting his arm. Squinting his eyes, he hung his head. "Your power slammed me. I knew then it was either I go or you would snap and teleport."

Guilt landed hard between Daegan's shoulders. He was losing his mind and putting people at risk again. What was wrong with him?

Casidhe.

"Do not do that again," Daegan ordered, but in a soft voice. He knew the level of Tristan's loyalty and shouldn't have been surprised. No one should take a risk for her but Daegan.

He hooked his hands behind his neck, walking in a frustrated circle. "Cathbad has her." Those words gutted him. He had no idea where to hunt, but … he couldn't think. His throat thickened with emotion as he thought of all the ways she might die.

"She has her sword," Tristan offered, but his morose tone admitted he doubted even with an ancient sword that she could have fought off Cathbad.

Daegan's stomach muscles twisted into knots. "I … " His voice broke. "I must find her."

Tristan leaned against the wall next to the hidden tunnel opening and rubbed his forehead. "I should have put an electronic tracker on Casidhe when I had a chance."

"No!" Daegan shouted at an empty room. All the maybes and should haves in the world could not fill the gaping hole widening in his chest. "She would not go down without a fight." He clenched his eyes shut, pausing, then opened them. "Something bad has happened to her."

What would Cathbad do to her? He wanted her alive to hunt the grimoires, but alive came in many forms.

That evil druid would torture her.

"*Boss!* Your power."

Daegan broke free of his nightmare. The room shook.

Cracks formed in the walls. He sucked back his energy, breathing hard.

Tristan stood pinned to the far wall until Daegan's energy dissipated. Face pale from the strain, he walked back to Daegan. "We'll find her. We'll start right now."

"How?" Daegan could barely speak. Clearing his throat, he said, "I don't have a scrying wall or dream vision or remote …"

"What about Reese, boss?"

"Yes. Good thinkin'." Daegan dropped his arms and called telepathically, *Quinn? I need Reese. Can ya find her?*

Hi, Daegan. Yep. She's with our team.

Guilt hit Daegan again. Was he putting someone else at risk? She was pregnant. But … she was out patrolling Atlanta.

Quinn asked, *What do you need?*

That shook off Daegan's hesitation. *Would she be willin' to do her remote viewin' in the Galway centre again?*

I'm sure she would. Are you sending Tristan?

Yes.

Quinn gave Daegan a spot Tristan could teleport to undetected. He added, *Once Tristan's here, I'll find him and send Reese back with him.*

Ya will not be joinin' her? Daegan asked, wondering what had changed for Quinn to stop hovering.

I know she's safe with you two and … she needs her freedom.

Daegan swore, *Ya know I shall protect her with my life as will Tristan. I do not expect her to be here long. I just need her to look from the centre again.*

Very well. I'll have her ready when Tristan arrives.

With Tristan standing patiently, Daegan hurried to explain, "I called to Quinn. He's sendin' Reese to do her remote viewin'." Daegan told him where to meet Quinn.

Panic building inside him, driving the urgency to find her. "Hurry, Tristan."

"I'm on it." Tristan's words floated in his wake of teleporting away.

Less than two minutes had passed when Tristan and Reese appeared. Her clothes were torn and her hair disheveled. "Who has Casidhe?"

"I fear Cathbad has her." Taking in Reese's bedraggled state, Daegan asked, "Were ya fightin' somethin' in Atlanta?"

She blew out a noisy breath. "Blasted demons, but I'm going to find the being producing them and get one problem off our backs as soon as I return. Okay, where do you want me?"

As Tristan had pointed out, all men had their own challenges with protecting the powerful women in their lives.

Daegan experienced a fleeting moment of happiness born of realizing he had his own special woman. He felt a warm spot in his chest and ached to have her near again. He'd wanted time to figure out how to bring Casidhe into his life, but it was so simple now.

He wanted her and she clearly wanted him.

They *would* have a future together. He would make that happen.

But Casidhe would not be back in his arms until he gave Reese a place to start her remote viewing. Pointing his hand at the back room, Daegan explained, "I believe the best place to search is next to the door she uses to enter her secret tunnel."

"Got it." Reese strode past Daegan and Tristan and across the back area.

Daegan told Tristan, "Step inside the doorway to the tunnel ahead of Reese so ya can protect that side of her. I shall watch her back."

"Done." Tristan bypassed Reese with a quick teleport,

then slipped through the doorway and hunched down at the bottom of the short stairs.

Reese stopped to scan the area and shoved her head into the opening. "This looks busted open. Must not be much of a secret anymore. I'm gonna sit on the top step, Daegan."

"Do ya need anythin'?"

She pulled her head back. "Not right now."

Sitting on the step, she twisted her shoulders back and forth, loosening up, then took a couple deep breaths. With her hands cupping her knees, her breathing slowed.

Daegan kept very still as it normally required a moment before Reese began speaking.

"Luigsech is hurrying through the tunnel, but the backpack slows her down some when she bangs into walls and has to duck to keep moving. When the tunnel ends, she's inside that big hollow tree again. She's pulling out small things to put in her backpack as if she's cleaning out the tree."

Reese went silent, which Daegan had seen happen before when she concentrated on what she saw.

Her lips moved with no words until she angled her head with a surprised look and began speaking again. "The Luigsech woman paused when she found a black velvet bag. She turned it up and poured a necklace into her hand, then she fastened the chain around her neck and dropped it down her shirt. She pulled on her backpack and ... she's heading back through the tunnel in this direction ... uh, what's she doing?" Reese murmured as if speaking only to herself. She leaned forward. "Oh, I see. She stopped halfway back to the centre and started pulling away rocks and dirt from one side. Uhm ... looks like she's opening up another escape route. Huh."

Daegan hadn't expected yet another escape tunnel, but neither should he be surprised.

Leaning slightly forward, Reese whispered, "Luigsech

dug a hole she could shove her backpack through then crawled in behind it. She's walking for a bit and ... she stepped into water up to her chest. Must have dropped off into a hole. I think her shoe is stuck and she's struggling to get her foot free. *Oh, crap!*"

"What?" Tristan whispered in a tense voice.

Daegan leaned past Reese and shook his head at Tristan, who mouthed the word *sorry.*

Reese must have still been deep into the vision, because she didn't notice the question. Her breathing picked up. She was fighting for air as if she tried to help Casidhe breathe.

Daegan could barely hold quiet himself. What was wrong?

Was Casidhe trapped and sinking deeper in water as they stood here? Should he interrupt Reese?

Before he could do anything, Reese began narrating her vision again. "Cathbad showed up. *Son of a bitch*! He can't get to her, though. Guess he can't crawl through the narrow areas Casidhe passed through. You'd think he would have majik for that. Maybe he doesn't trust going in there blind. He threatened to call her body to him. Said he could drag her involuntarily if she didn't come back on her own."

Fear rolled over Daegan when he'd never blinked an eye facing an enemy. But battling a physical enemy was easier than standing here helpless to save Casidhe.

He clenched his fists, but forced himself to remain still so Reese could find her.

"He can't do it," Reese uttered, sounding amazed. "Cathbad wants a book and thinks she has it. That's how he is going to call her to him with majik. Wow. She used her sword to free her foot and kept moving. Cathbad is shouting, but he's not trying to physically get to her in the tunnel. He's counting down from ten to give her a chance to come to him and telling her he will find her no matter what. At ten ... hah! The ceiling fell in and she escaped, but the fact that she's not getting pulled through all that right now must mean she doesn't have his book."

Daegan swept a look at the empty library. Good thing Tristan took her books to Treoir.

Clearing her throat, Reese talked on in a monotone. "Luigsech is out of the tunnel and rolling down a hill, then she catches her breath and runs to a road. It takes her a while to get there. She, uh, ... hitches a ride to a local airport, and someone helped her get into a ... shipping crate? Yes. That's exactly what they did. Shipped her as freight. Sneaky way to fly."

Daegan could see it all in his mind the way Reese described everything. Was Casidhe running away from Cathbad because Daegan and Tristan weren't there to help her?

He should have planned better to keep her safe. The minute he got to her, he was going to make damned sure she would not be in fear again.

Reese fell silent and her shoulders relaxed. She'd lost the tension of staying close to Casidhe.

Daegan's hope hit the ground. Reese could only do so much. She could not follow someone teleporting.

"Imagine that," Reese muttered. "I can see the airplane taking off and watch it fly for a while. Maybe hours. I can't see a benchmark in the air. The airplane landed."

Daegan had held his breath until she said she could still follow Casidhe. Good thing he'd been born an immortal or his heart might not survive the ups and downs of hunting anyone this way.

Reese quieted again, but she remained intensely focused for several more minutes before she opened her eyes. "I've reached as far as I can see to follow Luigsech traveling."

Daegan offered her a hand to step out of the tunnel entrance. Once Tristan joined them, Daegan asked, "What more can ya tell us, Reese?"

She described how Casidhe snuck out of the airport

in another city, then took off on foot with her backpack. Casidhe went to an apartment building next.

Reese scratched her head. "It sounded like Casidhe was speaking in code. She used the last name Hugh instead of Luigsech. She seemed to think the people inside would open their door to her, but they blew her off as if she was some stranger."

Daegan's anxiety over Casidhe's safety mounted. If Reese could get them close to the last location where she saw Casidhe, he would teleport there as soon as Tristan returned Reese to Atlanta.

Tristan asked, "Was there any landmark in the town she went to after getting out of the freight box, something that would make it easy for us to find her?"

Reese shook her head. "You have to hear all of this first. When Luigsech reached what appeared to be an apartment building in that city and the person refused to help her, she got upset that they wouldn't even feed her. She turned and made her way back into the non-residential part and walked over to a food truck. The guy waiting on her shouted something that sounded like, 'I know you. It's good to see you again.'" Reese shook her head. "Sometimes I can hear the simplest things and other times not so much, but it seemed like something interfered with me catching the whole conversation. Anyhow, the two guys in the truck got into an argument. Something about that truck was blocking my view of everything. Luigsech had paid for the food. She went around to the back where the door was open and stepped inside. I couldn't see her after that."

Daegan had no idea why Casidhe traveled that way when Tristan would have teleported her there. He paused and began connecting the dots, as Tristan called it. Casidhe had already been on her way somewhere when Cathbad happened to show up. She didn't ask Tristan to teleport her because she wanted to keep her journey secret.

"So nothing else after the truck?" Daegan asked, grasping at any explanation, but still coming back to the only one that made sense.

Reese held up a finger. "There's more. I stayed with it when everything went dark. After a bit, the truck came into view once more, but I could not see Luigsech until it stopped. Again, I have no marker for time, distance, or anything. In fact, when the truck pulled off the road, the land was still dark outside. The guy who had spoken to her opened the back and stepped in, then Luigsech jumped out. I thought she was going to run, but she turned around and he tossed her backpack to the ground. Then he closed up the back and drove off. She started walking. She eventually reached the top of a hill and raced down to a road on her left as if she knew exactly where she was headed. The dirt road wound around until it reached a single cottage. She did the same routine with the last name Hugh when she knocked on the door and the person said something about waiting above."

"Above what?" Anxious this was all going nowhere and more confused than when they started, Daegan clutched his neck, trying to hang on.

"I didn't understand that either at first," Reese admitted. She'd started walking as she spoke, as if unable to be still. "Luigsech seemed to know exactly where to go. She climbed a steep trail that came to a plateau about three times as long as this building. She walked to the end and sat down, staring at water. A lake, a bay, an ocean. I have no idea. After a bit, she half turned to look over her shoulder and stood up. This big figure I couldn't make out walked up."

"Was he an enemy?" Daegan would have Tristan teleport to the last airport Reese could identify and find someone who could point them in the right direction. Casidhe could be captured and terrified no one would find her.

Tristan stared in deep concentration. "You couldn't see the guy's face?"

"No. He was wearing furs and leathers, like something out of a historical period."

Sweat broke out on Daegan's forehead. "Could be a supernatural who dragged her off. Ya must know somethin' about where she is so we can save her, Reese."

"I don't think you need to save her."

"Why?"

Reese acted reluctant to share the rest but gave it up. "Luigsech smiled at the guy and called him by name right before he changed into a dragon and flew off with her to some mountains. They just disappear from view at one point as if being cloaked."

Tristan's jaw dropped. "What the hell?"

Daegan didn't understand. "A *male* dragon? Skarde is in my dungeon and the other one flyin' free is Brynhild." He pushed his gaze at Reese. "Ya said a name. What name?"

Reese had a puzzled look on her face. "It was odd. Sounded like she called him Herrick."

CHAPTER 14

BILE RAN UP DAEGAN'S THROAT and blood drained from his face. The walls started closing in on him. His voice came out strained. "No. It cannot be."

"Who is he, boss?"

Daegan forced himself to keep his power in check, fighting for a breath. "Skarde ... and Brynhild's brother."

Tristan muttered a curse.

"What's going on?" Reese asked.

Daegan couldn't answer her. His thoughts warped in all directions. He ran back over what Reese had narrated to them about Casidhe gathering her things from the tree. He'd believed the only thing that would keep her from him was danger. Cathbad. Queen Maeve.

None of this made sense. Casidhe knew the ice dragons?

She hadn't said a word to Daegan.

She'd packed to leave him. To go home. Her real home.

Every detail Reese shared flashed in his mind. He stumbled when recalling the tree where Casidhe kept possessions.

She'd put on a necklace before escaping.

He grabbed a thread, something to pull him from the hole he teetered toward. He rasped out, "Tell me about the necklace from the velvet pouch."

"Why is that important?" Tristan asked quietly.

Daegan swallowed, trying to pull himself together. "Casidhe told me while she was captive in TÅμr Medb she had listened to Queen Maeve and misjudged me. She admitted such and said she should have given me a chance to explain. 'Tis hard to keep my mind open to *any* explanation right now. Still, if the necklace does not have an ice dragon design, which would only be given to family or someone close, I shall allow her a chance to tell her side."

He could not bear to believe she had betrayed him.

His mind could see it clearly, but his heart refused to give up on her.

Reese explained, "It was a thick silver chain with a weird looking shape hanging as a pendant. In fact, it reminded me of ..." She turned to Tristan. "Daegan won't know what this is, but you remember those rings with a weave design that came apart and went back together like a puzzle?"

Tristan nodded, a sick look gathering on his face.

"That's what the pendant reminded me of. Half of a silver ring shaped with weird parts. Not enough to identify."

Daegan reached a trembling hand into his pocket, his eyes burning and denial screaming in his head. He pulled out his sister's ring.

Reese gasped. "Yes! Like that."

Words flew around Daegan's head, buzzing him like angry hornets. He couldn't move or speak.

Tristan's gaze held a mix of compassion and anger. He offered quickly, "Lanna said Casidhe would help you find the other half of Jennyver's ring. Sounds like she was spot-on."

Daegan's head felt two sizes too big. He'd suffered pain in many forms, but this slashed him from head to toe. An earth-shattering roar burst from him and shook the room. Muscles bulged across his shoulders. How could he have allowed himself to be tricked again? Worse, to have opened his heart to Casidhe?

No, she was the *Luigsech* woman. He would not allow himself to think otherwise.

Daegan's vision churned with fiery light. Claws broke through his fingertips and his dragon beat his insides, furious at their betrayal. Rabid thoughts screamed in his head.

This can't be true.

The evidence was damning.

And Jennyver. How could anyone but Jennyver have that half of her ring? Only someone who stole his sister.

Daegan held his head back, roaring with grief.

Ruadh felt the pain as deeply as Daegan. He opened his body to shift and allow his dragon to break free from the pain. Daegan had done this to them. No one should suffer but him.

Power shot free, spinning and pushing his body to expand.

"Daegan!" someone screamed.

Tristan's voice burst inside his head. *Stop, Daegan! Reese is pregnant. I can't teleport out.*

Crazed noises filled Daegan's mind.

Ruadh's voice smothered the others. *Stop. You kill innocent ones.*

Nooo, Daegan shouted, but Ruadh's words kept slamming his skull. He and his red dragon *protected* the innocent.

Raudh kept droning on in Daegan's mind, dragging him back from the brink of insanity.

He breathed in and out, now crouching and heaving as his body sucked all that energy back inside.

When he looked around, Tristan had Reese shielded behind him in a corner with both hands out forcing a kinetic barrier. Agony ripped his second's face.

Reese shouted, "Tristan, what's wrong?"

Daegan gripped his head. What had he done?

Tristan's voice came into his mind. *Daegan, you okay? What can I do?*

Dropping his hands, Daegan stood slowly. "'Tis safe

again."

Tristan lowered his kinetic shield and helped Reese to her feet. He asked her, "Ready to go back to Quinn?"

"No." She marched across the room. "Something is very wrong." When she reached Daegan, pale and shaking, she softened her voice. "I'm here. Let me help."

Daegan closed his eyes and took a shuddering breath. He could not lose his control again. Not like that.

Withdrawing his claws first, Daegan cleared his raw throat. "I am sorry for puttin' ya in danger, Reese. I ... was not expectin' what ya saw, but ya did me a great favor in comin' to help. I cannot thank ya enough. Please go back to Quinn and stay safe. There is nothin' more ya can do here."

She looked uncertainly from him to Tristan and back. "Okay, I'll go, but come get me if you need me again. I don't know everything, but it sounds like this Luigsech woman has pulled a fast one on you. I'll gladly help you find her and get your sister's ring back. If you think she's a demon, I can blast her, too."

Holding back the anguish waiting to rip out of him, Daegan forced his ragged words from a tight throat. "I shall keep that in mind."

Reese blew a curl off her forehead that fell back in place immediately. "Okay, Tristan. I'm ready to roll or ride." She brushed her hair back with her hands, muttering, "Hell, I don't know. Maybe teleporting is more like flying."

Tristan sent another worried look to Daegan, but gave Reese a quick nod, then the two of them disappeared.

Daegan cloaked the room and let out an inhuman wail. He shook his fists above his head. Neck and shoulder muscles strained from holding back his change.

He shouted, "*Why*? What wrong have I committed to deserve this knife in my gut?" Tremors shook the floor and walls. Pain wrenched his insides. He struggled between loss and fury.

How could he lose something he never truly had, though?

Luigsech had lied to him. The whole time. What had she wanted? What had she been doing here for the ice dragons?

Was there any way she could have known about Skarde?

She sure as hell knew about Jennyver.

Daegan had lost his family. He never thought he'd lose someone else that would cut him as deeply. No matter how hard he wanted to just forget about what he'd felt for her, the pain of never holding her again threatened to strangle him.

He had to pull himself together and be better. He had to shove a wall around those feelings and lock them deep.

Much easier said than accomplished.

He dropped his fists and lowered his head. He would never have someone in his life. Not after this. He could never risk trusting another woman even if he found one who possessed power.

Especially not with a supernatural.

Slowly, the structure calmed, but his insides would never be at peace again. From here on, his heart had no business interfering.

Once his control returned, his shoulders sagged. His body felt as if he'd been driven through a gauntlet with no weapon and fighting off battle axes. Every breath hurt.

He kept seeing Casidhe's smiling face. *Luigsech*, he reminded himself again. He had to chisel her out of his heart and couldn't do it with the name that had been his to hold.

How had she fooled him so easily?

Because she'd been taught by those who knew of the red dragon, taught by Herrick. She knew him better than he could have ever imagined. That cut deep.

She believed what Herrick's clan believed.

She knew the ice dragon clan hated him.

She'd convinced Daegan she cared for him intimately. Had he wanted someone to call his own so badly he'd made betraying him easy?

How could she belong to the ice dragons? The more he thought back over every moment with her, the less he understood. Why had she done this to him? She'd drawn him in close as a drunken moth to a dazzling flame then squeezed the blood from his heart.

He drove his hands through his hair and gripped hard, wanting to yank his mind out of this torment.

He had never appreciated Ruadh's presence more than right now and told his dragon, *Thank ya for stoppin' me from more damage.*

Ruadh said, *All pain heals.*

Only his dragon could bring what had happened into focus. Daegan had suffered before and would suffer again, but he and Ruadh would survive.

He had no idea how long he'd stood there before he removed the cloaking.

Tristan quietly said, "I'm back."

Daegan lowered his trembling hands to dangle at his sides. "I am ashamed of my reaction. I have never been so thoroughly deceived."

Tristan crossed his arms and stared out the front window of the centre. "She fooled me, too, boss. I'm sick over what she did to you." Huffing out a disgusted sound, Tristan shook his head.

"Did I harm Reese?"

"Nah. She's tough. She told me to come for her again if you needed anything she could do and to let you know she isn't saying a word about ... what happened."

Of all the anguish he felt over Luigsech, he was blessed to have those he cherished around him at his worst moment.

Tristan asked, "What do you want to do now?"

Daegan straightened to his full height. Fire churned inside him and flowed through his veins. He had people waiting on him. Depending upon him.

Speaking in a clear voice, Daegan strived to sound like the dragon king his people deserved. "I need that scepter in Luigsech's backpack. It must be delivered to the oracle, who can help me find the other grimoire volumes."

"Can we do all this without ... *her*?"

"'Tis the plan."

"I'm ready to do whatever we need."

Daegan had never had true loyalty from the dragon clans he'd battled beside to protect. Unlike those dragon shifters he'd known from birth, Tristan had proven an unwavering loyalty Daegan would always treasure. "We shall find Luigsech and Herrick. I may need ya to aid me in regainin' the staff from her backpack. I do not trust her to hand it over freely after holdin' my sister's ring all this time."

"Let's do this, boss."

"Once I find them, I shall not leave until Herrick tells me what happened to Jennyver. If he dares to deny me, he shall regret having lived so long. I am not in a merciful mood." Daegan would never harm someone who did not attack him first, but neither would he allow Herrick and Luigsech freedom to take a step from him until he had answers.

She had escaped Daegan for the last time.

He'd find a way to meet with the oracle alone this time. He was done with Luigsech.

He moved around and sat on the edge of Fenella's desk as he considered where to go next. "Reese's remote viewin' can only do so much. If I had time, I believe we could find Herrick and Luigsech, but time is fallin' through a crack as we speak."

Tristan drew his eyebrows tight and stared at the floor. "I doubt Storm could track a dragon flying across unknown land and through mountains without a starting point. Reese said they vanished in the mountains. I wonder if Herrick has the same ability to cloak his dragon like Brynhild does."

"I do not know." Daegan had never known Brynhild had such a gift until recently. "Storm would only be able to track them if we knew where Herrick landed. I fear that mountain range could run from horizon to horizon. Quinn once told me Lanna could find someone if she held a possession of the missing person, but she could not find Jennyver with the ring I carry."

Tristan snapped his fingers. "Wait a minute. Lanna might be able to find Cas, uh, Luigsech, though."

Daegan stilled, thinking on Tristan's words. "Ya think we can locate somethin' personal of hers in the cottage for Lanna to hold in her hands?"

Grinning, Tristan rubbed his hands together. "We have something better."

"What might that be?"

"Remember I teleported Luigsech's entire library to Treoir? That library is her most *prized* possession. Let's put one of those books in Lanna's hands."

Daegan inhaled a deep cleansing breath. "Aye. Lanna shall show us the way to our enemies."

CHAPTER 15

CASIDHE PREFERRED FLYING ON THE back of Herrick's dragon.

Like the rest of her existence, her preference meant nothing.

Her teeth chattered and her body ached from being battered around by wind while hanging from the dragon's claws.

Herrick hadn't smiled or said a word before tossing her the cloak he'd peeled off before shifting into his dragon and immediately taking to the air. He'd made a fast arc, swinging around to fly in just above the flat ground where she'd stood at the edge, watching the Tegernsee Lake.

She'd hooked her arms through the backpack straps and shoved her hands in the wrong sleeves of the cloak to wear it backward. She'd hurried to protect her face and chest, trembling at the possibility the dragon would throw her off the cliff.

She'd barely been ready when his dragon scooped her from behind, yanking her muscles.

Her stiff shoulders felt as if she'd been twisted into a noodle.

She couldn't feel her legs after flying all day. Herrick had taken a huge risk to fly during daylight. That showed just how angry he had to be. Darkness fell as his dragon finally approached the ward shielding Herrick's land from trespassers. The wide wings flapped slower as they passed through the ward. Inside the castle area where dark still shrouded the land, one of his men stood off to the side tending a fire.

She relaxed her body for the drop as the ground came up to meet her.

The claws opened. Wind blasted her down.

She tucked, hit, and rolled in a wobble, bouncing over the hard ground. The backpack dragged her to a stop.

Arms flopped away from her body, she lay there a moment staring up at the dark sky and trying to slow the dizziness.

His dragon screeched, flapping hard as it caught air then glided around.

Herrick was angry?

She was fuming mad. Standing, she shook off the cloak but left her backpack on. At this point, it felt like part of her body. She swatted hair off her face and snatched up the cloak, only so no one else would have to pick up behind her, and headed into the castle.

Her hands were frozen. Her face felt raw from the cold wind and her body hurt everywhere.

She'd reached the top of the steps when his dragon bellowed loudly, then a screech followed. Looking over her shoulder, she witnessed Herrick shifting back to human, then walking over to stroke Stian's head. He clothed himself in furs as he stood there chatting with his pet.

He cared more for a freaking griffon vulture than her!

She tried to yank the door open, but the heavy wooden covering had been built for someone the size of a Viking. No chance of being dramatic here.

Once inside, she tossed his cloak on a bench against a wall and strode over to the roaring fireplace.

"Do not think to run away!" Herrick bellowed as that heavy-ass door slammed for him, dammit.

She had her backpack on the floor at her feet and had turned for the fire to warm her backside. "I am not runnin' anywhere. I can barely walk after the last twelve hours."

His boots hammered every step he took. "You would be wise to watch your caustic tongue. I am not happy with you."

"Oh, really?" She crossed her arms. "Funny, because I'm just as unhappy."

He stopped abruptly and stared at her as if she wore her head backward.

The normally subdued Kleio came running down the stairs and into the crossfire.

"*Leave, seer!*" Herrick ordered, not taking his gaze off Casidhe.

"I have something you should hear."

"Did you not hear me?" he yelled, swinging around to her. "I said leave. Anything you have can wait."

"It is not what I have that is in jeopardy, but something of yours."

He drew up at that and seemed concerned.

Casidhe had a strange feeling the seer was drawing his anger, as if to free Casidhe of his wrath. What should she believe? Was this merely some trick to get Herrick out of here so the seer could get to Casidhe?

"What do you speak of, seer?"

Kleio wore her long hair braided in a thick rope down her back. Unadorned lavender eyes boosted her serious look. "Your prized possession may not last long enough to barter a successful trade."

Kleio's bold statement sent Herrick back a step as if she'd struck him with a club. "What ... what are you talking about?"

"Do not deny this treasure exists," Kleio said in a challenging tone.

What the devil was she talking about? Casidhe must be the only person to not know what treasure he possessed.

Herrick started to shake his head, then stopped. His

harsh voice fell off to a whisper. "How do you know of this?"

The seer gave him a censoring look most often saved for an annoying child. "Even after all this time, you question my ability? That is not the issue at this moment. Time draws near to make your trade."

What trade was this woman talking about?

Casidhe appreciated a moment to gather herself so she could better deal with Herrick, but she did not trust help coming from Kleio.

When neither one said a word, Casidhe found her backbone had thawed and stormed forward. "What are you talking about? What trade?"

Herrick ignored her, focused only on the seer. "Are you saying Skarde lives?"

Kleio said nothing as her gaze swiveled to Casidhe.

Herrick stared at Casidhe with confusion. "Have you found Skarde?"

Of course. Everything was about his brother. More hurt than angry, she lifted her chin. "I might have."

His face twisted into a vicious look. He bellowed and lifted her off the floor, shaking her.

Her survival sense kicked in to remind her she was pissing off an ancient dragon shifter. "Stop it! You're hurtin' me."

Herrick roared, "You know where my brother is and did not tell me?"

Kleio reached for Herrick's arm, pulling on the thick limb. "If you injure her, she will not be able to talk or serve you."

He dropped Casidhe faster than having grabbed a hot poker by the wrong end.

She stumbled backward, running into her backpack. For a fleeting second, she considered pulling out her sword. Then reality set in and reminded her Herrick had a bigger one and was still a dragon shifter. Got it.

Herrick wiped his mouth, then closed in on her. His face shifted with anger, but his voice rolled with suspicion. "What do you know of the red dragon? Is he the one who teleported you to see Fenella?"

Ah, damn. But then Casidhe realized for him to know about her teleporting away from Fenella with Tristan that meant Fenella and the squire families had been in direct contact with Herrick when they deemed it important enough.

They could reach him any time.

The betrayal continued to expand and take on new life.

Casidhe jutted her chin forward and straightened her stance. Pissed didn't begin to cover what she felt. "I'm not sayin' another word until I get answers."

Herrick's fists clenched. He reached for her.

Kleio spoke up quickly just before he touched Casidhe. "I have warned you of dire circumstances. Do you not care to keep your treasure safe?"

Herrick stopped so quickly it was almost comical if Casidhe could remember how to laugh. Not anytime soon.

He was standing there one minute and racing down the main hall toward his cavern at the back of the castle the next. His frustrated roar bounced off the halls.

Casidhe stared at him until he was gone. Her anger had a new target. "What was all that about, seer? What trade, what treasure, and why is it in jeopardy?"

Kleio glanced in the direction Herrick had disappeared. Seeming satisfied he was gone, she came back to Casidhe. "You can never go forward as long as you allow others to set your path."

"I'm so not in the mood for your cryptic comments, Kleio. I've had a miserable couple of days. I'm not interested in riddles. What the hell is goin' on here?"

Kleio sent another glance toward the cavern then suggested, "See for yourself."

CHAPTER 16

DAEGAN LOOKED UP AS LANNA'S soft steps entered the area where Garwyli trained her.

She announced, "I am here."

Straightening away from the window he'd been leaning against, he asked, "Do ya remember when Evalle was taken to the Scamall realm?"

"Of course." She clasped her hands in front of her.

"Ya could not see her then, could ya? But you told Storm to hurry."

Lanna's forehead drew tight with concentration. "That is true. When Storm handed me emerald chakra stone kidnappers ripped from Evalle's chest, I sensed her pain. I feared she would not survive, but ... I could not see her. Do you wonder about sister?"

"Yes. I will not rest until I know what the ring means when it jumps about. I wish ... to know if she lives or not. 'Tis not fair of me to ask that of ya, but 'tis all I can think about after ya said ya would see her dead or alive."

"I cannot see sister, because something hides her from me. I cannot say for sure she is alive or not."

While he still had no definitive answer, he felt comforted by the chance to close the gap between belief she had died and fear she still lived, but was trapped.

Tristan, who Daegan had sent to bring Garwyli, opened the door and held it open. The druid tapped his cane all the way over to Daegan. "Let's get on with it, dragon."

"As you wish, druid."

Garwyli chuckled and tottered away ahead of everyone. Daegan smiled to see the old guy looking a bit spry. Lanna seemed just as pleased, though he doubted she knew why.

Daegan had no idea how far back Garwyli's library stretched. The druid paused at the end of one long aisle and pointed his cane to the right. "The Treoir chronicles are settled over yonder. Lanna is a tremendous asset to Treoir." He glanced at her over his shoulder. "Ya have improved quickly. I am quite impressed."

She beamed under Garwyli's praise, which Daegan believed had to be earned.

Tristan lifted an arm, pointing down the aisle. "The books I brought in are way back there. Want me to teleport, grab one, and come back?"

"No," Lanna and Garwyli said together.

Tristan lifted both eyebrows. "*Ohhh-kay!*"

Lanna laughed. "Am sorry, Tristan. Is best for me to choose book."

"Hmm. That's cool. What if I teleport all of us back there?"

"'Tis a great idea, Tristan," Daegan said. "I, for one, do not wish to make that trek."

Garwyli scolded Daegan with a glare, but went along quietly.

Once Daegan reappeared at the rear of the library, he stood in a space with four heavy chairs adorned with thick cushions. A woven rug spread out twelve feet long beneath the chairs and a low table made of smooth wood.

Lanna volunteered, "I find nice place when I first read books from Garwyli's library. Is my favorite."

"What a wonderful *discovery*." Daegan had no doubt the old coot had created that for her without her knowing it. Garwyli wouldn't even look him in the eye right now.

Daegan stepped around, looking at books he could not recognize from the cover, but he knew the scents. One inhale and Casidhe's vibrant smile came to mind. This had been her happy place.

He could not think of her that way anymore. Not after what she'd done.

"Go on, girl," Garwyli urged as he walked over to a chair and settled. "Find yar book."

Tristan picked a wall to lean against.

Lanna stepped up beside Daegan. She said nothing and continued two more steps into Casidhe's library. She shook her head, mumbling something, then turned to Daegan. "You are not happy. Very ... hurt."

Daegan did not want to discuss Casidhe. *Luigsech*, he corrected himself. "I would prefer to only talk about findin' the woman who owns these books."

Garwyli made an "ahem" noise.

Looking chastised, Lanna walked through the row between shelves, running her fingers close to the spine of each book, but not touching any of those. She turned at the end and started up the next aisle.

Daegan stepped over to keep her in sight.

She seemed lost in thought until her hand stayed in one spot when she took a step forward. Backing up, she gently removed the book, then held it reverently in both hands with her eyes closed.

She stood that way a long time, so long Daegan regretted having put her on the spot.

Tristan and Garwyli made noises of moving around behind him.

Garwyli showed up next to Daegan, his hands propped on his cane, never taking his eyes off Lanna. Tristan stood behind Garwyli as if watching that the old guy did not fall backward.

Lanna lowered the book and walked forward to speak to Daegan. "I know where she is..."

Daegan's knees almost buckled. "'Tis great. Thank ya,

lass."

"Wait," she said quietly. "I know last place she was visible."

That did not sound promising. He held his questions to hear her out.

"Is mountain range."

"Reese told us that," Tristan admitted, sounding as ready to take off as Daegan.

Shifting a censuring glance his way, she asked, "Did she tell *exact* location in mountains?"

"Actually, no. She couldn't determine where the mountain range was in the human world."

"This *I* know."

"Truly, lass?" Daegan asked, awed by the young woman's power.

"Yes." Her gaze drifted to Garwyli.

Daegan took in the druid who said nothing, but his eyes and grim expression shouted something bothered him. "What is wrong, Garwyli?"

Sounding tired, the druid said, "Nothin' be wrong, dragon."

Lanna pressed her lips together and stared down as she spoke. "Garwyli not happy. He knows I must be there to show you location." When she looked up at her mentor, she said, "I do not say this for me. I know only one way for dragon king to find this woman."

She spoke with solemn confidence, not as the busybody she'd often been referenced.

Daegan had no desire to go against Garwyli's directive, but he had to ask, "Is this a problem, druid? If so, ya must tell me."

"As I said, 'tis no problem. I only worry for her safety." Old blue eyes swung to Daegan. "'Tis not meant to sound as an insult. I know ya are capable of protectin' her. But ya must protect her at all costs."

Garwyli was reminding Daegan of their conversation in the garden. Daegan said, "I will allow no harm to come to her even if it means turnin' back before I find the Luigsech woman. Ya have my word."

Tristan offered, "Mine, too."

After a deep breath, Garwyli told Lanna, "Ya shall go with my blessin'."

Her smile was one of appreciation, not of winning a battle. "I will return quickly."

Daegan's gaze drifted back to Garwyli's face where the old druid's steady, but grim, expression questioned if she would return at all.

Daegan meant his vow. When he had no idea if Jennyver still lived, an unrealistic thought at that, he could not allow his desire to find her prevent him from keeping Lanna safe.

Lanna cradled the book in the crook of her arm to carry with her. Once they returned Garwyli to his quarters, Daegan, Tristan, and Lanna walked toward the front doors of the castle.

Tristan brought up a point. "If Herrick knows something about Jennyver, how are we going to convince him to tell you, boss? His sister tried to kill you. Skarde would if he could. I'm betting Herrick might not be willing to talk before he goes dragon on you."

Lanna paid attention to everything said, but did not interrupt.

Daegan had been thinking on the same thing. "I have what Herrick will trade for."

"What will he accept?" Lanna asked.

"His brother."

CHAPTER 17

COLD WIND SLAPPED DAEGAN AS he stared at snow-dusted mountains stretching as far as the eye could see beneath a moon not yet full.

"Is not far," Lanna consoled. She hugged the heavy fur cloak around her. He'd covered her from the thick wool cap pulled low over her ears to leather-and-fur boots.

The lass might be cold, but she refused to show a weakness.

Tristan's gryphon stood next to them. His gryphon had flown out across the mountains, searching for any sign of a village where Herrick might be living.

He returned without any new information.

Skarde stood on Daegan's other side contained, muted, and protected by Lanna's majik. His fury seeped out, looking for purchase.

Daegan asked Lanna, "Where to now?"

She peeled a glove off one hand and reached inside her cloak. She had the book strapped there so it would not fall. She closed her eyes for a long moment.

Tristan spoke to Daegan telepathically. *You want me to carry Skarde so Lanna can be close enough to talk to you?*

No. Daegan appreciated Tristan's offer, but his second should not have to carry a man who had harmed his sister. Not unless Daegan had no other option.

Not that Ruadh would enjoy carrying the ice dragon shifter, but Ruadh would do as asked as long as Skarde remained wrapped in a bundle claws could hold.

Lanna opened her eyes and pulled her hand back out to slide into the glove again. "Valley is not far for gryphon or dragon. Is easier to find this valley if I fly with Tristan. When close, we land." She looked up at Daegan with eyes protected by clear glasses Tristan had suggested.

Daegan lifted his chin in acknowledgment. "I shall follow with Skarde."

The ice dragon made a noise, but too subdued by majik to be heard.

Once Daegan had Lanna secure on the gryphon's back, he shifted into his dragon. Ruadh lifted Skarde's body invisible to anyone not aware of the bundle, then used his rear legs to push off and fly, easily staying with Tristan's gryphon.

Lanna had been correct. It took only a few minutes for Tristan to make a slow sweep around a wide valley where nothing moved below.

No animals. No trees swaying in the brisk wind. Nothing except energy hovering over a wide area. A ward? What would it take to shield an area large enough to house Herrick and even a small clan? Herrick would not have survived so long without some form of clan.

Ruadh landed near Tristan's gryphon on a high ledge overlooking the valley.

A vulture Daegan had noted while flying, which had disappeared, now returned. It circled them, close enough for Daegan to make out an eagle-shaped head. Daegan had never seen a vulture that large or with a head similar to Tristan's gryphon.

Ruadh took note, but dismissed the bird as no threat and shifted to give Daegan the human body. He helped Lanna off of the gryphon, then Tristan shifted. Daegan clothed his second immediately.

"Did you see that weird vulture?" Tristan asked, pulling

his cloak close.

"Aye."

Lanna interjected, "Is scout."

Daegan dropped his gaze to her. "What scout?"

"Vulture not like other birds. Watched us fly. Eyes not natural." Spending no more time on the bird, Lanna said, "This where dragon and woman disappear." She pointed down at the empty area they had flown around.

Tristan waited in silence, but he kept his gaze moving, watching the vulture flying in a wide arc around them. It began screeching.

Lanna turned to watch the vulture, too.

Daegan had to make a decision on what to do next, but the vulture had gained his attention as well.

Lanna whispered, "It watches us."

The vulture broke out of the circle it flew and angled down into the valley where it disappeared in a blink.

"You find how woman and dragon disappear," Lanna announced.

"'Tis a ward," Daegan agreed.

"Can we breach it, boss?"

Lanna shook her head. "Would be dangerous."

Daegan agreed, but he had to get inside or bring Herrick out. Amazing that this ice dragon had found a way to survive all these years.

"Then what are we going to do?" Tristan asked, clearly impatient to get moving.

Lanna puffed out a white cloud of air. "We must wait."

Daegan had no idea what the ward hid. This would turn far more dangerous soon if that vulture really was a scout for Herrick. He spoke to Lanna. "I shall send ya back with Tristan."

Shaking her head, she repeated "*We* ... must wait."

But for what? If Herrick had a way to leave the ward

cloaked, Daegan's group could be attacked without a chance to shift into his dragon or for Tristan to teleport Lanna somewhere safe.

CHAPTER 18

REESE RUBBED A HAND OVER her hard stomach, which had yet to shape into a true baby bump. She'd never seen so many SUVs in such a small area. Even she and Quinn had shown up in one.

Evalle pulled Storm's Jeep into the lineup at Sweetwater Creek, a historical cotton mill site west of Atlanta that had burned during the Civil War.

Waving at Evalle, Reese asked Quinn, "How many demons have they seen in this area in the last hour?"

Referencing his telepathic communication, Quinn said, "Trey just updated me. There's been nine sightings in the last thirty minutes. They found one dead homeless person." He reached over to cover her hand, giving her an I-love-you-and-our-baby look.

Warmth spread through her soul.

She would not think about yesterday or tomorrow, just this moment. And she would not allow her heinous father to harm the man she loved.

She flipped her hand and squeezed his, determined to sound confident. "We're going to find I-zubrrali and stop this. Hopefully tonight."

He brushed his hand over her hair and shared a sad smile. "I know, but I worry that he may get to you."

"Not a chance. After that unexpected road nap, I'm super charged." She hadn't felt sick recently, but sudden exhaustion would hit her fast. To keep Quinn out with his people, she'd slept in the back seat of his ginormous sport utility.

Casper, a Belador ally, strolled up as Evalle joined them.

Reese reluctantly let go of Quinn's hand. They needed to have their game faces ready.

"Hey, Sunshine," Casper called to Evalle.

"Yo, Casper. I just love that nickname," she shoved back sarcastically. "Okay, how many do we have with us tonight and what do we know?"

"This is it," Quinn started.

"Really?" Evalle looked around. "What about all those vehicles?"

Quinn explained, "I have a contingent of Beladors keeping humans out of a twelve-acre area. Some are APD and others are part of the park service. They should be able to handle a demon trying to get out."

Evalle angled a confused expression at him. "Trey just told me on the way in that nine demons have been sighted here and they've evaded everyone who tried to take them down. That's not a lot to contain, but we could use extra bodies to contain them."

"It's 'cause we're thin," Casper volunteered. "Seven Beladors have gone to the healers just today."

"Shit," Evalle murmured. "Sure am missing Adrianna."

Reese heard the personal grief for a close friend beneath her quiet words. Evalle was not one to stand still when a friend was in danger. Waiting to find Adrianna had to be killing her.

Quinn lifted a hand to take the conversation. "We'll find her, Evalle. I sent for Lanna, but she left with Daegan to help him. The minute she returns, Tristan will bring her."

"Okay." Evalle sounded understanding, but she couldn't hide her disappointment.

A sand-colored Hummer came barreling in hot.

Sensing something odd, Reese glanced in Evalle's direction.

A ghostly-looking old man formed.

Doing a double take, Reese whispered, "Evalle?"

Evalle turned her way, which meant she stared through the ghost. "What are you doing here, Grady? In fact, how did you get this far outside the city?"

He frowned at her and grumbled, "I'm here to help find our witch. I jumped on that Hummer soon as I heard them talkin' on the radio about findin' y'all."

Now Reese remembered. That was Evalle's favorite Nightstalker. A good friend even if he was a ghoul who had died a long time ago. Nightstalker's were intelligence resources for supernaturals, but they rarely held any loyalty to one group.

"You need to hide," Evalle warned in a harsh whisper.

"Hmph." Grady turned invisible.

The Hummer had parked fast as if the driver owned this land. All four doors opened, spilling five big guys dressed in badass military looking gear.

Quinn shared, "The Belador team leader called to inform me Isak was headed this way. I said to let him pass."

Evalle grimaced in the direction of the Hummer and spoke to Quinn from the side of her mouth. "You know he's here for Adrianna, right?"

"Yes. I had hoped we'd have something to tell him before he found out."

"Let me talk to him first," she suggested.

Quinn nodded, which made sense. As Reese understood it, Evalle had known Isak longer than anyone, even Adrianna.

Reese had gotten to know Isak Nyght better while they were tracking Evalle's kidnapper. He'd known about nonhumans long before other humans. If not for him and his black ops team, she and Evalle might have been toast when a rogue group showed up hunting any nonhumans in the city.

He brought an extensive intelligence network with him when he became an ally of the Beladors.

With each powerful stride of that huge body, Isak sent the message he was not happy and would stop at nothing for what he wanted.

He smiled at no one as he strode over to Reese's group. "Where. Is. She?"

He'd spoken calmly, but each word carried a threat to anyone who delayed him from getting to Adrianna.

Evalle jumped in first and held up her hand. "Please don't go ballistic, Isak."

"I can't promise that."

"She's not here."

"I can see that, Sherlock," he snapped at Evalle. "Stop stalling."

Evalle looked sick at having to admit, "We were on top of a parking deck in Atlanta this morning and had to call in Sen. Some being showed up and took both of them, but ..."

"Then this being can't be one of your allies, right?" Isak asked so softly chills ran up Reese's arms.

"No."

"That makes him fair game." Isak gave a hand signal for the group in formation behind him and he turned to leave.

"Hold it," Reese snapped out. "We've been hunting Adrianna and Sen. We have intel."

Isak slammed to a stop and did an about-face. "What intel?"

"I used remote viewing to follow her, Sen, and the strange being through a bolt hole. I can't pinpoint where they are, but I saw enough to think they may actually be here in the Atlanta area, not another realm."

A muscle in Isak's jaw stopped flexing, but that couldn't be considered relief. He answered, "Good to know."

Before he could turn again, Evalle interjected, "Adrianna is our number one concern, but there seems to be more to this than what meets the eye. We need you to be in this with us."

"I'm on the hunt."

Quinn said, "Good. Then you agree to keep us apprised of all new information and not go off on your own, right?"

Isak said nothing.

"Give me a break, Isak," Evalle griped. "We need each other. Plus, we all still have to deal with the Imortiks and demons. You'll find information we won't, but we have supernatural resources you can't duplicate. Adrianna would expect you to join us in the search, not go off on your own. You'll be sick if you find out we missed saving her because we didn't work together."

Isak ignored all of Evalle's points, showing no remorse for his bullish attitude. "I'm deploying enough teams to cover the city and outlying areas. We're killing anything that isn't Belador or a known ally."

"*You can't do that, Isak!*" Evalle shouted. "We have non-human allies you don't know about and you risk humans being caught in the crossfire. We've had clueless citizens running up with their damned phones to video Beladors fighting Imortiks, which is why some of our warriors are out of commission with healers. They had to divide their attention while fighting, but they protected the humans. Remember that rogue black ops bunch that drew down on us yesterday? They're out there, too. You'll have a bloodbath."

"Then call your people back and leave the demons and Imortiks all to me!" Isak's voice shook with mounting frustration and no patience at being delayed for any reason.

Quinn always surprised Reese in these tense situations when he could speak in a voice of reason. "Everyone wants Adrianna back. Evalle's right that we should join forces. We have a woman with different gifts than Reese, who may be able to locate Adrianna. Work with us and—"

"Why isn't she here *right now*?" Isak demanded.

Quinn lost the effort to remain civil and snarled, "She's on another continent helping our dragon, who is trying to locate the grimoires to save this world." He leaned forward with power spooling around. "She's also my cousin, so back the fuck off."

So much for Quinn's reasonable voice, but Reese supported him a hundred percent. This was not the time to divide forces.

Isak and Quinn glared at each other in tense silence.

Then Isak turned and strode away, calling out, "Let me know if you find her. I'm going through the city until I find something."

Evalle hissed, "Grady? Come here."

The ghoul took shape. "What's goin' on?"

"A being none of us have ever seen grabbed Adrianna, but we think she's still in Atlanta. I'll explain more when I come by your area. Please put the word out with Nightstalkers in Atlanta and find out anything you can."

"You gonna owe me big time after this."

Evalle rolled her eyes. "If you need that Hummer to return to the city, you better get moving."

Grady jerked around at the sound of Isak's Hummer backing up to head out of here. He vanished and reappeared on top, grinning.

"Crazy Nightstalker better not get hurt," Evalle worried aloud.

Casper tipped his cowboy hat back and exhaled. "That went well. We'll end up with a civil war between humans and nonhumans in no time."

Evalle and Quinn had matching dejected expressions.

Reese took in all three faces. "Are we doing this?"

Quinn maintained his rigid posture as a leader and returned to the business at hand. "Yes, but we're only staying an hour tops. I just sent a telepathic message to Trey, informing him about Isak and his team so our people will not confront them, but I need to return soon." His gaze flicked past her to Evalle and Casper. "The good news here is that we have more combined power in our foursome than four Beladors. We'll be fine."

Evalle listened with tight lines across her forehead. She didn't seem to be as confident, but she popped out a quick smile. "Sure. We got this."

Quinn began directing everyone. "As always, it's better if we pair up. I'll take Reese and walk her east through the center of this area. You two cover this side." He pointed between him and back where the crumbled ruins of the brick mill stood.

Reese studied everything. Why would I-zubrrali set up here?

He hadn't been near water last time, so she dismissed the water to focus on the forest and remnants of the building. She still came up empty.

Who knew how a preternatural serial killer thought?

Evalle swung around, taking in the landscape in all directions. She turned back with her dark-brown ponytail flipping out of the way. "Not to argue, Quinn, but ... with so few people, maybe Casper and I should split up so we can watch both sides of you."

Casper stood with his boots apart and thumbs hooked in the pockets of his worn jeans. "I agree with Sunshine."

Evalle flipped him an annoyed glance.

The cowboy smiled as if proud of himself.

Reese took in the tense set of Quinn's lips. That man debated with how to do his duty and still keep everyone here safe. Hard to accomplish when their team of four had to spread out to cover the area.

Decision made, Quinn instructed, "Very well, you two parallel us. Casper, you don't have telepathy. How will you let us know if you run into a demon?"

"You'll hear it scream." Casper grinned, totally unconcerned.

Reese moved a hand to her stomach. "No time left to talk. I sense at least one demon."

Everyone turned deadly serious. Evalle and Casper split up.

Quinn asked Reese, "Which way?"

"Follow me."

He put a hand on her arm to stop her.

Without turning around, she repeated his words. "We have an agreement."

He gave her a gentle squeeze, just enough to let her know he was trying to do as he agreed, but would keep her safe. His fingers stayed a few more seconds as if undecided, then slid away.

Reese walked forward at a steady pace, not rushing, but not lagging either. When she threw quick looks to her right and left, she caught glimpses of Evalle's vintage tan BDU, or Battle Dress Uniform, shirt then Casper's gray T-shirt and black Stetson.

The deeper they went, the more the trees began to thin out.

Energy inside her churned faster.

Ugh. She whispered to Quinn, "I have more energy buzzing. Could mean multiple demons."

"Understood." His worry came through that one tight word.

She got it, but she could not sit in a protected room while her friends and others faced a growing army of demons. When no one thought she was listening due to sleeping, she heard one group tell Quinn the demons were turning into Imortiks faster every hour and Imortiks were harder to kill.

The way I-zubrrali, her damned father, whipped out demons, knowing they would be quickly possessed by Imortiks, she'd bet his goal was an army.

But how did he plan to control those monsters?

The energy heating her core ceased suddenly. Reese stopped walking.

"What's wrong?" Quinn asked, his gaze watching everything around her.

"My energy stopped humming."

His sharp blue eyes zeroed in on her. "That's good, right?"

"No. I have never had a demon fail to come for my energy. It's like crack to them. They can't make themselves back away. Something else is going on. Only someone more powerful can make a demon stand down."

"I-zubrrali?"

She swallowed hard. "Maybe. Probably. If he's shielding them from view, everyone out here is in trouble."

Loud noise erupted on Reese's left. Then on the right.

Quinn said, "My perimeter Belador team just told me they're fighting demons."

"They're coming," Evalle shouted, running up to Quinn and Reese with Casper arriving from the other side at the same moment.

Hands shoved up, Evalle spun with her back to Reese. She slapped kinetic hits at the demons rushing out from the forest. Quinn already had Reese at his back with his hands shoved forward creating a kinetic wall.

Casper raised his hands and shouted something like a war cry Reese didn't understand. Then a shimmering highland warrior took over Casper's body. This man had long brown hair, a bushy beard, a chiseled body bulging with muscles, and wore a Scottish plaid belted at his waist, which stopped above thick calves.

He lifted a sword and yelled, *"Ye vermin shall die!"*
Whoa.

Demons ran at them from all directions. Casper's alter

ego sliced a demon from right shoulder to its waist on the left. The demon turned into orange dust that floated away.

There were still too many.

Every demon that died and disintegrated into ashes still left a horrid sewage smell.

I-zubrrali had to be behind this ambush. Even a supernatural's energy would eventually become depleted.

Reese shouted, "Open a spot I can blast through!"

Quinn said, "No."

Evalle and Casper ignored her.

Reese turned and jumped up on Quinn's back.

He kept slapping kinetic hits at demons and yelled, *"What the hell are you doing?"*

"Be still and drop your kinetics to six feet high." She leaned down and pleaded, "Let me do the one thing I do best."

Quinn ordered, "Keep your wall up, Evalle. You and Casper protect my back."

Reese climbed higher on Quinn's back and hooked her legs around his neck, sitting on his shoulders.

Demons coming straight at Quinn looked up and drooled. Literally. They rushed in. He knocked them off their feet with his power, but more came right behind that wave.

Reese spun her hands together and waited until four had made it close enough. She went overhead and slammed a hit down in the middle of their group.

Power exploded. They turned to dust.

"Yes!" She fist-pumped.

Demons were leaping up and slapping at the top of Evalle's kinetic shield, trying to find a place to climb over. Their screaming banshee noise filled the air.

Reese took down another six demons with Quinn's help.

More were coming, crashing through the trees. How could anyone make that many?

Evalle said, "We have a new problem."

"What?" Quinn shouted.

"I see yellow ones showing up."

Demons surged on Casper's highland warrior.

Reese had two more coming at Quinn. Her heart tried to beat its way out of her chest. She hit the demons overrunning Casper then struck two rushing Quinn.

But that last hit was little more than a large spark. One not-yet-dead demon's body remained.

She now saw multiple yellow ones appearing at the back of the first attack. "Quinn. We can't beat this many."

"I want you out of here," Quinn roared.

"Not without you." She would not budge on that.

All at once, every demon, yellow or not, stopped moving.

Reese turned slowly, searching everywhere for I-zubrrali. He had to be here. Terror rolled through her. She clutched Quinn, frantic to keep him and the others safe. Damn her miserable father.

Evalle crowded closer to Quinn and whispered, "What's going on?"

Casper returned to his natural form and backed up to Quinn. "This can't be good."

Quinn said, "I think we have a firm answer on the demon origin."

Reese faced forward again, heart pounding as she searched.

I-zubrrali had to be here.

A misty veil formed and slowly fell away, revealing the greatest monster here.

There he stood in an all-white tunic and matching pants, holding himself as if all should fall to their knees in the presence of his superiority. He smiled at her.

She wanted to throw up. "Why are you overrunning this world with demons, oh, *sperm donor*?"

"You have a tart mouth."

If Reese closed her eyes, she'd think she was listening to someone with a professional speaking voice, one meant to calmly explain anything.

But with open eyes, she saw the bastard who had ruined her mother's life as well as Reese's. "I'll take that as a compliment."

He continued smiling and her stomach turned. "You got that flaw from your mother. She was fiery and full of words."

A small moment of pain crossed through Reese's chest, but she could not change that this demonic superbeing had stolen her mother away from her tribe in the Pacific Northwest and raped her.

Right now, he'd played this encounter so well that Reese was drained and unable to kill him. She whispered to Quinn, "Any chance of finding Tristan?"

He softly answered, "No. I don't know what this being has done, but I can't reach any of my Beladors not standing here."

Now that she had an idea of how I-zubrrali operated, she would have a trap they could set up quickly next time.

She had to keep him talking while she regenerated her energy.

First, she had to find a way to get everyone out of here safely.

"You haven't answered my question," she prodded, looking for any chink in his unholy armor.

"Why I make demons should be obvious. I always need followers, even more now than ever. When an Imortik dives into a demon I have created, the Imortik belongs to me as well."

Evalle cursed softly.

"What are you planning to do with your army?" Reese asked.

"Ah, child, I would enjoy sharing that, but with too much knowledge, you might step in my way." He enjoyed every word that came out of his mouth. "I have the feeling you wish to save your friends and the humans, though I do not understand that part at all. Still, if you want them to survive, I am willing to grant your wish."

Quinn gripped Reese's legs as if holding her firm to prevent her going after her father.

"So now you want to step in and be a dad? Give me nice things and make my life wonderful?" Reese put her hands on her thighs and leaned forward. "I'll play your silly game. What will it take for you to grant my wish and put down all the demons then slither back beneath the rock you came out from under?"

I-zubrrali maintained a neutral mask, but his eyes suddenly glowed even though they were black. "It is simple, daughter. I will give you a blood oath to destroy all my demons, even the ones possessed by Imortiks, and not make new demons for a thousand years. In exchange, give me the baby you carry right this minute. You can't birth that child alive, but I can take it from you and give the boy life. I'm making a generous offer."

Reese felt lightheaded, hot and cold, blood rushing fast through her ears. She put a hand over her middle.

The lives of all her friends, and Quinn, in exchange for her baby?

CHAPTER 19

A WEEK AGO, CASIDHE WOULD NEVER have stood in Herrick's great hall shouting at Fenella or Herrick, and definitely not a seer, whose power had always intimidated her.

Today, she'd had her fill. "What do you mean to find out for myself, seer? How can I know anythin' when all of you keep me in the dark?"

Kleio frowned, taking her time to reply. "To trust blindly is to allow others to take advantage of you."

Casidhe lifted her arms and looked up at the ceiling. "Give me a freakin' break! Is there no one in this universe who gives a damn about me?" She dropped her arms and stated, "I've had about enough of people dumpin' on me today. Either say what you mean or stop talkin'."

Kleio held her head as if it hurt.

Served her right.

The seer sighed. "This is not a time to be foolish."

"Oh, you mean arguin' with a dragon shifter who can smash me with one swat? Yeah, that wasn't my brightest moment, but I'm so done with everythin'. I don't freakin' care. Have you turned Herrick completely against me? Were you the one who convinced him to use me as bait for the red dragon?" Casidhe wished her words had come out strong and not bitter.

Sighing with pent-up frustration, the seer groused, "Do you not see what is going on?"

"Stop spewin' riddles. How can I see a damned thing?

I don't live here and I don't have your omniscient vision. Admit it. You turned Herrick against me," Casidhe railed, ignoring the sadness growing in Kleio's eyes.

Why wouldn't the seer come clean and tell her the truth?

Kleio's voice fell, sounding hurt. "I was the one who pleaded with him to send a warning to you and Fenella of danger coming to both of you. He only informed Fenella."

Truth, but Casidhe had no trust in anyone here. After all the years growing up around the castle, these people were strangers to her today.

A part of her wanted to take this great hall apart, make someone pay attention. Another part wanted to curl up in a corner and hide from all this, but that was the old Casidhe.

No corner here belonged to her.

She was on her own and not backing down. "You never wanted me here," she accused Kleio, daring the woman to deny it.

Eyes shiny with emotion, the seer said, "Oh, I did wish for you to be gone, but not out of any malice I hold against you. I have watched how Herrick has treated you since childhood. It was not my place to interfere, but I see that you will not survive if you do not stand on your own. And you cannot do that if you do not touch the truth with your hands."

Casidhe's head felt disconnected from her body.

Should she believe this woman or was Kleio so adept at fooling everyone that she thought she could spew any lie and everyone believed her?

Her miserable conscience and sense of fairness raised its head to ask questions.

What about the seer? Had Casidhe only seen this woman as a rival because of how Herrick turned to Kleio for whatever he needed and never gave Casidhe credit for her hard work?

Should she accept what Kleio was saying as truth?

If so, that painted Herrick as a monster.

Kleio glanced at the long hallway Herrick had run through to reach his lair in the mountain cave. She quickly turned back to Casidhe and leaned closer, speaking softly. "There is little time."

Casidhe lifted a hand with her palm flat forward. "Don't say another freakin' word if you can't tell me what Herrick is so worried about and some trade he's expectin' to do."

"You know the answer to the second question."

If Kleio had hit her with another riddle, Casidhe might have lost her mind. But the seer had said that as if she really expected Casidhe to know the answer.

She said the only thing Herrick should be worried about for a trade. "Skarde."

The seer canted her head.

Was that a yes from her? Casidhe rubbed her aching forehead. "Did you find Skarde?"

"No."

"I don't even know for sure if Skarde is alive," Casidhe admitted in an angry shout. Then she studied Kleio closely when she asked, "Have you had any visions about the red dragon comin' around Galway?"

Not a peep from the seer.

Dropping her hand to her waist, Casidhe took what she considered a don't-screw-with-me pose. "Okay, for argument's sake, let's say Herrick does plan to trade for Skarde and he still thinks the red dragon has Skarde. Now you say he has a treasure to trade. You make it sound like it's a loaf of bread about to spoil, so you clearly know what it is."

Kleio pursed her lips and released a noise of exasperation. "Use that mind of yours. What would the Treoir dragon king want above all?"

Reacting to Kleio's annoyed tone, Casidhe replied sharply, "I have no idea. Daegan is out fightin' Imortiks to save his people. He probably has a hell of a hoard, but he values his people the most. He ... "

Kleio remained stoic, not making a sound.

Casidhe walked around, thinking.

This should not be a difficult question. She sorted her thoughts out loud. "Daegan is desperate to save Beladors and humans bein' overtaken by Imortiks. I doubt Herrick has captured a Belador." She snorted at that idea. Daegan would have found the Belador by now.

Casidhe scratched her hair, wanting a bath and food. Unable to shake off her anger, she lost her patience and snapped, "If Herrick doesn't have a Belador, that leaves family. All of Daegan's family is in Treoir."

Kleio arched an eyebrow that questioned Casidhe's last statement.

Cold fingers climbed Casidhe's spine. She lifted her gaze to the seer. "What are you sayin'? Tell me now!"

"Nothing. I am forbidden from sharing visions without Herrick's approval."

That was the reason for the riddles.

Casidhe's face felt cold and bloodless. She could barely force out, "Does Herrick have one of Daegan's family?"

Was that even possible?

Why not? Herrick and Daegan still lived. So did maybe even Skarde.

Finally speaking, the seer replied, "Only Herrick can answer *that* question."

Hands damp, Casidhe wrung them just thinking about the implications. She whisper-shouted, "Where would he keep someone this long without any of us knowin' it?"

Once again, the seer answered her with a question. "Where is the one place none of us have ever entered?"

Stunned at the possibility Herrick might be holding a family member of Daegan's, Casidhe slowly turned to stare at the long hall leading to Herrick's cave.

His dragon's lair.

Shock had her shaking her head. "He has no one from today or Daegan would be tearin' this place apart to find that person. Who could Herrick have kept alive all these thousands of years? This is not a realm. It would have to be someone immortal, right?"

The damned ring chose that moment to vibrate.

Casidhe slapped her chest.

Kleio stared in shock. "What is wrong with you?"

"Nothin'."

The seer arched a stern look at that lie.

Casidhe narrowed her eyes and her voice hardened. "You have your secrets. I have some of my own." She had to find a way to prevent Herrick from going after Skarde until she had a chance to talk to Daegan.

She would not stand by and allow anyone to harm Daegan. He was the red dragon, but she had no idea what Herrick had been up to all these years. He had been planning a long time and Daegan didn't even know Herrick existed.

She would not lose Daegan to years of hate from an ancient war.

Kleio asked softly, "Where is the ring Herrick gave you before you left for college? Do you still have it?"

The question startled Casidhe. What did the seer know about this ring? Feeling irritable and smug, Casidhe pulled her hand from where she'd trapped the ring beneath her shirt and reached in to lift the chain.

Energy sizzled across her skin. A new and weird reaction.

"The ring now vibrates. That makes sense," Kleio murmured.

"I'm not even goin' to ask what you're talkin' about." Then she couldn't stop herself. "What exactly does this ring mean?"

"Find the owner of that ring, find the truth."

Nope. Kleio was incapable of a simple answer.

Inhaling deeply, Kleio hurried to speak. "You must decide for yourself where that truth lies. To believe the truth, you must first see it with your own eyes then touch it with your hands."

A noise drew Casidhe's gaze to the long hallway leading to Herrick's lair.

There he came stomping back with his dragon rumbling from deep in his chest.

Good. Casidhe positioned herself with feet spread apart, ready for a verbal throwdown with Herrick. He was too arrogant to speak in riddles.

"Now, back to you." He pointed a finger at Casidhe.

She crossed her arms. "What treasure are you hidin' that the red dragon would exchange for Skarde?"

His eyes glowed. "Do not dare to question me on anything. You have much to answer for."

Oh, hell no. Did everyone think to screw with her? "I have done a great deal for you, none of which you show any appreciation for, but that's beside the point. Tell me the truth and I might be able to prevent a bloodbath." Casidhe believed the red dragon could hold his own normally, but Daegan had the Imortik venom in him.

"Your insolence is unacceptable." Herrick's shouting had to be waking the entire castle.

"I have asked little from anyone," Casidhe plowed on, temper roaring. If she was to spend her last day on earth here, she would not go without getting to the bottom of this. "You never told me the truth about Fenella or that she was a member of the MacConnaugh squire family."

Herrick's mouth opened. That hit home.

Casidhe wasn't done. "I have been one-hundred-percent loyal. I have had no life while I spent every minute searchin' for anythin' that would find Skarde for you. But you have never told me the truth about who I am or my power. Your squire families fed me half-truths about the

Treoirs and the red dragon. Want to know how I know?" She didn't give him time to answer and kept at it, shouting, "Because Queen-freakin'-Maeve captured me and held me captive in TÅµr Medb. I was tasked with readin' books in her library from the time of dragons."

She paused for that to sink in.

Herrick looked dumbfounded and Kleio was clearly shaken.

Nodding, she kept on. "Yeah, that's right. I found a lot of conflictin' information, but I still would not question anythin' here. Not until after all the times I put myself in the path of danger to save Fenella, I find her relaxin' with her family. I knew right then I had been a fool. I had been used. She didn't need me." Casidhe drew in a deep breath and boomed out each word. "She. Had. *You!* Must be nice to have family."

The seer grimaced at that, but Herrick's face turned colder by the second.

Casidhe held his gaze. "You told me nothin' but half-truths about the Treoirs and my background. This is your chance to give me *all* the truth and redeem yourself."

That did it for Herrick. He stepped toward her, head lowered, and speaking in a deadly tone. "How dare you demand anything of me? A street urchin with *nothing* until I found you."

"Until you found me, which begs the question why you looked for me."

"You will pay for your impudence," he threatened.

She didn't know if everything she'd been through had crashed in on her or if she just did not care anymore. "Touch me and lose all hope of gettin' Skarde back."

Now that the words were out, she hoped like hell she could back them up.

CHAPTER 20

HAIR STOOD ON CASIDHE'S ARMS from Herrick's power rushing through the room. She couldn't take back what she'd said.

She wouldn't.

She needed something to hold over Herrick to get him to calm down.

Kleio had quieted the minute Casidhe announced she was the only one who could hand Herrick his brother.

Everyone else who lived in the lower quarters of the castle were not present, but Casidhe had no doubt the entire clan hid nearby, listening to Herrick's rants.

"Where is Skarde?" The raw emotion in his voice hurt to hear when he'd never shown anything close to it for her.

She held her arms tight across her chest and doubled down. "I'm not sayin' another word until you show me what you're hidin' in your dragon's lair. Or should I say the *person* you are holdin' prisoner." She read guilt in his eyes just as clearly as Latin text. "You said you had somethin' the red dragon would absolutely trade for. I foolishly thought you meant gold or other treasure, but I now know for sure he would not value somethin' so trivial as trinkets."

Shock widened Herrick's eyes before they narrowed into mean slits. He demanded in a rough voice, "You have become an ally of the red dragon? You betrayed *me* for that dragon?"

"I have betrayed *no one*!" Casidhe made clear. "*You*

raised me to find the red dragon. *You* sent me out with the Luigsech name, wavin' a flag to get the red dragon's attention. When he finally shows up, you do *not* get to accuse me of failin' to be loyal to you. I have been far more loyal to you than I have received in return."

Kleio's expression shifted with every word spoken. When Casidhe glanced at her to check the pulse of the room, the seer's proud gaze surprised her. That had been the last person she ever expected to nod and encourage her to keep speaking her mind.

"I. Want. Skarde!" Herrick ground out as if chewing bricks, just repeating the same words Casidhe had heard her entire life.

Did he think that would work with her right now?

Maybe, since she'd fallen into line every other time. She'd been through too much to fold now. She would never have a chance to be with Daegan until this all got straightened out.

Standing firm, Casidhe stayed the course, unwilling to answer another question from Herrick until he answered hers. She accused, "Your prize possession is someone dear to the red dragon. Who?"

"You will never know."

"Then you will never see Skarde again."

Herrick raged, "You will tell me where he is *now*!"

Kleio stepped forward. "I have always given you sound advice, Herrick."

He jerked to her as if he'd forgotten anyone else stood in the great hall with them. "What are you saying?"

"Every moment you spend arguing is one less minute you have to save ... your treasure."

Casidhe put it together. "Oh, hell! Is the person dyin'? If you let someone important to Daegan die and he finds out, he will destroy everythin' in his path to get to you."

"Only a fool would underestimate me." Herrick glowered at her.

Screeching erupted outside.

The man tending a fire when Herrick's dragon had dropped her off came running inside. "Sire! Your vulture is upset. I think it calls for you."

Herrick ran out of the room without hesitation.

"*Time is running out*!" Kleio yelled, panicking.

"For whom?" Casidhe asked yet again. "I need to know what's goin' on!"

The heavy door to the castle slammed open. Herrick made a prehistoric sound. "You brought the red dragon to my door!"

"Oh, no." Casidhe couldn't breathe. This would go downhill the second Herrick went out to engage him. She had to think fast as Herrick pounded across the room to her.

Kleio whispered urgently, "Use what you know."

Again, not clear.

Casidhe lifted a hand and said the only thing she could. "He's here to make a trade." If Daegan was here, then Tristan would be at his side. If Daegan did possess Skarde, he had only to send Tristan to teleport Skarde here.

Good logic, right?

What if Daegan did not have Skarde and had no idea where he was? If not, why was Daegan here?

Had he found a way to follow her?

She had to talk to Daegan first, no matter what.

Please let him have Skarde. That would actually push Daegan and Herrick to negotiate.

"You lie," Herrick accused.

As if she would admit to that? "Why would I lie? I did not bring him here, but he has a lot of people with gifts in his clan. He has a woman with remote viewin'."

Herrick angled his head at her.

Excellent. He had no idea what that meant. She pumped

her head to nod three times. "If the treasure you're holdin' onto is in jeopardy, what are you waitin' for?"

Herrick appeared to be in a dilemma.

"I want to see this person," Casidhe said, unwilling to argue more.

"No. You stay here."

"No!" Casidhe shouted back at him. "You need me. I want to know what you're tradin' with so I can make this work." Actually, she needed time to figure out what to do.

In a consoling, but compelling, voice, Kleio said, "You must hurry, Herrick. Death will end all trades."

He pushed all that anger in Kleio's direction.

She lifted a hand. "I am not the one who put you in this position. You wanted this day to arrive and it has come."

"You do not understand." This time, he sounded more weary than obstinate.

"Help us understand, Herrick." The seer kept trying to reach him without shoving too hard. "What do you have to show the red dragon?"

Casidhe rubbed her tired eyes then slapped her hands to her hips, beyond tired of this crap. "Daegan has figured out you have someone. I have no idea how he did, but he would not be here unless he knew." She hoped he came because he was worried for her, but then he'd really have to know this place existed.

To be honest, she had no idea how he found it or if he knew she was even here.

The vulture screeched again outside.

Kleio's voice shuddered. "Time is almost gone. You will have nothing."

Casidhe would never get this chance again to find out what Herrick had been hiding for so long. "If you don't want Skarde, say so now. I'll go out and convince Daegan you two have nothin' to talk about."

"*No!*" Herrick shook his fists in frustration then turned

for the long hallway and took off running.

Oh, no, he was not leaving her. Casidhe headed after him. Footsteps rushed behind her. Had to be Kleio.

When Casidhe reached the end of the hallway, she entered the infamous cave no one she knew of had ever ventured into. Herrick slowed and lifted his hand.

Kleio shouted, "Do not bar us from the room if you wish Casidhe to aid you."

Herrick stayed his hand then began moving it quickly, speaking terse words in a rapid pattern.

Once Casidhe and Kleio reached him, they stayed close.

As Herrick led the way downstairs, he continued his rant at Casidhe. "You have sided with a dragon that destroyed my family and all the other clans. I will never have more than Skarde again. I will not be denied my brother."

Casidhe would not waste breath trying to argue with him. She had doubts about the stories she'd been told of the red dragon's bloody rampage before Queen Maeve locked him away.

Herrick would believe nothing she said.

He made a last turn and entered a quiet room with two torches burning. It was like stepping back in time. Rough-carved stone walls surrounded the small cave room. Her skin pebbled with tiny bumps from the chilly air.

Please tell her this person was not a corpse.

He continued his one-sided argument. "You are wrong. I gave you the Luigsech name to protect you. Daegan would not kill someone he needed information from."

How was that consoling?

Casidhe kept her mouth buttoned tight. Arguing would slow them down. Curiosity was eating her up. How many secrets had she lived around for all these years?

The farther down they went, the more the ring quivered.

So this ring really was connected to the person he had down there? Another way he'd set her up. She'd been wearing part of what had to be a Treoir family heirloom around her neck.

He stopped talking when he reached a wall at the far side of the room and murmured soft words.

The stone disappeared to reveal a foggy gray cloud.

Casidhe stepped closer, but stayed behind him.

When the smoky barrier dissipated, it left behind a misty wall, which cleared to reveal a young woman with pale skin. Copper-red hair able to reach her waist draped along her prone body laid on a bed of marble.

Casidhe had no words. That woman belonged to Daegan's family.

Kleio gasped. "That's her."

Herrick turned to her. "You have seen her?"

"Yes. The vision that sent me to warn you." A tear ran down Kleio's cheek. "She begged me to help. She said you were killing her."

The ring inside Casidhe's shirt continued vibrating. She lost it and railed at Herrick. "How long have you had that woman here? Daegan's family? Are you kiddin' me? Is she even alive?"

"She lives." Herrick swung back to the image. "She remains in the same health she had when she entered."

"How can you know that?" Casidhe snarled at him, staring at the young woman. "How long, Herrick?" Casidhe felt sick.

"You may not be able to take her out of there, Herrick," Kleio warned.

"How can I trade her if I do not?" His agonized tone exposed how torn he was standing here.

He wanted Skarde, but he now feared handing over a body to Daegan if the woman did not survive leaving her cocoon.

Herrick just now realized that Daegan would hand him a body in return.

"You can't leave her there," Casidhe asserted. No person should have ever been trapped that way. The ring on her chain continued to act up. "Not unless you're willin' to bring Daegan in here to see her and let him make the decision to pull her out."

"The red dragon will never come in here!"

Casidhe's heart broke with staring at the woman. She thought she couldn't be any more disappointed and furious with Herrick, but he proved her wrong. "Didn't you have a plan to take her out when you found Skarde?"

"Of course I did, but ... now I am not so sure. I do not want Skarde harmed," he whined in misery.

He clearly hadn't cared that much about this woman or how Daegan would feel.

Casidhe couldn't continue another step until that woman was freed. If she died, then at least she would no longer be left in a living hell of being between this world and the next. If the woman had spoken to Kleio in a vision, which Casidhe believed had happened, then her spirit remained locked in that chamber.

Casidhe wanted this over with. "Take her out and I'll take her to the red dragon." The ring hummed faster with energy.

Herrick stepped closer to losing his mind every second. "You will stay here."

Unbelievable stubborn old shifter. "If you go out there with this woman, you two will battle before any trade is made. Daegan will think you are trickin' him. I thought you wanted your brother. Alive," she added. "What's more important right now?"

She must have gotten through to him. He walked over to the wall and pulled a small stone free that had appeared to be part of the solid wall.

He withdrew a scroll that smelled as old as the ones in Queen Maeve's library and rolled it out. That he did not take long to read it had Casidhe thinking he had reviewed the text many times over the years.

The woman in the chamber turned her head to Casidhe. Her greenish-hazel eyes opened.

Cold chills climbed Casidhe's spine. She did live.

The ring felt as if it would jump from inside the shirt. She breathed out, "Herrick?"

He ignored her.

Kleio said, "She lives."

Herrick turned slowly. His tanned skin lost half its color. His lips parted. He uttered one word. "Jennyver."

Casidhe's mind exploded with pieces of information on the Treoir family. Jennyver had been one of Daegan's older sisters.

Daegan would trade all he possessed to see her again.

He would also make someone pay dearly for what had been done to her.

Casidhe started trembling uncontrollably. "Get her out of there, Herrick." She didn't give a damn if she pissed him off. Bile ran up her throat at what had been done to Jennyver.

Heaving one deep breath after another, he didn't move.

Kleio supported Casidhe by telling Herrick, "You will have to live with your conscience later. Free this one now."

Seeming incapable of speech, he stepped over to the misty wall and began speaking softly at first.

Casidhe had no knowledge of the language he used.

Pausing to swallow hard, Herrick lifted his voice and spoke each strange word in a baritone that built energy with each syllable.

Power sizzled in the air and zinged around, dragging a silvery trail of crystals.

When Herrick reached the last words, he shoved his arm into the misty wall. It exploded.

Casidhe covered her ears and ducked away, but looked

around to find nothing tangible had blasted apart.

The ancient majik used to conceal and preserve the woman had reacted powerfully.

She hurried forward as wisps of smoke drifted away.

Jennyver shakily sat up and turned to lower her gown-covered legs down. She put a hand to her head and stared at Herrick. Her voice sounded as if she had a bad cold. "I dreamed of you ... killin' me."

"I never harmed you," he argued in a weak voice riddled with guilt.

Jennyver looked at Kleio next. "Are you dead, too?"

Kleio's eyes were full of tears. She shook her head and sniffled.

"Where am I?"

Herrick stared at the floor. "In my lair."

That really confused Jennyver based on her face. "For how long?"

Herrick opened and closed his mouth without speaking.

Casidhe held back tears and ordered, "She deserves to know. Tell her, Herrick!"

When he said nothing, Kleio shook her head in disgust and told Jennyver. "I know you are confused, but you have lived inside this space for ... many years. We want to reunite you with your family."

Wait until Jennyver found out her family was Daegan, who had also lived for two thousand years.

Casidhe clamped her lips shut, worried about shattering this moment. She wanted Jennyver to live even if it put Herrick and Daegan at war. This woman had her life stolen thousands of years ago. How inhumane to do this to any person.

Tears clung to Casidhe's lashes.

Not now. Not until she got this woman to her brother and got out of this hellhole.

What would Daegan think when he saw Casidhe with

Jennyver?

Would he jump to the conclusion that Casidhe had played a part in all this? No. He'd comforted her when she battered herself over making the wrong judgement about him without facts and evidence.

He would give her a chance to explain, especially if she was the one to hand him a family member.

Jennyver's hand trembled when she lifted it to her lips. "What of my father?"

Herrick whispered to Kleio, "Put her to sleep."

Shaking her head, the seer argued, "Not until you tell her the truth, Herrick."

Silent as a mule, he stared Kleio down.

The seer started forward.

Herrick blurted out, "This is your fault."

Kleio told him, "I would like to take credit for freeing her, but this is not my doing." She moved passed him to speak directly to Jennyver. "You have been in here for two thousand years in a deep sleep without aging."

Jennyver's lips trembled. She looked as if she would faint any second. Big fat tears started rolling down her cheeks. "*Nooo*," she moaned.

"How could you, Herrick?" Casidhe asked, her voice thick with emotion. "This is horrible."

Herrick glared at her. "Get out of here. Do not make me raise my hand to you."

Casidhe stared at Herrick as if he'd just butchered a baby, not moving an inch.

Jennyver blubbered out, "Are they all dead?"

Before Herrick could say another tainted word, Casidhe explained, "Your brother escaped TÅµr Medb not long ago. He still lives. I fear the rest of your family passed two thousand years ago."

Tears rolled down Jennyver's cheeks nonstop. "I was not with my father when he died."

That gutted Casidhe. She was glad to see the agonized expression on Herrick's face. He muttered, "Hurry up, seer."

Kleio ignored him. "We need to get her upstairs first." She asked, "Please, come with me, Jennyver, so we can prepare you to go out in the cold and join your brother."

"Daegan is here?"

Casidhe hated every minute of this. She would not say that Herrick intended to trade Jennyver for his brother. That would almost sound justifiable, which his actions were not. She explained, "We must take you outside a ward protectin' this castle, uh, cave. The red dragon is not allowed inside."

"I shall carry her," Herrick announced, clearly in a hurry.

Jennyver turned a searing gaze to Herrick and cleared her throat. "Do not touch me." That was the order of a woman born to authority. Before she struggled to stand, Kleio stepped over to offer her a hand.

By the time everyone returned to the great hall, Jennyver's hair was damp from sweating and she breathed unsteadily from the exertion.

Casidhe said, "She needs a cloak and boots."

Herrick scowled at her. "Do not think to give anyone here orders."

Unfazed, Casidhe replied in just as sharp a tone, "You are wastin' precious time." She ran to the bench by the door where she'd tossed aside Herrick's cloak earlier.

When she returned, she ignored his growling and held the cloak for Jennyver as Kleio kept the woman upright.

That blasted ring kept buzzing her skin.

She knew exactly what to do with it.

Casidhe stepped back and reached around her neck to unclasp her chain. When she had it loose, she dropped the agitated ring on her palm and offered it to Jennyver. "I think this belongs to you, but I never knew from where it came. I was told to keep the ring safe. The closer I came to you today, the more it vibrated. I never knew you were here and I'm gutted about what happened to you."

The woman stared for a second then lifted the half Casidhe offered and slipped it on a finger of her right hand. Energy buzzed around the ring and Jennyver touched it with a reverent look on her face as if saying hello to an old friend.

Herrick gave Casidhe a look that promised she would pay for her insolent attitude as much as her association with Daegan. He sneered, "Do not act so pious. You had nothing before I found you."

"I had self-respect," Casidhe countered. "I will have a hard time forgivin' myself for my part in this even though you kept it secret from everyone here."

Kleio stepped out of her boots. "You can wear mine, Jennyver."

As if dazed, which was understandable, Jennyver stepped into the boots. With her now properly clothed, it was time to hand her over.

Casidhe would be lying if she said she felt confident in Daegan's reaction, but she believed he would put gaining his sister above retaliating today.

Herrick ordered Casidhe, "You stay in here."

She managed not to shout no at him. "You would be wise to let me speak to the red dragon. He will not kill *me*."

That damn vulture was back screeching outside.

The door opened and Herrick's man stuck his head inside. Herrick strode to the door and stepped outside.

Kleio hurried to tell Jennyver, "He wants me to put you into a light sleep. I will make sure it wears off in one hour."

"*No! Not again!*" Jennyver took a jerky step back and faltered.

Casidhe and Kleio rushed to catch her.

Jennyver had every reason to balk at being put to sleep again. The woman might never trust sleep after this.

Casidhe suggested in a soft voice, "Why don't you just *pretend* to sleep to appease Herrick, but you will actually be outwittin' him."

The seer smiled her thanks.

"Why must I even pretend to sleep?"

Kleio explained, "Herrick knows what he has done is very wrong even if he has yet to admit it out loud. He will not trust you conscious outside this ward when he has no idea if you possess any powers."

Jennyver frowned then sighed. "I will pretend, but how will I leave?"

"He must carry you."

"His touch disgusts me," Jennyver muttered. "But I shall allow almost anythin' to reach my brother again." She wiped away a new tear. "I am strugglin' with grief and hope."

Kleio hugged her. "I understand, but stay strong so we may get you out of here forever."

Herrick returned, pounding heavy boots over the stone floor. "The red dragon is threatening to attack."

Kleio spoke in Jennyver's ear as Herrick closed in. The young woman went limp. "Catch her!"

Herrick caught her before she hit the floor.

Casidhe held so much anger against Herrick right now she might split in half if she didn't deal with it soon, but she couldn't wipe away a lifetime of caring for this clan. She would do all in her power to keep Daegan from harming the rest of those living here.

She would have time later for a discussion and for Herrick to answer for what she'd been through her entire life.

All of it would wait as long as Daegan got his sister back and both dragon shifters survived this meeting. This clan needed Herrick even if she no longer did.

Casidhe took a step, "You're not goin' without me."

"I don't need you. Daegan has Skarde with him."

CHAPTER 21

D AEGAN HAD STOMPED BACK AND forth more than he could take. "What makes ya think that bird can tell Herrick anythin'?"

Lanna had not moved since picking a spot to stare at the empty valley as if she could see into the ward.

Could she?

No. That lass would share whatever she discovered.

"Vulture came to us for message," Lanna explained, having not been the least bit concerned when the largest vulture Daegan had ever seen landed in front of them a few minutes ago.

Tristan stood with legs apart and arms crossed, ready for whatever came next. "You think he understood what Daegan said?"

"Yes." Lanna kept her gaze trained on one spot. "Vulture understand every word. Even what you say and I say."

Tristan's voice came into Daegan's head. *Maybe I shouldn't have said the ice dragons were cowards in front of the vulture.*

'Tis not a problem for me. Daegan paused to search for the bird, a dragon, anything. When he saw nothing, he kept pacing.

You think Herrick will come out, boss?

Lanna spoke up. "Is rude to talk in minds." She sounded annoyed.

Daegan paused. "Tristan and I apologize to ya, Lanna. We often speak telepathically to keep from alarming someone."

She angled a droll gaze his way. "I have seen much in life. Not so easy to scare."

"Good point and I apologize, too," Tristan said. "I was just telling Daegan maybe I shouldn't have insulted the ice dragons in front of that vulture."

"Did you not mean your words?" she inquired.

"I meant every word. First the female ice dragon tried to kill Daegan after making me chew off my hand. Then Skarde pulled his stunt in Treoir. I was hoping to piss off Herrick enough he'd come at us from the front and not our backs."

Lanna gave him a solemn nod.

Daegan changed the subject. "What are we waitin' for, Lanna? I trust ya to know more than many of us, but Tristan is as concerned for your welfare as I am."

"I will not be harmed. I trust dragon and gryphon. We must be patient to find answers you have waited long for. You told vulture to send out Herrick if he wanted brother. He will come soon."

"Soon," Daegan repeated sharply, his voice shaking. What could Herrick be waiting on?

"Is difficult, but worth this wait," Lanna said with understanding in spite of Daegan's short temper.

He felt every slow second as a stab to his soul. "I tire of delays every time I am close to learnin' somethin' of my family. And the idea of Jennyver close ... *I want answers now*!" Daegan had allowed as much time as he could for himself. Though it would be akin to tearing off an arm to leave, he had people depending upon him and would have departed by now if not for one question pounding his brain.

Was Jennyver alive?

CHAPTER 22

CASIDHE HAD A DEATH GRIP on Jennyver's cloak, keeping the woman from falling off the back of Herrick's dragon. A partial moon offered a smidgeon of light in this darkness.

Herrick had been insane when he shifted.

She would pay for gambling everything to be included outside with Jennyver.

She'd told Herrick she could prevent bloodshed. Daegan cared for her and would not leave if he believed Herrick held her against her will. She had not said that to Herrick, instead adding that since no one knew what condition Skarde was in, Herrick would be putting his brother at risk as well.

His dragon's body lunged, flying fast in undulating serpent-like moves. Casidhe leaned down closer and gripped even tighter to a thick scale to stay put, then released Jennyver's cloak with her other hand and wrapped that arm around the woman's waist.

Jennyver gave her a fearful smile of thanks.

When Herrick's silvery-blue dragon broke free of the ward protecting Herrick's land and people, energy zinged over her skin and Jennyver made a surprised noise.

Casidhe gasped at the sight of Daegan's powerful profile high on a mountain top. Her heart clenched with him so close. What she wouldn't give to be clinging to his red dragon instead of Herrick's right now.

Two more people stood with him. The tall male had to

be Tristan. What about the short female?

Who could that be?

And where was Skarde?

If Daegan had lied about bringing Skarde, there would be no stopping Herrick from attacking Daegan and fighting to the death.

Herrick's dragon circled around Daegan and his people, then passed them by and continued on.

What was Herrick up to?

Stian flew into view and took the lead only to the canyon floor. The vulture landed and brought its wings in, standing to the side like an odd sentry.

Casidhe waited for the dragon to lower its body with a wing in place for her and Jennyver to use for climbing off. She whispered to Jennyver, "Keep pretending."

Jennyver took a couple slow breaths then went limp again.

Once Casidhe was free of Herrick's dragon and held Jennyver, who slumped against her, Herrick shifted back to his human form. He decked himself out for a medieval war, including a huge sword in the sheath at his back.

Daegan, Tristan, and the small woman had teleported to the canyon floor a hundred feet away. The moon passed from behind clouds, casting an eerie glow over them, bright enough for her to take in the grim expressions.

She didn't think Herrick could do the same.

Striding over with an arrogant swagger, Herrick stopped to the left of Casidhe, who held Jennyver up on her right. He roared, "Where is Skarde?"

Daegan stepped forward, demanding, "Show my sister."

Until this very second, Casidhe did not truly believe he knew his sister was here. How had he figured that out?

When Herrick crossed his arms in a stubborn stance, Casidhe lifted her free hand. "Jennyver is here, Daegan."

Jennyver stood away from her and pushed the hood off

her face, smiling at her brother. Tears ran down her cheeks.

Herrick cursed, realizing he'd been duped. He grumbled out a string of words, which could be a spell, because light glowed around the three of them and that damn vulture.

Herrick would add Jennyver not being unconscious to the rest of his imagined transgressions Casidhe had committed. She would handle that later once Daegan had his sister safely in hand.

She could not look at Herrick. The hurt she could now see in Daegan's face stopped the breath in her throat. He looked every bit a warlord, but his pain sat clearly in his gaze even from where she stood.

Daegan called out in a voice raw with emotion, "Jennyver?"

His sister lifted a hand and spoke through tears. "I am here, Daegan."

Herrick roared, "Hand over my brother now! He had best not be harmed."

In answer, Daegan's face contorted into a deadly warning. "You have naught to accuse me of. I have kept your brother safe after rescuin' him from the Scamall realm. Your sister Brynhild attacked me just days ago. She fought to kill me. I spared her life as well when I could have struck her down. I have shown over and over that I am *not* the dragon who started the Dragani War. I would have brought Brynhild if she had not flown away."

Herrick lurched forward with a hand on his sword. "I want only Skarde. Hand him over."

Casidhe was even more disgusted with Herrick after that admission.

What would Brynhild think if she were here?

The small woman with Daegan turned and pointed at an empty spot next to her. A man Casidhe assumed to be Skarde appeared, but he could not move or speak. Only blink his eyes and mumble to prove he lived.

"Free him!" Herrick shouted.

"Send my sister first."

"*No!*" Herrick stood firm.

Casidhe fought off panic. Unless Daegan had healed the venom in his body, he would need Tristan to teleport Jennyver. He had to know better than to risk Jennyver's safety by trying to snatch her out from under Herrick. Daegan might have discovered his sister had been held here, but he could not possibly know what Herrick might have up his sleeve.

Herrick would retaliate if Daegan tried to trick him.

Plus, why do anything risky? Daegan held all the cards to win his sister back. He had Skarde.

Casidhe called out, "I will bring Jennyver to the middle and you bring Skarde."

Herrick's eyes burned bright blue and his pupils elongated. "You risk all by thinking to overrule me."

"I am *tryin'* to keep everyone alive, includin' Skarde," Casidhe retorted. She'd foolishly hoped to reach a happy medium between two rival dragon shifters who couldn't be more unhappy at the moment.

"Nay! Take your hands off her, *Luigsech*," Daegan roared, his voice burning with anger. "Ya shall *not* be welcome around my people ever again." His face twisted with being sick at heart then darkened into something far worse.

The mask of hate that dropped in place on Daegan's face stunned her.

"Daegan?" she begged in a strained whisper. His words had reached inside and clawed her heart into pieces. He couldn't mean what he said.

Daegan shouted in a voice laden with disgust, "I should thank ya for trickin' me, Luigsech. Your skulkin' about allowed me to follow ya to this place or I would not have found my sister. Move away from her. I shall bring Skarde and come for Jennyver myself."

Casidhe tried to speak, but emotion choked her words. Her hand fell away from Jennyver who weaved in place. Casidhe had expected Daegan to be confused, even angry, but he really believed she had betrayed him? She would crawl naked through fire to avoid hurting him.

How could he not give her a chance to explain?

How could he throw away the vow he'd made to her? They were going to be together after this. He told her how much he cared for her and ... she believed him.

Herrick accused Casidhe, "You lied again. You led the red dragon here!"

Casidhe's world crashed in on her. Blood rushed through her ears so loud she couldn't hear or deal with anything beyond her heart breaking open like a dam bombed to pieces. Unbearable pain flooded her chest. Tears clung to her lashes.

How could she lose him this way?

Daegan waved the woman to him and warned in a booming voice for all to hear, "My sister had better not be harmed beyond your repulsive actions so far, Herrick." He pointed at Skarde whose eyes were wide with panic. Skarde's body lifted off the ground and floated over to where Daegan stood. With a flick of Daegan's hand, Skarde's feet lowered to the ground.

Herrick lifted his sword. "If you have harmed a hair on my brother's head, you all shall die, starting with your sister."

Skarde stared wildly at Herrick and tried to make noises.

Daegan waited as the woman raised her hands at Skarde and spoke, but too softly for Casidhe to hear. When the young woman lowered her arms, she stepped back, her eyes locked on Daegan.

Skarde moved one arm as if testing it. His other arm was bound up as if fractured.

"You broke his arm?" Herrick raged.

"He broke it himself," Daegan snapped back.

Walking toward Herrick with Daegan at his side, Skarde used his good hand to grab the cloth tied around his mouth. He ripped it off and yelled, "*It is me, Skarde!*"

Jennyver took a step forward and jerked sideways to her right. She screamed and vanished from sight.

Casidhe lunged for her and grabbed air.

Everyone froze for a heartbeat.

Herrick stared, openmouthed.

Daegan roared, "*Jennyver!*" and sent a stunned Skarde backward with his kinetics.

Skarde started yelling and tried to run. "*No! I must—*"

The woman with Daegan flashed her majik and Skarde was immobile again, eyes crazed.

Daegan ordered over his shoulder, "*Get them out of here!*"

Tristan, the woman, and Skarde disappeared.

CHAPTER 23

"*Nooo!*" HERRICK HOWLED AND SHIFTED into his dragon in a blast of power.

Daegan changed into his red dragon even faster. Too shocked to think, he functioned on instinct alone, giving Ruadh the lead.

He couldn't believe he'd seen Jennyver. Alive and breathing. Within his grasp.

He'd considered sending Tristan to teleport her away, but he had made mistakes in the past he could not undo. As long as he held Skarde, he'd believed he had a safe way to regain her.

Why would Herrick yank her away?

Had she been real or had Herrick played a majik trick to force Daegan's hand with Skarde? Why would Herrick take that risk with his brother's safety?

Daegan couldn't sort through anything now.

Not when he and Ruadh had to survive this battle. Rage drove him to tell his dragon, *I want Herrick to hand over my sister.*

Ruadh replied, *Must win battle.*

Daegan agreed. They had to defeat Herrick so savagely he would have to give up Daegan's sister or die.

No more tricks. He refused to believe Jennyver had been a hologram or some other image. He'd seen her with his own eyes.

She lived!

His dragon flapped faster, lifting higher with every circle as they caught wind currents.

Herrick's ice dragon, the most powerful of that clan, could not equal Ruadh's speed in a straight line, but had no problem climbing quickly in sweeping circles, too.

Herrick had kept Jennyver all these years in some form, then showed her to Daegan long enough to rip his insides apart.

And Casidhe had helped him.

She'd shocked Daegan yet again when he thought she could do no more to destroy him. She'd been part of the ice dragon clan the whole time he'd known her. When he'd asked her about the Treoir family, she'd shared small amounts when she clearly had known so much more.

Such as his sister still being alive and with Herrick.

Could there be a greater betrayal for him? No.

He had no idea how Herrick had managed to keep a mortal alive that long. At the moment, Daegan didn't care. He only wanted his sister safe and to hold her again. To see a living member of his family a stone's throw away and not hug her gutted him.

Just as much as forcing himself to acknowledge that Casidhe had never truly cared about him. He would get over that eventually, but it would take a long time.

Some wounds never healed.

Ruadh swung wide and looked down, giving Daegan a view of Casidhe as she turned into a tiny speck. His last view of her as he'd shifted had been her falling to her knees and hands locked together pleading, while tears poured from her eyes.

He would be the greatest fool ever to take a step back toward her after today.

Herrick's dragon swept back and forth in wide slashes.

Ruadh kept an eye on their opponent.

As the ice dragon flapped hard below, Ruadh folded his wings and dove, jaws open to blast a raging storm of fire.

Herrick's dragon was not new to battles. He had fought with Daegan many times and knew how wily the red dragon could be. The ice dragon folded long silver-blue wings and rolled to one side, missing the fire.

Wings opening fast, Ruadh stopped the sharp fall and twisted then flapped around, now below the ice dragon. Ruadh flew straight up, a strain for his giant body, but it allowed for a direct attack.

This time his red dragon's fire hit its mark.

The ice dragon had been flying all these years, but maybe not in battle.

Herrick's dragon roared in pain and banked hard to the side, flying erratically without both wings healthy.

Daegan had not expected this battle to end so soon, but told Ruadh, *Take the ice dragon to the ground.*

Lunging forward with hard flaps, Ruadh blasted fire at the ice dragon's uninjured wing.

Herrick's dragon curled in on itself, falling before the fire struck. The silvery-blue dragon spread his wings fast, yanking to a stop and spinning to face Ruadh diving at him.

The ice dragon shot sideways, then back. One of Herrick's personal moves. It worked to give his dragon an immediate advantage too close for Ruadh to maneuver away from.

Ice blasted from above.

Even worse, the ice dragon had not attacked Ruadh's back but one wing instead.

Pain burst through Ruadh who kept his jaws shut against any sound, but Daegan felt the shuddering moan inside. He experienced the gut-wrenching agony just as Ruadh did.

They were spiraling down too fast.

Ruadh stretched his big neck around and puffed fire in short blasts at his frozen wing until the ice broke free. But the smell of burned wing surrounded them. Broken bones did not stop Ruadh from straining to open his damaged wing.

Daegan's red dragon would force a broken bone to move and hold the agony inside just to demoralize an enemy.

With incredible effort, Ruadh swooped around in a wider circle than before and lifted up to find Herrick's dragon. Moonlight glanced off the shiny scales, so much easier to find at night than the red dragon's body.

Ruadh flapped slowly in pain without making a sound, allowing their healing to flood the injured wing. The longer they flapped with one wing barely gliding up and down, the better to convince the ice dragon they were not injured.

Unlike Brynhild, Herrick's dragon had been battle-hardened. Much of those battles, Daegan had flown alongside the ice dragon siblings. He'd learned all their traits. Every ice dragon had been a worthy opponent, but none could take down the red dragon alone.

Daegan had never considered the chances of winning a battle between his dragon and the entire ice dragon clan.

Rather than spend his time proving his dragon was the deadliest, he'd built allies of every dragon clan, just as his ancestors had.

That lasted until someone impersonated his red dragon and attacked other clans.

He'd given every one of the ice dragons living today a chance to become allies. He'd done as Garwyli had said and tried his best to prove by his actions today he had not started the Dragani War. If Herrick and the others could not see past their blind hate, so be it. That would not change the way Daegan treated others.

He'd been willing to call a truce even if they could not be allies after trading Herrick's sibling for Daegan's sister.

They'd treated him as a fool. No more.

Ruadh spoke to him telepathically. *Battle must end.*

Yes. We will wait for the ice dragon to come down then

fight him to the ground.

Ice dragon fights to death.

Daegan considered what Ruadh was really saying. Either they fought to the death or they lost, because Herrick would not pull back.

All I ask is to do your best, Ruadh. I would like to take Jennyver home and need Herrick alive to get her back.

Ruadh said nothing, just angled around sharply as the ice dragon wove back and forth, slowly dropping above them.

They were coming very close to the canyon. If they fought too close, both dragons risked flying into a mountain if too caught up in the battle to manuever.

Herrick's dragon made a move first, dipping sharply as it came down at Ruadh.

The wing bones had not fully healed, but Daegan trusted Ruadh's ability to battle even when damaged. His dragon arched up as Herrick's came too close, blowing ice.

Ruadh's slow speed allowed for twisting fast and landing on top of the ice dragon, claws shoved into the dragon's neck and shoulders. The ice dragon roared an inhuman sound of pain.

Then something slapped Ruadh sideways, sending the red dragon tumbling over and over. Daegan lost sight of the mountains. Ruadh pulled out of the spin right as they banged against a narrow spot along the upper mountain range.

Daegan felt the hit in their side.

Rocks shot away from the broken peak.

What had knocked Daegan's dragon off Herrick's?

Ruadh found a spot and landed, then wrenched his neck to gaze up.

Two ice dragons flew across the sky, slamming into each other.

Brynhild? Where had she come from? Herrick hadn't

been interested in her at all.

One ice dragon wrapped up, spinning down like an arrowhead shooting toward a target. The other dragon whipped around and followed.

Daegan asked Ruadh, *Do ya want to shift and see if I can teleport?*

Ruadh lifted his head and opened wide jaws, blowing a shaft of fire high in the air just as the spinning dragon raced toward the flames.

Brynhild's dragon opened her wings and lunged to one side, but still caught some of the fire.

Ruadh told Daegan, *We do not run.*

True, but Daegan would teleport away to spare his dragon being attacked by two that might be able to kill his dragon together.

Pushing off, Ruadh flapped fast, flying straight up. His dragon wasted no time trying to catch currents with Herrick's dragon heading straight for them.

Rolling to the left, Ruadh looked as if they were evading, but flapped slowly enough to make that a lie.

Herrick's dragon flew in the same direction.

With both dragons flying parallel, the ice dragon started to swing wide jaws at Ruadh, but Daegan's dragon was ready.

Ruadh lunged at Herrick's dragon, ripping at every place his giant claws could slice into.

The ice dragon chomped hard, gashing Ruadh's shoulder.

Daegan said, *Use your tail.*

Ruadh lashed at the ice dragon with the sharp bones sticking up along his tail and wrapped up the ice dragon's tail.

Daegan felt the jerk of Herrick's dragon now focused on trying to free his tail. No chance.

They would both fall to the ground as they fought.

Ruadh never stopped attacking, taking advantage of the ice dragon's distraction. By the time Herrick's dragon realized how close they were to hitting the canyon floor, he shoved and battered his bony head against Ruadh's.

Daegan's dragon waited. When the bodies spun with him on top, he broke free, pushing away.

Too close.

Herrick's dragon slammed hard, shaking the rocks and ground as it bounced and flopped, then stilled.

Ruadh tucked his legs and wings, hitting just as hard, but rolling over and over until they hit a wall of rocks.

That unleashed a landslide.

His dragon remained tucked, allowing small rocks and boulders to rain down on them. When it all stopped, Daegan asked, *How bad are ya?*

No flying yet.

That's what Daegan had feared. Now he had two ice dragons ready to come in for the kill. He didn't think Herrick had died, but maybe his dragon was in as bad, or worse, condition than Ruadh.

Rocks began moving away from them quickly.

Ruadh lifted his head. *Loyal gryphon.*

Daegan was heartened to see Tristan, but called telepathically, *Watch for Brynhild. She is here as well.*

I'm watching, boss, but she's busy shouting at Herrick.

As soon as Tristan had enough rocks off that Ruadh didn't have to struggle to rise, Daegan asked for the human body.

Ruadh warned, *Do not trust ice dragons.*

I know. I shall take care. Daegan gritted his teeth through the shift. His back, arms, and legs had been beaten bloody and pain stabbed his injured arm, but Ruadh had suffered the worst of it and spent the time on the ground healing important areas.

Clothed in loose jeans and a soft long-sleeved pullover, Daegan opted for what Tristan called sneakers on his swelling feet.

"Damn, boss. You able to walk?" Tristan asked, no humor in his voice.

"Aye. For now."

"I got here as you and the ice dragon crashed into the ground." Tristan turned as Daegan caught up to him and fell into step.

Not seeing the pile where Herrick hit clearly, Daegan asked, "Is Brynhild still in dragon form?"

"No. She shifted and went after Herrick's dragon."

Brushing dirt off his face and out of his hair with his strong hand, Daegan said, "'Tis good to know she cares more for makin' sure her brother lives than killin' my dragon."

"What I heard didn't sound nurturing," Tristan muttered.

They neared Herrick, who had also shifted and sat on the ground with his head in his hands. Blood ran down his arms and from cuts on his face.

"*You disgust me*!" Brynhild yelled. "I hear your words. You care only about Skarde. Not me. You left me for a druid to capture. I spend two thousand years deep in ice pond."

Herrick lifted his head and spoke in gravelly voice. "I did not know you lived."

"Liar! You did not look. Red dragon tells you I live and you do not care. You are *not* my brother. Skarde is *not* my brother."

"Do not act like a child, Brynhild," Herrick shouted back.

She swung her arms wide and whipped them back at Herrick.

His body went flying fifty feet.

Daegan stopped. Tristan waited.

Herrick shifted into his battered dragon and roared ice at her. She called up a shield and held it in front of her. The ice shot off in different directions as it made contact.

Tristan whispered, "Looks like a new shield. Not the one I saw her use in Cathbad's cave."

Daegan nodded.

Herrick shifted back to his human form. "You are a fool. You stand with your back to the red dragon."

She flipped around, shifted into her dragon, and blinked out of view.

Watching her, Herrick stared as if he'd never seen her use cloaking before. Maybe he had not.

Daegan was done with both of them. "Enough, Herrick. I will fight ya for as long as ya wish, but we can end this right now. Give me Jennyver and I will bring Skarde back."

Herrick stared at them for a long moment. "I do not have her. She was stolen from both of us."

He shifted into his dragon and flapped away with crippled motions.

"Well, *damn*!" Tristan grabbed his head. He walked around a minute. "Now what, Boss?"

Everything from Luigsech's betrayal, to finding out Jennyver lived, to losing his sister again, and battling Herrick had drained Daegan of his rampage.

He said, "We go home." People would pay for today, but he was not defeated. Not at all. He pulled the other half of Jennyver's ring from his pocket. "We shall see what Lanna can do with this."

CHAPTER 24

CASIDHE LIMPED TO THE CASTLE from where Herrick's dragon had dropped her even higher off the ground this time. She didn't care.

Daegan hated her.

How could he care so much and turn his back on her like that? Yes, she understood his anger and hurt, but ... he should have asked her for the truth.

She'd never fill the hollow spot in her chest again.

In a span of days, she'd discovered Fenella had not been the sister of her heart, she had no clan, she'd been used her entire life, and lost the man she loved.

How easy it was to understand love when she'd been hesitant before. Nothing could hurt any more than losing someone she loved. She would grieve, but not this minute. Not when she had to survive Herrick's wrath.

She stumbled up the steps, catching herself before she fell.

The door opened and Kleio stood there, hope in her eyes. "Do both dragons live?"

Moving past the seer into the room, Casidhe said, "All three survived."

"Three?" Kleio hooked an arm around Casidhe, helping her toward flames dancing in the fireplace.

"Brynhild showed up." Even to Casidhe's ears, her voice sounded wooden.

"Did Jennyver go with Daegan?"

Casidhe stopped and made a sound that almost turned

into a moan of pain, but she clamped her lips shut. Blinking hard, she got past the tears. "No. She vanished."

Kleio released her to stand on her own. "What? How?"

"I don't know." Casidhe continued. "She was there one moment and vanished the next."

The heavy wooden door slammed open, shaking the castle. Herrick bellowed, "*Casssidhhee!*"

She turned around only long enough to glare at the man who had destroyed her world. Then she limped to her backpack.

Herrick growled and shouted, "*Do not turn your back on me.*"

Kleio wrung her hands and whispered, "Try to calm him, Casidhe."

Calm him? She wanted to strangle Herrick, but her hands would not reach around his thick neck. She hoisted the backpack to her shoulders.

She had to find Daegan, which meant convincing Tristan to talk to her first. Shit, Tristan had her books. She couldn't worry about that now, not when her every thought was consumed with reaching Daegan.

"You lost the woman and Skarde!" Herrick ranted as he closed the distance between them.

"In fairness, Herrick—" Kleio said in a soft voice.

"*Silence!*" Herrick slammed his huge boot on the floor. The castle walls shook. Sconces burst around the room. Glass scattered everywhere. The long table where they all took meals flipped over. He turned flaming blue eyes on the seer. "You did not put the woman to sleep. Get out of my sight. *Now!*"

Frozen in place, a hint of fear washed over Kleio's features.

Casidhe had never witnessed fear on that woman before. Herrick clearly only wanted to scream at her. Why put anyone else in danger?

Casidhe gave the seer a tiny head movement, encouraging her to leave and not make it worse.

Kleio got her back up. "Take care, Herrick. You are *not* my master."

"I am in this castle."

Shaking her head, Kleio walked away only to the stairs and stood on the bottom step.

With Casidhe as Herrick's primary target, he ignored Kleio's defiance. Shoving the force of his fury at Casidhe, he spoke in a threatening voice. "You were tasked to find the red dragon, not to side with the enemy and become close to him. Then you lead him here when you were told only to report when you found the red dragon."

Casidhe must have lost all her give-a-shit factor, because her mouth opened, and sarcasm came out. "I found the red dragon."

Kleio gasped.

Herrick's face turned bloodred.

Casidhe crossed her arms, ready for Herrick to unleash his anger on her and maybe leave everyone else alone. Resignation settled into her core.

The sooner they got this over with, the sooner she could leave here, find a place for a well-deserved breakdown, and start rebuilding her life. Also, the sooner she might convince Tristan to help her talk to Daegan.

An impossible task. Even if she called the number Tristan had given her to reach him or Daegan, all the person answering had to do was act as if they had never heard of her.

"You have brought *shame* to this clan," Herrick snarled, pointing his finger.

What a pile of crap. She took in a deep breath and shouted, "*Me?* I'm not the one who stole someone's life and kept her like damn chattel buried alive in a cave! How can you point at anyone after what you did to Jennyver? Look how you treated another dragon family then you want sympathy for losin' Skarde today?"

"You know nothing. You came from nothing and you owe me everything."

She felt like nothing right then. "I owe you zero. I've more than paid you for feedin' and clothin' me."

Herrick shook with so much rage, power zinged around the room.

Casidhe understood his frustration at losing Skarde and his trading chip, but she was just as furious. In the past two days, she'd lost all she'd believed in and had been at the mercy of every supernatural who took a shot at her. He didn't even care if she forgave him. He thought she'd just accept more crap and continue as ordered.

She'd lived a lie long enough. No more.

The pain in Daegan's face would forever be burned into her mind. She'd lost all she had to live for.

"You," Herrick snarled, leaning toward her. A rumbling came from his chest, which sounded more like his dragon than Herrick. "I trusted you with *one* job and you betrayed me. You betrayed this entire clan."

Oh, hell no. He was not laying this at her feet.

Unfolding her arms, she let them fall loose. "You can't seem to acknowledge all I've done for you since being a child. Not one time have you given me even a small bit of praise and you have *never* told me who I am or where I came from." She leaned forward. "You sent a warnin' to Fenella to protect *her*. Not me, because I never mattered. My safety never mattered. Nothin' mattered ... except gettin' Skarde back, did it?"

Herrick's fist curled tight, forcing veins in his muscular arm to lift. His words were low and chilling. "You do not question me ever."

Casidhe couldn't stop the avalanche of pain and anger driving her own sharp reply. "Oh, yes, I will. I grew up in the ten years I've lived away. I'm not a child anymore to accept everythin' dumped on me without question. I am owed answers. You set me up and got what you deserved. Don't think to blame me with your failure."

He held his arms out, shaking his fists, and dropped his head back. He roared over and over, rocking the castle.

Screams came from the kitchen.

Casidhe didn't know how to stop him. She hadn't thought he'd lose his mind and bring the castle down on the innocent clan.

All at once, he quieted, though heaving deep breaths. When he lowered bright glowing eyes, his voice shook. "I would kill another who betrayed me."

She swallowed. At least he'd said it as if he had another option. She only cared about one thing. She wanted out of here to find a way to speak to Daegan.

Herrick sneered, "You shall be punished, then you will live in the dungeon for one year ... *little girl.*"

Casidhe couldn't believe his words. He would steal what was left of her life?

No. She felt a calm wash over her at realizing she had nothing left to lose. She reached over her shoulder and curled her fingers, hesitating then pulled her hand back to her front. What if the sword didn't budge?

He'd watched her and grinned in triumph.

Herrick once told her the sword would come to Casidhe when it believed she'd earned the right to wield the ancient blade.

Kleio had told her she could go nowhere as long as others set her path.

A whisper ran through Casidhe's mind. *Honor my sword. It will honor you.*

Casidhe let her backpack fall to the floor to stand behind her. She dropped to one knee with her hand open and ordered in a confident voice, "Come to me, *Lann an*

Cheartais."

Nothing happened.

She stared at Herrick. His grin widened.

Her energy erupted in a strange noise again, stronger this time.

His smile fell.

A loud hiss sounded as the sword flew from her backpack, up in the air, then over her head to pause at her raised hand. She gripped the hilt. Power pulsed up her arm.

She stood, holding the sword in front of her face vertically, and declared, "You are mine."

Gold and black armor began forming over her shoulders and down her body, fitting every line of her body. Her power rumbled louder. Energy surged through her.

Herrick's mouth dropped open.

Raising her clear voice, she announced, *"No one* will ever use me again. I gave you loyalty and protected you with my life. I did not betray you, but you have betrayed me. Do not dare to think you will punish me or lock me away anywhere. I am no one's *little girl."*

NOTE FROM DIANNA

Thank you for continuing with me on this story journey. I deeply appreciate the wonderful reviews and kind comments I see posted everywhere. I'm not stopping until all nine books are out, just as I promised. You've been so nice about the cliffhangers, which are natural in an ongoing series where the core characters return to the same world in each book (much like a television series, except you won't have to wait a year for the conclusion of this series.) I'm a reader too and I always think of you first while writing. I'm honored you read the stories.

After the next three books, this entire Treoir Dragon Chronicles series will be complete.

Sincerely,

Dianna

MORE BOOKS

Thank you for reading my books. If you enjoyed this story, please help other readers find this book by posting a review.

For SIGNED PRINT copies of Dianna's books visit www.DiannaLoveSignedBooks.com where you can also preorder new books.

To be notified of all future releases, please join Dianna's newsletter at https://authordiannalove.com/connect

The complete 9-book series of Treoir Dragon Chronicles in ebook and audiobooks

Treoir Dragon Chronicles of the Belador World: Book 1
Treoir Dragon Chronicles of the Belador World: Book 2
Treoir Dragon Chronicles of the Belador World: Book 3
Treoir Dragon Chronicles of the Belador World: Book 4
Treoir Dragon Chronicles of the Belador World: Book 5
Treoir Dragon Chronicles of the Belador World: Book 6
Treoir Dragon Chronicles of the Belador World: Book 7
Treoir Dragon Chronicles of the Belador World: Book 8
Treoir Dragon Chronicles of the Belador World: Book 9

**The hardback print versions of
Treoir Dragon Chronicles**

Treoir Dragon Chronicles of the Belador World: Volume I
Books 1-3
Treoir Dragon Chronicles of the Belador World: Volume
II Books 4-6
Treoir Dragon Chronicles of the Belador World: Volume
III Books 7-9

*Note: Hardbacks can be ordered/preordered signed and
personalized from* www.**DiannaLoveSignedBooks**.com

Reviews on Belador books:

"…non-stop tense action, filled with twists, betrayals,
danger, and a beautiful sensual romance. As always with
Dianna Love, I was on the edge of my seat, unable to pull
myself away."
~~Barb, The Reading Café

"There is so much action in this book I feel like I've
burned calories just reading it."

~~ Goodreads

"…shocking developments and a whopper of an end-
ing... and I may have exclaimed aloud more than once…
Bottom line: I really kind of loved it."
~~Jen, top 500 Reviewer

"DEMON STORM leaves you breathless on countless
occasions."
~~Amelia Richard, SingleTitles

"...Its been a very long time since I've felt this passionate about getting the next installment in a series. Even J. K. Rowling's Harry Potter books."

~~Bryonna Nobles, Demons, Dreams and Dragon Wings

"As much as I am impatient for each installment these stories are so worth the wait."

~~ Rosemary, Goodreads

"This adventure win or lose is going to change things for Evalle and her friends. Brava Ms. Love for another fantastic ride."

~~ In My Humble Opinion

AUTHOR'S BIO

New York Times **Bestseller Dianna Love** once dangled over a hundred feet in the air to create unusual marketing projects for Fortune 500 companies. She now writes high-octane romantic thrillers, young adult and urban fantasy. Fans of the bestselling Belador™ urban fantasy series will now have the new Treoir Dragon Chronicles of the Belador™ spinoff. Dianna's Slye Temp sexy romantic thriller series wrapped up with Gage and Sabrina's book–Fatal Promise–perfect for bingers! She has new League of Gallize Shifters paranormal romance series. Look for her books in print, e-book and audio. On the rare occasions Dianna is out of her writing cave, she tours the country on her BMW motorcycle searching for new story locations. Dianna lives in the Atlanta, GA area with her husband, who is a motorcycle instructor, and with a tank full of unruly saltwater critters.

Visit her website at www.**AuthorDiannaLove.**com or www.**DiannaLoveSignedBooks.**com

A WORD FROM DIANNA…

Thank you for reading my new *Treoir Dragon Chronicles of the Belador™ World* series. I have been excited to give you this spinoff series for a long time.

As always, I must thank my wonderful husband and partner in this journey, Karl. He is the greatest gift in my life and you readers are another one!

Nothing happens without a good team. High five to Jennifer Cazares and Sherry Arnold, very early super readers who help me hand you the cleanest book possible. You are so valuable.

I am fortunate to have Jodi Henley, who is an amazing content editor. She sees the books first then it goes through a gauntlet of reads before you receive the book. Judy Carney has only gotten better and better over the years. Stacey Krug is a tremendous aid with proofing and always ready to read. Joyce Ann McLaughlin is invaluable when it comes to beta reading as she listens to the audio file. Her ear is far sharper than mine, for sure. I am so happy with my wonderful audio narrator, Stephen R. Thorne, who the fans chose – they were right!

Hugs and a big thank you to Candace Fox, Kimber Mirabella, Leiha Mann and Sharon Livingston Griffiths, who are wonderful about reading whenever I need it and so supportive in other ways.

I can't say enough great things about my awesome early review team - they just keep rocking big time!

The incredible Kim Killion never fails to create terrific covers for me (I love my covers for this series and am so jazzed to reveal them) and Jennifer Litteken has saved me more than once when it comes to formatting (a shout out to DD, too).

I could go on and on, because I appreciate every reader and would love to thank you in person. But … I keep hearing "write faster," so I'm jumping back into my cave.

Dianna

www.ingramcontent.com/pod-product-compliance
Lightning Source LLC
Chambersburg PA
CBHW050952180726
48291CB00006B/1797